THE RETIREMENT

A JON SUMMERS NOVEL

★ JEFFREY THRALL ★

Editing, design, and distribution by Bublish

ISBN: 978-1-647047-38-2 (paperback)
ISBN: 978-1-647047-37-5 (eBook)

DEDICATION

For Marilyn

ACKNOWLEDGEMENTS

Many thanks to my sons, Jon and Mike, for their help with research and the story. Special thanks to Jon for allowing me to use and develop some of the characters from his Shattered Soldier series he's developing, allowing for the expansion of the Summers universe. Thanks to Mike for his artistic input as we talked about interior layout, cover layout, and author pictures. Thanks to my wife, Marilyn, for putting up with my many moods through this journey, as well as for her editing skills and recommendations. Thanks to the rest of my family and friends for their support and encouragement through all my ramblings in creating this storyline. Tom, Tracy, Mark, Carol Ann, Katie, Stacy, Kay, Barb, Ken, Harry, Nancy, and Dawn—you guys are the best. Lastly, thanks to my publishers for their guidance, help, and creativity in bringing this project to fruition.

CHARACTER LIST

Law Enforcement:

Michael J. Trask – Assistant United States Attorney.

Cassandra (Cassie) Summers – Jon Summers's niece; assigned to the US Attorney's Office; Matt Summers's oldest child.

Tina Ramsey – Trask's senior assistant.

Glenn Grey – FBI agent in charge of the New York office.

Martin James – Franklin County Sheriff.

Abigail (Abby) Crogan – Stephen Summers's girlfriend; part-time deputy.

Brady Jasper – Franklin County Sheriff's Deputy.

Eugene Sanderson – FBI Assistant Director for Critical Incident Response.

Scott Preston – Inspector with the Royal Canadian Mounted Police.

Intelligence Community:

W. C. Putnum – Retired admiral; Deputy Director of the NSA.

Tommy Mitchell – CIA case officer in charge of a covert action team.

Kayli (Kay) Wiedenkeller – CIA analyst assigned to the team; daughter of former Navy SEAL Al Wiedenkeller.

Justin Summers – Jon Summers's middle son; former Navy SEAL listed KIA; working as a covert CIA operative.

Ryan O'Keefe – Justin's partner; son of Patrick O'Keefe; Sarah's half-brother.

Joseph DePalma – Member of Justin's CIA team; expert in technology.

Military:

Lt. Commander Stephnie Smith – Naval Intelligence.

Lt. Commander Bryan James Kingston – Son of Richard Kingston; mother is Fiona Ericson and a hostage.

Ensign Edward Johnston – Commanding officer of SEALs sent to help the FBI.

Chief Mike Skier – Second-in-command of the SEALs sent to help the FBI.

Kidnappers:

Ron Hapke – Julie's ex-boyfriend; former Town of Lakeview police officer.

Servati – Second-in-command on the island.

Richard Kingston – Former admiral; convicted of treason, serving time in Leavenworth Disciplinary Barracks; planned kidnapping as a means of escape.

Andrea Handcock – Former aide and lover to Kingston; convicted of treason and serving a life sentence.

Hostages:

Nancy Summers – Matriarch of the Summers family.

Julie Summers-Romero – Jon Summers's younger sister.

Sarah Summers – Sean Summers's wife; Becky O'Keefe's daughter; she is a doctor.

Raymond Jonathan (RJ) Summers – Son of Sean and Sarah.

Patricia (Patty) Louise Summers – Daughter of Sean and Sarah.

Emily Summers – Matt Summers's youngest daughter.

Hector Summers-Romero – Julie's oldest child.

Alexandra (Alex) Summers-Romero – Julie's youngest child.

Mark Wells – Retired NCIS agent involved in the arrest of Kingston.

Judy Demmer – Former Air Force officer who helped arrest Kingston.

Tiffany Rice – Marine Corps colonel Kingston holds responsible for his arrest.

Josh Ericson – United States senator from Hawaii; married Kingston's ex-wife.

Fiona Ericson – Kingston's ex-wife; successful businesswoman.

Amy O'Leary– United States senator from Maryland.

Ben Fortum – Kingston family attorney; previously defended Richard Kingston.

Sue Ellen Del Monte – Congresswoman; powerful Democratic leader.

Franklin Del Monte – Husband to Sue Ellen.

Eric Hennen – Congressman; powerful Republican leader.

Arthur Alexander – Senator; older gentleman.

Civilians:

Jon Summers – Former Navy SEAL; retired admiral.

Matt Summers – Jon's younger brother.

Karen Summers – Matt's wife.

Sean Summers – Oldest son of Jon and Nancy Summers; Sarah's husband.

Stephen Summers – Youngest son of Jon and Nancy Summers.

Becky O'Keefe – Sarah's mom; friend of the Summers family; a doctor.

Bill Gateway – Sarah's grandfather; friend of the Summers family; a retired general.

Kevin Gateway – Sarah's uncle; CEO of the family business, Webber Media.

Timothy Gerard Evans – Alias for Patrick O'Keefe, former IRA gunman and CIA operative; retired to the Bahamas.

George Ellison – Retired Marine Corps general.

Charles Naylor – Retired Army general.

Allen Wiedenkeller – Retired Navy master chief petty officer; Kayli's father.

George Reardon – Retired Army sergeant major.

Chet Shomakker – Retired Marine Corps sergeant major.

Walter Samcevic – Retired Navy SEAL; author.

Maggie Crogan – Owner of the Mohawk Tavern and Grill; full-blooded Mohawk.

Fred Crogan – Maggie's father; Mohawk tribal leader.

Isaiah (Issy) Upton – Owner of a marina in Bluffton, New York.

Nathan Crogan – Maggie's oldest child and Army veteran.

Sandy Monroe – Nationally known reporter on a major TV network.

★ PROLOGUE ★

WOLVES

Algonquin Park
Ontario, Canada
July 17, 2010
0800 hours

The water lapped against the rocky shoreline in a soft and relaxing rhythm. A gentle breeze tousled the silver fur of a large alpha wolf as he drank from the lake—pausing to look up only after catching a peculiar scent. He stood perfectly still, elevating his snout into the air. The scent was unfamiliar— and close. The alpha female behind him released a low growl, indicating she perceived a threat.

The alpha male lowered his nose, staring over the water at the man sitting in a canoe. He knew this man. Every day for the last several weeks, the man had watched them, always keeping a respectable distance. Today was no different.

One of the other members of the pack also started growling, signaling danger. The alpha glanced over his shoulder. Members of the pack were focused to the right; that was the same direction the scent was coming from. He turned back to face the man in the canoe, who watched the pack intently.

The man was doing something he'd always wanted to do—volunteer to help the Ministry of Natural Resources research the Source Lake wolf pack they'd been following since late April. The pack had come to accept his presence and no longer ran away every time they sensed him near. He noticed the alpha female caught the scent of something to the west, and he guessed it wasn't food by the way she was acting. Meanwhile, the alpha male was watching him intently. The man allowed the canoe to drift closer to where the pack was drinking along the shoreline; he'd learned that if he sat quietly, the pack would go on with life uninterrupted.

When the last member of the pack moved forward to drink the cool water from the lake, there was a metallic flash from the trees to the west. The man watched the area, but he didn't see the metallic flash again. His curiosity was piqued; that was the same direction the alpha female's attention was directed. He waited a minute and then turned his attention back to the pack. The alpha male was still watching the man in his canoe as the last of the pack finished hydrating.

Suddenly, the man saw the flash again. This time, it was followed by the sound of metal clashing against metal. In unison, the pack sprinted for the cover of the forest. The man in the canoe looked to the west, eyes searching again for that metallic flash. Just as soon as he'd begun to assume that he and the wolves were worrying for nothing, there was a different kind of flash, and the air exploded with the sound of gunfire. Spires of water erupted around the canoe, causing it to capsize and send its occupant into the lake.

The gunfire stopped. Two young men clad in camouflage clothing stepped out from the cover of the trees, each carrying an assault rifle equipped with a scope. One laughed, taking off his camouflage hat and revealing bushy, dark hair. He pointed to the capsized canoe, saying something quietly to his companion that inspired more laughter. They reloaded their rifles and fired again at the capsized canoe. When both rifles were empty, they lowered their weapons, laughing again.

"I don't see a body floating anywhere, do you?" the bushy-haired man asked his partner, who shook his head, reloading. "Don't see him swimming, either. Must have gone under when we hit him with the first burst."

"Probably, but the profile on this guy said he was a good swimmer. You stay here and cover me while I go beyond those trees over there to make sure he didn't come ashore." He pointed down the shoreline to where several windfalls leaned into the lake. "Chances are you're right and we got him, but we're being paid well for this. The boss won't tolerate any mistakes. Let's make sure he's at the bottom of the lake."

His friend nodded. "I hate the woods; I just want to get out of here. Get to it, and we can be back to Toronto by dinner."

"Hey, I'm a city boy too." The second man laughed. "The sooner I'm out of here, the better."

The second man moved off toward the windfalls about fifty yards away, carrying his rifle with its muzzle pointed up. He moved as close to the shoreline as he could, but on several occasions needed to sidestep large rocks or climb over a fallen tree.

The first man smiled, watching his partner struggle to get over to where the trees were leaning into the water. He considered it a relief to get out of the Canadian wilderness and back to the United States, as the idea of having killed a man in a foreign country wasn't one he liked. As his friend disappeared into the forest, he focused his attention on the capsized canoe, which was drifting offshore. There was still no sign of the man they'd been sent to kill.

A sudden sound of crashing branches and a scream drew the man's attention back to the forest. A second later, there was the sound of a rifle being fired, then silence. He raised his rifle, pointing it in the direction of the disturbance. For every second that passed without a sound from his partner, the man felt his panic rise higher.

Looking along the shoreline, he yelled, "Leo? You okay?"

There was no response to his hail.

"Leo? Come on, man. Don't mess with me. Leo?"

His calls were met with silence. He looked around but saw no movement from where his friend had disappeared into the forest. A low growl from behind him caused him to swing around, rifle up and ready. Twenty feet in front of him was a large gray wolf, crouched low to the ground, teeth bared. Behind the wolf were several more canines—smaller, but just as menacing. The alpha didn't move forward, but held his ground, continuing to growl his warning.

The man had no way of knowing he was too close to the pack's den— that he was being warned away by the pack leader—and so he pointed the rifle at the threat in front of him and pulled the trigger.

There was a click, but nothing else happened.

He felt the panic starting to move up into his throat as he realized he hadn't changed the magazine after emptying it into the canoe. Reflexively, he ejected the empty magazine, reaching for one of the loaded magazines he kept in his vest pocket. He fumbled trying to insert it because it was backward. There was movement in his peripheral vision, and he was hit hard by something big. A scream followed, echoing across the lake.

CHAPTER ONE

REVELATIONS

FBI Offices
New York City
July 18, 2010
0930 hours

The Joint Weapons Task Force consisted of agents from the Federal Bureau of Investigation, the Bureau of Alcohol, Tobacco, Firearms and Explosives, investigators from the New York City Police Department, and the New York State Police. Their mission was to intercept weapons and explosives entering the country through the Port of New York and build criminal cases against those involved. The previous night, a New York City Transit officer had made a routine stop at Kennedy Airport, stumbling onto an explosive smuggling operation. Two suspects were taken into custody by the officer and his partner, and the NYPD called the task force due to the involvement of military-grade explosives. When the suspects resisted, one of the transit officers ended up in the hospital. Backup arrived quickly, subduing the two men who were still resisting when brought into the building.

A records check determined the suspects were tied to a nationwide gang known for smuggling drugs and weapons into the United States. The FBI notified the Department of Homeland Security and the United States Attorney's Office. Because of the implied threat to national security, Homeland Security was looking at issuing one of their many alerts, while the US Attorney's Office sent representatives to monitor the interrogation.

Michael J. Trask was the assistant United States attorney who drew the assignment that Sunday morning. Trask's reputation for being thorough when building his cases preceded him, as did his impressive record of winning most of the cases he worked on. He was a good listener, with a quiet and unassuming manner, and was a straight shooter when it came to dealing with investigations, investigators, witnesses, and suspects. His firm-but-fair attitude made him popular with defense attorneys, although they were more inclined to deal with him out of court. They, too, liked to boast about winning records.

A call at home had notified him of the arrest. He wanted to arrive at the FBI office before they brought the suspects in. Trask asked one of his assistants, Tina Ramsey, to respond with him, because she was an excellent notetaker. She would be an asset to him while he conducted his own investigation. His boss had directed him to bring one of the new attorneys the Department of Justice hired right out of law school, but he hated being a babysitter. He wasn't happy about being called in on his day off, and this made his mood even fouler, but there wasn't any other option. Ramsey and the new attorney met him at the FBI offices to save time. She was younger than Ramsey and seemed nice enough. He'd been told her name over the phone but hadn't bothered writing it down, as she was to observe and nothing more. Knowing her name wasn't important.

Trask smiled while watching the agents bring in the two suspects. Both men—one was rough around the edges, with shaggy, dark hair, missing teeth, and tattoos, while the other was bald with a full beard—were in handcuffs, according to procedure.

Trask glanced at the new attorney shadowing him for the day. She stood silently with a steno pad in hand, eyes on the subjects as their handlers moved their handcuffs from behind their backs to in front of their bellies.

What came next unfolded so quickly, Trask nearly couldn't follow it.

The bald suspect, temporarily uncuffed, slipped free of his handler. He was at once pursued by the two handlers and another agent. The first to reach the suspect was met with a fist to the face, and before the others could respond in kind, the suspect yanked Trask's new attorney by the wrist and reeled her up against his chest.

Trask began to panic when he saw several agents draw their weapons. He and the supervising agent exchanged concerned looks. A quick glance over his shoulder revealed Ramsey was safely behind him and the responding agents.

The suspect slowly backed away from the gathering agents who were ordering him to release his hostage. The expression on the young attorney's face changed from surprise and fear to one of anger. The man's arms were around her, pinning her arms at her sides. She initially stepped backward with her captor as he moved in the direction of the door, making the escape easier. As though realizing this, Trask watched as the woman's head dropped, her legs going limp, much like a toddler throwing a fit.

The suspect was suddenly dragging the young woman. There was a look of surprise on the man's face. It appeared that he and the pursuing agents hadn't seen what Trask had and assumed the woman had passed out. But Trask knew better, watching the young woman's hands ball up into fists. Suddenly, her legs pushed her body up hard. She deliberately pushed her head back, catching the man in the nose. He howled in pain. As his captive came back down, she drove the heel of her right foot into the top of his, and he screamed again, loosening his hold, allowing her to twist partially free. Their feet and legs intertwined, causing them to fall to the floor, the new attorney on top. When the suspect tried to get up, she brought her right arm around, catching him in the throat. The blow was not fatal, but it slowed the man significantly, allowing agents to subdue and drag him away.

"Get a paramedic up here!" shouted the supervising agent, who was now kneeling next to the young lawyer. He redirected his attention to her. "Are you okay, young lady?"

She propped herself up, rubbing her temple. Trask knelt beside the two of them, utterly shocked over what had just unfolded. Up close, he had to admit that this new attorney was pretty, with strawberry-blonde hair and blue eyes. There were no tears as she responded, "I think I'm okay, except for this bump on the back of my head."

They watched as four agents dragged the suspect off to the waiting interrogation room, blood flowing freely from his nose as they moved him quickly past the small group gathered around the woman on the floor. The suspect was no longer resisting. The supervising agent took her hand, moving it away so he could see the back of her head.

"What's your name?" he asked, parting her hair so he could see her scalp. There was some swelling, but no cut. She winced slightly as he inspected the injury.

"Cassie Summers—and can you stop touching that? It hurts like hell!"

"I imagine it does," responded the supervising agent. "After all, you broke his nose."

Trask turned, looking at the supervising agent, who handed the young woman the cold pack from a first aid kit. It was a good thing the agent had asked for the new attorney's name, because Trask hadn't remembered it. He glanced behind him and saw both his assistant and an FBI agent scribbling notes. When he turned back around, Cassie winced as she put the cold pack on the back of her head.

"That was a pretty gutsy move you did, Cassie," said the agent. "Where did you learn to do that?"

She smiled at the agent. "My dad was worried about my sister and me growing up, so he had my uncle teach us some self-defense tactics. He was in the Special Forces. I also had a cousin who was a Navy SEAL who taught me some stuff. I guessed if he got me out of this room, my chances for survival would decrease, so I couldn't let that happen."

A smirk crossed the agent's face. "You're pretty smart for someone your age. It looks like your uncle taught you more than just defensive tactics, because your evaluation of the situation was spot-on. Tell me, what's your cousin doing now? I could use him to teach my people a few things."

The expression on Cassie's face became very serious. "He was killed during a training accident. My family doesn't believe it, but…"

Nothing more was said, but both the agent and Trask exchanged looks.

Trask finally spoke. "Cassie, let's get you off the floor. Do you think you can stand?"

Cassie nodded, and Trask helped her up. Even though she seemed stable, he helped her to an empty chair in the next room, followed by the agent and Ramsey. Trask asked Ramsey to stay with Cassie as he and the senior agent walked back into the other room.

"She was good back there," said the agent. "I haven't seen her before."

"It's her first day on the job," responded Trask. "She was sent along last minute to observe. Right now, you know as much about her as I do."

The agent looked at the attorney next to him for a second, then grabbed the arm of another agent walking by. "Go get some basic information on Miss Summers in the other room. Do a quick background check on her and give Mr. Trask's office a call to see what they have as well. Michael, I'll let you call and let them know we'll be in touch, so they're not surprised. I don't expect to find anything, but it would be nice to know more about the person who just kicked my suspect's ass."

Trask laughed. "I blew her off this morning, so I better know more about her than I did five minutes ago or I'll get *my* ass kicked. I'll have my office forward everything they have."

The agent went off to do as he was told while Trask and the supervising agent moved to observe the interrogation.

Summers' Cabin
Adirondack State Park, New York
July 18, 2010
0930 hours

Nancy Summers walked out to the front porch of the main cabin and rested her elbows on the railing of the deck. Several other cabins lined a dirt path, which led to the boathouse perched on the edge of Shadow Lake. After her in-laws passed away, the camp was passed to Jon, his brother, Matt, and his sister, Julie. They kept it as rustic and simple as they could. There was electricity in the main cabin and boathouse, but the other buildings in the complex were off-grid. The electricity was a recent addition from when Nancy's mother-in-law discovered the wonderful world of computers. Nancy smiled, thinking fondly about her in-laws. She missed them.

The sound of an approaching motorboat drew her attention. Jon, her husband, was in Canada on an extended vacation. Ever since their middle son, Justin, had been reported dead in a Navy SEAL training accident, she and Jon had been at odds with each other for the first time in their marriage. Nancy knew about the type of accidents Navy SEALs experienced in the line of duty—even in training. Her husband, Jon, had been reported missing and presumed dead during a training accident himself for almost ten days before a Navy destroyer picked up both his team and some former POWs they rescued from Vietnam.

Nancy simply couldn't believe her son was dead. Not without a body. Not without undeniable evidence. She wasn't buying the Navy's training accident explanation. Besides, Jon didn't defend the Navy, which meant he didn't believe them either. She knew he was looking into Justin's death himself, likely using all the contacts he'd made over the years—as he should. Her issue was he wasn't talking to her about what he suspected. She knew he was trying to protect her, but it wasn't protection she wanted. All she wanted was the *truth*.

Nancy shielded her eyes from the early-morning glare off the water, trying to make out the boat headed toward the island. She suspected it was her daughter-in-law and the kids coming back from town. Sarah had taken them to pick up some groceries and hopefully meet her mother and grandfather, who were driving up from Albany.

She glanced at the other cabins on the compound. They were quiet. Everyone else was likely still asleep. Julie and her two kids were not early risers and probably wouldn't poke their heads out of their cabin until after ten o'clock. Matt's youngest daughter was there, too, and had worked late on her doctorate thesis in astronomy the night prior; Nancy didn't expect to see Emily until closer to noon, as she'd brought along her telescope and had spent a good portion of the night working. The stars, she'd claimed, were so clear and vivid compared to where she lived in Chicago, which she appreciated as a junior professor of astronomy.

Nancy's in-laws had been given the deed to the island—which was four square miles and located in the middle of Shadow Lake—from a local businessman who operated several resorts in the Adirondack State Park. Her father-in-law was a teacher and worked summers at one of the resorts, keeping it a success, so the businessman rewarded them with the island getaway and a cabin. Because many of the lakes in the area were connected by rivers, creeks, or channels, they would be able to commute to their summer jobs via boat. They started with one cabin and expanded each time the family grew. It now was a complex of four cabins, each able to comfortably house a family of eight, a boathouse, and two maintenance sheds that were the size of small barns. There were two towns within an easy boat ride of the island: the town of Dartford, located on the lower end of the lake, and the village of Bluffton, snuggled in the upper bay.

With the island being located at the center of a lake, the family kept several motorboats on-site, along with a large collection of canoes and kayaks for the kids and grandchildren. That morning, Sarah had taken the pontoon boat in case her mother and grandfather arrived, allowing for plenty of room on the return. The pontoon boat was a large, lumbering beast they used to haul big loads to and from the cabin. Jon's father, Ray, had purchased the boat years ago, after one of the locals had charged him an exorbitant amount of money to transport lumber out to the island when he was building one of the cabins. Within a week, Ray found and purchased the boat that was billed as a party boat. It was used for that purpose, as well as for hauling untold amounts of supplies and building materials. Sarah had learned to handle each of the boats like an expert, and that morning looked to be no different as she steered the vessel up to the dock, aligning it perfectly.

Having watched Sarah's approach, Nancy left her position on the porch and headed to the dock to help carry anything Sarah had picked up on her visit to Bluffton.

As she walked down the rocky path from the main cabin to the dock, her grandchildren came running toward her. RJ, short for Raymond Jonathan, was seven years old and in the lead. He was being followed by his five-year-old sister, Patty. Both had their father's strawberry-blond hair and fair skin, but Patty was the spitting image of her mother.

"Slow down, kids," said Nancy to the swiftly approaching children. "You know the rules. No running on the island."

"Okay, Grandma!" blurted RJ, racing passed his grandmother.

Patty stopped to hug Nancy's leg, squeezing tightly. "Love you, Grandma."

The respite was short-lived; the girl released her grip, racing off after her brother.

"Walk!" said Nancy with a raised voice, watching after her grandchildren. Both waved over their shoulders, continuing to run up the hill toward the cabin. She shook her head, smiling. When she turned back toward the dock, she saw her daughter-in-law grinning and shaking her head while tying off the boat.

"It's good to see someone as ineffective as I am. I'm constantly telling them to walk around the island, but they're so excited to be here. They only have one speed, and the only one they listen to is Dad."

Sarah looked ashamed she'd brought the subject up. Nancy smiled at her, waving a hand to dismiss the comment. "You're a hundred-percent right, Sarah. Jon has a way with them when they're here. This is his world, and they know it."

"I'm sorry, Mom," Sarah said softly. "I shouldn't have brought it up."

Nancy leaned over and hugged her daughter-in-law. "Sarah," she said, "I still love Jon, and we're not getting divorced unless one of us does something stupid. He knows something about Justin he's not sharing. A little time apart will let both of us cool off."

"The kids keep asking when he's coming to the island. I don't know what to tell them anymore."

Nancy forced a smile. She was having the same problem and was feeling the same frustration. She took a bag of groceries from Sarah and said, "I'm in the same boat. Say, weren't your mother and grandfather supposed to be along by this time?"

The question seemed to change the mood; Sarah was suddenly beaming.

"It appears the general," Sarah answered, referring to her grandfather, who had been a general in the Army, "remembered they make some first-class wines here in New York State, so he and Mom detoured to purchase some. They should be here by late afternoon."

Nancy laughed. "Wait until he sees all of the wine we have stashed here on the island."

Both women started up the hill to the main cabin, chatting happily.

Upton's Marina and Boat Sales
Bluffton, New York
July 18, 2010
0930 hours

Isaiah "Issy" Upton scratched his three-day-old beard while watching the group load several large crates onto his biggest pontoon boat. They'd rented it from him a short time before and were all strangers. He'd lived in Bluffton his entire life, leaving for only two years to serve in the Army during the Vietnam War, so he didn't consider himself an expert on people by any means. He wasn't comfortable with this group. They seemed to be on edge and had paid cash for the boat, not even bothering to haggle. They'd accepted his first price, paid in brand-new twenty-dollar bills, and claimed the crates they sought to transport contained construction materials for the Summers' place on the island.

Issy didn't think they looked like construction workers, and their cargo was in unlabeled crates. Not that he knew what the typical construction worker looked like, but this group looked to be dressed more for camping. There were fifteen men and five women, all dressed in long pants and boots. Nope, they didn't look like construction workers. If he guessed, they looked more like soldiers, because they wore those pants with all the pockets. The other thing that bothered him was Mrs. Summers hadn't mentioned anything to him about this. Even young Sean's wife hadn't said anything when she was in town earlier.

He stepped out of the shop and walked toward the man who was in charge. He was a good-looking kid—at about five feet nine, he was about three inches shorter than Issy but was arguably in better shape—and was in his late thirties or early forties.

"May I help you, Mr. Upton?" Ron Hapke asked, eyeing Issy.

Issy didn't care for Mr. Hapke, because he didn't smile and conveyed an attitude of superiority, but there was no avoiding this interaction. Issy nodded at the crates being loaded into the pontoon boat. "Mr. Hapke, those boxes look pretty heavy. You want me to get you some help for them? I'll call a couple of my guys if you want."

Mr. Hapke scowled. "We're all set, thank you, Mr. Upton. We won't be too long here."

"I just thought I'd see if we could help," said Issy. "You sure you won't need help on the other end?"

Hapke's scowl didn't leave his face. Just as he was about to respond, the cell phone in the man's pocket chirped, indicating he'd just received a text message. Hapke kept his harsh gaze fixed on Issy while he pulled the phone from his pocket and looked at the screen. The message read, "Stay cool, get rid of him."

Hapke put the phone back in his pocket. The message had been sent from an unknown number. Looking around, he didn't see anyone who might have sent the message moving about the street between the marina and the line of stores opposite it. The sender had to be the mysterious, faceless person who'd hired him to put this job together. They both seemed to have the same goal of getting even with Jon Summers, which was why he'd taken the job. The money was excellent, and the bonus of getting even with Summers's sister was an incentive. There were larger things at work here he didn't care about, and the fact he'd never met the person who hired him didn't bother him. Contact was always over the phone, and the voice was always scrambled, so he couldn't even say if it was a male or a female.

"Thank you for your offer, Mr. Upton," answered Hapke, "but we're all set."

"Suit yourself, Mr. Hapke." Issy looked at one of his employees, who was working on a nearby boat for a tourist. "Eddie, I'm going for coffee."

The man looked over at Issy and waved. "Okay, boss! We got it under control."

Issy looked back at the leader of the group. "You have a good day now, Mr. Hapke."

Hapke didn't respond, turning away to watch his people put the second of two RIBs into the water. The first one was already in the water, outfitted with two outboard motors attached to the stern. Issy made a mental note and headed across the street to the Mohawk Bar and Grill on the corner of Lake and Adirondack Streets. He looked over his shoulder, noticing Hapke was watching him.

Mohawk Tavern and Grill
Bluffton, New York
July 18, 2010
0935 hours

The woman sat at the table facing a large window overlooking the street, with the marina and dock beyond. She had all the trappings of a tourist so as not to arouse the suspicions of the locals. Her cell phone revealed her last outgoing text message: "Stay cool, get rid of him."

The marina owner—Mr. Isaiah Upton—clearly realized something was up, but Ron Hapke had done a good job of ending the conversation. Hapke wasn't her first choice to lead this mission, but he had the right motivation: he hated Jon Summers and the Summers family. He was also greedy and easily manipulated, which made him an acceptable choice, just not her first one. Regardless, her boss insisted he was the best fit, even though he had a reputation for being hot-tempered and a loose cannon. Not a good mix for an operation such as theirs. He appeared to have successfully completed the first phase of the operation in Canada by selecting two of his more ruthless men to complete the job. They'd sent a text that it was done.

Isaiah Upton walked past the woman sitting alone near the window, not noticing she was watching him. The Mohawk Tavern and Grill was the only restaurant and saloon within the village limits and, like many of these older establishments, was expansive enough to take up most of the small block. At one time, it'd been a hotel. It no longer served that purpose, and the rooms on the second floor served as the residence for the current owners. The entire first floor consisted of the restaurant and tavern.

Issy walked up to the counter, taking a seat on one of the stools. The food there was excellent, and the coffee was the best in the county as far as Issy was concerned. Even better than his wife's coffee, but he wasn't about to say that out loud. Maggie Crogan, who owned the Mohawk, was his wife's best friend, and he didn't want to cause any trouble at home.

Maggie was a full-blooded Mohawk and a matriarch in the local American Indian society. Issy didn't know the culture well, but he understood Maggie was a good friend and good neighbor. She ran the restaurant with the help of her five children, as well as her father, who added his own brand of Native American flavor to the place.

Brandi, the youngest of the five kids, walked out from the kitchen when Issy took his seat. She was young—seventeen—and a typical teenager. She was the spitting image of her mother. She nodded to Issy, pouring a mug of coffee and placing it in front of him without saying a word. He came in often enough that everyone knew what he wanted at any given time of day.

"Thank you, Brandi," he said, looking around the room. This was when he noticed the lone woman by the window being the only other customer. She sat at the window overlooking the marina and dock beyond and had her cell phone out in front of her. "You're too kind to an old man."

"And you're too predictable, Mr. Upton," Brandi said with a giggle. "Can I get you anything else?"

Upton smiled. She also had a sense of humor like her mother. "I'm looking for Abby or Stephen if they're around. I need to ask them something."

"Abby took Mama to church, but I think Stephen is out back with Grandpa," Brandi answered. "I'll go get him." She smiled at the older man and turned to enter the kitchen. She pushed open the two-way door, raising her voice. "Nathan, I'm going out back to get Stephen for Mr. Upton; I'll be right back."

As quick as she'd disappeared beyond the swinging door, the head of Nathan Crogan popped into sight through the pass-through window. "How are you doing, Mr. Upton? Can I get you anything?"

Issy shook his head, smiling at the young man. "Doing good, Nathan. Brandi already got me my coffee," he said, holding up the full mug. He took a sip. *Good and hot.*

Nathan nodded, grinning. "Just call me if you need anything, sir. I'm just getting the lunch special ready."

With that, Nathan's head disappeared.

Maggie had done well after her husband died of cancer. He'd been older than her and served in Vietnam. The doctors told her that the cancer was caused by his exposure to Agent Orange. He was a shrewd real-estate investor and left Maggie and the kids with a small fortune. Maggie's tastes were simple, so she pooled the money from the investments and opened the Mohawk. Because she wasn't afraid of hard work, she made that a success and lived a comfortable life. She passed her work ethic on to her kids, and they made a good living here in Bluffton. Nathan, like his father, served in the Army, spending a tour in Iraq. Stephen was the youngest of the Summers boys, from out on the island. He had been seriously injured in a helicopter crash in Iraq and made Bluffton his year-round home, having taken up with the oldest daughter of the Crogan family, Abby. They had known each other since they were kids, as Stephen's grandfather Ray and Abby's grandfather Fred were friends. Both the Summers boys, Jon and Matt, spent quite a bit of time with the old Indian. He taught them how to track, hunt, and fish.

The sound of boat motors coming to life shifted Issy's attention out the window. The big pontoon boat was headed out to the Summers' place, easing away from the dock and moving slowly into the channel. Along with all the crates, he counted five people on board. Hapke certainly was pushing the capacity of the boat. The other fifteen people were divided into the two RIBs, following the pontoon boat out of the marina.

"You wanted to see me, Issy?"

Upton jumped when he heard Stephen's voice. He was so focused on the boats leaving his marina, he never heard the boy walk in. Behind him stood old Fred, who nodded a hello to Issy. The old man didn't talk much. Stephen was tall, with a full head of shaggy, light-brown hair and had grown a beard since he arrived two years before. Fred was about two inches shorter than Summers, with long dark hair laced with the occasional streak of gray that fell to the middle of his back. He had a solid build, and his weathered face gave him the look of the wise old Indian from the Western movies. No one knew exactly how old Fred was, but Issy guessed him to be in his seventies. He also guessed he was teaching the boy how to be stealthy.

"Sorry, Issy, I didn't mean to scare you." Stephen's smile was warm and friendly.

Issy returned the smile, noticing the woman near the window had turned to face them. When she saw old Fred, her mouth dropped open. He was quite a sight if you didn't know what to expect. Fred didn't respond in any way, but it was obvious he saw the woman's reaction. When the woman realized she was gawking, she turned away. Fred glanced at the two men, his eyes sparkling with delight. He winked but didn't crack a smile.

"Stephen," Issy managed to say while stifling a laugh, "is your mother having some work done out on the island today?"

Stephen thought for a second or two before answering.

"I wouldn't think so . . . it's Sunday. Besides, Uncle Matt and Aunt Karen are supposed to come today, as well as Sarah's mom and grandfather. She wouldn't schedule any work with so many people showing up."

Issy pointed to the three boats headed out of the bay into the lake. "There are three full boats of people and materials headed to the island right now. I thought that seemed funny because your mom would have said something to me about it. If they were working for her, why would they rent a pontoon boat? Wouldn't your mom have sent hers?"

Stephen's eyes narrowed as he peered through the window at the pontoon boat cutting across the lake. The boy wouldn't lie to him—that Issy knew—and besides, everything he'd said made sense. Something wasn't adding up. She would have told him about any major project and made sure that Stephen, Sean, or Matt would have been there to supervise. Issy knew Matt would be leaving New York City later that day and Sean was scheduled to arrive tomorrow. With Jon and Nancy separated, he guessed this was an issue for Stephen.

It was Fred who broke the strained silence. "Call your mother, boy."

Stephen nodded, walking over to the cash register, where a phone hung on the wall. He took the handset and quickly punched in the number for the island. The line was busy. He replaced the handset, giving the other two men a worried look. He knew everyone's cell phone on the island would be off. He would have to wait.

FBI Offices
New York City
July 18, 2010
1000 hours

Cassie sat alone in the senior agent's office. It wasn't a small office, but it wasn't huge either. She held the ice pack on the back of her head while running through the events of the morning one more time. She received the call to come into work early. They had wanted her to observe Trask while he worked with the Joint Weapons Task Force. She had been informed this was to be her permanent assignment. She wasn't assigned to be the lead attorney, but she was excited by the assignment nonetheless—so much so that she hadn't minded coming in on her day off. Her parents had spent the weekend with her and were leaving for their cabin. She would see them next weekend and would have quite the story to tell.

The ice pack must've been working because the bump on the back of her head seemed less painful. She reminded herself to thank her uncle Jon the next time she saw him. A smile crossed her face as she remembered the scream of pain the man had made when she broke his nose. She'd proved she wasn't defenseless, and he was now charged with attempted escape and attempted kidnapping. The smile disappeared when she remembered her uncle's advice: *Don't ever get overconfident; that will get you killed.* Was she being overconfident? It was something to talk to her mother about. Her father would just worry.

Hearing voices coming down the hall, she pushed those thoughts aside. She recognized Trask's voice and that of the lead FBI agent, but not the third.

Trask poked his head in. "Cassie, would you come with us, please?"

He waited at the door while the FBI agent and the third man continued down the hall.

Cassie collected her purse and jacket, then joined them walking down the hallway. As their strides fell in sync, Trask asked, "How's the head?"

Cassie placed the ice pack back on her head as they moved. "Still a bit sore, sir. I think I'll have a headache for a while."

Trask snickered. "I must tell you, young lady, you put on quite a show in there. A room full of FBI agents, and the new assistant US attorney kicks a violent felon's ass. It certainly made my morning."

Cassie grinned—which in turn made her head hurt, causing her to wince with the pain.

The two men in front of them entered another office. Cassie and Trask followed them into a space that was considerably larger than the one she'd just left. Not only did this office have the typical desk and workspace, but it had a credenza and large conference table.

This new player was someone of importance.

The owner of the office held out his hand. "Miss Summers, my name is Glenn Grey. I'm the special agent in charge for the New York office of the FBI."

Cassie shook his hand, managing a weak smile that she hoped distracted from the fact that she was feeling a little overwhelmed. Grey appeared to be in his early fifties. He was a good-looking African American man with short dark hair that had just enough gray to make him look distinguished. He was tall with a medium build and a nice smile. Cassie's immediate impression from his tone and body language was he only dealt with facts and was skeptical about everything else. She knew she needed to make a good first impression with him, or her working relationship with the FBI would suffer.

Grey motioned to the chairs in front of the desk. "Please, take a seat. Make yourselves comfortable." He moved around the desk to his own chair and added, "Miss Summers, I know your uncle. I worked with the admiral some years ago on a case involving the Navy. He's an interesting man. I like him, even if he is a bit scary."

"How so?" Trask asked.

Grey looked at Cassie, as if to ask permission to speak plainly. She shrugged, and Grey smiled broadly. "Admiral Jon Summers is one of the best minds in the field of intelligence I've ever met. He's a former SEAL and Medal of Honor recipient and as crazy as they come. He used himself as bait to lure out and help us capture one of the biggest spy rings in our history. He was wounded in the process but still managed to keep most of the operation under the radar. If you're a bad guy, he's one of those people you don't want to come after you, because he *will* find you, and *when* he does . . ."

Trask grinned, raising his hand to stop Grey. "I don't think I need to hear any more on the matter." He gave Grey a pointed look, smirking. "Besides, I don't want to have to look into any of your past misdeeds, Glenn."

Grey laughed, folding his hands on his desk. "I was going to say *bring you in.* We got most of our bad guys alive, at least the main players. The ones who didn't make it decided their own fate."

Cassie noticed a picture that hung on the wall behind the desk. In the picture was a group of six people—five men and one woman—in front of a large aircraft with United States Air Force markings on it. One of the people in the photograph was a younger Glenn Grey, and another was her uncle, dressed in dirty camouflage khakis, leaning on a crutch.

Grey noticed her looking at the picture and gave her an approving smile. "Your actions today, young lady, show you might be as crazy as your uncle."

Cassie was shocked by the comment. "I'm sorry, I don't understand wha—"

"I don't mean that in a negative way," interjected Grey. "You showed great courage and ended a situation that was heading south quickly. If the suspect made it outside with you as a hostage, there could have been a more tragic ending to the incident. As it is, the suspect was so shaken by what happened that he waved his rights to an attorney and confessed to smuggling explosives into the country."

"Getting his ass kicked by a girl really messed with his ego," added the senior field agent, smirking. "He did a lot of talking to us before reality set back in and he lawyered up."

"Did he say who the explosives were for?" asked Cassie, taking the ice pack off her head and setting it on an empty chair.

Trask answered, "There's something going on up in the Adirondacks— that's where the stuff was headed. Some big operation. This guy was rambling on about a prison break of some kind. There are several prisons in the Adirondack area, and we've given them all a heads-up about the plan."

Grey furrowed his brows, visibly skeptical. "But I don't believe there are any high-profile prisoners in any of those prisons. The suspect specifically stated that the goal was to use the explosives to break out a high-profile prisoner."

"A gang member, maybe?" asked Cassie, trying to feel productive.

"No," answered Grey. "They're just the delivery guys on this one. They were paid to transport the explosives; they weren't part of the break."

There was a knock at the door, and another agent walked into the room. He handed Grey a piece of paper, closing the door quietly as he left. Grey looked at the paper, frowning.

"It seems," he said, "we have a Canadian Mounted Police inspector on his way to see us. They're working the case of an American who has disappeared in a park in Ontario that may be related to our explosives."

Both Trask and Cassie raised their eyebrows, looking at the SAC with interest.

Trask asked, "How so, Glenn?"

Grey frowned. "They're faxing their files, but it has to do with the potential escape of a high-profile criminal somewhere in upstate New York. They mention a place in Franklin County named Shadow Lake."

Cassie's heart sank. Her family was spending the weekend at their cabins on Shadow Lake.

Summers' Cabin
Adirondack State Park, New York
July 18, 2010
1015 hours

The boats came from different directions—three from the south and two from the north. All five were identical military-style RIBs. They were fast, each outfitted with double outboard engines and carrying a cargo of armed personnel. Two of the boats landed at the main dock, while the other three beached themselves at various locations near the cabins or the boathouse. The armed occupants raced ashore, weapons ready.

Nancy saw the group moving up from the dock. The sight of armed intruders on the island sent her out to the front of the cabin, screaming a warning to the other cabins. The closest of the interlopers raised his weapon, firing at Nancy, dropping her to the porch.

The man quickly reached the cabin, bounding up the steps, and found his victim at the same time Sarah did. The young woman, shockingly, showed no fear. She stared at him with ire in her eyes, moving to help the fallen woman. On the other side of the large picture window, the man saw two young children. They stood still, as though frozen, and watched their mother help their fallen grandmother with tears running down their terrified faces.

A quick examination showed no visible bullet wound. Nancy was conscious but obviously stunned. Sarah moved her mother-in-law's top just enough to examine the skin around her left shoulder. There was a deep-red bruise, indicating Nancy had been hit by some type of projectile designed to incapacitate rather than kill. For that, she was grateful, although she guessed Nancy would be sore for a while.

The other intruders moved quickly from cabin to cabin, collecting the others on the island. Emily was the second to be found, after Nancy. She was sleeping at the time of entry and didn't resist. She was bound behind her back using a zip tie and then escorted toward the main cabin, barefoot.

The intruders entering the cabin where Julie and her kids were staying weren't as lucky. The first man to enter through the door was taken by surprise. Julie lunged at him, knocking him off-balance and pushing him into the wall. But the second intruder, a woman, punched Julie in the face, knocking her to the floor. Julie was prostrate, stunned and bleeding.

Julie's twenty-year-old son, Hector, went after the woman, only for the third intruder to strike him down with a well-placed jab of a rifle butt. He ended up on the floor next to his mother, bleeding from a cut on his hairline. Alex, Julie's eighteen-year-old daughter, had been told by her older brother to climb out a window and hide in the heavy forest on the far end of the island. She made it out the window without incident but was grabbed and subdued by two armed men as soon as her feet hit the ground. She struggled but gave up when she realized she was no match for her larger and stronger captors. All three were bound in the same fashion as Emily and walked to the main cabin.

The hostages were ushered to the main sitting area overlooking the lake. It was a large, two-story cabin that included a fireplace, a kitchenette, and multiple bedrooms both on the top and bottom stories. A single chemical toilet was located downstairs.

When the others were brought into the cabin, they found Nancy sitting in one of the easy chairs in the living room with a makeshift ice pack on her shoulder. It was clear that she'd been crying, and Sarah was hovering over her. RJ and Patty sat on one of the sofas, looking scared and holding each other as they watched the procession enter the cabin. Two armed intruders stood guard over them.

Emily was sat on the couch next to RJ and Patty. Meanwhile, Julie, Hector, and Alex were thrown down on the second sofa. The two men watching the captives remained, while the others left to continue their search of the complex. There was the sound of a dog barking, immediately followed by gunshots, then silence. The hostages exchanged horrified glances, knowing the barking dog had been Kuma, their family pet. The family's wide eyes and worried expressions indicated they were at war with what had just happened: Had Kuma been shot and killed, or had the one-hundred-pound Akita gotten away, chased off by the first gunshot? Kuma had been Justin's dog, adopted by Jon and Nancy after their son was reported killed. He was a good dog, gentle and friendly with the kids, and responded well to the rest of the family. It would be like losing a family member to discover that he'd been shot.

Sarah moved to the couch where Julie and her children were. "I need some supplies from the kitchen or bathroom to help these people."

The guard closest to her looked at his comrade and spoke. "What was that?"

The second guard, who was standing in front of the big picture window in the room, shook his head. "Don't know, can't see a thing. The intel report on this place said there was a large dog here. I'm guessing that's been taken care of."

Patty started to cry softly. "Kuma . . ."

Both guards gave her an irritated look.

Emily, her hands still tied behind her back, gently moved closer to the two children while angrily looking at the armed men. Patty cuddled close to the young woman, while RJ still held his sister's hand.

"I still need some help here to stop the bleeding on this head injury," blurted out Sarah, trying to get the guards' attention.

This time, both guards looked at her, but neither responded. Nancy glared at the two men, starting to get up out of the chair she was sitting in, when the man closest to her turned, pointing his weapon at her. "Lady, my rifle isn't loaded with rubber bullets. If you move, I'll shoot you, and I promise it'll hurt more than the last time."

Nancy indignantly followed the man's orders. "RJ, honey, come take this ice pack from Grandma and take it over to Aunt Julie. Mommy will show you what to do with it."

Without a sound or hesitation, RJ climbed off the sofa, taking the ice pack from Nancy, and carried it over to Sarah. She quietly told RJ where to place it on Julie's face as she tended to Hector's injury. RJ did as he was told, smiling at the encouragement given by his mother and Julie.

The door suddenly opened, and a female intruder walked in, laughing.

"What's so funny, Servati?" asked the guard closest to the door. "What was all the shooting for?"

The woman looked around the room, a big smile on her face. "Perkins was checking one of the barns on the island and that big dog listed in the intel reports surprised him. He tried to shoot the dog, but it got away into the woods."

Patty gave an audible giggle of approval, while the rest of the captives smiled at each other. The three intruders looked annoyed but said nothing.

"The boss is on the pontoon boat with the others; let's make sure we have room for everyone."

In the distance, the sound of a powerful motor from a large boat carried over the lake.

FBI Offices
New York City
July 18, 2010
1045 hours

Cassie's concern over the mention of an issue at Shadow Lake was obvious. Grey was quick to assure her the information was specific to a prison break and there were several prison facilities in the area. He was sure her family was in no danger. With her present, he put in a call to the New York State Police and the Franklin County Sheriff's Office. He also sent his senior field agent to check on the interrogations. The state police issued an alert to all its substations and units currently on patrol in eight counties of upstate New York. Being Sunday, the Franklin County sheriff, Martin James, was not in the office. The dispatcher told Grey they would contact him and have him return the FBI's call as soon as he checked in. In the meantime, they, too, were putting out the alert to the deputies on patrol.

Grey peered across his desk at the young woman and offered her a look of reassurance.

"You see," he said, "everything is fine. All the law enforcement agencies in the area are on top of it. I don't see anything happening there, especially now, since we've intercepted the explosives."

Cassie smiled weakly. "Then why am I not reassured, Agent Grey?" she asked, unable to disguise her worry. The only way she'd feel better might be to see her family for herself, to call them, even. "I really want to believe you, but I just don't believe in coincidences."

"Now you sound like your uncle." Grey laughed. "He said that on more than one occasion when we worked together."

Grey glanced at the picture on the wall, prompting Trask and Cassie to do the same.

"Where was that picture taken?" asked Trask.

"There was a time not too long ago I couldn't answer that question. It was in the Philippines in 1995."

"It looks like your uncle was injured in some way, Cassie," Trask said, nodding again at the photo. In it, Cassie's uncle had blood splattered over his clothes and face.

"Not injured—wounded," Grey corrected.

"What's the difference? Isn't that just semantics?"

"To be wounded suggests external harm, whereas injury can be accidental or even the result of self-affliction." Grey turned his attention to Cassie. "Your uncle was wounded while he rescued the people who were being held hostage."

Trask raised an eyebrow. "That was *when?*"

Grey smiled. "I already told you: in the Philippines in March of 1995."

Trask's eyes widened, the significance of the date sinking in. Grey held the man's gaze but said no more. Trask looked at his subordinate, who had returned to pressing the ice pack against the back of her head. "Cassie, did you know?"

Cassie smiled, knowing that she'd just gained more credibility with her boss, thanks to Uncle Jon. Grey was referring to the rescue of World War II veterans from the Philippines in 1995. She hadn't known her uncle was part of the rescue, although she wasn't surprised. He was involved in so much more than the family was aware of that very little surprised her anymore.

There was a knock at the door, and the senior field agent entered carrying a folder. Grey looked at him, and the agent answered the unasked question. "These guys appear to be just couriers for the explosives. They know very little, except they were supposed to meet some people in Dartford. We've passed this on to the Franklin County Sheriff's Office and the Dartford Police

Department. They're checking, but they have no high-priority prisoners in custody there."

Grey turned to Cassie. "What can you tell me about Dartford, Miss Summers?"

Cassie thought for a couple of seconds. "It's a resort town, both summer and winter. The lake is good for fishing, and there's plenty of game for the hunters. It has a couple of bars, a marina, and a police department of three: two full-time and one part-time. It's a pretty quiet town, all things considered."

Grey stroked his chin. "This doesn't make any sense to me. Everything is pointing to something big happening in the Shadow Lake area—a prison break is what's described, but there's nothing high profile on the radar in that area. It just doesn't make sense."

"Can I worry now?" asked Cassie with a serious tone.

Grey ignored her comment, looking back at his senior field agent. "What else do you have for us?"

The man smiled weakly and said, "They identified the missing American in Canada from yesterday. They're flying the RCMP representative in on a military flight tonight with some of the details, but their current information points to the same thing as our interrogations here. Something big is about to happen in the Adirondack area of New York."

Grey took the folder handed to him, opened it, and began to read.

His eyes widened.

"You're right, Cassie—this isn't a coincidence."

Summers' Cabin
Adirondack State Park, New York
July 18, 2010
1100 hours

Nancy's shoulder was in pain. The bruise had deepened, turning into a welt. Her hands were now secured behind her back with a plastic zip tie, and the discomfort of the position aggravated her shoulder even more.

The intruders had found every cell phone on the island, turning each one off. The landline that ran into the main cabin rang off and on, but the intruders ignored it. Before long, several large boats arrived at the dock, and people began moving heavy items.

Nancy could hear voices outside but couldn't make out what was being said. She looked around the room and saw fear in everyone's eyes. Sarah worked on her sister-in-law and nephew, bravely tending to their injuries; she'd already cleaned both of their faces and had been allowed to get some ice from the kitchen to reduce the swelling. She was so cool under pressure, Nancy thought, and reminded Nancy of her mother. It bothered her that Sarah was a prisoner again, just as she had been fifteen years before, when she and her family had been prisoners in the Philippines. Now, her grandchildren were also prisoners, and that angered Nancy more than anything. No child should go through this. She wished she and Jon weren't having trouble, wished that he were here with them, because he would know what to do.

The door opened, and two men with rifles walked in, followed by an old man, his hands secured behind his back like everyone else in the room. He looked familiar, but Nancy couldn't place where she knew him from. A few seconds later, another man entered, his hands bound the same way. He was followed by a female whom Nancy recognized as a politician from Washington, but the name escaped her. The next person through the door was also a woman. This time, Nancy immediately recognized her as Senator Amy O'Leary. O'Leary recognized Nancy as well, moving toward her after being pushed forward by one of the guards. Another man, whom Nancy also recognized as a politician, entered behind O'Leary. He was followed by another old acquaintance, Fiona Ericson. Following Fiona, two more male prisoners carried Fiona's husband, Josh.

Josh Ericson had been one of Jon's teammates thirty years before, during Jon's first deployment to the Philippines after graduating from Annapolis, and was wounded on a mission, losing the use of both legs. He had gone on to be a successful businessman in Honolulu after his medical discharge and was elected to the United States Senate in 2000 and reelected in 2006. Being the junior senator from the fiftieth state and a Republican, he was gaining notoriety as one of his party's leaders. Ericson had been friends with his wife, Fiona, since he had lost the use of his legs. She had been married to a man who had tried to kill Jon. That man was in prison. Fiona divorced him when she learned of the murder attempt and the fact he had had an affair. Nancy knew Fiona's father-in-law had supported her during the divorce and endorsed her courtship and marriage to Ericson. His son's dishonor affected the entire family. Even though there were three other children, the old man had apparently had a fondness for his former daughter-in-law. Perhaps it was her quiet dignity that had appealed to him—but either way, upon his death, he'd left Fiona her former husband's share of the family fortune. No one objected.

Nancy struggled to her feet when she saw Josh being carried in. The guard closest to her turned, pointing his weapon at her. She raised her hands, nodding at Josh. "Put him in the chair—I can use the floor."

There were a few seconds of strained silence as Nancy and the guard stared at each other. Nancy was surprised by how calm she was with a rifle pointed at her. The guard didn't respond but ordered the two men carrying Josh to place him in the chair. Nancy exhaled a quiet sigh of relief, repositioning herself on the hard wooden floor.

As soon as she'd sat down, the cabin's front door flew open yet again, and two more female prisoners were led in by Servati.

Nancy looked to the captives following Servati. It had been years since she'd seen either of them, but she recognized Tiffany Rice and Judy Demmer. Both women recognized her in turn.

The hostages were corralled into the center of the room. One of the men carrying Josh smiled at Nancy. She recognized Mark Wells. What did a retired NCIS agent have to do with the rest of them? What common denominator did all of these people share?

Only one thing—or person, rather—came to mind. Jon!

She had the terrible feeling something from Jon's past was coming back to haunt them, threatening her family.

United States Disciplinary Barracks
Fort Leavenworth, Kansas
July 18, 2010
1005 hours

The guard held Richard Kingston up at the door to his cell until the radio squawked the entire way to the meeting room was clear. He then allowed him to move out into the hallway. This section of the military prison was for prisoners in solitary confinement. Kingston had come to enjoy the solitude away from the other inmates; he didn't want to interact with them, and the fact one or more of them might try to kill him for his past sins reinforced that feeling every day. He'd passed information on to an organization that had paid him well, and Americans had died because of what he'd done. The government called it espionage, but he looked at it as a simple business transaction. He found it strange his fellow inmates would have a code of ethics regarding killing and would want him dead; after all, many of them were in here for doing the same thing. They weren't convicted of betraying their country, though. That alone put a target on his back. He guessed it wasn't that he didn't want to interact with his fellow inmates as much as it was that he didn't want to tempt them to do what they all likely wanted to—which was kill him.

The pair moved silently down the corridor, passing the other cells in the block. Another guard stood at the end of the hallway, where the bars on a closed sliding door blocked their way. There was a loud alarm blast as the barred door suddenly began to open, allowing them to pass. The second guard led the way through, followed by Kingston, then the first guard. On the other side of the door, two more guards stood at their posts behind a desk. Once they passed through the doorway, the alarm sounded again, and the large steel bars began to close behind them. The two guards remained with him while he navigated through several more doors and was brought to a small visiting room.

The room was empty, except for a telephone that sat on the table in the center of the room. The guards at the disciplinary barracks were all Army personnel, and a staff sergeant was at the entrance to the room.

"Kingston," said the sergeant politely, "the call from your lawyer's office is on line one. Once you're in and settled, just pick up the receiver and push the flashing button."

Kingston hated being treated like a child by the guards, but he knew they took the same attitude with every other prisoner. They showed little emotion when they dealt with him, but Kingston suspected if he were ever caught by the other inmates, he could expect little, if any, help from any guards. He had fallen from grace, and no one in this institution could be trusted to help him.

Kingston smiled. "Thank you, Staff Sergeant."

He entered the room, closing the door behind him, and took a seat on one of the chairs at the table. He picked up the receiver, pushed down the flashing button, and said, "This is Richard Kingston."

"It's good to hear your voice, Admiral," said a pleasant female voice on the other end. "How are you feeling?"

"It depends on your news about my appeal," Kingston replied stonily.

"All the witnesses have been subpoenaed, and we will be presenting your case later today. We expect a quick ruling on the case. We have some powerful witnesses on your behalf. You should be optimistic about this."

"Any estimate on how long the jury will be out?"

"Our best guess is it won't take more than two days. We expect the prosecution to try to fight it, but we have some surprises ready for them. Believe me when I tell you we're ready for anything. I'm quite confident this appeal for you and Lt. Handcock will be successful."

Kingston smiled at the mention of his former aide and lover. Andrea Handcock, too, had been sentenced to life in prison for her part in the attempt to help a Japanese crime syndicate take over the Philippine island of Mindanao. He hadn't seen her in over a dozen years, but they kept in touch by letter. Her picture was one of the few personal items he maintained in his cell. Even after everything that had taken place, she'd stood by him. His senior aide, Stephen Williams, had rolled over, testifying against the two of them at their court-martials. He'd apparently struck a deal and was sentenced to twenty years in a medium-security prison down south. He ended up dying in prison of a suspected heart attack six months ago. Kingston knew better; medium security worked both ways.

"How is Andrea?" asked Kingston.

"She's in good health and spirits, Admiral," responded the voice on the other end. "She's looking forward to seeing you after you're both released."

"The other issue I asked you to look into?" Kingston asked while he thought about Handcock with a smile.

"As requested, the relationship with that firm has been officially terminated as of yesterday. We're just waiting for the final details on that meeting."

Kingston's smile broadened. Based on all the coded phrases, he should be out of this hellhole in a couple of days, reunited with his lover, and on his way to a nonextradition, third-world country where he could live out his days in luxury with the money he'd stashed away.

The people who'd put him here were about to pay with their lives. Those who were not currently held prisoners would spend the rest of their lives looking over their shoulders. Overall, the plan was working. The people he hired were worth every penny. Best of all, they had taken care of his nemesis.

Jon Summers was finally dead.

Summers' Cabin
Adirondack State Park, New York
July 18, 2010
1130 hours

The main cabin was now flooded with hostages, including children. Nancy conducted a quick head count and came to a total of nineteen.

Despite the main cabin being a relatively large space, it was clogged by people sitting on the floor, occupying the furniture, or standing watch with rifles. Everybody except for the children were restrained, their hands tied behind their backs. Interestingly, the only adult who was not bound was Sarah. She was allowed to attend to all of them and their needs. Nancy suspected they knew Sarah was a doctor, which meant they'd done their share of research and planning. This was not a random act.

Josh quickly assumed the role of leader, making sure everyone knew each other.

Nancy recognized Mark Wells, whom she'd met years earlier in Annapolis. He was an old friend of her husband and a retired NCIS special agent. Josh introduced Congresswoman Sue Ellen Del Monte and her husband, Franklin. She was one of the most powerful Democratic leaders in Congress and was always on television, which was why Nancy recognized her. Next, he introduced Congressman Eric Hennen, an equally powerful Republican representative, followed by Democratic Senator Arthur Alexander from Montana, the elder statesman of that legislative body. Nancy knew O'Leary, the junior senator from Maryland from her time in Annapolis when Jon filled in as the superintendent of the Academy. Nancy suspected O'Leary had tried to seduce her husband but knew him well enough to know that didn't take place.

Apparently, all the politicians had been attending a dinner at Ericson's when they were taken captive. Rice was currently a Marine Corps colonel serving at the Pentagon. They'd all met Tiffany at Sean and Sarah's wedding and knew she had something to do with Jon's mission in the Philippines in 1995. She was taken from her home while she slept. Demmer was also part of the Philippine mission. She left the Air Force and was working as a computer executive near Washington. She, too, was taken from her home in the middle of the night. The last to be introduced was Ben Fortum, who was Ericson's attorney in Virginia. He was taken as he drove to work. Nancy introduced her family, and they settled in to try and figure out what was going on.

The tone of the conversation was low, so the guards were ignoring it to this point.

"I'm guessing this has something to do with Fiona's ex-husband," commented Fortum. "Too many of us here were involved in that."

"Who's your ex-husband, dear?" asked Congresswoman Del Monte, who appeared to be openly irritated.

"Easy, Suzy," Fiona's husband responded defensively. "Whoever it is, they're looking for some leverage with who they grabbed. Just take it easy so we can all figure this out."

Josh smiled, making eye contact with Franklin Del Monte. His wife was hotheaded on the floor of the House of Representatives and looked to be no different here. She was a bulldog that got things done but wasn't known for her tact. She and Josh had tangled before, so he knew that Franklin was her opposite and would keep her calm.

"Fiona's ex is Richard Kingston," answered Ericson. "He was involved in some nasty business a few years back—"

"Wasn't he the admiral convicted of treason over the attempted takeover in the Philippines back in 1995?" interrupted Alexander.

Congressman Hennen grunted in disgust, glancing around the room in search of everyone else's reaction to Alexander's statement. He saw little support.

"Can it, Eric," scolded O'Leary. "Fiona was as much a victim as all those hostages. She's not responsible for what her husband did, so don't get indignant about this. It's not the time or place."

"And besides," interjected Alexander, "she's here with us. I tend to agree with Mr. Fortum's theory because, as I recall, Mrs. Summers's husband led the rescue. That would make this little gathering either a bid for freedom or someone trying to get even."

Hennen scowled. "The wife of a traitor—why are you defending her?"

Sarah had been moving past the congressman, checking everyone. She stopped in front of the man, making eye contact. "Mr. Hennen, I was one of those hostages, and several people with us here helped save me that day. I would recommend you keep your mouth shut if you can't be helpful, or I'll be forced to gag you."

"Young woman, I—"

Sarah held a finger to her mouth to silence his protest. "The alternative, Congressman, is a lot more painful, because you're making yourself part of the problem." The young doctor and the congressman stared at each other for a few seconds. Nothing more was said.

"Well spoken, young lady," commented Alexander. "I believe that would make you the general's granddaughter. Is that right?"

Sarah returned the old man's smile. "That's correct, Senator, and thank you."

"Say, where is Jon?" asked Demmer innocently.

"He's dead!" replied a voice from the doorway. The hostages turned to see who had made the statement, moving in unison. Nancy was surprised to find Ron Hapke on the other side of the dialogue.

"Ron?" Julie stumbled over her words. "Wh-what are you doing here?"

Hapke grinned at Julie and Nancy's surprise. "I was hired to do a job that's allowing me to get even with you and that half-assed hero of a brother of yours," he declared, and the whole room burst into frantic muttering. "Right now, the Canadian police are dredging a lake looking for his body. They found his canoe full of bullet holes, and it's only a matter of time before they find his corpse. I finally got even with the son of a bitch."

Julie fired a glance at Nancy, who shook her head, telling her not to reply. Julie then glanced at Ericson, who also nodded, but with a sly smile. Ron Hapke wasn't nearly as informed on the subject as he thought.

CHAPTER TWO

UNKNOWN AGENDAS

FBI Offices
New York City
July 18, 2010
1230 hours

Cassie and Trask sat alone in the conference room next to Grey's office, going over her statement. Ever since Grey had informed her that the missing American the RCMP was searching for was her uncle Jon, she'd been holding back tears. They found his canoe capsized in the lake where he was doing some research on local wolves. There were over twenty bullet holes in the hull, so the Mounties rightly suspected foul play. The RCMP also said there were suspects in custody, but there was no body. They were doing a search of the lake with the park rangers in hopes of finding the remains and would be sending a representative to the New York FBI office late that evening to share information.

Ramsey entered the conference room with a coffee for both herself and Trask and tea for Cassie. Trask looked up when she set his coffee on the table. "Grey said he had an idea about what might be going on. Has he shared anything yet?"

Ramsey shook her head. "He hasn't said a thing—but something is definitely going on. He's calling everyone in and is burning up the telephone lines to DC. I called our office. They have nothing on the radar to warrant this kind of activity."

Before Trask could say anything, Grey entered the room, followed by several agents.

"Good, you're all here," he said, looking at Ramsey, Trask, and Cassie. "Have a seat, Miss Ramsey. I need to bring you all up to speed."

Ramsey found the nearest chair, taking a seat along with the agents funneling in behind Grey, and the room fell silent, awaiting his briefing.

"I don't believe," Grey began, "in coincidences. So, when we were told that the missing American in Algonquin Park up in Ontario was Cassie's uncle, I started to check on some things. I just got a call regarding an inquiry I made to Washington. It appears several high-ranking politicians are missing, including Senator Josh Ericson, who is a very close friend of Miss Summers's uncle. They used to be in the Teams together. It seems Ericson married the ex-wife of my most famous arrest, Richard Kingston."

Cassie and Ramsey both looked confused. Trask eagerly jumped in to fill in the blanks.

"You were both kids at the time, so I'm not surprised you don't recognize the name. Kingston was charged and convicted of treason back in the late nineties. He provided information that led to the taking of American veterans as hostages and to the deaths of American servicemen in the Philippines."

"The rescue Uncle Jon was part of?" asked Cassie.

It was Trask's turn to look confused. He glanced at Grey in a silent plea for backup, which Grey then provided.

"Many people don't realize that there were two rescues in March of 1995. The first group was ambushed by mercenaries hired to take over the island of Mindanao. The second was led by Miss Summers's uncle and included the arrest of Kingston and both his aides for passing information. There were other charges levied against Kingston as well. He was a known rival of Admiral Summers. I'm having checks done on other people who were involved in Kingston's arrest. I have a bad feeling I know where the prison break is going to take place and am concerned more people may end up missing. I'll have a complete list of the missing politicians within the next thirty minutes, as well as an update on others I suspect are in danger."

"You don't think . . ." Trask trailed off in disbelief.

Grey held his gaze. "I'm not saying anything yet, Mike. There are just too many things not adding up. We'll talk again in thirty minutes."

Upton's Marina and Boat Sales
Bluffton, New York
July 18, 2010
1250 hours

Issy stood working on an outboard motor just outside his shop. The motor was old but well maintained. He pulled the cowling off and immediately saw he was going to have to fabricate a part. There was a small machine shop in the back for just that purpose. It would be an easy fix but would take some time because of the fabrication.

The sound of outboard motors made him look up. Three boats were coming down the channel. One was the large pontoon boat he'd rented out earlier that morning. The second appeared to be another pontoon boat— though not his—and the third looked to be one of the RIBs the group had brought themselves. He guessed they were returning for another load of materials for whatever project Mrs. Summers was working on. It wasn't any of his business, and Stephen wasn't hopping in his boat to run out there. He guessed he would hear through the grapevine what was going on.

Issy walked back into the shop to talk to his mechanic about the part he needed. When he reached him, his attention was directed back out to the docks by his employee.

"What the hell are they up to boss?"

Issy turned to see the pilot of the first pontoon boat come in perfectly between two smaller docks. He hopped off the craft, leaving it drifting between the docks. The second pontoon boat repeated what the first had done, the pilot dropping something on the seat by the wheel just before jumping off the craft and onto the dock.

Issy stormed out of the shop, followed by his mechanic. "Hey, you tie them boats up!"

The two men ignored his order, jumping into the waiting RIB. When they did, Issy's eye caught one man carrying a handgun. Time seemed to slow. He looked to the other men, realizing that all three were armed. That slowed his movement toward the dock. The strangers didn't even acknowledge Issy or his mechanic, and soon enough, the RIB powered up and sped off into the channel.

"That's damned strange," commented the mechanic. "I think the second boat belongs to Goodwin Marina down in Dartford."

Issy didn't look at the man. "You grab our boat and tie her off. Check her for damage."

"Got it, boss," said the man as he walked off as directed.

Issy quickly moved to the end of the dock, grabbing the side of the second pontoon boat before it drifted too far away to reach. He took the bow painter and tied it off, then moved to the stern of the boat, repeating the process with a rope there. He turned to look at his mechanic, who finished tying off their pontoon boat. The man nodded he was all set. Issy stepped onto the boat, looking for anything that might explain the strange behavior. On the seat by the wheel was a large manila envelope. Izzy could see writing on it, so he moved closer. He froze when he saw *Franklin County Sheriff* printed in big block letters.

Issy looked at the mechanic, who had walked up next to him. "Go get Abby Crogan and tell her this is a sheriff's department issue."

Mohawk Tavern and Grill
Bluffton, New York
July 18, 2010
1300 hours

Abby was waiting tables when the mechanic came into the restaurant. There wasn't a big crowd, as it was Sunday, but there were a few customers, including a woman nobody had seen before sitting beside a large window overlooking the marina. The mechanic asked her to come with him. Abby asked her mother, Maggie, to take her place and left with the mechanic.

Maggie arrived at the table beside the restaurant's largest window and addressed the woman sitting there. "I'm sorry, ma'am; my daughter's a part-time sheriff's deputy, along with working here. Small town, you understand. What can I get for you?"

The customer returned Maggie's smile. "No problem," she said, gesturing to the docks and marina beyond. "I just love the quaintness of this place. I'll have the turkey club and an iced tea, unsweetened, with lemon if you have it."

"You got it. Are you vacationing here?"

The woman nodded. "I needed some peace and quiet—too much time in the city."

Maggie grinned. "Peace and quiet we got," she said, putting away her notebook with the woman's order written on it. "Let me put in your order and get you that tea."

As Maggie moved off, the woman pulled out her cell phone and began to type a text message. The operation was running ahead of schedule and things were as they should be. Her only concern had to do with the team from Canada—they hadn't checked in. She knew from her sources in Ontario that they'd completed their mission of finding and taking care of Jon Summers, but moments after issuing that report, they themselves went silent. Not a big concern. They were instructed to be discrete after completing their task. She was confident they would turn up. It was time to set the next phase of the operation into motion, and that's what her drafted text message was for.

She hit send and smiled.

New York State Thruway
Woodbury, New York
July 18, 2010
1315 hours

Karen Summers was glad she was driving instead of her husband. It would be about a four-hour drive to the cabin from Cassie's apartment, and she enjoyed the trip. Besides, Matt had just received a text that seemed to upset him. His entire demeanor changed after he read it the first time, and she'd caught him rereading the same message, growing more withdrawn by the minute. She asked him what was wrong, but he didn't answer. She guessed it was about one of the girls. He admitted to being overprotective and tended to overreact until he could work through the issue. The ringing of Karen's cell phone—attached via Bluetooth to the car speakers—brought Matt back to reality.

Karen pushed the button on the car's steering wheel, answering. "Hello?"

"Momma." It was Cassie's voice. She sounded stressed. "Is Daddy there with you?"

"I'm here, baby," answered Matt. "What's wrong?"

"Where are you guys?"

"On the thruway, headed to the cabin," answered Karen. "How was the big emergency at work?"

There was a second of silence before Cassie replied, "It's getting bigger. Have you guys heard from Emily or Aunt Nancy at all today?"

Karen glanced at her husband. He had a pained look in his eyes at the mention of their youngest daughter.

"Nothing today, Cassie. Your sister was probably up all night stargazing and doing research for her thesis. Your aunt Nancy has her hands full with RJ and Patty, and Aunt Julie got up there yesterday, but they probably slept in, too. Why do you ask?"

There was more silence.

"Just curious, Momma," Cassie said, before hastily adding, "this emergency could have repercussions for that area of the state is all. I'll call them. Let me make sure everything is okay on the island before you get there. Daddy, I have some bad news. It's about Uncle Jon."

"What about your uncle Jon?" asked Matt in a serious tone, taking Karen by surprise.

"Daddy, he's missing." There was no hesitation this time, only concern in Cassie's voice. "The Canadian police are looking for him. They found his canoe capsized in Ontario but haven't found him yet."

"Why'd they notify *you*, baby?" Matt's voice was cold, all business.

"Matt!" Karen said, her tone more sympathetic. "Honey, fill us in. Tell us everything."

"Does it have to do with this emergency you're working on?" asked Matt.

Again, there was hesitation on Cassie's part before she answered. "One of the FBI agents I'm working with knows Uncle Jon, and this case of his disappearance came across his desk. He let me know."

Matt's tone softened. "Look, baby, I'm sorry if I sounded harsh. The news just took me by surprise. We'll try your sister and your aunts, too. Did your FBI friend have someone I can contact about my brother?"

"I'll ask, Daddy, but for now, that's all the information we have. The Canadian Mounted Police are sending a rep down tonight with some info on the search. I'll see if they'll let me sit in on the meeting and then call you."

"Thank you, baby." Matt's voice was quiet and soft again as he spoke.

Karen glanced at her husband. "We'll call you when we get to the cabin in a couple of hours, kiddo."

"Thanks, Momma. Love you guys."

Both Karen and Matt responded to their daughter's last statement, saying their goodbyes. Karen hung up, glancing at her husband. He was already texting someone, which she found to be quite irritating. What else could be so important?

Mohawk Tavern and Grill
Bluffton, New York
July 18, 2010
1340 hours

The woman stood at the register, paying for her turkey club and unsweetened iced tea. The Mohawk Tavern and Grill was a pleasant restaurant, and the food was good. It was too bad she'd be leaving in the morning, as it was a nice place to spend a couple of quiet summer days. Her phone pinged, indicating that she had a new text message. She returned the smile of the young man at the register, thanking him for the meal, and walked out the door.

After exiting the Mohawk, she looked across the street at the gathering crowd of people around the boats. It was starting, and she needed to get to her perch so she would have a good view of all the excitement.

She took her phone out of her purse and looked at the message. The next phase of the operation had started and would be well underway in the next couple of hours. She smiled with satisfaction, putting the phone away.

Evans' Residence
Nassau, Bahamas
July 18, 2010
1345 hours

Timothy Gerard Evans, Esquire, was not his real name, and he wasn't really a lawyer. He didn't have any real clients and had no college education, much less a law school degree, but his cover was so good, you would never know any of it was fabricated. He'd logged enough time in courtrooms to be able to pass the bar in the Bahamas and three states. He played golf with members of the Bahamian Parliament, drank whiskey at the club with judges, exchanging stories of courtroom derring-do, and regularly consorted with the rich and famous who came to visit Nassau, its beaches, and casinos.

He had been in the Bahamas since December of 2006. Before that, Timothy Gerard Evans was just a name on paper. His employers were many in the past, but the last helped him put this retirement package together. He was always well paid for his services over the years, and Evans felt they were more than generous with their retirement terms. There was no monetary settlement, but they let him live and fabricated the cover he now enjoyed. He'd wisely salted away money from previous employers who were even more generous and had since invested it wisely. Now, he was worth about seventy-five million dollars and could afford the retirement of his choice. He was a man who'd done bad things to earn that kind of money, and if his former countrymen or former employers knew he was alive, he would be hunted down and killed.

Even though he lived an extravagant lifestyle, he flew under the radar. He stayed away from controversy and public office. When he courted the rich and famous, he did so from the shadows, where the paparazzi didn't venture. He was rarely alone and yet often felt lonely, as he was as good as dead to everyone he cared about, including his family. That kept them safe. And so he lived in a world of many acquaintances but no close friends.

At this moment, Evans was heading from the pool to the main house, where he could get to a secure telephone. When he'd received the text, he'd been slow to react. The verbiage of the text message would've been ambiguous to anybody but him, and that proved it'd been sent by possibly the only person that Evans was frightened of. A man who saved his life in a far away, violent land. A man to whom he owed much and whom he thought he left in his long-buried past. A man who could be dangerous, not only because he'd figured out where he was, but also because he was a professional. This man knew they'd both killed others for what they believed in.

How did this man find out where he was and his identity? He even texted his cell phone number. How did he know how to reach him? Evans guessed he would find all that out momentarily.

When he got into the house, he walked directly to his private office, closing the door. He dropped into the chair behind the large mahogany desk, staring at the phone for a minute, wondering if it was going to tell him how all this had taken place. He finally picked up the receiver and punched in the number linked to the sent text messages. The phone rang twice before it was answered.

There were several long moments of silence before a voice said, "Sorry to drag you away from the beach and the bikinis, old man, but I need your help."

Evans had to smile. This voice from his past almost sounded cheery.

"How did you find me? I'm dead!" he said, and there was a chuckle from the other end of the phone.

"At the moment, so am I. So we must both be in hell." It was Evans's turn to chuckle, both for what they'd done in the past and how true that statement was. "You are family," continued the voice on the other end. "Did you really think I wouldn't look into your death?"

"I wasn't sure," Evans replied evenly.

"I suppose it helped that I'd stumbled upon the truth of your death—or fake death, rather—while looking for something else."

Evans paused, intrigued. "Did you find it?"

"As a matter of fact, I did. Finding you was the bonus. I assume you're in that lavishly decorated office behind that mahogany desk."

"How do you know . . ." Evans stopped, realizing he was underestimating the caller. To do that would be a mistake. He was more than capable of tracking him down and of even entering his estate without being detected. He'd been trained to do these things long ago, usually with deadly results. Evans took a breath before saying, "I've retired from that line of work, you know?"

"Retired from being a solicitor or being a terrorist?"

Evans laughed out loud. He knew the statement was meant as humor and took it as such.

"You know the answer to that," he replied. "I grew tired of killing the day you dragged us all out of that godforsaken jungle. I knew then I needed to get out of the business. What happened in the years after that only solidified the decision. Sorry, I can't help you."

"Check your email."

"What?"

"I thought you'd retired—not gone deaf. I said check your email."

Evans opened his laptop, which was on the desk beside him. The screen came to life, and he quickly pressed a few keys. He knew better than to ask how this person had gotten his contact information.

While logging into his email account, Evans asked, "May I assume you've had someone hack into my computer as well as my bank records?"

There was a laugh. "Are you implying that I'm a dinosaur and couldn't do it myself?"

Evans smiled, for that's precisely what he was insinuating. "If the shoe fits."

"Frankly, Councilor," the voice said, "I couldn't care less about your computer or your bank records. What I do care about is communication and being able to get ahold of you when I need to, such as now."

Evans opened his account and found a message waiting for him. It was, of course, from the man on the phone. He read the message, anger rising with every word.

"You're not serious. Not again," said Evans. "You're leaving me no choice here, are you?"

"Look at the attached video."

Evans moved the cursor to the attachment and clicked on it. It took a few seconds for the video to cue up. There were two men, bound and blindfolded, leaning against a log in what appeared to be a forest. Evans could hear animal like growling, and a large patch of gray fur moved in front of the camera. Evans couldn't make out what it was. It wasn't human. There were more growls, and then a question. When the two men didn't answer, a hand reached over and dropped something on their legs. Almost immediately, the screen was filled with gray fur again. This time, Evans could make out several of the creatures. The growling was louder, then the fur was gone. You could see the two men clearly again. Both men were talking freely and answering the question asked earlier. The video suddenly went black. It was over.

"Interesting interrogation technique," said Evans, focusing back on his caller. "Where do I meet you?"

"You don't, Councilor. You'll have another email within the hour. It'll give you all the information you'll need for your little part of the plan. No killing until the mission is completed."

"Are you implying that I have no control?" Evans asked seriously, no humor involved.

"I am not implying, I'm stating a fact," the voice answered. "No emotional responses while we're doing the mission. When it's completed, get in line to take your shot if you want, or you could just return to your retirement."

"Damn you!" was the only response Evans could muster. He hung up, staring at the phone, mind flooded with questions he couldn't find answers to. Either way, one thing was clear—and that was that Evans didn't have a way to get out of this.

Calhoun's Marina
Point Breeze, New York
July 18, 2010
1405 hours

It was a typical Sunday afternoon, with all the summer boaters coming in and out of the shop. Kay didn't mind working Sundays; it kept her busy on a day meant as a day of leisure. She was not big about going to church and enjoyed the hustle of the marina in good weather. Like her two partners, this was just a front, giving them some extra cash and making them look respectable. It also filled the time between their runs overseas. A busy Sunday afternoon here at the marina also served as a respite from their adrenaline-filled adventures when they traveled.

Kay was half Japanese, and in this western New York hamlet on Lake Ontario, she was a novelty. Not because she was a pretty, Asian girl in her late twenties, but because she was single. This made her the target of every single male between fifteen and seventy-five in Orleans County, as well as some of the married ones. Most of the single girls went off to college or to the nearby cities of Rochester or Buffalo. If they didn't do that, they would likely be engaged to be married right out of high school.

It seemed just about everyone in this area of New York owned a boat, and most of them used Point Breeze as the place to launch them and gain access to Lake Ontario. Kay cashed out two eighteen-year-old boys, who then asked her out on their small boat after buying fifty dollars' worth of merchandise. She thanked them but said she worked all day. She smiled while watching the two dejected kids walk down toward the dock.

The phone behind the counter rang. She picked it up and said, "Calhoun's Marina, this is Kay, how may I help you?"

There was a moment of hesitation before a very confident male voice said, "I'm calling in regard to the boat for sale by Mr. Noah and Mr. Quint."

Kay froze.

The use of "Mr. Noah and Mr. Quint" served as the initiating protocol used by the agency to cryptically announce a new assignment.

This brought her back to reality.

It had been a while since they'd been sent after someone overseas. The last assignment had been a little rough, and Tom Mitchell, their boss, had confided in her he thought the team needed a rest. This assignment was coming sooner than she'd expected, and the voice on the line currently wasn't Tommy's. Something wasn't adding up.

She initiated the counter phrase. "I'm sorry, those gentlemen just lease space here, you may want to contact them by email."

"I already have, Kayli Ann," replied the voice in perfect Japanese. "Have them both check their email immediately."

Kay instantly began to panic. This was not part of the normal routine, and the man on the phone had just called her by her proper first and middle name. Without thinking, she asked in English, "Who is this?"

There was a laugh on the other end of the phone. When the man responded, he was still speaking in Japanese. "It's a ghost, Kayli Ann, but a friendly one. Have them check their email and listen to this message. I know your calls are recorded."

Kay couldn't believe what she was hearing and knew she should hang up and run. Their cover had been blown, but if she kept him on the phone, she just may learn something else from the caller. It was a gamble she was willing to make.

"If you want to wait, I think I see them pulling in."

There was again laughter on the other end of the phone, and this time the response was in English. "I know they're in the warehouse out back. Have them check their email; they'll know what to do. Don't worry, Kayli, you're safe. Your father would never forgive me if I let anything happen to you."

The last statement sent Kay into a full-blown panic, and to make matters worse, the line went dead. She hung up the phone and looked around the store. One of the summer clerks was on the floor, helping a customer. She waved the girl over to the counter.

"Suzy, get Bob in here from outside, and the two of you work the store. I've got an emergency I must talk to the guys about."

The girl nodded, watching Kay rush out. Kay wondered if she looked as stressed as she felt.

Upton's Marina and Boat Sale
Bluffton, New York
July 18, 2010
1405 hours

Marty James stopped his squad car on the street, as it was impossible to get into the parking lot with the gathering crowd. He was already irritated because the FBI tracked him down on his day off to discuss a potential prison break in his county. That call ruined his day of fishing with his grandchildren, and now this. It didn't matter what happened because this was such a quiet area of the state. Minor incidents were a big thing and drew a crowd. A boat rented out of a marina in Dartford showing up at a marina in Bluffton certainly wasn't the crime of the century, if it was a crime at all, but you wouldn't know it by the crowd of locals that showed up.

The crowd was being held back by a couple of the local firemen. He could see Deputy Brady Jasper and the part-time girl, Abby, by the boats. He knew Issy Upton was the one who had called this in; Sherriff James considered Issy a pain in the ass. He tended to call for little things, tying up his deputies' valuable time. And why wasn't the part-time girl in uniform? Issy probably sent for her, and she called this in. James would have her badge if that was the case.

James slammed the door to his car and began walking around it. Jasper heard the car door close, apparently, and walked out to meet his boss. The firemen parted the crowd to let the sheriff through.

"Brady, did Issy call the part-time girl in for this?" asked James, not bothering to hide his irritation, and Jasper nodded.

"Sure did, boss. She called this in once she got here and saw what we had."

"Good, so I can fire her ass," said James, starting to walk to where Abby and Issy were standing on the dock. "A boat in the wrong marina isn't worth all this commotion."

Jasper grabbed his boss's arm as he marched past him. "Calm down, boss. There's more to this than just that. She wouldn't have called you for just that, and I certainly know better than to allow it."

James gave his deputy a puzzled look. "What is it then?"

Jasper nodded toward the boats at the end of the dock and said, "It'll be easier to show you."

James was at the end of his rope but had learned to trust his subordinates. He followed Jasper to the end of the dock where Abby stood next to Issy.

"Afternoon, Marty," commented Issy. "Nice day, don't you think?"

"Sheriff," acknowledged Abby with a nod of her head.

Jasper handed Sheriff James a pair of latex gloves, and for the first time, he noticed that both Jasper and Abby were each wearing them. He put them on, and Jasper handed him the manila envelope left on the boat. The sheriff gave his deputy a puzzled look.

"You're going to want to open it, boss," said Jasper. "You won't be happy. It's self-explanatory."

James focused on the envelope while doing as his deputy requested. He pulled out what appeared to be a letter and several eight-by-ten pictures. Names were written on the back of each picture. He read the letter.

> *Dear Sheriff James,*
>
> *Enclosed you will find pictures of the people we are currently holding hostage. Please be assured that they will remain safe if the federal government does exactly as requested. Your office, the FBI office in Washington, and the White House will all be getting an email today at 3:00 p.m. exactly. In that email, we will lay out our terms for the release of these hostages, which will be nonnegotiable. As you can see, we have selected our hostages carefully by the number of high-profile people currently being held on Shadow Lake in the Summers' cabin. The others are important only to us in a sentimental way from an old court case related to our goal.*
>
> *Sheriff James, please do not be so bold as to think that you can take the hostages back by force. That will only get some or all of them killed. To prove our point, we have already killed Rear Admiral Jonathon Summers on Source Lake in Algonquin Park, Ontario. Please feel free to check with your counterparts in Ontario to confirm that. Admiral Summers's death was preordained for our little operation. You hold their lives in your hands.*
>
> *I look forward to our further communication at 3:00 p.m.*
>
> *Yours Truly,*
> *Richard Kingston*

Sheriff James looked at the three people standing next to him. "You all read this?"

Deputy Jasper and Abby both nodded, but Issy shook his head, reaching out for the envelope hopefully. "No, I called for Abby when I found it, because it didn't look right, but never did read it. Can I read it now?"

James grunted in response, putting all the material back into the envelope and handing it to Jasper, who in turn put it in a plastic evidence bag. Issy's hand fell to his side, lips pressing into a thin line.

"Who boarded the boat?" asked James, looking at Issy.

Issy smiled. "Just me, Marty."

James grunted again, then said, "Call for the crime lab."

"Done, sir," answered Abby. "They're already on the way."

"Get more backup units here and to Dartford. Call everyone in. This is big enough we'll need all available personnel."

"Already being done, boss," chimed in Jasper. "Dispatch is calling all our people in, and the state troopers are responding both here and to Dartford. Dartford PD has an officer at Goodwin Marina and is securing the scene there. We're also having them run this guy, Richard Kingston."

James looked at his senior deputy. "Any idea where these pictures were taken?"

"The Summers' cabin, sir," answered Abby without thinking.

James turned and looked at the young woman. "And you know that how?"

Abby didn't answer, giving him a weak smile in response, and James waved a hand a moment later, piecing it together. "Of course you would know. I forgot that you're engaged to Stephen. He's the youngest of the Summers boys, right?"

Abby nodded silently, and James realized she must've been very worried on the inside.

He cleared his throat, looking at the envelope. "That means these are recent pictures."

"Yes, sir." Abby added, "Did you notice all of their hands are bound by flex-cuffs in the pictures?"

James hadn't noticed that fact but couldn't let the part-time deputy know, so he just nodded. He heard vehicles approaching and turned to see another patrol car pulling up, followed by a New York State Police car. He turned back to the young woman.

"How long will it take you to get into uniform? I need you to do the initial report here and take charge of this scene. I need Deputy Jasper somewhere else."

Abby smiled proudly. "Give me ten minutes, Sheriff."

James looked at the young woman, motioning for her to go. Abby took off at a run and crossed the street, entering the Mohawk.

James turned to his deputy. "She lives in a bar?"

"Her family owns the place, boss," answered Jasper. "They live on the second floor. We never have any problems there; they run a clean operation."

James nodded. "She's good, Jasper. I suppose I'll have to learn her name now and stop calling her 'part-time girl.'"

He looked at his deputy, and a smile passed between them.

Mohawk Tavern and Grill
Bluffton, New York
July 18, 2010
1420 hours

The woman watched from a distance, taking pictures and looking like a typical tourist. The first text message was delivered. The second would be delivered in forty minutes. Then all hell would break loose. She entered the restaurant a few minutes before taking a seat at the same table near the window, placing her camera bag and expensive digital camera where it could be seen. She was at the table less than a minute before a woman she knew to be the owner came over to wait on her.

"Back so soon? What can I get for you this afternoon?" asked Maggie.

The woman returned Maggie's smile. "I'll have a Coke, please."

"Can I get you a piece of pie or something else?" asked Maggie, looking the woman over. She really hadn't taken notice before, but something big was going on across the street, and this woman seemed intrigued by it.

"Apple pie, if you have it," answered the woman politely.

Maggie pointed to the camera. "Taking many pictures?"

The woman nodded. "I'm an amateur photographer, and this area is so beautiful. I've probably taken close to a thousand pictures. Too bad I leave in the morning. Have to be back in New York by two for a meeting."

"Well, I hope you enjoy the remainder of your stay here in Bluffton. Let me put your order in, and I'll be back in a minute with your Coke."

When Maggie moved off, the woman looked back across the street at the scene. More police cars arrived, as well as more spectators to be handled. This would turn into a circus, which would work in her favor.

While she watched, a noise from behind her drew her attention. She turned to see a young woman in uniform walk through the restaurant and out the door. She was followed by a young man in civilian clothes. She recognized the young woman from her visits to this restaurant. Things were moving fast; they were calling all their reserves. She knew the young man; he was one of the people she had been watching.

Calhoun's Marina
Point Breeze, New York
July 18, 2010
1420 hours

Kay, Ryan, and Justin listened to the recording for the second time. The three of them huddled around the small desk in the warehouse office. Kay, who was usually very calm, looked scared and uneasy. When she came back to get them, she was visibly shaking. They sat her down at the desk and listened to the recording.

"What do you think?" asked Kay. "Is our cover here blown?"

"I don't know the voice," said Ryan O'Keefe, looking at his partner, Justin Summers.

Both Justin and Ryan were thought to be either dead or missing. That helped them in their current job. They both worked for the CIA, and their job was to hunt down terrorists threatening the United States and her allies. Justin was a former Navy SEAL who was captured on a mission and listed as killed in action. After his escape from captivity, he was recruited by the CIA for this project and teamed up with Ryan, an Irish national. Together they became the agency's go-to guys for this type of job. Kay knew Justin before he went missing, and they met in a chance encounter after he returned. She was hired by the agency as an analyst and assigned to the project. They worked out of this western New York location because of its proximity to the Canadian border, which gave them multiple travel options when they needed to leave on a mission. It was tough on Justin, as his family only lived thirty miles away in Rochester, but he'd managed to keep himself under the radar—or so he thought.

"I know the voice," said Justin, returning Ryan's gaze. "We're not in danger of our cover being blown."

"But there's something else?" said Ryan, recognizing apprehension in Justin's voice.

"Check the email, Ryan. I'm sure all the explanation we'll need will be there."

"My email or yours?"

"It won't matter," answered Justin, "the message will be the same on both."

Ryan pushed his chair over to a second desk with the computer. Meanwhile, Justin focused on Kay. "I know the voice, Kay, and he's a friend. I don't understand the ghost part, but we're not in danger."

"Justin, the part about my father . . . and he knew I was part Japanese, that I would understand the language . . ." She looked up at him, wide-eyed. "How?"

Justin gave Kay a reassuring smile, brushing her dark hair out of her eyes. "Nothing he does or knows surprises me. The fact he knows Ryan and I were back here means he's been here and none of us recognized him."

"You're telling me I know him?"

Justin nodded, but before he could say anything else, Ryan burst out with, "Holy Jesus! Guys, you need to see this. I mean *now*."

Kay and Justin looked at each other, surprised by Ryan's reaction. They both moved over to where they could look at the computer screen themselves. After a few seconds, Kay exclaimed, "Oh my God! I don't believe it. This can't be true."

Justin said nothing but could feel his face growing red with anger. He glanced back at his friend and partner and saw the concern in Ryan's eyes.

"I'm okay, Ryan—but you know I'm going to have to help. I'll explain it to Tommy."

"If he knows this much about us, you know he's been here."

"More than once," responded Kay, continuing to read.

"And probably not legally," Ryan added with a chuckle. "How'd we miss it? We're supposed to be the best at what we do."

"Apparently he's better at it," commented Kay. "You're not going on this mission alone, Justin."

Justin stepped back, looking at his two friends. "I can't ask you guys to be part of this. This is a family matter."

Ryan pointed to the email. "This is *my* email, not yours, and this doesn't look like a cry for help to me. You don't think he included me for a reason, do you?"

Kay looked at Ryan and smiled, realizing where he was headed with this. "No, it doesn't look like he's asking for help, does it? It does look like a set of orders, though. Like it or not, Summers, you're stuck with us on this."

Justin smiled at his two friends. "But we keep it just between us. I'll let Tommy know; I owe him that much. This is off book because it's personal. You two pack everything we need while I call Tommy."

Justin turned, walking toward the door. This was impressive. How had he missed being discovered?

FBI Offices
New York City
July 18, 2010
1430 hours

Grey waved them into his office while he continued talking on the telephone. Trask allowed Cassie and Ramsey to sit before he sat down. Two agents accompanied them, sitting as well.

"Thank you for the information, Sheriff James," said Grey. "We'll have agents on their way to you within the hour." There was a pause as Grey listened to the sheriff on the other end. "No, we have no intention of releasing him. We'll be in touch with the Army to make sure he's secure, and between them and the US Marshal Service, I'm sure there'll be additional security placed on him."

Grey waved one of the agents over and handed him some handwritten notes. He pointed to something on the paper he'd circled and looked to the agent for acknowledgement. The man nodded, taking the paper and racing out of the office.

"You too, Sheriff," said Grey. "We'll talk again after the email is delivered. Thanks for the heads-up."

Grey hung up and let out a long sigh. He looked at Cassie, jumping right into an explanation. "We figured out what's going on, and its bad news. We have a group that's taken multiple hostages, including members of your family, Miss Summers."

Cassie didn't respond, but her posture seemed to stiffen.

"Your sister is one," continued Grey, "as well as your aunt Nancy and aunt Julie. Your cousins Hector and Alexandra, Sarah Summers, and her kids are all being held. I'm sorry to have to be the bearer of this type of news."

Trask leaned over and put his hand on Cassie's arm. "I'm sorry, Cassie. I really am."

Cassie took a deep breath before she spoke. "Where are they being held, Agent Grey?"

Grey sighed again before answering. "They're being held in the cabin owned by your family on Shadow Lake. There are also some members of Congress being held, as well as some people who were involved in a case I worked."

Cassie seemed to be getting over the shock, the professional attorney returning. "Did the suspects say why they're being held hostage?"

Grey smiled; there was a cool professionalism that enveloped the young woman. He couldn't say too much at this point because a lot of it would be conjecture. Besides, he wasn't sure how much information to give her, considering it was likely that she would be excused from working on the case. After a few seconds, he decided to say, "It's connected to the case I worked on with your uncle. Some of the hostages are people I worked with or were witnesses. I can't really say more than that."

Cassie held Grey's gaze. "This is your prison break, isn't it? It's connected to what we're working on here?"

Grey nodded. "Yes, Cassie, I believe it is."

There was a brief silence before anyone spoke. Cassie turned to Trask. "Sir, I believe I must exclude myself from this case," she said, reading Grey's mind. "My closeness to it could jeopardize any case the government may try to build."

Trask nodded. "I understand, Cassie, and you taking this step before having to be told to is commendable."

"I also know, sir, that I just started with the office, but I need to take some time to be with my family during this crisis. What do I need to do?"

"You just go and be with them. I'll make all the arrangements. If I need you, I'll contact you on your cell."

Cassie nodded, turning back to Grey. "I want to thank you, Agent Grey. You've been kind. Is there anything you can tell me about this I can share with my family when I see them?"

"Cassie," started Grey, sounding a bit apprehensive, "they claim to have killed your uncle Jon in Canada. They knew where he was. You can share they have given us a written note stating he's confirmed to be dead."

Cassie sat in silence for a moment and then smiled. "But there's no body?"

Grey only shook his head.

"Well, I had better go," Cassie said, rising from her chair. Grey and Trask also rose.

"This agent will make sure you get home," said Grey, looking at the agent still in the room. "If I get more information to share, I'll get it to you through Michael here."

Cassie nodded, saying goodbye to both Trask and Ramsey, and then followed the agent out the door. When the door closed, Trask said, "She took the news about her uncle pretty well."

Grey smiled, staring at the door. "Like the woman said, there was no body."

Mitchell Residence
Arlington, Virginia
July 18, 2010
1450 hours

Tommy Mitchell sat in the living room of his condominium and stared at the ceiling.

He'd just hung up from talking to Justin Summers, who was taking his team to Shadow Lake to help his family, who was apparently in a hostage situation. He silently cursed whoever contacted Justin. Over the phone, he was informed that it'd been an anonymous voice on the phone and an untraceable email directly to his team that had sent them on this mission. How was that possible when he'd taken great pains to keep his team's existence a secret?

Someone *knew* about the team.

And how would the Summers family react when they found out Justin was alive? Being listed as killed in action, he'd had no contact with his family for over three years. Now the team was enroute to see what they could do to save Justin's family. This would put them in harm's way and potentially ruin their effectiveness for tracking down terrorists. Mitchell guessed Justin's father probably knew about him and tracked him down. Justin told him the person who contacted him said the Canadian police were investigating Jon Summers's death. He'd believe that if he weren't in this business.

The doorbell rang, causing him to jump. He wasn't expecting anyone. It was Sunday, and things were quiet. He walked to the door, opening it. Standing in the doorway was an older man dressed in casual clothes, flanked by two men looking like official security people. Mitchell didn't want any company. He needed to figure out how to minimize the damage to his operation if his team was to break cover.

"May I help you?" he asked, voice clipped. He didn't bother disguising the fact that he wasn't in the mood to entertain company, even for the sake of politeness, but when the old man standing at his doorstep held up an ID wallet that confirmed he was with the NSA, that all changed immediately. Now, he was even *less* interested in this business.

"Captain Mitchell, my name is Putnum." The presentation of the ID was accompanied by a knowing smile. "May we come in and talk for a bit?"

Mitchell flashed the older man an irritated look. "I'm afraid now is not a good time, Mr. Putnum. I'm busy. Maybe you can contact me at the office tomorrow."

Putnum's smile disappeared, though he continued to hold his ID up for Mitchell to read. Mitchell noticed the title *Deputy Director* on the ID, but before he could react, Putnum continued. "I'm afraid it's not an option, Captain. I'm here on business. We can talk here, or these gentlemen will be happy to take you into custody so we can talk someplace more convenient to me."

Mitchell didn't like being threatened, but the look in the old man's eyes told him this was no idle threat. He stepped back and motioned for the three men to enter. One of the security people entered first, quickly doing a visual scan of the room. He was followed by Putnum, who commented, "I would like to speak to you about the reason for your team being contacted by an outsider."

Mitchell's mouth dropped in shock.

The president of the United States sat behind his desk in the Oval Office, his arms folded across his chest, listening to one of his advisors speak about the email. They had debated the contents of this email for the last fifteen minutes. The director of the FBI was on speakerphone with the president and two of his aides. The president said little, except to clarify points covered in the email.

"We can't have these people kidnapping politicians anytime they want something," said the first aide. "If we let it go, then the next individual or group that wants to hold this country hostage to get what they want will do the same thing. Mr. Director, I say you send in your HRT people as soon as possible."

The voice on the other end of the line sounded more cautious. "It may come to that, but before I authorize anyone going in, we need more intel on this group. Who are they? Is this Richard Kingston making a bid to escape or something bigger? Do they have intel as far as our resources? They've shown they have drug and gang connections, so is this act purely criminal or something more sinister? Richard Kingston was privy to who knows how many of this nation's secrets. Could this be a bid by someone to get ahold of those secrets?"

"Or his old business associates trying to get him out of prison?" added the president's other aide.

"No," exclaimed the first aide, "it doesn't matter who they are or what's going on here, we need to stop it *now*. We need to show them we mean business. We need to kick their ass back to wherever they came from!"

The president sat up straight, placing his hands on the desk, looking at his aide. He didn't approve of the use of that type of language, even behind closed doors. His posturing was all that was needed to convey his disapproval. He leaned forward, resting his elbows on the desk, and said, "Enough of this debate."

The aides fell silent, though it clearly pained them to do so.

The president took a deep breath, thoroughly considering his next words. When he was ready, he spoke directly to the FBI director. "Sam, how long to get this intel you need?"

"We should have most of it by morning. NSA has already contacted us and has information to share. Their deputy director was involved in Kingston's capture, as was our agent in charge of our New York office. Both should be in upstate New York by that time. We're also taking precautions at Leavenworth by isolating Kingston even more to make sure he isn't calling the shots from there. We're doing the same with his coconspirator where she's being held. By morning, we'll have enough info to know if this is a threat to national security or if it's just an attempt to break a federal prisoner out of Leavenworth. It'll also give us enough time to get HRT and our other assets in place. Until then, everything is buttoned down tight. We have until Tuesday night to release Kingston or attempt a rescue. I suggest we use that time to our advantage."

The president asked, "You're saying not to be rash in our reaction?"

"Yes, Mr. President," responded the director. "They expect us to use some—if not all—that time before we take action. All I'm saying is we look at all our options."

The president shook his head, thinking for a few seconds.

"Sam, they have some key members of Congress being held hostage up there on that island. People who know their own share of top-secret material, and Colonel Rice is on her way to a promotion to general and a posting with NMCC. There are also innocents being held hostage—children. I can't give an order that would get them hurt or killed. Now, what about this admiral they killed?"

"Summers is recently retired," the director went on, "highly decorated, Medal of Honor recipient, and former Navy SEAL. He was in Naval Intelligence and authored one of the initial reports on 9/11. He was doing some scientific research up in Canada. They found his canoe all shot up and capsized in a lake, Mr. President."

"Damn," responded the president. "Kingston has a long reach. Do they have any idea why they killed him?"

"Kingston and Summers were old Academy rivals," the director said without hesitation, "and Summers was part of the team that drew Kingston out and arrested him. Summers also served with Senator Ericson, who married

Kingston's ex-wife. Mr. President, they haven't found Summers's body yet. The RCMP is sending an investigator with copies of their files to the New York scene to see if they have any information that'll help our people."

The president let out an audible sigh. "Sam," he said, "none of these options available are acceptable to me. Get me some better ones."

The president turned to look out the window so that his aides couldn't see the worry on his face.

Summers' Cabin
Adirondack State Park, New York
July 18, 2010
1800 hours

They remained huddled in the center of the cabin's living room. Hennen and Del Monte had been arguing with each other nonstop. They'd apparently carried their partisanship from the House floor to this situation without even knowing it. They didn't see the chuckles from their captors, or the disgusted looks from their fellow hostages. Ericson quietly passed the word to allow this to continue because it focused the guards on those two, ignoring the rest of them.

Ericson may have been mustered out of the Navy in 1979, but he retained many of the skills that made him an excellent Special Forces operator. He was cataloging numbers of the force holding them captive, what weapons they were equipped with, their chain of command, and the level of training they appeared to have. He found there was a great deal of help with this in the persons of Wells and Rice. Both knew weapons and tactics well. Demmer and Alexander were skilled to mentally catalog and retain all the data they were collecting. Demmer was a systems information specialist in the Air Force whose job was just that—the cataloging of information. Those who worked with her found she could retain almost as much information as the computers she worked with. Alexander was a human catalog of information going back to his childhood; he was able to absorb and retain vast amounts of information down to the smallest detail.

Fortum and O'Leary concentrated on placing names with faces, a skill they were good at. Ericson thought it important to know the names of their captors, should they be able to acquire that information somehow. He smiled to himself when he thought about calling them Goon One, Goon Two, etc. It wasn't original, but he felt it fit in this case.

Nancy, Julie, and the rest of the family had been asked to pick up on any conversation that might take place in their presence. Ericson explained the smallest bit of information might be important. He recognized Julie was angry—the leader of their captors was an old boyfriend, after all, but that came with the advantage of knowing a vestige of what was going on and who was in charge here. Ericson spoke to Julie, asking her to put her feelings aside and keep Hapke focused on her and distracted—and Julie was determined to make that ruse work. Ericson didn't doubt her for a second.

They were surprised when the woman named Servati came to get Nancy and Emily, removed their flex-cuffs, and walked them out of the cabin. They were gone less than fifteen minutes and returned carrying frozen food from the boathouse. To Ericson's surprise, he discovered Emily could judge distance well. She shared the distances between cabins and the tree line around the compound. Ericson didn't share with his fellow hostages how serious things were, because he truly felt several of them were targeted to be killed. He now felt there was a chance to get at least some of them out alive. There was the beginning of a plan. They would fight to the end.

Mohawk Tavern and Grill
Bluffton, New York
July 18, 2010
1800 hours

Matt and Karen sat in a dark booth in the far corner of the tavern. They had arrived about an hour before to find Cassie waiting for them. She was given a ride up with a team of FBI agents who were transported from New York City by military helicopter. The agents were a preliminary team *sent up* to assist the local police in arranging a perimeter to contain the situation. They were to do the groundwork for the federal authorities to take over the crime scene sometime after midnight with the arrival of the main FBI contingent.

Matt had discouraged an attempt to send a team in to rescue the hostages, but it was obvious they would do this against his recommendations. They felt they knew the land well enough. After all, they'd talked to Stephen for most of the day, and with one of their deputies having spent a great deal of time on the island, they had access to firsthand knowledge of the property. Despite all that, Matt still protested, but it fell on deaf ears. He was tired of arguing and left Cassie and Stephen to echo his protests. The sheriff and the state police were willing to listen to the two younger members of the family. The FBI agents seemed happy to sit back and watch.

Matt sipped his glass of beer.

His wife looked at him and said, "You're angry, honey . . . Why?"

He held the heavy glass mug in both hands, focusing on his wife. "The sheriff just dismissed my opinion without even considering it. At least he's listening to Cassie and Stephen. I guess I'm just feeling old and not needed. He even told me I didn't have any tactical experience."

Karen laughed. "Honey, he's right—you don't have any tactical experience. You're a computer executive. Besides, the kids will get the point across to the sheriff. He's not a stupid man, after all."

Matt looked at his beer, setting it down on the table.

"I'm not stupid, either, Karen," he said, voice calm. "We've been here for a little over an hour, and I already know they suspect there's about forty armed individuals holding Emily, Nancy, and the others on the island. I also know the sheriff is planning a rescue attempt before dawn, using his people and state police special operations units. I don't know any this from an official briefing—I heard it on the streets of Bluffton. The operational security on this is for shit."

"Did you get that opinion from hanging around your brother?" asked Karen with a smile.

"No," said a voice from behind her, "from Raymond. He always had a good grasp of the natural order of things."

Both Matt and Karen looked up to find Fred Crogan approaching them, followed by his daughter. Matt rose and threw his arms around the old man, giving him a hug. He gave Maggie one as well. Karen followed suit.

"Have a seat, paleface," joked Fred. "You're in my home, and I'm going to feed you."

Maggie hit her father on the shoulder, and he just smiled.

"Sorry," Fred amended. "You're in my daughter's home, and she'll feed you."

Matt laughed but did as he was told. Fred slid in next to Matt, and Maggie was next to Karen. Almost immediately, plates of stew appeared from the kitchen and were placed in front of the four people in the booth. While they all started to eat, Karen asked, "Fred, you referred to Matt's dad . . . I don't understand what you meant . . ."

The old man smiled, looking at the younger man next to him.

"Raymond knew that if you wanted to keep a secret in this town, you tell no one. You don't even say anything to family. It's a small community, and everyone knows everyone else's business. It's the natural order, the nature of a small town."

United States Disciplinary Barracks
Fort Leavenworth, Kansas
July 18, 2010
1700 hours

Kingston knew the operation was underway because the corridor outside his cell was quieter than normal. They had taken his neighbors out of their cells for their scheduled exercise periods, and they had not returned. They also increased the patrols of the corridor, and the guards were traveling in pairs. A civilian, probably FBI, had briefly looked in his cell when he toured the cellblock. Kingston smiled, thinking about what was taking place back east. He was even happier over the news the first part of the operation was successful. He only wished he was there to pull the trigger. But that didn't matter now—Jon Summers was dead, and he himself would soon be free.

Kingston paid good money for this chance, but it was worth it. He'd made millions and banked it wisely, so he could afford the cost. He would use his entire fortune if it freed him from this place. He could always make more money, but not from here. This was a good plan, and his people on the outside were most efficient. He sprawled out on his cot and grinned.

Upton's Marina and Boat Sales
Bluffton, New York
July 18, 2010
1935 hours

Justin Summers and his team arrived at Bluffton and, following the directions of the local fire police, parked where the media were being told to park. Their plain, white, unmarked Chevy van was filled with their equipment and gear.

The crowds weren't huge, but Justin guessed that would change before morning when the word of the incident spread; the authorities couldn't keep it under wraps for long. On the way, they made a quick stop at one of several small motels near the marina and booked two rooms under aliases. They could've walked the rest of the way from the motel, but they needed to maintain their cover for as long as they could. Driving up in a van and announcing they were a news crew from Buffalo seemed like the best approach.

Kay never went into the field with them, but both Justin and Ryan felt she would be a good addition. It wasn't an official mission and should be relatively safe being in the United States as opposed to where they normally operated. Besides, she looked the part of the pretty reporter and knew how to ask questions. Justin took on the role of videographer because he could hide his face behind the camera while Ryan was playing producer. Ryan would be able to move more freely through the community to do research. He could charm people with his good looks and Irish accent. Ryan headed to the Mohawk to see what information he could come up with, leaving Justin and Kay to go straight to the marina.

Shortly after arriving, Justin noticed two people coming out of the secured area of the marina. He touched Kay on the shoulder, nodding in their direction. "Family. Talk to them."

Without hesitation, Kay placed herself at the entrance, microphone at the ready. The two were headed right for her—a young woman and a young man. Kay immediately knew the man to be a Summers because he looked so much like Justin. A quick glance over her shoulder told her Justin's camera was up to cover his face.

She took a deep breath and raised the microphone. "I'm Kayli Kimura from the *New York Cable News*. Do you have any comment about today's events?"

Behind her, Justin laughed when she used her mother's maiden name. She thought that was more believable than Kayli Wiedenkeller. She knew her father would forgive her.

The woman didn't respond to her question except to give her a fiery look as she stormed past. The man held up his hand and said, "No comment at this time, thank you."

They passed quickly, and Kayli turned to look at Justin, who'd already lowered his camera. He was laughing, and she looked a bit hurt. He held up his free hand to stop her from saying anything. "Look, you did great—and the name was a great improvisation. It makes you more believable with your cover."

"You're not mad? It just came to me at the spur of the moment."

Justin managed to bring his laughter under control. "Just let us know next time, Kay. We don't need to get caught in something that'll jeopardize all three of us. Besides, you did so well with this that we'll have to start calling you Ninja Girl. I know you know how to defend yourself."

Kay smiled at Justin's reference to her father. She nodded, then, at the back of the woman she'd just tried to interview. "Who was that woman? She looked at us like she wanted us dead."

"My cousin Cassie. She was in law school last time I checked," answered Justin, sounding a little choked up. "The guy was my brother Stephen. He looked pretty upset, too."

"At least he was polite. What do you think the news was that got them so upset?"

Justin watched his brother and cousin cross the street and enter the Mohawk. "I'm guessing the authorities are going to try and storm the island, putting the hostages in danger. That would be enough to make the two of them that angry. Trust me, if Cassie was that angry, her not saying anything was being polite."

Kay nodded, noticing Justin looking around the gathered crowd.

"You stay here and see what information you can come up with," continued Justin. "I'm going back to the van to see if I can eavesdrop and find out anything else."

Kay nodded. She handed him back the microphone and made sure her press ID was displayed prominently. Justin looked at her, smiling, then they both separated.

Mohawk Tavern and Grill
Bluffton, New York
July 18, 2010
1945 hours

The woman sat at the table, slowly stirring the straw in her iced tea as she watched the two young people storm into the restaurant. They didn't look happy, and the locals all gave them a wide berth as they moved through the crowded room. She smiled, typing something into her cell phone, thinking, *what did we do before the age of electronics?* She remembered carrying pens and notebooks to take notes in. That was so cumbersome and inconvenient. This was so much more practical, and it even corrected one's spelling.

The reaction of the two family members confirmed what she'd already suspected: the sheriff's office planned an assault on the island sometime after midnight. This was expected, and they were ready. She finished up the text to her man on the island and hit send. His orders were specific, and he knew the consequences of not following them. He got what he wanted already, so now the money was all that mattered to him. Greed was his weakness. She guessed he wouldn't live to collect the money. He was, after all, expendable.

Upton's Marina and Boat Sales
Bluffton, New York
July 18, 2010
1950 hours

Abby finished her initial report and processing of the scene. There weren't many fingerprints found on the boats, but they would investigate the few that were. They knew the name of the man who rented the boat from Issy, and a background check revealed he used to be a policeman from the Rochester area of New York. She made a call and spoke to the current chief of police in Lakeview, finding out Ron Hapke had been a SWAT officer and had tactical training. This worried her some but didn't faze Sheriff James at all. He met with the FBI and the New York State Police. They were putting together an assault team to go in under the cover of darkness after midnight and were counting on the bad weather forecast to help cover the assault and the rescue of the hostages. They were also counting on surprise, but Abby wasn't as optimistic. She added the numbers and guessed there were up to forty people on the island. If true, that was too many to take by surprise. She'd watched Stephen and Cassie storm off, which meant that Sheriff James told them of the assault plan. She knew that wouldn't make them happy and didn't dare return to the Mohawk to rest. Besides, she was assigned to the assault team due to her knowledge of the island. She would do as ordered but couldn't put herself in the position of arguing with Stephen. For now, it was best to quietly blend into the crowd at the marina to find someplace to rest for a few hours.

Canadian Air Force C-130
Over the Canadian/United States Border
July 18, 2010
2235 hours

Inspector Scott Preston sat silently in his seat with his eyes closed. The flight had been delayed due to waiting for a late passenger to arrive. When he did, Preston cracked an eye open and saw a man that stood just under six feet tall and looked to be older than him by about ten years. He looked fit and wore forest camouflage fatigues, right up to the boonie cap on top of his head. He boarded with what looked to be two packs, a small duffel bag, and a black helmet. What puzzled Preston was he carried a knife strapped to his right leg. There were no identifying unit patches on the uniform like the flight suits of the crew. The crew also carried no weapons. While it didn't seem right to Preston, he didn't question anything because this was a military flight, and he was just a passenger. They were, after all, headed to a friendly country.

He thought about the case he was working; it was concerning that they hadn't found a body yet. The two men in custody had emptied several clips each into the canoe they'd found floating on the west side of the lake. They had also found a paddle near shore, but no corpse, which his knowledge told him should've risen to the surface already due to the buildup of gases in the body cavity during decomposition. That being said, Source Lake was a difficult lake to dredge because it was so deep, and they decided to use a camera system to search the bottom. There was a summer camp on the other side of the lake, and the last thing they needed was a young camper finding a floater when they went swimming. The cottagers also told them of the other treasures they might find at the bottom. An aluminum canoe loaded with full cases of beer had been sent to the bottom years before by a couple of staff men from that same summer camp. That had happened decades before, and it wasn't really known whether it was fact or myth. He imagined the crew searching the bottom if they came across that find. At least the beer would be cold.

The most troubling aspect of the case, however, had to do with the way the suspects were discovered at the lake. After shooting up the canoe, they were bound and blindfolded in the victim's camp and claimed to have been attacked and knocked unconscious by wolves or some other large animal after killing their target. This was, of course, preposterous. Someone else had to have been at the campsite. When they regained consciousness, they found themselves restrained and blindfolded, saying the wolves were in the camp nudging their bodies, nipping at their arms and legs, licking their faces, and sniffing all around them. One even claimed the animals urinated on him more than once. He thought he heard a voice whisper in his ear, asking who had sent them, and the two started to babble everything they knew about the plan. The animals finally stopped, and they began to shout for help. A park ranger found them safe the next morning when he came to check on the man doing the research.

The evidence showed wolves had indeed been in the campsite all around them. Tracks, patches of gray fur, and even urine were present at the scene. There was no evidence regarding who left the suspects bound and blind-folded, however. Wolves didn't tie men up and certainly wouldn't have blindfolded them. The police and the rangers asked if it could have been their target, but both suspects were adamant that they'd killed him. They never saw him surface after they shot him. They said the canoe was a good fifty yards from shore. If he was alive, he certainly would've *had* to surface. The rangers knew the victim was a retired schoolteacher from the United States and seemed capable of the research he was there to do. He even helped the rangers on several occasions, impressing them with his knowledge and skill outdoors. There was evidence someone else had been in the campsite recently, probably a woman. Smaller boot prints, a woman's scarf, and longer hair in the tent were found, but nothing less than a week old. These discoveries certainly didn't suggest the presence of someone capable of incapacitating two full-grown men. The puzzle pieces weren't fitting together, and Preston kept running them through his mind, hoping to find the piece he was missing. Now this mess in the United States seemed to be related.

"Inspector Preston." The voice brought him back to the present. He sat up straight, opening his eyes. The navigator stood before him, smiling. "Sir, the pilot wondered if you'd like to spend some time on the flight deck?"

Preston managed to smile as he gathered his thoughts. "I'd love to; it's my first time on one of these planes."

Preston stood up, now fully aware of his surroundings, and followed the officer toward the front of the aircraft. They passed the other passenger—the one who had rendered the flight late—and the crew chief on their way to the open door and the ladder to the cockpit. The crew chief was checking to make sure the cargo they were ferrying to an American base in Georgia was secure. The other passenger leaned over one of the packs, checking it carefully. The duffel bag was open, and Preston could see it contained what appeared to be a shiny medal cylinder. The other pack leaned against the seat and looked full and heavy. Preston was drawn to the second large knife, whose sheath was attached to the left shoulder strap of the pack. The crew chief stood nearby, watching the man's progress. When they walked by, the passenger looked up, smiling at the two men.

"Having a nice flight, sir?" asked the young navigator of the other passenger. The tone of voice was more than just being polite; there seemed to be an aura of respect in the addition to the word "sir" used by the young officer.

"The flight has been very comfortable, Lieutenant. My compliments to the major," responded the passenger. The man obviously knew the pilot. He then surprised Preston by speaking to him. "Enjoy the tour, Inspector. I think you'll find it quite interesting."

Preston took a good look at the man, seeing a sincere smile on the face looking back at him. He couldn't help but return the smile. The man knew he was a policeman. How? They were never introduced. They went through the door leading to the flight deck. The navigator motioned for Preston to climb up the ladder. Preston did as he was told, while the young officer closed and secured the door behind them. He couldn't remember whether the door was open or closed throughout the rest of the flight.

It wasn't a long climb, and when he reached the top, he found himself in an area full of electronics. Sitting forward of this compartment were three men. The pilot, the copilot, and the flight engineer were seated in the glass-enclosed dome that was the cockpit. All three men were friendly while he was shown what everything in the cockpit was for. He was surprised to find they had a bunk in this area of the aircraft. It made sense when they explained the duration of some of their flights could be days in this age of midair refueling. At one point, there was a slight shutter to the aircraft. The crew didn't seem worried, so Preston thought nothing more about it. The pilot was speaking to air traffic control, and the copilot explained that they were crossing over into United States airspace and were being handed over to the NORAD controllers in Rome, New York. Preston looked down at the earth below them and thought how beautiful all the lights looked in between the clouds. Above them, the moon was in its last quarter, providing some additional light in the darkened cockpit. The flight engineer pointed out concentrations of light and began identifying cities. The copilot reached for several switches, and the aircraft again generated a slight shutter.

This peaked Preston's interest, so he asked about it. "I could feel the plane shutter a bit. What was happening?"

"It was a routine adjustment because we're about to begin our descent into the New York City area," answered the flight engineer.

The pilot, who was on the radio almost constantly, turned and explained they were given a priority approach and landing clearance because of Preston's mission. The FBI would be meeting him at the airfield and taking him to the scene of the hostage crisis in upstate New York. It had been determined the case he was working on was related. The pilot told Preston the navigator would be taking him back down to the cargo area because they would be on the ground in less than thirty minutes.

Preston thanked the crew and followed the navigator back down the ladder. He felt a blast of cold air when the door was opened and was handed a flight jacket and a blanket by the crew chief when he entered the cargo hold of the aircraft.

"Sorry for the change in temperature, Inspector," explained the crew chief. "We had a pressurization issue down here, sir. The compartment cooled off quite a bit, but these will keep you warm and toasty."

Preston took the jacket and put it on as he looked around the cargo hold. He looked at the navigator, asking, "Where's the other passenger?" The other man was nowhere in the compartment. The packs were gone, as well as the duffel. The shutter of the aircraft, the cold temperature in the hold, and the missing man—this didn't make any sense.

He looked the navigator squarely in the eyes, waiting for a reply.

"What man are you talking about, Inspector? You're the only passenger we have on board tonight."

Preston watched the young man's eyes twinkle back at him and was taken by the broad smile that accompanied the look. This would be the entire crew's answer, and being military personnel, he had no authority to pursue his questions with them.

Again, Preston eyed the navigator, making his suspicions quite clear. "Did we just drop a spy into a friendly nation?"

The young navigator continued to smile, turning and heading for the door to the flight deck without another word—however, that alone was answer enough. The crew chief put his hand on Preston's shoulder and motioned to where he had been sitting before. "Have a seat, Inspector. I think the thin air up here must be affecting you. It happens all the time if you're not used to it."

Preston saw a similar twinkle in the crew chief's eyes, accompanied by a broad grin.

Mohawk Tavern and Grill
Bluffton, New York
July 18, 2010
2245 hours

The Mohawk was closed every Sunday by ten o'clock, but not tonight. Maggie told Sheriff James she would stay open all night to make sure his deputies, the state police, and the dozens of other law enforcement officers would have someplace to get food, coffee, and rest, if needed. Besides, with the influx of the media in the area, she was making enough money to make up for the free food she was giving the police.

Fred watched the crowds growing around the marina and could see Issy camped out in his office to make sure his interests were looked after. He shook his head, looking up at the stars and the moon from his place on the Mohawk's rooftop. The sky was starting to cloud up. The weather forecast predicted heavy thunderstorms after midnight, but Fred guessed they would arrive closer to morning. Without streetlights, the stars seemed to jump out at you. The half-moon put out enough light to cause the trees to cast shadows. If you weren't used to the woods, it would look spooky and ghostlike.

He was not alone on the roof tonight. Matt joined him, as did Matt's daughter Cassie, and nephew Stephen. It reminded Fred of the days when Ray would bring the boys here and Fred had taught them all how to tell time by the stars and tell them stories. They weren't telling stories tonight, though; they were all worried about loved ones.

"I can't believe Abby agreed to guide the rescue team in," said Stephen, while Cassie pointed out a shooting star. "She doesn't agree with the plan because she feels there are too many hostiles on the island."

"Then she'll be their best chance of getting away safely," commented Fred.

"They're estimating up to forty armed intruders on the island, Uncle Fred," said Cassie. "They're sending in half that many. Sounds like a fool's errand to me."

"I'm afraid she'll get hurt, surprise or not," added Stephen. "They're assuming they have automatic weapons and some police or military training. The leader is a former Lakeview cop."

"So much for operational security," chuckled Matt.

Fred smiled at Matt's comment. "Abby is a warrior, and it's not in the stars for her to die on the island tomorrow. She has a full life ahead of her, and she'll be back."

"How can you be so—" Stephen stopped midsentence, watching a shadow pass in front of the moon. "Did you see that?"

"Something moved across the moon," added Cassie. "It was too big to be a bird. It almost looked like a parachute."

"It was a cloud," stated Matt flatly.

"That was no cloud, Dad," protested Cassie, "you need new glasses."

"It's the spirit of the Wolf Clan coming to take revenge on those who have transgressed on our sacred ground." Fred was looking unusually proud of himself.

"I think the two of you have been smoking some ceremonial herbs," said Stephen as he carefully got up and stepped past the two older men to get to the open window in a nearby dormer. "I need to get down to the bar to help Nathan with the crowd."

"And I'm going with you," said Cassie, carefully following her cousin, "because you're going to make me a very large, strong drink."

The two older men watched until the cousins disappeared into the open window. Matt looked at Fred and asked, "Spirit of the Wolf Clan?"

Fred smiled, continuing to look at the stars. "Be respectful, paleface; I'm a medicine man, a mystic, of the Wolf Clan, of the Mohawk Nation. Besides, it was just as good as your cloud explanation."

"Better," answered Matt with a chuckle, "because it's somewhat true. I have a feeling that some very nasty things will be happening on that island come morning."

It was Fred's turn to laugh.

CHAPTER THREE

SPIRITS FROM THE PAST

Stewart Air National Guard Base
Newburgh, New York
July 18, 2010
2330 hours

Preston disembarked the C-130 an hour later, still upset over being lied to about the other passenger having been on the aircraft. He guessed the man had parachuted out over American airspace, and he wasn't sure what to do about that, because he was here in the United States to help the FBI with a possible terrorist case that might be connected to his. Did this mean he was indirectly involved in espionage against a friendly power? Either way, he didn't want to have to lie to the people he came to work with. So, he made a call to his supervisor after getting off the aircraft. The call took a few minutes, and his boss made a call of his own. The result made Preston feel better. They were not dropping spies into the United States, and the RCAF would be tracking down who the other passenger was. He was to be open about this with his FBI contacts, so as not to create other issues.

Preston was forthcoming about the incident when he met the lead agent, Glenn Grey, after disembarking from the plane. Grey smiled, saying nothing surprised him anymore, as they traveled in a caravan of government SUVs speeding north on the New York State Thruway.

Preston was in the SUV with Grey, Trask, the US attorney assigned to the case, and the attorney's assistant. They shared with him what was going on at Shadow Lake and how it related to the case he was investigating. He in turn shared the details of his case.

"Wolves in the campsite, Inspector?" asked Trask. "Are your people sure about that? It doesn't seem logical."

Preston grunted, thinking prosecutors in the United States were no different than those in Canada. He looked at the man. "Park rangers there confirmed the story of the two men. We found wolf DNA in several places in and around the campsite. Fur, urine, scat, and such were found all around the area. It really unnerved these two hard cases; they couldn't stop talking."

"But wolves don't tie people up," interjected Trask. "How do the park rangers explain that?"

Grey chuckled, and Preston gave him an irritated glance.

Preston took a deep breath before saying, "The two suspects are adamant they killed their target. They never saw him surface after filling the canoe with holes. There were twenty-eight, to be exact, mostly on the starboard side and bottom. Our first thought was they missed and were attacked by Mr. Summers. They never saw what hit them because they were knocked unconscious. We do have evidence of another person—smaller, likely a woman—being in Mr. Summers's campsite possibly a week before. But even so, this person wouldn't have been big enough to take these two guys out. Mr. Summers was an accomplished canoeist, according to the rangers, but other than that, we only knew he was a retired teacher. Today, you tell me he was in the Navy and this man Kingston had him killed."

"I don't mean to sound like I'm questioning your investigation," Trask explained apologetically, "but some pieces of the puzzle just don't fit—such as animals being responsible for tying up and blindfolding two full-grown men."

"Tell me about it," commented Preston. "I was trying to put those puzzle pieces together on the flight here when I ran into the other situation."

"The mystery passenger?" asked Trask, and Preston nodded.

"My experience tells me it's related to this whole thing somehow, but I'll be damned if I can figure it out. He would have parachuted out somewhere near where we're headed, if my calculations are correct."

"Using wolves is an interesting interrogation technique," said Grey, bringing the conversation back on track.

"That can't be true," interjected Trask. "Who would use a vicious animal to interrogate a suspect? How could you control them?"

Grey grinned in response. Preston answered.

"Wolves can be vicious when they need to be, but they're social by nature. We think they were prompted to be near the suspects and lick and nip at them. We found traces of canned stew on their clothing. We also found traces of human urine along with wolf urine on the clothing of one of the suspects."

"Ew!" The lawyer sitting next to Trask in the back seat wrinkled her nose. Trask looked surprised. "What?"

Grey's grin turned to a knowing smile. Again, it was Preston who answered.

"We think the person who tied the men up urinated on the one suspect to mark his territory, if you will, and in turn, the alpha male of the pack did the same thing. The human urine didn't belong to the suspect, at least not from that part of his clothing. We haven't been able to provide a DNA match to it."

The attorney sitting next to Trask turned her head and smiled, blushing as she did.

Trask shook his head. "Damned interesting. I think I'd be talking and telling whoever this was my life's story."

Preston smiled at the response, turning to Grey to add, "Mr. Summers was in your Navy. What was his job when he worked for them?"

Grey held the gaze of the Canadian investigator. "Admiral Summers was a Navy SEAL and worked for Naval Intelligence."

Grey watched several of the missing puzzle pieces appear and fall into place for Preston—though there was no change in the man's expression. Grey leaned forward to the two agents in the front seat. "Billy, see if we can get a copy of Admiral Summers's personnel jacket from the Pentagon, at least the part that's not redacted. Make sure it contains a recent picture and have it waiting for us when we reach Bluffton. Also see if they can provide a sample of the admiral's DNA to the inspector's people for comparison."

"Yes, sir!" replied the man in the front passenger seat of the SUV, picking up his cell. Grey turned to see a sly smile on Preston's face and a look of shock on Trask's.

"What are you saying, Glenn?" asked Trask.

Grey smiled. "Do you believe in ghosts, Mike?"

Mohawk Tavern and Grill
Bluffton, New York
July 18, 2010
2345 hours

It'd been a long day. Of course, the crowd was normally lighter, even now during the peak of the summer tourist season—but that night, the place was packed and would probably remain that way throughout this crisis. Police, federal agents, reporters, locals, and even just the curious seemed to have moved in. Everyone waited for the next tidbit of news about the fate of those being held hostage on the island.

Stephen was glad he came back down off the roof to help Nathan because the bar was still busy, even so late into the night. Maggie had decided to keep the place open until 2:00 a.m. He and Nathan would retire after they closed and cleaned the bar. Maggie called in all her staff due to the increased business, setting up shifts to accommodate the temporary change in hours. Stephen's aunt Karen also jumped in to help and was working in the kitchen with Maggie. They planned on keeping coffee and food available all night for the police and fire personnel working across the street, and if they sold a meal or two to the curious along the way, so be it. Nathan's brother, Jared, and his sisters, Brandi and Hannah, were opening in the morning, leaving Nathan and Stephen free to see if the scheduled rescue attempt would be successful.

Sarah's family finally arrived. Her mother, Becky, and her grandfather were scheduled to be in earlier that day, but when news of the hostage takeover on the island reached them, they diverted to Syracuse, where they met a private jet carrying Stephen's brother, Sean, Sarah's husband, and her uncle, Kevin. They were now sitting in a corner of the bar with Matt, Fred, and the rest of the family. Stephen guessed they were in the process of bringing the new arrivals up to speed, although he knew his uncle Matt and Fred were planning something. They seemed to know more than what they were telling everyone else.

"Too bad about the people on the island being taken hostage." The comment brought Stephen back to reality. It'd been made by a man of about thirty who had been in and out of the bar a couple of times that night. He spoke with a bit of an accent, which made the man memorable. This time, there was an Asian woman with him. He recognized her as the reporter who tried to talk to him and Cassie as they left the marina earlier.

Stephen asked, "How can I help you?"

"Are you still serving food?" the man asked politely.

"Yes. I can find you a table."

The man smiled, shaking his head. "No thanks, the order will be to go. Our cameraman is manning the remote feed, and we better eat with him, or we'll have a bit of a snit, if you know what I mean."

This brought a smile to Stephen's face. He produced a couple of menus from under the bar, handing one to each of them. It took less than a minute, and they ordered three meals to go. Stephen wrote the order down, asking, "Can I get you something to drink while you wait?"

The man smiled broadly. "That would be nice." He gestured to the woman sitting on the stool beside him. She nodded her approval. "The young lady will take something fruity with rum, and I'll take an Irish beer of any kind, if you have one. We won't tell the cameraman. He can't have one; he's on duty."

"You English?" asked Stephen, placing the food order on the computer behind the bar.

"Gawd, no!" exclaimed the man. "I was born an Irishman. Right now, I'm an American citizen doing an honest job."

Stephen saw the woman smile at that comment. He guessed it was because the man wasn't quite telling the entire truth. He made the drink for the reporter and handed it to her. She thanked him and took a sip. Her eyes opened wide when she realized how much rum was in the drink, and she thanked him again. He handed the man a bottle of Guinness from the cooler below the counter.

"Thanks," said the man. "You Yanks need to learn how to drink a good beer. Room temperature is the way to do that, not chilled."

It was Stephen's turn to smile.

"You should have asked; my uncle only drinks his at room temperature. I could have gotten one for you."

"Next time." The man returned Stephen's grin. "Do you think they'll mount a rescue operation in the morning?"

At this, Stephen's smile disappeared. "Couldn't say. Being a reporter to the end, are we?"

"Actually, I'm the producer," said the man, his accent now showing a bit more. "She's the reporter. Nothing personal, man. We're just doing our job. I'm just gathering background information and such for the story. It's big news right now."

"Are they giving you a hard time, little brother?" asked a voice from behind Stephen. He turned to find Sean standing there, looking very serious. He had several empty beer bottles in his hand.

"No, big brother, they're just doing their job," replied Stephen sarcastically, looking back at Ryan and Kay.

Ryan raised his eyebrows, sizing up Justin's brothers. The resemblance was uncanny. Justin told him if he wasn't careful with the family, the ranks would close quickly and getting information from them would be impossible. It appeared that the door had just been slammed in his face. They would have to rely on locals for their information, and that would be tough, seeing as he spoke with an accent, Kay didn't look like she came from Bluffton, and Justin couldn't do it because someone might recognize him.

Kay stepped up to try to lighten the mood. "You make a mean drink," she said to the first brother, Stephen. "I promise, no more questions. Make me another one of these and I promise to keep my producer quiet as well."

Kay got her drink, but the mood between Stephen and the pair didn't get better.

Mohawk Tavern and Grill
Bluffton, New York
July 18, 2010
2355 hours

The woman finished the text and got up from the table, putting her phone in her jacket pocket. The restaurant and bar were both packed and a gold mine of information. The locals seemed willing to talk to the media, mostly about how terrible this incident was and how nice Mrs. Summers and her family were, even though they weren't from Bluffton. She knew anything she got from the locals needed to be taken with a grain of salt. The same with the conversations between the reporters and other media types as they compared notes. More important were the quiet conversations between the members of law enforcement taking their breaks in the restaurant. She felt she was getting a pretty good picture of what was going on.

As she stepped onto Lake Street and into the cool evening, she looked up and noticed the stars that were there earlier were gone, covered by clouds. The weather called for heavy rain overnight, and it seemed likely the local authorities would try their rescue when the storms came. She'd overheard the conversations and knew a rescue was planned for some time before dawn. For now, it was time to walk toward her hotel just around the corner to get some sleep before all the excitement started. She would be leaving in the morning after passing on some last-minute information to her team on the island. She needed to be ready for the next phase of the plan, and that meant she couldn't be in Bluffton much past noon.

The team on the island was expendable, although they didn't know that. Their escape plan was only on paper. If they managed to get off the island, there would be no cars waiting for them. They would be on their own. They didn't know who she was, just that there was a contact in the village keeping track of the authorities and their plans. They also didn't know who hired them because that was done over the phone and the computer. Hapke thought she was a fifty-year-old man from New York City. She made sure he would never find out the truth, even if he did survive.

She took her phone out when it chimed, touching the screen to light up the display, and read the new text message that popped up. They would be ready to ambush the rescue party when it came. Good. She typed as she walked, indicating she received their message. Returning the phone to her pocket, she continued, smiling to herself as she turned the corner toward the hotel.

United States Disciplinary Barracks
Fort Leavenworth, Kansas
July 18, 2010
2300 hours

Kingston lay on his cot, smiling. The plan was working. He managed to make out some of the hushed whispers from the guards. There were hostages being held in New York State, and an email was sent to the White House demanding his release. The hostages included his ex-wife and her new husband

and some high-ranking politicians. It couldn't have worked out better. The best news was the confirmation that Jon Summers was dead. Having his body on the coroner's slab would make him feel better, but he was still ecstatic. The guards wondered if he'd sent the email, because he had not been near a computer in weeks. The computer IP address was traced to Fort Leavenworth by the FBI. They were now investigating guards who came in contact with him to see if one of them was an accomplice. They were nervous and making the mistake of talking too much around him.

There was an FBI team on-site, joined by a team from the United States Marshals Service. Kingston guessed they would be moving him before the end of the day tomorrow, or the marshals wouldn't be here. Yes, the plan was working, and he and Andrea would both be free and making up for those years behind bars. They would disappear and live comfortably ever after. His freedom would soon be secured, and those who put him behind bars would be punished. He closed his eyes, the smile remaining on his face.

Upton's Marina and Boat Sales
Bluffton, New York
July 19, 2010
0005 hours

The van Ryan and Kay climbed into was parked on the road next to the marina. It was packed with electronic equipment and a transmission tower that made it pass for a TV news vehicle. There was even equipment allowing it to send video and audio signals, but not to a TV station. The tower was up, and Justin was working on several things. Kay climbed into the back, taking the empty seat next to Justin, and opened a large plastic bag, pulling out a take-out container. He took it, placing it on an empty workspace in front of him. Ryan, who had hopped into the empty passenger seat of the van, handed him a large Styrofoam cup with a cover on it. Justin gave him an annoyed look as he took the cup.

"Sorry, man," said Ryan with a shrug, "they don't allow alcohol to go at the Mohawk. You were right about pushing for information. Your older brother shut things down quickly when he thought we were harassing your younger brother. Even Kay's charm and pretty smile didn't get us anywhere."

Justin looked to Kay, who said, "It was a tough crowd for sure."

Kay exchanged another take-out container with Ryan for another large drink, and all three began to eat a late dinner. Between bites, Ryan asked, "Did you pick anything up on this fancy gizmo they gave us to play with?"

Justin smirked, taking a paper napkin from where Kay had placed them and wiping his mouth before saying, "This thing can do most anything. I can tell you from the radio and cell traffic that the good sheriff and the state police plan to launch a rescue around 2:00 a.m. I can tell you there are those on the sheriff's staff who have advised against this, but he doesn't want to turn this over to the FBI at dawn. I can also tell you that every media outlet here knows about this, although not the specific timeframe."

"That's not good," said Kay as she took a sip of her drink.

"If they know," interjected Ryan with a thoughtful look, "then it's a good possibility the buggers on the island also know."

"They do," responded Justin, "or at least, I think they do. There are signals from cell phones here going to phones on the island. They're not voice transmissions—probably text messages, so I don't know what the content is. They're talking to each other on a regular basis."

Kay raised an eyebrow. "So, someone here is talking to someone on the island?"

"More than one someone, Kay. There's at least two—maybe three—different cell phones here in Bluffton and two on the island. One of the cells on the island is also sending out messages to other cell phones as well. They're all outside this area, and many of them seem to be in transit."

"We need to figure out who here in Bluffton is sending out information," stated Kay, thinking out loud.

"You said 'in transit,'" noted Ryan. "Do we know where they're going?"

Justin's expression became serious. "Here. They're on their way *here*."

All three of them exchanged looks, thinking of the implications of Justin's answer. The equipment in the van was tied into the computers at their home office in Langley, Virginia, so they were able to track the other cell signals via their GPS chips, no matter where they were in the world. A beeping alarm on the console in front of Justin told the three of them someone was transmitting a signal.

"Where from?" asked Ryan simply.

"The island—and it's a text message," answered Justin.

Just then, Justin's cell, which was sitting on the console, went off. The screen lit up with the notification of a new text message.

"Oh my God!" exclaimed Kay.

The three of them exchanged nervous looks before Ryan said, "This has got to be a coincidence. This is too much."

"Only one way to find out," said Justin simply, picking up his phone. All three crowded around the console so they could read the message on the small screen. He pulled up the new text message, which read, "Are you in Bluffton yet?"

They all looked at one another. Finally, Kay stated the obvious. "It's from someone on the island."

"But who?" asked Ryan.

"And how'd they get my cell number?" added Justin.

"Answer it, Justin," Kay suggested. "Maybe we can draw out more information."

Justin typed, "Yes, who is this?"

The console beeped again, indicating that Justin's message was on the way. Less than thirty seconds later, the alarm went off again, followed by the chime on Justin's cell. Justin touched his screen, bringing up the text message.

What they read chilled their blood.

"Stop the rescue!!! Ambush!!!"

Upton's Marina and Boat Sales
Bluffton, New York
July 19, 2010
0030 hours

Matt, accompanied by his nephew Sean and Sean's mother-in-law, Becky, arrived to meet with the sheriff. He was grateful the crowd of reporters thinned out considerably, so they weren't questioned entering the marina. They were offered seats in the small showroom, and Issy, who refused to leave his business at the mercy of the sheriff's office, popped out of the back room and offered them coffee. Matt and Becky took Issy up on his offer, but Sean declined, pacing nervously about. He wore a T-shirt that exposed some burn scars he received on September 11 at the Pentagon while rescuing victims from the attack. The deputy assigned to them stared at the scars, but Sean didn't seem to notice.

To everyone's surprise, Abby entered the showroom and walked over to Sean, giving him a hug as she said, "I'm so sorry, Sean. Sheriff James wants to end this quick and won't listen to anyone."

Sean returned the hug and gave his brother's girlfriend a kiss on the cheek. He then, cupping her shoulders, pushed her back to look at her. He smiled and nodded at her in her uniform. "Deputy Crogan, you do look good."

Abby blushed, and Sean pulled her close, hugging her again. This time, he whispered, "Whatever happens, Abby, you take care of yourself."

She and Sean released, and she went over to Matt, who repeated the hug with her and added, "I'm going to tell you the same thing Sean just said— you take care if he decides to go through with this."

"Stephen?" asked Abby as she released Matt and hugged Becky.

"He's fine," answered Matt. "He's helping your mother with the crowd. He and your brother will be here in the morning when you get back."

Before they could continue the conversation, James walked in, followed by Deputy Jasper and a New York State Police captain. The look on his face told them this appeal was going nowhere. The man looked irritated to have to be there with them.

"What can I do for you folks?" asked James, remaining polite. His tone left no doubt as to how he felt.

"Sheriff James," started Matt, "my name is Matthew Sum—"

"I know who you are, Mr. Summers, and I'll save you the time by saying we're going in. Nothing you can do or say will stop that from happening."

"Sheriff," Becky said, "do you think you have enough intelligence to launch a rescue attempt? Don't you think gathering a little more information on the bad guys might be prudent?"

Matt cringed when he saw the sheriff's face twist into a rictus of ire, as though Becky wasn't making a common-sense proposal but rather suggesting he grow wings, take flight, and rescue the hostages himself.

"And you're *who*, ma'am?" asked the sheriff with an edge to his voice.

Becky took a deep breath. "I'm Dr. Rebecca O'Keefe, Sean's mother-in-law."

The look on the sheriff's face said everything and more, but he decided nonetheless to follow up with an explanation. "Dr. O'Keefe, I assume you're a practitioner of medicine, so I won't waste your time because it's so expensive." Becky's face flushed, and both Matt and Sean went pale. "I don't tell you how to treat your patients, so please don't presume to tell me how to do my job. You have no experience with law enforcement."

Becky's face was bright red. "You're right, Sheriff James. I have no law enforcement experience, but I do have experience as a hostage," she went on, almost without thinking, and the sheriff's posture went rigid, "and I know what can happen when even true professionals don't have the right intelligence. You owe it to the hostages and to your own people to make sure you have accurate information. I—"

The state police captain stiffened at the "true professionals" comment, and James got just as flushed as Becky.

He interrupted her with a clipped, "That's quite enough, Dr. O'Keefe. I think we're done here." He turned to Abby, adding, "Deputy Crogan, escort these people out of here."

Sean stepped up to within inches of James.

"Look, Sheriff James, you may not think much of us, but the man behind this is ruthless and most certainly has anticipated your attempt to rescue the hostages. All we're asking is for you to wait a bit longer until we know what he has waiting for you on the island."

"Get out of here, boy, before I arrest your ass."

James was so angry, he clenched his fists until his knuckles were white.

"Get them out of here, Crogan," the sheriff added. "Now!"

Abby took Sean by the arm, leading him away from her boss. Sean's gaze remained on James until they were outside the showroom, being led to the street. They walked to the fire police checkpoint at the entrance to the marina. Becky said, "Well, all things considered, that went well—at least we're not in jail."

"I'm not taking his side," said Abby, "but you pushed his buttons with that 'true professionals' comment."

Becky reached out and put her arm around Abby's shoulder. "I know. Unfortunately, it's true. If the man goes in, people are going to get hurt or worse, because his ego won't let him wait. I'm pretty sure the man who orchestrated this has probably accounted for an early rescue attempt."

Abby looked at the woman next to her and said, "I'm going with them; I'll make sure everyone gets out."

Becky looked at her son-in-law. "I wish your father was here. He'd take that arrogant son of a bitch out behind one of the boats and kick the shit out of him."

There was a chuckle from Matt, who was walking a few steps behind them. "And if your ex-husband were alive, he would have shot him where he stood."

Becky looked over her shoulder in surprise at the comment. She withdrew her arm from around Abby and slowed until Matt came up even with her. She took his hand and squeezed it. "You're right about that, Mr. Summers. Are you saying you'd agree with that course of action?"

Matt looked at her with a half smile on his face and shrugged.

Upton's Marina and Boat Sales
Bluffton, New York
July 19, 2010
0130 hours

James was upset over the meeting with the Summers family and couldn't sleep. His strike team consisted of his deputies, a State Police Special Operations Response Team, and several FBI agents. They were trying to get some rest before they would have to get ready for the rescue. The team consisted of twenty-two people, including Abby. He knew she felt it was ill-advised to attempt a rescue, but she assured him she would do as she was ordered. He asked the FBI to get some information on Dr. O'Keefe—he was curious about her comment about being a hostage before and felt that might be important if he had to deal with her again later—and they assured him they would have the information when they returned.

The rescue team was scheduled to arrive on the island about 4:00 a.m.— not that it would matter, because the forecast was for heavy rain and thunderstorms. Hopefully the weather would cover their movements.

James continued to be bothered by the comments from both the Summers boy and his mother-in-law. The elder Summers was strangely quiet but obviously wanted them to hold off going in. Why? He approached the entrance to the marina, noticing there was only one reporter and her cameraman near the barricades set up by the fire police. He decided it was a good time to get a cup of coffee from the Mohawk. The stuff Issy was trying to pass off as coffee was swill. James smiled, thinking he hadn't ever seen Issy drinking it. He always went out for his.

The smile on his face disappeared as he reached the barricade and a reporter asked, "Sheriff James, do you think your security has been compromised?" At this, he balked, looking the reporter in the face. She added, "You know, due to the information getting out that you're launching a rescue attempt at dawn?"

James stopped dead in his tracks, again looking the pretty, young reporter squarely in the eyes. The man next to her had the camera up but wasn't the man he'd seen with the camera earlier. He looked around and saw one of his deputies and a trooper headed toward him and motioned for them to hurry over.

"No comment, Sheriff?" asked the reporter. "I thought you might be worried, because if we have that information, so might the people holding the hostages."

The deputy and the trooper arrived.

"Take these two into custody," Sheriff James ordered. "Take them to the showroom—and I want one officer to stay with them."

"You can't do that, Sheriff," protested the cameraman in an Irish accent. His lack of concern and respect was infuriating to James. "Freedom of the press and all that."

James ignored the protest, gesturing for his subordinates to take action. "They're not to talk to anyone until we return. Understood?"

The two law enforcement officers nodded, escorting the news people toward the building. James's smile returned, and he nodded to the two fire policemen manning the post by the barricades. They, in turn, chuckled.

As instructed by the sheriff, the deputy stayed with the news people after they were ushered into the darkened showroom. Their camera and other equipment were placed on a table near the door, and they were allowed to sit in a couple of folding metal chairs nearby. Nothing was said between them. The deputy didn't notice the small light on the camera, indicating the device was on. The news people were quiet and that, after all, was all he cared about.

The door opened, and Abby came into the showroom, looking at her coworker. The deputy nodded, saying nothing. She made her way to the news people.

"Where'd you get the information about the rescue?" she asked. Her tone was neutral but direct, and she shifted her gaze back and forth between the reporter and the cameraman. She settled her gaze on the young reporter and added, "You can tell me here or we can go into the backroom, and I guarantee you'll tell me there."

The reporter looked surprised by the comment but said nothing. It was the cameraman who spoke.

"I don't think you'll do that," he replied evenly. "Doing so would cost you your job—and besides, our sources are confidential."

Abby leaned down so that only the news people could hear what she said. "Listen to me carefully. I have family on that island, and if anything happens to jeopardize this rescue, I'm coming back to kick your ass, then hers, and your confidential source's ass. Damn the job. You better pray it doesn't come to that, because you'll talk to me then."

Abby looked at the deputy guarding the two and nodded. She then headed toward the door. The deputy called her to wait, and the two of them stepped outside. As soon as the door shut behind their backs, Kay and Ryan looked at each other.

"You were right," said Ryan, "she is a fiery one."

There was a chuckle on the other end of the miniature earpiece each of them wore. The deputies hadn't noticed they were wearing them, and their cell phones sat on the desk with the camera, well within range of the Bluetooth devices they wore under their clothing. The system allowed them two-way communications with Justin, snuggled safely in the van.

"As much of a treat as it would be to see her kick your ass," Justin said with a chuckle, "we need to stay focused."

Ryan smiled. "I'd rather see her try to kick Kay's butt."

Kay turned, hitting Ryan on the shoulder. "The man said *stay focused.*" Ryan jumped back in mock fear as Kay turned her attention to Justin, asking, "Do you think the sheriff will back off on the rescue attempt?"

There were a few seconds of silence before the answer came over the earpieces.

"No."

Summers' Cabin
Adirondack State Park, New York
July 19, 2010
0230 hours

The living room was dimly lit, and most of the hostages were sleeping. There was a guard by the door to the front porch, who was dozing, and another by the entrance to the kitchen, who was wide awake. He ignored the hostages for the most part but was alert to any sudden movements. The hostages were either lying on the floor or on the furniture. Their restraints had been removed, and they'd been allowed to get blankets and pillows to sleep.

Nancy was awakened by the sound of soft crying behind her. Next to her, Emily was curled up and cuddled with RJ, both sleeping soundly. On the couch above them, little Patty slept in her mother's arms. In the dim light, Nancy could see Sarah's eyes were open and she was looking in her direction.

Nancy silently mouthed, "Who's crying?"

Sarah shrugged and motioned that it was coming from behind Nancy. Nancy rolled, slowly sitting up. The guard by the front door jumped awake. The man looked around the room and then settled back down into his chair. The sentry by the kitchen was not as lax, exchanging a guarded look with Nancy before going back to looking out the front window into the black night.

Nancy made a show of fluffing the pillow she was using and then decided to lie back down, finding herself facing O'Leary, tears rolling down her cheeks. Behind O'Leary, Nancy could see Ericson lying awake, his wife sleeping in his arms. A roll of his eyes told Nancy he wasn't happy with the crying.

"What's wrong, Amy?" Nancy whispered, giving Josh an irritated glare over the crying woman's shoulder. Ericson smirked in return.

"Oh . . ." O'Leary busied herself wiping away tears. "I didn't mean to wake you. I'm so sorry."

"You didn't wake me, Amy." Nancy kept her voice even, despite Josh continuing to make faces behind O'Leary's back. "Why are you crying?"

"Because he's dead," O'Leary said, the tears starting down her cheeks again.

It was all Nancy could do not to reach over the poor woman and hit Ericson in the head because of the look he gave her. Instead, she put her hand on O'Leary's shoulder.

"Who's dead, dear?"

The expression on O'Leary's face scared Nancy. Her eyes got big and round with anger. If the light were better, she guessed the senator would be flushed with color. O'Leary wiped the tears away again and whispered, "Jon's dead! Your *husband* is dead. Don't you feel anything?"

Nancy guessed the look on her face must have been one of shock. She had forgotten O'Leary once tried to seduce her husband and guessed the woman didn't know he told her about it. O'Leary obviously wasn't over the relationship from the summer Jon was at the Naval Academy as acting super-intendent. O'Leary went along on several adventures with Jon while hunting a vicious serial killer stalking the Chesapeake Bay area. Jon was a guest on her sailing yacht when O'Leary tried to seduce him in the shower. Nancy knew her husband could resist most anything, but she was truly amazed he managed to resist O'Leary's advances. She was a beautiful and determined woman who was used to getting what she wanted. That was probably why she still felt the way she did. Jon was the one that got away.

Nancy glanced at Ericson, who gave her a look indicating she shouldn't an-swer the question. She flashed him her best *go to hell* look, focusing on O'Leary.

"Look, Amy, I know about you trying to seduce Jon back in Annapolis . . ."

"Oh my God!" blurted out O'Leary in a raised whisper. Behind Nancy, Sarah chuckled out loud. O'Leary's look of anger was replaced by one of fear.

"Quiet over there!" ordered the sentry by the front door. The sentry by the kitchen shifted slightly but said nothing.

Nancy took a quick look around while she waited for the two guards to settle back down. Josh's smirk was back on his face, and he was making a definite effort to avoid her stare. He obviously didn't expect her to know about Amy and Jon. She knew if the man looked at her, he would start to laugh. He obviously approved of how she was dealing with the woman be-cause he wasn't trying to warn her off—or was he just being chicken? She decided she would deal with her old friend when this was all over.

Both guards settled. Nancy gently squeezed O'Leary's shoulder. The woman jumped as she looked into Nancy's eyes. "Look," said Nancy, "if nothing else, Jon and I have had an honest relationship all these years, and I trust him, even with you." O'Leary shuddered but relaxed as she saw the gentle determination in Nancy's gaze. "Jon told me about the boat while we were still at Annapolis. As far as him being dead, I have only one question: Where is the body?"

"Huh?" O'Leary clearly didn't understand where Nancy was going with this.

"Hapke said he was dead, but they were still looking for the body. That's a big assumption to make considering who you're talking about. And besides, Ron Hapke has made a life's career underestimating Jon. Since they haven't heard from the two guys they sent to kill Jon, my guess is they'll find their bodies before they do Jon's."

O'Leary didn't respond except to sniffle.

"Now," continued Nancy in a more forceful tone, "pull yourself together, woman, and remember you're a United States senator. Jon must have seen something in you, or he wouldn't consider you a friend."

Sarah chuckled again; this time, she was joined by several others. There was also the sound of voices and movement outside of the cabin. They all strained to listen to see if they could make out what was going on.

The silence was finally broken by Ericson, who whispered, "Sounds like they're deploying their people. I'm guessing a rescue attempt is on the way. They seem to know they're coming."

"Not a good sign," commented Rice.

They all remained quiet, and most began falling back to sleep. Nancy finally made eye contact with Ericson, who just smiled at her and shrugged his shoulders. She flashed an angry glare at him, and he just repeated the shrug. She put her head down on her pillow and found herself staring into the smiling face of Amy O'Leary.

"Thank you," whispered the woman next to her.

Nancy thought what she really wanted to do was strangle the woman.

She returned the smile. "You're welcome."

Summers' Cabin
Adirondack State Park, New York
July 19, 2010
0245 hours

The weather was dry, but Hapke knew that was going to change. Some heavy weather was due to roll in just before dawn, and that was when he guessed the sheriff would try his rescue attempt. While it wasn't raining, he was moving his people into position, and they would be ready when the rescue landed. The text he just received from his contact said the rescue force would be leaving in about thirty to forty minutes. The contact confirmed the boats were ready and twenty-two law enforcement officers would be conducting the raid. Part of the rescue team was said to be a New York State Police SORT team, but Hapke had trained with them and knew their tactics. There was nothing to worry about there. The FBI agents were predictable, as were most of the deputies. Only a few personalities remained unknown. The part-time female deputy was relatively new, and she was only being allowed to come because she had knowledge of the island. He wasn't happy about that and gave orders to have her neutralized quickly. She was to be the only female on the rescue team and shouldn't be difficult to spot.

The route the rescue team was following stayed close to shore, avoiding open water until they were directly opposite the widest point of the island. This meant they would be exposed in the open for the shortest distance. Hapke was pleased with this inside information. It made his job easier. Now he would use this knowledge against his opponents and would keep them from rescuing his prisoners. He needed them to get away so they could let the FBI know how well fortified the island was to allow time for the rest of the plan to work. Once he got the all clear that Kingston was free, he and his people would use their escape plan—and each would be a million dollars richer.

Hapke had put together a fifty-person team for this operation. All were ex-police special services or ex-military, none of whom were bothered by working on either side of the law. He had forty with him on the island; two had been assigned the Summers hit in Canada, and the others were assigned a mission even he wasn't aware of. He'd never actually met his contact. There was a video conference with a shadowy figure with a disguised voice, but nothing in person. Since then, all contact had been over text message or email. The money was good, and the intelligence was dead-on when it came to target movements and opposition strength. He already made sure Summers would never bother him again, and next he would take care of the meddling sister.

He heard Servati giving orders to a group to be deployed around the cabin in case any of the rescue team made it past the ambush. There would be nine for that, including the two guarding his prisoners, Servati, and himself.

Servati was a former Army military police specialist and an excellent tactician. She wasn't bad to look at, either, and didn't mind sleeping with the boss, so she stayed warm and dry while the others put up with the foul weather. *Benefits of the job*, thought Hapke, smiling. He refocused and checked his cell. Another message would come when they left, but nothing yet. They were ready.

Upton's Marina and Boat Sales
Bluffton, New York
July 19, 2010
0330 hours

Most of the officers were armed with shotguns or M16s, but the SORT team members carried newer M4 carbines used by special operations teams. They boarded four small powerboats—each different, but all shallow-draft craft to allow them to get in close to shore. Every officer wore body armor. The SORT team had decided not to wear their helmets and was going with baseball caps instead. All badges and other reflective material had been removed from their uniforms, and each member seemed to be focused on the mission.

Sheriff James decided that the first boat to land would be the one carrying most of the SORT team, so it left first, slowly hugging the shoreline. James figured that with their tactical experience and training, they were best suited for the job of securing a landing area. He was in the second boat with the rest of the SORT team, an FBI liaison, and Abby. The last two boats carried his deputies and several more FBI agents. He was surprised the FBI consented to the rescue attempt, but they'd told him they, too, wanted to end this early. The senior FBI agent spoke to Washington, who agreed freeing such high-level hostages was the priority.

As the second boat pulled away from the pier, her vibrating phone made Abby jump. She took it out of a pocket on her tactical vest, seeing she'd received a text. She pushed a button, displaying the text: "Communications compromised. They know u r coming. Setting ambush. Tell sheriff."

Abby read the message once and then reread it. James was watching the last boat slowly ease out of the marina. He turned, seeing the look on her face.

"What is it, Crogan?" he whispered.

She didn't say anything and instead simply handed him her cell phone. He took it and read the message. Abby guessed he read it a couple of times because it took a few seconds for him to respond.

"Do you know the number this comes from, Crogan?"

"No, sir. I have no idea whose number that is."

James showed the message to the FBI agent and a state police lieutenant. The FBI agent looked up from the cell and asked, "Do you think it could be from one of the family members who want us to hold back?"

Abby considered the question seriously for a few moments. "I can tell you it's not from Stephen, but beyond that, I can't say. I just don't know."

The FBI agent holding the phone typed a quick response and hit the send button.

"There. We'll see what response we get."

The agent handed Abby her cell phone and smiled like he'd just won the lottery. James, conversely, couldn't hide his irritation. He distrusted federal authorities, like most local law enforcement did. It only took a few seconds before a different phone vibrated. This time, it was James's cell. He took it out and answered, "This is Sheriff James."

"Sheriff," a male voice responded, which James didn't recognize, "tell that idiot from the FBI that your operation is compromised. How else could I have your cell number? You should have listened to Dr. O'Keefe. She knows what she's talking about."

James looked at the FBI agent and held out his cell to the man. "It's for you."

Back at the showroom, Ryan and Kay made themselves comfortable while they watched the four boats carrying the rescue team disappear into the darkness. Deputy Jasper now oversaw the command post and was standing in the showroom with the deputy assigned to watch the news crew.

"I'm Brady Jasper. I'm the deputy in charge," he said. "As soon as I know they've landed safely on the island, Sheriff James told me to release you. I'm sorry we had to detain you, but you did have information you weren't supposed to have."

Ryan grunted, saying nothing. Kay looked up at Jasper.

"Brady," she said, "don't you think it's just a bit curious that we had the information in the first place? No one even questioned how or where we got it."

Brady smiled at Kay. "We're guessing it was hard work on your part, ma'am. Besides, it hasn't surfaced anywhere else. Our communications are scrambled; no one can monitor us."

"That's a lie!" Justin's voice came over the earpieces Ryan and Kay wore. Kay, being less experienced in the field, jumped. Thankfully, Jasper didn't seem to notice. "They just can't shut up out there on the lake. They're broadcasting every turn and move they make."

Kay smiled at Justin's comment; Jasper assumed she was smiling at him.

"Ma'am, I'm going for coffee—can I get you something?"

"No, thank you, Brady," answered Kay. "We're both fine."

"He didn't offer Ryan anything, Kay," said the voice in the earpiece. "Go for it. Maybe he'll take you on an early breakfast date."

Ryan snickered softly. Kay gave him a dirty look.

"Suit yourself, ma'am," said Jasper, smiling. The other deputy followed him, and both stood outside for a moment.

When the door closed, both Ryan and Justin began to laugh.

Kay said, "You're both assholes, you know that?"

The laughter continued, and Kay even joined in. It was Ryan who brought them all back to reality. "Well, we tried to stop them, but they'll have none of it."

"How can they be so narrow-minded?" asked Kay. "They'll get themselves killed before this is over."

"Ego is a bigger enemy sometimes than the enemy themselves," commented Justin over the earpiece. "Whoever sent us that text also sent a text to Abby. I can only assume it was another warning because a message was sent in return. That prompted a verbal warning to Sheriff James's cell. The caller was a male—I can tell you that much—and definitely came from the island."

"You think one of the hostages managed to keep their cell?" asked Kay.

"How would they know to contact us?" Ryan countered.

"Senator Ericson sits on the Senate Intelligence Committee, but you're right, Ryan—there's no way he'd know about us. And yet, the voice is familiar," Justin commented, pausing for a few seconds to mull it over. "But he can't be there . . ."

"Who?" Kay and Ryan both asked at the same time.

Justin didn't know what to say next because neither of his friends would believe him.

Gulfstream G650PO
Somewhere over Pennsylvania
July 19, 2010
0345 hours

Mr. Evans had dozed off and was surprised when the copilot woke him up. He owned the Gulfstream and employed the crew as an insurance policy. Even though most people thought he was dead, there was still the possibility of a former employer or enemy finding out he'd entered a new life and trying to end it prematurely. The Gulfstream had the range and speed to give him a head start if he felt he needed to leave someplace quickly.

"Mr. Evans," said the copilot, "there's a call for you, sir, on the satellite phone."

Evans rubbed his eyes, sitting up straight. The seats on the plane were comfortable, and he was sure that'd help him sleep. He nodded to the copilot, thanking him. The copilot headed back to the cockpit. Evans picked up the phone hanging on the cabin bulkhead next to his seat and said, "Hello?"

"Where are you now?" asked a voice on the other end. He recognized it immediately as the voice belonging to the man who'd started him on this adventure.

"Somewhere over the East Coast of the United States," answered Evans, forcing his mind back to full alertness. "If I were to guess, over Pennsylvania or New York. I'll be there by dawn, depending on traffic."

"They're going to attempt a rescue at about that time. You sure about that timeframe?"

"Give or take an hour," Evans said with a grunt. "Depends on customs at the airfield where we land. They're an unknown. I have a car waiting, so once I'm clear of customs, it's supposed to be a thirty-minute drive. Any chance the rescue will be successful?"

"No. Too much information has gotten out. They know the rescue is coming, down to the exact time. The rescue team is outnumbered about two to one."

Evans let out a sigh, thinking about how his peaceful retirement could be a thing of the past if he followed through with the plan. The trouble was, there was no other choice—he had to get involved.

"Are you getting soft on me, Irish?" the voice asked.

"You're a bastard, you know that?" replied Evans, with a certain hardness returning to his voice. "You know this could jeopardize my life by landing me back in prison. You know I don't have a choice. You just keep your end of the deal."

"Mr. Evans, your secret is safe with me. You know me well enough to know I'll keep my end of the deal or die trying. Besides, you're the only one out there I can trust to do what you've been asked to do and do it right."

"That doesn't make you any less of a bastard." Evans smiled, leaning back in his seat.

There was a chuckle from the other end of the phone. "Then there are two bastards working on this little mission. Welcome aboard, Irish."

The connection went dead, and Evans slowly hung up. He smiled to himself, closing his eyes. They just might get away with this.

Rescue Boat Two
North of Summers' Island
July 19, 2010
0515 hours

James wasn't happy with the weather; it had become overcast, and a light rain started making it almost black. The upside of the bad weather moving in was it should cover their insertion onto the island, giving them the element of surprise. He unconsciously reached under the raincoat he was wearing and touched the butt of the Berretta forty-caliber pistol in the holster. In twenty-eight years of law enforcement, he'd never had to draw his weapon in anger, but he guessed that was going to change shortly.

While the boat moved forward, he could see Abby staring out into the blackness, in the direction of the island. Her eyes were wide, jaw set. Every muscle in her body seemed coiled as tightly as a spring. She looked ready. The sheriff knew she was opposed to this rescue due to the numbers indicating the kidnappers had over thirty bodies on the island and the fact that her boyfriend's family was there. She felt the operation could backfire and hostages could be killed. She hadn't minced words when she shared her opinion with him.

James leaned over, saying quietly, "Take a deep breath and relax. You'll do fine."

"The boats are making too much noise," she responded without turning to face him. "They can hear us coming."

James smiled. She sounded like her grandfather. The man was like a ghost. You could never hear him coming or going. The Sheriff's Office used him because he could track anything in any kind of terrain. James had been told Abby was almost as good. He smiled at his deputy.

"The weather will cover our approach and the engine noise. We'll be fine."

"We should paddle the boats in, Sheriff."

"Jesus, Crogan," an FBI agent replied. "You'd think you were a full-blooded Indian or something. We'll be fine, and the boats will take us in. Now drop it."

James could feel the anger radiating from his deputy, even in the dark. He should warn the agent that he'd just insulted a full-blooded Native American, but a mental picture of the man being scalped flashed through his mind. A smile crossed his face. He didn't like the man much either.

North Shore
Summers' Island
July 19, 2010
0530 hours

The shadow moved silently along the north shoreline of the island. His pace was slow and deliberate; most of all, he was silent. He would move a step or two, stop and listen, and repeat the process. The rescue boats were making their way along the north shore of the lake. Even the rain didn't mask the sound. It wasn't that the motors were loud—they weren't—but they were mechanical and the sound they made didn't belong in nature. That made it stand out.

The kidnappers set up three forward observation posts that would alert two assault teams to the rescue team's landing site. From there, they planned to drive them back to the boats, showing them exactly how tough it would be to rescue the hostages.

The vestige froze, hearing a noise. He blended into the shadows between three trees and watched as two men came down a path toward him. They were on their way to relieve their friends in one of the OPs. They talked softly, moving down the path toward him. Every word they were saying could be heard, and it was obvious the taller of the two had a slight limp. Their noise discipline, except for the conversation, was pretty good, seeing as they made little noise as they moved. They passed within feet of the trees, not seeing him. It would have been so easy to reach out and kill one, then the other—but there were other plans this morning. His job was to keep people alive.

They passed by him. His movement toward where the landing might take place continued. The boat noise changed as they started across the open water of the channel between the island and the mainland. It wouldn't be long.

Rescue Boat Two
Approaching Summers' Island
July 19, 2010
0550 hours

The fog was quickly rolling in over the water. It hadn't started as a heavy fog but was turning out to be just that. The first boat was approaching the island. The trooper who was steering was using a pair of night vision goggles, for what good they were in the ever-increasing fog. James and the lieutenant in charge of the SORT team conferred all the way in. The FBI agents kept to themselves but still monitored the conversation between the two policemen.

The radio chirped, letting them know the first boat had dropped off their cargo and was backing out of the landing area. Everything on the boat became eerily quiet except for the sound of the outboard engine, which was running just above idle. The leader of the landing party on the first boat gave the okay for the second boat to come in, and the boat immediately moved forward slowly. The north shore of the island suddenly appeared, and the boat ran aground, making a soft grinding sound on the rocks.

The state police lieutenant was the first off, his weapon at the ready. He was followed by another trooper, then by Abby, James, and the rest of the landing party. The two FBI agents were the last off the boat, giving the all clear signal to the boat driver. There was the sound of scraping again as the engines increased power gently, and the boat eased away from the shore, quickly swallowed up by the fog.

The lieutenant gave the okay for the next boat to land via radio.

When that transmission was acknowledged, it became evident the first team was nowhere in sight. Some quick radio chatter determined the second boat strayed off course and landed fifty yards to the west of the first team.

"I say we move inland and rendezvous with the rest of the rescue team there," said the senior FBI agent.

"No," said the lieutenant, "we move east to link up with the rest of the team and move forward from there. Do you agree, Deputy Crogan?"

Abby kept her attention focused on the thick forest, saying, "I do, Lieutenant. They have a larger force defending the cabin, and we're more vulnerable to attack in smaller groups. Look at what us Native Americans did to Custer when he split his forces."

Abby couldn't see the smiles of satisfaction on the faces of her boss or the senior trooper, but the chuckles of other members of the landing party were certainly audible in the darkness. No one needed to see the reaction of the FBI agent; his silence said everything.

The lieutenant gave the order to move out along the shoreline to link up with the first section. They moved slowly and in single file. The radio told them the third boat dropped their section of the rescue team and was backing out. It also told them the first and third sections had successfully linked up, setting a perimeter. They heard the lieutenant tell the ranking officer of those sections they would be linking up within the next ten to fifteen minutes, about the same time the last section would be landing.

Abby was surprised by how loud the boat engines were. Even on idle they put out a good deal of noise. She heard what she thought was a twig snap inland from her and immediately stopped, straining to hear more. Nothing. No more noise. Just silence, except for those moving with her.

James moved up, passing her. "What is it, Crogan?"

"Thought I heard something, sir," she responded, still straining to hear.

Out in the fog, ahead of where they stood, there was a loud crash, and shouts echoed across the stillness. They all knew what happened, but the radio confirmed the third and fourth boats collided. The lieutenant got them quieted down, and in less than a minute, it was determined there was no damage to either boat. More importantly, no one was hurt. The third boat moved off, headed to where the first and second boats linked up midchannel. The fourth boat continued in to drop the last of the rescue team.

They were approaching the perimeter set up by the first and third sections just as it started to rain. Lightly, at first, but the intensity was quickly increasing. The heavy forest protected them slightly, but the men still in the boats would be drenched. The lieutenant radioed they were approaching the perimeter and was told to come in. The fourth boat was four minutes from landing.

There was a sudden noise to their right, about twenty yards into the woods.

Abby immediately stopped, crouching down. James heard the noise as well and moved next to the young woman. The trooper who had been immediately behind Abby joined them, and James motioned for the others to move on by. There was another noise in the brush.

"Something big," whispered the trooper. "Deer, maybe?"

James commented, "Yeah, probably a deer."

Abby focused on the area where the noise had come from. "Could've been a deer, but to my knowledge, there are none on the island. There's more food for them on the mainland, so they swim there if they get stuck here when the ice goes out. Probably a human."

"Exactly what are you saying?" asked the trooper, sounding puzzled.

There was the sound of another branch snapping, then the sound of something metallic—like the bolt on a rifle being pulled back. All three of them knew what that meant.

James grabbed the shoulder of the trooper's BDU shirt.

"Get everyone behind that perimeter; we'll cover you."

The trooper nodded, moving off to hustle the last few people along. As soon as the last of the landing party moved to within twenty feet of the perimeter, both James and Abby raised their rifles, firing into the underbrush.

North Shore
Summers' Island
July 19, 2010
0615 hours

The bullets fired by Sherriff James and Abby had been aimed in the right area—they were just too high, whizzing over the heads of their targets. The bullets also came from an unexpected location. The perimeter set up by the rescue team was more to the east, about fifteen to twenty yards from where the gunfire came from.

The leader of the kidnappers' first assault team was surprised they had been flanked by the rescue team. He ordered his people to return fire. This, in turn, brought fire from the perimeter, where most of the rescue team was located. The kidnappers quickly adjusted their positions, and within less than a minute, they were in a full-blown firefight with the rescue team from two directions.

As the intensity of the firefight increased, Abby and James found themselves cut off from the others. In short order, the kidnappers' second assault team reinforced the first, and the rescue team's perimeter came under heavy fire, making it impossible for them to get through. The fourth boat was landing when the firefight started, and one of the deputies was killed instantly when a bullet struck him in the head. Because the boat was out in the open, several more deputies were wounded, and the radio calls for help began.

The chatter on the channel was nonstop. Panicked voices escalated to frantic shouting, making it almost impossible to understand. It took the state police lieutenant several minutes to bring this under control so he could direct a cohesive defense of their position. It became evident they would not be able to rescue the hostages. It looked like all they could do to get themselves out alive. The lieutenant ordered the fourth boat to withdraw with their casualties and the other three to come in to withdraw the rest of the rescue team.

Abby and James disengaged from the firefight, and she led him down a path toward the east end of the island. James managed to radio they were separated and would be looking for the boat at the alternative pickup site. James figured their communications were being monitored, and his transmission was code that he and Abby would fend for themselves on the island. The rest of the rescue party knew to withdraw and not wait for them. He also hoped the transmission would draw some of the defenders away from the ambush. Abby's knowledge of the island, as well as the deteriorating weather, would be to their advantage.

The skies opened, and the rain came down in buckets, accompanied by a huge thunder and lightning show.

Upton's Marina and Boat Sales
Bluffton, New York
July 19, 2010
0625 hours

A convoy of black government SUVs pulled into the marina just as the firefight started on the island. Two dozen federal agents exited, descending on the showroom. They listened to the frantic radio transmissions from the rescue party while the agent in charge—a Black man in his fifties—sought out Brady Jasper to be brought up to speed. While the two men spoke, the FBI agent noticed the news crew being detained sitting in the corner.

Kay and Ryan saw the FBI agent nod in their direction. He walked toward them.

"We could be in trouble, Justin," Ryan said just loud enough for their partner in the van to hear but not loud enough to be otherwise overheard. Beside him, Kay shifted in her seat, facing the opposite direction.

"The FBI is here and taking over," she said, turning her head so Jasper couldn't see her talking. "Their senior agent just noticed us."

Justin's voice was even. "Stay calm. They've got a disaster in the making on the island. You two are the least of their worries."

Jasper reached them and smiled weakly. "You two can go, but you can't leave town. We've got some issues, and the FBI will want to talk to you. I checked, and I know you booked a room in the motel around the corner, so be either there or someplace else nearby. I'll chase you down when they want you."

Jasper motioned for them to leave, and as Ryan made a show of picking up the camera, Kay discreetly placed a bug on the desk they had been sitting at. They would still have ears in the building. They were going to be spying on a sister federal agency. They left knowing they were being watched by everyone at the marina.

"Come right to the van, guys," said Justin over their earpieces. "This is getting bad."

**North Shore
Summers' Island
July 19, 2010
0635 hours**

The firing was sporadic due to the heavy rain and fog. All the boats managed to land together, helping the withdrawal. The kidnappers tried to close in to see if they could capture any of the rescue team but were met with heavy cover fire from the SORT team. The rescue team withdrew without any more casualties, the heavy rain and fog helping cover them. The kidnappers were monitoring the rescue team's radio transmissions and knew one of the FBI agents was killed and another wounded.

The radio also confirmed the rescue team suffered total casualties of two dead and five wounded. Meanwhile, they hadn't lost one man, not even one wounded. They also picked up on the fact that two members of the rescue team had been separated and were on their own, probably heading east from the landing area.

While the main assault force moved in, confirming the rescue team had indeed left the island, smaller teams were sent out to find the two individuals and kill them. Based on the radio transmissions, they knew it was the sheriff and the female deputy. Hapke gave the okay to terminate them. There were four teams of two moving east about twenty-five yards apart. All were armed with automatic weapons and grenades. They moved slowly and deliberately through the thick underbrush, like hunters driving their prey. The fog and heavy rain made for an eerie dawn as the skies brightened some but not enough to help them in their search. They knew their quarry was ahead of them even though they couldn't see them. They just needed to be patient.

About a hundred yards ahead of them, Abby and James crouched behind a fallen log. They knew they would lose any confrontation if they engaged their pursuers. Abby was able to determine there were at least three teams of the kidnappers hunting them. James knew once the kidnappers determined the rest of the rescue team was gone, more personnel would be tasked with finding them.

"We're going to run out of island soon," said James as he peeked over the log. The rain was heavy, the fog obscuring his view.

"We need to get to the hill on the east end of the island," said Abby, checking her rifle. "The terrain gets rougher as you go up, and it'll be easier to defend if we have to make a stand. The steep slope and rocks might also discourage them from pursuing us, because it'll take time they don't have."

"Let's go, then," said James, moving away from the log, "before they cut us off."

James led off, keeping low. Abby looked over the fallen log, counting to herself. She saw nothing through the rain and fog and, when she reached five, headed off after her boss. She stayed low and went about ten feet when there was a bright flash of lightning and the roar of thunder. Both Abby and James froze for several seconds. Rain cascaded from the sky.

With the flash of lightning, one of the teams was able to make out a shadowy figure. James stood erect, with the lightning exposing his position. The team immediately opened fire in his direction, radioing the other teams. Both James and Abby dropped to the ground, bullets flying wildly over their heads. Abby crawled up to the sheriff.

"You hit?" she asked when she reached him.

"No," he answered, shaking his head. He pointed to a large tree, and they both crawled to it, as it afforded them more cover than where they were on the ground.

A second team started firing in their direction, but they didn't know exactly where they were because bullets were impacting to their north.

"They're trying to keep us pinned down," commented Abby. "We need to keep moving."

James pointed to a path. "You lead off and stay low. I'll be right behind you."

Abby nodded. She started off, keeping low to the ground. When she got to another large tree about ten yards away, she took cover, turning to signal for James to follow. When he reached the tree, they looked at each other and took a deep breath. James motioned for Abby to move off again. The firing from their adversaries was wide. They were focused on the wrong place. They certainly weren't keeping them pinned down. When Abby moved off, he kept watch in the direction they came from. Two figures appeared out of the fog just beyond where they were moments before. He needed to buy time for his deputy to get away.

Abby almost made it to a fallen tree when she turned to see James raising his rifle to his shoulder. Her mouth opened to warn him not to fire because it would give away their position, but it was too late. James quickly let loose with several three-round bursts. This was followed quickly by a hail of incoming bullets in his direction. Abby stopped, hesitating to go back to her boss to help. He ducked safely behind the tree, waving her on. There was a momentary lull in the incoming fire. James left the cover of the tree at a full run.

Abby turned to run in the other direction when she heard two thumping sounds, followed within seconds by bright flashes of light and a deafening noise. Abby thought she heard a scream but couldn't be sure because of the ringing in her ears. She was lifted off her feet and thrown off the path.

Abby lay still on the ground, her face looking up at the treetops of the forest canopy. She blinked rainfall out of her eyes and arched to gauge her ability to move. There was no sharp pain, so she guessed it'd been the force of the explosion that had knocked her to the ground. She couldn't hear anything due to the ringing in her ears. Her rifle was missing; she must have dropped it when she was thrown off her feet. The baseball cap she had been wearing was gone too.

She shook her head, trying to focus, and assessed her situation. It took a few seconds, but she decided she hadn't been wounded. She rolled over onto her left side and spotted her rifle about five feet away, just off the path. Beyond that, she could see James lying on the ground. He was moving but obviously wounded. The ringing in her ears was beginning to subside, and she was starting to hear sounds. She could hear voices but couldn't make out what was being said or where they were. She started crawling toward James.

**Shadow Lake
Off Summers' Island
July 19, 2010
0650 hours**

The lieutenant put his SORT team into one boat, sending the rest of the rescue team back in the other three. The SORT team was intact; they suffered no casualties. The remaining deputies would be needed for other duties, so even though they volunteered to stay, he sent them back. He'd never tell them the choice was because he felt more comfortable with sending his team, and his team alone, as he was more familiar with their training. To say that out loud would be an insult, and they had already proven their mettle under fire.

The boat sat silently about two hundred yards off the north shore of the island. The heavy rain soaked all the men right through their rain gear and other protective clothing. The temperature was in the low sixties, but the dampness was bone-chilling. He was proud of his guys; not one of them complained. You could see the treetops over the fog, and the lieutenant thought it looked like one of those horror movies when you approached the mysterious island through the fog only to find it filled with monsters. It certainly had been an island of death for them. Whoever tried to warn them off was right about that. He hoped that would now change; someone on the island was trying to help them, and it was time to listen.

Summers' Island
Adirondack State Park, New York
July 19, 2010
0655 hours

Several of the enemy search teams had an M203 grenade launcher attached to one of their weapons. When James had fired at the team in the middle of the formation, they each fired a grenade at his position, creating a blast that downed James with shrapnel wounds and sent Abby flying into the air. When they found James, he was in obvious pain. They searched him for weapons, taking his sidearm and a pocketknife.

A second team intercepted Abby, who was crawling toward her boss. They searched her as well, taking her pistol and a small sheath knife she had attached to her belt. When they finished, they backed off and let her continue to her boss on her hands and knees. Several chuckled, but none commented.

Abby reached James. After doing a quick check, she realized all his serious wounds were to his legs. "Get me a first aid kit," she demanded, looking up at the armed men gathered around her. The men just looked back at her; a few smiled, but none responded or produced a first aid kit. She counted her captors, making mental notes. There were eight gunmen. These were not ordinary criminals; she guessed they were mercenaries, meaning the police were outgunned. She needed to get the word out somehow.

"What do we do with them?" asked one of the men. "This one's hurt pretty bad," he added, kicking James's boot, "and I sure as hell don't feel like carrying him anywhere."

The question was directed to a man in command. He looked down at Abby, who was now cradling James's head on her lap, and smiled. "Then you and your partner stay here and finish the job. You know what Hapke ordered."

Abby didn't need anyone to explain the statement. She casually tried to look for a way for her and James to escape, but with him semiconscious and probably unable to walk, there were few options. She wasn't going to leave him.

Four of the gunmen turned and disappeared into the fog. The rain let up for a few minutes, but it would be coming again—Abby could hear it moving across the island. The remaining four gunmen sought shelter from the heavy rain under some low-hanging branches nearby. After a couple of minutes, the rain lightened up just a bit. One of the four moved in close to Abby and James, pulling his pistol out.

"I've got this," he said without emotion. "Then we can get in where it's dry."

Two of the gunmen moved about fifteen feet down the path while the last moved next to the man with his pistol out. Abby refused to be intimidated by these thugs, even though she didn't expect to survive more than a minute. All four men looked at her, and she met their gaze defiantly. The intensity of the rain began to increase again, blending the greens and grays of the forest into a blur. She looked at the two men down the path just as the forest seemed to reach out and grab the one farthest away. There were some muffled noises, and the man dropped to the ground. A greenish-gray shadow moved quickly to the next man, and within seconds, he too dropped to the ground. Abby couldn't believe what she was seeing. Her eyes must have given away her surprise, because both of the gunmen next to her turned, raising their weapons to meet the threat.

Flame erupted from the mysterious shadow, followed by a series of gunshots. Both gunmen collapsed near Abby's feet and didn't move. The closest man looked back at her with lifeless eyes and a bullet hole in the center of his forehead.

The figure down the path took his time checking each of the fallen gunmen before approaching Abby and James. Abby took a deep breath and controlled the fear. She couldn't defend herself, but she wouldn't leave her fallen comrade. She checked the sheriff quickly. He was still unconscious, so at least death would be painless when it came. Her mind was racing, thinking of all the people she wanted to have the chance to say goodbye to before her time came, when she suddenly realized she was looking at a pair of boots.

She looked up and was struck by how quiet and peaceful the weather had gotten. The rain had stopped. The loud chorus of rainfall had been reduced to the steady pitter-patter of rainwater dripping off the forest canopy above and hitting the forest floor.

In front of her stood a man dressed entirely in camouflage, from his boots all the way to the floppy hat on his head. He cradled a rifle in his left arm in such a way it reminded her of one of those pictures of the frontiersmen who carried their muskets like that. For some reason, Abby thought it looked almost natural. The man's face and hands were painted shades of green to match his clothing. He had appeared out of nowhere and moved so fast. He took out four heavily armed men in seconds and didn't even seem to be breathing hard.

They didn't have a chance, yet there didn't seem to be any aggression in his posture as he stood before her. A smile began to appear among the green face paint. It was a warm smile, not threatening. For some reason, she was reminded of the smile of the Cheshire cat in the movie version of *Alice in Wonderland*. She laughed out loud. Still cradling the rifle in his left arm, he extended his right to help her up. She knew she would be all right.

CHAPTER FOUR

ENLIGHTENMENT

Upton's Marina and Boat Sales
Bluffton, New York
July 19, 2010
0715 hours

The fog wasn't as bad in the bay where the village was located. The rain continued but appeared to be letting up some. The temperature was in the low sixties, which was not bad, even for this area, but the combination of the rain and fog made for a dampness that chilled you no matter how many layers of clothing you had on you. For Kay, this seemed to be especially the case. They'd returned to the van from the marina forty-five minutes earlier, and she still couldn't stop shivering. Both Justin and Ryan made fun of her while she curled up in a blanket.

The news wasn't good. As suspected, the rescue was doomed from the start because the force holding the hostages had good intelligence about the law enforcement response. Justin managed to isolate the frequencies they were using. They were encrypted, and he didn't have the equipment to hack past that encryption. If he were able to do that, then they might stand a chance on the rescue.

Ryan shook his head. "Two dead and five wounded," he said. "I guess it could have been worse. Whoever tried to warn them certainly knew what they were talking about."

"Now they've got two missing as well," added Kay, pulling the blanket a little tighter around her. "I wouldn't want to explain this one."

There was a quick transmission from the SORT team still off the island, trying to contact the sheriff and his deputy. There was no response.

"It's useless," commented Ryan. "They should just give up and come back. Those two are probably lying dead out there somewhere." Ryan was surprised by the look Kay gave him. "What'd I say?"

"Ooooh!" exclaimed Kay in frustration. "It's obvious you just don't get it. What kind of man are you, anyway?"

Kay looked at Justin for help with this. He'd been in the teams and understood exactly what point she was trying to make. He returned her gaze and shook his head. Ryan saw the exchange and frowned, asking again, "What?"

"In the United States military, we're trained not to leave any man behind," explained Justin, seeing Kay becoming more frustrated. "The commander of the state police team doesn't want to leave two unaccounted for behind, not even their bodies."

Ryan thought for a second, nodding. "I can accept that. Not having a military background and being brought up in Northern Ireland with the IRA and the Brits shooting at each other, it makes sense to me. You don't leave your people to the devices of your enemies. Kay, why didn't you just say that to begin with?"

Kay sighed in frustration, again turning away and looking out the front window of the van. A black suburban was coming toward them with tinted windows and government plates. It slowed as it approached the line of news vans parked next to the marina. Because of the weather, there were only a few people outside. Nothing was happening that was newsworthy enough to brave getting wet. They all knew the rescue team had set off but didn't know how miserably they had failed, or they would have been storming the marina for information, no matter what the weather. As the suburban passed by, Kay noticed two official-looking gentlemen sitting in the front seat. She could see that there were people in the back seats, but no more than that because of the tinted windows.

Ryan noticed Kay had become distracted. "What do you see?"

"Looks like more FBI," answered Kay, watching the suburban pass by. "With the number of government cars pulling in the last couple hours, they seem to be pulling out all the stops."

Justin grunted, and Ryan chuckled, watching Kay lean forward to try and keep the vehicle in sight.

"They're looking for something or someone. They were slowing down."

"You know the FBI," said Ryan with a grin. "They have a higher opinion of themselves than I find is warranted. They're well organized but overly cautious for my taste when it comes to this sort of thing."

"This from Mr. Leap Before You Look," added Justin, laughing.

Kay smiled just as the back door to the van opened. All three of them jumped in surprise, recognizing their boss, Tommy Mitchell. Mitchell smiled at their reaction to his presence.

Summers' Island
Adirondack State Park, New York
July 19, 2010
0745 hours

The climb up the hill was steep and, with the load she was carrying, exhausting. Abby was soaked through all her clothing, even though the rain was reduced to a drizzle. The higher she climbed, the less dense the fog was, so visibility was better. The forest was thick with brush on this side of the island, so anything that made it easier to see was a godsend. She strained with each step, wondering how her savior was doing. He was carrying James as well as weapons and other equipment from their four tormentors.

He said nothing, using sign language to indicate they shouldn't talk. He checked her for injuries and then did some quick first aid on James, who was still unconscious, stabilizing him. He worked fast, seemingly familiar with this type of situation. He policed the bodies of the four hostage takers, keeping any item looking like a weapon. Smaller items were carefully placed in two small packs. He left personal items but took any food and water they were carrying, putting them in the packs as well. To Abby's surprise, he left one of the men alive, spending a few minutes treating his wounds.

They left the attacker conscious but in pain, heading east, then circling around in a wide path in the opposite direction. He stopped several times to allow Abby to rest and to check on James's condition. Eventually, they came to a hill on the west side of the island. They were now about three-quarters of the way up the hill, and Abby was ready for another rest stop. Abby guessed that whoever this guy was, his pace would have been faster if she wasn't with him. She looked ahead and saw he easily navigated over some rocks and around a deadfall. She shook her head, looking down to where she was placing her feet. She knew for a fact the other side of the hill was easier to climb and wondered why he'd chosen this side. It dawned on her they would be harder to follow, but then again, the men who ambushed the rescue didn't seem the type to be motivated enough to climb this side of the hill unless extra cash was involved. She concentrated on where she placed her feet and hands as she navigated the rocks and went around the deadfall. When she made it around the fallen tree, she smiled to herself with pride. This wasn't easy, and yet here she was, climbing something this steep while carrying well over half her weight. This was quite an accomplishment. She looked around to see where to head next.

Her smiled disappeared when she couldn't see the man who had rescued her anywhere. He wasn't ahead of her, up the hill, or to her right. She couldn't see anything to her left because of the deadfall but turned and looked back in the direction she had come just in case she had missed him. Nothing, he was nowhere to be seen.

She jumped when something touched her from behind, letting out a muffled scream. She found him behind her with his finger to his lips, indicating she needed to be silent. She put her right hand to her mouth to stifle any further sound without thinking. He helped her put down the extra weapons she was carrying and then helped her take off the pack. He motioned for her to stay where she was. Then, picking up his rifle, he disappeared around the deadfall.

Curiosity piqued, she picked up her rifle and moved to the edge of the cover afforded by the fallen tree and looked around. The man moved slowly down the hill. Every so often, he would stop and move the brush around or brush the ground with a branch or his hand. She realized he was erasing any sign of their ascent up the hill. He was assuming there was someone who could track them and was making it as difficult as possible. This was not his first time in a situation like this.

Abby came back around the deadfall and sat down, allowing herself to fall back against it. She looked up at the cloud-filled sky and allowed the light rain to fall on her face. She closed her eyes, thinking about the nightmare she was living, and exhaled a deep breath, waiting for a second before opening her eyes again. When she did, she noticed the brush was exceptionally thick in this area of the hillside—and that James was nowhere to be seen.

Just as she started to get up, her newfound partner reappeared, helping her to her feet. The twinkling blue eyes calmed her as she stood. Her savior was about six feet tall with a solid frame but didn't scream youth. His demeanor could be best described as mature calm. He noticed her confusion, and as if reading her mind, he put his finger to her lips and motioned for her to follow him. He picked up the pack she had been carrying and one of the weapons and nodded toward the end of the fallen tree, where the rest of their belongings were stowed.

As prompted, Abby picked up the remaining weapons, and moved off after the man.

The deadfall was a large tree, and when it came down, it appeared to have pulled part of the hillside in the form of a large rock with it. She followed him around the rock and, to her surprise, found him pulling a sheet of camouflage fabric aside, the way one might open a door. He motioned for her to enter. She'd spent a lot of time on this island and never heard of a cave or outcropping on the hill that could be used for shelter, but he seemed to be leading her into one. When she entered, she felt the fabric of the makeshift door; it seemed to be heavy nylon. He allowed it to close, and she could see a dim light on the other side of what appeared to be another layer of fabric. She shivered, thinking of going into a damp cave, but at least it wouldn't be raining.

He raised the second layer of fabric, and she moved past it. It was the same as the first layer—camouflage nylon—but she could see what looked to be ropes hanging off the ends. The word *parachute* came rushing through her mind. The cave went forward for a short distance and turned right, where the light was coming from. The first thing that struck her was the smell of coffee. She was still shivering from being wet but didn't feel the dampness she expected. She followed him into the cave and, when she made the turn, was shocked to find a small, well-lit cavern about twelve feet by fifteen feet. It was warm, and she saw James resting comfortably on a cot by the far wall.

"Some people had a tree house when they were kids," said the man, breaking his silence at last, "but my brother and I had this cave. It kind of brings a new meaning to the term *man cave*, don't you think?"

With all the camouflage clothing and face paint, she hadn't recognized him, but she knew the voice almost immediately. Abby dropped everything she was carrying, threw her arms around his neck, and hugged him.

Summers' Cabin
Adirondack State Park, New York
July 19, 2010
0750 hours

They hadn't eaten a solid meal since the day before, and all the canned food from the cupboards was running low, so Hapke decided it was time for some food to be prepared. There were plenty of eggs in the refrigerator to feed the hostages, but there were also his forty hired guns to feed. After speaking to Nancy, Hapke decided to send her to the boathouse, where there was a big chest freezer and another large refrigerator filled with food. The electricity for the island came via underwater cables running from the mainland to the boathouse and then through aboveground wires to the main cabin. The family long ago decided to store their extra food in the boathouse, mainly because there was room for the large freezer and refrigerator. It also kept curious critters away from the cabins.

Nancy took Emily and young RJ along to help her carry the food back to the kitchen. She and Emily chose food that would be easily prepared for a large group, so they each carried several bags. RJ carried every loaf of bread they had stockpiled, while Nancy and Emily carried the heavier items. Hapke sent two of his people with them who were never more than a few feet away. Neither offered to help carry any food, looking relaxed, moving with their captives.

They entered the back door of the cabin near the kitchen, placing the bags on the large table in the center of the room, and while Emily began to unpack and organize their wares, Nancy walked RJ back into the living room. The news of the foiled rescue was no secret because their guards boasted openly about how easy it'd been to squash the effort. They also knew the local sheriff and one of his deputies, a female, were chased down and killed by their captors. This left the group demoralized, so when Nancy came in, whistling and carrying a bouquet of wildflowers, she drew several annoyed looks. She returned RJ to sit on the sofa next to his sister, continuing to whistle. She caught Ericson's attention and held up the flowers in a gesture to him. He returned her gaze with a puzzled look.

"You go out to pick up food, and you have time to pick flowers?" Sue Ellen Del Monte scoffed sarcastically.

"No, Congresswoman." Nancy smiled back at her pleasantly. "I do believe these were left by an admirer."

"Humph," grunted the congresswoman. "One of the guards, probably."

Julie and several other people chuckled at the comment, drawing a vindictive glare from the politician.

"While Mr. Hapke has offered to entertain me in the past," Nancy replied, keeping a polite smile while looking at the politician in a way that made it clear she'd crossed a line, "he is not gallant enough to think of flowers."

Nancy said no more on the subject, because her sister-in-law had dated Hapke for almost a year after her husband's death. She stopped seeing him after she found out how brutal the man could be. Nancy instead turned her focus to Ericson. "Josh, do you remember the young officer in Subic Bay who used to leave me those exotic flowers he found in the jungle?"

Ericson looked confused. "I do, but what does that have to do with this situation?"

"Oh, probably nothing." Nancy smiled at her old friend with a confidence he remembered from better times. "The flowers were just left in the same way. They're fresh cut, in a vase—or, in this case, a large mason jar. They're from a meadow on the far side of the island. It's the only place here they grow. The forest is too dense."

The puzzled look on Ericson's face was replaced with a sly smile. While many in the group still looked confused or even indifferent about the conversation, several who'd known the Summers family shared in Ericson's response to Nancy's statement.

"Ooorah!" whispered Rice.

"God save them!" added Demmer.

"Amen!" said Wells with a chuckle.

Ericson looked back at Nancy, winking. She nodded in response; no one saw the tear running down her cheek.

Upton's Marina and Boat Sales
Bluffton, New York
July 19, 2010
0750 hours

The three boats that returned said it all.

Ambulances backed up to the docks, unloading the frantic medical teams meeting the boats as they arrived. The coroner's van sat ominously off to the side of the parking lot, and two members of the coroner's staff stood patiently by while the wounded were unloaded; the members of the rescue party they were there to pick up were not in need of medical attention.

Grey stood off to the side while emergency crews off-loaded the wounded. The crowds gathered early, knowing something happened because the firefight could be heard in both Bluffton and Dartford. The fact that they'd returned without the hostages and a boat short started the rumor mill in full overload.

Agent Grey was concerned about security when they arrived and thus had put out an immediate call for additional manpower. Agents were coming from all over the East Coast, and he pulled in additional troopers and deputies from nearby counties to help control crowds and traffic. He was keeping Jasper and a newly arrived state police major close by to help coordinate those tasks. The state trooper was off arranging extra security at the hospitals the wounded were being ferried to, but Brady was standing nearby like a dutiful hunting dog, ready for action. Grey felt bad about that analogy, but the deputy made it clear he wasn't comfortable leading his department with an incident of this magnitude and was perfectly happy to have Grey calling the shots. His knowledge of the area and its residents thus far proved invaluable.

Inspector Preston also stood nearby. He brought another whole set of questions to the table. Both Grey and the Mountie knew it would only be a matter of time before the murder in Canada and this kidnapping were linked.

Grey watched the first of the ambulances start to pull away from the docks, and as he watched the red flashing lights, he began looking at the people crowding the area. Among them, he noticed an FBI agent hand a manila folder to the RCMP investigator. He guessed the file with the background information he'd requested for Preston finally caught up with them. The siren on the first ambulance kicked in when it made it to the street in front of Upton's Marina. Grey frowned, narrowing his eyes at the ambulance's display.

There was no need for the siren. The use of such felt performative, more for the gathered media and their cameras than to expedite their trip to the hospital. A quick look in the direction of the crowd confirmed his suspicions, as there was a flurry of activity among the gathered reporters and cameramen.

There was also a government SUV parked next to one of the media vans. Grey didn't recall any of his people radioing that they were going to be out with any of the media, and yet he saw a familiar face and stopped where he was. The man he was watching made eye contact with him, nodding in acknowledgement.

"Holy shit!" blurted Deputy Jasper, staring at his cell phone. The look of astonishment on the deputy's face was enough to bring Grey's attention back to the dock.

"What is it, Deputy?" he asked, and Jasper looked up, the expression of shock on his face not changing. He then held out his phone for Grey to take.

"It's from Abby Crogan."

Grey took the cell and looked at the screen. There was a text message from the missing deputy that read, "We are safe. Sheriff wounded but alive. Assume radio and cell communications compromised. Will be in touch."

Grey read through it several times before looking at Jasper. "Deputy, your thoughts on this message?"

Jasper managed to regain his composure. "Sir, Abby knows this area better than any of the rest of us. She's resourceful and is the best tracker in the department."

"Make your point." Grey's voice was calm, but it was obvious he didn't want a profile on Abby Crogan.

Jasper just smiled at the FBI agent. "She's found someplace safe for them to hole up, and I'm guessing she'll get back to us with some more info on the bad guys as soon as she's able to."

Grey was silent for a moment. He then looked over at the agent standing next to Preston and motioned for him to come over. "Do we have the cell phone of the commanding officer for the New York State Police SORT team out there on the lake?"

"Yes, sir."

"Send him a text message that Sheriff James and his deputy are safe and I need him back here to help plan an assault. I need them to return as quietly as possible, and let him know that our communications are being monitored.

I want the suspects to think we still have a trained strike team out there, ready to come in at a moment's notice. Get that out now. Go!"

The agent left, and Grey turned to Deputy Jasper. "May I send a message to Deputy Crogan?"

Jasper nodded, still smiling. Grey typed on the small keyboard: "I am Agent Grey of the FBI. Stay put for now and let us know if you have any info on the suspects."

As soon as he hit send on the message, Preston walked over. He looked concerned and held the open folder in his hands. "Glenn, this man is the one who was in the plane, the man who disappeared."

Grey looked over at the open file and saw that there was a picture of a man in a naval officer's uniform. He recognized the man in the picture. The two policemen exchanged a silent glance, indicating they connected the two cases. The cell in Grey's hand chirped. Grey looked down at the screen.

"Glenn, just like Mindanao."

Grey looked toward the crowd of reporters and again saw the government SUV, but this time, the familiar face was gone.

This case was getting very freaky.

Bluffton Motor Court
Bluffton, New York
July 19, 2010
0800 hours

Justin had been surprised when Tom Mitchell opened the door to the van—and he was even more surprised when Admiral Putnum walked up behind Mitchell. An old friend of the family, Justin was taken aback by both the admiral's presence and the fact that he wasn't surprised to see him alive. Putnum seemed to have a working knowledge of what Justin's team's mission was, as well as insight on their history.

They had been relieved at the van by another member of their team, Joey DePalma—also known as Joey D—who worked out of Mitchell's Langley office. Joey was a technology specialist and just the sort of person you wanted working the van. Joey was given the rundown of what was taking place and what frequencies to monitor, settling in quickly.

Mitchell wanted to speak to the team in private, so they headed to their motel room, and on the way, Justin wondered what Mitchell's visit was about. He suspected his boss wasn't happy about his team responding to this incident, as it might compromise their integrity and effectiveness—and yet he'd been surprisingly calm since his arrival. Considering Mitchell was the sort of leader who never yelled at subordinates, his mask of calm wasn't the positive omen that might've been coming from somebody else. Besides, Putnum's presence indicated that something was wrong. Seeing as the CIA wasn't chartered to operate domestically, their being here meant breaking a few laws, and if Justin had to make a guess at what this little meeting was going to be about, that's what he'd bet on.

The government SUV pulled into the parking space in front of their hotel room—room number four, specifically—and Mitchell moved up next to Justin as they got out of the vehicle and made their way inside.

"Sorry about your dad," he said, in a hushed tone. "And for the record, I do understand why you're here, with your mom being held hostage and all." Justin decided to stay quiet and not tell his boss what he suspected. Mitchell cleared his throat and added, "After we debrief the admiral, he and I are going to go make nice with the FBI. He knows the agent in charge and is going to unofficially offer our help, since you've managed to track some of the hostage takers' communications. I guess he worked with him on some assignment in the Philippines back in the nineties."

Justin smiled, opening the door. This information explained why Putnum was here. As they entered the room, they froze. On the far side of the small space, four men sat around a table and appeared to be playing cards. There was also a female voice coming from the bathroom. Before Justin could respond, he was hit in the jaw and knocked to the floor.

Upton's Marina and Boat Sales
Bluffton, New York
July 19, 2010
0800 hours

Evans remained unnoticed and obscure in the flurry of activity in and around the marina. He entered the Mohawk, finding the coffee strong and to his liking. He ordered a breakfast of fried eggs, ham, and hash browns to go and returned to his rented car. When his private plane landed at the Adirondack Regional Airport, there was an envelope containing some written instructions and photographs waiting for him at the car rental desk. He spotted one of the people from the photographs when he went in for the coffee and the take-out order.

After returning to the car, he watched as a government SUV stopped a news van around the corner from him, pulling the crew out. He recognized two of the people in the crew and shrank behind the steering wheel so he wouldn't be seen. He found it funny the government was spying on their own people, but then he, better than most, knew why that was taking place. The crew got into the SUV with their CIA handler and an older man he assumed was CIA or NSA, driving off. He chuckled to himself, again thinking this was as close to the old days as he wanted to get.

When he sat back up, the first ambulance hit the road, its siren wailing when it passed his parked car. There was no traffic to speak of, and the police had the crowds controlled, so the EMT driving the ambulance was clearly showboating for the media.

He positioned himself so he could see the entrance of the Mohawk and immediately saw his target leaving the restaurant. She, too, watched the ambulance as it left, although her look was more of amusement. She got into a red Ford sedan and slowly pulled out of the parking space, eventually driving past him, paying too much attention to the goings-on in the marina to notice that he'd been watching her all along. He waited until her vehicle made a turn before pulling out to follow her. She was headed to the airport, so he didn't have to rush; he could lay back and do a proper job of tailing her.

Evans took out his cell and smiled. This call would upset his contact, but then again, this man had called him and interrupted his retirement. He did so miss the Bahamas. The phone rang once before it was picked up.

"I told you to text—you know the phones are being monitored."

"I know," he responded, not bothering to disguise his Irish accent. "But you didn't tell me I'd know the team doing the monitoring. They know me, you realize."

There was a chuckle on the other end of the phone. "Then we're keeping it all in the family."

"The package you left me at the airport . . . the third picture in the folder, featuring a female target . . . she's headed back to the airport now. I'll follow her, but how will I know where she's headed?"

There was another chuckle before the man on the other line said, "Were you always this difficult? How did you survive in this business?"

Evans smiled. "Because I was meaner than the others. Now, it's a legitimate question, how will I know where she's heading? I know you don't want someone else doing the dirty work."

"No," said the man on the other end, laughing openly now. "Only you or I get to do the dirty work on this one."

"Then since I know you're not available because of where you are, I guess that leaves me to do the dirty work alone. I'd appreciate not being put in contact with those CIA types watching the FBI. Too close for comfort."

"Not to worry. Someone will be in touch once that information has been determined. You'll know just where to go. Mr. Evans, you have a good trip now. Remember, we don't do anything until they're all together."

"Ah, the pot calling the kettle black. Keep your head down, sport."

Both men hung up.

Bluffton Motor Court
Bluffton, New York
July 19, 2010
0805 hours

Justin looked up to see who'd hit him. There was movement in his peripheral vision, which he realized was Ryan making a run to defend his friend. He was stopped only a few feet away by a tall-standing man, who cornered Ryan, expression furious.

"You son of a bitch," the man said, voice shockingly familiar to Justin. "We all thought you were dead!"

It took a second for Justin to focus on the face of his older brother, Sean. To his right, he identified his younger brother, Stephen. Stephen was the person moving to meet Ryan. It would have been an interesting confrontation: marine versus an Irish street fighter.

He erased the thought from his mind and refocused on Sean.

"Well, I may be a son of a bitch, but I had to come to help get her and your family off the island alive," responded Justin.

Sean extended his right hand to his brother. Justin took it, being helped back to his feet. For the first time, he noticed everyone in their party made it into the room. Ryan and Kay both wore cautious looks on their faces, while Mitchell looked flat-out worried over the fact that Justin's cover was officially blown; his family now knew for a fact that he was alive, and he couldn't possibly fake his death twice. This reunion could influence his efficiency in his current assignment. Putnum smiled, seeming to enjoy this little event. The two men who were never far from Putnum's side remained stoic. Justin figured Putnum knew more about what was going on than he was letting on.

Sean surprised Justin by throwing his arms around him, giving him a hug. "Damn, it's good to see you, little brother."

A third pair of arms joined the hug. Stephen added, "And if you ever do this again, I'll kill you myself."

The three men stood in the center of the room with everyone watching. The only one who didn't seem touched by the reunion was Mitchell, who still looked worried by the events currently unfolding. Finally, he said, "It's too bad your father isn't alive to see this."

"Who said he isn't?" said a female voice as the bathroom door opened. "You obviously don't understand who you're talking about."

Becky walked over to where the three young men were huddled. They broke up as she approached, and she immediately slapped Justin on the back of the head. "That's for putting your mother through hell. Now give me a hug, and welcome back to the living."

Justin put his arms around his brother's mother-in-law. She squeezed him and kissed him hard on the cheek.

"Damn, it's good to have you back with us, young man," she said, releasing him from the hug only to grip his shoulders, holding him at arm's length. She looked him up and down the way any mother would, giving him a once-over. "You're as handsome as ever. Wait until I get ahold of that bastard of a father of yours. He obviously knew you were alive to call you back here for this. At least he told your uncle Matt to be on the lookout for you."

Becky nodded toward one of the four men at the table.

"What the hell is going on here, anyway?" blurted out Mitchell, only to fall silent when Putnum placed a hand on his shoulder. His outburst drew everyone's attention, even the four cardplayers. They immediately went back to their game, while Becky kissed Justin one more time on the cheek and moved off to hug Putnum.

"Admiral, it's so good to see you again. As always, you come riding in with the cavalry to save the day. I assume he called you, too?"

Putnum chuckled. He released the woman he had met on the Nimitz so many years before and said, "It's good to see you, too, Rebecca—and yes, I got a call as much to warn me as to get me to send in the good guys. It seems an old nemesis is rearing his ugly head again."

"What the hell?" blurted Mitchell again. "Am I the only one here who doesn't know what's going on?"

Becky released Putnum and moved over to Mitchell, extending her hand. The look of surprise at the gesture was only topped by the reaction to her introduction. "You must be Tom Mitchell. The war hero said you would be the angry one. I'm Becky O'Keefe."

The look Ryan gave Justin didn't go unnoticed by Becky.

Mitchell tried to retract his hand, but Becky held on tight. "What?" he said. "I—"

"Don't feel bad, Mr. Mitchell, you're in good company." Becky smiled. "Jonny's pretty good at keeping secrets, even from the CIA, it seems." Before Mitchell could respond, she moved on to Ryan. "That would make you Ryan O'Keefe."

"Yes, ma'am," replied the young Irishman, blushing as she kissed him on the forehead.

Becky took a step back and looked at him, smiling. "You're as handsome as your father, God rest his soul." *Becky* seemed confused by the look Ryan gave Justin but continued, adding, "You have a half sister being held hostage on the island, as well as a niece and nephew. I'm glad you're here to help bring them out."

Before he could answer, she moved on to Kay. "And you must be Kayli."

Kay nodded. "I am—and how do you know us?"

The look Kay gave Becky was not harsh but certainly demanded an answer. Becky's response was to smile. "I'm assuming you inherited your mother's looks because the master chief is an ugly son of a gun. You've inherited his feistiness, though."

Kay looked truly surprised. "You know my parents?"

"Your father helped pull some other people and me out of a jungle a few years back. I'll always be in his debt."

"Damn!" blurted out Kevin Gateway from the table where he was playing cards. "I think the old man's cheating!"

"Which old man?" asked Matt. "I think we all qualify for that category?"

"He's referring to me, Matthew," responded Bill Gateway. "I'm by far the oldest here."

"That you are, General," Matt said, laughing.

"But I'm not cheating," continued the elder Gateway. "Maybe my partner is, though—after all, his people own most of the casinos in this state."

Fred snickered, locking eyes with the man. "White men, always blaming their lack of good card playing on the house. Maybe there's a reason we own all the casinos in the state."

They all burst into laughter.

Matt rose, looking at the crowd at the door. "Why don't we go over to the Mohawk, where we can bring all of you up to speed and not be so cramped while we do it?"

Everyone agreed and started out the door, back into the fog and light rain. As they moved, Becky leaned over to Stephen, saying, "Your dad has Abby and the sheriff in a safe place on the island. She's unhurt, and he's playing doctor with the sheriff."

Mitchell's head snapped around at the comment of Stephen's father being alive. Kay and Ryan had a similar reaction, though less pronounced. Becky made eye contact with the CIA man, smiling.

Hidden Cave
Summers' Island
July 19, 2010
0915 hours

James was regaining consciousness and felt something rough and moist moving across his face. He slowly opened his eyes, seeing the large snout of an animal with a mouth full of teeth. An animal's tongue was licking his face.

His first thought was that he was about to be eaten, so he jumped to a sitting position.

The pain in his legs was immediate and severe.

"Jesus . . ." He closed his eyes and collapsed back down, trying to cope with the pain. Through it all, he could hear what sounded like a dog whining.

"Kuma, stop!" came the sound of a familiar voice. "Leave him alone. Back up!"

James opened his eyes to find Abby leaning over him, giving him a reassuring look as she said, "Sheriff, you're okay. We're safe in a cave on the west side of the island."

He glanced around at the rock walls of the cave. He also noticed electric lights and the smell of hot food in the air. He motioned at everything around them, brows furrowed in a way that clearly said, *Where are we, and what is going on here?*

"I don't have an answer," responded Abby to the unasked question. "I know the most about this island, and even I didn't know the cave existed. They've somehow managed to run electricity here and some other comforts."

James looked behind Abby, seeing the large brown-and-white dog who had licked his face. He guessed the animal to be over a hundred pounds with a kind face, upright ears, and a curled tail. It cocked its head, whining.

"That's Kuma," said Abby, raising James's head slightly and putting a cup of water to his lips. Some of the cool liquid missed and ran down his chin. He would never have believed how good water could taste.

"He's the Summers' dog," continued Abby, wiping his chin with a cloth. "He must have gotten away when they took everyone hostage."

He looked down at his legs covered with a blanket. "The pain . . . What happened?"

"There was an explosion, and you took some shrapnel to your legs. Can you sit up?"

He nodded, and she helped him up to a sitting position. He was ready for the pain this time, so it wasn't overwhelming. Abby placed some pillows and blankets behind him to cushion him from the hardness of the rock. For the first time, he realized he was on a cot. Abby went over to the small stove across the room and ladled some hot liquid from a pan into a porcelain cup. She brought him the cup, and James quickly realized it was a small serving of chicken noodle soup.

"How'd we get here, Abby?" he asked as he blew on the hot liquid to cool it. He gave another nod at the general direction of the cave—the lights, the stove, the cot. The whole area was set up in a way that served as a perfect off-grid camp.

"The enemy was in possession of grenade launchers," Abby said. "They fired at us, causing the explosion. While you were unconscious, four men of the enemy force were assigned to finish us off and were about to do that when this ghostly shadow came from deep inside the forest. He used a knife to pick off two and a captured rifle on the others." Abby paused, sighing. "He saved my life. Your life, too. He took the two of us—carrying you—here, and we've been hiding in this cave ever since. You've been out for three hours."

James sipped his soup, shaking his head. "So, we were all but done for?"

Abby nodded. "Then he came out of nowhere. It's like he was part of the forest, taking out all four in less than fifteen seconds. I couldn't believe what I was seeing. He killed three and left the fourth to be found by his comrades. He stripped them of all their weapons and ammo."

James followed her hand gesture to a neatly stacked pile of rifles, handguns, knives, and ammo by the opposite wall. All the rifles were fully automatic and, he assumed, ready for use.

The sheriff looked at his young deputy. "Exactly who was our savior, Abby?"

She looked at her boss with surprise. "You mean you don't know?"

"I wouldn't have asked if I knew, Deputy."

Abby smiled. "Jon Summers, sir. Apparently, he and his brother have been working on this little hideaway for years."

"Didn't they say he had been murdered in Canada by these lowlifes?"

"Apparently the report of his death was exaggerated, sir."

James flashed Abby an irritated look, saying, "So he took out four of these guys here and who knows how many in Canada when they came after him. Who the hell is this guy, anyway?"

"He's a SEAL, sir. He's retired from the Navy, but he served as a SEAL."

James thought for a moment before asking, "Just how did he get here without anyone knowing?"

"I don't know, sir, but there is a camouflage parachute helping to hide the entrance to the cave."

James grunted. "And where is he now?"

Abby tried not to look too smug. "He outfitted himself with some weapons and told me he was going to go recon the kidnappers' positions."

James looked at the young woman, saying nothing. He noticed one of the captured rifles was outfitted with a noise suppressor. Abby followed his gaze, then looked back at her boss. "Sir, he's been passing info to our people in Bluffton ever since he arrived."

James laughed. "But none of us were listening, were we? I bet they are now."

Summers' Cabin
Adirondack State Park, New York
July 19, 2010
0935 hours

The radio traffic had increased to a frantic level over the past twenty minutes. Something was wrong, as evidenced by the panic in the voices at the other end. The guard by the front door shifted nervously, while the second guard paced in and out of the dining room. Nancy, Julie, and Emily made a large breakfast and were feeding their captors in shifts when the initial radio call came in. Everyone seated at the table grabbed their weapons and scrambled out of the cabin, leaving only the two guards with the hostages. The two men herded them all into the living room and made them sit in a group in the middle of the room.

"What's happening?" asked Alexander, leaning close to Ericson, who was still seated in the chair and conferring with Wells and Rice.

Ericson knew the senior politician well enough to know that he was just being curious and not self-serving. The man served his country during the Korean conflict, though not in combat. He leaned close to the elder senator and said, "Our hosts had one of their teams attacked, and they've taken some casualties."

A thin smile crossed the old man's face. "Too bad; I was just getting to like them."

They huddled close enough for the entire group to hear, so smiles crossed several faces. There was another flurry of radio traffic.

"I didn't understand a word of that," said Hennen.

"It appears that the team they left to finish off a couple of our would-be rescuers was hit," said Frank Del Monte, his arm around his wife's shoulder. "Three dead and one wounded, with the two deputies missing." They all looked at the man with surprise. He blushed. "I'm in the communications business, and I understand that gibberish pretty well."

There were more smiles around the group as Ericson finished the explanation.

"Apparently," he went on, "the two captive deputies are missing, which means either they overpowered the team or someone helped them escape."

Ericson's gaze landed on Nancy, who smiled weakly. Before anyone could respond, the front door burst open without warning, causing most of them to jump. Hapke stormed in, followed by Servati and two more of his men. He grabbed Julie and dragged her to her feet. Hector rose to defend his mother but was met with a fist. Hapke struck the young man squarely in the jaw, knocking him back into Wells. Both men fell into a crumpled heap among the remaining hostages.

"Stay down, boy," chided Hapke, pointing at Hector, "or I'll kill you just like I did your father."

There was a stunned silence while the horrified hostages all looked at their antagonist.

Julie struggled while she protested. "Hector was killed in an automobile accident!"

Julie was clearly no match for Hapke, but he backhanded her across the face for good measure, ensuring her cooperation. When her body surrendered to his overpowering strength, he said, "That's what everyone thinks, but the driver of the truck was paid off and didn't survive the crash to tell any different."

Julie started weeping, so Hapke pressed his advantage. "Who else is on the island!"

"No . . . no one!" Julie said, sobbing. "Just us here and the people you brought!"

Hapke slapped Julie again, blood appearing on the side of her mouth. Hector started to rise again, but Wells and Emily held him back.

"Stop lying!" Hapke's voice showed how close to being out of control he was. "Who is on the island?"

"No one, I said!" Tears were freely flowing down Julie's cheeks. "Why don't you believe me?"

Hapke shook her one more time. Nancy began to get up, her gaze steady on the crazed man. "She's telling you the truth." Hapke watched the woman slowly move to where he stood, putting her hands on her sister-in-law's arms. "Everyone who was on the island when you landed is in this room. There was no one else."

Hapke shifted his fervent look from Julie to Nancy. For the first time, she realized Servati and Hapke's other people had their weapons trained on her. Nancy took a deep breath, remaining calm, keeping her gaze on their leader. His attitude seemed to be returning to normal, realizing they were telling him the truth. He released Julie, and she turned, collapsing into Nancy's arms.

"Then who attacked my people?" Hapke seemed to ask everybody present.

No one responded. The back door to the cabin flew open and several of Hapke's men carried in a wounded man, placing him on the table. There was a half wall separating the living room from the dining room, with several large beams serving as supports for the second-floor bedrooms. Servati grabbed Sarah, dragging her to her feet and over to the dining room table and the wounded man.

Sarah didn't have to be told what to do; her training and instincts kicked in. She began to pull gear and clothing off the man so she could see the wounds to evaluate what needed to be done. Everyone in the room remained silent as the young doctor went about her work. She turned and looked at Servati and then at Hapke.

"Well, Doc?" asked Servati.

Sarah looked at her and then, ignoring her, turned to Hapke. "Your man's been stabbed. Several times and by someone who knows how to use a knife. He'll live but won't be able to walk until he has surgery." Hapke saw Ericson smile at the doctor's description of the wounds. He was about to say something to the invalid when Sarah continued, "I can bandage the wounds and make him comfortable, but he needs surgery. There's tendon and muscle damage that needs to be repaired, which can't be done here. I need someone to get my medical bag out of my cabin, and there's a large red backpack hanging in the boathouse that's a first aid kit—I'll need that, too."

Hapke didn't hesitate, turning to one of his people. "You! Go!"

The man didn't say a word and was out the back door of the cabin just as his wounded comrade began to regain consciousness. Sarah asked for some water, and Emily was escorted to the kitchen to get it. As the doctor helped the wounded man drink some water, two more of Hapke's men came in the back door. One handed a pouch to Servati. She opened it, looked inside, and then held it out to Sarah. "It's morphine, Doc, to help him with the pain."

Sarah looked at the woman but didn't reply. It was obvious her statement wasn't a request, so she took the pouch, setting it down in front of her, next to the wounded man. She checked the man's pulse.

"You're going to be okay. Nothing vital was damaged, but you won't be up and around for a while. I have something for the pain, and then you need to rest."

The man nodded, looking around. He spotted Hapke standing nearby and weakly asked him to come closer. Sarah quickly prepared a syringe of morphine for the wounded man as he said to Hapke, "He came out of no-where . . . had a knife . . . we couldn't do anything."

Hapke's face could've been carved from stone. "Was it one of the deputies?"

The man shook his head, while Sarah injected the pain medication. "They were both down . . . one wounded, one a prisoner. They couldn't do a thing. Our attacker had a green face, almost like he was part of the forest . . . it was more than camouflage, like his skin was all green. Green face, green hands, everything!"

Hapke's nostrils flared. "And he killed the others but not you?"

"He . . . he took my weapon and shot the others . . . It all happened so fast . . ."

The morphine was taking hold, so Hapke grabbed the wounded man by the shoulder, shaking him. "Stay with me, man. Who was he?"

"He . . . he was . . . like a ghost. All gr-green. He . . ." The man's eyes fluttered, and it was clear he'd be passing out soon. "He said that if we all left n-now he . . . he'd let us l-live. Other . . . otherwise he'd k-kill us all . . ."

The wounded man quietly slipped into a drug-induced sleep, allowing Hapke to look at the people gathered around the table. The expression on every face showed fear. The back door opened, and the man rushed in with Sarah's medical bag and the first aid kit.

"I'll need room to work on this man, if you don't mind." Sarah's tone was that of the professional doctor.

Hapke told Emily to stay with Sarah and left one guard to keep an eye on them. The rest of them moved closer to the back door. Hapke watched Nancy lead Julie back to the group, sitting her down next to her children. She stopped crying, glaring at the former policeman. He grinned, turning to Servati.

"No one is to be outside our perimeter alone. No one! Understand?"

Servati acknowledged the order with a nod.

"I want two four-man patrols," continued Hapke, "moving around the island, looking for those deputies and whoever rescued them. There are only three of them, and at least one's wounded. They can't be hard to find. I want the rest ready to defend this complex when the FBI makes their attempt at a rescue."

He looked over at the gathered hostages, seeing a mix of fear and shock on their faces. Ericson met Hapke's gaze, and the kidnapper saw no fear, not even contempt or hatred. The man seemed to be assessing him more than anything else. Hapke walked over to the group, followed by Servati.

"You seem pretty smug, Senator." Hapke smiled. "I wouldn't get my hopes up about a rescue. There's only one man out there with a wounded sheriff and a female deputy. Not a rescue force to be worried about. We'll know about any rescue attempt before the FBI comes in, just like we did the locals."

Ericson returned the smile. "First, I'm not being smug—more like realistic. There's a lot of history in these woods, a lot of ghosts." He paused, holding Hapke's gaze. "Anything can happen out there. Your man described a man with a green face, appearing out of nowhere, like he was part of the forest. Sounds like a ghost to me. You are in Indian country, after all—land of the Mohawk, I believe."

"If you're trying to scare me, Senator, forget it," responded Hapke indignantly. "There are no ghosts out there, no little green men from outer space, no Indians. Like it or not, you're here for the duration, so stop your mind games."

Hapke turned and headed toward the door, glancing at the man being tended to on the table. Before he left, he turned to look at Ericson, who just smiled back.

"Remember, Mr. Hapke," he said, smirking. *"Ghosts."*

Hapke slammed the door behind him, making several people jump, including several of the guards. Alexander chuckled.

"Josh, you certainly know how to tell a good summer camp ghost story."

Ericson looked at Nancy, winking, then turned to the elderly senator. "It's not a ghost story, Art."

Julie had seen the exchange between her sister-in-law and Ericson, and her mood shifted. "Jonny's here."

Outside, the velocity of the rain increased, causing Hapke's people to run for the cover afforded them by the cabins and other buildings in the compound. No one saw the shadow moving through the fog.

Mohawk Tavern and Grill
Bluffton, New York
July 19, 2010
1015 hours

Grey, Trask, Preston, and Ramsey entered the restaurant, shaking the rain off their umbrellas. The rain and fog were increasing again, making it feel damp and cold even though the temperature was mild. The place was crowded, mostly with media types, and their presence was immediately noticed. They spotted an empty booth in the corner, heading for it. Almost before they were settled, a young lady with a big smile met them, taking their orders for coffee. She returned within a minute with four steaming mugs and some menus.

"Nice place," said Preston once they were alone. "It reminds me of this place up in northern Ontario . . . I'll bet the tavern is through the door behind us."

Trask turned to look. "Can't tell, the door's closed," he said. "It's probably too early for it to be open."

The waitress suddenly appeared. "Agent Grey?"

Grey raised his hand like a schoolboy, meeting her gaze. "That would be me."

"There's a phone call for you, sir," said the young woman pleasantly. "You can take it back in the bar. It'll be quiet there."

"Do you know who it is?"

The girl shrugged. "No, sir, but my brother's in the bar. He'll get you the phone."

Preston saw Grey's apprehension, which went unnoticed by Trask and his assistant.

"Hey, let me go with you," said Preston. "I just love these places. Since I'm not here to have a beer, it might be my only chance to see the place."

Grey smiled, nodding. The two men excused themselves, following the waitress to the door behind their booth. The door closed quietly behind them. The young man behind the bar was certainly related to their waitress; he had the same pleasant smile. He nodded to the two men, saying nothing. The tables in the back of the room were pulled together, where a large group of people were talking quietly over coffee and pastries. A number looked familiar, including the two journalists who had been held earlier in the day by the Sheriff's Office. He looked back to the bar and over to where an older man sat with his back to the door, sipping a cup of coffee.

Grey started to the bar, walking up next to the man. "Can I assume you're my phone call, Admiral?"

The man turned, answering with a grin. "It's good to see you, too, Glenn—and I see you brought the Mounted Police for backup."

Both men exchanged a surprised glance as the old man held out his hand to Preston. The Canadian policeman took it. "I'm W.C. Putnum, Inspector Preston, deputy director of the NSA, and an old friend of Special Agent in Charge Grey, here. I hope the flight down wasn't too disturbing. Jon can have that effect on people."

"How'd you know?" asked Preston, releasing his grip and looking suspiciously at the old man.

"It's his job, Scott," Grey said, "and the admiral's the best at it. So . . ." He paused, eyes locked on the admiral. "He's alive and here, isn't he?"

"Alive and on the island," said Putnum. "He's already put down four of the bad guys, saving Sheriff James and Deputy Crogan."

A frown weighed at Grey's mouth. "How do you know this?" Putnum gave Grey a hard look that put the agent's doubt in its place. "Okay, then," Grey went on. "We got a text from Jon, too. No details."

"Three dead and one wounded," said Putnum quietly. "That brings them down to thirty-six effective people for us to deal with."

Grey raised his eyebrows at the number, then looked at Putnum. "Why are you here, Admiral?"

"It seems a CIA team beat you here." Putnum grinned. "I came with the team's handler to keep them out of trouble. They've been monitoring all communications from a van outside the marina. I'll make sure they share what they have with you."

"The news crew?" asked Grey.

"It seems that Jon's middle son, Justin, is on that team. He got wind of this little family problem and brought the team here to help spring the hostages."

Grey's brows furrowed, and again, he frowned. "Admiral, didn't I read Justin Summers was killed on a mission overseas? He was a SEAL or something, correct?"

Putnum took a sip of his coffee, choosing his words carefully. "I know this will come as a shock to you, Agent Grey, but it appears our government lied about his status after that last mission."

Preston laughed, while Grey shook his head. "And, of course, Jon figured it out."

"After 9/11, Jon was assigned to some pretty sensitive stuff and spent a lot of time overseas. The CIA guessed he would find out, so they actually leaked it to him so as not to compromise the team. During that time, Inspector Preston, it seems the good Admiral Summers led an Army team in to rescue a crew from a Canadian Air Force plane that made an emergency landing in territory controlled by the Taliban. I believe last night, some members of that crew returned the favor."

Both policemen shook their heads.

"Look, Glenn," said Putnum, "in about thirty minutes, one of your assistant directors is going to land here and take over. The family wants to cooperate. So does the CIA and NSA, but your bosses can't know we're here. We'll feed you the information we get, and you can pass it on."

"Who's coming?" asked Grey.

"Gene Sanderson," answered Putnum.

Grey rolled his eyes.

Linda's Cafe
Adirondack Regional Airport
July 19, 2010
1035 hours

He sat alone at the table, sipping his coffee and watching the twin-engine plane rolling down the ramp toward the runway to take off for Boston. He didn't know how they were going to find out her destination but guessed some strings were being pulled. Everyone owed his contact favors, and he seldom called them in, so when he asked, people tended to help him. The plane reached the runway, hesitated for a few seconds, then turned and started to gain speed. It slowly lifted off the ground, gaining altitude.

His cell phone rang, and he looked at the number on the caller ID. It was one of several numbers he had been given. He smiled; the call was right on time.

"Timothy Evans, here," he said, answering. "I assume you have the information I need."

"Mr. Evans," said a female voice he recognized. "Mr. Smith is in the woods hunting but requested I contact you at this time with your information."

Evans's heart sank, hoping she didn't recognize his voice. He'd been disguising his voice, using a proper British accent, in the effort of concealing his identity.

"So, he's going by Smith now, is he?" he commented. "And would you be Mr. Smith's secretary, young lady?"

He could almost picture her smiling. "You can call me Rebecca, Mr. Evans, and I'm one of Mr. Smith's associates. Have we met before, sir?"

Maybe she did recognize his voice.

"I doubt it. I do most of my business with, uh . . . Mr. Smith over the telephone. He only calls me when he has serious legal issues to deal with."

"Then you're an attorney, Mr. Evans," responded the pleasant female voice. "That's good, because Mr. Smith needs a good attorney, with the business he allows himself to become involved in. He asked me to pass on that the young lady you asked about is booked on a JetBlue flight out of Boston to Dulles International Airport in Washington. From there, her destination is unknown."

Evans found himself thinking out loud. "That can't be her final destination . . ."

"Mr. Evans." The woman's voice brought him back. "Is there anything else I can help you with?"

"Sorry, Rebecca." They had met in his previous life and had married. He found himself wanting to see her, but knowing that couldn't happen, he cleared his throat and said, "Mr. Smith has asked for my help chasing down an old girlfriend who wants something. I apologize for allowing myself to get distracted. It was nice making your acquaintance. Maybe someday we can meet in person."

There was a laugh on the other end of the phone.

"I'm not surprised he's having trouble with an old girlfriend. My experience with Mr. Smith is he has far too many of them. It's been nice talking to you as well. You never know, maybe someday we might meet face-to-face . . . maybe when I need a good attorney. I have your number now, after all."

There was a chuckle, and the line went dead. Evans took a deep breath, feeling good she hadn't recognized his voice. He forced himself back to the mission at hand. Smith asked her to make the call intentionally. The son of a bitch was playing with the two of them, probably thinking it a sick joke. He smiled to himself. It *was* pretty funny.

Upton's Marina and Boat Sales
Bluffton, New York
July 19, 2010
1100 hours

The assistant director in charge of the FBI's Critical Incident Response Group, Eugene Sanderson, arrived and was listening to a briefing from Grey of what had transpired thus far. They sat in folding chairs in the marina's small showroom, and he looked around, wondering how the local sheriff lost only two men on his attempted rescue. He watched Issy walk out of the maintenance shop in the back, through the showroom, and out into the yard.

Sanderson motioned for Grey to pause his briefing. "Agent Grey, I know you haven't been here much longer than me, but who was that?"

Grey looked to Deputy Jasper, hinting he should answer the question. The deputy cleared his throat and said, "Uh, that's Issy Upton, sir. He owns the marina, sir."

"Why is he still here?" asked Sanderson indignantly.

Jasper looked like a scolded puppy. "Because it's his place and he's letting us use it."

Sanderson didn't respond. He just stared at the deputy in silence. Jasper returned Sanderson's gaze, adding, "Sir, you can be as critical as you like about us up here in the Adirondacks and how backwoods we may seem, but the fact of the matter is he's also the only witness we have who's spoken to the suspects. Because Sheriff James wanted to ensure his cooperation, he allowed him to continue his work here."

Sanderson said nothing but continued to look at the deputy with annoyance. Grey found himself respecting Jasper's courage to remain unyielding to one of the most powerful men in the law enforcement community. Personally, Grey didn't care for Sanderson, due to how he'd achieved his current position. Sanderson had been with the bureau for some time, working in some high-profile areas, but he didn't have the credentials others did to be placed in charge of such a critical area of the FBI's operations. He had a reputation for climbing over others to get to the top, which was neither admirable nor respectable. Grey guessed the man planned to use this situation to further his career even more.

"Agent Grey," Sanderson began, shifting his gaze to the FBI agent, "this is now exclusively an FBI operation."

"Yes, sir," responded Grey to the obvious.

"This marina will be our command post, and all civilians and local law enforcement are to be escorted outside the perimeter, which will be secured by our agents. All local law enforcement is to be assigned perimeter duties."

Grey could see the anger in Jasper's eyes, but the man said nothing.

"We have a New York State Police SORT team working with the Sheriff's Office," Agent Grey said. "Where would you like them?"

Sanderson gave Grey an eye roll. "They're local law enforcement, Agent Grey, and already had their shot at this. The rescue will be effected by FBI hostage rescue and SWAT personnel. They can work the perimeter as well."

Grey closed his eyes for a second and could already see the issues that were bound to arise when these orders were conveyed. He opened his eyes again and looked at the man who'd just taken command.

Sanderson was staring directly at Jasper as he spoke. "I want all observation of the island to be handled by FBI teams, and I need some boats up here to ferry the rescue teams across the lake. The street out here needs to be cleared—get the media moved back."

Several of Sanderson's assistants busily scribbled in notebooks. Grey snorted; the orders weren't that detailed and didn't deserve that kind of attention. He guessed his status on scene was now that of just another supervisory agent, so he stood back and listened.

"All press briefings will take place at that motel down the street," continued Sanderson. "That'll move them far enough away to keep them out of our hair. Now, what's the status on the two deputies hiding out on the island?"

Grey answered, "Sheriff James and Deputy Crogan are in a safe place on the island. There's a third party helping them."

"Who?" asked Sanderson, looking directly at Grey.

"They haven't said in their text messages, sir," answered Grey. "That's how they're currently communicating with us; all communication is being monitored by the hostage takers on the island. We know they're able to monitor radio and cell communication, probably with a scanner or radio tuned to those frequencies. Text messages appear to be safe at this point. We do know Sheriff James has been wounded, though."

For all of Sanderson's professional achievements, he lacked the intuition to pick up on the microexpressions exchanged briefly between Jasper and Preston the moment they realized that Agent Grey wasn't revealing everything they knew about Jon Summers—that he was alive, specifically, and even participating indirectly with their mission.

Agent Grey smiled, keeping his expression even.

If Sanderson was going to do things his way or not at all, then he wasn't a true ally. It was a risk, however. If Preston or Jasper decided to adhere to blind conformity, they'd rightly correct Agent Grey right now, revealing the truth.

"Inspector Preston." Sanderson focused on the Canadian. "Any word on the search for Mr. Summers's body?"

There was a stilted pause that had Agent Grey holding his breath.

Preston cleared his throat. "No, sir," he said, and Grey exhaled at last. They were on the same side, then. "And I spoke to them just before the briefing, in fact. They're talking about suspending the search."

It was Grey's turn to smile; Preston had already spoken with his people in Ontario and had called off the search because they knew exactly where Summers was. Preston had indeed followed Grey's lead when it became obvious Sanderson was only going to complicate things.

"Is there any chance that our missing body might be our Samaritan on the island?" Sanderson asked Grey.

Grey tried to hide his surprise. Perhaps Sanderson wasn't so blind after all. He gave the assistant director a bland smile. "That's always a possibility, sir. He is familiar with the area, and his family has lived on that island for years."

"How would he have gotten here?" Sanderson asked no one in particular. "He was a schoolteacher. I doubt he would have made it here that quickly. No, our third party must be a local or another family member."

Grey decided to give his superior a chance to amend his assumption. "Sir, he was also a Navy SEAL and a Medal of Honor recipient. I wouldn't rule out—"

"I don't care what he used to be, Agent Grey." The words sliced through the tension between the two men. "Nor do I care how highly you regard the man. The fact remains that he's probably dead. If he survived the attack in Canada, there's no way he could get back down here without going through customs and our knowing about it."

"But sir . . ." Grey took a deep breath, trying to stay calm. "You need to know—"

"I'm not going to argue the point, Agent Grey!" Sanderson cut him off. "You have your orders."

Grey was about to press the argument but stopped when Preston put a hand on his shoulder.

"You have your orders, my friend, and you also have a back channel to pass the correct information through."

Grey looked at the Canadian for a few seconds, then at his staff from the New York City office. All the expressions said the same thing. When Grey left to follow his orders, they all followed him out.

Upton's Marina and Boat Sales
Bluffton, New York
July 19, 2010
1115 hours

Sanderson walked out of the marina's showroom, taking a deep breath. The rain had stopped, and the fog seemed to be lifting off the bay, but the heavy overcast remained, making the village of Bluffton look dreary and depressing. He looked at the street and wasn't surprised Special Agent Grey had already put his agents to work clearing the media from the area.

Grey was currently standing next one of the vans, talking to an older man. He briefly made eye contact with the man, who smiled. Sanderson thought the man looked familiar but was distracted when he heard the door of the showroom open behind him. He turned to see the deputy United States attorney and his assistant coming up behind him.

"It's a miserable day to be doing this, Mr. Trask," Sanderson commented, smiling at the young lady. Trask didn't look happy. Sanderson knew the reason was all the shuffling of responsibilities he was doing.

"We could have some issues with the New York State attorney general," said Trask, responding quickly. "They could contest jurisdiction. That state police major looked pretty upset when he left."

Sanderson grunted. "Jurisdiction is ours," he said. "Several of the hostages are serving representatives of the federal government, and others were transported across state lines. That puts jurisdiction firmly in our hands."

"But the Summers family and some of the guests were here in New York State at the cabin when this started. It appears the other hostages were brought in after they were taken prisoner. They do have a prima facie case that they have the initial jurisdiction. It could muddy any plans you have on making a rescue, if they push this in court. Local judges, even federal ones, could be more sympathetic to them than us in this case."

Sanderson thought for a moment. He didn't agree with Trask, but the attorney did make a good point. Sanderson didn't need anyone trying to stop him from doing what he felt he needed to. He looked at Trask.

"I see your point, Mr. Trask. I want you to deal with the state attorney general's office directly. We need to stop any jurisdictional turf war from keeping us from accomplishing our final goal here. Set up with Agent Grey and use him as you see fit in stopping this thing. You both have existing relationships with the New York people, and that's where I need the two of you now. Leave your assistant here to help advise me on the legal aspects of our mission. You'll be right down the road if she needs any help."

With that, Sanderson dismissed Trask, ignoring the angry expression on the man's face. Sanderson didn't care if he ruffled the feathers of the United States Attorney's Office. He needed people near him who would help him, not throw up roadblocks. He took out his cell, turning his back on Trask to make a call.

The little group outside the marina showroom didn't take notice of the old man by the van. Grey moved on to complete his tasks, but Putnum stayed to watch the exchange. The body language spoke volumes for him since he couldn't hear what was said. It was obvious Trask didn't care for Sanderson or how he was doing business. When Sanderson turned his back on Trask, the latter's expression told Putnum there were issues in the hierarchy of the team planning the rescue. It was time for him to do some research of his own.

Hidden Cave
Summers' Island
July 19, 2010
1125 hours

James woke to find Abby pacing back and forth in the cave. She wore a worried look and kept glancing at the entrance to their small sanctuary. James hadn't realized he dozed off and the pain subsided to a dull ache. If he moved, he would get a jolt of pain, but only for a moment. He guessed it'd been one of those moments that brought him back to consciousness. Abby noticed he was awake.

"How are you feeling?" she asked, coming over to check on him.

"Only hurts when I move." He smiled weakly. "What are you pacing for?"

Abby checked him for a temperature like she'd been instructed and then looked to his bandaged legs. "Jon's been gone almost three hours. I'm worried he's in trouble. The rain let up, and the fog has lifted here on the island."

James looked at his deputy. "He's taking his time and being careful," he reassured her. "These Special Forces types are invisible because they don't rush and make stupid mistakes. If he did what you say, then it's the kidnappers who have to worry."

She smiled. "No fever, and the bandages look good. And thanks, Sheriff James."

James returned her smile. "What are you thanking me for, Deputy? You're the one taking care of me."

"You're a good boss, Sheriff. You always keep things in perspective and your people's spirits up."

Abby saw James's eyes widen and turned around to find a man in green camouflage from head to toe standing in the cave entrance. He cradled an M4 carbine in his arms, equipped with a suppressor, and had a pistol strapped to his side. There was also a combat knife inverted on his backpack strap. He had just appeared without making any noise and looked every bit the Special Forces commando one might see online.

Kuma had sensed Summers's arrival and stood next to him, tail wagging.

Summers took off the boonie cap, revealing camo paint well up onto his bald head. He smiled at the two of them, and his white teeth stood out from all the shades of green.

"How's the patient, Abby?"

"Not bad, thanks to you," answered James on behalf of his deputy. "I have to ask—how'd you get here without customs knowing you'd crossed the border?"

Summers set his M4 next to the other weapons by the wall. "I hitched a ride with some friends who legally flew over the border and then over here."

"And you just happened to exit the aircraft as it passed over the island?" added Abby, expression a hybrid of shock and admiration. "I'm assuming the parachute we're using as a door to the cave was yours?"

Summers shrugged his shoulders in response, smirking.

"What about the men who were sent to kill you?" asked James, turning serious. "They were found at your campsite, but no sign of you. I assume you questioned them. They have rights, you know?"

Summers looked at the sheriff, giving him a slight smile.

"I could care less about their rights," Summers replied frankly. "They are alive because I wanted to know why they were trying to kill me. I didn't torture them, if that's what you're worried about. I will admit to scaring them a bit, though."

"How?" asked Abby innocently. Jon guessed this tactic would serve her well as an investigator.

"People have fears about the wild, so I exploited them. I invited some of my research subjects into the campsite." Summers scratched Kuma behind the ears to indicate what he was referring to. "They became very talkative after that—but they were never in any danger. I stayed close by until the rangers got there."

James looked at Abby. "I guess I missed something here?"

"Jon was in Canada doing wolf research," Abby explained, and as James pieced it all together, he looked at Summers, then at Kuma, and began to laugh.

"The big bad wolf. This is too much," he said, and Summers gave him a puzzled look. James pointed at Kuma. "When I came to, that dog was licking my face, and all I saw was his teeth. Scared the hell out of me—thought I was about to be eaten. This is too much."

All three of them started to laugh. As they did, James's cell phone rang. He pulled it out of the holster he carried it in, looking at the screen, not recognizing the number the caller ID displayed. He showed the display to Abby, who shook her head. Summers leaned over and looked as well.

"It's a Virginia area code," he commented. "Answer it—but don't give them any information over the phone."

James nodded and pushed the talk button. "Marty James."

"Sheriff, this is Eugene Sanderson of the FBI. I'm so glad to hear your voice. Are you and Deputy Crogan, okay?"

James looked at Summers, who just nodded to go ahead and answer. "We're safe, Mr. Sanderson. Why are you contacting us?"

"I'm the assistant director in charge of the FBI's Critical Response Group and wanted to assure you that we're doing everything possible to get you and the hostages out of there," Sanderson said. "Can you tell us where you're located so we can get a team to you and extract you off the island?"

James didn't even look at Summers for a response. "Mr. Sanderson, you do understand these communications are being monitored, right?"

There was silence on the other end of the phone for a few moments.

"Sheriff, we understand you're feeling the need for security, but I don't think these people are that good. We think you're being helped by someone who was on the island when the hostage takers landed there. If you let us know who that is, we can make sure you're safe with them."

James looked at both Abby and Summers. Both shook their heads at Sanderson's last statement, and James couldn't help himself. "You know, Sanderson," he said, "you're an idiot. Don't bother calling me back."

James disconnected the call.

Summers' Cabin
Adirondack State Park, New York
July 19, 2010
1130 hours

The laughter from the dining area got all the hostages' attention. They were celebrating something, but most of the hostages didn't hear what. Hapke and Servati came out of the dining area laughing and gave the hostages an amused glance. They then disappeared out the front door, continuing their celebration outside.

"What's going on?" asked Congresswoman Del Monte, stretching her neck to look in the next room.

"A man named Sanderson from the FBI was trying to get information from the local sheriff over an open channel," responded her husband, Frank. "Sounded like he gave our friends in the other room quite a bit of information about himself."

"Sanderson's a pompous ass," Alexander added with a grunt. "The man has a huge ego, and every decision he makes is self-serving. If he's in charge of the rescue, we may be here a while."

"Isn't the sheriff one of the policemen they're looking for?" asked Fiona.

"Yes, and he's a fast learner," answered her husband. "He may be stranded somewhere on the island because he didn't listen, but he's clearly listening to someone now, as he didn't give up his location over the air."

Wells chuckled. "And put Mr. Assistant Director in his place, too."

"Unfortunately, Mr. Sanderson gave these guys information they could have only guessed at," commented Ericson from his chair, "and that's what they're so happy about. The government response is now predictable."

At this, everyone in the room went silent, and the mood turned pensive.

Mohawk Tavern and Grill
Bluffton, New York
July 19, 2010
1135 hours

The two FBI agents had thought it was funny, even laughing out loud at one point, when Grey asked them to help hide the news van behind the

Mohawk. The laughter stopped when they realized the people they thought were reporters were employees of another government agency spying on their operation. Grey told them they were now in charge of security for a joint operation with the CIA and NSA and were to answer only to him. He assured them this was coming from the highest levels of the bureau, but they were not to share this with any other agents on the rescue assignment. Since they had come with Grey from the New York office, they were fine with the orders.

The van was backed quickly behind the Mohawk and wasn't missed by the other news crews in the confusion of everyone else being moved. The two FBI agents created a short-lived traffic jam on Lake Street, keeping everyone's attention, while Justin moved the van off the side street and into place by the garage. Stephen moved a box truck the Crogan family used in one of their business endeavors so that it blocked the driveway and sight of the van. With Joey DePalma's help, the van was back up and running within minutes and this time connected directly with NSA in Maryland. Grey and his two agents were surprised at how quickly this had taken place.

DePalma was placed in charge of the van and all its electronics, and the first thing he did when they went operational again was give Grey a transcript of the cell phone conversation between Sanderson and Sheriff James. Grey smiled as he read through it. He looked up at DePalma, who was sitting in the open door of the van, and said, "This van does all this? I'm impressed at where all my tax dollars are going."

DePalma grunted, waving his hand dismissively. "Don't be impressed. Without the connection to NSA, it's just a typical surveillance van. It's better than most, I'll give you that, but still limited on what it can do. You won't be as happy with the next set of transcripts."

DePalma handed Grey another stack of papers—this time, transcripts of radio communications between the various posts the kidnappers had on the island. These revealed that they were adjusting their defenses based on Sanderson's call because they now knew who they were facing.

DePalma could see the anger rise in Grey's face.

Mohawk Tavern and Grill
Bluffton, New York
July 19, 2010
1140 hours

Sanderson screamed in anger when Sheriff James hung up on him. He didn't tolerate insubordination from his own people and certainly wasn't about to let a backwoods sheriff make a mockery of him with such a flagrant display of disrespect. He ordered two agents to follow him, with Tina Ramsey in tow, as he stormed across the street to the Mohawk. He'd calmed down some by the time he reached the front door but was still red-faced, with his hands curled into fists, and visibly angry.

The restaurant was crowded with locals and media who jammed in because it gave them the perfect view of the marina and the activities taking place there. With no vehicular or pedestrian traffic any longer on Lake Street, someone coming through that entrance brought a hush to the customers gathered there. This just made Sanderson angrier.

There wasn't an empty seat in the place, and every spot at the counter was taken. There were a few waitresses moving around, but Sanderson focused his attention on the young woman who was standing behind the cash register. She looked Native American, and his people told him the Mohawk was operated by a Native American family.

He moved deftly through the crowd, with the attorney and two agents trying to keep up. The girl saw him coming and looked back over her shoulder, saying something to someone out of sight in the kitchen.

Sanderson reached the cash register. "I would like to see Maggie Crogan, young lady!"

Brandi held the man's gaze, not showing any emotion. If she was afraid or intimidated, Sanderson couldn't tell—and intimidation was what he'd intended. The door from the kitchen opened behind Brandi, and she smiled without looking.

"May I help you, sir?" asked Nathan from behind his younger sister.

Sanderson could tell they were brother and sister and knew his initial tactic wasn't going to work. Both wore the same polite smile, so he decided to try something else.

"My name's Eugene Sanderson," he said, displaying his ID card and badge, "and I'm the assistant director of the FBI's Critical Incident Response Group. I'm here to see Maggie Crogan. I'm looking to see if she's been in touch with her daughter, Abigail."

"So you've rescued her from those bastards on the island?" Nathan asked politely, raising his brows. "Because if not, I'm not sure she'll want to speak to you. She's just a little busy with family business."

There was absolute silence in the restaurant, and every word had been overheard by every customer present. Sanderson's anger became even more evident when he heard laughter behind him, his ears reddening. The young man deliberately hadn't used his title or name when addressing him, which was an open slight. He was further embarrassed when the Lake Street door opened again and Agent Grey entered, followed by Deputy Jasper. They quickly moved up behind Sanderson and his party.

"Director," Grey said quietly, "we need to talk; I have some information for you."

Sanderson gave Grey an irritated glance before turning back to face Nathan, who still stood politely behind the counter. "When I'm done here, Agent Grey. I need to speak to Maggie Crogan, one way or another."

Sanderson was shocked to see Nathan look around him and directly at Grey. He was even more surprised when Grey nodded and Nathan smiled broadly. He couldn't yet piece together exactly what was going on, but it felt like they were indulging him the way two parents might a toddler in the midst of a tantrum.

Again, Sanderson's face radiated with heat. Before he could retaliate, however, Nathan nodded toward the back and said, "If you would come with me, Mr. Sanderson."

Nathan didn't rush, first checking to make sure Brandi was going to be all set covering the restaurant. He then motioned for Sanderson and everyone to follow him.

Sanderson turned to Grey, asking, "What the hell is going on here, Grey?"

Grey's look was serious, but his tone betrayed his pleasure in his superior's discomfort. "I was looking to tell you myself, sir, but now I think you're going to find out for yourself."

Sanderson sensed his subordinate didn't care for him and gave him an aloof look as they followed Nathan to the door leading to the bar.

"Sir," said Grey, "I need to talk to you before we go in there."

Sanderson didn't even look back. "Not now, Mr. Grey. I need to talk to this Crogan woman. Maybe she can control what's going on, if no one else can."

Nathan was already through the door, and Sanderson, Ramsey, and the two agents followed close behind. Grey turned and looked at Jasper, shaking his head in disgust.

"Hey, man," responded the deputy with a shrug and a smile. "You tried to warn him."

Grey answered with a grunt, and the two men followed the others into the bar.

Sanderson was surprised to see a large group gathered around several long tables pulled together on the far side of the room. Toward the center of the group was a woman Sanderson guessed to be in her early fifties with long dark hair. On either side were two older men. To her right was a man with long hair that was graying. He had the look of a Native American who had spent most of his time outdoors. To the woman's left was the older man he saw standing next to the van along Lake Street earlier. He still looked familiar, but Sanderson couldn't place a name or where he knew him from. As he started to approach the group, he noticed Inspector Preston sitting at the end of the table with another woman, laughing and enjoying himself. This made Sanderson hesitate. He tried to process what was taking place. He decided he would take it up with their Canadian guest later. He refocused, continuing his passage toward the tables, only to find his way blocked by a man he didn't notice before.

"May I help you?" asked the man, not moving or yielding to Sanderson.

Sanderson looked impatient as he said, "I'm here to see Mrs. Crogan."

"In regard to what, if I may ask? We're kind of busy." The man didn't retreat from his position between Sanderson and the table.

Visibly irritated, Sanderson again pulled out his ID and flashed it to the man. "My name is Eugene Sanderson, and I'm assistant director of—"

"Ah, the big man himself," interrupted the man before him, without flinching. "There are a number of us here who would like to talk to you as well."

Matt extended his hand as a matter of protocol. Sanderson looked from the man's face to the extended hand and back again without showing any sign of reciprocating the gesture, and eventually Matt retracted his hand.

"So, what do we call you, Mr. Sanderson? Special Agent, Director, Mister . . . I assume using 'Gene' would be out of the question?"

Sanderson was giving this man a serious look over. He was taller, and he guessed him to be in his fifties. He looked reasonably fit, having a businessman look about him. Sanderson decided he would allow no disrespect from this group and decided to set the relationship right from the start. "It's Director Sanderson."

A slight smile appeared on the man's lips.

"Well then, I'm Matthew Summers. My friends call me Matt, but you can call me Mr. Summers. My family owns the island where the hostages are being held, and many of us in this room have family members being held there. Why don't you have a seat? Let's see what we can do for each other."

Matt motioned for Sanderson to take an empty chair across from Maggie. When Sanderson started to sit down, Summers pulled up an empty chair, sitting next to him. Grey found a chair for Ramsey and then one for himself. Jasper also found an empty chair, and they all sat down. The two FBI agents Sanderson brought along remained standing a few feet behind the group.

Sanderson looked to the end of the table, where Inspector Preston sat watching the drama at the middle of the table.

"Inspector Preston, you seem to have made yourself comfortable here in the bar."

The Canadian policeman ignored the intended barb. "I go where the case takes me, Director Sanderson. I'm here hoping to get more information on my case. It seems that we've had a breakthrough on our end."

"What on earth are you rambling on about, Preston?"

Preston just shrugged, sensing Sanderson's discomfort. "It seems," he said, speaking slowly for dramatic effect, "that our two cases are more connected than ever. It appears we've located our victim."

Sanderson's head snapped around, glaring angrily at Grey. Before he could say anything, Jasper interjected by saying, "Hey, man—he tried to get you to stop before you came in here so he could tell you. It's your own fault for being in such a hurry."

There were a few chuckles throughout the room.

Sanderson's anger and embarrassment were quite evident. He moved his gaze away from Grey and tried to refocus on why he had come. Matt met his gaze, watching as the FBI executive controlled his anger.

"Director Sanderson," started Matt, "you came here to meet with our hostess, so allow me to introduce Mrs. Maggie Crogan, Clan Mother of the Wolf Clan of the Mohawk Nation. Next to her is Fred Crogan, her father, one of the Hereditary Chiefs and Medicine Man of the Mohawk Nation. Everyone else in the room has a stake in what is taking place, so you can address all of us. I will act as spokesman and keep this meeting in order. After all, we all want the same result—the safe release of all the hostages."

Sanderson's anger was not subsiding, but he did have it under control. He shifted his gaze from Summers to Grey and back again. His face was still flushed when he said, "Mr. Summers, I'm not comfortable speaking about ongoing rescue operations in front of all these people."

"Director, if you wish to speak to me," said Maggie quietly, "it will be in front of everyone in this group or not at all."

Sanderson saw the look of determination on the woman's face and gave in.

"Okay, then," he said, "but don't complain if you get embarrassed. I would like to ask you to contact your daughter and ask her to keep her and the good sheriff under cover while the professionals take care of the situation. We're equipped and ready to go in and take the hostages back by force if necessary and I can't have them getting in the way."

Sanderson saw no reaction on the part of the older members of the group. Several of the younger members looked angry, and one young woman looked ready to say something, but true to his word, Matt kept the group under control with a wave of his hand. The young woman kept her seat and remained quiet.

Fred leaned forward. "The implication is that my granddaughter and Sheriff James are not professionals. Mr. Sanderson, that's a cheap tactic on your part to bait us into reacting to your comment to get information, and I resent you and your methods. Besides they're not the ones you need to be concerned about."

Sanderson held Fred's gaze. "And who should I be worried about, Mr. Crogan?"

The old man allowed a smile to cross his face. The group remained silent as his brows raised knowingly. "You really don't understand, do you?"

"Understand what, Mr. Crogan?" Sanderson said, balking. "You're talking in circles."

Fred chuckled and put his hand on the shoulder of the older man next to him. "I think you had better read the man in, Admiral."

Sanderson suddenly realized who the older man was. He was looking at Admiral W. C. Putnum, Deputy Director of the NSA, and realized he was being evaluated. He had already made the mistake of not recognizing someone higher in the chain of command.

Putnum leaned forward. "Mr. Sanderson, do I need to introduce myself?"

Sanderson shook his head. "No, sir, Admiral Putnum."

"Good, then we can skip the formalities. Would you and Special Agent Grey step outside with me? Matt, Maggie, and Fred, will you come out with us as well?"

"Sure thing," responded Fred, who appeared to be the group's spokesperson.

"Tom," continued Putnum, "bring your team; I want to introduce them to *Assistant Director* Sanderson."

The man sitting next to Putnum acknowledged the comment and rose, starting for the back of the room. Sanderson got to his feet, looking at Grey with a pleading expression. Grey leaned over and whispered something into Sanderson's ear and the FBI executive paled and nodded.

While they filed out the door, Cassie came over to where Ramsey was seated, taking an empty chair. "How'd you luck out to get assigned to the big man from the FBI?"

Ramsey shook her head. "Trask is running interference with New York State, and that left me to work with *Mr. Personality* there. He's a bit of an egomaniac, but it's a rush being so close to the action. How are you holding up? I mean, with family being held hostage on the island and all?"

Cassie evaluated her coworker, deciding not to tell her everything she knew.

"Families have secrets," she settled on saying, "and I'm finding mine is no different."

"Who was that man Sanderson seems scared of?" asked Ramsey.

Cassie didn't trust Sanderson, and because Tina was now working with him, decided again not to tell her everything. "He's a friend of my uncle Jon. I'm not sure what he does. I do know he's not here officially."

"So what's the breakthrough in your uncle's case? Is he safe?"

At this point, it was obvious Ramsey was fishing. Cassie decided for the third time not to share all her information. "I don't know about safe," she said. "I'm not sure Uncle Jon ever does anything safe. Inspector Preston thinks he may be alive because they haven't found the body. It's a theory they're floating. That's enough for me to be hopeful."

Before Ramsey could ask another question, one of the two agents waiting for Sanderson came up and told her they were to return to the marina. Ramsey reluctantly agreed to go back with them, saying her goodbyes to Cassie. While Cassie watched them walk out, Stephen came up next to her.

"Friend of yours?" he asked.

Cassie turned, smiling at her cousin. "Coworker, but I find myself not trusting her. It's scary—I'm finding myself not trusting anyone outside the family on this thing."

"Welcome to the club, cuz—but don't worry, I think the admiral and your dad are about to turn Sanderson away from the dark side."

Cassie smiled, but she still wasn't sure that was the real issue. She felt there was something else wrong.

Outside, Sanderson was doing his best not to show his anger when he realized that the CIA had been spying on an FBI operation. He didn't say anything while he watched Joey DePalma work the electronics in the van, and he instead looked at the three-person team that had masqueraded as the news crew.

"Admiral," Sanderson began, "I really must protest the CIA's involvement in this. It could compromise our operation."

Putnum looked at Sanderson. "That's exactly why Tom and I are here. This isn't an official visit on our part."

Sanderson looked puzzled.

Mitchell answered the question Sanderson didn't ask. "Director Sanderson, I'm Tom Mitchell, and I'm the case officer for this team. We were contacted by Admiral Summers, who managed to escape the murder attempt. He somehow crossed the border and is on the island. They were monitoring communications, and we can tell you two things at this moment. First, the subjects on the island are monitoring your communications and can react to anything you do. Secondly, we suspect there are people here who are feeding them information about your movements and plans."

"How do you know this?" Sanderson's tone was more concerned than accusatory.

"The team has been recording all communications since they arrived yesterday, and we're now tied in with NSA, so we're even more capable of monitoring their communications; we're hopeful that we'll figure out who's monitoring your operation soon."

Sanderson thought before he spoke. "You're offering to work with the FBI?"

Putnum smiled. "Gene, they've been working for you since I arrived," he said plainly, spelling it out. "They just can't be legally recognized as CIA or NSA assets."

"That goes for our help as well," said Matt. "We don't want to work against you."

"Mr. Summers, I can appreciate your concerns due to your family members involved," Sanderson said, sounding sincere for the first time, "but they kidnapped representatives of the United States House of Representatives and Senate. We'll get them all out—believe me when I say that."

"You really don't understand what's going on here, do you?" said Putnum.

Sanderson gave Putnum a long, hard look. "Admiral, I have a traitor who is trying to gain his freedom by holding members of Congress hostage. It seems obvious. Everyone else is collateral damage."

"You really are a stupid white man," said Fred. "Things are not what they seem here."

Putnum and Fred exchanged glances, and the latter continued, "What do you know about Dick Kingston?"

Sanderson's face flushed at the comment, but he kept his cool as he answered.

"He was caught selling information to the Japanese underworld that tried to take over the island of Mindanao back in 1995, I think. He was captured by the FBI and sentenced to life in prison. Pretty straightforward, Mr. Crogan. Nothing too sinister. He's a bad man trying to force the United States to free him. We think he has money salted away from his dealings with the Japanese. Neither we nor our counterparts in Japan have had much luck finding those funds, though. He did a good job of hiding the cash."

"What do you know about the hostages?" asked Fred.

"Not much," answered Sanderson as he turned to look at Grey. "Special Agent Grey never ordered a workup on the other hostages. That's been done now, and I should have it in the next couple of hours."

Grey didn't respond but looked at Putnum, who did. "Gene, you really need to take time to listen to people. You came in here making assumptions and were so busy trying to show everyone who the boss was that you missed a significant amount of intelligence that was there for the taking."

"Director," said Mitchell, "all the material you are about to be told is classified and can't be shared with anyone, not even your staff."

Sanderson looked at Mitchell with surprise but nodded. He was even more surprised when it was Grey who started to give the briefing.

"When you look at the list of hostages," Grey began, "it's a who's who from the case against Dick Kingston. Senator Ericson was a disabled vet turned successful businessman. He lost the use of his legs when Dick Kingston called off an extraction of a SEAL team from Vietnam in 1978."

Sanderson cocked his head. "We were out of Vietnam long before that—you must have the date wrong."

A quick look at Putnum told Sanderson he'd made a wrong assumption and needed to be quiet and listen.

Grey continued, "Senator Ericson still had contacts in Naval Intelligence and started running an unofficial surveillance on a suspected group of Japanese nationals living in Hawaii who were known to have ties to the Japanese underworld. This was while Naval Intelligence was looking into naval officers being solicited for information on ship movements and tactical responses to defend some of our allies along the Pacific Rim."

"And Richard Kingston was on the suspect list?" asked Sanderson, glancing at Putnum to make sure he was okay asking the question.

"Correct," answered Grey. "Senator Ericson has since married Kingston's ex-wife. Their friendship started when the then Mrs. Kingston started visiting the wounded Master Chief Ericson in the hospital in Subic Bay in 1978. They reconnected in 2001 and were married in 2005. They are both on the island as hostages. The other members of Congress were at their house at the time of the abduction, and we think they're the collateral damage in this case."

Grey watched Sanderson for a reaction to this theory. He couldn't tell if the FBI executive agreed with it or not, but the man nodded in a way that suggested he understood. Grey accepted the nod, expanding on his briefing.

"The Naval Intelligence investigation was a small one but included a young Air Force officer. That young officer was Captain Judy Demmer, who is currently a hostage on the island. The officer leading the investigation was Jon Summers, who was a captain at the time. It was no secret he and Kingston were rivals at the Naval Academy. Kingston hates Summers so much that when his SEAL team was rescuing some POWs whom the Vietnamese government knew nothing about, Kingston secretly cancelled the extraction."

"The same SEAL team Ericson was on?" asked Sanderson, looking for the connection.

"Yes, sir," answered Grey. "When the Japanese mafia tried to take over the island of Mindanao in 1995 and took a group of American vets hostage, the president put together a task force to expedite the release of the hostages and plug the hole in our defenses in the area."

"Where are you getting this information?" interrupted Sanderson, looking more than a little confused. "That attempt to take over Mindanao was led by a radical Muslim separatist group that was killing other separatists as well as local Philippine officials. You're not making sense."

Grey smiled. "The Japanese mafia was trying to set up their own little kingdom in the Pacific using that separatist group as a front. I was the FBI representative assigned to the investigation led by Summers, which included then NCIS Special Agent Mark Wells. Tiffany Rice was then a marine captain assigned to Kingston's command and was sent on the second rescue attempt by Kingston. She wasn't supposed to return from that mission but surprised Kingston by doing just that. Both Wells and Rice are on the island."

Sanderson had the look of a man deep in thought. "Obviously, there's a definite pattern to who the hostages are," he commented, eyeing Grey and Putnum. "Shouldn't *you* be worried about being on Kingston's list?"

"He is," interjected Putnum, "as am I. I took command from Kingston when Glenn and Mark arrested him for treason in his compartment on board the ship. He was leading the battle group sent to rescue the hostages and transmitted the landing locations of both rescue attempts. Glenn has agents following up on us over the past several weeks to see if they can find if we were under surveillance by these guys. My guess is we were, but they couldn't get a clear shot at either of us because of where we both work."

Sanderson nodded in agreement. "Probably not, Admiral. How about the rest of the hostages? Are they connected in any way?"

Grey again took control of the briefing. "Benjamin Fortum was Kingston's attorney during his trial. He remains the Kingston family attorney but was fired by Richard Kingston years ago. Kingston's father passed away just last year, and Fortum is executor of the estate. It's quite a sizable fortune, with Richard Kingston being written out of the will altogether. I'm guessing for him to be included as a hostage that there's some animosity there. We mentioned the politicians, and the rest are members of the Summers family. The leader of the hostage takers is a former law enforcement officer and no friend of Summers. He was forced off the job for trying to provoke an incident with Summers in 1995, just before he left to head the investigative team in the Kingston case."

"There is one more person we're still trying to chase down," said Putnum, sounding concerned, "and that's George Ellison, a retired Marine Corps general and old friend of Summers. He and his wife retired to run a small horse farm in Virginia and neither has been heard from in two days."

"You suspect foul play?" asked Sanderson.

Putnum looked concerned but apparently refused to be pessimistic about his friend's condition. "George is very capable of taking care of himself," he replied. "I would just like to know he's safe."

"And he was part of the investigation?"

"He almost shot Kingston as he reached for a gun," answered Grey. "Now I'm wishing he had—we wouldn't be dealing with this today."

Sanderson gave Grey a disapproving look but said nothing.

"Gene," said Putnum, "your challenge will be to get the hostages out before Kingston gives the order to kill them."

"He wouldn't do that," responded Sanderson with a frown. "It would be suicide to kill that many high-profile politicians, plus women and children."

"Trust me, sir," Grey said pointedly, "he'd do that in a heartbeat if it would cover an escape attempt to get him out of the country."

Sanderson thought for a second before saying, "He's in Leavenworth. How's he going to get out of there?"

"My guess is they'll create a situation to get him moved," responded Putnum. "They need him moved out of the prison and more into the open to even try to break him out. These guys on the island are military trained, probably mercenaries. They beat off a well-armed rescue attempt, including a trained SWAT team."

"Our people are better." Sanderson didn't sound like he was bragging; it was more like he was stating a fact. "We'll get them out."

"What about my brother?" asked Matt.

"He needs to stand down," answered Sanderson without hesitation. "No matter what his experience. With all due respect, we do this for a living. We're the professionals."

The laughter surprised Sanderson. His face lit up with shock, then went several shades redder with anger. Before he could protest, Putnum spoke for the entire group in saying, "You would have no way of knowing this, Gene, but hostage rescue is Jon's specialty. In the mission that was mentioned in 1978, he and his team evaded capture in the Mekong Delta and brought out four POWs, even with the botched extraction. In 1995, he was the one who led the rescue mission on Mindanao and brought out all those captured vets. I apologize for the laugh at your expense, but you really did walk into it."

Sanderson took a moment, processing what he had been told, and eventually looked around the group. He saw no malice in the faces of the people around him and decided to join in on the levity for a moment.

"I still need him to back off and just feed us on-site intelligence. One man can't get all those people out."

Justin grunted, and everyone turned to look at him. He said nothing.

Agent Grey cut in, saying, "We've been texting him. To our knowledge, the hostage takers don't have the capabilities to intercept that type of message. However, we do know they're monitoring both radio and cell frequencies, so we can't communicate with him that way. That's why Sherriff James hung up on you."

Sanderson nodded and then looked at Matt. "Can you give my people an idea of the general layout of the island?"

"Not a problem," responded Matt almost cheerfully. "I'll come back with you and give you whatever information you need."

Joey DePalma poked his head out of the sliding door of the van and asked for help. Kay and Ryan both responded without being asked. Justin remained behind Mitchell to monitor the meeting with his boss.

"No, Mr. Summers, that won't be necessary," replied Sanderson, obviously hesitant to have a civilian inside his headquarters. "For security reasons, I'll have my people come to you. Nothing personal—I just want to keep my operations as secure as possible."

"So far, I have to say your security sucks, Mr. Sanderson," said Fred, speaking before Matt could. "They seem to know what you're doing as fast as you decide what to do."

Sanderson, obviously irritated by the comment, bristled. "That all happened before my division took control, Mr. Crogan. I think you'll see a change in the way business is being done. Freeing hostages safely takes time and can't be rushed."

The old man grunted. "Let's go back to what you're going to do with Kingston. The premise of their whole operation is to get him out of prison and free him. How are you going to stop that from happening? So far, he's engineered this entire thing and has you all jumping just like he planned. It's like an evil spreading its tentacles and controlling this entire nightmare."

"Evil, Mr. Crogan?" sneered Sanderson. "I mean, really, it's not that melodramatic. It's just a group of henchmen trying to get their boss released."

A sly grin crossed Fred's face. "You misunderstand me, Mr. Sanderson. I'm not talking about a theological or supernatural evil; I'm talking about real evil that resides in each of us. Kingston can manipulate fears, moral weaknesses, and even our strengths to get what he wants. History is filled with men and women like that. And Dick Kingston? He's very good at it."

"You make him sound like Adolf Hitler, Mr. Crogan," countered Sanderson. "Frankly, I don't see any comparison. If that were the case, he never would have been arrested."

"I agree, Mr. Sanderson, there's no comparison to Hitler." Fred was quick to respond, not skipping a beat. "We both know the circumstances for Hitler coming to power, and they were unique to his situation. I do compare him to Charles Manson, though. He easily manipulates people, even from prison, and gets them to do exactly what he wants them to."

"What exactly is your point, Mr. Crogan?"

"Keep him in Leavenworth where he is." Fred's tone was serious but not demanding. "He can't be sprung from there. If you move him anywhere else, that's when they'll make their play to free him. All he can do from prison is attempt to call the shots, but with you controlling his communications out of prison, that would be difficult—if not impossible. We also have them monitored pretty well from here, so you can react in time before they have a chance to do anything."

Sanderson was quiet, thinking about what the old man had just said. He took his time contemplating his answer.

"You make a good point, Mr. Crogan. I can't promise they won't move him—that decision would be made above me—but I can advocate against it. If they do decide to move him, I can control the who, when, and where of that operation, so they will have no way of knowing where he's taken."

Both Fred and Matt looked as if they were about to say something when DePalma came to the door again. "We've got a message coming in." Everyone sat up a little straighter as he added, "It's from the hostage takers."

Justin was at the van in seconds, followed by Mitchell. The rest of the group crowded closer as the CIA team went to work. DePalma worked on keeping a clear signal while Ryan and Kay made sure the recording and decryption equipment were working. Justin was on his phone talking to their contact at the NSA in Maryland.

"It's a text message," said DePalma, "so it'll take a few minutes to decipher, but we have a clear signal."

"NSA's tracking the source of the transmission," added Justin. "All they can tell at this point is it's not local."

Sanderson looked at the rest of the group. "See? There's nothing mysterious here. They're just getting directions from whoever is planning this little jailbreak. They're up against the wall and they know it."

Sanderson seemed pleased with himself, making a show of broadcasting just how happy he was by grinning from ear to ear. At this, Mitchell spoke for the first time, looking at the FBI executive with ambivalence. "Let's wait and see what we have first, Sanderson. Don't celebrate too early."

Sanderson flashed an angry look at the case officer, upset over the obvious lack of respect in front of all the others. He started to say something, but DePalma turned to face them, looking a bit shocked. He held a paper copy of the message and handed it to Mitchell. As Mitchell read the message, he too seemed overcome by surprise.

He said to Putnum, "You're not going to believe this."

He handed the paper to the older man, who in turn read it without comment. His face was stoic, not giving away any hint of emotion.

"What's it say?" demanded Sanderson, trying to move around so he could read it over Putnum's shoulder. Putnum gave the FBI agent a cold look, and the man stopped dead in his tracks. Sanderson shifted nervously as Putnum raised the paper and read the message again—this time, out loud for everybody to hear.

"The message says," stated Putnum, looking around the group, "that Hapke is not to deal with the FBI, CIA, or NSA directly, but rather is to speak only to Fred Crogan as intermediary."

All eyes shifted to the old man, whose expression, for the first time since the start of the incident, represented a sense of genuine surprise. Sanderson started to say something but stopped when Putnum raised his hand.

"It states further," continued Putnum, "that Hapke knows what to demand and that he make it clear the hostages will die if those demands are not met in the prescribed amount of time."

The room was silent. No one said a word while absorbing the message.

It was Justin who eventually broke the silence. "The sender was at Boston's Logan International Airport."

"But the information originated here," said Mitchell, "and it's from someone on the inside. They are aware of the three government agencies present and must know Fred plays a leadership role in the community, or they wouldn't have picked him as intermediary."

Sanderson was speechless for the first time.

"What do you think about my theory concerning evil now, Mr. Sanderson?" asked Fred as he left, not waiting for an answer.

★ CHAPTER FIVE ★

UNWANTED GUESTS

The rain returned a few minutes before noon and was coming down hard. The fog was also moving back in quickly, obscuring visibility across the bay. Sanderson ran from the Mohawk toward the marina showroom, noticing two black government SUVs out front that hadn't been there before. He wasn't expecting any additional agents; they were all being deployed to prearranged locations around the lake to conduct surveillance of the island or stage for the rescue. A quick glance behind him showed the old man was keeping up. The rain didn't seem to bother him like it would most people. When they entered the showroom, he immediately saw the owners of the SUVs.

On the other side of the room stood a group of eight men in camouflage military uniforms clustered around a single female officer in a service khaki uniform of the United States Navy. Sanderson was already upset due to communications from the island indicating that someone in Bluffton was passing on information to the hostage takers. He wanted to say it was probably one of the locals but deep down knew it was probably someone from outside the town. More than likely someone who had responded to the kidnapping. Which meant he'd have to deal with the group huddled on the other side of the room—they were a distraction he didn't need.

The female officer walked toward him. It was obvious from her posture he wasn't going to get a break. "Director Sanderson," she began, extending her hand for a handshake, "I am Lieutenant Commander Stephnie Smith."

Sanderson took her hand, shaking it. The officer was a pretty woman in her thirties. She looked fit under the uniform and wore her brown hair pulled back. She wore no jewelry to speak of, except an Academy ring. Her demeanor and body language spoke of confidence.

Sanderson thought he knew why she was in Bluffton. He smiled slightly while mulling over his response. "To what do I owe the pleasure of your visit, Commander?"

Smith's eyes followed Fred as the old Indian walked past, but she directed her response to Sanderson. "I'm here with all the information that Naval Intelligence has on the Kingston case to assist you in your investigation, Director."

"I appreciate that, Commander," responded Sanderson, watching the old man stop in front of each man in the clustered group. "I'm sure it will be helpful, since the original case was started by that agency. Who are the men you brought with you? Analysts?"

Sanderson enjoyed watching the female officer flush; her eyes flashed her distaste for the comment, but she remained in control. "They are volunteers from SEAL Team Two in Little Creek, Virginia. My boss wanted to offer their assistance in the rescue of the hostages. He thought with their special skills, they might be able to sneak in, secure the hostages, and protect them while your teams move in on the kidnappers."

Sanderson shook his head while he watched Fred take his time looking at each man.

"Commander, I don't think so. Using troops in a police operation on American soil is illegal. I'm not going to put my career on the line because the Navy is embarrassed one of their former officers is trying to arrange an escape from prison while serving time for betraying his country."

The immediate response from Smith was for her to turn bright crimson, but before she could say anything, Crogan chimed in with, "Take her offer, Sanderson. These men are warriors. I'm guessing you're going to need them."

Shocked by the comment, both the FBI agent and the naval officer watched the old man walk past, go through the door, and disappear into the heavy rain.

Logan International Airport
Boston, Massachusetts
July 19, 2010
1225 hours

Evans slid into the empty seat at one of the gates, casually checking the airport terminal to see if he could spot the surveillance team he was replacing. His Gulfstream arrived about thirty minutes before and was met by a car that brought him directly to the terminal, and he was escorted through a back door, avoiding security altogether.

There was a text message saying his target was booked on a later flight to Dulles, so he decided to spend more time observing her, learning her habits and maybe even a weakness or two. Guessing the size of this operation, something that simple could come in handy. He sat back, waiting to see if he could spot the surveillance.

Evans took out his cell, typing in the prearranged phrase, telling the puppet masters of this little drama that he was in place. He hit send and waited. The target was in the gate seating area across the way from where he settled. She found a seat next to an outlet, and her laptop was out. She appeared to be working on something. After years of hiding, he had a keen sense of the tells people gave off when doing surveillance work.

Movement caught his eye, and a maintenance man who had been taking his time repairing a wall-mounted map of the concourse was suddenly picking up his tools and casually moving off. That behavior wasn't suspicious, necessarily—it was the way he carried the tools that caught Evans's eye. This man was not a tradesman; he held the tools awkwardly, like he was unfamiliar with them. A mistake if you're tasked to watch a subject, especially if they're a professional.

To his left, a young couple sitting in the next section slowly got up and moved down the concourse. The young woman was on her phone, and for an instant, her smile gave way to a serious look. Nothing big or overt, but the smile reappeared looking more forced than before. While they walked away, the young man who was a part of the couple deliberately glanced at the target and then looked around to see if he could find the team taking his place. Another mistake—and Evans found himself wondering how long these people had been in the business.

For his part, Evans was absorbed in the magazine he brought along with him, so all the young man recognized when his eyes passed over him was a middle-aged businessman reading. While Evans pretended to read, he caught no other movement indicating additional members of a surveillance team. He guessed with short notice, Smith's team only had three people in place and someone monitoring the many cameras that watched the ebb and flow of humanity each day at Logan International Airport. Evans also guessed that part of the surveillance wouldn't end just because he was in place. He glanced at the target, who was deep into her work on her laptop. Either she was very good at this and chose to maintain her anonymity or she had no idea she was being watched. Evans wasn't sure yet but guessed it to be the latter. She was too absorbed in what she was doing.

Upton's Marina and Boat Sales
Bluffton, New York
July 19, 2010
1230 hours

Sanderson watched as Commander Smith and her SEAL team walked out to their black SUVs in front of the showroom. He smiled as the rain came down harder. Smith turned, giving Sanderson a final resentful look before disappearing into the vehicle.

Sanderson had been adamant he would not accept the military's help in this negotiation. That's exactly what this was—a negotiation, not a military operation. He had plenty of agents trained in both surveillance and tactical operations, all experienced and already in place. He saw no need to bring in eight trigger-happy cowboys to complicate the operation.

He didn't know or care where they were headed but guessed they would be close by until he could get his superiors to recall them. He knew things were more complicated with both the NSA and the CIA close by, but he also knew with Admiral Putnum taking an interest in the case, he would hold both of those agencies to all current standards and protocols. His biggest concern was about who Kingston's inside man was. Whoever they were, they were close enough to monitor the movements of his people and pass them on to the hostage takers. With the CIA team working in tandem with NSA, hopefully they would be able to track down the informant before they could do any real damage to his operation. He guessed they were in place for some time and were local because they had passed on the information about the initial rescue attempt.

The command post was typical of most he worked in the past. They brought in their own secure communications, leaving the local phone open to avoid any tapping of the lines or eavesdropping on the part of the media. Most of their communications were done by encrypted cell and radio, so Sanderson had little fear of the hostage takers being able to monitor their back-and-forth transmissions. He smiled again while he watched the two black SUVs pull out of the marina parking lot and onto Lake Street. The fog was coming in quickly because of the heavy rain, and the two vehicles quickly disappeared.

Sanderson murmured, looking around to see if he could find the old Indian to prep him for his meeting with the hostage takers when they called. He finally found him standing just outside the main entrance to the showroom under the overhang, keeping dry. Sanderson grabbed a passing FBI agent, pointed to the old man, directing the agent to bring Crogan to him. He watched while the agent went to the door, poking his head outside.

Sanderson had started to smile when another agent came up behind him and said, "Sir, we have the kidnappers on the line, and they're asking specifically for you."

Sanderson turned around, brows furrowed. He decided if they knew the CIA and NSA were here, why wouldn't they know he was here as well? He smiled and pointed to the phone on the desk closest to him. "Can I take the call on this phone?"

"No, sir," answered the agent. "It came in on our secure line."

Sanderson was stunned, wondering how they could have that information. Only agents assigned to the command post and the most senior field agents knew about the secure line. He suddenly realized Fred was standing next to him and had seen his reaction. The old man's expression said everything—the leak was right there in the command post and was not a local, as originally expected. Someone close to Richard Kingston had penetrated the FBI.

"Don't you think you should take that call?" asked the old man without any fanfare.

Sanderson walked over to the communications panel set up by the far wall of the showroom and pointed to a headset. "Can I use this one?"

"Yes, sir," responded the agent seated in front of the bank of electronic equipment, punching a couple of keys. "It's live now."

Sanderson picked up the headset, placing it over his left ear with the small microphone in front of his mouth. "This is Assistant Director Sanderson."

"Let's set the ground rules, Mr. Sanderson," the electronically disguised voice began, setting the assistant director on edge. "In any future conversations we may have, you will need to answer us in thirty seconds, or we will disconnect and kill a hostage. Do you understand?"

Sanderson stayed calm, trying to redirect and take control of the conversation.

"Who am I speaking to? You know who I am. It would be nice to know with whom I'm negotiating."

Sanderson couldn't tell if he was speaking to a male or female, but he assumed he was speaking to the former policeman they identified as the leader of the group.

The voice asked again, "Do you understand the ground rules, Mr. Sanderson?"

"Am I speaking to Ron Hapke?" asked Sanderson evenly and calmly. "If I am, I know you understand our methods and playbook. You also know this won't end well if you don't negotiate on the up and up with us. How about it? Cut the pretense, and let's talk about getting everyone out without anyone else getting hurt."

While he spoke, other members of his negotiations team gathered nearby so they could hear the dialogue. Sanderson would have preferred one of them was talking to the hostage takers, due to their training. He could easily be baited into saying the wrong thing, and it was critical in hostage negotiations to keep your cool. That was why he never volunteered for the job.

"Mr. Sanderson," responded the voice, "you have thirty seconds to confirm that you understand the ground rules, or we disconnect and we kill the first hostage. What will it be? Will we continue our conversation, or will someone die? Maybe we should kill one of the children to drive our point home."

Sanderson looked at his lead negotiator who said, "I'd answer to buy time, sir. We still have other options, but we need to keep them talking."

With the negotiator's support, Sanderson didn't hesitate. "I understand your rules."

"Repeat them back to us," demanded the voice.

"I respond when you call within thirty seconds, or you disconnect and kill a hostage."

"See? That wasn't so hard, was it?" The voice was almost hypnotic in its rhythm. "Now we know you have your negotiation team there with you and we can't stop them from listening, but we'll only talk to you, so don't try to pawn us off on one of them. If you do, we will go back to the ground rules. Do you understand?"

Sanderson looked at the lead negotiator, who didn't look happy, but all the man could do was nod. They were between a rock and a hard place, and there wasn't time to strategize for a clever loophole or other way out of this.

"I understand—and I also understand that you feel you can change the rules as we go."

Sanderson had deliberately added the last statement. The negotiator standing next to him gave him a thumbs-up.

"You really *do* understand the rules, Mr. Sanderson," said the voice. "Now, here's what you need to do. You need to send Fred Crogan out to the island to speak to us. Send him over within the hour in a nonmotorized boat of some kind. I'm sure you can find a rowboat, or maybe a canoe. He is a Native American, after all. We'll give him our terms for the release of Richard Kingston and Andrea Handcock from prison, and he can bring them back to you. Rest assured we'll be able to monitor everything you're doing regarding this little negotiation we're involved with."

The negotiator scribbled notes onto a pad of paper, handing it to Sanderson, who then read those notes out loud over the phone. He started by asking, "How can we be sure that Mr. Crogan will be safe?"

"You have our word."

"And how can I accept that if I don't know who I'm speaking to?"

"It's all part of this game we're playing, Mr. Sanderson," responded the electronic voice. "We have to trust you, and you have to trust us. The only thing each of us knows for sure is each side is trying to gain the advantage over the other. We have the hostages on the island, and you have the island surrounded. You try to rescue the hostages and we kill them. Action and reaction on both sides—or move and countermove, like a game of chess. We'll talk more later today, after we've spoken to Mr. Crogan."

"How will I contact you if I want to talk to you?" asked Sanderson, trying to buy some more airtime. "What if I have information I need to pass on to you?"

"Bye!" was the only reply, and the line went dead.

It took a moment before everyone realized the caller had hung up.

"I want to know how they got this line!" demanded Sanderson, putting the headset down. "Trace it back and see where the call originated from and get me another secure line in here!"

No one said anything, but there was a flurry of activity while agents scrambled to comply.

Sanderson looked at the negotiations team. "Your thoughts?"

The lead negotiator stepped forward, answering on behalf of the group. "We'll do a full evaluation and have it ready within half an hour, but my immediate thoughts are whoever was on the other end was careful not to use the singular when referring to their side of the negotiations."

Sanderson looked at the man questioningly. "How so?"

"They always used the words 'we' and 'us,' never referring to 'I' or 'me.' And I don't know if you noticed the slight hesitation before you were answered each time, but that could be one of two things: it might have been a delay in their communications hookup from the island, or it could indicate that there was a group listening and preparing their responses. Give us a few minutes to confer, and we'll have more for you."

Sanderson nodded, looking over to his second-in-command. "Get Grey over here, now!"

"Yes, sir!" responded the FBI agent, moving off with his phone to his ear.

Sanderson looked around the room, searching for Fred, but did not see him anywhere. He asked the gathered agents if any of them had seen where the old man had gone. One agent stated they saw him leave the building immediately following the comment about Native Americans and canoes. This was followed by a few comments about ruffling the old man's sensitivities, along with some chuckles and snickers from the gathered crowd. A stern look from Sanderson sent them all out to find the old man. Alone for a few moments, Sanderson smiled to himself, knowing where the old man had gone on his own. He knew he was about to learn a new lesson in trust.

Summers' Cabin
Adirondack State Park, New York
July 19, 2010
1240 hours

Nancy sat on the floor next to her sister-in-law and her children. They had all heard the conversation between Hapke's people and the FBI. They quietly passed on the context to their fellow hostages and debated what was to come. They were interrupted by laughter from the dining room. Hapke seemed pleased with his phone call with the FBI, slapping several of his people on the back enthusiastically. He noticed he was being watched by the hostages, deciding he would address them directly.

"Don't look so depressed, love," he said to Julie. "If all goes well, I'll be completely out of your life by sometime tomorrow."

Julie didn't respond, looking at the man defiantly. She knew if she said anything, she would probably put them all in more danger than they already were.

"Nothing to say, love?" goaded the hostage taker. "Too bad. We'll get our demands out today, and if all goes well, we're out of here by tomorrow. If not, you won't know the difference because you'll all be dead."

There were a few gasps of surprise and a few tears in response to that statement, but for the most part, the hostages said nothing. Hapke noticed the invalid senator looked the most defiant, so he directed his next comment to him.

"You don't seem to upset about facing death, Senator."

Ericson's reply was cool and even, and his eyes never left those of his captor. "I can't walk because I've faced death before—more than once—and I'm still here. I have no illusions I may not make it out of here, but I'm prepared to die. Are you? I make no threats here, but you're involved way over your head in this little escapade. You have no idea who you can trust or turn to when your little plan goes south—and trust me, my friend, it *will* go south. Between right now and tomorrow is a long time with some very dangerous forces being brought into play. Your boss could care less about you and your people. What happens to you once he's free? You must have an exit plan, but he has no intention of allowing you or your people out of here. His real plan here is to use all of you as a diversion while he disappears into the fog. He's a brilliant tactician and manipulator with no moral conscience whatsoever. No, my friend, the fact I may be dead by tomorrow doesn't bother me as much as the fact that your boss might be on the loose as we speak. You don't scare me because you're just a pawn in this chess game."

There was silence in the room while Ericson spoke, but when Hapke reached for the pistol at his side, there were a few gasps of surprise. Hapke's hands shook as he started to pull the weapon out of its holster. The back talk had infuriated him, which he conveyed through the sort of glare that made it clear he was contemplating killing the man right then and there. But there was something about the way the senator looked back at him that made a shiver run down Hapke's spine. The senator wasn't falling for his show. He was dangerous; Hapke could see it in his eyes. He may not be able to walk, but Hapke guessed if he were within arm's reach of Ericson, the man would grab him and crush the life out of him before his people could react.

A little voice in the back of his head told him he needed to kill this man, but his orders were to the contrary for at least another day, lest it jeopardize the objective of the operation. He slid his pistol back into its holster, turned, and walked out of the cabin, followed by Servati and several other kidnappers. There were questions about their plan now. He needed to check their exit plan to make sure it was still in place.

Ericson scored a victory. He'd placed a seed of doubt in the back of his adversary's mind.

After Hapke stormed out with his inner circle in tow, the hostages let out a collective sigh of relief. Most understood how far Ericson had pushed Hapke and considered him lucky to still be alive.

Ericson gave Nancy a pointed look. "You're right—the man's nuts. He was actually considering shooting me."

"Josh, I told you he's not stable," said Nancy. "You shouldn't push him like that. Next time, he might not restrain himself."

Fiona, who'd been quiet for most of their captivity, spoke up. "That's because Richard knows exactly how to control his minions," she said confidently, referring to Kingston. "He has something on this man that keeps him in line, even though he may not know him personally."

"You make your ex-husband sound like he's evil incarnate," said Del Monte. "He can't be all that bad."

"He is!" responded a good many of the hostages in unison.

Whether Sue Ellen Del Monte was daunted by the response she received, she didn't show it. "Josh, you mentioned dangerous forces being brought into play. I assume you weren't referring to the FBI?"

Ericson looked at his fellow representative and answered solemnly. "Richard Kingston will stop at nothing to get out of prison, so he has put some extreme plans into play. It's obvious his people have infiltrated one or more agencies responding to our kidnapping, or we wouldn't still be here. He has also targeted some key people responsible for his imprisonment, and several aren't here, which means they're either dead or alerted to his plan. I know one for sure is alive and will respond to help get us out."

Ericson didn't explain, but Nancy and the rest of the family were smiling.

"That individual won't be alone," continued Ericson, "and, because of his current station in life, won't be bound by the rules like the FBI. You need to do exactly as I say, when I say it, Sue Ellen, and don't stop to question what you're told."

Del Monte looked puzzled but didn't say a word. Her husband, Frank, leaned closer to her and whispered, "Just stay close to me, dear, and do what I do."

Franklin Del Monte looked over to Josh and nodded. Ericson smiled.

Mohawk Tavern and Grill
Bluffton, New York
July 19, 2010
1300 hours

Commander Smith sat with her eight-man SEAL team. They had left the marina and found parking spots for their SUVs up the side street from the FBI command post. She intended to feed the men and find a place for them to hole up while she fought through the bureaucratic red tape preventing their involvement in the rescue.

What she didn't like was how much they stood out in uniform. She guessed half the patrons in the restaurant were from the media and antici- pated she would be approached shortly, asking about military involvement in the rescue. Her story of being Naval Intelligence sent there to help would only go so far, seeing as her men all wore the Naval Special Warfare Trident on a patch above their left breast pocket. This would tell any reporter worth their salt they were SEALs and probably not there to pass on intelligence to the FBI.

Because her team insisted on sitting with the building's exit in view, she was left to sit facing the counter and the kitchen. Currently in view was the waitress who'd taken their order speaking to a young man from the kitchen. The girl pointed in their direction, saying something to the young man. He nodded before seemingly giving her instructions. She disappeared into the kitchen. The customers at the table next to theirs were obviously from the media, drawing Smith's attention with their whispering. She suspected they were about to get bold enough to ask what the Navy was doing in Bluffton, and she couldn't blame them; if she were the reporter, she'd want to know why a team of SEALs was in town.

"Excuse me, Commander." The voice made her jump. "I think I can find a table more private in the other room."

Once she looked up, Smith saw the young man from the kitchen standing next to her. He had a gentle smile, making her feel at ease. She also noticed his appearance had thrown off the timing of the reporters. Without bothering to consult her team, she agreed to be relocated to a more private space.

The young man from the kitchen nodded at her, then gestured to the rest of her team as he said, "If you would all grab your drinks and follow me to the bar area, I think we can find someplace more private for your group, where you won't be bothered."

All eight members of the SEAL team brightened up at the notion of heading to the bar, even though they knew they wouldn't be able to drink. Smith grabbed her diet soda, following the young man through the maze of tables in the restaurant's side of the building. A quick glance over her shoulder revealed the SEAL team was right behind her, as were a couple of the reporters. They reached the door to the bar to find their waitress waiting there. For the first time, Smith noticed the resemblance between the young man and the waitress. The waitress opened the door, motioning for them to follow her. Smith stepped aside, allowing the SEAL team to follow the young woman. She waited to deal with the reporters.

After the last member of the team was through the door, Smith started to step out to block the reporters, only to have the young man push her through the doorway with the team and say, "Don't worry, Commander, I'll handle them."

Smith found herself in the tavern of the Mohawk with the door closed behind her. It was darker than the main dining area of the restaurant but about the same size. She took a moment to get her bearings, noticing that there were other people on the other side of the room. The waitress smiled at Smith while she moved to the last open chair at the table.

Smith returned the smile and asked, "Is that young man your brother?"

"Yes, ma'am. That's my brother Nathan."

"Thank you both for getting us away from the press out there. I think it was about to get ugly."

Brandi's face blushed a bit, acknowledging the comment before scurrying off back to work. Smith took another look at the group across the room. They seemed to be as curious about the naval personnel as she was about them. She guessed they had to know the owners of the tavern to be seated here, away from the craziness of the dining room.

The only chair left at the table had her back to the door again. Her training went against sitting in a place without a view of the building's entrance and exit, but Smith knew that if a threat came through the door behind her, there was nowhere better to be than with these men. She had nothing to fear.

The team talked and joked about being moved to the tavern, discussing how rustic and eighteenth-century it looked. They were pleased with the change.

There was some commotion from the group at the other end of the room, and Smith noticed a puzzled look cross the chief's face. She looked over her shoulder, noticing two men joining the group. One handed a folder to a man sitting with his back to them.

She looked back toward Chief Mike Skier. "What's the problem, Chief?"

"Sorry, Commander," answered Skier, still looking troubled, "but I think I know that guy who brought in the folder."

"Good," replied Smith, "maybe he can tell us what the hell is going on here."

The chief shook his head, still looking troubled. "The problem is, Commander, he was listed as KIA several years ago. His whole team was ambushed on a mission, a few made it back, but he was killed. A burned body was found with his dog tags on it."

"May I ask how you know all that, Chief?" Smith asked, giving him a skeptical look.

"I was on that team, Commander. I was wounded and made it back. Something funny, though—we all thought there was more to our being ambushed. His old man's an admiral or something and went searching for him for a couple of years, then suddenly stopped."

The color drained from Smith's face when her past came rushing back to her in a flood of memories. It was the chief's turn to look at her skeptically.

"Chief, this is important," she said, locking eyes with the man. "His last name wouldn't be Summers, would it?"

The chief nodded. "Yes, ma'am. His name is Justin Summers. His father was—"

"Admiral Jonathon Summers," Smith said, finishing the man's sentence, "former SEAL, Medal of Honor recipient, my former commanding officer, and . . ." She paused, eyes dropping to the floor, deep in thought. "And the man who saved my life."

The entire team leaned forward to hear Smith's explanation.

"My last year at the Academy, the admiral was acting superintendent and stopped me from being murdered by a serial killer."

"I remember that," said one member of the team.

"Urban legend says the asshole tried to outswim the admiral," said another.

Smith found herself smiling. "No legend boys. He did try—but he didn't succeed."

There was laughter all around the table.

"Did the admiral really punch him out, ma'am?" asked the young ensign.

"As did the Coast Guard rescue swimmer who jumped in to help."

Smith noticed the eyes of the team were looking at someone behind her, so she stopped talking. She turned to find three men walking up to their table. It took several seconds for the face of the man in front to register, but when it did, Smith found herself standing up and snapping to attention. The SEAL team followed suit, not knowing why. The entire room was silent.

Justin stood behind the two older men. He made eye contact with Skier, nodding. The second man who was just in front of Justin was familiar to Smith, but she couldn't place where she had met him before. The old man in the lead smiled broadly.

"It's good to see you again, Commander," said Putnum.

Summers' Cabin
Adirondack State Park, New York
July 19, 2010
1315 hours

With Sheriff James and Deputy Crogan on the loose, Hapke was keeping his security perimeter tight. His contacts within the federal government gathered in Bluffton hadn't given him any information on the third person loose on the island, except to say there were possible local connections. The team he'd sent after Summers hadn't reported back yet, as well as the team sent after the retired general in Virginia. He guessed both teams were keeping a low profile after completing their part of the mission. Having the Canadian police in Bluffton looking for a connection between what happened to Summers and this operation was encouraging. Hapke wasn't worried but also didn't want to take any chances. His patrols were called back within the defensive perimeter they'd established around the compound, but not before placing motion sensors along some of the paths on the island.

The perimeter extended around all the cabins and boathouse but didn't include the two storage buildings. Hapke checked these buildings personally and found them to contain tools, two ATVs, and two snowmobiles. The larger of the two sheds also included a work area with several unfinished projects. His people wanted to use the ATVs, but there were no batteries for any of the vehicles. It wasn't worth the time to search for them or force the information out of the family.

"Any word on when the old Indian might arrive?" Hapke asked, walking with Servati and two men in front of the main cabin. "He should have been here by now. I want to keep this operation on time."

"Nothing yet, Ron," answered Servati, adjusting her tactical vest.

Hapke covered his eyes, looking out over the fog-covered lake. "Pass the word to our sentries to keep an eye out for him; I don't want anyone shooting him by mistake when he comes out of the fog."

"No chance of that," came a voice from the porch of the main cabin above them. "They might also want to look for the canoe beached next to the boathouse."

Instantly, Hapke's men and Servati rushed up the stairs, rifles poised at the broad chest of an old Native American man.

Fred sat in an Adirondack porch chair between the door and the large picture window that allowed those in the living room of the main cabin a stunning view of the lake. The old man looked up with a grin that enhanced every wrinkle in his weathered face. He wore a checkered flannel shirt under a green, waist-length raincoat, jeans, and a well-used pair of boots. His long, salt-and-pepper hair fell over his shoulders. Hapke thought the man looked every inch the Indian he remembered in pictures from when he was in school. The dark skin, the look of someone who lived outdoors, the long hair, and the defiant eyes were all there. His teachers described them as a noble people, but Hapke had feared the pictures as a child, choosing to believe the Hollywood version instead.

This man claimed to have walked all the way from the boathouse—if he were to be believed—without being seen by any of Hapke's people. A shiver ran down Hapke's spine, forcing him to control the fear surging from his subconscious. Fred recognized the look in the man's eyes. His grin broadened.

"How long have you been here?" demanded Servati, her rifle still raised at Fred's chest.

The old man turned to look at the woman standing in front of him. His grin disappeared, replaced by a polite smile. "About fifteen minutes."

Suddenly, the radio on Hapke's hip crackled to life. "Patrol three to command," a voice on the other end said. "We have a canoe beached on the west side of the boathouse. Our man's not here—he must be on foot somewhere in the compound."

Servati sighed, keying the transmit button on her radio's lapel mic. "We have him at the main cabin," she said, making eye contact with the old man again. The smile on his face may have been polite, but it certainly wasn't friendly. "Tighten up security out there."

With that, she motioned for the old man to stand, and he complied. She took him by the shoulders and spun him around to face the wall of the cabin. "Put your hands behind your head, old man."

Fred responded immediately to her command, and she started to pat him down, looking for weapons.

"Don't worry, young lady," he said, glancing at Hapke as he spoke, "I left my scalping knife and tomahawk at home."

Hapke took a step back, fear showing in his eyes. It was all Fred could do not to chuckle at Hapke's reaction.

Servati didn't skip a beat while she continued her search. When she finished, she stepped back and addressed Hapke. "He's clean, Ron. No weapons."

The two hostage takers who had been pointing their rifles at Fred relaxed, lowering their weapons. Hapke slowly stepped between them, addressing the old man. "You take pretty big chances for someone your age, old man. One of my people could have shot and killed you on your way up here, and then your friends inside would be worse off, with no one to take our demands back."

Fred turned so he faced Hapke. "I was in no danger, Mr. Hapke. I walked within ten feet of some of your people and they didn't even know I was there. They, on the other hand, need to be more alert, because there are warriors out there better than I."

Hapke grunted. "The FBI sent the lady officer and SEALs packing—and I know you referred to them as warriors. I don't have to worry about them. The FBI, HRT, and SWAT teams are too predictable. Don't get me wrong, they're good, but we know their tactics, and that gives us the advantage."

Fred raised an eyebrow, absorbing the information.

Hapke continued, "You don't need to worry about what my people are doing. Just carry the message back to Director Sanderson. If all goes well, we'll be done with our business by tomorrow evening and no one else will get hurt."

Fred could tell the man was lying. He had every intention of killing those hostages. He shrugged his shoulders and said, "This is Mohawk land, protected by the spirits of my ancestors; they are the ones you have to worry about."

Hapke laughed. "You're the second person today to try and scare me with ghost stories, old man. That crippled senator said pretty much the same thing."

"Sounds like a smart man," said Fred coolly.

Hapke shook his head. "I don't believe in ghosts, and ghost stories don't scare me. Let's get down to business."

"You've been warned," the old man said with a sigh, but he clasped his hands in front of his belly and raised his brows in a way that indicated Hapke should start talking.

Hapke stepped closer, lowering his voice. His crew raised their rifles, aimed at the Indian's chest in open warning. "Here are our demands—"

"After I see the hostages," interjected Fred.

Hapke glared at the old man for a moment. "You're here to take back our demands, nothing more. Seeing the hostages wasn't part of the agreement."

"If I don't see that the hostages are alive and unhurt, that doesn't happen."

Hapke flushed at the man's defiance. "Then we'll just kill you right now."

Fred shrugged. "The deal is I see the hostages and then I'll deliver your demands. If you kill me, that's only going to hurt your position in this negotiation. It's your call, Mr. Hapke."

Hapke glared at the old man. His body language told Fred he was controlling the rage building up inside him. It also told him that Hapke was just indecisive enough to take advantage of at some point. He responded emotionally, and that could be used to any rescuer's advantage.

"Ron . . ." Servati brought the man back to reality. "There's no harm in him seeing the hostages. It could also work to our benefit."

Hapke looked at his female counterpart. "You're right. He can see them."

Hapke turned, and the two men behind him stepped back so he could open the front door. Fred followed him into the room, followed by Servati and the two other hostage takers. Hapke gently pushed Fred back against the wall of the cabin.

"Not too close, old man. You wanted to see them, not touch them."

Fred recognized Nancy and the members of her family. They were huddled near the couch, facing the window. He also recognized the politicians, who he'd seen on television or read about. He assumed the rest were either the family of the politicians or the people Grey told him were involved in the arrest of Richard Kingston. There were nineteen hostages in total, and all looked none the worse for wear. He guessed the ones more formally dressed were from the dinner party.

Nancy made eye contact. "Fred, it's good to see you."

Fred nodded and smiled. "You look like you're holding up, Nancy. Is there anything I can get you?"

"Out of here?" replied Nancy, trying to read into the old Indian's visit.

"Senator." Hapke addressed Ericson. "It appears the old Indian shares your affinity for ghost stories. He tried to scare us off with talk of marauding spirits."

"I tried to warn you," replied Ericson, making eye contact with Fred. The two men appeared to be sizing each other up. They nodded slightly to each other, maintaining eye contact; a shiver ran down Hapke's spine as he observed the exchange.

"That's what he said," commented Servati, looking at Fred. The old man just shrugged his shoulders.

"The spirits saved my life once," Ericson said, keeping eye contact with Fred. "I haven't been able to walk since, but I survived."

"Have faith, Senator," answered Fred. "Those same spirits are with you now."

"That's enough about spirits and ghosts, old man." Hapke was starting to look irritated with the conversation. "There's nothing like that here."

Fred smiled ever so slightly at both Ericson and Nancy. "I beg to differ, Mr. Hapke. These ghosts know this forest extremely well. You'd do well to heed their warning to you."

"That's enough," complained Servati as she grabbed Fred by his raincoat, pulling him toward the door. "You've seen the hostages, as requested. Time to leave."

"Thank you, Fred," said Nancy, watching the hostage taker drag him toward the door.

Fred planted both his feet, stopping Servati cold. She turned to order the old man forward, but said nothing when she saw the look on his face. The old man shifted his gaze from the hostage taker to the hostage, giving Nancy a smile and simple nod. He then walked past Servati, breaking her hold on his raincoat, going through the doorway and onto the front porch. The female hostage taker followed right behind him, the two gunmen behind her, and Hapke bringing up the rear.

Nancy and Josh looked at each other.

Fred had just confirmed what they suspected. They now knew who was out in the woods stalking their kidnappers. Their hope was renewed.

Outside, Fred stopped, waiting for Hapke. When Hapke closed the door, Fred said, "I'm satisfied they're all okay. Now I'll take your demands to the FBI."

"You got big ones, old man," commented Hapke. "Did you give the FBI this much trouble?"

Fred looked the hostage taker in the eye. "I don't care for Mr. Sanderson any more than I do you, Mr. Hapke."

Hapke smiled. "Good, then I know you'll deliver the message and give the correct information. Richard Kingston is to be removed from Leavenworth and sent to Dulles International Airport. Andrea Handcock is to be removed from the Federal Penitentiary in Bedford Hills, New York, and sent to the same location at Dulles. We'll be monitoring their movements, so no tricks. This needs to happen by 9:00 a.m. tomorrow, or we kill a hostage. We'll be expecting a call from Admiral Kingston by 9:00 a.m.—or else. We know there'll be feds all over the place, so we'll let them fly the admiral and Miss Handcock where they need to go to catch a plane to a nonextradition country."

Hapke stopped to allow Fred to digest what he'd been told, only to find the old man staring at him. This made him nervous.

"Did you get that? I'm not going to repeat it."

Fred repeated the instructions word for word, then asked, "And what happens to the hostages once all of your demands are met?"

"They'll be released, and we'll be gone. We'll have no need for them, and there's no need for anyone else to get hurt."

Hapke shifted nervously. The body language didn't speak of confidence. The reality was that nobody could be sure what Kingston would or wouldn't do.

"Do you trust Richard Kingston, Mr. Hapke?" Fred asked. "He betrayed his country for money, so who's to say he won't betray you? Who's to say he won't leave you here alone to fend for yourself and clean up his mess?"

Hapke laughed, shaking his head. "No you don't. I'm too smart for that type of mind game. We've already been paid, and the money is in the bank. Trust me, we'll be out of here once we hear from Kingston."

Fred smiled at the last statement. "Mr. Hapke, I don't trust you, and I don't trust Mr. Sanderson. These are good people you're holding hostage, and they're the only reason I've allowed you to involve me in this. I promise you this—if anything happens to any of them, you won't be safe anywhere in the world."

"A threat, old man?"

The look Fred gave Hapke sent a visible shiver down the man's spine.

"No, young man, not a threat—a fact of life," said Fred. "And it would be a decision that would shorten yours considerably. Do you have any more instructions, or can I go deliver your message?"

Hapke shook his head, waving the man off. Fred went down the stairs, followed by two of Hapke's men, heading toward the boathouse and his canoe.

Hapke turned to Servati. "That old man comes back here, you have him killed," he said, turning to walk away, only to hesitate, adding, "Send a squad to check the boats and make sure we still have an escape plan in place. I don't want any surprises at the last minute."

"Sure thing, Ron. I was going to do that anyway."

Hapke walked back into the cabin. Servati smiled. Her boss didn't trust the man who was paying for their services, but then again, could you really trust someone you had never met?

Hidden Cave
Summers' Island
July 19, 2010
1330 hours

Sheriff James woke up with a start when he heard female laughter. He had fallen asleep after the call with Sanderson. His legs throbbed, but he didn't feel too bad other than that. Jon did a pretty good job of bandaging his wounds and stabilizing both legs. There was also a good supply of ibuprofen in the cave, and while it didn't kill the pain, it certainly made him feel better.

"Sorry I woke you, Sheriff." Abby's soft voice came from across the cave. "Jon's putting camo paint on me, and it tickles."

James looked across the cave and found Abby sitting on a stool under a light. She was dressed in the same camouflage, fatigue-style uniform Summers wore, right up to the combat vest. Her pistol was strapped to her leg in a tactical holster, and her knife was attached to the web belt around her waist. Her dark hair was tied back, and she looked up at the roof of the cave, allowing Jon to access her full face. He leaned over her, applying various shades of green and brown to her dark complexion. A quick look around showed her uniform hanging above the stockpiled weapons she and Jon brought to the cave.

"Why are you dressing like a soldier?" asked James, feeling a little concerned about the combat outfit. "You are a deputy sheriff, after all."

Jon was the one to reply.

"Oh, she keeps reminding me about that, Sheriff, don't you worry. We're just going out to do a little reconnaissance work, and I don't want her to stand out like the flashing strobes on the top of your patrol vehicles. Hapke has pulled all his people into a tight defensive perimeter since I took out the four guys who were trying to kill you. He's not taking any chances, but every defense has weaknesses," he said, painting another splotch of green on Abby's cheek. He rose, then, and addressed Sheriff James directly. "It's up to us to find those weaknesses before our guests arrive tonight."

"Guests?" James's brows furrowed. "We have people coming in tonight? Not Sanderson, I hope. The man's an idiot."

"No, the FBI isn't that reckless," Summers replied with a laugh. "Let's just say some visitors are coming and Hapke and his people won't be happy."

"Jon." James became deathly serious. "You can't go out and kill them all. I mean—"

"Ah, all done!" Jon said, acting as if he hadn't heard James speaking. He stood up, stepping away from Abby, who pulled a boonie cap down over her eyes. She turned to James and opened her arms, as if to invite comments.

"How do I look?"

"My God," responded James. "You look like a Navy SEAL in that getup."

"She's supposed to, Sheriff. If it makes you feel better," Jon went on, pausing for a few seconds, "she's going along as my conscience."

"Conscience?"

"To make sure I don't kill them all," Jon replied bluntly. "I can't promise I won't kill anyone, because my mission is to keep the hostages and the two of you safe—so if one of Hapke's men jeopardizes that, then trust that I will act accordingly."

"But she looks like . . ." James searched for the words.

"I know," responded Jon before the sheriff could finish. "But right now, stealth is our biggest advantage, and with all the bells and whistles that come with a law enforcement uniform, what can I say? She has the natural skill to move through the forest silently. With a little training, we'll make that a tool she can use while working for you."

"Okay," James surrendered, at last. "I can live with that—as long as you can justify whatever you do."

Jon smiled, but his tone was serious. "And how do you justify the taking of hostages to free a man who betrayed his country for money? Throw in the fact that a good number of those hostages are my family, and the rules of engagement get a little fuzzy."

James thought about that for a few seconds. "I can see your point and appreciate your restraint."

The men looked at each other for a few moments before Jon turned away and started to get ready to leave.

"Sheriff, we'll leave a rifle and pistol within reach. You shouldn't need it, but just in case. You have plenty of water on the off chance we're gone for a while. We'll holler in before we enter so you don't shoot us."

James laughed but understood Jon's meaning. Abby placed the weapons and spare ammunition next to where James was lying. As she started back to grab a couple of milk jugs filled with water, James grabbed her arm and looked up into her painted face. "What do they call that stuff he put on your face?"

"War paint!" Jon said from the other side of the chamber, both his expression and tone perfectly serious.

Upton's Marina and Boat Sales
Bluffton, New York
July 19, 2010
1415 hours

The canoe carrying Fred Crogan glided to a stop at the dock, where Sanderson and several of his aides stood waiting. Fred grabbed the dock, stuffing the paddle under the thwart and stern seat of the canoe.

"So, what are the demands?" asked Sanderson without even a hello. Fred looked at him, then stood, keeping his center of gravity low while stepping onto the dock. He lifted the boat out of the water, unsurprised by the lack of help he received, and balanced the hull on his knees.

"What were the demands?" repeated Sanderson.

"Unless you all want to end up in the lake, I suggest you move," responded Fred politely, ignoring the question a second time. The dock was wide enough for the men to have taken a step backward and not be in the way, but they moved somewhat overdramatically toward the shore end of the dock. Fred continued cradling the canoe on his knees. He gently set it down on the dock, turning it over, and proceeded to wipe his hands off on his jeans before walking toward his reception committee.

Before Sanderson could repeat his question a third time, Fred began to relay Hapke's demands in detail. This took Sanderson's aides by surprise, who were scrambling to get their notebooks out and write down what was said. Fred repeated himself several times because the aides couldn't write as fast as he passed on the information. When they finished, Sanderson motioned for them to follow him, and they headed toward the boat showroom.

"Mr. Crogan," the FBI executive asked, "what's your assessment of Ronald Hapke?"

Fred thought carefully. "He's an insecure sociopath. He's not a real brave man, hiding behind his well-armed men. He's certifiably nuts. The hostages are in true danger if he's in command. His second-in-command is a woman. She's a pretty cool customer, but just as dangerous."

Sanderson stopped short of entering the marina's showroom. "What's your opinion about Hapke following through with his threats if the demands aren't met?"

"He'll kill the hostages without hesitation," answered Fred. "Like I said, the man's nuts."

Sanderson looked at his aides. "That's what I was afraid of," he said, waving them through the doorway. "Get inside and pass this information on to headquarters. I'm sure they'll want to move forward with the plan we were discussing earlier, and they'll need to move quickly if we're to meet the hostage takers' timeline."

The aides rushed off, leaving Sanderson alone with Fred. The old man looked at the FBI agent curiously.

"You're going to meet their demands? That'll be a mistake. You give up a certain amount of control by removing Kingston from the safety of prison. Hapke had information from our conversation that took place just before I left for the island. Someone here is passing him that information."

Sanderson didn't look surprised. He smiled and asked, "You don't care for me much, do you, Mr. Crogan?"

"You haven't given me much reason to."

"I find myself in a unique position," said Sanderson, thinking out loud. "I have someone in the inner circle here passing our every move on to the hostage takers, and I find I can't trust the chain of command going up or down because I have no idea where the leak is—and it could cost the lives of nineteen people and the release of a traitor."

"That's why you get paid the big bucks, Mr. Assistant Director," Fred said, returning the FBI agent's smile, but Sanderson only shook his head.

"I'm a by-the-book type of guy, so it's killing me to have to ask you to pass a request on to Admiral Putnum."

The two men huddled outside the showroom for almost ten more minutes before Fred left grinning ear to ear.

Mohawk Tavern and Grill
Bluffton, New York
July 19, 2010
1415 hours

Putnum, Matt Summers, and Mitchell spoke outside, as the rain had let up for the last hour or two. The temperature had managed to climb into the low seventies but wasn't likely to go much higher without the sun sneaking out between the clouds.

"They're safe where Jon has them holed up," Matt said to the other men. "The cave's away from the cabins on the other side of the island and can't be seen through the forest. The tree cover on the hill is intermittent, but the entrance is still well hidden. Knowing Jon, he's improved on the natural cover, making it impossible to see."

Putnum grunted, smiling as Mitchell added, "If I can get Justin and Ryan in there, we can get the sheriff and the deputy out. Then we can concentrate on the hostages."

Matt was all business, showing no emotion to what Mitchell just said. During his career, he was routinely part of strategy sessions and thus took the brainstorming exactly for what it was. His tone in response to the comment was not critical but blunt. "To my knowledge, Justin and the other kids aren't aware of the existence of the cave. It was something Jon and I were using as a getaway, our private sanctuary away from the family."

"Kids . . ." Mitchell grinned, shaking his head at Putnum. "Some of them just never grow up, Admiral. You have a cottage in the mountains, and you build a clubhouse to get away from the family at the cottage."

Putnum smiled, grunting again, but said nothing.

Matt ignored the comment, adding, "Besides, I don't think we have enough time to bring them out and then go back for the hostages, do we?"

Mitchell thought for a moment, then nodded his agreement. "You're probably right; time is an issue. We have to find a way to get a team on the island and secure both the hostages and the remainder of the first rescue team."

Putnum was distracted by movement on the street. From where they were standing by one of the back entrances to the Mohawk, the tree-lined sidewalks along Gold Street visibly ran between Lake Street and South Road in town. Five men walked slowly down the sidewalk, talking among themselves. They were not young; there was a lot of gray hair on their heads. They walked casually, so as not to draw attention to themselves, but their expressions were anything but casual—each man's face and body language showed a sense of purpose. They all looked fit for their age, and each man's eyes scanned their surroundings.

A faint smile crossed Putnum's face, and he motioned for one of Grey's agents to come over. The man complied. Putnum quietly said something to him. He raced off in a direction to intercept the five men. Summers and Mitchell stopped their brainstorming, trying to figure out what the admiral was up to. Putnum said nothing to explain his actions, but rather stood silently, waiting for the FBI agent to complete his mission.

In less than a minute, the agent was returning from around the truck with the five men in tow. The man just behind the agent was doing all the talking and complaining.

"And the FBI has no right to stop us! Like I told you, we're here visiting friends in the area and decided to come to town to see what all the excitement is about."

"And your friend lives on an island in the middle of the lake?" asked Putnum evenly, trying to maintain a serious look.

The man he was addressing squinted through the darkness of the overcast afternoon, then balked. "Admiral!" he exclaimed, a look of genuine surprise on his face. "What the hell are you doing here?"

The smile Putnum had been suppressing finally burst free, and he grabbed his former colleague, giving him a hug. "We've been worried; I have people looking for you," he replied, stepping back to give the man a once-over. "You look well. What happened? Where have you been, George?"

"Whoever they are, Admiral," said George Ellison, "Jonny gave me a heads-up. They sent a two-man team to get me. The wife is safe at Quantico, and they're cooling their heels with some friends of mine there. We haven't told the FBI yet. Jonny said to only trust Glenn Grey, but his office said he was up here. Have you seen him?"

"Turn around, you old hothead," said Grey. He and Preston had just walked out of the rear entrance of the Mohawk.

Ellison turned and smiled. "The base provost at Quantico has the two guys who tried to grab me, Glenn. They're not real mobile now."

Grey took the extended hand of the retired marine general and grinned. "I assume they talked after you persuaded them to do so."

Ellison chuckled, shrugging his shoulders. "Hey, shit happens, man— and I can't help it if they couldn't shut up. The provost took their statements."

"You didn't use a pack of timber wolves to interrogate them, did you?" asked Preston.

Ellison looked at Grey, silently requesting an introduction. Agent Grey gestured to the man standing beside him and said, "Inspector Scott Preston, Royal Canadian Mounted Police, I'd like you to meet Major General George Ellison, United States Marine Corps, retired. George isn't quite as subtle as his friend Jon when it comes to matters like interrogation."

The two men shook hands.

"He really used a pack of wolves as an interrogation tool?"

Preston nodded. "And they're still talking."

There were chuckles all around the group. Ellison stepped back and motioned toward his four companions. "For those of you who don't know these gentlemen, let me introduce them. The good-looking gentleman on the left is Brigadier General Charlie Naylor, US Army, retired. Next to him is retired Marine Corps Sergeant Major Chet Shomakker, and that mean-looking son of a gun in the back is retired Army Sergeant Major George Reardon. The gentleman on the end is retired Master Chief Petty Officer of the Navy, Allen Wiedenkeller."

While hands were being shaken all around, only Putnum noticed how Mitchell reacted to Allen Wiedenkeller's name.

Grey got Putnum's attention. "Fred Crogan's returned from the island. He's reporting to Sanderson and should be over shortly."

Putnum nodded, looking at Ellison. "You guys couldn't have better timing. There's a lot going on, and we may need your help."

"Where's Jon?" asked Ellison. "I expected him to be here."

Putnum looked at his old friend. "He's on the island, George. Jumped in last night, from what we can tell. He's killed three bad guys and wounded one. He's pulling all the strings from a cave somewhere on the island."

"Damn!" exclaimed Shomakker in disbelief.

While they were speaking, Ryan opened the side door to the van and exited. He carried a piece of paper in his hand and gave it to Mitchell. Mitchell read the message, and the look on his face suggested he wasn't happy with the news.

"Bad news, Tom?" asked Putnum, and Mitchell nodded.

"Two calls were made from a burn phone inside the FBI command post: the first to a burn phone at Logan Airport in Boston, and the second call to another phone on the island. It looks like Sanderson has a sieve for security over there." With that, Mitchell looked at Grey, addressing the agent. "You need to let him know there's one hell of a leak in his organization."

"Fred's on his way over with something in writing from Sanderson," answered Grey. "Let's wait and see what it is before I go running in there."

Mitchell looked back at Putnum. "Your people are monitoring the phone in Boston to see what comes from that end. If it calls anyone, they'll trace it."

Putnum nodded, looking up at the sky, which had grown darker than the previously silver overcast, descending to a deep shade of periwinkle. "We have to do some planning. Let's go inside before it starts to rain again."

He started in, followed by Mitchell and the rest of the group.

Kay and Justin exited the van by the side sliding door. When they did, they didn't see Al Wiedenkeller stop, nor did they see the look of surprise on his face. Ellison turned around to see why Wiedenkeller had stopped in his tracks and followed his gaze to where the two young people were talking to DePalma. His jaw also dropped at what he saw. The two men looked at each other and together started to walk toward the van. Ryan saw this and opened his mouth, trying to say something, but Ellison pointed at him and then motioned for him to be silent by placing his finger on his lips. The look on Ellison's face told Ryan it would not be a good idea to do other than directed.

Kay and Justin were unaware of the men behind them but sensed something by the expression on DePalma's face. Kay wheeled around to find herself facing none other than the man who was her father.

"Daddy!" she said, clearly flustered. "I . . . uh, I—"

"Kayli . . ." Wiedenkeller stayed calm, despite noticing the gun and federal badge on his daughter's belt. "Why are you here?"

Kay swallowed hard. "I'm working, Daddy. I work for Tom Mitchell."

Justin didn't turn around yet, hoping he would go undetected, but when Wiedenkeller turned his attention to him a second later, it was clear to Justin that he hadn't accomplished what he'd hoped.

"And you!" Wiedenkeller said. "You work for Mitchell, too?"

Justin forced a smile, turning around. "Master Chief, I can expla—"

The rest of the sentence died in his mouth the second he turned around and realized that he was facing an unsmiling George Ellison. Justin snapped to attention, but that wasn't enough to garner Ellison's approval.

"The master chief asked you a question, Mr. Summers," said Ellison flatly.

Justin was shaking, and it took every ounce of strength to control it. "Yes, sir, General. I do work for Mr. Mitchell."

"With everything you put your mother through, the two of us should take you out behind this dumpster and beat the shit out of you, boy," Ellison replied evenly, as though he was speaking about a matter of fact.

"With all due respect, General . . ." Justin glanced at Kay and noted that she looked as uncomfortable as he felt. "It'll take both of you to do that, sir. I'm here to help rescue my mother and the rest because Dad contacted me."

A smile crossed Ellison's face. "Then we'll let your mother deal with your father. Get over here boy and give me a hug. It's good to see you alive."

Admiral Putnum watched the reunion from the window, smiling while he watched Wiedenkeller hug his daughter. Both men welcomed Justin back from the dead.

Logan International Airport
Boston, Massachusetts
July 19, 2010
1445 hours

Evans closed his phone and exhaled. He glanced across the terminal at his target; nothing had changed. She, too, was on her cell and intently working on her computer. He slowly moved his head from right to left to scan up and down the terminal. No one else seemed to be giving the woman any mind, so he felt comfortable there was no danger in conducting his surveillance so close to the target.

Evans took a minute to reflect on the phone call he received. He wasn't happy he put his newfound anonymity in jeopardy, but his contact was right—this was a desperate situation. It was still unnerving, however, reopening this part of his life, which he'd left behind so many years ago. All the tradecraft and instincts came back far too easily. The phrase "it's like riding a bike" sprung to mind, and he had to smile. How was it that even this line of work was a matter of muscle memory? Perhaps it wasn't a bad thing that he'd been contacted by the man pulling all the strings. Evans was, after all, in the business of knowing things most didn't—and he did owe the man a great deal. He would ride this out and then, with any luck, fall back into peace and obscurity.

Movement across the terminal brought him back to reality. The woman put down her laptop and stood up. She was on her phone again, stretching as she talked. Evans found her attractive and wasn't surprised she was involved in this operation. His job was to follow her and determine exactly who she worked for and what part they played in this whole mess. He didn't even know whose side she was on. He hadn't been asked to kill anyone yet and guessed that wouldn't be an issue here. That was what people usually hired him to do—kill people—and he was very good at it, but the people he was doing this for wanted her alive. Besides, the man who tracked him down was very capable of killing and wasn't the type to ask someone else to do his dirty work.

Evans opened his own cell phone, typed a text message, and hit send. How had they survived in the old days without technology? His current handlers needed to know she was on the phone again. What they did with that information wasn't his business. Possibly, there was some way to know who she was calling, but he couldn't be sure. His cell phone chirped. They had acknowledged his message. The woman sat down, closing her phone. Looking around the terminal, she was searching for anyone watching her. The subject's eyes looked right passed him and up the terminal. Evans smiled; he hadn't lost his touch after all, even after a few years off. She sat back, comfortable in the fact she wasn't being watched. He shifted his weight. *Too bad she's wrong.*

Upton's Marina and Boat Sales
Bluffton, New York
July 19, 2010
1445 hours

The rental car pulled up to the entrance of the marina and was stopped by two armed FBI agents. The driver's side window rolled down, revealing a naval officer in his early thirties behind the wheel. He held up his credentials for the two agents to inspect, but neither bothered to look at them.

"Sorry, sir," said the first agent. "No admittance. You can join the other naval personnel across the street in the restaurant if you want."

"Other naval personnel?" asked the man, still holding his credentials up. "What other naval personnel?"

"Not my business, sir," answered the agent. His partner looked in the back window of the vehicle, doing a casual inspection. "You can ask them when you join them."

The officer's tone hardened. "I'm not with them; I'm the son of one of the hostages. If you looked at my ID, you'd see my name's Kingston. I've been told to see Assistant Director Sanderson regarding my parents."

The agent's eyes widened, clearly nervous. At this, he finally leaned over, looking again at the offered credentials. He leaned back and raised a small portable radio to his lips, quietly speaking into it. The radio crackled, followed by something unintelligible.

The agent looked down, mortified. "Sir, you can proceed through and park your car in front of the showroom just over there. Someone will meet you there, sir."

Bryan Kingston fought the urge to say something to the agent, deciding it wouldn't help him get his mother and stepfather out of their current predicament. He followed the man's instructions, parking the car where he was directed. When he stepped out into the light rain, he put his combination cap squarely on his head and waited as a very serious-looking female agent came out of the showroom.

"Please follow me, sir," she said, leaving before he could agree. He followed her inside and over to an office in the corner with the door closed. She knocked, and someone inside bid them enter. He followed her in.

The office wasn't big enough for the six people crammed in it. Two men dressed in tactical gear stood in front of the desk and turned to face him as the door closed. They, too, looked serious, and their dress made them look a bit intimidating. Sitting next to them in the only side chair in the room was a young woman who was obviously not an agent. She looked very professional, and Kingston thought her to be a lawyer. He also guessed the man sitting behind the desk to be Assistant Director Sanderson, who didn't bother looking up as he said, "What can I do for you, Commander Kingston?"

"I was notified of my mother and stepfather's kidnapping by DOD, and they suggested I might be of assistance to you, Director. They sent me up here to help."

"Help?" Sanderson finally looked up. "Help how, Commander?"

Kingston didn't respond to the question; instead, he gave the FBI agent a puzzled look. Sanderson looked back down at what he was writing on the legal pad. "You here to help your mother, who's a hostage, or help free your father, whose people have made her one?"

"Excuse me?" The surprise in Kingston's voice was genuine. The room went silent.

Sanderson sighed, again looking up from what he was doing. His body language was that of a man whose precious time was being wasted. "They didn't tell you?"

"Tell me what, Director?" Kingston asked, swallowing hard. Now it was he who felt that his precious time was being wasted. "Your statement doesn't make any sense. My fathers in prison, and we haven't spoken in years. My mother and stepfather are my concern here."

Sanderson maintained eye contact, studying Kingston openly.

After a few tedious seconds, it appeared Sanderson decided that Kingston was telling the truth. He ripped the top piece of paper off the legal pad he'd been writing on and began to fold it as he said, "The men on the island who are holding your mother and stepfather hostage are doing so in a bid to free your father from prison. I'll take you at your word that you know nothing about it, but surely you understand I can't have you around this command post. The less you know about our operations, the better."

Kingston started to smile, as though catching on to an elaborate joke, but the severity of the people in the room dampened all humor. His smile slid off his face. "You're not kidding, are you?"

For the first time, Sanderson showed a sense of empathy. "No, son," he said, shaking his head slowly. "I'm not—and it's only a matter of time before the media finds out the reason for the kidnapping. When they do, and if they find you here, you won't have a free minute to yourself. It's bad enough the media saw the other Navy personnel here."

"What Navy personnel, if I may ask, sir?"

"I really can't comment on that, Commander. Last I heard, they were in the restaurant across the street. Feel free to ask them yourself why they're here."

"Do you have a name, sir?"

Sanderson seemed to balk at Kingston's audacity. "You seem like a man who's used to getting his questions answered," he commented, and before Kingston could follow up, the assistant director added, "Smith, a Commander Smith. She seemed very competent."

Smiling, Kingston responded, "She is, Director. She's one of the best."

Sanderson didn't respond, standing to face the officer. He handed him the folded paper. "There's a little motel down the street where we've set up a briefing area for the media. Take this note to Special Agent Grey there, and he'll keep you under wraps and informed. After speaking to him, he'll pass on any pertinent information you might have that can help us in any rescue we attempt. He'll also keep you informed of our progress."

The assistant director was passing him off. Kingston understood the logic of such a move, considering the circumstances, but it still chafed. He nodded, forcing himself to swallow the upsurge of indignance he felt in his chest. "Thank you, Director."

Sanderson looked at the young man. "Have a good day, Commander Kingston."

Kingston took the note, staring blankly at Sanderson. It was hard to believe this was the way a family member of one of the hostages was being treated. Without another comment, he turned, starting for the door of the showroom. He heard a few muffled remarks regarding his last name from the agents who were standing with Sanderson but chose to ignore them. Because of his father's arrest and conviction for treason, he'd been fighting an uphill battle his entire career in the Navy. It was a burden he chose to bear, although he never got used to it. He exited the building and didn't even notice the rain had intensified.

He took a deep breath, starting the car. The engine came to life, and when he reached for the gearshift, he realized he was still holding the folded paper. He took another deep breath, his anger starting to subside, and opened the note. As he read, his eyes widened. The anger was replaced with panic, so he read the note again. Kingston took another deep breath, bringing all his emotions under control. He turned, looking back into the showroom. He was startled to find Sanderson standing by the window, arms folded across his chest, looking serious and staring back at him. A shiver ran down his spine. He continued to watch Sanderson while he maneuvered the rental car out of the marina parking lot. The FBI agent's posture remained unchanged.

Summers' Island
Adirondack State Park, New York
July 19, 2010
1455 hours

The weather had worsened since they'd left the cave, but Abby hadn't noticed the rain soaking through the layers of camouflaged clothing she was wearing until she'd gotten so wet that her socks were sodden inside her boots. She had a new appreciation for what everything was used for when Jon outfitted her like she was going on a combat mission. She had on her own ballistic vest under the uniform, and with the pack, combat harness, boonie cap, and painted skin, she looked every bit the soldier.

She was already an accomplished outdoorsman, but Jon had taught her things in the last hour that she'd never dreamed of learning. When he moved through the woods, he was as silent as a tiger, even in the wet underbrush. Every move was slow and deliberate, and he was never in a rush to get to the next cover point. He'd cleared the trail between the cave and their destination already, which had originally been riddled with booby traps and motion detectors laid out by the hostage takers. Jon had rearranged them strategically—they now covered the obvious route around their original coverage area. If she had to get back to the cave fast, Jon had told her to use the trail. The hostage takers wouldn't use the trail and would be slowed down by their own devices. She smiled to herself, thinking about how simple he'd made it for her to return to the safety of the cave and at the same time slow their adversaries down. She was glad he was on her side.

Summers also taught her sign language as they traveled through the thick underbrush. He told her from the start there would be no talking from the time they left the cave until they returned. He showed her the basics before they left, and she picked up on more as they went.

Abby huddled under the cover of a fallen tree to the left of the trail leading out into the clearing near the boathouse, feeling proud of herself. Summers had picked the position for her—a place just inside the tree line in a copse of maples, affording her cover not only from their adversaries but from the worsening weather. It offered her a good line of sight over the tall grass and wildflowers populating the field down to the lake. There was once a lumber camp here on the island, which explained the grassy clearing. Except for the complex of cabins the Summers family built, everything was pretty much as nature had left it. There were a series of trails through the heavily wooded island that could not be seen from the air, otherwise there was no hint anyone lived here.

Jon had left Abby some time before, crawling into the tall grass. She was able to watch him for a while, but he was out of sight now, closer to the boathouse. The goal was to get a message to the hostages. Jon had guessed the hostage takers would be bringing one or more of their hostages out to get food from the freezer in the boathouse to feed everyone. He planned to leave a message there for Nancy. Abby's job was to cover him if something went wrong—and after working with him for the past day, she felt sorry for the hostage takers if something did go south.

Thunder grumbled in the distance, and the rain was getting worse. Water dripped off the brim of Abby's boonie cap. The fog rolled in from the lake, the wind picked up, and the clouds darkened, indicating a storm was brewing. She quietly reached behind her, pulling out the poncho Jon had insisted she bring along. How did he know? Maybe he was guessing and got lucky, though she doubted it. More than likely, he'd prepared her for the basics, given the weather. Abby silently covered herself with the poncho, settling back to watch the trail from the boathouse. It was impossible to predict what would come next—and while Abby knew, instinctively, that Jon was competent enough to pull this off, she still couldn't shake the terrifying idea of what this operation would look like without him. What if, somehow,

Hapke beat him to the punch? Jon wasn't young, after all. All she knew was that there were people in that cabin counting on her, and she'd do whatever she could to back Jon up. Everything else was up to fate.

Summers' Cabin
Adirondack State Park, New York
July 19, 2010
1455 hours

Hapke came in the back door of the cabin, brushing the water off his clothing. He took off the black baseball cap he was wearing, shaking the water off that as well. Servati and the two-man detail that always accompanied Hapke walked in behind him, repeating his actions. As he entered the living room, the hostages shifted nervously, their gazes following him. He walked to the window, looking out over the lake. The clouds were dark, roiling with thunder. Lightning flashed in the distance, followed by a thunderclap loud enough to rattle the windowpanes.

Hapke turned, looking at Nancy. "With this weather, my people will need something hot to eat. You'll make it for them."

Nancy didn't answer, returning the man's stare with one equally disdainful.

"Did you hear me?" asked Hapke, volume rising.

This time, Nancy forced a smile. "I heard you," she said softly. "I'll have to go down to the boathouse to see if what's in the freezer is enough to feed a group this large."

"No!" Hapke barked. "You're not leaving the cabin, and neither are they."

With that, he pointed back and forth between Fiona and Julie. Both women looked surprised that they'd been singled out.

Nancy decided to push her luck. "Why, Ron?" she asked, recruiting the shock value of referring to him by first name. "We're on an island. You have enough people to make sure we can't get away, and even if somehow we did, we'd have to cross the lake without a boat, and that effort wouldn't get us very far. Julie and I know where to go, so we're the best choice to go get the food."

"That's the point," said Hapke, eyes bulging. "The two of you already know what's in the freezer. You don't need to be going to cause us trouble."

He looked around the group of hostages and said to Servati, "Take her, her, and the senator as well."

Hapke pointed to Emily, Rice, and O'Leary. Each looked worried, shifting nervously where they sat. Almost haphazardly, Hapke then also gestured toward Sarah. "Take the doctor, too; they seem to keep a lot of their emergency supplies in the boathouse, so maybe there's more there she can use. And take the two brats, too."

"It's about to storm!" objected Sarah loudly.

Hapke ignored the comment, turning back to Servati. "Take four people and go to the boathouse with this crew. I want you to bring back enough food and supplies to last the next twenty-four hours."

"Ron, we don't need this many people," Servati replied. "I can get our people to—"

"These people aren't on the list!" Hapke replied coldly, and everybody in the room went silent at the admission. His meaning was clear: these people weren't important enough to be kept alive. "So," he went on, "if anything happens, you know what to do."

Hapke turned, walking into the kitchen, leaving Servati to follow orders.

Mohawk Tavern and Grill
Bluffton, New York
July 19, 2010
1455 hours

Admiral Putnum followed Fred into the Mohawk's kitchen and found Maggie, Karen, and Nathan working hard over the stoves along with two other employees. The added business because of the hostage situation on the island was keeping them busy throughout the day and for extended hours at night. Maggie was using all the help she could get, and extra food was being delivered to keep up with the demand. That meant some long days, so when Karen volunteered, her help was welcomed.

Fred and the admiral came into the kitchen after Maggie sent a message via one of the waitresses that another naval officer had entered the Mohawk and was sitting at the counter. They spotted Maggie and Nathan almost immediately after walking in and joined them near the pass-through window.

Maggie nodded at the pass-through window. Seated at the counter was a lieutenant commander in a rain-drenched uniform. He had a glass of milk in front of him and a piece of cherry pie. He was looking around the restaurant like he was in search of someone.

"He's been here about ten minutes," said Maggie. "He asked Brandi about the other naval officer. He's not with Commander Smith but seems real interested in finding her."

"We need to get him away from the media," said Putnum. "That's Richard Kingston's son, Bryan, and he's here because of his mother. We need to . . . Damn! How long has the older guy sitting next to him been here?"

Maggie didn't even look out the window to see whom Putnum was referring to. "You mean the one trying to charm Brandi? He's been here for about an hour, asking all sorts of questions about the Summers family. He says he's a writer, but he's asking the wrong questions for being a reporter. He's just a bit creepy. I was about to have Nathan chase him out."

A scowl crossed Fred's face. "Let *me* throw him out."

Putnum chuckled and reached out, touching Fred's arm. "He's not a reporter, but he does write. Whether or not he's a writer is up for debate, and creepy isn't a good descriptor for him. Scary fits him well, though."

Fred looked at Putnum, who leaned close to say something quietly. Fred nodded as Putnum spoke, then said, "I'll give you two minutes."

Maggie and Nathan went back to work and were ignoring the two men. Putnum left the kitchen the way he came. Fred crossed his arms, watching the two men at the counter. The young officer was busy looking around the restaurant and wasn't paying any attention to the man next to him. The old man was tanned, with a full head of hair that was gray around his temples. His full beard was grayer than his hair, and he wore a pair of wire-rimmed glasses he looked over when he spoke. His smile oozed charm, and Brandi was laughing at his every word. Fred took a deep breath and walked out the two-way door from the kitchen.

"Brandi, hon, your mother needs you. I'll take care of these gentlemen."

Brandi looked up at her grandfather, still laughing at something the man said. "Sure thing, Grandpa."

Brandi walked away, leaving Fred with the customers. Fred stepped up to the naval officer and asked, "How are you today, Commander Kingston?"

"Huh? Oh, fine, sir—" Kingston stopped when he realized he'd been called by name and blinked back at the old Indian in open shock.

"The name's on your name tag, son. I'm not psychic," said Fred. "I do know you're looking for someone, though."

Kingston's look remained serious. "And I bet you know where to find her, old man?"

Fred held the young man's gaze, deciding that his attitude was defensive rather than malicious. He looked down at the untouched plate of cherry pie. "Something wrong with my daughter's pie, Commander?"

Kingston looked down at his food, as though he'd forgotten it was there, and instantly picked up a fork. "No, sir, I'm just a little preoccupied at the moment."

Fred allowed the hint of a smile to cross his face. "Look to your right, Commander. Do you see the gentleman by the door over there?"

Kingston did as he was told and recognized the older man standing there. He looked back at Fred. "He looks familiar. What about him?"

Fred picked up the untouched pie, grabbing the fork out of Kingston's hand while he was at it, and took a bite. For a few seconds, the commander only stared, flabbergasted by the old Indian's audacity.

"I recommend," said Fred, preparing to take another bite, "taking a casual walk to the exit where that man's standing. Don't do anything to arouse the media hounds out here; they're already watching you because of the uniform. A nice walk over to that door, and my friend can reunite you and the woman you're looking for."

Kingston maintained eye contact with Fred as he lifted himself off the stool and backed away from the counter. He slowly turned, walking to where Putnum stood by the door. Putnum knocked softly, and the door opened. The two men disappeared, the door closing behind them. With that settled, Fred turned to face the man who had been flirting with his granddaughter. He took another bite of the pie.

"Well, that was mysterious," said the man, an interested look on his face. "How would I find out where the commander went?"

"It's no mystery, Commander Samcevic," answered Fred with a grin. "Just depends on why you're here."

Fred continued to eat the pie Kingston left behind. Walt Samcevic carefully looked the old Indian over. A cautious smile crept onto his face. "I don't have a name tag on. That would make you clairvoyant, or you've read one or more of my books. What do I call you? If I call you 'Chief,' I could be accused of being racist."

Fred laughed mirthlessly, finishing his pie. "Somehow, Commander, I don't see that particular accusation bothering you. With all the controversy you've stirred up in Washington during your career, I bet you consider being accused of racism benign." At this, the man's eyes widened behind his wire-rimmed glasses. "They call you the 'ultimate warrior' in your books. You do have the look of a warrior—an old one, but a warrior, nonetheless. You can call me Chief if you want, because I am one. I don't stand on ceremony, so most people call me Fred."

Samcevic's smile broadened. "Okay, Fred, call me Walt. That ultimate warrior crap was my publisher's idea to sell books. It stuck, but I was just one of the guys when I was with the teams. That was Richard Kingston's son, wasn't it?"

Fred put the empty plate and fork in a large plastic bin under the counter, maintaining eye contact with Samcevic. He didn't answer the question, but rather repeated one of his own from earlier. "Why are you here, Walt?"

Samcevic gave a sigh of resignation. "Josh Ericson is a former teammate and good friend. I've met Jon Summers over the years, and anything I can do to help either of them is my number one mission in life."

"Can I get you some pie, Walt? It's my daughter's recipe. Cherry or apple?" Fred asked, and the older man nodded politely, with a fleeting glance toward the door Kingston had walked through moments ago. "I think you'll appreciate a few things I've got to say. Don't worry about the commander. He'll be just fine."

"Yes, please," said Walt. "On both accounts: the apple pie and your company."

"Settle in, white man," said Fred. "There's much to say."

Summers' Cabin
Adirondack State Park, New York
July 19, 2010
1505 hours

Sarah, Emily, Rice, and O'Leary grabbed ponchos—originally stored for the children in the main cabin—and began putting them on. Rice had been sleeping when the kidnappers showed up and was still in her pajamas, while O'Leary had been at a formal event and was in an evening dress and heels. Nancy had found her boots, but there wasn't anything they could do about the gown, which seemed ridiculous when paired with the blue disposable poncho.

O'Leary joked about how she wished she'd been sleeping like Rice at the time of being whisked away and held hostage. The women laughed. Rice tugged at her sweatpants and had to agree that they were the preferable garb in the scheme of things.

Servati put together a five-person detail, in which she was included. All were equipped with the same M4 carbine assault rifles and light packs with ammunition. She checked each of her prisoners, making sure they were ready to go. They were picked because they were not the high priority prisoners their employer wanted to keep out of harm's way. If anything happened during this errand, Hapke had ordered her to kill them. She had no problem doing that. She told her people to check their weapons, then gave the order, and they all left the safety of the main cabin.

Summers' Island
Adirondack State Park, New York
July 19, 2010
1505 hours

Abby made herself as comfortable as possible. The wind-driven rain hit the windfall she was using for cover, and the thunder was getting closer. She used the poncho to make a small shelter to avoid getting wet.

The fog was still rolling in with the weather. Visibility was deteriorating. It was heaviest on the water but was starting to move onshore from the lake with the wind. She still could see the boathouse, but the cabin complex, which was up a small rise from there, was obscured. There was a glimpse of light from where she knew the main cabin to be. The back door was open. She strained to see through the fog and could make out figures moving from the cabin and down the hill toward the boathouse.

She suddenly caught movement to her right. She looked, seeing Kuma come through the tree line about fifty yards away, moving toward her. His nose went up in the air, as though he'd caught the scent of something. Facing the trail and the lake, he stood erect. The rain, surprisingly, didn't seem to bother him. The dog apparently smelled whoever was coming down the path from the cabin. Like her, he watched them with curiosity.

Abby knew the cabin was separated from the boathouse by about one hundred fifty yards, so she looked through the scope on her rifle to see if she could make out who was on the path. A quick count showed eleven potential targets, all dressed in ponchos or rain gear.

Targets? She caught herself thinking the word, trying to convince herself it was okay. Her training had been to prepare her to use her weapons for defense. This wasn't defensive. They were all targets because she was looking at them through the telescopic sight of a rifle. She just needed to determine which were friendly and which were hostile.

The first two were small and headed to the boathouse. Children? The next two looked to be female, and she recognized Sarah by the way the children minded her, stopping when they got too far ahead. Abby guessed the other to be Emily because the woman looked to be the right size and age. With the hoods of the ponchos up, it was impossible to see their faces.

The next target was also female; under her poncho, there appeared to be a formal dress of some type. *Hostage.* No question there. The target after that was male and carrying a rifle. *Hostile.* After that was another female with no weapon that could be seen. Probably a hostage. Immediately behind her was another armed male. Abby designated him as hostile as well. The remaining three were way behind the first group. She designated each of them as hostile.

Were they far enough back they could possibly get this group away from their captors? Where was Jon? Somewhere ahead of her in the meadow, she guessed. She hadn't seen him since he disappeared into the tall grass. Could he see what she was seeing? He'd done this for a living, so she guessed he did. They would need the hostages to know they were there, so when the time was right, they wouldn't hesitate to come into the forest and meet her.

Abby pulled the small penlight she used at night and pointed at the children who were proceeding down the path. She began slowly pushing the button on the end of the light, turning the device on and off. It gave off a gentle red beam that she hoped would be seen by the hostages but wouldn't draw too much attention to her position. She did this for several minutes, whispering to herself for the kids to see the flashing red light. The children suddenly stopped and were looking her way.

RJ had seen her signal and stopped his sister. The two adults quickly caught up with them, and all four stopped to look in Abby's direction. They started walking again, slower this time, staying close together. She kept signaling.

To her right, Kuma barked, scaring her and causing her to jump. *Oh God, no! What else could go wrong?*

Summers' Island
Adirondack State Park, New York
July 19, 2010
1510 hours

They stepped out of the open door into the driving rain. Servati exited first, followed by two other hostage takers. They waited outside the door, watching as their charges exited, starting down the path. The children led the way, followed by everyone else. O'Leary was complaining as she walked, holding up her long dress so she wouldn't trip over it. Rice brought up the rear, followed by a guard.

The thunder shook the building, but the lightning was still way off. Servati and the two kidnappers who stepped out first didn't lead off but waited to bring up the rear. They were taking their time, and the pace being set by the children was putting them farther behind. Rice noticed this, recognizing the possibility of getting at least the children into the woods and possible safety. There was no way to communicate the opportunity to Sarah, Emily, or O'Leary without giving the plan away. She noticed the fog was rolling in off the lake, closer to the boathouse. That would provide better cover for them if she could create a diversion. She picked up her pace.

Up front, RJ and Patty got far enough ahead that Sarah was calling for them to hold up. They were happy to be out of the cabin and didn't seem to care about the storm. RJ jumped in puddles on the pathway, trying to splash mud on his sister, when she stopped, looking at the tree line where the path from the boathouse entered the forest.

"Look, RJ! Fireflies!"

"Patty, fireflies don't come out in the rain," responded RJ, stopping next to his sister. She pointed, and sure enough, RJ could see a faint red light flashing on and off close to the ground. He knew they weren't fireflies and recognized Abby's signal from when they would play in the woods. Abby was in the woods, and she was a deputy. She could help them escape.

Less than a minute later, Sarah and Emily came up to the two children. RJ pointed out the red light in the forest and said he thought it was Abby.

Emily said, "Abby does carry that red penlight with her."

Sarah looked back and saw O'Leary and the guard following her were slowly getting closer. She was trying to keep her dress as clean as possible in the weather. Behind them, Rice was catching up and looked to be waving them on. In an instant, she realized the marine officer was telling them to run. Servati and Hapke's other two men were about fifty yards behind her, and Sarah recognized the opportunity. She turned back and told the kids to start walking forward but to stay with Emily and her.

While they walked, she turned to Emily. "When I give the word, you grab RJ and I'll grab Patty, and we're going to run to where that light is."

Emily stared nervously at Sarah. "We're not 'on the list,' Sarah," she said quietly, eyes as wide as saucers. "Hapke doesn't have any reason to keep us alive. Any funny business, and we're as good as dead—"

"We're as good as dead either way," Sarah responded. The sound of thunder funneled into the silence following her words, her admission. "They are going to kill us either way. This is our only chance."

Emily was scared, and she had every right to be, but Sarah could see the determination in the young woman's eyes. She nodded, feigning a smile of confidence. They suddenly heard a dog barking. There was Kuma at the tree line, his tail wagging.

There was a sudden flash of light and a deafening clap of thunder.

Summers' Island
Adirondack State Park, New York
July 19, 2010
1515 hours

Servati and the two men with her were casually walking down the path behind the group. She wasn't worried because the area between the cabins and the boathouse was secured. They posted sentries around the area to ensure the sheriff and whoever was with him couldn't disrupt their plans. While they walked along the path, her companions exchanged stories about places where they'd experienced weather like this. She smiled, listening to them try to top each other.

She suddenly realized that they hadn't seen a sentry since they left the shelter of the cabin. She scanned the area ahead of them, seeing the children stopped and waiting for their mother. Her other two guards were ahead of her, but the column was spread out along the path. Damn, they were too far back to prevent the first group from running if they decided to, and there were no sentries in sight.

Servati pulled out her portable radio and keyed the transmit button.

"This is Servati," she said. "Where are my sentries along the path between the main cabin and the boathouse?"

After a few moments, a reply squawked over the radio. "Come on, Servati, it's pouring rain out there."

"Where are you?" she demanded.

"We're in one of the smaller cabins, trying to stay dry. There's nothing out there, anyway."

"We're out here with prisoners, you dipshit! Now get your ass out here!"

Before the sentries could answer, Servati heard a dog bark inland from where they were. Again, she strained her eyes, seeing the black-and-white dog standing by the tree line. She was about to say something to her two companions when there was a blinding flash of light and a deafening boom of thunder. She was looking up when the lightning flashed and so was blinded for several moments. By the time she regained her vision, things changed.

The first group of hostages ran to the tree line, the two adults carrying the children. There was a third person by the senator, dressed in dark clothing, attacking her guard. The last hostage was attacking the man guarding her, and from Servati's vantage point, appeared to be winning the contest. She knew she needed more help.

Summers' Island
Adirondack State Park, New York
July 19, 2010
1520 hours

At the moment the lightning struck, O'Leary had been looking down and retained her vision as a result. When she looked up, she saw Sarah and Emily had picked up the kids and were running for the tree line. A voice from her past told her not to hesitate and to follow them. As she started to run, the man behind her grabbed the poncho, pulling her back. She cursed herself for having tightly secured the poncho up, as she could've easily slipped out of it otherwise.

While she was being pulled back, the earth next to her rose, moving passed her. It was a sight she couldn't explain. It looked like something wild had just emerged from the depths of the forest's foliage. The man behind her let go. She stumbled backward but managed to stay on her feet. She turned and realized that Rice had surprised her guard, managing to throw him to the ground. She pinned his shoulders with her knees and hit him with her fists.

Amy focused on the guard next to her. He was on the ground, his head turned, with blood flowing freely from his nose and mouth. Kneeling over the body was a man dressed in camouflage and covered in mud and grass; his face was dark, smeared with mud and something green. He was putting a knife back in its sheath. She drew in a breath, remembering the wounded hostage taker babbling about a green man who'd attacked them. Then there was that voice again, colder than she remembered it.

"Amy, run!"

She picked up her dress and started to run after Sarah and Emily. There was a muzzle flash from the tree line; she heard gunfire. She glanced back at the man who saved her. He raised his rifle and fired at the pursuing guards. She couldn't be sure, but she thought she saw one drop.

Summers' Island
Adirondack State Park, New York
July 19, 2010
1520 hours

Rice was closing in on O'Leary and the man who was guarding her. Sarah and Emily stopped and looked back, and Rice did her best to signal them to run. The look on Sarah's face told her that the doctor understood, but then again, she'd been in this position before.

The lightning flash took her by surprise. It was the perfect time to try an escape. Her vision had been impaired temporarily by the lightning, but she didn't hesitate. She stopped in the middle of the path, and when the guard behind her bumped into her, she grabbed his poncho, using his own momentum to throw him over her hip and onto the ground. Before he could react, she hit him twice on the windpipe and then repeatedly in the face. She heard screams from behind her, and Servati and the two men with her stopped. The men were raising their rifles. A rifle sounded from behind her. A second rifle was sounded from about twenty feet away. She counted two rounds and saw one of the guards fall. The rifle fired again, two more rounds, and the second man fell. Servati stood there for a second with a disbelieving look before she scrambled behind a tree for cover.

Rice turned, looking behind her to see a man in full combat gear. She heard men yelling from the cabins—more of Hapke's men were coming. She grabbed the rifle of the man she had killed, quickly moving back to kneel next to the man covering her. He handed her a bandolier full of ammunition, as well as a backpack and web belt from the man he'd taken down. There was a pistol on the belt. He had also taken the man's rifle and slung it over his shoulder. He motioned for her to head for the tree line, then raised his rifle and fired a couple of rounds at Hapke's people who were responding to the gunfire. She fell back, thinking nothing had changed since she'd first met this man.

Summers' Island
Adirondack State Park, New York
July 19, 2010
1520 hours

Abby was in a full-blown panic when Kuma barked. When the lightning and thunder struck a few seconds after that, she screamed and jumped. She normally wouldn't have reacted that way, but the tension of the moment needed to be released. Thankfully, she'd recovered quickly, and saw Sarah and Emily running her way, carrying the two kids. She would make sure they made it to the cover of the tree line.

She was about to fire at three kidnappers bringing up the rear when she saw the woman in a long dress get caught by the guard behind her. Out of nowhere, Jon rose, taking the man down. She couldn't see what he did, but the man stayed down—lifeless. She could also see the last woman had turned on the guard watching her. She was now hitting him on the ground.

Abby raised her rifle to her shoulder and fired at the three guards running after the escaping hostages. They stopped, raising their rifles toward her muzzle flash. She was about to fire again when she heard Jon's rifle go off, and one of the men dropped. Jon fired again, and the second man dropped. The female guard stood for a few seconds, looking as if she couldn't believe what was happening. Abby fired a couple of more rounds in her direction as she jumped behind a tree. Hapke's people started to come to life, flooding down the path, moving to where the woman had taken cover. The hostage who had taken out her guard retreated about twenty yards beyond Jon, dropped to a knee, raised a rifle she must've stolen, and opened fire on the hostage takers, giving Jon cover to withdraw.

Jon, in turn, repeated the maneuver, allowing her to withdraw. While they repeated this tactic, working themselves back to the tree line, Abby collected her gear, moving over to the path where Sarah, Emily, and the kids had taken cover. There were several hugs between Abby and the family, but they were short-lived as the gunfire drew closer.

Abby looked around, finding the woman in the long dress hiding behind a tree not far away. "I'm Senator Amy O'Leary," the woman introduced herself.

Abby's face gave away her surprise. They had freed one of the politicians. "Come with us, ma'am," said Abby. "Please keep as low as you can and stay on the path."

A rustle in the bushes made them all jump, but there were screams of elation from the children when Kuma joined them, licking their faces with a hello. Abby did a quick head count to make sure she had everyone.

Both Jon and the other woman were at the tree line, firing at the approaching hostage takers. The opponents returned fire; 5.56 rounds struck trees, sending bark flying into the air like shrapnel.

The woman who was withdrawing with Jon came up to them and introduced herself to Abby. "I'm Colonel Tiffany Rice, Marine Corps. Abby, you're supposed to get us out of here—like, now."

Abby looked over to where Jon was kneeling and firing. He glanced at her and waved them on. "What about—"

"He's going to lead them away from us. You lead, and I'll bring up the rear."

Abby nodded, knowing that arguing would waste valuable time. She led the way, followed by the band of rescued hostages. As they crept out of sight, Rice looked back, seeing Summers still holding his position and firing. She wondered how long he could hold them back.

★ CHAPTER SIX ★

SCHEMERS AND BELIEVERS

The scene in the dining room was one of chaos. The orders to those responding to the attack were indecisive. There was no organized response, and there was the sound of panic on the radio. Panic can be contagious, and it seemed to be spreading among the hostage takers engaging in the fight to get the escaped hostages back. The gunfire had started sporadic but reached a crescendo, leading to a full-fledged firefight.

When Hapke spoke, his voice was raised; he was showing the stress of command and wasn't wearing it well.

The hostages listened with interest and relied on Ericson to interpret what was happening. The senator smiled as he listened to the hostage takers' defense unravel. According to the radio chatter, they'd all escaped. There were casualties—that was apparent—but he couldn't tell how many for sure. He could hear Servati on the radio, so she wasn't one of them.

As he quietly relayed what he was hearing, the morale of the group took an upturn. He didn't have the heart to tell them he guessed this was the work of one or two people—rather than the success of the FBI's involvement—but at least six of them had been freed.

Hapke noticed Ericson smiling and quietly speaking to the other hostages. Anger rose in him; he fought back the panic.

"Zero one to zero two?" he said into the radio.

"Zero two on," answered Servati.

He hesitated before he spoke again, maintaining eye contact with the senator. "Get everyone back here except one team."

"What?"

"Consolidate our people around the cabins and get someone down to the boathouse to get those supplies back here. Send one team after the group that got away. And get everyone else back here—now!"

There was silence on the other end of the radio.

"Servati," Hapke went on, "we need to make sure they can't come after the rest of the hostages. Do what I say. Send one team after them and get everyone else back here to consolidate and reinforce our position."

The chatter started up on the radio again, and Ericson heard Servati barking orders.

The panic was gone, but there was still desperation in their voices. Ericson knew it was because something unknown was out there and was turning their piece-of-cake mission into something else—something they hadn't expected and certainly didn't seem prepared for. The hostage takers would be more dangerous now, so Ericson knew he had to keep a lid on what he and the other hostages did so as not to antagonize them.

Ericson watched Hapke's face flush when he deliberately smiled at the man's frustration. He looked around and saw that his fellow hostages were looking for an explanation of what was happening. His smile disappeared when he started to explain. "We need to stay calm and do nothing to upset these people. They're extremely dangerous right now, because they're scared, and that makes them unpredictable."

"But there's a rescue team out there," observed Del Monte. "They should be trying to get us out of here soon."

"I'm not scared of these guys," added young Hector, looking at his mother and aunt sitting at the end of the sofa. "Besides, I have a score to settle."

Nancy and Julie both started to say something to the young man but stopped short when Ericson held up his hand. "Young man." His voice was quiet but hard. "You put your personal feelings aside. Our first goal is to keep all of us alive. Do you understand?"

Hector looked at his feet but didn't answer.

"I asked if you understood, boy. Do you?"

"Yes, sir."

"You have every right to be upset, son, and you may even get your chance to avenge your father's murder. Let's get everyone out of here first."

Hector nodded, then took his mother's outstretched hand, squeezing it.

Ericson looked at Del Monte. "Sue Ellen, they're consolidating their positions, which will make it harder to get us out without a bloodbath. We have to remain calm and not make our rescuers' job more difficult by angering the bad guys."

The congresswoman nodded shyly, smiling at Nancy, indicating she understood whom Ericson was talking about.

Del Monte's husband spoke up next. "They just confirmed that four of their men were killed in the skirmish out there. One was killed by Colonel Rice when she escaped, and three were killed by this guy in green. He's freaking them all out. Killed one hand-to-hand, according to the report, and then calmly fired four rounds, all hits, killing two more before they could fire their weapons. He's spooked the hell out of this Servati woman."

"Motherfucker!" expressed Hector out loud without thinking. His mother reached over and slapped him on the back of the head. She leaned over and whispered, "Be respectful when you speak about one of your uncles!"

Hector's eyes grew big as he turned to look at his mother and his aunt. They both nodded to his unasked question. He glanced at Ericson and thought he saw the hint of a cruel smile on his face.

Mohawk Tavern and Grill
Bluffton, New York
July 19, 2010
1530 hours

Kingston was surprised at the activity in the bar of the Mohawk. There was an entire second operation being run there. There were representatives of the

FBI, CIA, local police, and the Navy. He was most surprised to find the old man who took him in was the deputy director of the NSA.

He handed the note Sanderson had given him to Grey and was surprised when he was put in a pool of resources that were mostly family members of the hostages. They could be trusted. Kingston found it to be a very different situation.

"Do you know what was in the note?" asked Grey, looking over a pair of reading glasses.

Kingston nodded. "I thought he was just being condescending, but it looks like he's got a serious problem."

Grey handed the note to Putnum, who read through it quickly, then looked at the FBI agent. "You know he's asking you to run a separate rescue operation."

Grey nodded. "Yeah, and just when I was getting used to hating the man, he becomes sensible."

"You and I need to make a phone call," said Putnum, "but we should get Sanderson here to be part of that conversation. Someone in his operation is feeding all their plans to the hostage takers. Glenn, only Sanderson, no one else connected to that operation, can be part of this."

Grey opened his mouth to express his agreement, only to be disrupted by Justin, who rushed through the back door with Mitchell on his heels. "We have news!" Mitchell declared earnestly. The others gathered at his side, eager for an update.

Mitchell looked at Putnum and Grey. "There's been a firefight on the island."

"Who started the—" Becky jumped in, stopping just as quickly when her father put his hand on her arm.

Justin spoke up. "From what we can tell from the transmissions, it looks like they were moving some of the hostages to the boathouse to bring food and supplies back in the middle of this storm. We can't be sure what exactly took place, but the transmissions indicate that some of their security took cover from the rain, allowing enough of a gap for the hostages to escape."

"Justin," Matt said, "Tom mentioned a firefight. Was anyone hurt?"

Justin shook his head. "Six hostages got away clean. It wasn't until their security tried to stop them that all the fireworks started."

"The volume of fire heard over the radio was unbelievable," said Mitchell. "At times, it was so heavy you couldn't understand what was being said."

Justin picked up where he left off. "We can say for sure that Sarah, RJ, and Patty got away."

Becky turned, hugging her father.

"They also indicated Emily was with them."

Matt put his arms around Karen and Cassie, giving each a gentle kiss on the forehead. All had tears in their eyes.

Mitchell continued, "We're not as sure who the other two hostages are. We suspect that one might be Colonel Rice because they talked about a female hostage jumping her guard, taking his weapon, and joining in the firefight."

There was a grunt from the back of the room. Ellison said simply, "Good marine."

"The last hostage appears to be a woman—one of the politicians," Mitchell finished, trying not to smile at Ellison's comment. "We'll have to wait until the island contacts us to know who that is."

"Tom," asked Putnum, "any word on casualties?"

"The hostage takers lost four men from what we can tell. Two in hand-to-hand combat, which is why we think the one hostage was Rice. One of the rescuers was described as rising from the ground, taking one guard out—also hand-to-hand—and shooting two more while covering the escape. The hostage takers are all freaked out, describing a green man or something like that. They sound panicked, Admiral."

Fred stood, turned, and looked at Matt. "Spirit of the Wolf Clan."

Matt nodded. Things were now getting interesting.

Hidden Cave
Summers' Island
July 19, 2010
1550 hours

The rain let up some; it was now only a mist, but the lightning and thunder continued. A heavy fog rolled in from the lake and rose from the forest, masking their ascent up the hill. They were all wet from the rain, but spirits were high among the escaped hostages because they were away from their captors. When they reached a wooded ledge on the steep hill, Abby called a halt and waited for everyone to catch up. They took cover behind a fallen tree while Abby made sure they hadn't been followed.

"We need to get under cover," said Rice, bringing up the rear. She knelt next to Abby. "We need to get to wherever you are hiding out and get these people dried out."

Gunfire echoed from the forest below them. Abby flashed Rice a smile from under all the green paint on her face. "Just making sure they're not following us."

Rice looked down the hill and was struck by the beauty of the heavy mist rising from the forest. She'd almost forgotten why they were on this hill when another exchange of gunfire rose from the forest to remind her that they were still in danger.

"Hey," said Emily, touching the foliage next to her, "this is cloth. How'd this get here?"

Abby smiled, motioning for Rice to follow her. She silently moved back by Emily and observed her six charges. Emily was looking at Abby, eyes wide and questioning as she held the remnants of the parachute between her fingers. RJ had moved next to her and was examining the fabric she was holding. Patty watched but was cuddled close to her mother, shivering. O'Leary settled next to Sarah, shivering as well. She was too preoccupied by the sporadic gunfire below to notice what Emily was talking about.

"It gets stranger," said Abby. "Stay behind me."

She approached the rock face of the hill, moving aside the brush and fabric that covered the cave entrance. She smiled at the collective gasps of surprise from behind her.

"Sheriff," she said loud enough for the wounded man inside the cave to hear. "It's Deputy Crogan; I'm coming in with friends."

"Come ahead," answered a voice from inside. "Nice and slow, Crogan."

Abby turned, pleased with the look of surprise on all six faces.

Upton's Marina and Boat Sales
Bluffton, New York
July 19, 2010
1555 hours

Sanderson and his team had been taken entirely by surprise with the escape of six of the hostages and the resulting firefight. They weren't only monitoring the hostage takers' pursuit but were recording everything. The ferocity of the storm was so intense, it created interference over the hostage takers' radios, but the level of fire could be heard clearly. While they pieced together what was taking place, there were comments on the number of casualties suffered by the bad guys. His IT specialist tried to clear up some of the interference but was having little success.

"Sorry, sir," said the man without looking up from his work. "This storm is just putting off too much electricity to make it any cleaner."

Outside, lightning flashed and thunder boomed as the storm passed overhead. Rain pounded down outside the safety of the showroom.

"What's the final update on the pursuit?" Sanderson asked, looking at the storm raging outside. How could men fight in this kind of weather and still be effective? He wouldn't have believed it possible, but he was listening to proof of it now over the radio.

"Sir," his IT specialist replied, "since the engagement started, six of the hostages have been freed. We know two of them to be the children, but who the rest are, we can only guess. Transmissions indicate the hostage takers took four casualties, all dead. We have no information on any friendly casualties. They are pursuing the rescuers east on the island in what appears to be a running firefight."

"They're heading east?" asked Sanderson looking at the man.

"Yes, sir," answered the tech man. "East on the island, away from the cabin complex."

Sanderson looked at one of his tactical people. "What's on that end of the island?"

Two SWAT commanders leaned over a table covered with maps and aerial photographs. The one closest answered, "There doesn't seem to be much but trees. The cabins are located on the east end of the island, so there isn't much territory east of them. There's a meadow to the north, and beyond that is the area where the first rescue team landed and was ambushed. Most of the island is to the west, and that's where the high ground is. I'd be headed there to make my stand."

A smile crossed Sanderson's face. There wasn't much island to the east, and that was where the pursuit was being led. The door to the showroom opened, and all of them looked up to see one of Agent Grey's rain-soaked agents standing there. Sanderson guessed there was a development he needed to attend to in the back room across the street. He looked at the group gathered around the radio console and told them he needed to step out for a minute to consult with Grey and his team, as they would need to release some information to the media shortly. He left specific directions for each of them to carry out during his absence. He then followed the agent out into the storm.

Hidden Cave
Summers' Island
July 19, 2010
1630 hours

The children were wrapped in blankets immediately. Emily found the stock of canned goods and started heating up some soup to take the chill off. They also found dry clothes, though most were in men's sizes and were military-style BDUs. Emily joked with Sarah that Uncle Jon found a place for all his old uniforms. O'Leary was the first to change, getting out of her long formal dress, and then replaced Emily at the stove to give her time to change, too.

Sarah checked Sheriff James's wounds. A moment later, she was joined by Abby, who showed her the wounds under his bandages. Sarah smiled, commenting on how professional a job her father-in-law had done, and then started to cry. All the pent-up emotion flowed out of her like a waterfall. She put her head on Abby's shoulder, hugging her as hard as she could.

"You going to be okay?" asked Abby, trying to smile.

Sarah released her hold on Abby. "You forget I've been through this before. I needed to get that out of my system so I can do what's needed to get my children out of here. Say, where did the old man come up with this place?"

All Abby could do was shrug her shoulders in response. Emily came out from behind a poncho that had been made into a makeshift changing room. She was wearing desert camo pants and a navy-blue sweatshirt with a gold SEAL trident on the left breast of the shirt.

Emily smiled at the two women when she came out and modeled her new ensemble, making everyone in the cave laugh. O'Leary joined in, modeling her outfit. She had forest camo pants with a matching shirt, which she'd left open, displaying the red top she had been wearing with the formal dress.

"I think these are Justin's," said Emily, looking sad when she and the senator went back to the soup they were heating up. "They're smaller than the rest of the military surplus back there."

"I don't think he would mind," commented O'Leary with a sympathetic look. "You are family, and this is an emergency."

"It just seems funny with him gone and all." Emily's statement sounded melancholy.

Sarah looked at Abby and nodded a thank-you. She rose, moving toward Emily. She put her arms around the young woman, hugging her gently.

As she released her grip, she said, "Then wear them with pride; he would expect that."

The two women were quiet for a few moments before Sarah turned to her children. "Come on, kids—let's go see what dry clothes Grandpa and Uncle Matt have stashed away that might fit us."

Summers' Island
Adirondack State Park, New York
July 19, 2010
1630 hours

The rain subsided, and the storm passed over. The aftermath left a heavy overcast and fog that clung to the forest. Moisture dripped off the trees, giving the mistaken effect that it might still be raining above the canopy. It felt like moving through an enchanted forest one might see in the movies, or so the four-man team pursuing the escapees thought.

They knew two things and transmitted them back to Hapke. They knew there was only one person performing a rearguard action, allowing the escapees the opportunity to get away. There was also nowhere else to go, because they were only a couple hundred yards from the end of the island. They had escaped only to run into a dead end. If they were to get away, they would have to swim, and Hapke didn't think they would do that with children.

There was a muzzle flash from a heavy thicket of small trees down the trail, and two rounds whizzed over their heads. All four men dropped, returning fire, riddling the thicket. The patrol leader told his men to hold their fire. They sat for a minute with no response. Checking his map, the patrol leader found there was a booby trap on the trail just before the thicket to slow down rescuers. He directed his men to split up and take opposite sides of the trail to avoid it. They moved forward slowly and cautiously, alert to any resistance to their front. The first man stood on one side of the trail, with his partners on the other, rifles up and ready for action. The leader held back, contacting Hapke on the radio.

"We're moving in on the escapees," he said into his voice-activated mic, his rifle up in a vain attempt to cover his comrades. "We're moving around the trap set on the path on the easternmost point of the island and expect to have the escapees back in custody shortly."

"Roger that," came the response. "Keep your head down."

The man laughed. "Don't worry—"

Two explosions shook the forest, knocking the man to the ground. Brush fell to the forest floor on either side of the path, having been cut by the shrapnel from the booby trap. One of the men caught in the explosion was screaming for help.

"Base One to Patrol One," squawked the radio. "What was that?"

The patrol leader was trying to get to his feet when he saw a figure standing in the center of the path, watching him. He couldn't distinguish any features to help him describe the man, except that he was wearing head-to-toe green camouflage.

"Base One to Patrol One, what's your status?"

One of his comrades continued screaming while he answered the base. "There's been an explosion. Three men down. He's . . . he's here on the path." He paused. "I'm gonna get him."

He raised his rifle, firing in the direction of the figure on the trail. The rounds impacted short of their intended target, sending up a spray of dirt between him and the man standing on the path. His weapon emptied, and he screamed as he ejected the clip, reloading. He pulled back the slide, charging the weapon, still screaming. When he raised his weapon to fire, the figure fired his weapon a split second before he could.

The patrol leader's weapon fired wildly. The rounds fired by the man in green found their mark, knocking him to the ground, bleeding and badly wounded.

"Patrol One, Base One, what's your status?" repeated the radio.

The patrol leader was sprawled face-first and prone in the mud. At first, he felt nothing except the sensation of being out of breath, but he knew he'd been hit. When he tried to move, white-hot pain pulsed through his body, causing him to scream involuntarily, activating his microphone. Somebody grabbed him and flipped him over. The movement was enough to turn that white-hot pain into a wave of agony radiating out from his core, and he let out another scream.

The patrol leader fought to focus through the pain. Standing over him was the green man, who was pointing his rifle at the hostage taker's head. Only now did the patrol leader realize his partner was also screaming, lying someplace out of sight in the mud. Unbeknownst to the patrol leader, his microphone had tripped, so it was continually active when he had been rolled over. This had not been accidental.

"You're . . . you're all green. Who . . . who are you?" gasped the patrol leader, pain cutting through his consciousness. "Oh my God—it hurts!"

There was no emotion to be found in his antagonist's green-painted face. His rifle remained pointed at the patrol leader.

"It doesn't matter who I am," the green-faced man said. "You just need to know you shouldn't be here. You should have left when you were told."

The hostage taker moved slightly, screaming in pain again. "Give me something for the pain . . . please . . . it hurts so much. Are you going to kill me? I don't want to die. Please don't kill me, please—"

Jon raised the muzzle of his weapon and knelt next to the wounded man. He started to strip the man of his weapons and ammunition, causing the man to scream again. Finishing, he leaned in close to the open mic. "You all should have left the island when you had the chance. Now, none of you will."

"Oh my God," moaned the wounded kidnapper. In the background, his fallen comrade continued to scream.

Summers' Cabin
Adirondack State Park, New York
July 19, 2010
1640 hours

Hapke peered back at his people gathered around the table, seeing the same emotions in each of their faces he himself was feeling. Shock, fear, and panic could be seen in every pair of eyes. The cabin was completely silent during the entire series of transmissions, and there was no doubt everyone, including the hostages, heard them. The screaming of their wounded comrade could still be heard, so Hapke ordered everyone to switch to an alternate channel. He sent one of his people out to pass the word, along with orders for each of his people to check in with the base station once they had made the change. He also sent word for Servati to check in with him.

The messenger left the cabin, and within minutes, the men began checking in. As they were taking roll call, Hapke noticed Ericson was watching him intently from the other room. Hapke felt himself flush, turning away to look at the man running the radio console next to him. More of his people were checking in, and the radio operator was taking roll as they did. The whole reason he'd come to this island and signed up for this job was because he'd been promised it'd be an easy mission with a quick escape—and seeing as they'd already defended against the first rescue attempt without even breaking a sweat, he'd thought this was a no-brainer. Plus, the intelligence they were getting from within the federal response was right on-target. How was it that he'd lost six of his people, possibly more, and with another seriously wounded, to a couple of local cops running around the island? One of them was supposed to be wounded. Now he had taken more casualties, with an entire four-man team being ambushed by this phantom man in green. He was missing something, and he needed to find out what.

Hapke glanced again at the hostages. They were huddled together, not paying attention to what was happening—except for the crippled senator. He was intently watching the goings-on in the dining room. He wore a smug smile on his face that Hapke wanted to rip off, but something told him it would be a mistake to try. Still, he knew something, and Hapke was thinking it was time to ask the good senator a few questions.

"Zero Two to Base One." Servati's voice came over the radio. "I've switched to the alternate frequency and have sent a ten-man patrol to see about the pursuit team. They'll check in shortly."

"Roger that, Zero Two," answered the radio operator, looking at Hapke for any orders to pass on. Hapke thought for a second, shaking his head.

"Tell Zero One that we're consolidating our positions to concentrate on the cabins," Servati transmitted. "We're moving food to the main cabin and should have everything in place within thirty minutes."

Hapke nodded and told the radio operator to have her report to him as soon as she was done with the consolidation. Hapke looked over at the hostages. Ericson was still smiling and watching everything. They were going to have a talk.

Upton's Marina and Boat Sales
Bluffton, New York
July 19, 2010
1640 hours

Sanderson's meeting across the street with Grey was short, so he was back in the command post in time to hear the latest firefight over the radio. Nothing was said by those gathered around the communications set as they continued to hear the screaming of the wounded coming from the speakers mounted on top of the console. No one said a word while listening to the haunting voice of an unidentified man speaking to the wounded kidnapper. Even the psychologists stopped scribbling on their legal pads to stare at the radio. There was no emotion in the voice, no anger, no rage. It was as if the person was just passing on a fact, and that's what made it sound so chilling.

"I can't take the screaming anymore," said Ramsey, covering her ears and finally breaking the silence. "How can someone inflict that kind of suffering on other people?"

Sanderson motioned for the agent manning the console to turn the speakers off. "Start scanning other frequencies; they'll have to change in order to communicate."

The agent acknowledged with a nod and went right to work. Sanderson turned to find several agents snickering at the young attorney's reaction. They stopped when it became obvious their boss did not approve.

"I need to know your thoughts on how this affects our tactical options," Sanderson said to his two SWAT leaders.

An agent dressed in forest camo answered, "The fact the hostage takers are consolidating their perimeter will make it more difficult for us to rescue the hostages without an all-out fight. When their firepower was spread out, we could have slipped a small team into the cabin where they're holding the hostages, neutralized the guards, and held off the rest until our teams could get in to effect an arrest. Now their people are too concentrated for us to even try."

"I agree with that assessment, sir," said the second agent. "The only upside is we should be able to put teams on the rest of the island because they'll be confined to the one area."

"What about the booby traps the hostage takers have set?" asked the agent in charge of the bomb unit. "We know they've set a number of them out there, and that will make any progress slow until they're cleared out."

"Is there any way we can contact Sheriff James or his deputy? I'll bet they have an idea where the booby traps are," said another agent. "That way we can bypass all the traps, allowing our people to move into the interior of the island and our EOD people time to dispose of any unexploded ordinance that might still be out there."

"I don't think they're the ones we need to be trying to contact," said one of the SWAT leaders. "Whoever this man in green is, he's the one we need to get ahold of. He's turned their own traps around on them. You heard the radio transmissions—they knew that there were explosives rigged on that trail, and yet they set them off. That was no accident. This guy knows what he's doing and rigged them to go off when these guys walked where they thought it was safe. He's the one we need to contact."

"Who is this man in green?" asked Sanderson. "Anyone have any idea who he is and how we might contact him?"

There was silence around the group for almost a minute before one of the agents cleared his throat and said, "Well, he's not from the first rescue team—we've accounted for all of them, including the sheriff and the deputy."

"How about one of the locals?" offered another agent. "I'll bet it's one of them."

"With Special Forces training?" asked one of the SWAT leaders. "That's what this guy must have. He's good at tactics and guerilla warfare and is not likely to be your run-of-the-mill local."

"How about family?" asked the other SWAT leader. "The Summers family has a history of military service—it could be one of them."

"They're all accounted for," said the first SWAT leader. "But what about a friend?"

"They haven't contacted us to help," offered yet another agent. "Doesn't that make them guilty of obstruction and give us some leverage to make them cooperate?"

They all looked at Ramsey, the only legal representative present, who didn't hesitate to answer. "Technically, yes, we could make the case for obstruction. The only problem being this person has saved the sheriff and the deputy and so could be considered working with law enforcement. Besides, he doesn't seem to scare easily, so threatening to prosecute him probably wouldn't work."

"We know he's killed," said an agent, thinking out loud.

"To save lives or in self-defense," Ramsey fired back. "We need to find out who this person is and then contact him to get the information you want. I'm telling you, trying to threaten this person to get his cooperation won't work."

There was silence again while the group stood around the console. No one seemed prepared to take the conversation further, so Sanderson decided to put an end to it. "You all need to come up with the answer to this. Check the background of every local if you have to. We need to know who's on that island. Who's missing from around the lake? What Summers' acquaintances are unaccounted for and might be capable of doing this? We need these answers yesterday, people. We don't send anyone in until we know where the booby traps are. We can't afford to lose more people through carelessness or poor planning, but we're still under the gun to get those hostages out alive. Get to it."

All the gathered agents rushed to follow directions and chase down leads. Sanderson hated sending his people on a wild goose chase but knew it was necessary until he found out who was sending the hostage takers their intelligence information. He turned to his IT man sitting at the console and snapped, "Did you find that other frequency yet?"

Mohawk Tavern and Grill
Bluffton, New York
July 19, 2010
1640 hours

The storms had passed and the fog was lifting, leaving just overcast skies to emphasize the bleakness of the situation. Word of the firefight spread through the bar like wildfire, and many gathered to listen to it over the speakers at the van. There was silence among the gathered crowd for two reasons. First, Joey DePalma kept the volume as low as he could so passing strangers wouldn't be drawn to the noise. They did their best to block the view from the street, but it was a public road, and the media were still all over the village, searching for stories. Second, most of those gathered had not been in combat and were awed by what they were hearing. Men were dying several miles down the lake and they were casually listening to it. Several walked away from the van when the screaming of the wounded started, not needing to hear any more. When Jon made his last transmission, several people, including Grey, seemed to stiffen.

"He can't kill them all," said Grey to Putnum. "The odds are against him, and he hasn't broken any laws or done anything we can't justify to this point."

"He did come back into the country illegally," quipped Ellison, grinning. "If you can't get him on that, then I'm sure Inspector Preston can."

There were a few chuckles, and even Grey managed to smile.

Putnum looked at Mitchell. "They'll have to change frequencies now, Tom."

Mitchell nodded and turned to DePalma. "Keep monitoring and recording this frequency but start scanning others in the same range."

"But why keep monitoring this one?" asked DePalma, starting to search.

"Because," said Justin, who was in the van, helping his teammate, "they'll send a rescue party out for the wounded, and we may pick something up because the mics are still live."

Joey D nodded, and the two men continued to work.

"I know that was Uncle Jon," commented Cassie, cuddling into her father, "but that statement scared the hell out of me. I can't imagine how that left the bad guys feeling."

"Right now, most of them are questioning the wisdom of taking on this job," said Wiedenkeller, his arm around his daughter as well.

"It'll work on most of them because they'll start to question their leadership," Naylor added. "I'm guessing they were all sold a bill of goods about how easy this job was going to be."

"And now they have a bunch of dead and wounded," finished Ellison. "This isn't what they signed up for. It was supposed to be easy money."

"I don't understand how the hostage takers set off their own booby trap, though," said Kay, looking at her father for an answer. "I mean, they had to know where it was. Weren't they the ones who placed it?"

Samcevic answered before Wiedenkeller could. "We used to do it all the time in Nam. We would find the booby traps the VC put out for our guys, and we would move them to the trail that they used to get around them, and that's where Summers learned it. He was there, and from what I'm told, he was a good point man."

"But not as good as you, though—right, Walt?" Ellison said with a laugh, and Samcevic just smiled back at the retired marine.

"We got it!" shouted Justin. "We got the other frequency!"

Mitchell went to the van to check on what Justin and DePalma had found while the rest of the crowd began to break up. Kay and Ryan joined them as they began to monitor and record the second frequency. Putnum stepped over to where the active-duty Navy personnel had been standing together. He spoke to Smith and Kingston briefly and then walked off with the group of retired servicemen.

Smith turned to Johnston. "Ensign, I need you and the chief to be available to meet with the admiral with us in about an hour."

"Yes, Commander," replied the young officer. "If I may ask, ma'am, who are those old guys the admiral is walking off with?"

Skier leaned forward, speaking quietly. "Sir, you know we've told you there are times you need to just keep your mouth shut and just watch, listen, and learn."

Johnston nodded, remaining silent.

"This is one of those times, sir."

Smith smiled. "Ensign, the only people I feel safer being with other than you and your team are those old guys. Listen to the chief."

Smith turned, walking back into the Mohawk, stifling a laugh.

Logan International Airport
Boston, Massachusetts
July 19, 2010
1650 hours

Evans had moved twice—once to go to the bathroom, and once to get a cup of coffee from a nearby café—but his target remained in the same place, working on her computer. She had picked a seat next to the wall at the departure gate for her flight. If his intelligence was good, and it had been thus far, her flight to Dulles was leaving in an hour and a half. He'd checked the monitor when he went for coffee and confirmed it was scheduled to leave on time.

He glanced up and down the terminal to check on what was going on. It was crowded, but nothing out of the ordinary was happening. That is, until his target suddenly sat up straight, scowling at her computer screen. She typed frantically for a few minutes and then settled back into watching the screen. Evans guessed she was emailing or chatting with someone, because her look remained serious. She began typing again. He could see anger on her face, her entire demeanor changing.

Evans set down what he had been reading and took out his phone. He brought up his text messaging and began to type. "Target agitated and communicating with unknown people. Something has happened, and target appears to be sending detailed communication."

He hit send, picking his magazine back up. He glanced around the terminal again. He remembered the good old days, when he was happy to use a pencil and paper to get a handwritten message out. Now everything was electronic and happened instantly. His phone chirped, indicating he'd received a text message. "Big firefight: Six hostages escaped, including name you know. Six dead, two wounded."

Evans stared at his phone for several moments, then looked across the terminal at his target. Whatever Smith was up to was working. The woman's whole persona changed and could only be described as intense. It was visibly noticeable, and Evans guessed she would now be more alert to what was going on around her. He would have to work harder to blend in.

His cell phone chirped again, and he casually read the text. "Target is dangerous; DO NOT break surveillance, but caution emphasized."

Evans smiled at Smith's sudden concern for his safety. It was not characteristic of the man to say this to anyone because of his history, but Evans guessed it to be sincere. They were alike in many ways, and in another time and place would have been good friends, but life hadn't led them in that direction. He dealt with dangerous people all his life and knew overconfidence could be deadly. He would not make that mistake here; the stakes were too high.

He typed his response. "You insult me, Mr. Smith, and you know me better than that."

Less than thirty seconds later his cell chirped one more time, and the message was simple. "Sorry."

Evans quickly looked around the terminal to see if anyone was watching him. He saw no one checking his target. She was still communicating to someone using her computer and hadn't noticed him, although she was paying more attention to those around her at the gate.

Something was wrong. Smith was not the person he was communicating with; he never would have apologized to him. Who was sending the messages and speaking for Smith? He would be more cautious in how he approached this job, but he would continue.

Mohawk Tavern and Grill
Bluffton, New York
July 19, 2010
1700 hours

The doors to the tavern opened, and the room quickly began to fill up. Putnum decided they couldn't monopolize the tavern for their planning and scheming without raising the curiosity of the locals who frequented the venue or attracting the media. The Crogan family was more than willing to keep it closed, but Putnum and Mitchell were concerned. They planned to use the open tavern to gain intelligence. Besides, Putnum guessed the revenue from the bar being open would more than pay for the food and hospitality the Crogan family was providing his little band of conspirators.

Putnum didn't send Smith and the SEALs away. Instead, when he met with them, he found them civilian clothing to wear and put them to work gathering information. They would not be making an initial assault on the island. With the security issues Sanderson was having, he wanted to keep the team close. Putnum also contacted the commanding general at Fort Drum near Watertown, New York, to put several of his infantry and aviation units on alert in case they would be needed. He contacted Bryan Kingston's chain of command and was having a special delivery made overnight with the help of the Air Force and Fort Drum. This whole situation would come to a head tomorrow, and he wanted to be ready to ensure a positive outcome. He couldn't trust that would happen if everything was run through the command post across the street.

On the second floor of the Mohawk, the real planning for the evening was taking place and would end with a trip to Dartford just before midnight. It was going to be a long night, and Putnum decided he needed to have a little something to eat, so he sat down at a table with Gateway, Kevin, and Becky. They looked at a menu, and suddenly Ensign Johnston appeared in front of them dressed in a polo shirt and blue jeans, asking them for their order. Kevin and Becky looked surprised, glancing at Putnum, who smiled.

"You'll have to pardon the naivety of my children, W.C.," remarked the general. "They seem to have missed the fact that Johnston and two of his teammates are now running the bar and that Miss Wiedenkeller and Mr. O'Keefe are back in their guise as reporters, mingling as patrons."

Kevin took a quick glance around the room. "I'll be damned, Dad. When'd you notice that?"

The general chuckled. "I may be old, son, but I'm not blind and senile—yet. Mitchell has been slowly moving his people into place and looks to be running his own little intelligence operation here in downtown Bluffton."

"I don't understand, Dad." Becky looked around the room, seeing the same thing her brother had. "Why would they need to do that?"

Becky was looking at Putnum for an answer, but it was her father who spoke. "The media may be a pain in the ass for the FBI and those of us in public service, but they are professionals and extremely good at their jobs. The job is to gather facts and information. They are also human, and when speaking to peers, discuss that information."

Both Becky and Kevin smiled at the last comment, and Kevin finished his father's statement. "And Tom has conveniently created the opportunity to gather some of that information."

Becky wrinkled her forehead, asking, "Is that legal?"

Johnston shifted nervously, and they all remembered he was still standing there. Before anyone could give him an order, Cassie and Fred walked up, both looking serious, taking the last empty chairs at the table.

Fred addressed Johnston. "Son, bring a round of drinks for everyone here, on me."

Johnston gave the old man a puzzled look. "But you own the place, Mr. Crogan."

"No, I don't," Fred said, almost indignantly. "My daughter does, but they'll put it on my tab." He then glanced at the bar and saw the two other SEALs working behind it. He rolled his eyes. "Where's Nathan?"

"Oh, he and Stephen are on an errand with Mr. Upton," Johnston answered innocently. "The boys and I are helping out until they get back."

Fred looked at Putnum. "You're kidding, right?"

The smile he received in return told him that he wasn't joking. He turned back to Johnston, still looking serious. "Son, you get everyone's drink order—I'll have a whiskey, neat. Then bring everyone the stew special to eat."

"Careful, Johnston," said the general. "It may not be legal to sell Indians liquor in this county."

Johnston hesitated for a second, looking at Fred.

Fred replied, "Boy, do as you're told, or I'll have to scalp you. I'd scalp the old General over there, too, but it looks like someone beat me to it."

There was laughter all around the table, and Fred was about to say something when a husky female voice broke in. "Excuse me, Dr. O'Keefe and General Gateway, but could I have a moment of your time?"

Everybody turned to see a well-dressed, attractive woman in her late forties standing before them. Becky and Bill immediately recognized Sandy Monroe, newswoman. They had been hostages together in the Philippines in 1995. Everyone else recognized her as one of the anchors for one of the national network's morning shows. Both Becky and Bill rose, moving to meet her. Becky gave her a hug, kissing her on the cheek; Bill followed suit. This caused everyone else at the table to rise.

"Sandy," said Bill, gently holding the woman's hands, "it's wonderful to see you, but we're not giving interviews just yet."

Monroe shook her head. "No, I heard you were all here, and I wanted to say how sorry I am to hear about Admiral Summers's death. I didn't think anything could kill him after the Philippines."

Members of the group looked at each other, betraying what they knew.

Monroe, ever the reporter, read the room immediately. "You mean he's not dead? But the word out of Canada is—" She stopped cold, knowing they were likely being eavesdropped on, and smoothed the lapels of her red fleece peacoat. "Anyway, I also wanted to give you all a heads-up that someone is feeding information to all the networks," she said, keeping her voice low. "We'll all be breaking stories within the hour about exactly who the hostages are and that this entire fiasco is a bid to free Richard Kingston. They'll be bringing a lot of what took place in the Philippines into the open for the first time." No one said anything, so she sighed and added, "Look, I wanted you to know before these other guys find out who you are and hound you to death."

"Thanks, Sandy. You're a good friend," Becky said, giving the woman another hug.

"And you're not looking for anything in return?" Fred asked suspiciously.

"No. Friends look out for one another. Nothing more." They all nodded, and Monroe turned to Putnum, studying his features. There was something about him that was familiar. "Excuse me, sir, do we know each other?"

"No, Miss Monroe. I don't believe we do."

Hidden Cave
Summers' Island
July 19, 2010
1730 hours

The forest below her had fallen silent. There were no more sounds of gunfire echoing up from the thick timber stands. The heavy overcast kept the dampness of the storms earlier in the afternoon from escaping, so Rice stayed under her poncho, trying to keep warm. It really wasn't cold; the temperature was about seventy degrees, but the humidity made her feel chilled. The poncho helped keep her body heat in, as well as keep her camouflaged. The slope below her was dense with trees and underbrush and was rocky. The path through it was hard to find coming up from the forest floor and easily defended from her position if necessary.

Behind her, somebody came out of the cave. Rice turned to find Abby carrying plates of steaming-hot food. Abby handed her a plate and then sat down next to her under the cover of the windfall.

Rice smiled. "Spam and mac and cheese—comfort food, even here."

Abby returned the smile. "The place is well stocked with dried goods and canned food. Emily and I made enough for a small army, so there's seconds."

Rice managed to give a thumbs-up as she shoveled a spoonful of mac and cheese into her mouth. "Mmmm . . . that's good," she said, swallowing. "Beats the hell out of MREs."

"They have those stashed in there, too," Abby added, laughing. "Any sign of Jon?"

Rice shook her head, swallowing another mouthful. "Sorry, I haven't eaten much since they grabbed me. Don't worry about the admiral—I'm sure he's fine. He'll be along as soon as he feels it's safe."

"He's outnumbered like forty to one," Abby said, playing with the food on her plate, and for a moment, they were both quiet. She didn't need to say what they already knew, but she did anyway. "He can't fight them all."

Rice motioned for Abby to eat. "It's a good thing he doesn't need to," she said, turning to gaze at the forest. "He knows this terrain, so he just needs to take them on one at a time. Do you know his history?"

Abby shook her head as she ate. Like Rice, it seemed she hadn't realized how hungry she was until food was at her disposal.

Rice thought for a second and then told her story.

"He was awarded the Medal of Honor for facing odds greater than that in Vietnam, and he probably should have been awarded another for a rescue he did in the late 1970s. I'm not supposed to know about that, but ever since my first encounter with him in the Philippines, I've had an interest in why he does what he does. He takes on the odds but isn't reckless with his safety or the safety of the people who work for him."

"He leads from the front, that's for sure," commented Abby.

"He has to get his family out before these guys kill them," continued Rice, "and he's not going to do something stupid like get hurt or killed before he's able to do that."

"Do you really think they intend to kill the hostages?"

"Yes." The answer came from the ledge above them.

Both Abby and Rice jumped and were surprised to see a familiar figure above them on the ledge. A smile sliced through the dark camouflage paint on the man's face. "The whole idea of grabbing who they did was to eliminate who Dick Kingston perceives as his enemies. Unfortunately, most of them are innocents." He shrugged, adding, "Sorry to scare you ladies, but I seemed to have stirred up a hornet's nest down there, so I took the long way back."

"Jesus, Jon!" blurted Abby. "You scared the hell out of me!"

Rice exhaled deeply. "Man, have I lost my edge; I never heard you coming."

Jon motioned for them to stay down and out of sight and then disappeared back up the ledge for a minute. He returned carrying some additional weapons and gingerly made his way down to the cave entrance. Rice grabbed the extra weapons he was carrying, and he put down a pack filled with handguns, knives, and ammunition. Before he could say anything, Abby threw her arms around him, hugging him. "You're crazy, you know that?" she said softly. "But now I know where Stephen gets it from."

She released him, and he smiled at his youngest son's girlfriend. Jon and Rice exchanged glances.

"I didn't want to get shot coming in from a direction you didn't expect me."

"I still should have heard you coming," said the marine. "I've been inside too long—I need to get back in the field."

"You did pretty damn good earlier this afternoon," commented Summers. "You both did. We didn't take any casualties; they took eight."

"Eight?" said both women.

Summers showed no expression; they both knew enough not to ask more questions.

"They're a bit busy down there at the moment and won't be after us for a while," said Jon. "Why don't you two help me carry in these weapons and ammunition? I want to see the grandkids, get a bite to eat if there's any left, and take a nap."

Both women smiled, helping him pick up the rifles. They disappeared into the cave.

Summers' Cabin
Adirondack State Park, New York
July 19, 2010
1800 hours

They had been cooking for over an hour to feed their captors. The easiest thing to make was spaghetti and meat sauce for everyone. They were cooking all the frozen ground beef from the freezer, and there was plenty of macaroni and bread to go around, so nobody complained about being hungry.

Julie and Alex were helping Nancy in the kitchen. Nancy was used to having Sarah or one of Matt's girls help, and things generally went well. Neither her sister-in-law nor her niece were comfortable in this kitchen, and it showed with how long it took them to prepare the meal. The kitchen was hot and the ventilation poor, so Alex complained more than she helped. She was being a typical teenager who didn't want to be there. The fact that there were guards with guns standing in the doorway was probably the only thing keeping her from sneaking off. Julie worked hard but was visibly uncomfortable being so close to Hapke, who stayed in the next room. She'd become more emotional with the revelation of how her husband really died. Hector was a decorated policeman they thought had died in an accidental car crash. To have Hapke admit to killing him had been a shock to everyone. Nancy guessed Julie was feeling guilty she dated his killer for a time. She moved over to where her sister-in-law stood stirring a pot of sauce on the propane stove.

"Are you doing okay, kiddo?" Nancy asked, checking on some of the cooking meat.

Julie shook her head, and Nancy could see tears forming in her eyes. Her voice was a rasp when she said, "I slept with him, Nancy . . . I slept with that monster a year after he killed Hector with that car crash."

"Mom?" Alex stood behind the other two women, frozen and visibly in shock. There was a look of revulsion on her face. The tears Julie had been holding back let loose, streaming down her cheeks.

"Alex . . ." Nancy's voice was calm but direct. "Your mother had no way of knowing what that man had done. In some way, I'm sure the sick bastard thought it was funny, but you can't blame her—she didn't know."

Nancy held her niece's gaze, and the teenager's look finally softened. She rushed to her mother and threw her arms around her. Nancy fought back tears herself watching the two women crying. Julie hugged her daughter, looking at Nancy while mouthing the words "thank you." After a moment, both Julie and Alex regained their composure and stood over the pot of sauce, watching it bubble.

Alex looked over to her aunt. "What will Uncle Jon and Uncle Matt do when they find out about Mom and Mr. Hapke, Aunt Nancy?"

"I expect they'll draw straws to see who'll deal with the man. I don't give him much of a chance of getting out of here with his life."

"They'll kill him?"

"If I don't kill him first," said Julie. Her voice was clipped, emotionless—stating not a threat, but a promise. The look on her face let both Alex and Nancy know she was serious.

Hidden Cave
Summers' Island
July 19, 2010
1800 hours

Summers was greeted by hugs and kisses from all the freed hostages when he entered the cave with Abby and Rice. Eyebrows rose when the kisses from O'Leary were a little more passionate than expected. Summers managed to pry himself loose from the senator and check on the condition of Sheriff James. He spent several minutes detailing the running firefight when he drew the pursuers away from the escapees. James thanked him for not killing all four of the men but editorialized he would have understood if that wasn't possible.

Abby took control of the weapons he brought back with him—cleaning them with a small bottle of CLP and stockpiling them with the rest.

"When did you find this cave, Uncle Jon?" asked Emily, handing him a warm plate of macaroni and cheese. "In all the years we've been coming here, I didn't know this place existed. When I get ahold of my cousins, I'll slap them silly for not showing me this place."

Jon smiled. "Be easy on them, Em—they couldn't tell you because they didn't know about it either."

"Then who did?"

"Just your grandfather, your dad, and me. We found it when we were playing as kids, and your grandpa helped us build it into a fort. It was our place to go hide and play. I used to come here a lot after returning from Vietnam and leaving the Navy. As we got older, we made a few improvements."

"Electricity," chimed in Abby. "That's quite an improvement."

Jon nodded. "It was hard running the cables and getting everything wired up. Matt did most of the wiring, and no one questioned the two extra circuits in the breaker box in the boathouse because he controlled the work being done. We never left any of that work to you kids—even Stephen, and he lives here year-round."

Abby and Emily looked at each other, still trying to grasp that no one in the family knew about the cave.

Abby spoke first. "So, no one knows about this place?"

Jon grinned. "I'm going to guess your grandfather does, because he and my father had few secrets, but you know Fred—I'm guessing he's told no one."

"I would have thought you would've told the boys," said Emily. "I mean, this place is such a guy thing."

Jon chuckled at his niece's comment. "Your dad and I made an agreement that we would eventually tell all of you when the time was right. I think that's been done at this point."

Sarah brought her father-in-law a hot cup of tea. As he took it, thanking her, he noted the sad look on her face. "Why the long face?"

"I was just thinking of Justin and how he would have loved this place, Dad."

A strange smile crossed Jon's face. "You'll find that out this evening."

Sarah's brows furrowed as she thought about her brother-in-law, casting a confused look at Emily, who shrugged.

Jon reached for Sarah's forearm, holding it softly. They locked their eyes. "Justin's not dead like everyone thought, kiddo. It's so unfair that you two weren't told this until now, but clearly, it looks to be a family tradition to fake our deaths at some point."

"What?" Sarah asked shrilly, face pale.

"Sean, Stephen, and Justin will be here tonight with some friends to help get everyone out of this cave and back to the mainland," Jon confirmed.

Everyone in the cave turned to look at Jon, who seemed to be ignoring their response. He went over to where the clothing and supplies were stored, pulling out a small pillow and blanket. They all watched while he made himself a bed near the wall of the cave that was free of anything else. He took off his web belt and combat harness, placing them near the pillow.

Sarah, Emily, and the children quietly approached, looking very somber. Sarah asked, "Justin's really alive?"

Jon nodded as he fluffed the pillow. Sarah grabbed her father-in-law's arm and pulled him close. As Emily joined the hug she whispered, "Aunt Nancy's going to kick your butt, Uncle Jon."

Jon kissed both of them on the forehead, and they released their hold on him, returning to the others. He looked at his two grandchildren, who moved next to him, giving him hugs.

"RJ," he said to his grandson, "can you make sure they wake me up at nine o'clock?"

"Is Daddy really coming?" RJ asked hopefully.

"Sure is," answered Jon, hugging the two children back. "And when he gets here, he'll be taking you, Patty, and your mom away from the bad men who kidnapped you."

"I love you, Grandpa," said Patty, quietly hugging him again.

"I'll make sure you're awake at nine," said RJ, returning his grandfather's smile.

Both children gave him one last hug, and then Jon lay down on the blanket, head on the pillow, and covered his face with his boonie cap.

On the other side of the cave, O'Leary said, "Damn!"

Sarah and Emily noticed a tear in the woman's eye and exchanged a curious glance, remembering the senator's conversation with Nancy the night before.

Abby just rolled her eyes.

Mohawk Tavern and Grill
Bluffton, New York
July 19, 2010
1900 hours

Justin loaded the equipment they would need into the back of two vans. They had to be as quiet and discrete as possible, seeing as much of the media was just on the other side of the wall. He found it funny he was selected to be part of the team to go to the island and secure the hostages. The entire team was off the books, and he guessed the main assault force was going to be made up of more than the FBI SWAT teams. He'd heard Putnum speaking to Washington and knew the man would get approval for whatever he had in mind—it would just take time. Justin focused on checking the equipment, making sure everything was in order.

"You look pretty healthy for a dead man."

Justin turned to find Mike Skier standing behind him. The bulge under the light jacket told Justin he was wearing a ballistic vest beneath his civilian clothes and likely working as part of the security detail Putnum set up.

"Mike," Justin acknowledged his old teammate, "you look pretty good for a guy who was going to leave the Navy a few years back. What changed your mind?"

Skier moved next to Justin, leaning on the van. "It seems some friends of mine were listed as missing and presumed dead on a mission a few years ago. Because I made it back, I felt guilty and stayed in. Figured the least I could do is keep these young officers from putting themselves in the same situation. What about Scotty?"

Justin closed his eyes for a moment, thinking about Ensign Jimmy Scott, who had been their second-in-command. Scotty was a bright kid with a lot of potential. He and Justin were captured on that last mission. Both were tortured, and Scott had eventually died due to injuries sustained from that torture. Justin still had nightmares about that time of his life.

"Scotty died while we were being held prisoner," he said softly. "They beat us almost daily and questioned us in some unique ways. One day, Scotty didn't come back."

"Then how do you know he's dead?" The tone of Skier's voice was angry and bordered on accusatory.

Justin's eyes flashed a warning, but his voice remained even. "Because they hung his fucking body outside the cage they were holding me in so I could look at it every day for over a week—at least I think it was that long, as there was no way of knowing without a window to tell me when it was night or day." At this, Skier's face went pale. "When I escaped, they told me I had been gone for over two years. I had no concept of time after the first couple of weeks. Nothing they ever trained us for prepared me for what Scotty and I were put through."

"How'd you get away?" Skier's tone had softened.

"What'd they tell you about that mission?"

"Just what they briefed us on, and when the rest of us got back, they just told us that Chief Thompson was really a bad guy and led us into that trap. I stayed in to get a crack at him. I have a guy at Naval Intelligence who's keeping an ear to the ground about Thompson. If he surfaces, he's assured me a shot at the asshole."

Justin scoffed. "Mikey, your intel guy either isn't worth a crap, or he's leading you on."

Skier looked puzzled at Justin's reaction.

"You might as well retire, buddy," continued Justin, "because I killed the son of a bitch when I escaped."

Skier was slow to respond—first with a blank look of nonunderstanding, which was then slowly replaced by a look of surprise. Finally, a cruel smile crept across his face. "I assume, then, that you did the job right. Was it painful?"

"I don't really know, Mike," said Justin after a few seconds of silence. "I just know it was something I had to do. I can tell you he knew who I was before he died. I needed him to know that—for both Scotty and for the team."

There was an awkward silence before Skier asked the question he'd been wanting to ask since he first saw Justin earlier that day.

"Who knows?" Skier sounded uncomfortable. "I mean, obviously Captain Mitchell knows because he's your boss, but what about Cory and Shelly?"

Justin thought of Shelly Mitchell-Hayes and her husband, Cory Hayes. Shelly was Tom Mitchell's daughter and had been Justin's fiancée until he had been listed as killed in action. Cory had been a shipmate and teammate of Justin's. They'd been married two years after he'd been taken prisoner. Shelly now managed the tavern she'd worked in when they were engaged, and Cory left the Navy and was working as a civilian contractor. They still lived in Virginia Beach. Justin did his best to forget that part of his life, but it all came rushing back.

"Justin . . ." Skier saw the confusion sweep across his former teammate's face. "You okay, buddy?"

"I'm fine." Justin nodded, holding up his hand. "No, they don't know. They can't know."

"I think they deserve to know." Skier's tone was factual, with no sign of emotion.

Justin shook his head. "No, if only for Tom's sake. Shelly would never forgive him. I can't have Cory and Shelly second-guessing their relationship or what they did. They were told I was dead; I'm satisfied to leave it that way."

"Come on, Justin. Give them more credit than that," said Skier, but Justin shook his head in a way that made it clear this conversation was over. "So, they told no one?"

"They apparently told my father, because he tracked me down for this."

Skier chuckled. "The admiral does have a reputation among the teams. Even when he was overseas in Iraq and Afghanistan, there were rumors of him going off the reservation. Saving an aircrew here and a patrol there—not singlehandedly, mind you, but the rumors were out there. The scuttlebutt was he was looking for you. Made quite a name for himself among the rank and file when he was around a battle zone. They weren't used to seeing someone of his reputation still sticking his neck out like that. I heard they finally pulled him off his assignment over there and sent him home. That must be when they told him because the rumors stopped at that point."

Justin shrugged his shoulders nonchalantly. "That sounds like Dad, all right. Say, how about you give me a hand with the rest of the equipment?"

Skier looked at Justin for a few seconds, then threw his arms around his old teammate, giving him a hug. "It's good to have you back, buddy."

United States Disciplinary Barracks
Fort Leavenworth, Kansas
July 19, 2010
1800 hours

Kingston rested on his steel detention bunk, reading a week-old newspaper article on the economy and how it was being affected by the slump in the housing market. He spent all but two hours of his day there, in his cell. He was kept isolated much of the time, with few visitors stopping to see him. His ex-wife hadn't taken the time to see him since he'd been imprisoned. There were the occasional reporters looking for a story, and one author visited several times for research purposes. Now, his new lawyer was the only regular visitor, and his children only saw him occasionally. His father had come to see him several times before his death; the last time was to tell him that he'd been removed from the old man's will.

Kingston was not bothered by the solitude. It was helpful in his planning. He'd set everything in motion years before, with the help of coded messages sent to friends and allies on the outside. Not everyone had abandoned him, and now was his time to show those who put him in here he was smarter than they were. He proved in the Navy he was a master tactician and able to outwit his foes over the years.

The one exception was Summers. He'd grossly underestimated the man and had paid the price for it. It was a heavy price, but his revenge on Summers was slow and deliberate. He'd cost Summers a son—killed in combat—and a marriage. Kingston had rejoiced the day he received word that

Nancy Summers had separated from him over the loss of their middle son. Kingston was only giving Summers a small taste of what he'd been through when he was convicted of treason and imprisoned.

That didn't matter much now. Summers was now floating dead in a Canadian lake, the victim of a mysterious assassin. The same should be true of that marine, Ellison, who'd almost shot him. He should be lying dead on a farm in Virginia. Ellison would have known before he died that he shouldn't have listened to the NCIS agent and killed him anyway. He was told in the last message he received that his people couldn't get close to Agent Grey, of the FBI, or Admiral Putnum due to the tight security around them. He didn't care; after tomorrow, they would spend the rest of their lives looking over their shoulder. That was enough for Kingston. The rest of the conspirators involved with his arrest would be killed by the man he selected to oversee the kidnapping. There might be innocent people there as well, but he didn't care. If they were with either the Summers family or his ex-wife, they wouldn't be all that innocent. The man he'd put in command was a coward and psychotic. When everything would begin to fall apart—and it would, because the FBI was efficient—he would kill all the hostages. This man and those with him were expendable and would be sacrificed to provide a smoke screen for his actual plan. Kingston's key people were good at their jobs and knew when to leave to meet him.

He heard footsteps out in the corridor, followed by the whine of a door at the end of the cellblock being unlocked. He prepared himself, because it might be time. His lawyer was an unwitting accomplice. He carried the coded messages to those on the outside, thinking they were going to family contacts. Little did his lawyer know his ex-wife and the cripple she married would be dead by this time tomorrow. When Fiona married Ericson, he'd been in a rage for weeks. She'd married one of the men who helped to put him in prison.

The footsteps in the corridor stopped outside his cell door, and he heard the buzz of the lock. The door swung open. Standing outside were seven uniformed Army guards. They carried expandable batons but no other weapons. He remained on his bunk, watching the first two guards enter and do a quick sweep of the room. They were followed by two more guards, one carrying several ditty bags and the other carrying a set of hand and ankle irons. Kingston smiled. His plan had worked. Then, two officers entered the cell. One was a second lieutenant who Kingston knew to be the shift commander. The other was the major who was the deputy commander of the disciplinary barracks. He oversaw what was taking place.

"Pack all of his belongings in the bags," said the major, "along with two complete changes of clothing. Come on, Kingston—stand up. You're going on a trip."

Kingston responded slowly, first moving to a sitting position, then standing next to his bunk. One of the guards moved in close and motioned for him to put his hands on top of his head. He complied, and the guard immediately patted him down to make sure he didn't have anything on his person that could be used as a weapon. When that guard stepped back, the other carrying the shackles moved in, and they both began to put them on their prisoner.

"May I ask what's going on, Major?" Kingston asked politely.

"You're taking a trip this evening," the major responded. "I'm sure you're aware as to why we're doing this, aren't you, Mr. Kingston?"

"I have absolutely no idea. What's going on?"

A quick survey of all the guards' faces showed Kingston not one of the men believed him. He couldn't let on that he knew anything, just in case this was a ploy to get information. All the scenarios showed he would be moved, and if that indeed was the case, he knew he just needed patience and he would be free shortly. Kingston stood quietly as the guards finished putting the shackles on.

"Seriously, Major, I have no idea what you're talking about," Kingston added with his best impression of innocence, but the officer only grunted in reply, looking around the cell to make sure his men completed their tasks. Kingston looked down at his restraints, allowing his tone to sound a bit angry. "Has my attorney been notified about this?"

The major looked at the prisoner with disdain. "You're being moved by executive order, and your attorney is being notified as we speak. He's been asked to be available to travel as well. He'll meet you at your destination in the morning."

"I'd feel better if I could talk to him now."

The major ignored the request and looked to his subordinate. "Bring him now."

The lieutenant responded with a "Yes, sir!"

The guards took Kingston's arms, leading him out the door. The shackles didn't allow him to move fast. No one noticed the look of satisfaction on his face while they slowly moved down the corridor.

Logan International Airport
Boston, Massachusetts
July 19, 2010
1945 hours

The hum of the twin engines as they taxied for takeoff—rather than the roar of people jockeying for a position in the many never-ending lines of the airport terminal, or the frenetic energy wafting off those late for their flight—was a relief. Indeed, the comfort and solitude of the G650 was quite refreshing.

Right after Evans boarded his plane, he poured himself a glass of Connemara Irish whiskey, settling on the couch in the rear of the aircraft to reflect on his day. He was exhausted and planned on getting some sleep during this flight.

He stayed with his surveillance of the target until he was sure she was on her plane and the jetway had been pulled away from the aircraft. He didn't want to take any chances she might be able to disembark before the aircraft left the gate. When he checked in to say that the target's plane was being wheeled away from the gate, he was told to go to a gate farther down the terminal and check in with the agent there. When he did, he was surprised with how fast he was ushered outside onto the tarmac to a waiting car.

From there, he was driven directly to his plane. He checked in during the short drive and was told via text that his plane had been cleared to Dulles International Airport outside of Washington, DC. A surveillance team was already in place to pick up the target. The instructions he received were specific, and he knew walking away would be pointless. The organization displayed by the people Smith—or whoever this was—was staggering. They were cool—and, for the most part, professional. Aside from the initial teams he'd spotted in Boston, he guessed there were others he did not. Given the time to prepare for the target's arrival at Dulles, he guessed the teams there would be hard to spot. Smith was not a man to cross, and besides, he had a personal interest in this. No, he was hooked and there was no backing out.

The whine of the engines increased, and Evans felt the G650 turn, increasing speed. He glanced out the window across from him and saw the scenery outside move by faster and faster. In a few seconds, the nose of the aircraft lifted off the runway, and then he felt the sensation of the whole plane rising. They were off the ground and on their way to Dulles.

He looked around the cabin and sighed. He was alone on the plane except for the pilot and copilot. He downed the last of his whiskey and sprawled out on the couch. He told the pilot he was going to get some sleep and to wake him when they arrived at Dulles. He fell asleep almost immediately.

Oceana Naval Air Station
Virginia Beach, Virginia
July 19, 2010
2000 hours

The two C-17 Globemaster III military transports sat on the tarmac under heavy guard. The cargo was loaded onto both aircraft and had been secured less than an hour before. The aircraft crews were currently receiving their final briefings. The operation was waiting for the last of the personnel to arrive and would leave as soon as they were there. Standing near the ramp of the first aircraft, a Navy lieutenant looked around nervously. This was his cargo and his mission, so he naturally wanted it underway as soon as possible.

The call was last minute, but then again, in this line of work, it often was. The men they were waiting for needed to be called in, allowed to pick up their equipment at the Little Creek Amphibious Base on the other side of Virginia Beach, and then be shuttled here to Oceana. This had to be important, because the number of guards around the aircraft doubled since his arrival with the cargo. They were all heavily armed, and none looked to be in a good mood.

He asked the three officers assigned to the security detail if they had any information about what was happening. The first two said they didn't know anything, and the third said nothing, just looking at him and walking away.

Two black SUVs came from around one of the hangers, moving slowly toward the aircraft. They were stopped by one of the security people, who spent some time at each vehicle, speaking to whoever was inside. The lieutenant assumed the man was checking IDs. When he finished, the two vehicles continued toward the aircraft. The SUVs stopped where he was standing, the doors opened, and men exited each vehicle. They were dressed similarly to him, but he could tell they were all shooters based on the way they carried themselves, the quiet confidence brought on from training and experience. They unloaded several duffel bags from the vehicles, which quickly moved off when they finished.

The lieutenant recognized one of the men. He was an officer he worked with in the past. He was a SEAL, commanding an eight-man squad. The second officer, also a lieutenant, waved an acknowledgement to him. They approached one another, exchanging greetings.

"Do you have any idea what's going on?" asked the first officer.

The SEAL shook his head. "No, I was hoping you could tell me. I'm guessing this thing in New York might have something to do with this, but I was told I'd be briefed in flight."

"That's what I was told, too. New York doesn't make sense, though. They don't use people like us in domestic situations."

"How long you been here?"

The lieutenant checked his watch. "Going on two hours now."

His counterpart nodded. "When we were loading for the trip here, scuttlebutt came down the chain of command that this is big. The orders are coming from the top. Word is the FBI has been compromised and they need to have a plan that's foolproof. Apparently, the hostages are high-ranking political subjects, and we already have boots on the ground up there. It makes sense to send both of our units. Who's better suited to do a rescue from an island?"

The lieutenant noticed the flight crews returning from operations and motioned for his friend to take notice.

"It shouldn't be long now," replied the SEAL officer.

The loadmaster for the aircraft came jogging up to them.

"Sirs." The senior enlisted man fired off a casual salute. "As soon as the rest of your people get here, we'll get underway."

Before either officer could respond, the man boarded the aircraft and began to check the cargo, making sure everything was tightly secured one more time. It wasn't long before they heard the roar of jet engines starting up. An unmarked coach bus pulled out onto the tarmac from between two of the buildings. It only took a minute for the bus to reach the two aircraft, coming to a stop between them. The door opened, and twenty-seven sailors exited as fast as they could. Each carried a duffel bag, and they formed two lines next to the bus, their duffels sitting on the ground next to each man. The lieutenant walked over, giving directions. When he finished, the men picked up their gear, walking up the ramp of the aircraft they were assigned to. The eight SEALs boarded the aircraft the lieutenant was on. When the last man boarded, the ramps came up, and the huge transports began to taxi.

Upton's Marina and Boat Sales
Bluffton, New York
July 19, 2010
2030 hours

Sanderson called a meeting of all his key people to pass on the news. His entire staff, plus the US Attorney's Office, was present. Each looked anxious for the meeting to start, as they were anticipating approval for a rescue for first thing in the morning. The men who put the assault plan together sat near the maps on the table, smiling smugly. They all were briefed on their aspect of the mission to rescue the hostages, but no one knew the entire plan. That was about to change.

"We received the green light to go in first thing in the morning," said Sanderson to the group, telling them what they wanted to hear. A cheer went up among the agents gathered around the table. "We start at seven in the morning, hitting the island at seven-thirty. Because our explosives and ordinance disposal unit are worried about IEDs, we've decided on a daylight assault. I don't want any more casualties than necessary."

There were some moans from around the room, as they had been debating a daylight assault versus a night assault most of the day. Both plans had advantages and disadvantages.

"We're missing some of our assault boats," commented his communications man. "We're four short and don't have enough to send all our teams in right now. I've sent out some inquiries to see what happened to them, but I'm getting pushback from our people in supply, saying all available boats have been sent and they have no more. Without those boats, we can't mount a full assault. Some boats will have to come back to get the remaining teams."

"My god, man," said the junior tactical advisor. "We're on a lake, and you mean to tell me we can't come up with four more boats?"

A hard look from Sanderson silenced the agent. He knew his outburst was out of line. Sanderson said nothing to him but looked toward Grey on the other side of the table. "Agent Grey, would you follow up on that issue?"

Grey nodded, expression serious. "I'll chase the missing boats down, sir."

Sanderson turned to his senior tactical advisor, giving him a nod. He then provided the group with a detailed description of the assault that was to take place in the morning. They would use the RIB assault craft to take them to an inlet to the west of the cabin complex and land there. It was an isolated cove on the island with heavy forest for cover that would allow them to organize once the assault teams were on the shore. It also allowed them cover to move east and assault the cabin complex. Heavy fog was expected in the morning and would help provide cover for the landing. There were several questions regarding the assault, but they were quickly answered, and the briefing ended after forty-five minutes.

Sanderson looked around the room. Now that they had been given the green light to move, the tension in the room was easily sensed. He knew his people would do their jobs and there would be a successful conclusion to the operation. He looked at Ramsey. "Do we have any word from Mr. Trask and his dealings with the state attorney general?"

"No, sir, he's still in Albany, and I understand that New York State has contacted a federal judge about the jurisdiction issue. He'll be busy for some time on that topic."

"Then when we end this tomorrow, the issue of jurisdiction will be a moot point," Sanderson said with a smile. There was some laughter around the room. "One more thing, people," Sanderson added, his tone serious again. "Despite my objections, Richard Kingston and his coconspirator, Andrea Handcock, are being moved from their current locations in prison to an undisclosed facility near Washington."

The room fell silent.

"We have to be successful tomorrow. We can't let this guy get away with this."

Everyone in the room stood quietly for a moment. Eventually, the meeting began to break up. No one noticed Grey speak to the senior tactical advisor and walk out with him.

Summers' Cabin
Adirondack State Park, New York
July 19, 2010
2200 hours

Nancy was exhausted. She finished the last of the dishes and cleaned off the kitchen counter. Alex dried the dishes while her mother put them away. They spent over four hours cooking all the food their captors brought from the boathouse. Both Alex and Julie looked as tired as she felt when they finished.

The guards didn't bother them while they went about their tasks, and Nancy guessed this nightmare would be coming to an end soon, one way or another. They served food to the other hostages and would now take a few minutes to feed themselves while they finished in the kitchen. Nancy looked out the window, noticing the ground fog hanging low over the meadow between the cabins and the tree line. She loved this weather on the island because it meant the fog would be low among the trees as well, giving off that enchanted forest look. It was beautiful, and she and Jon used to walk in the forest on nights like this. She missed those walks.

It also meant the fog on the lake and along the shoreline would be thick and impossible to see through. Even as tired as she was, she knew something would be happening tonight. It *had* to happen tonight. She guessed it would be more like a horror movie than a fairy tale. Some nasty things would be coming out of the fog.

Her thought process was interrupted by Servati when she entered the kitchen. "Are you done in here? It's time to go back with the others."

Nancy gave their female captor an exhausted look. "We're just now eating. Can we please finish?"

Julie and Alex didn't even acknowledge the woman's presence—they just kept eating the food they had put on the plates in front of them. Servati didn't show any emotion, shaking her head as she said, "You can take your food with you, but I need you back with the others."

The three women looked at each other, hesitating.

"*Now*, ladies!" Servati's voice hardened. The three women took their plates and were escorted out to the living room to join the others. As they walked through the doorway from the kitchen to the living room, they could see Hapke and several other kidnappers busy working on some incoming communications. Servati took note of the look of hatred all three women gave the man. Julie and Alex settled on the floor next to the couch where Hector was asleep. Nancy settled on the floor next to the chair where Josh was, receiving a hug from Fiona sitting next to her. Most of the hostages were sleeping, or at least trying to. The room was dark, the only illumination coming from the equipment the kidnappers were using in the dining room.

Servati moved back to the kitchen doorway. She continued to watch the hostages to make sure they were going to settle and was startled when Hapke appeared next to her. He motioned for her to follow him into the kitchen. She took one last look at the hostages and then followed.

"They'll be coming in the morning," he said quietly. "Our contact has them coming in west of here at that little cove. They're hoping to use the fog and heavy forest to get in here, but we'll be there to meet them when they try to land. They won't stand a chance."

"What about the hostages?"

"They're in the process of moving Kingston, so the plan's working. The hostages die, just like the plan says."

Servati had no problem with killing if it was needed, but it looked like everything was falling into place. She didn't see the need for senseless killing. "Once he's away, do we need to kill the hostages? It'll just bring more heat down on us."

"If they're moving him, then he's all but gotten away, so if we want to get paid, the hostages die. We do as we're told. Understood?"

Servati gave him a quiet nod but otherwise didn't reply.

Hapke continued, "I'm guessing our employer doesn't expect us to survive this little mission, but I for one plan on leaving this island alive. You take two people and secure our boats. That'll leave me with twenty-six people to ambush the FBI. That should be more than enough to set the ambush since we have surprise and excellent cover."

"How many teams are coming?" asked Servati, looking back at the hostages. They had all finally settled.

"Eight teams in the initial assault and two in reserve."

"Jesus!" Servati exclaimed, looking surprised. "That's almost a hundred agents on the assault with another twenty-four in reserve. We can't stop that. These guys are the best of the best, and once they land, we'll never be able to hold them."

"That's the key—they can't land. We hit them while they're still coming in, while they're out in the open on the water. With all that confusion, they'll send their reserves to the cabin here, but we'll blow it and take care of the hostages. We hightail it to the boats and escape across the lake."

Servati didn't answer.

"With the cabin being blown and hostages killed, they'll be too busy to follow us for a while," continued Hapke, sounding more than just a little proud of himself. "I bet it buys us an hour or more. That's enough time to get to our transportation in Dartford and get out of the area."

Servati nodded, and a smile crept across her face. "It just might work. Damn, it might work."

Servati kissed her boss hard on the lips, not caring if anyone saw her. Everyone on their team suspected they were sleeping together, so why should she care? Now it looked like the two of them might get out of here alive and rich. She left the cabin to get her two volunteers and secure their boats.

Mohawk Tavern and Grill
Bluffton, New York
July 19, 2010
2230 hours

As soon as word got out that the FBI was going to officially launch their next rescue mission, the media returned to their news stations, networks, and newspapers to prepare their next reports. This left the Mohawk Tavern and Grill surprisingly empty for the first time in twenty-four hours.

There were thirty minutes before the networks announced this entire fiasco was a ploy to win the release of Richard Kingston from prison. There wasn't much debate between the conservative and liberal media outlets because Kingston was convicted of murder and treason and no one wanted to defend the man. The only debate was whether he should have been put to death after his conviction, and that was being downplayed with hostages' lives on the line.

Sandy Monroe sat alone at the bar. She sipped her drink and watched a competing network on TV while mulling over a few things she'd noticed since her arrival in Bluffton. First, the comment she'd overheard about Jon Summers possibly being alive—no one had denied it. Next, there were also a lot of faces that didn't look like members of the media or like they belonged to the FBI. She looked at the young man behind the bar—he didn't fit. He was too clean-cut for a rural bar. She would have expected longer hair and maybe some facial hair. No, he wasn't right for Bluffton, but he did make a mean drink. She ordered another.

While the bartender was making her drink, a couple sat down at the bar next to her. The woman was pretty, and the man was handsome; she thought they looked good together, but they didn't seem to fit here, either. The man looked familiar, but Sandy was positive they hadn't met before. Movement behind her made her jump as another man moved up to the bar on the other side of her.

He looked at her, smiling meekly. "Sorry, ma'am, I didn't mean to startle you."

Sandy held his gaze. "That's okay. Everyone's a little on edge with all this business."

It was a bit strange that nobody else had ordered a drink yet. She glanced at the couple and found them both watching her. Her instincts told her this was trouble and to run, but the reporter in her said she was going to get a story out of this.

"Miss Monroe," said the man beside her, "my name's Bryan Kingston."

Sandy felt the panic rise into her throat, and when she glanced at the man on the other side of her, she noticed the gun under his jacket for the first time.

"Please, Miss Monroe," continued Kingston. "You have nothing to fear. We're not here to do you harm. I have nothing to do with my father's bid to escape justice."

The words he chose piqued her interest. "Then why are you here, Mr. Kingston?"

She thought the man looked far too serious for someone his age. She guessed it made him look older than he should.

"Miss Monroe, I'm Commander Stephnie Smith with Naval Intelligence. Commander Kingston's here because his mother is one of the hostages. That's not why Chief Skier and I are here—well, not exactly, but their safe release is paramount."

Sandy looked from the woman to the man with the gun under his jacket. He smiled pleasantly, nodding. She looked back at Smith. "I assume you're here to help with the rescue, Commander?"

"The FBI has refused our help, but Admiral Putnum has other plans for us."

"Putnum?" Monroe looked as if a lightbulb had gone off. "The old guy with the Gateways. He's the deputy director of the NSA. I knew I'd seen him somewhere."

Smith nodded her head, saying nothing.

"So," Monroe went on, "I assume there's an operation underway to rescue the hostages, or you wouldn't be here talking to me. How soon does it take place?"

"It's been underway for some time," said Kingston. "Some of the hostages have already been freed."

"I knew it—you guys already have boots on the ground. How many troops do you have on the island?"

"One," answered Smith.

Sandy was shocked by the answer and was silent for a moment before that lightbulb went off again. "Jon Summers," she said. "Damn, he is alive."

"You already know the first rescue attempt was ambushed, and the sheriff and one of his deputies are missing, right?" Smith surmised, and Sandy nodded. "He saved them and has been hiding them somewhere on the island. He and the deputy freed six of the hostages, including a Marine Corps colonel. The hostage takers have taken some casualties and now have consolidated their position on the island."

"Won't that make it tougher to get the rest of the hostages out?"

"There's always a danger that something can go wrong in one of these operations, but with the team that's been assembled, those odds should be reduced and make rescue easier."

"I know this guy, Sanderson. He's a by-the-book type of agent. I doubt he'll approve anything that might be the least bit out of the ordinary."

Neither Smith nor Kingston responded. Instead, they merely maintained eye contact with Sandy, whose mind raced as she put together what the implications of the silence meant. "Sanderson doesn't know, does he?"

There was more silence.

"Jesus!" said Sandy, clapping a hand over her mouth. "Putnum's running his own operation . . . The military's going in, aren't they?"

Kingston looked at Smith, a smile finally crossing his face. "Well, that clinches it—she knows, and now we have to take care of her. We can't have her talking."

Sandy hesitated, becoming very serious. "Is this where you make me disappear and lock me away? That's not legal, you know—and neither is using the military for something like this."

Kingston laughed, shaking his head. "Nothing that dramatic, ma'am. Besides, if we even contemplated such a thing, we'd get our butts kicked by Admiral Summers. We can't take the chance you'll talk to anyone, so as of now, you're embedded with one of the rescue teams. You'll be coming with us for a boat ride."

Sandy blinked in disbelief. She saw Smith grin at her reaction, but before she could comment, the bartender brought her two drinks. She looked at the young man behind the bar silently for a few moments, still shocked at what she had just heard.

"Um, excuse me," she said at last, "I only ordered one drink."

The young man didn't look up as he said, "You'll need both drinks if you're coming with us, ma'am. If you think it'll help, I can make one to go."

Summers' Island
Adirondack State Park, New York
July 19, 2010
2330 hours

Servati and her two companions made their way to the base of the rocky hill that dominated this side of the island. This was where they'd stashed the inflatable boats for their escape. It was a short ride across the lake to the mainland, and then a walk through the forest to where their ride would be waiting. If their luck held out, it was a good plan.

Servati was on the lookout for whoever freed the one group of hostages, because they could be a threat to that plan. So far, there was no sign of them; they were probably holed up for the night somewhere safe.

The ground fog and overcast sky made the forest seem eerie. She was walking point, and for all her experience, she felt more on edge than she knew she should. She guessed all the talk of spirits by the old Indian, the firefight with the man who seemed to rise out of nowhere, and now the fog all contributed to how she felt. She tried to clear her thoughts and focused on the task at hand.

Servati brought one of the other female hostage takers with her, along with one of the men, who was only slightly wounded. She signaled for her two companions to stop and then set up security while she checked the boats. They complied while she cautiously moved forward on the trail to where the first boat was covered with brush. The outline of the craft was clearly visible under its camouflage.

Servati slowly and quietly uncovered the boat, seeing that the gear they kept inside looked undisturbed. Satisfied everything looked in place, she allowed herself a smile for a few moments, but that quickly disappeared. Something didn't look right. The boat looked like it settled low to the ground; it shouldn't have. They'd brought five of the craft because they were collapsible, lightweight, and fast. Each was outfitted with outboard motors to propel it the short distance to the mainland. There was enough room to comfortably accommodate eight people. They wouldn't need all five boats.

Servati touched the tube on the side of the boat and immediately knew what was wrong. The tough material gave way, because there was no air in the tube. Instinct made her look back down the trail. Both of her companions were still in place, providing security. She let out her breath, clearing her head again. There was no reason for the fog to freak her out so much, but it was. There were still four more boats to use—more than enough for those who were left—but curiosity made her check to see why the tubes were not inflated like they should be. It took less than a minute to find out why. The tubes were slashed in several places by something very sharp, probably a knife.

Panic rose in her throat, tightening her chest, and she checked her security, again. They were still in place. She forced herself not to panic further, moving on to the next boat. She quietly uncovered it, finding it to be in the same condition. All the gear in the boat was undisturbed, but the tubes were slashed. She moved to the third boat, realizing that it too was sitting low under the brush that covered it.

Her worst fear had been confirmed: the boats had been discovered by whoever freed the hostages, and he'd known just what to do to disable them. From where she stood, she could see the remaining boats. Her panic was now out of control, showing clearly on her face.

Whoever this was could have used the boats to escape at any time, but didn't. That meant there was no intention of leaving the island. *He was here to fight.* That wasn't good news, because he obviously knew what he was doing.

The fog clung eerily to the forest floor, and every noise made by the frogs and insects suddenly overwhelmed her. When she heard a noise behind her, she jumped and let out an audible scream, wheeling around to see her security team disabled. Her male counterpart was on the ground in a crumpled heap, and something big had the female, whose arms were flailing about, attempting to fight back. She was gasping for breath but unable to get any.

Servati wanted to run but forced herself to stay, raising her rifle. Before she could fire, something hit her hard from behind. She suddenly couldn't breathe; something grabbed her around the throat. She, too, found herself fighting to get free and breathe again. She dropped her weapon, trying to reach behind her head, but couldn't get ahold of whoever grabbed her. She tried using her elbows to strike out, but the blows were easily deflected. She couldn't contact what had hold of her.

Her vision began to blur, and her eyes watered as she gasped for any air she could find.

The woman on her security team surrendered, dropping to the ground alongside her male counterpart. Whoever had a hold on the woman had seemed to just drop her. All she could make out in the dark was a shape. The fog seemed to rise from the forest floor around it. It was moving toward her. She tried to scream, but there was no noise. Her lungs began to hurt, straining for air. She tried kicking what was behind her, but to no avail. She vainly tried to take in some air. The last thing she remembered was the dark, looming figure in the fog coming to get her.

Municipal Pier
Dartford, New York
July 19, 2010
2330 hours

The boats slipped quietly into the water, and the motors were attached to the rear of each. Equipment was unloaded from the vans that had transported the team and placed in the boats. Everyone who exited the vans was dressed in woodland camouflage and carried weapons. For all the activity, there was surprisingly little noise. There was no one about, but a lone sheriff's deputy stood nearby to keep away anyone who might question their presence. All four boats were ready in about ten minutes, but the team took their time. This was new to several of them. There were fifteen members of the team, all kept busy applying camo paint to their faces. Each boat had a crewman whose job it was to load the cargo of medical equipment and communications gear as well as check the engines. The engines had been modified with a muffler system to cut down on the noise, but on a quiet night like this one, there wasn't much that could be done to keep the noise from traveling.

The team took a few minutes to check their personal gear and weapons. They looked every bit like the professional strike team. The thirteen males and two females each looked serious when they boarded their assigned boat, settling in for the thirty-minute ride out to the island. They needed to land without being detected by the hostage takers if their part in the mission was to succeed. The mission was to rescue all the hostages, alive, and evacuate them from the island. With the current situation, the odds of that happening were extremely low. This team's job was to change those odds, but the problem was they were currently doing so without the authority of the FBI or any other federal agency. That authority would come before morning, each member of the team knew that, but they were currently on their own.

The boats started up; they were surprisingly quiet for the size of the motors. Each slowly pulled away from the pier, disappearing into the fog blanketing the lake. The deputy stood next to his car, listening to the sound of the motors growing softer and softer. He looked at his watch and then back at the fog-covered lake. They took twenty minutes to set up and slipped away into the night. The vans that delivered the team drove past him on their way back to Bluffton. He got back into his car, deciding to find a place where he could catch a couple of hours of sleep. It was going to be a busy morning.

Hidden Cave
Summers' Island
July 19, 2010
2355 hours

Servati came to slowly, vision a blur. She tried to open her mouth for air but couldn't, realizing her mouth had been taped shut. Her eyes finally focused, and she found herself face-to-face with a little girl she recognized as the girl who had been a hostage.

Servati had been propped up against something damp and cold, with her hands bound behind her back. It was uncomfortable, being seated the way she was. Her eyes darted about, trying to get an idea as to where she was. It looked like a cave, but there was electricity—lights whirred overhead that she was sure weren't battery operated.

There were other people close by. She recognized the senator and the girl who was helping in the kitchen and was surprised to find that the girl carried a sidearm. Servati's legs had been bound with large zip ties, and her two companions had their hands and legs bound as well, with duct tape over their mouths.

She looked back at the little girl.

The child cocked her head and said, "RJ, this lady's awake now."

Servati suddenly found the face of the seven-year-old boy in front of her. His expression was curious—there was no fear in his eyes. It was as if the boy knew she couldn't do anything to him. She thought he was going to poke her, but he didn't.

"Mom, the lady Colonel Rice put to sleep is awake."

Within a few seconds, a woman was in front of Servati, hands on her chin and moving her head while she examined her throat. Servati recognized Sarah as the doctor from the cabin. Servati resisted, recoiling from the doctor's reach.

"You can resist all you want, but all I'm trying to do is to make sure you're breathing okay with your mouth covered. They used a sleeper hold on you. Just checking to see if there's any damage. Do you understand?"

Servati nodded, allowing the doctor to continue her examination.

"Does this hurt?"

Servati shook her head.

"How about this?"

She shook her head again.

"Does it hurt to breathe?"

Servati shook her head one more time and noticed the senator was helping to move the sheriff in front of the three captured kidnappers. The doctor looked back at the wounded law enforcement officer.

"You have one minute, Sheriff, then you're back on the cot."

The sheriff grunted, taking a long, serious look at his three prisoners. "Looks like my deputy is getting better at keeping Admiral Summers from killing potential prisoners." All three of the hostage takers shifted nervously, looking at each other, then back at the sheriff. This caused the man to smile. "Just to keep things straight, I'm placing the three of you under arrest, mainly for your own safety. You're being held for suspicion of being involved in murder and kidnapping. You have the right to remain silent, the right to be represented by an attorney during questioning . . ."

Sheriff James continued to recite their Miranda rights from memory. Their eyes told the sheriff they couldn't believe what he was doing and almost looked defiant. When he was done reading them their rights, he added, "Now, I said I placed you under arrest for your safety, and I'm serious about keeping you safe. This is because the man who captured you has a very different perspective on this than I do. You see, your friends are still holding members of his family, and he has no qualms about extracting whatever information he needs from you, but I have to follow the rules. I don't think he cares about the rules. Personally, if I didn't need you guys myself, I wouldn't care how he went about getting the information he wants, because you killed friends of mine. But I do have a job to do, so now you're under my protection."

"Sheriff," Sarah interrupted quietly. "Time's up. I need to check those wounds to make sure you're not bleeding again."

James gave the young doctor a frustrated look and then glanced back at the three prisoners. "Now, the three of you behave. If you try to escape or cause any trouble, this pretty young lady here will be forced to shoot you. Since you held her hostage, I don't think that would be beyond what she's capable of."

James was helped back to the cot he was confined to by O'Leary and Sarah. The three prisoners turned their eyes on Emily. She just put her right hand gently on her pistol, grinning ever so slightly. Three sets of eyes grew large with fear.

CHAPTER SEVEN

INDIANS IN THE MIST

Shadow Lake
Adirondack State Park, New York
July 20, 2010
0015 hours

The four boats slowed, and the engines cut out. They glided silently in the thick fog, staying close enough together they could see the boat next to them. They had an idea of where they were on the lake because of the GPS in each boat but couldn't see any landmarks or detect any movement on the water.

Ellison was in command, having the most experience leading this type of mission, and no one questioned Admiral Putnum's decision when he'd set up the command structure for this little group. Charlie Naylor was second-in-command, and the actual combat team was made up of Wiedenkeller, Shomakker, Reardon, and Samcevic. Justin, Kay, and Ryan were tasked with getting any intelligence they could to link the kidnappers to Kingston and the bid to free him. Matt, Becky, Kevin, Sean, Stephen, and Nathan were to collect all the freed hostages and get them to a pickup point. Stephen and Nathan had been deputized and given the additional task of being responsible for any prisoners that might be taken. Given the company they were keeping, they didn't think that would be too likely.

The GPS showed them to be two hundred yards off the northwest tip of the island, but they were concerned about what awaited them on the shore after the first rescue attempt had led to an ambush. They were pretty sure they would be able to land without being detected but didn't want any surprises. Justin and Ryan prepared to go over the side and swim in to make sure the landing area would be secure for the rest of the team. While both Wiedenkeller and Samcevic had done this regularly when they had been active with the teams, they were retired and out of practice. Justin and Ryan had done this type of thing more recently in their work for the CIA. They were going to swim in. Justin would rather approach submerged, but Ryan hadn't ever done this in the dark.

The two men slipped into the water and started for shore at a slow, comfortable pace. They each carried a pistol, extra ammo, and a knife—nothing more. Samcevic gave them a hard time for not carrying a rifle and other gear, but Justin defended their decision, citing his partner's lack of experience and the fact those who did have the experience were too old. There were some indignant grunts, but the complaining stopped. The water was cold, but neither man complained. They checked their heading on a waterproof compass and disappeared into the fog.

Washington Dulles International Airport
Cargo Terminal
July 20, 2010
0015 hours

Evans managed a quick nap before returning to following his target around the main Dulles terminal for about forty minutes. She got into a car that met her at the curb and took her away from the passenger terminal. He anticipated her next move and was taken back to his plane, which had been assigned a parking spot on the tarmac with some other private jets just outside a large white hanger. The crew was bunked out in the rear of the plane. They fueled it and made it ready for takeoff before parking their aircraft between two corporate jets. The location gave Evans a direct view of the front of the hanger he would need to observe.

He was surprised at how much pull his contacts had. He'd been told his contacts would get him anything he needed, and so far, they had been true to their word. The man who started him on this adventure hadn't directly contacted him in some time, so Evans guessed he was in the thick of things. Part of Evans wanted to just walk away, because Smith already lived up to his end of the bargain, securing him what he wanted. There was a time in his life when he could have done that, but there was something in the way Smith always treated him. Evans thought about how hard it was to describe their relationship. The words "good, old-fashioned respect" came to mind. Even though they started out as enemies, this mutual respect between them managed to come to the surface, defining their relationship.

Movement on the tarmac brought Evans back to reality. Three black SUVs pulled up in front of the hanger, parking near the far side so they wouldn't block the main hanger doors. He picked up a small pair of binoculars, looking at the people getting out of the vehicles. He counted six, eight, nine, eleven people wearing US Marshal windbreakers and one female in an orange jumpsuit with handcuffs and leg irons. Evans quickly switched out the binoculars for an expensive digital SLR camera. He took several pictures of each of the individuals to send to his contacts. He watched as two of the men opened the small side door, walking their prisoner inside.

He continued to snap pictures, documenting everything taking place. He suddenly stopped, recognizing the only female wearing a US Marshals jacket as the woman he was tailing. He cursed under his breath. Smith had him following a *federal agent*. What was he getting himself into? Evans was confused for a few seconds, fear forcing his common sense to doubt himself while his mind raced. The fear was quickly set aside, because he knew he had to trust Smith. He smiled to himself, continuing to take pictures. The whole operation was about to get very interesting.

Fort Drum Military Reservation
Wheeler-Sack Army Airfield
July 20, 2010
0020 hours

They landed at Fort Drum about ten o'clock, but the operation was so rushed they had to wait for the trucks to transport the cargo. The two big flatbeds arrived just after eleven o'clock, and the cargo was quickly off-loaded from the aircraft and secured to the flatbeds. By the time they covered the equipment, it took over an hour.

Security was tight, like it was in Oceana. Armed soldiers were everywhere. Adding to all the activity was an enfilade of helicopters staged near the Globemasters. Both naval officers would have preferred to have deployed by helicopter, but a helo deployment would have given away the element of surprise. The SEAL officer commented to his counterpart that it looked like the Army was preparing their own air deployment because of the preparations they observed.

They'd been met by the commanding general when they'd landed and were surprised to see that he was present again when they prepared to leave his base. The general provided them with trucks needed to transport the extra equipment they carried, as well as several armed Humvees with drivers to carry the naval personnel who would be guarding the equipment. An additional platoon of men in armed Humvees were assigned as additional security, citing the importance of their mission. The two junior officers just looked at each other, thanking him for his courtesy.

They left the airfield, heading southeast, following the lead Humvee through the gate and security. There, they were met by four state police cruisers that took over the front of the column, red lights flashing. They went down Route 26, crossing the Black River, turning left at Route 3. According to the directions they were given, they would remain on Route 3 until they reached Dartford. If all went well, they would be in Dartford and ready to off-load their cargo within the next three hours. Plenty of time to be ready for whatever was planned for dawn.

As the convoy turned east from Route 26 onto Route 3, two men came out of the all-night gas station at the intersection. They watched as the heavily armed Humvees escorted their deadly cargo away from Fort Drum and toward its destination. Both men had served their country.

"'Bout time they grew some balls to go after these assholes," said the man in the John Deere baseball cap.

His companion grunted. "They'll need some Special Forces in place to save the hostages. These guys are good, but unless they're inserted in the dark, most of the hostages will be killed."

One of the soldiers manning the fifty-caliber machine gun on top of one of the Humvees looked at the two men, who waved. The man gave them a nod.

"You don't think they've already done that?" asked the man in the John Deere cap.

"The military's not making the calls here. The politicians are. They'd screw up anything and sacrifice these guys and the hostages if it made them look good. The whole situation's fucked up."

"Then we just have to hope that someone else is calling the shots. Someone with a brain and a little backbone."

The last Humvee passed the two men, and the convoy disappeared down the dark road.

Summers' Island
Adirondack State Park, New York
July 20, 2010
0045 hours

The fog hung thick along the shore when Justin and Ryan slowly crawled up onto dry land. Justin motioned for Ryan to stay still, and they hid quietly behind a fallen tree for a few minutes, listening for any movement that might indicate they were expected. The only things they heard were the songs of the crickets and frogs, as well as the occasional hoot of an owl.

Satisfied none of the kidnappers were close, Justin got up and motioned for Ryan to follow. He stepped over the fallen tree, taking another look around. Finding nothing out of place, he opened the waterproof bag he was carrying and began to set up the communications equipment stored there.

"You know, Justin," Ryan said, voice just above a whisper, "I don't know why Putnum is sending these old men when we had a perfectly good SEAL team sitting in the pub."

Justin looked at his friend and shushed him.

"I mean, all these guys are retired or they're amateurs," Ryan went on, speaking quieter than before. "No offense, your uncle knows nothing about military insertions, and Gateway is a publisher. I know why we brought my stepmother along—there could be a need for a doctor—but a good medic would have sufficed. And look at Samcevic. He's sixty-five if he's a day, and he's the most arrogant son of a bitch I've ever met. And the rest are all retired . . ."

While Ryan continued to ramble on about their situation, Justin finished putting the device together and clicking the mic twice to indicate it was all clear. He blocked out Ryan's droning and concentrated on any sounds coming from the fog. He heard the engines starting up and smiled. They were approaching at a slow speed, which helped reduce the noise, but Justin knew that if he could hear the engines, then so could the kidnappers. He focused on what other sounds he could hear and there was nothing. The crickets, frogs, and night birds were silent. The lapping of the water along the shore was the only other sound besides the engines on the boats. Even Ryan had shut up.

The second the thought crossed his mind, Justin whirled around, drawing his pistol.

A large dark figure was standing behind Ryan, with one arm across his chest to hold him still and the other pressing a knife against his throat. Justin couldn't make out who this dark figure was visually—but when he heard the man speak, his voice made a shiver run down Justin's spine.

"Mr. O'Keefe talks too much."

"Sorry, Justin." Ryan was struggling to get the words out. "He came out of nowhere, an—"

The knife touched Ryan's throat, and he went silent.

"Like I said," the man behind him reiterated, "he talks too much."

"At least he makes enough noise for all of us to come in without being heard," said a voice that was clearly female. A second dark figure appeared from the trees, this one holding a rifle and pointing it at Justin. He lowered his pistol, and the woman lowered her rifle. He turned back to look at the dark figure holding the knife to Ryan's throat.

"It's nice seeing you, Dad. How long have you been there?"

"Justin!" a female voice from just inside the forest's darkness said. "Justin Summers, you're alive!"

A camouflaged-clad figure came rushing out of the woods, throwing her arms around him and kissing him on the cheek. "Stephen will be speechless when he sees you. Everyone thinks you're dead."

"It's good to see you, too, Abby—and Stephen already knows."

Justin touched his jaw, causing Abby to giggle. Ryan had been freed by the older Summers and stood there, rubbing his throat. "The man could have killed me!"

"Not likely." Abby responded by slapping Ryan on the shoulder. "I've seen the man work enough over the past twenty-four hours to know that if he wanted you dead, we wouldn't be talking."

Ryan looked embarrassed. "Well, he could have hurt me."

"Not even close, dude," said Justin, grinning at his friend's expression.

All conversation stopped as the first boat landed and Ellison, Matt, and Nathan piled out. The other three boats quickly repeated what the first did, and the team unloaded the packs carrying additional supplies and equipment.

"What the hell did you bring, George?" Jon asked his old friend. "It looks like you packed to go on a Caribbean cruise. What is all this stuff?"

"We figured you could use some food and ammunition. There's comms for the whole team, plus extras, knowing you had freed a few hostages, but most of it is medical supplies the Flower Child insisted we bring along."

Becky, who was standing behind them, punched the retired marine's shoulder.

"I only let *him* call me that. You watch yourself, marine."

There was a tone of levity in her voice, so Ellison took the hand she used to hit him, kissing it gently. "I say the nickname with a great deal of respect and reverence, Doc. After all, in this business, we all have a call sign or nickname."

"Yeah, and what's yours? It's not Teddy Bear, is it?"

Jon and some of the others quietly chuckled, knowing Ellison would be frowning at their reaction.

"The general's a big John Wayne fan," commented Jon. "His men started calling him 'Duke' in Vietnam and the nickname stuck."

"I feel like I'm in a bad G.I. Joe movie," Becky said, giggling.

"Then you must admit that 'Flower Child' is an appropriate call sign," said Jon as he gently put his hand on her shoulder. "This isn't your first mission, Becky. And besides, it's just corny enough to fit."

Becky threw her arms around her old friend, giving him a hug. "I'm glad you're safe, Jonny. We were all so worried."

Jon kissed her on the cheek gently. "We need to get going, kid," he added, softly pushing her away. "Let's get you up to headquarters."

"Headquarters?" asked Ellison.

"Oh, you have no idea, sir," said Rice, moving past Ellison. "This is just the beginning. Skipper, I'll lead the way."

"Skipper?" Ellison asked jokingly.

"It's a long story, sir," commented Rice, moving off into the forest. She was followed by several members of the team.

"Come on, Duke," Becky said to Ellison, "walk me safely through the woods, big guy."

"I have a feeling this is going to be a long mission." Ellison sighed, following Becky.

Next in line were Matt and Kevin. Jon and his brother embraced and exchanged greetings quickly. Jon never questioned why his brother was with the rescue team, but he looked at the rifle he carried with a raised eyebrow. Matt said, "The same man who taught you to shoot also taught me."

"Ditto," responded Gateway, "as well as a few other people in my life."

Jon shook his head, watching the two men move by. He and Stephen exchanged nods as his youngest son passed. Jon noticed the last of the boats was backing out and they were headed the long way around the island back to Bluffton. He pulled Justin and his team out of the line, looking at the three of them as he said, "I need the three of you to bring up the rear. There's probably no one on this side of the island, but just in case."

"Yes, sir," answered Justin instinctually.

"You okay with this?" Jon asked Kayli.

The young woman looked surprised by the question. "I've had weapons and self-defense training."

"That's not what I asked." Jon tried not to sound condescending. "I forced you into your first field assignment that will involve combat. You've worked as an analyst to this point. You ready for this? Everything will be the real deal—you can get hurt, or worse."

There were a few moments of silence while Kayli processed what he said. "Sir, thank you for your concern, but I'm good to go."

"Good girl," responded Jon, his tone upbeat. "You're your father's daughter. Thank God you inherited your mother's good looks."

Ryan grunted.

"And you, Mr. O'Keefe, are just like your father. He talks too much, too. He's a good man in a fight, but he does like to talk."

"My father's dead."

Jon stifled a laugh, turning to address Justin. "Follow about five minutes behind me and head up the hill. I'll meet you about halfway up and take you the rest of the way in."

"Take us where? Dad, there's nothing up there but rocks."

"Oh, ye of little faith."

The three CIA operatives looked at each other. When they looked back, Jon had disappeared into the darkness.

"How does he do that?" asked Ryan.

"He's a SEAL," said Kayli, putting her hand on Ryan's arm. "He's trained to be a ghost. He's also one of the legends of the service, and legends tend to live up to the hype. My father used to tell stories about his team and what they did in Vietnam. It was part of the mystic of the SEALs. Then, when they served together once back in the nineties, all he said was that the stories were true."

"You mean he's crazy?"

"You have no idea," commented Justin.

"You think he knows about my father?" asked Ryan.

"He does," replied Justin and Kayli in unison.

Upton's Marina and Boat Sales
Bluffton, New York
July 20, 2010
0100 hours

The briefing started on time, and Sanderson felt it seemed to be going well. His lead tactical planner, Agent Herb Stanley, was currently going over the plans for the assault on the cabin complex. They would land the entire assault team just west of the cabins, work their way inland, surround the cabins, and move in. The plan called for fast movements and immaculate coordination.

Sanderson looked around the room; everyone was taking notes. He didn't care about this plan—the operation had ceased to be his for the time being, and he was focused on the new and more immediate task of identifying who was leaking information to Hapke. Everyone present was a key player in the response to the kidnapping, had been vetted at the highest levels, and should be above reproach—and yet one was a traitor.

Putnum had told Sanderson there was more than one person feeding information to the hostage takers. One of them was now out of the area. Grey had been tasked with checking the backgrounds of the team in the room to see if there was any indication as to who the traitor might be. To help, Sanderson changed the responsibilities of his regular security people, and Grey brought in people from his New York office to fill in. All of Sanderson's people were on the suspect list, and it killed him to think he'd missed something that important.

The only man on his staff that was currently cleared was Agent Stanley, the man doing the briefing. Sanderson trusted him to plan any operation and was relieved he'd been cleared.

Stanley had been told to plan two assaults. Now, he was describing the first, which involved their SWAT teams surrounding the complex and freeing the hostages after neutralizing the hostage takers. The heavy fog on the lake would cover their approach and insertion onto the island, and they calculated a ninety percent chance of freeing all the hostages unhurt—providing their insertion went undetected. The second plan was a simple frontal assault on the cabin complex from the lake. The plan was much simpler and more direct, but the chances of freeing the hostages unhurt were considerably less.

"Why aren't we inserting on the east end of the island?" asked one of the team leaders. "It's much closer to here. There would be less time on the lake and less of a chance they would hear us coming."

Agent Stanley answered, "We know Hapke's team has placed booby traps on the east side of the island. It would slow our approach getting the explosives cleared, as well as increase the chances of us being detected. The area we've chosen to insert you is thick forest, and there's little chance of them setting the types of traps we've seen them use already."

Another team leader asked, "We know that Sheriff James and a deputy have managed to free some of the hostages. What are the chances we'll be getting some intel from them?"

"Sheriff James is wounded, and two of the freed hostages are children. We've told them to lie low until we get there. They've given us what intelligence they have, but with their limited resources, the safe play is for them to lie low."

"The rumor is there's someone else on the island helping them. I don't want some amateur putting my team in jeopardy. Anything on that, sir?"

"I have no confirmation of that. We've all heard the rumors, but in our conversations with Sheriff James, there's been nothing to indicate they have any help."

Sanderson hid a smile. There were people in the room who knew different, but no one disputed what was just said. He especially thought the amateur comment quite poignant. There were a few more questions, but this part of the briefing concluded, and Stanley introduced Tina Ramsey from the United States Attorney's Office. Ramsey spoke briefly to the group about the need to follow all protocols when apprehending kidnappers so none would go free on technicalities. When she finished, she looked at Sanderson and nodded.

"Now, we'll be landing on the island at seven a.m.," said Sanderson, stepping forward to conclude the briefing, "which means the boats will be pushing off from here by six a.m. You've been getting ready for this since we've arrived, so have your people get some rest. They're going to need it. Any questions?"

There were none, so he dismissed the meeting. As everyone stood and started to leave the room, Sanderson counted at least five of his people who went right to their cells and were either talking to someone or texting. He frowned, wondering which one was the traitor. His concern only deepened when he saw the agent in charge of their communications was one of them.

"Why the long face, sir?"

Sanderson turned to find himself facing Ramsey. She looked concerned. He'd let his emotions show, which was embarrassing.

"No reason," he answered, "just nervous about the upcoming operation."

"You have every right to be concerned—there's a lot at stake here. Any word on what they're doing with Kingston?"

Sanderson forced a smile. Ramsey was a good kid and didn't deserve to be the recipient of the complaint he wanted to air. "You know as much as I do on that one. Your bosses in the Department of Justice are having him moved just in case. The woman involved in the case as well."

"Andrea Handcock."

"Huh, yeah, her. They're moving them both but haven't told us where. They're worried about potential leaks." Sanderson flushed with anger, realizing he said too much already. *No one was supposed to know there was possibly a leak.*

"Our office in New York passed on that they were moving them to Washington to be placed under guard by the Marshals Service. I was wondering if there was any word on them changing their minds. It's safer keeping both where they were; no one could break them out of prison."

Sanderson flushed even more after being told that the Department of Justice trusted a young attorney with information that they didn't trust an assistant director of the FBI with—it was a slight at best and disturbing at worst. Still, it wasn't her fault, so he remained pleasant.

"No, the plans haven't changed—at least as far as I'm aware. You should get some sleep, Miss Ramsey. It's going to be a long day."

"Thank you, sir. I think I'll take you up on that offer and go back to the motel for an hour or so if you don't need me."

Sanderson shook his head. "You go right ahead. I'll need you thinking clearly a little later this morning."

Ramsey smiled at the senior FBI agent and excused herself. Sanderson watched her walk away for a few moments and then turned his attention back to his communications man. He was still on his cell phone.

Summers' Cabin
Adirondack State Park, New York
July 20, 2010
0115 hours

Most of the hostages were asleep, and the guards were dozing as well. Since Hapke's people consolidated their perimeter, there were more of them in and out of the main cabin. Ericson was keeping track of their comings and goings as a matter of security, in case of a rescue. He didn't want anyone ambushed when the good guys came through the door, and he knew they were coming.

Being held hostage, he was spending a lot of time reflecting on his life, and this moment was no different. He considered himself a realist, and when he'd lost the use of his legs, he hadn't allowed himself to dwell on that setback for long. He literally picked himself up and learned to live with the disability. He continued to be a very successful businessman and, as a United States senator, was well respected on both sides of the aisle. He became reacquainted with Fiona, and they were immensely happy in their marriage together. But at this very moment, he found himself frustrated with his disability. It didn't allow him the movement to do what he was trained to do.

A commotion in the dining area caught his attention. A quick glance told him that he was the only hostage awake, so he strained to hear what was being said. The back door opened, and Hapke walked into the cabin. Ericson pretended he was asleep like the others. He sensed the man wasn't stable and didn't want to give him any reason to unravel. That would come soon enough.

"We received a message, boss," said the communications man.

"What's the message?"

"The FBI is going to start their assault at zero seven hundred. They'll be coming ashore at these coordinates."

The communications man showed him a notepad with the written message and a longitude and latitude on it. Hapke just stared blankly back at the man. The communications man continued, "It indicates the little cove to the west of us. It's heavily wooded but offers plenty of cover for us to ambush them."

Hapke smiled. "Good. We'll take care of them before they land and catch them while they're still in the water with no cover. Then take off from the other side of the island. Is there any word from Servati yet?"

The communications man shook his head. "Nothing, boss—but then again, she knows they're monitoring our communications."

Hapke nodded, glancing over at the hostages. He remained quiet for a few moments before saying, "Spread the word. We'll leave our guests here at zero five thirty and set the ambush for the FBI. I want all these buildings ready to be turned into toothpicks. Do you understand?"

The communications man nodded.

"I don't want any survivors here," continued Hapke. "None! Shoot them all and then blow the cabin. Clear?"

The communication man nodded again, this time adding, "If that's the case, sir, we need to verify that our escape route is secure. Shouldn't we contact Servati and our friend on the outside to make sure everything's ready and in place? They'll be after us big-time once they know we've killed everyone."

Hapke looked agitated, shaking his head. "No, no, no! Servati would be the first to lecture me on radio discipline during an operation. If she needed help, she would contact us. She's set and just waiting for us to do our job.

Make our last communication with our contact verifying the vehicles are in place. Now, get busy, we have a lot to do."

With that, Hapke marched into the kitchen and out of sight. The communications man looked frustrated, but he did as he was told.

In the living room, Ericson thought about everything that had been said. He now knew what they intended to do with them, but for some reason, he didn't feel the need to be concerned. He wouldn't share that information with his fellow hostages due to the panic that would almost certainly ensue. Besides, he felt confident something would happen before then. There was something big and mean and nasty out in the woods, and he guessed Servati already met it—that was why she hadn't checked in. She was too efficient, after all.

Whatever it was, it was getting bigger and meaner and nastier while they waited here in the dark. It was out there, watching and waiting. It would be coming for them soon, and they had no idea.

Mohawk Tavern and Grill
Bluffton, New York
July 20, 2010
0130 hours

Putnum was dozing off and on as the operation progressed. He was not one to micromanage his people, and he knew Mitchell and Grey to both be very capable. He wasn't surprised when they disturbed him from his catnap with an update. A quick look around revealed the only people in the tavern were those working on their team or members of the family.

"There's been a development," said Grey as he moved all the way over to the wall across from Putnum. Mitchell slid in next to Grey.

"Joey intercepted another text message sent to the hostage takers," interjected Mitchell, "from here in Bluffton."

Cassie appeared out of nowhere with two mugs of coffee. She placed one in front of Putnum, and the old man smiled, motioning for her to sit down next to him. There were no objections as Grey continued the briefing. "The hostage takers have the FBI's entire rescue plan, so my guess is they'll walk right into a trap."

"Or so the hostage takers think," said Mitchell, smiling. "Our team is on the island, and they've contacted Admiral Summers. They haven't given us their plans yet, but we'll pass on this information, so they have it."

Putnum sipped his coffee. It was hot and strong, bringing him fully awake. He looked at the two men across the table. "You both know as well as I do that Jon and George will tell us their plans only after they've executed them. With a leak in Sanderson's operation, they won't take the chance there's not a leak in ours as well."

Both men nodded, laughing. Only Cassie looked concerned. "From a legal standpoint, that could be a problem," said the attorney. "I mean, the US Attorney's Office would have a cow if they proceeded without having any plan run by them."

"Two things, Cassie . . ." Mitchell did his best not to sound patronizing. "The first thing being that if family was involved, do you think your uncle would care about the rules?"

Cassie shook her head.

Mitchell continued, "He's the type of guy you want doing this kind of job, and George Ellison is cut from the same cloth. They'll do what they must to bring the hostages home safely. All of them."

"The second thing," chimed in Grey, "is that your boss volunteered to go to Albany. He knew about this second operation and allowed Tina Ramsey to be assigned to Sanderson, no matter how it looked. He has an idea about what's going to take place, but because he's in Albany talking to the attorney general, he can't be responsible for what he doesn't know."

"Plausible deniability," Cassie surmised.

"Exactly—and with you on leave because of your connection to several of the victims, and Ramsey being kept out of the loop, the US Attorney's Office is in the clear."

"Uncle Jon could get away with murder," commented Cassie, "but he won't because that's not who he is. What's his fail-safe?"

"His what?" both Grey and Mitchell asked together.

"He would have something in place to make sure he wasn't crossing the line of committing a criminal act. I know him, and he has a good idea of where that line is, but he'd have a plan B in place to ensure that didn't happen."

All three men smiled, but it was Putnum who spoke. "You're a smart kid, Cassie; I think you'll go far. Jon's using the sheriff and Deputy Crogan to gauge how far he can go. They already have a few prisoners, and believe it or not, they've been Mirandized. They're not lawyers, but they are professional law enforcement. Part of the team that's been sent in have been deputized to help with the prisoners and any more they may pick up."

Cassie shook her head. "Admiral Putnum, sir, you don't fight fair."

"Young lady, I've discovered you don't win battles or wars that way."

Hidden Cave
Summers' Island
July 20, 2010
0135 hours

The cave became crowded with the sudden influx of people. Ellison and his team entered only long enough to drop off the medical supplies Dr. O'Keefe brought. They then joined Jon outside the entrance and sat checking their equipment for their upcoming mission. Stephen and Abby enjoyed a quick embrace and then turned to the prisoners. They found Nathan squatting in front of the three prisoners, looking them over carefully.

He looked up at his sister and smiled. "You know Grandfather warned them."

"When?" asked Abby, looking surprised.

Nathan looked back at the prisoners. "When they wanted someone to pass their demands to besides the FBI, they requested Grandfather. He came to the island, and they treated him without respect or dignity. They have no honor, or they wouldn't be doing this with children, so Grandfather told them to leave and they could keep their lives. They didn't, so he sent Stephen and me. They're your prisoners, but if they try to escape, we'll deal with them in the old way."

The eyes of all three prisoners grew large with fear, looking to Abby for an explanation.

"The old way?" questioned Abby.

"Your grandfather is one of the hereditary chiefs of the Mohawk," chimed in Stephen. "He blessed us before we left and charged us with bringing these trespassers to justice. If not Sheriff James's way, then the old way."

Abby looked at Stephen for an explanation, only to receive a wink in return. She looked back down at her brother, who was staring intently at the prisoners as he said, "Nope, I hope they try to escape, or at least give us trouble."

Fear was plain on each of their faces. Abby turned away so they wouldn't see her grin.

Becky gave Sarah and each of her grandchildren a quick hug and then went to work with Sarah on Sheriff James's wounds and getting him ready to travel.

"You're lucky, Sheriff," Becky said. "It's a good thing Jonny knows something about bullet wounds. He stabilized you quick enough that you're in pretty good shape. We'll give you an IV to get some more fluids in you and then we'll carry you off this rock. You'll be in the hospital a couple of days and then home for a while."

"I'm sorry, Doc . . . I mean when we had words yesterday."

James found this funny because the doctor in front of him didn't look anything like the woman he'd met the day before. The pretty, petite, fiery woman whom he exchanged words with was replaced by a woman dressed in combat fatigues with her face painted. She was all business, and her hands seemed to be gifted, quickly working to replace the bandages.

"You've done this before, Doc?"

"I've been a doctor for a while. You're not my first patient, Sheriff," Becky said with a grin, dodging the obvious question. James decided that was enough for now. He now knew there were two teams here on the island. One to free the remaining hostages, led by Summers and Ellison. The second to escort the freed hostages and his prisoners off the island, led by Matt and Sean. He didn't know why, but he wasn't giving the hostage takers much of a chance. The intensity of the people he saw thus far was nothing like what he'd experienced when he was a young man in the service. They were on a mission.

Matt was quick to find his youngest daughter in the cave when he entered. He wasn't surprised to find her in a set of camouflaged fatigues and carrying a weapon. When she saw him, she threw her arms around her father. "Daddy, what are you doing here?"

"Because you're here," Matt answered, hugging her back. "Can't let your uncle Jon do all the work. It's our island, after all."

Emily giggled. "Except you kept a few things secret. Nice hideout from the kids."

Matt started answering the barrage of questions that followed about the cave, and Emily eagerly listened to every word, keeping an arm around her father. She noticed three final people enter the cave, and she stiffened. Her arm dropped to her side, and Matt watched as she deliberately weaved through the crowd of people toward the three new arrivals. With the look on his daughter's face, he knew what was about to happen but decided not to shout a warning. He grinned in anticipation.

Emily reached the three people and stood before the man in the center. There was recognition in his eyes, but before he could say anything, Emily balled up her fist, striking him square in the jaw, knocking him back against the wall of the cave.

"Damn, Em!" said Justin, wiping blood from his lip as he pushed himself away from the wall. "All your sister did was *slap* me. Why'd you have to go for a punch?"

Emily threw her arms around her cousin and kissed him on the cheek. "You son of a bitch, making us all think you were dead. Your mom's going to *kill* Uncle Jon for keeping this from her all this time!"

"Come on, you two." Sean took his cousin away from his brother, giving her a hug. "There isn't time for this. Justin, get that comm equipment passed out and set up. Dad wants to get going."

Justin nodded to his brother. Sean looked down at his cousin. "Thanks for helping them get out, Em."

"Look who came to take us home—you and Daddy."

"Family first," said Sean, hugging his cousin one more time.

Emily turned back to Justin, who handed her a radio headset and said, "Since I see you're carrying a weapon, you'll probably need one of these. This is Kayli—she'll show you how to use it."

The two cousins hugged one more time, then Justin grabbed Ryan by the arm, leading him farther into the cave. They stopped next to the cot where Sarah and Becky were working on the wounded sheriff. Sarah looked at her mother, who simply nodded.

Sarah then stood up and hugged Justin. "You're in so much trouble," she said to her brother-in-law, "but you'll get off easy. I'll deal with you later." Then, she turned and looked at Ryan, who shifted his weight uncomfortably.

A warm smile slowly crossed her face as she leaned forward and hugged the young man in front of her. "So, you're my brother, Ryan?"

Ryan was speechless and just nodded. Sarah stepped back and looked him up and down one more time. "I see him in you, Ryan," she said. "Welcome to the family, and thanks for coming to get us out."

Ryan blushed under all the camo face paint, causing Justin to grin. Ryan reached out and gave Sarah another hug.

With all the excitement inside the cave, O'Leary couldn't find the person she wanted to speak to. She correctly guessed Jon would be outside with the rescue team. Since she knew some of them, she wasn't surprised that they were all business—checking weapons and equipment. Jon had his back to her as she approached. He didn't even turn around when he said to her, "Hello, Amy."

"How do you know when I'm here?" she asked.

Jon turned to face her, but it was Ellison who answered. "Because he can smell you coming. You do have a unique smell, Senator."

O'Leary looked at the retired marine, smiling politely. "Do I smell that bad, General?"

"Actually, quite the opposite, Senator. You smell very feminine—quite appealing in another circumstance, but all of us could smell you the minute you stepped out of the cave. It's not a smell that belongs here. Not bad, just out of place."

"I couldn't smell her," said Walt Samcevic with a grin, stepping closer.

"That's because you're older than the rest of us, old man," said Reardon. "Being a swabbie, I'm guessing it's too many years smelling the salt water."

"You're being too hard on Mr. Samcevic, George," teased Rice. "It's all the times he's had his nose broken."

Samcevic smiled. "Don't mind the critics, Senator, they're actually my biggest fans."

O'Leary laughed, turning back to Jon. "You've really put together a charming crew."

"They'll get the job done."

O'Leary was silent, looking at Jon. She put her hand out, gently touching his face as she said, "Be careful of what you do today, because neither Josh nor I may be able to protect you. I know it's family there, but I don't want to see you hurt. Let the FBI do their job."

Amy had seen that look in Jon's eyes once before, when he had dealt with a situation years before. There was no anger or emotion there; they looked cold and determined. She knew her comments had fallen on deaf ears. He leaned forward, kissing the senator gently on the cheek, and whispered something, causing her to blush.

He then leaned back and looked at Wiedenkeller. "Get everybody together, Master Chief. We need to move out."

Mohawk Tavern and Grill
Bluffton, New York
July 20, 2010
0145 hours

Assistant Director Sanderson stood next to Admiral Putnum and Agent Grey, listening to the latter's report on the progress of where they stood in the investigation into the leak. He was pleased to learn that Grey had finished vetting most of the senior-level members dealing with the tactical part of the operation.

Due to how quickly the investigation progressed, those tactical advisors stood next to the three men during Grey's report, and Sanderson was oddly satisfied by the look of surprise on their faces at hearing they had all been vetted again. It wasn't their ignorance that was satisfying but that his judgment and trust in them was well placed.

Sanderson looked at Grey, who continued to speak. The man ran a good operation and had locked the area down without creating too much animosity with the locals. They were standing behind the Mohawk near the van, and Sanderson's people were also surprised they were using the tavern as a secondary command post. Sanderson was impressed at what Grey had accomplished with Putnum's help.

The night was cool, so they were all wearing light jackets. The fog was heavy on the lake, moving inland to surround the buildings in the village. Even in the rear of the Mohawk, the fog not only obscured visibility, but left everybody without the appropriate clothing feeling bogged down and uncomfortable.

When Grey finished up his briefing, several of Sanderson's men looked nervous.

"So, if we have a mole in our command structure somewhere, then you're saying the hostage takers already know our plan for the rescue," said one of the agents, and Grey nodded in response. "And they'll be waiting for us when we go to land on the island?"

This time, Grey didn't respond.

The agent's eyes widened, piecing it together. "You're using us as a decoy while you send in another team."

Grey's eyes locked on him. "Yes, we are," he said calmly, "and I know that sucks, but the truth is that until we identify the leak, we can't trust anybody."

The agents' faces were wide-eyed and shocked. A few even went pale. The gravity of the situation was heavy and unrelenting. But despite that, Sanderson smiled. He understood exactly how they felt.

"You're not using the SEAL team that's here, are you?" asked another of the agents after a few moments of charged silence. "That would be illegal, and you know that."

Grey stared at the agent, who shifted nervously. "Our command structure has been infiltrated and has made us all but ineffective. While we are actively pursuing this investigation and rescue, you need to understand that we are by no means in command here. Our friends in the CIA and the military are here to support us, but they aren't in charge either. There is a very limited pool of people who we're sure haven't been influenced by Kingston, and all of us are working with them to resolve this situation by the order of the president. We are part of a bigger team and are to work together, like it or not."

The gathered agents looked at Sanderson for direction.

"I couldn't have said it better, Agent Grey," he said. "You all know me and know how I feel about outside interference. Our job is to get the hostages back alive, but with someone in our camp passing on all our plans, that isn't going to happen. We know we have an issue, and we're working to correct it, but that's a slow process, because we all have to have our backgrounds checked again."

"And who's doing that?" asked one of the agents with an indignant tone.

"We are," answered Grey sharply, causing the agent to look at his feet. "And all of you have been cleared, or you wouldn't be here."

The radio in the van came to life, causing everyone to look in that direction.

"Pathfinder to Whiskey Charlie Papa, all comms are up. Request permission to proceed?"

DePalma poked his head out of the van, looking at the gathered group of FBI agents. He then locked eyes with Putnum, who just nodded. DePalma disappeared back into the van.

"Pathfinder, you have a go. I repeat—you are cleared to proceed."

"Roger that, Whiskey Charlie Papa."

The gathered FBI agents shifted their gaze to Putnum. The senior agent spoke on behalf of the whole group when he said, "You already have a team on the island, don't you? You sent in the damn SEALs."

Putnum stared back at the agents neutrally, taking his time. "No. You presume we don't care to obey the laws of the United States. We both know I can't use troops without approval. While I have taken steps to get that permission, I don't have it yet. The team on the island is not active military, but they are more than capable of getting the job done."

The agents shook their heads, and a few even had the audacity to openly scoff. The spokesman decided to press the issue with Putnum. "You do realize that it's illegal to use NSA and CIA assets on this as well? You may have compromised this investigation."

Putnum didn't hesitate to shut the man down. "Compromised? NSA and CIA aren't compromised by some spy passing information on to the kidnappers. I may have assets from both agencies on the team in support capacities, but the team leader is under the direct supervision of Sheriff James and his people. That makes it a local operation with the primary focus of freeing the hostages. When I get permission to use available military units to assist with that mission, I fully intend to use them. You can investigate whatever is left when we're done with that mission, including how a man in federal custody was able to hatch a plan that completely crippled your operation."

There was silence among the gathered agents as they all tried to avoid Putnum's gaze.

It took a full minute before one of them built up the courage to speak. "We all know that Sheriff James is wounded, so who's your team leader?"

Putnum smiled, knowing the reaction he was about to get. "Jon Summers."

There were looks of shock and confusion throughout the group. The senior agent finally spoke up. "You must be mistaken; Jon Summers is dead."

There was laughter from a group near the van. Standing among the gathered family working on the rescue with Putnum was Scott Preston. He looked at Fred as he spoke. "And they talk about us Canadians being naive."

Washington Dulles International Airport
Cargo Terminal
July 20, 2010
0200 hours

It'd been almost two hours since there had been any activity around the hanger. Evans caught himself starting to doze when he noticed an aircraft approaching the hanger on the taxiway. It was a small jet—probably a Lear.

He forced himself to full alertness on the off chance it was coming to the hanger. If it passed by, he was going to wake the pilot to watch for a period while he got some sleep. There were three of them in the aircraft, after all.

When the jet drew closer, Evans was able to determine it was a Lear but was surprised to see United States Air Force markings on the side. He guessed this was indeed the plane he was waiting for. He quickly checked his camera to make sure it was ready and raised his binoculars, watching the aircraft approach. He didn't have to wait long for activity, because the small door on the side of the hanger opened and about a dozen people walked out. They were dressed in tactical gear or in US Marshals jackets, and they were all heavily armed with a variety of automatic weapons. Evans shifted his attention to the group of marshals spread out in front of the hanger.

The woman he had been following was again in the front of the group, hands on her hips, looking impatient. The badge clipped to her belt and the automatic pistol made him shiver like it had earlier when he first saw her with this group. He didn't like this part of the business, especially following a federal agent.

When he scanned the other federal officers, he noticed a new face—another female agent who stood back near the door. He hadn't seen her before, which was a surprise; Evans didn't remember seeing a second female agent earlier when the SUVs had come and gone. She too had a badge on her belt and carried a gun. Something wasn't right, but he couldn't put his finger on what.

The Air Force jet pulled in front of the hanger and came to a stop by the group but didn't shut off the engines. The door to the aircraft opened and the steps were lowered. Two heavily armed soldiers exited, taking up positions facing the marshals, weapons at the ready. An officer, armed with just a pistol, exited the aircraft while carrying a clipboard. He nervously looked around, making sure things were secure. While Evans snapped pictures of the scene, the officer walked over to the first female marshal, and the two began speaking. The marshal took the clipboard and produced a pen from her jacket pocket. She signed the page on top, and when the officer lifted several other pages, she signed again and again. This process was repeated several more times before the officer was given back the clipboard. He then appeared to rip several pieces of paper off, handing them to the marshal. He turned toward the aircraft, shouting an order.

Two more armed soldiers exited the aircraft, one only carrying a pistol. The soldier turned and helped a man in an orange jumpsuit down the steps. The man was in shackles, making it difficult for him to come down the steps without help. Evans had never met the man but immediately knew who he was. He was witnessing the exchange of Richard Kingston from military custody to the US Marshals Service. Kingston had been caught and charged with treason and had been fortunate enough to get life in prison and not a death sentence. Things had changed since then, and Evans guessed he wouldn't be so lucky now.

Kingston made it down the steps, stopping once he was on the tarmac. He stood up, looking around to get his bearings. He was still strikingly handsome and in excellent shape, even after his years in prison. The man grinned, focusing on the officer and the female marshal. It didn't look like he said anything to his guards, but he complied when they urged him forward. The two soldiers were met by three marshals and the exchange took place. The keys to the shackles were handed over, and the soldiers returned to their aircraft. The marshals hustled their prisoner to the hanger door and disappeared. The officer and the last two soldiers boarded the aircraft, the steps were retracted, and the door was secured. Evans heard the engines of the Lear power up, and the aircraft began to move. He continued to watch it move back onto the taxiway. When he turned his attention back to the hanger, the last of the marshals were going inside.

Everything was suddenly quiet again.

The entire exchange had taken less than ten minutes, and a quick look around revealed only the Air Force jet retreating down the taxiway. There was no one else in sight. Evans stared at the door to the hanger—something wasn't right. He wasn't sure what, so he started to look through the pictures he had taken on his digital camera. There had to be something in one of them that would tell him what was amiss. After twenty minutes, he stopped and stared at the picture he had taken of the woman who had arrived two hours earlier in the orange jumpsuit and shackles.

Evans stared at that picture, memorizing the woman's face: pale skin, dark-brown eyes, shoulder-length hair with a distinct line of silver running from her temple. Nothing stood out about her particularly. No, the only lack of continuity—the only thing that might be wrong—was that there hadn't ever been two female agents. He would've recalled that.

Who was this second agent?

He scrolled back through the camera's log, stopping to study the second female agent as soon as she cropped up. The first agent—the one signing the papers—was tanned, with a tight blonde bun at the base of her skull, and a stern face. This second one, though, she . . .

Evans paused, blinking.

The second agent had pale skin, dark-brown eyes, and shoulder-length hair with a silver streak running through it. That wasn't a second female agent—it was the prisoner, dressed up as a federal agent.

These people weren't with the Marshals Service.

Evans jumped as the large door to the hanger started to open, taking him by surprise. The lights were on inside, and there were a few armed men dressed in tactical gear checking the surrounding tarmac, making sure everything was clear. While the door opened wider, a large private jet started to inch forward. Evans guessed it could carry up to twenty passengers, plus a crew of three, and there was likely enough room for the team of fake marshals. A quick glance around told him there was nobody else watching this—except for him.

As the jet began to pull out of the hanger, Evans shrank down in his seat—effectively shielding himself without compromising his view. He peered into the lighted cockpit, only about fifty yards away. He didn't recognize the pilot, but the man sitting in the copilot's seat was none other than

Richard Kingston. The man was smiling and laughing as the plane cleared the hanger; he certainly wasn't being transported as a prisoner.

The plane turned, blocking Evans's view of the cockpit, and the few guards remaining on the ground quickly boarded through the open door of the aircraft. The steps were retracted, and the door secured, allowing the plane to move off the tarmac and onto the taxiway.

Evans jumped again as the large door on the hanger began to close on its own.

The whole thing only took seconds.

Evans was immediately on the phone with his contacts. This time, he was speaking with a man, and Evans briefly told him what he'd observed before reading off the tail numbers of the aircraft he was watching pull away. He was asked if there was anyone near the hanger. There was supposed to be a team of federal marshals still there. While Evans watched the large door of the hanger close tight, he told his contact he saw no one. He was told to wake his aircraft crew up and stand by. The line went dead, but Evans didn't find this strange at all. He was involved in something much bigger than he anticipated. He again wondered what he had allowed himself to get into.

He left the cockpit and woke the aircrew, telling them to ready the aircraft for departure. While they began to stir, his cell rang. The voice on the other end was someone Evans hadn't spoken to yet. The tone told him it was someone important—probably the decision-maker for whatever drama was unfolding.

"Mr. Evans, I know you probably want out of this little case of espionage, but I need you to continue to follow the aircraft you just observed leave the hanger."

"Where's Smith?" he demanded. "I need to talk to him."

"He's not available. He's involved in another part of the operation."

"How about Rebecca? Can I speak to her?"

"No, she's with Smith."

Evans didn't respond immediately. He sat down in one of the seats in the passenger cabin to collect himself. The man on the other end of the phone continued, "I gather you're surprised by that fact, Mr. Evans. Don't worry, she's still the rebel you remember. For her, it's all about family, something I think you understand."

There was something in this man's voice that told Evans he knew the truth.

"Then you know who I am, sir?"

"I know Smith isn't really Smith and you're not really Evans. Last names don't really matter because you both are who you are. You're both dangerous and you're both on a mission."

"And what, by chance, do I call you, sir?"

The proper British accent slipped into one that might have originated in Belfast. There was a chuckle on the other end of the phone. "So, all pretense is gone, eh, Mr. Evans? You can call me W.C. Like I said, last names don't matter. So, are you going to follow that aircraft, or do I call in favors elsewhere?"

"And if I don't, you tell my enemies who I really am?"

"Nothing of the sort. Your past is just that—your past. I'll appeal to your relationship with our mutual friend and even your relationship with Rebecca. I won't use your past; you've paid your dues."

There was a moment of awkward silence before Evans responded.

"W.C.," he began, deciding he'd speak plainly, "you don't seem like the type of man to let my past go. Why would you pass on that opportunity?"

The man laughed. "Oh, you're so right, Mr. Evans. But my loyalty to our mutual friend prevents me from pursuing my instinct when it comes to your background. Much like your relationship with him, there is respect and trust between us. I wouldn't compromise that for anything."

"Honesty, I'm impressed, W.C. This is not something I would expect from someone in your position. I assume you're in a position of great power and know how to wield it."

"The less you know about me, the better, Mr. Evans. My main goal now is the mission and its successful completion. Getting you to cooperate and follow this aircraft would make my job so much easier, but your saying no would not make it impossible."

"I'll finish this because I gave my word to our friend, but out of curiosity, how would you do this if I refused?"

There was a laugh on the other end of the phone, then it went dead. Evans sat for a few moments, then put the phone down on the table next to him. The response—even if it'd only been laughter—had answered his question.

Summers' Island
Shadow Lake
July 20, 2010
0215 hours

The patrol moved silently through the forest. It looked surreal with the fog lying thick on the ground, seeming to cling to the trees. Fireflies danced in and out of the fog, adding to the enchanted feeling. All five men were spooked due to everything that had taken place since their arrival on the island. Their senses were overloaded with the fog obstructing their vision and the forest's dead silence, and so they moved slowly down the path. They expected to find someone behind every tree and log, overreacting to every sound.

These men were tasked with providing an outer perimeter security patrol a hundred yards into the thick woods surrounding the cabin complex. They were apprehensive, having seen what happened to their counterparts who were unfortunate enough to escort the hostages who escaped. Servati and her team hadn't been heard from in several hours, and they guessed they were gone as well. They didn't want to be on this patrol.

The radio squawked. "Hapke to Patrol One, come in!"

The patrol leader motioned for his men to stop, raising the radio to his lips. "This is Patrol One, sir."

"Bring it back in—we're getting ready for the next phase."

"Roger that, sir. Over and out."

The entire patrol seemed to give off a collective sigh of relief. They looked nervously around them one more time.

"This place is scary."

"I know, you expect them to pop up right out of the fog. I for one am glad we're out of here."

"It's like they're not human by the way they do things—appear out of nowhere and kill our guys, then they're gone."

"Shut up, you guys," said the patrol leader, "and follow me back to the cabin. They're nothing but a bunch of freaks."

The squad leader started off toward the cabins and didn't see several of his people make faces at him. They followed him single file, looking carefully around while they left the forest for the meadow. Once they were out of sight, the shadowy figures seemed to rise from the fog next to where the patrol had been standing. One of them, Becky, looked around at her companions and saw most of them putting knives back into their scabbards. She looked at Jon as he put his away less than ten feet from her. He shrugged his shoulders, smiling weakly. He then motioned for the group to move out.

She turned to Reardon, who had been tasked to keep her safe. "You guys *are* scary—they were less than two feet from us and none of you moved. Why the knives?"

Reardon motioned for O'Keefe to move out behind Jon.

"Scary we are, ma'am. We take pride in being ghosts to the enemy. Freaks, we're not. The knives were to make them suffer if the boss gave the word."

Becky knew better than to press that conversation and followed the rest of the team into the fog.

Summers' Cabin
Adirondack State Park, New York
July 20, 2010
0230 hours

The flurry of activity outside piqued Ericson's interest.

He glanced around and noticed Nancy was awake. Everyone else was sleeping. Hapke was huddled with his communications man in the dining room, whispering instructions while the man nodded his understanding. Every now and then, Hapke turned, looking to where the hostages slept, ensuring they weren't being overheard.

"I'm leaving six of you," he said. "You shouldn't have any trouble finishing your end of the job."

"Understood, sir."

"Good. Give us two hours to get in place, then finish the job here. I need them alive as long as possible in case the FBI demands proof. They'll be coming at about seven, and we'll hit them before they land while they're in the open on the water. We're taking their boats, so you need to be there."

The communications man nodded.

"I'm assuming Servati has fallen prey to whoever's out there, but if you hear from her, let me know right away."

The communications man nodded one more time. Hapke patted the man on the shoulder and then left out the back door. The communications man looked at the hostages and, satisfied they were asleep, went back to his business.

Nancy leaned close to Ericson, concerned about what she had heard.

"Josh," she whispered, "they have no intention of letting us go. We have to do something."

Ericson's jaw tightened, knowing she was right. But little did she know, there was hope for them yet. "Do you trust your husband?"

Nancy's brows furrowed. "I don't understand what you mean."

"It's a simple question: Do you trust your husband?"

Nancy looked at her old friend to see if he was serious. Ericson's eyes told her he was, and his gaze calmed any fears she might have been feeling. It was all business, cold and calculated. She knew this look on her husband's face. She'd seen it years before in a confrontation with Hapke in a mall parking lot. It was one of the few times she'd ever feared Jon. Not fear for herself, but fear for others and what he might do. There was no fear this time—more the feeling of relief they weren't alone.

"I trust him. What do you know that I don't?"

Ericson didn't answer right away. He first looked at the guard and the communications man to make sure they weren't listening. Neither seemed to notice the two hostages talking.

"By now, Jonny knows these guys have someone on the inside and is planning his own rescue. To me, these guys leaving six men means the rescue will come sooner rather than later. We need to be ready to help him when he comes. What does he know about this cabin that they don't?"

Nancy's expression was blank while she processed the question. She cocked her head, asking, "Josh, how on earth would Jonny know they have a spy in the FBI?"

The corners of Ericson's mouth curled up. "That's what your husband does. He knows things you wouldn't expect him to know and does the impossible against unthinkable odds. My guess is he'll be here within the hour."

Nancy didn't respond.

**FBI Offices
New York City
July 20, 2010
0230 hours**

Trask sat at the desk with his head in his hands. He was exhausted. It had been a long day since he arrived back in the city, and he wasn't even in his own office. He came directly to the FBI offices and was working with a multiagency team to follow up on the background checks of everyone involved in the incident at Shadow Lake. He shook his head, trying not to laugh. In his own mind, he'd just reduced the taking of close to twenty hostages to free a convicted traitor to a simple incident. He was more tired than he thought.

Sanderson's insecurity of trusting those other than the ones already on his team played into Putnum's plan to follow up on the backgrounds of everyone involved at Shadow Lake. Sanderson thought Trask was in Albany arguing with the New York State Attorney General about jurisdiction, when he really was in the New York field office of the FBI, supervising the background check process. Trask had in fact met with the attorney general, but there was no argument or discussion about jurisdiction. New York State was helping with the record check process, supplying manpower to help the FBI and other federal agencies with the task.

They were taking a break, and Trask opted to stay at the desk he was using to try to relax for a few minutes. It wasn't nearly long enough to make a difference, but the change in routine was nice. They were working in teams, starting their checks by looking at Putnum's record and working their way down the chain of command. They even checked the backgrounds of those on the island, including Summers, who was supposed to be dead. Each team in turn reported to Trask with their findings. It wasn't a fast process, but they were being thorough. The team coming in consisted of two FBI agents and two state police investigators. They were bringing in only two files to be reviewed.

"Mr. Trask," said one of the FBI agents, "we were tasked with checking out Inspector Preston, the Mountie. Sir, he's the real deal. Been with the RCMP for twenty years and rated one of their top investigators. Everything checks out, sir. He's squeaky-clean. The RCMP even sent a copy of their entire investigation on the attempted murder of this Summers guy. The man's crazy. He had two full-grown, professional mercenaries crying because he convinced them they were going to be eaten by wolves. They spilled their guts to him. You know the rest, sir."

Trask couldn't help but chuckle, thinking about how he'd met Cassie and her comments about her family. "I wouldn't want to make an enemy out of either man," he replied, and the entire investigative team chuckled in unison. "Anything else on Inspector Preston?"

"No, sir, he's definitely one of the good guys."

Trask looked at the two state troopers. "Our investigation looks to be pretty normal —with just one small anomaly, though. When we did an internet search, we came up with an obituary for someone with the same name from the same hometown as our subject."

"Who?" Trask asked, and the investigator answered by way of handing him the manila folder he was carrying. Trask's eyes grew large.

"As you can see, this individual is from Roundup, Montana, sir."

There were again chuckles from the rest of the team.

The investigator added, "That individual was killed in an automobile accident several years ago, and we're having problems following up with the local authorities because, as you might guess, Roundup is not a big place."

The chuckles grew into open laughter, but a look from Trask brought the room back to silence. When he spoke next, his voice mirrored the austerity of his demeanor. "Son, you do what you have to and verify this. The sooner the better. I don't believe in coincidences, and you may have just found our traitor."

"Sir, we have the Montana Highway Patrol enroute to wake the local authorities and chase everything down. It'll just take a little time."

"Time we don't have." Trask's tone was serious. "As of right now, all four of you are working just on this. Keep an open line with the Montana authorities and use the entire weight of the federal government to get this done. We're not in this to make friends, so I don't care who you have them wake up! Understood?"

The team answered with a collective "Yes, sir!" and exited the office. Trask picked up the phone on the desk, and the tired voice of the secretary who was guarding the outside office answered. Trask gave her directions. "Connie, get me Glenn Grey right away. It's a priority."

"Yes, sir."

The phone line went dead, and Trask looked down at the file one more time.

His hands were shaking. They hadn't found the traitor where they thought they would.

Summers' Cabin
Adirondack State Park, New York
July 20, 2010
0245 hours

Walt Samcevic rested the high-powered rifle on a log and looked through its night vision scope, adjusting it slightly while looking for targets. He quickly found three by the back of the cabin and vainly searched for the fourth.

"Damn," he cursed through his teeth. "I can't see the fourth outside man."

"He's down in front of the cabin, out of sight. You won't be able to hit him. They'll have to take him down when he comes back around."

Sean was acting as his spotter. He had drawn the assignment partly because of his knowledge of the cabin complex, but also because he had experience from his time in the Navy.

"Commander, you have one target at two hundred fifty yards, a second at two hundred sixty yards, and the last at three hundred yards moving toward us."

Samcevic grunted as he sighted the closest target one more time. "You've done this before, haven't you, boy?" He glanced over and saw the smile on the young man's face. He smiled as well. He could appreciate working with someone experienced. "I understand you were wounded on 9/11 at the Pentagon?"

"Yes, sir, I was burned pretty bad."

Samcevic zeroed in on the third target, who was moving toward them. He guessed the man was headed to the cabin.

"But you got those burns running into the fire, not away from it." Samcevic glanced at the young man next him, who continued to do his job as though Samcevic wasn't there. The retired SEAL was impressed by how disciplined his partner was.

"Does it matter, Commander? I ended up getting discharged because of it. Hey, target three is going into the cabin."

Samcevic shifted back to target three. Sure enough, the man opened the back door to the cabin and was going in. He turned his attention to the two targets he could still see.

"It does to me, boy. Means you were going to help, not going to safety." Samcevic's right hand left the trigger guard of the rifle and touched the mic near his throat, activating it. His hand then returned to its original position on the rifle.

"I must have been lost, sir."

He grunted at the young man's response, speaking next into his mic. "Pathfinder, this is Overwatch, you have an additional target inside the cabin. I repeat, you have an additional target inside. We only have two in sight at the rear of the cabin."

There was a single click over the frequency, acknowledging the message.

Summers' Cabin
Adirondack State Park, New York
July 20, 2010
0250 hours

They watched the sentry in the front of the cabin move out of sight. When he was gone for sixty seconds, Jon moved forward, followed by Ellison, to the panels that enclosed the bottom of the front porch of the cabin. Jon touched the edge of the tallest panel and, as if by magic, the panel opened, exposing an entrance to what appeared to be a room.

While Ellison covered the direction the sentry had gone, Jon covered the hill along the side of the cabin.

Almost immediately, Justin and Ryan crossed the open space between the tree line and the cabin, disappearing underneath the porch. They were followed by Kay and her father, then by Becky and Reardon. As Reardon passed Ellison, he tapped him on the shoulder. Ellison checked the direction he was covering, and seeing it clear, he disappeared under the porch. He touched Jon on the shoulder, and Jon followed Ellison. The panel closed behind them. It was as if no one was ever there.

At the tree line, Naylor and Shomakker covered the infiltration, standing ready to move if needed. They watched when the sentry started back around the cabin and readied themselves for what was to come. Someone keyed their mic twice over the communications system.

"Overwatch copied," said Sean. "Starting the countdown now."

Bluffton Motor Court
Bluffton, New York
July 20, 2010
0250 hours

The first deputy arrived immediately when the call went out. He was followed seconds later by a New York state trooper, and they locked down access to the motel. Several more units followed before the FBI SWAT team arrived. They moved fast, gaining access to room number eight.

The results were disappointing for the crowd they drew. The room was empty, having been cleaned out, and looked like it was wiped down. Grey and Sanderson stood outside while their investigators moved in to see what evidence they could find.

"I'm glad this is over," commented Sanderson. "Now I can go about my job the way I should and get those people out."

Grey looked at the assistant director and decided to say nothing. He knew the background checks would continue, because if there was one traitor, there could be two, or possibly even more. Putnum wasn't taking any chances. Like Sanderson, he guessed they found the leak, but he also knew they had to be sure.

"At least I know now it wasn't one of mine," said Sanderson, "but how did she get past the record checks? I mean the actual person's been dead for over three years. The people who did that background check will be answering to the attorney general in the morning."

Grey couldn't help himself and smiled ever so slightly. "We did the background check for the Department of Justice."

Sanderson's nostrils flared, his jaw tight. He turned to face the movement in the corner of his eye, spotting Cassie approaching, looking concerned.

He openly scowled and turned toward Grey. "Damn it to hell, what does she want?"

Cassie walked up and ignored Sanderson, looking directly at Grey. "Agent Grey, I was told you wanted to see me. I'd like to know what could be so important to be summoned here at three in the morning."

Cassie motioned to the drama unfolding in front of them. The look on Sanderson's face was priceless. It was a mixture of surprise and anger. Grey knew enough not to smile and thought carefully about what he was about to say. Sanderson still hadn't figured out he wasn't in command of this incident scene anymore.

Agent Grey smiled politely at Cassie. "Miss Summers, your boss has been back in my office in New York supervising the follow-up on the staff combing through the backgrounds of all of us here, looking for the leak."

Sanderson's mouth dropped. Cassie grinned at his reaction. She again motioned to the scene behind her.

"I assume that's what this is all about?"

"I thought Trask was in Albany?" protested Sanderson. "Why wasn't I told? I'm the assistant direct—" Sanderson stopped before he finished his protest because he knew the answer and didn't want to be embarrassed in front of this young woman.

"That is what this is all about. It appears Tina Ramsey isn't really who she says she is. The real Tina Ramsey was killed in an automobile accident just after she was offered this job. How DOJ missed the switch, or how the death was missed during the background check, will be under investigation for years. Kingston appears to have been planning this for some time."

"Do you have her in custody?" asked Cassie.

Sanderson jumped into the conversation by inquiring, "Are you asking because of your personal attachment to this case or as a member of the US Attorney's Office?"

Cassie looked at Sanderson, letting him know she wasn't happy with the question, and at his side, Agent Grey shook his head.

"Mr. Sanderson," Cassie said, "the question was strictly professional. This leaves you without legal counsel at a critical time in your operation."

"So the question is, Miss Summers," continued Grey, "do you feel you can step up to the plate in Ramsey's absence? More specifically, can you represent the US Attorney's Office without prejudice or conflict?" Sanderson started to object, but Grey held up his hand, cutting him short to add, "That question comes from both Mike Trask and Admiral Putnum. They both feel you can handle the job until Mike can get back here."

Sanderson was red in the face, his fury clear, but kept his mouth shut, realizing this decision had been made above him. Cassie looked contemplatively back at the scene behind her, then at Grey. "I can handle the job, Special Agent Grey. My only question is, would you be comfortable with me doing the job?"

Grey just smiled.

Summers' Cabin
Adirondack State Park, New York
July 20, 2010
0257 hours

The room was larger than one would expect. It not only encompassed the entire area under the front porch but extended under the front part of the cabin. It was weatherproof and was used for the storage of important items. There were several four-drawer, fire-resistant filing cabinets, as well as a large steel gun safe. They all wore night vision gear, so no light was necessary, and because they were below the hostage takers in the cabin, they enforced strict noise discipline. Justin was surprised to find yet another secret spot his father had kept from him—first the cave, and now this.

Jon opened the gun safe and took out several small pistols, placing them in his rucksack. Using hand signals, Ellison asked him what he was doing. Jon pointed to where the hostages would be and indicated the weapons were for them. Ellison nodded, smiling. Justin investigated the safe as his father started to close it. It was filled, and he was almost certain he saw an M1 Garand, Browning M1919, and other World War II–era weapons.

Jon then moved toward the back of the cabin, and the room became smaller as the floor sloped up the hill the cabin was built on. Justin watched as his father began to remove a floor panel that revealed a trapdoor in the floor. Justin realized this was not a new room. The construction materials didn't look new, so he wondered why he hadn't ever known about this place. He was tapped on the shoulder and turned to find Ryan had opened what looked to be a wardrobe that was filled with old clothes, including uniforms. There was another tap on the shoulder, and he turned to find Becky motioning for him to pay attention. He looked toward where his father was and saw he was halfway through the trapdoor. They closed the wardrobe, moving forward.

Summers' Cabin
Adirondack State Park, New York
July 20, 2010
0300 hours

Nancy couldn't relax enough to so much as doze after figuring out what Hapke's people had planned for them. At least Sarah and the kids managed to get away. Jon would protect them—though she didn't feel there was much of a chance of him getting the rest of them out.

He was only one man, after all—and against how many?

Nancy didn't understand Josh's optimism, though she had to admit it was infectious. She couldn't help but wonder what he'd meant by bringing up her husband, and her trust in him, which she'd always thought was obvious.

One of the guards from outside came in and began talking to the communications man. They weren't paying attention to the hostages. A quick glance at the man guarding them revealed to Nancy that he'd dozed off.

There was a creak in the floor of the master bedroom. Nancy glanced at Josh, who was peering back at her, wide-eyed. He'd clearly heard it too. He then smiled at her, as if to say *I told you so.*

Mohawk Tavern and Grill
Bluffton, New York
July 20, 2010
0300 hours

Sanderson stormed up to the van and was about to protest loudly about how he avidly disapproved of being left ignorant of important developments within his own mission only for Mitchell to hold up his hand, keeping him silent. Putnum was on the phone, and the body language of the agents present told Sanderson he needed to calm down. He took a deep breath and listened to Putnum's conversation.

"Yes, sir. . ... No, I don't think that's necessary. With what you've authorized and what's already in place, we'll be able to resolve this issue quickly come daylight. . ... I understand, sir. We already have an operation underway to ensure that doesn't happen. Our priority must be the hostages, but we're ready to move forward with that as well. . ... No, sir. There are no guarantees for a hundred percent success for either operation. Our recommendations were forwarded and not followed by the Department of Justice, and now we're in a deeper hole than when we first became aware of this about forty hours ago."

Sanderson raised his brows in open question and looked at Mitchell while he mouthed the question, "Who is Putnum talking to?"

Mitchell shook his head and motioned for Sanderson to pay attention.

"I'll say it again, sir, there are no guarantees. We have boots on the ground, sir, and until we have confirmation on the second situation, we're continuing to track the location of those involved. Your permission for the use of the additional assets will help more than you know. . ... It shouldn't have been allowed to get this far, sir, but Mr. Kingston planned this to include most of the options. He didn't know there were some extra cards in the deck, and that's working against him. Yes, sir. . ... Yes, sir. . ... No, sir, I'm in contact with the Marshals Service, and as soon as they confirm the second issue actually exists, I'll get your permission to start the second operation. . ... Yes, sir, I have a team on-site as we speak. The operation is ongoing."

Sanderson's eyes grew wide when he realized Putnum had a team on the island. Who was he speaking to? He was about to ask when Grey and Cassie walked up. He checked his question when Mitchell gave the two newcomers the same quiet signal.

"Again, sir, if they had listened to our recommendations in the first place, we wouldn't be in this situation right now. It's hard enough the man planted people in our ranks over the years, but to have our own people work against us is intolerable. . ... Yes, sir, I will pass that on to Assistant Director Sanderson. He won't be happy, but that may be some consolation. . ... Yes, sir, that I can promise, sir. . ... That's what we do, sir. That I will guarantee, no matter how long it takes. Thank you, Mr. President. . ... Yes, sir, I'll keep you informed."

It was all Sanderson could do not to balk at hearing "Mr. President."

Putnum put the handset back into the van, turned to look at the group gathered close around him, and said, "It looks like Dick Kingston has escaped. The Marshals Office has lost contact with their protection detail at Dulles."

"Damn!" muttered Cassie.

Mitchell sighed, hand over his mouth, while Grey swore quietly under his breath. Their worst fears had been confirmed. Sanderson looked blankly at Putnum, all but paralyzed by his sheer disbelief.

Putnum met his gaze. "The president wanted me to tell you how sorry he was that they didn't listen to your recommendation not to move Kingston from Leavenworth. There's no way he would have escaped from there."

"You mentioned you might be working on another operation. Might that have to do with tracking Kingston?" Sanderson dared to ask, and Putnum smiled before excusing himself, leaving the entire group standing there.

"Damn him!" said Sanderson, a vein bulging at his temple.

Mitchell shook his head. "You don't get it, do you, sport?" he said, giving Sanderson a clap on the back. "The man's protecting you."

"Protecting me from what?"

"For an educated man, you really are thick," said Cassie. Sanderson gave the woman an angry look. She ignored him, continuing, "Whatever it is, it's probably illegal, and he doesn't want you near it because you would either try to stop it or would get fired."

Sanderson looked at the attorney—seriously at first—but a smile slowly crept across his face. "Oh, is that all?"

Public Dock
Dartford, New York
July 20, 2010
0300 hours

The convoy, led by two state police cruisers, pulled into the parking area next to the dock to find a sheriff's car waiting for them. The trooper in the vehicle leading the convoy got out and spoke briefly to the deputy, who pointed to the boat launch. The trooper shook his head and motioned at the flatbed trucks behind him. All the deputy could do was shrug his shoulders.

A lone figure got out of the Humvee behind the trooper cars, walking up to join the conversation. "What's the problem?"

The trooper looked at the naval officer, shaking his head. "Sorry, Lieutenant. This is the only public boat launch in town, and it's going to be tough unloading those things here."

The lieutenant pointed to a boat lift in the marina next door. "What about that? We can use that to off-load our equipment."

"That marina is owned by the mayor," said the deputy. "He's not a big fan of the sheriff and isn't really cooperative with us. He's even pulled his police force in for the night. He doesn't want to have anything to do with getting the sheriff out of his predicament. Small-town politics."

The lieutenant pulled out a phone. "I don't have time for this bullshit," he said, quickly dialing a number. The call was picked up after only one ring. "Sir, I have a small problem."

57 Hidden Cove Lane
Dartford, New York
July 20, 2010
0305 hours

The mayor of Dartford prided himself on keeping a strict schedule. Both he and his wife had turned in by 10:00 p.m., the way they did every night, and didn't even pay attention to the news of the day's events.

Sheriff Marty James had opposed and beaten his brother-in-law for sheriff, so he figured the man was just getting his due. The mayor had been approached to make his marina available for the rescue effort, but he had refused. There was going to be no helping Marty James, and he didn't know the others being held hostage. It was no skin off his nose.

The phone rang, and he rolled over to look at the clock. Who on earth would be calling the house at three in the morning? He guessed it was the police chief whom he'd given strict orders to stay out of this ongoing circus.

The mayor answered on the second ring. "This better be important, or I'll have your job, you son of a bitch."

"I don't think so." The voice on the other end wasn't one the mayor recognized. It was also not intimidated in any way. "Mr. Mayor, this is Admiral

Putnum, and I'm with the NSA. I need to talk to you about something important."

"I don't give a damn who you are. Do you know what time it is?"

There was a knock at the door, and the doorbell rang.

"Honey, who is it?" asked the mayor's wife. "What's going on?"

"You need to answer the door, Mr. Mayor," said Putnum flatly.

The phone was a cordless one, so the mayor was able to take it with him. "You can't intimidate me. I'm not just anyone, you know."

There was a laugh from the other end. "I know *exactly* who and what you are, Mr. Mayor, and it's not about intimidation. It's about need. Now, answer the door."

The last statement sounded like the man was used to getting his way. When the mayor approached the door, there was another knock.

The mayor spoke while opening the door. "I don't care who you are or who you work for, I—"

The mayor found himself facing a deputy sheriff, a state trooper, and a very serious young man in a military uniform carrying an assault rifle.

"I can tell by your silence, Mr. Mayor, that we've reached the intimidating part of our conversation. Are you ready to listen while these gentlemen explain your options to you?"

From behind him, the mayor's wife called out, "Honey, who's at the door?"

Summers' Cabin
Adirondack State Park, New York
July 20, 2010
0305 hours

The trapdoor had been hidden by a rug in the master bedroom of the cabin. Jon was the first one through and quickly made sure that they were alone. The others came through one by one. Because everything was made of wood, there was the occasional creak, but nothing that would draw attention. It took several minutes for everyone to get inside, with Justin being the last. He passed his pack up to Ryan and then climbed through the trapdoor. They were all wearing night vision gear, and Justin looked to his father for directions. Jon motioned for him to close the trapdoor. Justin did so, covering it back up with the rug.

Jon took a minute to line his shooters up before they entered the main rooms of the cabin. Several of them drew their handguns from their holsters and attached noise suppressors. They had gone over the plan several times, and Jon placed his most experienced people where he knew they were needed. With several inexperienced people on the team, this wasn't the time for hesitation. Jon looked at his people, and each gave him a thumbs-up, indicating that they were ready. He activated the mic on his headset and whispered, "Green light."

Summers' Cabin
Adirondack State Park, New York
July 20, 2010
0310 hours

The high-power sniper rifle Walt Samcevic was using was also suppressed, but in the silence of the night, the noise still carried. His first shot dropped the sentry closest to the door. While he zeroed his scope in on his second target, Sean gave him the range, and he adjusted the rifle accordingly. Seconds later, the second round fired, downing the target—just in time, too, as the enemy was aiming his own rifle right at them, having seen their muzzle flash. The impact of the round threw him back about five feet, where he was now lifeless on the ground.

On the other side of the cabin, the third sentry reacted to the sound of the first shot. Though suppressed, it was obviously a gunshot. The man started to raise his rifle and move up the side of the cabin. Catching movement to his left, he turned to meet the threat. He was struck by two rounds from Shomakker's M4. The man dropped as fast as his two companions. Naylor and Shomakker moved silently out of the tree line toward the cabin.

"Team three is clear," came Samcevic's voice over the radio.

Naylor and Shomakker looked at each other. It was Naylor who spoke. "Team two is clear."

Summers' Cabin
Adirondack State Park, New York
July 20, 2010
0310 hours

It seemed like hours since Nancy had heard the creaking floor in the other room. She'd looked at Ericson, who had put his finger to his lips, telling her not to say anything. Everyone else in the room had been, and still was, fast asleep.

Ericson motioned for her to stay calm and stay down. She started to think about how someone could have gotten in the other room. *The trapdoor.* She had forgotten about the trapdoor. They never used it and hadn't shared its existence with any of the kids, so it was easy to forget about. Midway through the thought, she was abruptly pushed to the floor by Ericson, who also covered his wife's sleeping body with his.

There was a flurry of movement from the other room. It seemed to be in slow motion. Dark silhouettes came out of the bedroom, looking like ghosts in the darkness. The first turned into the living room, the second to the dining area, a third to the kitchen, and a fourth to the bathroom. There was a series of popping sounds, and a cry of pain. This was followed by the sound of something metallic being dropped and the thud of something heavy hitting the floor.

There were gasps of surprise as the others woke up. Two more shadowy figures moved past where they were lying on the floor and started up the stairs toward the second story, rifles at the ready. The figure who had entered the living room moved past them, covering the two going upstairs. Nancy couldn't see them but could hear them going from room to room. The entire process took about thirty seconds.

"Clear here," said a voice with a thick Irish accent from the balcony above.

"Clear," said another voice from the kitchen.

"Clear," reported yet another voice from the bathroom and master bedroom.

"Clear—and their communications are secure." This time, the voice was recognizable, and Nancy knew it belonged to George Ellison. Just as she felt a rush of newfound hope, she heard somebody else's voice. Another voice she recognized.

"Teams two and three, copy that the exterior is secured," he said, and Nancy went still, understanding Ericson's questions from earlier. "Pathfinder to Fort Bluffton, all hostages are secured—no casualties."

That voice belonged to her husband.

Summers' Cabin
Adirondack State Park, New York
July 20, 2010
0312 hours

With Jon's transmission confirming that they were set inside, Samcevic glanced over at Sean and gave him a broad smile. The younger man was still intently doing his job. He did exactly what he needed to do and was now checking to make sure that no one was coming back to help those in the cabin.

"Your job's done here, kid. Time to go get the others."

"Aye, aye, Commander." Sean put the spotter scope back in his rucksack and looked at his partner. With that, Sean silently backed out of their position and disappeared into the dark forest.

Samcevic listened closely—there wasn't a sound. "Team three to Pathfinder," he said, speaking into his mic, "my very stealthy partner has moved on to his next assignment."

Summers' Cabin
Adirondack State Park, New York
July 20, 2010
0312 hours

Nancy sat up, looking around for the first time since Ericson had pushed her and his wife to the floor. The sentinel assigned to guard the front door was now folded over himself, with two holes in his forehead.

Those rounds could've struck them if they'd been sitting up.

Nancy looked to her husband, who was standing by the downed guard. He was watching her but remained cool and professional as he said, "Everyone stays down and quiet until the doctor can check you all out."

Nancy realized for the first time that it was Becky who was checking the hostages for injuries. This wasn't a normal rescue. Jon and George were both retired, and the FBI certainly wouldn't have let Becky come along. Several of the other rescuers looked to be older than Jon.

Jon smiled as he spoke into the mic. "Copy that, boss. I'll let you know the pickup point."

His intensity softened when they exchanged a look of relief, both knowing the family was okay. Then she realized he was holding a pistol, and it was him who'd shot the guard. In all the years they'd been married, she knew he was trained to do this but never thought she'd ever see him kill someone.

"Jonny!"

"Uncle Jon?"

Julie and Alex had jumped up and raced to Jon, hugging him. He struggled to keep the pistol in his hand out of the way while his sister and niece latched on, smothering him.

"Did you kill him?" Hector asked solemnly, nodding at Jon's pistol.

Jon gave a nod of his own in reply. Julie and Alex looked down at the dead kidnapper but didn't release their hold.

"They killed my father, you know."

Jon looked down at Nancy, who gave him the sort of look that suggested he approach this topic with circumspection. He glanced at his sister, finding her crying. "I know, Hector. Emily told me. Your uncle Matt and I will take care of that. Here, take your mother and sister and get them ready to move out of here in a few minutes."

The young man said nothing, taking his mother by her shoulders and leading her to the couch. His sister followed, hugging her uncle one more time. Nancy managed to get to her feet and went to help Ericson, who waved her off. Fiona had her arms around her husband, and it was all too obvious he didn't want any help from friends. She turned, smiling, just in time to see the two men coming down the stairs. She immediately recognized the first man, and turned toward her husband, raising her hand to strike him across the face.

"You son of a bitch—"

Jon caught her raised hand and drew her in close to him. "Go to him, damn it. We can settle this later."

Jon's eyes twinkled as he spoke to Nancy. She broke free and rushed over to Justin, almost knocking him over. Jon took a quick glance around the room. Kay was busy collecting anything she could from the communications area to save as evidence. Ellison was policing the bodies of the dead kidnappers to see what he could find. Becky was being helped by Reardon and Wiedenkeller, checking the hostages. Justin was buried in family, as Julie and her kids joined Nancy in welcoming him back from the dead. Ryan looked back at him and just shrugged.

Jon finally put his pistol away. "Ryan! Justin! Get outside and help teams two and three with perimeter security. We can't have the bad guys coming back and taking us by surprise."

A huge grin made its way across Ryan's face as he reached into the crowd and grabbed Justin by the collar. "Come on, boyo, we've got work to do. You can reacquaint yourself with the family when we don't have people trying to kill us."

Justin struggled to free himself from his mother and aunt, nodding at his father. He kissed Nancy gently on the cheek, moving toward the door. Ryan followed, still grinning. Kay smiled at the two of them when they walked by her.

"Kay, you all set?" asked Jon.

"I'm with her, Jon," answered Ellison. "We're packing up some hardware she wants to process."

Jon nodded, and they continued their work.

Nancy came back over to her husband, voice low. "You're a bastard, you know that?"

"You've known that for years, my dear."

Nancy smiled and then threw her arms around her husband, kissing him. When she released him, some of the camo paint had rubbed off on her face. "Thanks for getting him back. I knew you had something up your sleeve."

"Nothing until you got kidnapped."

"You know that we were told you were killed in Canada, right?"

Before Jon could answer, Naylor entered the cabin, walking up to them. "Nancy, good to see you alive."

Nancy turned, smiling at the man. "I can't tell you how good it is to see you, Charlie."

Naylor turned his attention back to Summers. "Jon, they have all the cabins wired to blow, and we found several of their wounded in one of the smaller cabins. Some of them are in bad shape—what'd they run into?"

Nancy gave her husband a serious look.

"Oh," said Naylor. "Look, Jon, they've rigged each of the buildings in the complex to blow with C4. Nothing EOD out of Drum can't handle. Between them and the FBI, they'll make short work of it, but it's not safe to keep these people here in case they can detonate them remotely from their location."

"Fine," said Jon. "Send someone to a safe distance, where they can radio that we'll be using the alternate extraction point and that we'll need that special evacuation team."

Naylor smiled at Summers. "Justin's already working on that."

Jon should have guessed that Naylor was one step ahead. Charlie was the best the Army had to offer in the way of a multilevel thinker, even if he'd retired the year before. He also didn't stand on ceremony when something needed to be done.

"Jon, I really think Becky should take a look at a couple of these guys in the other cabin."

Jon nodded his approval, and Naylor moved off to get the doctor. When Becky moved by, with Reardon in tow, Jon grabbed her pack harness. "We can't take any of them with us, and you're not staying. The FBI will be in to bring them out, and you can radio in what the injuries are and what they'll need."

Becky just stood and looked at Jon for a second. "Don't take this wrong, Jonny. These men are in that cabin because they're the ones you didn't kill. They also took members of my family hostage and hurt people I love. I'll make them comfortable and do what I can to help—nothing more, nothing less—but I am not leaving without my family." With that, she turned to look at Nancy. "You okay? I hear you got hit by a rubber bullet when they took this place."

"Just a bruise; I'm fine."

"I'll take a look at it nonetheless when we stop to let the others catch up, just to make sure there aren't any problems."

Without another word, Becky disappeared out the door. Nancy looked at her husband and hugged him again. "Now I think I understand the nightmares."

"Let's get these people out of here," said Jon, back to business. "We've been here too long already."

Mohawk Tavern and Grill
Bluffton, New York
July 20, 2010
0320 hours

They had been listening to the operation for ten minutes and were amazed that the hostages were already being moved to a rendezvous point. Sanderson showed no signs of emotion during the operation. The blow-by-blow account over the radio demonstrated that these were not amateurs doing what he felt his people should be doing. They—whoever *they* were—had done this before. Based on the damage they'd done, he guessed there were at least six more dead hostage takers. His people couldn't have done it any more cleanly.

Putnum was again on the phone with the White House, partly to let the president know that the hostages were in friendly custody and to get permission for the next phase of the operation. For his part, Sanderson knew there was a cabin full of wounded prisoners waiting for him and explosives for his people to clean up. He would be grateful for the help of EOD out of Fort Drum. The fact that they set booby traps around the island didn't make him happy either. Clearing those would be a monumental job in and of itself.

He and Putnum took a minute to discuss the possible escape of Richard Kingston. Both men were upset their superiors hadn't listened to them. Putnum assured Sanderson a plan B was already in place—and working. They would track the man down and return him to custody.

As soon as Putnum was off the phone, he gave Mitchell the order. "Spread the word—we have a go from the president. All plans and teams are approved."

Mitchell nodded, taking out his phone.

CHAPTER EIGHT

EXTRACTION

Public Dock
Dartford, New York
July 20, 2010
0400 hours

The boats were in the water, the crews feverishly putting all the bells and whistles where they belonged. The bells and whistles for a Special Operations Craft—Riverine or SOC-R—were a variety of miniguns, machine guns, and grenade launchers, which made the thirty-three-foot, forty-knot craft very popular as an infiltration and exfiltration craft for special operations teams. The intention of this process was to bring the hostages back without allowing the hostage takers any opportunity to intercept them.

The mayor of Dartford jumped in without hesitation to help after the phone call. He ran the lift himself, getting each boat off the flatbed and into the water. He was still on the dock, offering to help in loading the boats, much to the chagrin of the crewmen.

Putnum's phone call had worked wonders. The New York State Police SORT team had arrived at about 3:40 a.m. and now stood watching the process unfold before them. They were told they were going back to the island to help retrieve the hostages and arrest the hostage takers. After their earlier experiences, they stated their apprehension to their superiors. The rumors were that there were spies in the FBI camp, and they didn't want to be part of another botched rescue attempt. Their captain assured them they would be working with the best HRT people in the business and that there was nothing to worry about. Watching the boats being put together and the men sent to work with them, their concerns seemed unfounded.

A series of black SUVs pulled into the lot. Another group of armed men in uniform exited the vehicles. Unlike the group that was with the boats, their faces were already covered in camouflaged paint, except for three: two women and a man. The officer in charge of the boats immediately stopped what he was doing, running up to the man, coming to attention, and saluting. The salute was returned, and some words were spoken. There was laughter, and the new arrival patted the young officer on the back, who then trotted toward the boats. The men he arrived with moved off to join the others, except for one, who stayed with the two women.

The newcomer was now focused on the SORT team, standing near their vehicles. He started their way, followed by the two women and the face-painted man.

"Good morning, Lieutenant," said Kingston. "I'm Commander Kingston with the Navy's Special Boat units, and this is Commander Smith with Naval Intelligence."

The state police lieutenant stepped forward, accepting the handshake. "Nice to meet you both. Why is the Navy here in Dartford? Aren't we a ways from the ocean?"

The tone of the question was neutral, so Kingston answered in the same fashion. "The president has approved the limited use of the military in extracting the hostages and apprehending the hostage takers. We obviously aren't professional law enforcement, so your team has been assigned to us when we go in. We can't have any arrest jeopardized because we've been a little overzealous in doing our job. You're here to make sure we use the proper restraint."

"And Miss Monroe—is she here to help you maintain your restraint as well?" The lieutenant pointed to the reporter standing behind Kingston.

She answered for herself. "Lieutenant, I'm kind of their prisoner, because I know too many of the players in this little drama. For example, Mr. Kingston here is the son of the man who made all this possible. But don't worry, he's really one of the good guys. He's here to get his mother out, nothing more. The whole alphabet soup of government agencies is here, and they want your team to make sure these Navy SEALs don't get overzealous. Lieutenant, I don't envy your job."

The state policeman looked at Kingston, who just smiled weakly.

At this point, Smith added, "Our job, Lieutenant, is to land you and these other teams on the island and take off any hostages who've already been freed."

"Freed? By whom? What about Sheriff James and Deputy Crogan? They wouldn't let us go back to get them and—"

Kingston held up his hand, stopping the man. "They were freed about an hour ago, and Sheriff James is wounded. We have two doctors on the island, however, and he's in good hands. Deputy Crogan will join you when you land. Some old friends are on the island and have made all this possible."

"Old friends?"

"Commander Smith and I met most of them when we went through the Naval Academy together."

"Then they're military," he deduced, clearly skeptical.

"Not anymore," answered Smith.

The lieutenant raised his brows. "Mercenary then?"

Kingston shook his head. "Retired."

"What the . . ."

"Oh, you have no idea, Lieutenant," said Monroe, laughing. "These guys are the ones who bring a whole new meaning to the word *nightmare*. They're ghosts come back to haunt these would-be hostage takers. Men long thought dead—or hoped to be, by their enemies—including Richard Kingston. I could tell you stories."

"Most of which never took place," said Smith, chastising Monroe with a look.

"Or are gaps in someone's service record," the state policeman added, laughing. "I'm a marine, Commander, so I understand."

The comment brought a smile to both Kingston and Smith. Kingston motioned the man in the camouflage paint forward. "Lieutenant, this is Chief Skier. He'll introduce you and your people to the other guys on the team. The chief is with SE—"

"We're with the Franklin County Sheriff's Office SWAT team," interrupted Skier.

The SORT team lieutenant looked puzzled. "Franklin County doesn't have a SWAT team, Chief."

"They do as of about two hours ago, sir, when they swore us in," said Skier with a grin.

Summers' Island
Adirondack State Park, New York
July 20, 2010
0400 hours

They moved away from the cabins, walking for about fifteen minutes through the thick forest. When they crossed a well-used path and were in the thick undergrowth on the other side, Jon called a halt, and the former hostages were huddled together behind a pair of windfalls that formed the shape of a V, offering them cover. Hector and Fortum had helped carry Josh, who was frustrated without a wheelchair. Wells was given weapons taken from the dead kidnappers and now helped with protection of the little group.

When they settled in their current location, the rescue team produced ponchos, which were set up to protect the former hostages from the dampness that came with the thick fog clinging to the forest floor. Becky continued to check the hostages for any major medical issues, finding nothing. She ignored all conversation, going about her business, now assisted by Nancy, Julie, and Fiona. Josh had been made comfortable on the outside of the group, with Hector nearby to help him.

"Why don't they just take us out of here?" asked Sue Ellen. "I mean, it can't be that hard, right?"

Hennen chimed in, saying, "I agree with Sue Ellen. They need to concentrate on getting us out. They have a plan. I mean, we are members of the senior leadership in Congress! Don't they have orders from the president to get us out of here right away?"

"Eric and I never agree, but he's right. Whoever oversees these men needs to get us out of here."

Frank Del Monte couldn't contain himself anymore. "The two of you need to get over yourselves! You're no more important than anyone else here who was taken hostage. There's another whole group out there that we have to meet up with. We all go out together when they say we go—not before."

Sue Ellen looked down, not able to meet her husband's gaze, but Hennen wasn't afraid of lashing out. "You have no right to speak to me that way, Frank!" he said. "I'm—"

"Oh, shut up, Eric," interrupted Alexander. "You're being an insufferable ass. Just sit there and be quiet."

The younger politician looked hurt. "Art, I—"

"Just *shut up*, Eric," Alexander repeated. "Haven't you figured out these people aren't law enforcement or military? We're no longer hostages because they came to help us when no one else could or would."

Ericson smiled, adding, "There's also a well-armed force of kidnappers out there that outnumbers our rescuers. While there's no doubt in my mind these gentlemen and ladies could handle them, they're currently split into two groups. They stand a better chance of getting us all out once we have everyone together."

The conversation stopped when one of their rescuers approached them.

Congresswoman Del Monte's eyes grew large when she recognized Walt Samcevic. She knew him from her early years in Congress, when she was just a member of the House Armed Services Committee investigating some misuse of funds by different branches of the military. Samcevic's unit had been one of those under investigation, and he retired early because of the hearings. If Samcevic recognized her, he gave no indication. He knelt next to Ericson and said, "How're you doing, Chief?"

"Fine now, Walt, thanks to you guys."

Nancy quietly moved over to Samcevic, followed by Julie, and both women kissed him gently on the cheek.

"Thanks, Walt," said Nancy. "I know you didn't have to do this."

"Yeah, I did. This old sailor pulled me out of the jungle more than once. It's time to return the favor. Besides, if your husband won't give me an interview about his past, then working with him will give me insight on what makes him tick. I'll write that book one way or the other."

"Careful, Walt," Nancy said with a chuckle. "You know what they say about putting your head in the lion's mouth."

Samcevic smiled at the response, and Julie added, "I'll speak to him—the most he'll say is no."

"Bless you, Julie. Will you marry me?"

Julie giggled, kissing him on the cheek again. "Thanks, but one crazy in the family is enough."

It was Samcevic's turn to laugh. "Julie, honey, your whole family's nuts, just in case that slipped by you. That's why I love you guys, though." At this, Samcevic turned his attention back to Ericson, pulling an unopened bottle of Wild Turkey bourbon out of his pack. "Jon gave me this for you and the rest of your merry band here. He thought it would fight off the dampness."

"How long until we move out, Walt?"

"That depends on how long it takes the kid to get back with the others."

"The kid?" asked Nancy. "What kid?"

Samcevic smiled and maintained eye contact with Ericson as he answered. "That would be your oldest son. The one who walks through the woods without making any noise. He's gone to get the other group being led by your brother-in-law. They could be a while, because they have the wounded sheriff, the kids, and even some of the kidnappers."

"Kidnappers?" Ericson's brows shot toward his hairline. "Am I hearing you right?"

Samcevic shrugged his shoulders. "Listen, Jon's keeping the more civic-minded in his family happy. We've all had a good laugh to see him so restrained. It appears that son number three is dating a deputy sheriff. Nice girl—Native American, pretty. She felt having a kidnapper or two of our own might be nice. This is a family affair, after all."

Ericson smiled more at Del Monte and Hennen's reaction than at what was said. The two of them looked positively scandalized.

"You mean this isn't an official rescue?" asked Sue Ellen.

For the first time since he came over to the group, Samcevic looked directly at the congresswoman. "No, ma'am, it's not. It's more like the Wild West. The FBI was infiltrated by this bastard, so they can't make a move without the bad guys knowing, and the president must get approval to send in the military. Unfortunately, they picked the wrong place to take hostages. The family that owns this island is more than capable of taking care of business, but they also have some good friends willing to help." Sue Ellen didn't answer and just looked at Samcevic as he continued. "We'll get you out, ma'am. All of you. Just be patient. This is what we do."

Samcevic cracked open the seal on the bottle in his hand and took the top off. He took a short pull of the whisky inside and handed the bottle to Ericson. He did the same, and then both men looked at young Hector, who was shivering.

Ericson held up the bottle. "You ever had this before, son?"

Hector shook his head.

"Just a sip, boy. It's going to burn a bit going down."

Hector took the bottle and didn't hesitate. It took a couple of seconds, then he coughed and put his arm up to his mouth. Everyone in the group laughed while Hector handed the bottle back to Samcevic, who said, "At least he's not shivering anymore, Chief."

There was more laughter, and even Hector managed to smile. Samcevic offered the bottle to Sue Ellen. "Ma'am?"

She took the offered bottle, inspecting it. "What? No Scotch?"

"Sorry, ma'am, I'll know better next time."

"Thank you for everything, Commander."

Summers' Island
Adirondack State Park, New York
July 20, 2010
0420 hours

Hapke watched as his people built their positions. They'd moved all the heavy armament to this location, and he'd given strict orders not to damage or destroy the boats the FBI would be using. They would need them to escape. There were just over twenty people with him, plus the six in the main cabin, who were fit enough to fight. The wounded would be left behind, naturally, as they would only slow the rest of them down—and besides, nobody other than he and Servati had any good information about where they were to head when they left the island.

With that being said, he officially had to assume that Servati was dead; they hadn't heard from her in quite a while. That meant access to their boats was compromised and they needed the ones being used by the FBI.

Hapke didn't care if his people got away. That would mean there would be more money for him. He arranged for tickets for him and Servati to a nonextradition country with liberal banking laws under the assumption that he could leave on his own if necessary. He just needed the rest of his people to hold together long enough to finish this part of the mission. There was, after all, safety in numbers. Whoever was on the island was picking off individuals and small groups. From this point forward, they stayed together.

He took cover behind a tree and sat down, laying his rifle across his lap. He pulled out the burner phone and nervously typed out a text. "Where do we stand w/ assault? R U able to get extra exfil boats? Pls ans ASAP."

He hit send and sat for a minute, looking at the phone before deciding to type and send a follow-up text. "Will be done w/ mission as of 0500. Exfil compromised, repeat, need more boats, imperative. Pls respond."

This was his fourth message without an immediate response. He was beginning to get worried. He took a quick look around. His people were still hard at work.

About fifty yards behind him, two shadowy figures watched what was going on with great interest. They were sent out to locate the main force of the hostage takers and get information about the defenses they were setting up. Naylor used a small pair of binoculars he carried in his rucksack to pinpoint the activity, checked a small handheld GPS device, and wrote what he observed down in a small notebook. Reardon was next to him, rifle at the ready because of how close they were to their adversary.

Even they didn't notice another set of eyes, hidden behind some fallen trees, watching the scene. Their sole focus was only on one man—and he was busy sending text messages.

Interstate 87
Starbuckville, New York
July 20, 2010
0420 hours

She had been driving for three hours and was taking great care not to draw attention to herself along the way. That meant staying at the speed limit, not rushing, and taking breaks whenever she felt tired. They would find out sooner or later she wasn't who she pretended to be, and they would be after her, knowing she was the one passing on the information to Hapke.

The woman who had posed as Tina Ramsey considered the man an idiot, but armed with what she and her sister had passed his way, he'd managed to hold the FBI at bay for almost a whole day.

Her cell chirped, indicating she'd received a text message. She picked it up and took a quick look, only to toss it back on the seat next to her, focusing on her driving. It'd been from Hapke. She didn't care what it said—the man was on his own now. Kingston had never intended on the man or his people surviving the island phase of the operation. They only recruited him because of his hatred for Jon Summers and his family. He was expendable, along with his people. They accomplished what was intended, and she now needed to get to the plane waiting for her and get out of the country to meet Rick and her sisters. They had already won.

White House
Washington, DC
July 20, 2010
0420 hours

The president sat on the sofa in the hallway outside his bedroom. His staff encouraged him to sleep, but with everything going on, he was having trouble relaxing. He moved out into the hallway so he wouldn't disturb his wife. He wasn't happy with what was taking place and didn't want to go back to the situation room. The reports made it look like things were getting worse. He needed time to think without others making recommendations, or worse—second-guessing themselves.

The hostages were free, technically, but still on the island—and as such, they were all still arguably in danger. The FBI was compromised and ineffective in ending the situation. And now they'd learned the leak was from the Department of Justice—which meant that not only was this situation compromised from a legal standpoint, but so was any case this young woman worked on previously. Justice was still assessing the damage there.

Even more, a traitor to his country had escaped federal custody and was on the loose, having executed the team of US marshals assigned to guard him. He was said to currently be in an airplane somewhere, and they didn't know exactly where he was headed or if he was still in US airspace. That situation alone was a political disaster because the FBI, CIA, and the military advised him against the move for that very reason. He listened to political advisors and members of Congress, all of whom gave advice based on political—not practical—motives. Now he'd approved the limited use of military assets to help extract the former hostages. It was a good thing this was his second term, because he would never get reelected after this.

The phone on the table next to him rang, and the Secret Service agent standing closest to him started to reach for it.

The president stopped him, picking up the receiver. "Hello?"

"Mr. President," said the switchboard operator, "the conference call you requested is ready."

The president was instantly speaking to his last two predecessors about his predicament and asking for their advice. The man he'd followed was a Republican, while the man who had preceded him was in his own party. He was surprised when both men gave him similar advice: stay away from the political types and trust the professionals. His immediate predecessor expanded on his feedback, saying, "I found Admiral Putnum to be very competent. He was one of the clear heads in 9/11. He sees the big picture and can manage the most difficult situations tactfully. If he's managing this for you, then you'll come out on top."

"He managed the original Kingston investigation for me," said his other predecessor, "and did it quietly and without a fuss. The bastard never got the media coverage he was hoping for because of how resourceful Putnum was. If he has a plan B to track Kingston, let him run with it. He'll get it done. Trust him, Mr. President."

The president was silent for a moment before he said, "The man leading this ground unit, they say his name is Summers . . ."

"Jon Summers? He's alive?" His immediate predecessor sounded puzzled.

"The briefs you sent said he was killed in Canada. He's on the island?" the Republican predecessor said, his Texas drawl activated.

"Yes. He wasn't killed like we were told, and instead he hitched a ride on a Canadian Air Force plane. He parachuted onto the island and has been interfering with the kidnappers ever since."

"Hot damn!" responded the Texan.

The other former president laughed. "You have nothing to worry about if he has the hostages, Mr. President. He'll get them out—and God save the kidnappers if they try to take them back."

There was a chuckle from the Texan. "Y'all might want to give the man a call and remind him you need prisoners to connect these sons of bitches to Kingston. These guys kidnapped his family. If I were him, with his skills, I just might want some payback. Not that I blame him at all."

The other one added, "If it were me, I'd be mad as hell and would be making them pay dearly. Then the history between him and this Hapke fella sure would make me worry. I certainly wouldn't want Summers coming after me. I know what he did the first time he went after Kingston. I agree, you should consider that call."

The president didn't respond to either of his predecessors. He was deep in thought. Most of the rescue team had no connection to the government anymore, therefore, there was no formal control. Apprehension began to rise in the back of his mind. Had he made the right decision?

Dartford Island
Adirondack State Park, New York
July 20, 2010
0430 hours

The four boats silently beached on the east side of the island, having made the short trip from the public dock in Dartford. They weren't worried about being detected because the owner of the cabin on this island wasn't in this weekend. They decided to land here and wait because they were away from Dartford and the inquiring eyes of its citizens and the media.

With the boats being as crowded as they were, this also gave them a chance to spread out and relax before they were needed. Kingston assigned the New York State Police SORT team to work with the two SEAL teams on some basic police procedures for taking prisoners into custody. The reverse was also true if the hostage takers refused to surrender and resisted. SEALs didn't allow much resistance when they encountered a hostile force, and the SORT team needed to know how they would respond if any was offered by the remaining hostage takers.

Monroe watched the interaction between the troopers and the SEALs with unbridled interest. She also kept a close eye on Kingston while he checked with his crews, making sure the boats were ready.

Smith smiled, watching the reporter make her mental notes. "Are you planning a news story on this little adventure, Miss Monroe?"

Monroe jumped, startled, not realizing Smith was so close. She quickly settled, returning Smith's smile. "It's a reporter's dream, Commander.

Kidnapping, murder, escaped villain, dead hero back from the dead . . . this is some prize-winning stuff. I'm not naive enough to think I'll be able to air much of this. I was with the admiral in the Philippines in '95, and very little of that made it to the news."

Smith shook her head. "That man's a mystery, even to us. I served as his aide for a while, and he still amazes me every time I'm with him. He's as unpredictable as they come; I never knew what to expect from him from one minute to the next."

Monroe let out a chuckle. "He's not *that* unpredictable, Commander. He leads from the front and always moves toward the gunfire. I've seen him in action. People follow him because he doesn't expect them to do anything he wouldn't do. He breeds a fierce loyalty in his subordinates because they know he'll go the distance for them."

Smith nodded in agreement. "All true, but there's just something about the man. It was an adventure working for him."

Monroe gave the commander a nod, believing that statement fully, and then pointed at Kingston, who was working on one of the boat's guns. "So, what's his story?"

The attitude change spoke volumes to Monroe. The Naval Intelligence officer went from straight-backed respect to something softer, perhaps even a little more sentimental. "He's a good man," she said. "And a good officer. If his people know what his father did, they don't care. He's made his own way in the Navy not despite his father, but because of him. He does his job well and has earned the respect of all of us who know him."

Monroe didn't hesitate with her next question. "How long have you been in love with him, Commander?"

Smith looked directly at Monroe and didn't hesitate either. "Ever since he took a bullet for me in the Academy. We've stayed in touch, but we both have careers that don't allow us to pursue, well . . . you know."

Monroe sighed. "We do make sacrifices for our careers, don't we?"

"He stopped a killer from taking me as his next victim. The man shot him, and he gave Admiral Summers the time he needed to get the son of a bitch. He spent two months in the hospital and still finished with his class on time."

"The Chesapeake Bay Killer." Monroe looked at Smith sympathetically. "You were the female midshipman he tried to take, and Kingston is the one who was shot? Holy shit!"

"Connecting the dots, Miss Monroe?"

"Yes," she responded, shaking her head, "and I shouldn't be amazed that any of you are here either. The more I hear, I wouldn't expect anything less."

Gulfstream G650PO
Off the Georgia Coast
July 20, 2010
0430 hours

Evans had been dozing in the cabin of the aircraft when he felt the presence of someone moving down the aisle. He opened his eyes to find the pilot walking by, headed to the bathroom in the rear of the airplane. After he passed, Evans sat up, stretching. He was a little stiff, but the stretching seemed to take care of that. He looked out the window into the passing darkness and couldn't tell where they were or where they were headed.

The moonlight revealed the heavy cloud cover below them. His guess was Kingston was headed to South America. That's what he would do if he were in the man's shoes. And he *had* been in the man's shoes on more than one occasion. Through a brief break in the clouds, he could see the reflection of the half-moon off the water below. They were over the ocean, then. That confirmed his suspicion about their direction of travel.

"Mr. Evans." The pilot came out of the bathroom, surprised to find Evans awake. "I'm sorry if I woke you, sir."

Evans looked at the man, smiling. "It's okay. I won't get much sleep until we finish this little errand."

The pilot's expression turned serious. "If you don't mind me asking, Mr. Evans, exactly what is our little errand? I know we're following another plane and we're getting directions from someone . . . I'm assuming they're American?"

Evans looked at the man. He knew better than to tell him anything, but these types of questions were inevitable. His flight crew was loyal to him, but they weren't stupid. They were curious if they were in danger. "I'm doing a favor for an acquaintance from years ago," he chose to say, maintaining his smile. "It's something I must do to even an old score. It's nothing that will put you in danger or have you doing anything illegal."

The pilot's ears went red. "That's not my concern, sir," he reassured Evans. "You pay us well, and you're a good boss, so I can honestly say we're not worried about either one of those things. We're both ex-Royal Air Force, sir, and the information we're being fed from the voice on the other end of the radio rings of a military operation. At least, the people feeding us the information appear to have a military background."

Evans didn't answer, as he had no idea who was feeding them the information about the flight path of Kingston's aircraft. He could only assume his pilot was right.

"I know you may not be able to answer me, sir, but I thought you ought to know our feelings on the matter."

"I have to be honest," Evans replied, "I don't know who's passing us information. I can only say my acquaintance was in the American military, so I must assume his contacts were too. Their intelligence has been spot-on thus far, which would support your theory. If the two of you have any misgivings about this, we can separate when we land, wherever that may be. No hard feelings—and you still have a job when I return home."

The pilot shook his head. "No, sir, like I said, that's not an issue. We're just thinking of keeping you out of harm's way. Like I said, you're a good boss, and we're trying to look out for you."

Evans smiled at the comment. "Where were you when I was younger? For now, let's stay on task. Just let me know if anything seems out of place in the information you get. I trust my acquaintance—not necessarily who's on the other end of the radio."

The pilot nodded. "Very good, sir. You go ahead and get some rest. I think we're going to be in the air for a while. If anything comes up, we'll wake you."

The pilot disappeared back into the cockpit, leaving Evans alone with his thoughts.

Sleep, yes . . . he needed sleep. Evans guessed he would take the pilot's advice and try to do that. Sleep came hard to him because he didn't trust too many people in his life. Because of the nature of the trip, he didn't expect he'd get much on this trip either. As a rule, he didn't sleep well when he traveled. Too many enemies in his past. Evans did trust his contact—they had a bond that was impossible to break. Reclining in the seat he was in, he thought about where they might be headed. Exhaustion won; Evans was asleep within minutes.

Upton's Marina and Boat Sales
Bluffton, New York
July 20, 2010
0445 hours

Sanderson sat alone in a dark showroom, watching his teams prepare for the upcoming assault on the island. They seemed to be working with a renewed purpose now that the identity of the spy had been revealed. *Spy*—the word had a nasty ring to it, but it seemed so appropriate. No one knew if they would catch up with the woman who successfully posed as Tina Ramsey for so long before she got out of the country. She had probably changed her appearance and identity before she left. With the head start she had, he didn't hold out much hope of catching her. Speculation was they would be going overseas to get her. That was a mission he wouldn't be part of; he was in command when it took place. He hoped they would at least allow him to exit gracefully.

Someone standing next to him scared him, making him jump. His heart settled when he realized it was Cassie and she was holding two cups of coffee. She placed one of the cups in front of him and sat down in the empty chair next to the desk. "Sorry, Director, I didn't mean to startle you. They said you like two sugars in your coffee."

He nodded, raising the mug. "Thanks, Miss Summers. I guess I was distracted. This has been a messy operation. Sorry if I've offended you during this craziness. I'm glad to hear that your sister is safe."

Cassie watched as the man took a sip of his coffee. She shrugged her shoulders. "You were doing your job, Director. I know it was nothing personal, but then, I'm not the one in the family you'd have to worry about."

Sanderson looked out the window and grunted. "I know—your uncle."

"I'm sure Uncle Jon would want a word with you, but he'd be in line behind my dad. Emily's the baby in the family, and Daddy's just a tad overprotective."

Sanderson grunted again, looking at the young woman.

"Finally, something in this whole mess I understand. A father's love for his daughter. You'll pardon me if I sound cynical. I'm guessing I'll be looking for a new job shortly. A spy in my operation . . . sounds like career suicide to me."

"I wouldn't be too sure. You might be a bit of an arrogant ass, but you are effective at what you do. Your people know their job, and now that we don't have anyone passing our plans to Hapke and his people, we should make quick work of the ones that are left. Putnum says you're the best at what you do, and you had no way of preventing what took place here. Trask tried to tender his resignation, and they wouldn't accept it. I doubt they'll go after your job if they didn't want his. The people who did the background on this bitch might have to worry, but not you."

Sanderson turned, looking at Cassie again. She was leaning forward, looking into her coffee as if it were a crystal ball.

"So, what's your legal advice for our little assault this morning?"

"God save them if they resist the assault teams."

Summers' Island
Adirondack State Park, New York
July 20, 2010
0500 hours

Hapke was panicked. He hadn't heard from his contacts in several hours and knew an assault from the FBI was imminent. He checked his people's positions and now moved back into the forest to try his contact again. They had promised him that he and his people would be extracted before any assault could take place—but that would have to be *now*. He guessed they would start moving teams into place by about six o'clock, with the assault to start at seven, if the original information he'd received was still correct. But that was the problem: there was no way of knowing if the timetable was the same.

His pace quickened, and his anxiety rose. He noticed the ground fog in the forest thicken, making it look more eerie than earlier. That only increased his nervousness. He typed a quick text message on his cell phone while he moved. He hit send, taking a quick look around to get his bearings. The forest seemed to be getting thicker, if that was possible. He thought he saw movement behind every tree and bush. He looked back down at the phone in anticipation of an answer, but there was none.

Something suddenly hit his legs, knocking them out from under him. He managed to hang onto the phone when he hit the ground hard, knocking the breath out of him. His lungs hurt, and he struggled to breathe. He'd landed face-first and was lying prone. With a jolt, he realized he was missing his rifle. The fog closed in around him, disrupting his focus and spiking his anxiety levels. He looked at his phone again—no response.

A sinking feeling came over him. They had been left to their own devices to escape. The man who was paying for their services should be safely out of the country by now and was leaving them to occupy the FBI. All this time, he and his people were expendable in Kingston's eyes. His heart sank even further.

He put the phone in his shirt pocket and began reaching around with both hands, looking for his rifle. He'd drifted away from his people's positions, and now more than ever, he realized they needed to take the FBI assault boats intact for any of them to escape. To make matters worse, the men he'd left to kill the hostages hadn't checked in. Something else to be anxious about. He needed those men to ensure a quick victory over the FBI assault force.

Hapke was starting to breathe normally again and forced himself to his knees. The fog was still thick as he moved slowly around, feeling for his rifle. He needed to get back to his men. His right hand landed on something smooth—it felt like leather, like a shoe or boot. Before he could think about it anymore, he was grabbed by the back of his harness and pulled up.

In the blur of the moment, he thought he saw a man in a World War II Army combat uniform standing in front of him. Before he could focus, he was hit repeatedly in the face. He tried to raise his arms to block the punches, but they were knocked away. He was hit again and again and could feel something warm running down his face. In the haze that surrounded him, he guessed it to be blood. He landed against a tree and was hit once in the stomach, but because he was wearing a ballistic vest, the blow was cushioned. His mind told him now was the time to fight back, while his attacker was assaulting a protected portion of his body. Before he could react, the blows shifted to his sides—not protected by the vest—and back to his face. He reached for his holster to pull his pistol but found it empty. Something hit him hard in the groin, and the pain seemed to take over his body, causing him to drop all his defenses.

Suddenly his attacker grabbed him by the throat, and he found it hard to breathe again. He focused through the fog and found himself facing a man in a steel helmet—not one of the modern Kevlar ones, but a World War II–era helmet to match the uniform of the man standing before him. The man's face, while familiar, wasn't someone he knew. He was being held by one hand, but the pain from the last blow was so intense he couldn't fight back. He was hit several more times in the face, bringing him to a state of near unconsciousness.

The voice was deep and even. "The old Indian warned you about the spirits in these woods. You've hurt my family and brought bad medicine to this island."

Hapke could barely speak but managed to whisper, "Who . . . who are you? Why are you dressed like that?"

A strange smile came over his captor's face. "This is my island, and you came here to do harm to people I love. I'm one of the spirits who inhabits these woods—and this, my friend, is what I wear to war. Unlike you, I served my country honorably. You placed members of my family in danger. It's time to pay the price."

The words faded into darkness as Hapke started to lose consciousness. He tried to scream himself awake, but nothing came out. The last thought that crossed his mind was that the pain was excruciating.

Summers' Island
Adirondack State Park, New York
July 20, 2010
0520 hours

The glow highlighting the eastern horizon went unnoticed in the thicket where they had taken refuge. The forest was so thick there that even on a clear day, without the fog or overcast, it would've been hard to know the sun was just starting to come up.

Nancy couldn't sleep and kept watch to make sure everyone else was getting rest, or at least what would pass for it until they could get off the island. Jon gave her an extra shirt he had in his rucksack to help keep the chill off. She made her way back around to Fiona and Josh. Most everyone in the group had fallen asleep. Even in these rudimentary conditions, the relief of being rescued seemed to lift the tension that had kept most of them from sleeping since their ordeal started. Josh was wide awake, while Fiona dozed with her head on his lap.

"No sleep while there's a mission on, Master Chief?" asked Nancy. She could see the half smile on his face, even in the dim light.

"I helped train both Jon and Walt, and here they are with a bunch of their friends pulling us out of this mess. I never would have thought this could happen."

"Not even with Dick Kingston?"

Ericson looked down at his wife to make sure she was asleep. Her breathing confirmed she was. "The man is a master tactician, that's for sure. This whole scheme to get him out of prison must have been in the works for years. He went after everyone who was involved in his arrest and conviction and either has them here on this island or has tried to kill them. As usual, though, he underestimated Jon. All he did was make him angry."

Nancy giggled at the thought of her husband questioning the men who tried to kill him.

"Justin said he used a pack of wolves to question the men Dick sent to kill him. Do you think there's any truth to that," she asked, "or are they just exaggerating?"

Josh's smile broadened.

"Nancy, I've seen your husband in the worst of times, and all I'm going to say is, if he left them alive, they're very fortunate. He's not a stone-cold killer, but he has on more than one occasion taken a life. Using a pack of wolves to interrogate somebody is an innovation, and I imagine a very effective one."

They both started to laugh, stopping short at the sound of metal on metal coming down the nearby path. Josh instinctively drew Fiona closer to him, which woke her up. He covered her mouth, so she remained quiet, but her eyes showed her alarm. Jon materialized out of the fog and knelt next to them. "Don't worry—it's Matt coming in with everyone else. We'll let them rest for a few minutes, then go meet the bus, so to speak."

Fiona looked more at ease. "Thanks, Jon, but you didn't have to tell us personally."

"I can't have the master chief here trying to jump everyone coming down the trail," he replied, and Fiona laughed. "And you know he would to protect you."

"Always the gentleman, huh, Jon? Will this keep Richard from escaping? As far as I'm concerned, he can rot in Leavenworth."

She sensed a change in Jon's demeanor. "Sorry, Fiona. He's already escaped. They tried to move him, and he got away after the Army turned him over to the Marshals Service."

Fiona's eyes widened, her face going pale. She knew all too well what he was capable of and didn't want to think what could happen to her family.

"How many dead?" asked her husband solemnly.

Jon hesitated, looking at Fiona. Her eyes pleaded for an honest answer. "They found the entire Marshals security team dead in a van just outside Dulles Airport."

"How many?" asked Josh a little more forcefully.

Jon sighed in resignation. "Twelve."

"Oh my God!" exclaimed Fiona, covering her mouth.

"Don't worry, he won't get away," Jon reassured them. "Neither will the person who was passing Hapke information. We'll get them all."

Josh looked at Jon, his expression severe. "You're just being optimistic, Jon. If he made it out of this country, it could take years just to track him down. How the hell could they let this happen?"

Ericson saw a strange smile move across Jon's face. "Josh, it's best you don't know how this will unfold. But he won't be free long," he said with certainty. "You just have to trust that some of us know what we're doing."

The tension broke when Becky came over and knelt next to Jon. Josh stifled a laugh, looking at the doctor dressed in camouflaged fatigues and face paint. She looked very much like a proper soldier. Knowing her background, Josh found it funny, drawing a look of irritation from her. She kept her focus on Jon. "Matt has the sheriff on a stretcher being carried by the prisoners. He's stable, and everyone's in good shape."

"Prisoners?" asked Josh, his tone changing.

Jon just smiled at the question, while Becky ignored it, adding, "The whole column is in pretty good shape; Sarah did a good job of prepping them."

Jon couldn't help but grin—as much at his old teammate's reaction to Becky's report as to Becky's professionalism in giving it. Though, he really should've known. As a doctor, Becky was used to high-stress, life-or-death situations.

"Thanks, Flower Child," he said. "Get whatever help you need to get the entire column ready to move. We'll meet the extraction team after first light. Too much can go wrong with a group this size if we try to extract in the dark. I don't want any mistakes."

"Won't a daylight extraction be more dangerous? I mean, won't it expose our position?" asked Josh. "After all, I do have some experience with this type of operation."

Becky looked at Jon, scowling. "Was he always this much of a pain in the ass?"

This brought laughter from both Fiona and Nancy. Jon looked at Josh, grinning, then back at Becky. "You have no idea, Flower Child. I want to move out in thirty. Get whatever help you need to have them all ready."

With that, Jon silently disappeared into the fog, leaving Becky to answer the inevitable question of, "Flower Child?" Josh stared at her. "He gave you a call sign?"

There was muffled laughter again from Nancy and Fiona.

"Jonny's called me that for years," said Becky. "George coined it as my call sign."

"George? George Ellison?"

The laughter was no longer muffled. Sean came out of the fog, followed by Samcevic, both stopping next to Becky. Nancy jumped to her feet, hugging her oldest son. Sean looked down at his mother-in-law. "Need any help here, Flower Child?"

More in the group joined in the laughter. The group began to stir as the two columns began to mix. Josh gave Sean an irritated look. "I suppose they gave you a call sign, too?"

Sean smiled at the senator, then looked down at his mother-in-law. It was all Becky could do not to laugh out loud. She put her hand on Sean's arm and said, "I'm all set here. Thanks, guys."

Rice had moved up behind them. She smiled, knowing what was going on. "Come on, Hemingway, bring your partner. Pathfinder wants to brief us all."

Samcevic looked at his former teammate, grinning. "Hemingway. I like that, don't you?" His grin seemed to broaden. "Come on *He who walks silently through the forest*, we have to take an early meeting."

As they disappeared into the fog, even Josh was laughing.

Summers' Island
Adirondack State Park, New York
July 20, 2010
0525 hours

The hostage takers worked on their ambush preparations for several hours. They were fully briefed on the fact that their biggest priority was to commandeer the assault boats to facilitate their escape off the island. They'd taken losses they weren't supposed to, and things had gone nowhere near as smoothly as promised. Now, they were fighting for their lives just to get off this island.

After talking among themselves, the general view was to screw the hostages and simply get off the island. The prospect of getting paid for this job was dimming with each passing hour, and now the best they could hope for was getting out of this alive and without incarceration.

The two men in the prepared position to the extreme left of the line were taking a break, talking about that very topic, when two more of their compatriots joined them.

"Hapke's missing," said the first of the newcomers ominously. "No one's seen him in over twenty minutes, and he's not responding on comms."

"What do you mean he's missing?" asked the senior resident of the position.

"He's not in his hole. We have a couple of guys looking for him nearby, but seeing as he's not responding on comms . . . I've got a bad feeling about this."

"He couldn't have just disappeared."

"The last we heard from Hapke was several hours ago, when he confirmed he hadn't heard back from his informant," the second newcomer said anxiously. "In fact, he was starting to panic about it."

"Damn! Nothing's been right since Servati disappeared. She kept Hapke focused and seemed to make things run right. I think he ran."

Several of the men nodded in agreement. They were interrupted by another man running up to them. He was out of breath. "The men left . . . left behind to kill the hostages . . . all dead. They're all dead. We also lost contact with Simpkins and Burke."

"Where were they?" asked the man who had been leading the discussion.

"They headed west to check our flank there. They were on the air one minute and not responding the next. I'm guessing they ran into something out there—it's not like them to just fall off the grid."

Everyone was silent while they absorbed the latest report. Fear of capture or worse began to take seed. The man who had been leading the discussion was an Army and police veteran, and Hapke placed him in the group's chain of command. Everyone looked to him for a decision. He looked back at the pleading faces around him. They all knew they were facing murder and kid-napping charges at minimum, probably worse. They needed to get off the island as quickly as they could—and then get out of the country.

"How many active people do we have right now?"

"Twenty-one," somebody answered. "We left all the wounded back at the cabins."

"Get them all here right now. We do everything as a group. No patrols, no separate recons, no missions. Right *now*. It's safety in numbers."

There were nervous nods all around.

"The team that they sent to get the hostages has to be a small one," their leader added, thinking out loud. "Probably no more than six to eight. They'll be headed for their extraction point, and I'm guessing that'll be west of here. We move in force, meet them at their extraction point, overwhelm them, and use their boats. We've either been left as a sacrificial lamb, or our contact with the FBI has been found out. If we wait here, we're dead for sure."

Everyone nodded in agreement.

"Get everyone here, and we'll move out as soon as we brief everybody."

Two of the kidnappers left to collect everyone else.

Summers' Island
Adirondack State Park, New York
July 20, 2010
0530 hours

Hapke was about a quarter of a mile north of the position where his men were currently meeting, with his hands zip-tied around the truck of a tree. He was sitting on the forest floor, with the fog swirling around his waist and tears rolling down his cheeks.

Ten feet away, the mysterious figure crouched, staring back at him, saying nothing. He held a bayonet to an M1 Garand rifle, throwing it at the tree Hapke was tied to. It thudded into place inches above Hapke's scalp.

"You can't do this to me," blurted Hapke. "I have rights!"

The figure dressed in World War II combat gear continued to stare at him as he got up, removed the bayonet, and reassumed his previous position. All the while, he didn't reply. The bayonet was then thrown into the tree one more time, landing so close to Hapke's head that it shaved away the top of his hair.

"Stop that! Just stop that!" demanded Hapke, voice shrill. "You can't intimidate me like this! I used to be a cop, and I know the law. I have rights. You can't do this to me."

His captor retrieved the bayonet from the tree once more, smiling slyly as he pushed the metal World War II–era helmet higher on his head. "And while you were a cop, you had my son-in-law killed. Right now, you're on my island, and here, we follow my laws." He paused to stare daggers at the man tied to the tree. "And guess what? Here you have no rights. I'm here to collect a debt you owe. On top of that, you threatened my family on my island and tried to kill my son."

The tears continued down Hapke's cheeks. "Who are you?"

Without looking, the soldier threw the bayonet into the tree again.

Hapke flinched, trying in vain to wiggle away.

"You know who I am. Take a good look. You saw my picture in my daughter's home when you were seeing her after you killed her husband. You'll pay for that. That's something I can't forgive. Guess how you'll pay?"

"I'll kill you!" Hapke declared, sobbing.

The soldier's smile turned cruel. "You know I've been dead for sixteen years. What part of this don't you understand? You can't hurt me—but you, on the other hand, are going to suffer for your sins."

"But . . . but you were an old man when you died," Hapke said, crossing the threshold, leaving reality behind, without even knowing it. He'd just admitted he was dealing with a ghost. The volume of tears increased from a trickle to a cascade.

"The old Indian told you about the ghosts in the forest. This is my forest, and this is my war face. This is the face you deal with. You hurt my family, and now you have to pay."

Hapke was desperately trying to fight his way back to reality. "You're not real! You're just my imagination! You can't hurt me! You—"

The figure threw the bayonet again, but this time directly at Hapke.

The kidnapper let out a scream that would be heard on the entire west side of the island. The bayonet was protruding from the tree, sliced directly through his ear. The soldier was suddenly next to him, whispering something to him. Hapke could feel the man's breath on his neck. The voice was cold, menacing, and sent a shiver down his spine. "They're coming for you. You know what to do. If you don't, we'll meet again."

The soldier stood, taking the bayonet out of the tree. He ran the blade across Hapke's chin, causing his jaw to clench and eyes to close. The soldier then placed the bayonet into its scabbard on his web belt and disappeared into the fog-shrouded forest. The last ounce of sanity Hapke had been clinging to finally eluded him, and he began to sob uncontrollably.

Summers' Island
Adirondack State Park, New York
July 20, 2010
0540 hours

Most of the kidnappers heard the scream. It wasn't close, but it was close enough for them to hear it clearly.

"That was Hapke!" exclaimed one of the men who had just arrived.

"Do we go look for him?" asked one of the others.

"No," responded the new leader, "they either have him or he's dead. That means they've been watching us and these positions are compromised."

Two more men arrived.

"Did you hear that?" asked the first.

"The old Indian was right—this place is haunted," added the second.

It was too late to reverse the fear spreading throughout the group. Any initiative they thought they had was gone, they just didn't realize it yet.

The sound of their former leader's scream lingered in all their minds.

Summers' Island
Adirondack State Park, New York
July 20, 2010
0540 hours

Ellison and Wiedenkeller were standing with Jon when they heard the scream. Naylor, Reardon, and Shomakker had just brought in two more prisoners and reported the kidnappers were getting ready to move out of their current positions.

Jon sent Ellison and Wiedenkeller to investigate while the others started the column moving toward the rendezvous point with the boats. They knew they wouldn't have long, so they moved quickly but cautiously in the direction the scream came from. Within minutes, they could hear someone crying. Shortly after that, they found Hapke bound to the base of the tree.

They were cautious, making sure it was safe to approach the restrained kidnapper. There was always the worry of ambush by the other kidnappers.

Hapke saw them. "Save me!" he had the audacity to say. "Help!"

Seeing no one around, the two men dashed in and had their first look at the man who had been leading Kingston's scheme.

"His hands are zip-tied behind the tree," said Wiedenkeller, pulling out his combat knife.

Hapke started to scream. Ellison grabbed the man by the throat and squeezed, noticing the man's ear was sliced in half and bleeding profusely. Hapke coughed and sputtered for air, but his screaming stopped.

"Listen carefully, asshole," said Ellison. "You may not remember me, but we met a few years ago when you tried to hit my friend at a Marine Corps range. He taught you that you can't fight if you can't breathe. I maintain that you can't scream if you can't breathe. Nod if you understand." It was an effort, but Hapke managed to nod. Ellison loosened his grip. "Now, my friend here is going to cut the zip tie. You fight or try to run, you die. Understand?"

Hapke nodded. "Y-y-yes . . . just get me out of here . . ."

Ellison let go of the man's throat; there was no fight left in him. Wiedenkeller easily cut the zip tie with his knife and stood Hapke up. The man was still crying as the retired SEAL put the man's hands behind his back and applied a new zip tie.

"Who tied you up here?" asked Ellison as he searched the kidnapper.

"Sum . . . Summers did," mumbled Hapke. "He caught me, then tied me to the tree."

Ellison shook his head, brows furrowed. "We've been with Jon. He wasn't out here in this direction. Couldn't have been him. Besides, he probably would've killed you for killing his brother-in-law."

"It wasn't . . . it was the father. Julie's father," he said, and everybody present went still and silent, waiting for Hapke to finish. "He . . . he told me he would get me if I didn't tell the truth . . ."

Hapke continued to babble as Wiedenkeller pushed him in the direction they needed to go. He looked at Ellison, shrugging his shoulders. "The man's off his rocker. His own guys probably did this."

Ellison shook his head. "The man's gone wacko. Jon's father passed away just before we went to the Philippines back in 1994. He's not making any sense."

As they moved off to join the others, Hapke continued to ramble on about anything and everything, oblivious to those around him. He left all reality in the forest behind him.

Summers' Island
Adirondack State Park, New York
July 20, 2010
0545 hours

Jon started everyone down the trail toward the lake. With a hostile force of twenty-plus people looking for them, they couldn't be caught napping. If they needed to engage, he wanted it to be at the extraction point. It seemed likely that the enemy was after the boats, so the rescue team would engage the bad guys by the water, where they would have the advantage.

Naylor and Reardon took point and reported all clear so far. Justin and Shomakker were acting as flankers on the left side of the slow-moving column, between the kidnappers and them, so there were no surprises. Everyone else spaced themselves out along the column for the protection of all.

Sheriff James, being carried by the prisoners, led off the column. Over Abby's objections, Jon connected each of the prisoners with a rope tied around their waist. She had been overruled, and even Sheriff James agreed with Jon. The prisoners were strangely compliant, and James confided to Abby he suspected that Jon had spoken to them about the penalties for resisting.

Next came the former hostages—some of whom, like Rice and Wells, were armed and helping to protect the column from further assault by their former captors. Ericson was being carried by Hector and Fortum, with Fiona right behind them. Sue Ellen and Frank Del Monte made a comical trio with Hennen, while O'Leary and Alexander stayed close to the Summers family, helping with the two children. Sarah stayed close to James because of his wounds, and Becky monitored everyone else. Because of James and Ericson, the pace was slow and easy. Fortunately, it was going to be a short trip.

Jon stood with Sean and Samcevic as the last of the family moved out. Nancy hesitated a moment, but the look on her husband's face told her it was time to leave. Jon watched as she followed the last of the column down the path. Wiedenkeller's voice and call sign came over the earpiece of the radio, saying that he and Ellison were coming in with another prisoner. Within seconds, the two men came out of the fog—dragging Hapke along with them.

Hapke's hands were bound behind him, and tape was over his mouth. When he saw Jon standing before him, his eyes filled with fear, and he tried to break away. His struggle was short-lived when Wiedenkeller kicked his feet out from under him, dropping him to the ground.

"Stop that," ordered Wiedenkeller, "or you'll have to be carried out of here!"

"What's that all about?" asked Samcevic.

Ellison smiled while he said, "It seems old Fred Crogan talked to him about the ghosts that live in the forests when he came to get demands for the FBI."

"He thinks he was visited by the admiral's father dressed in full combat gear. Said he was threatened and told to tell 'the truth.'"

Jon raised an eyebrow, saying nothing.

Ellison continued, "The man's been babbling incessantly. Won't shut up, hence the tape over the mouth. He did admit to killing your brother-in-law, though. Gave names about who he was working for and everything."

Jon looked at Wiedenkeller, who confirmed the same. He knelt down next to Hapke and squeezed his cheeks with his right hand. The kidnapper winced, but his full attention was now on Jon, who said, "You say you met my father?"

Hapke nodded frantically, tears coming down his face.

"He was dressed in World War II combat gear?"

More frantic nodding.

"You know he's been dead since 1994?"

Hapke's eyes widened. He looked away and nodded one more time.

Jon paused thoughtfully before saying, "Al, get him up with the other prisoners. Tell Steven and Nathan that if he tries anything—and I mean anything—shoot him." Jon's eyes then dropped to Hapke, still on the ground. "Do you understand what I just said?"

Before Hapke could respond, Wiedenkeller dragged him to his feet and was leading him down the trail. The frantic kidnapper looked back, his eyes telling the men he understood all too well what Jon had just said.

"Ghosts," Ellison said with a grunt. "The man's flipped. He obviously couldn't have seen your father. He's delusional."

"Makes for a good story, though," said Samcevic, laughing. "At least from an author's perspective."

Jon looked at his oldest son, who smiled back at his father.

"Oh, I don't know guys," he said, turning down the path, "I've met some of old Fred's ghosts myself, and I'm sure this one seemed real to Hapke."

Sean laughed.

Mohawk Tavern and Grill
Bluffton, New York
July 20, 2010
0545 hours

Putnum was listening to the communications intently. The hostages were rescued, and the two columns were joined. There were over twenty armed kidnappers ready to move, if not already moving. He guessed they would meet near the extraction point like Summers anticipated. He knew it wouldn't be pretty, but he also knew who would win. He trusted Ellison and Summers implicitly, and he either knew every man who volunteered to go in personally or knew of them due to their reputations. His "dream team" was on the island and ready for anything. Being a good poker player, he'd stacked the deck in his favor. The kidnappers needed to surrender. Putnum knew they wouldn't, but they needed to.

Sanderson was transmitting on all the known frequencies the kidnappers had used, requesting a peaceful surrender. He was using a script developed by Cassie to comply with the needs of the US Attorney's Office. There was no reply, and he didn't expect one, since each kidnapper was looking at life in prison. Sanderson and Cassie were not present at the Mohawk, being across the street at the marina, giving the assault team last-minute instructions.

Mitchell had been standing by the van, monitoring communications, when he was handed a piece of paper. He read what was written on it, then turned, walking over to Putnum, who was speaking to Fred. He handed Putnum the piece of paper and stood by, quietly waiting. Putnum took his time reading and handed the paper back when he was done.

"What do you think, Tom?"

"It's overdue, sir. Do you want me to pass the word?"

Putnum nodded. "Any word on the other operation?"

"He looks to be heading toward the islands in the western Caribbean or South America. The Air Force is keeping their distance but has marked both aircraft. We'll know where they land. I have our assets in that region on high alert. He won't get away, sir. That I promise you."

Putnum nodded again, pursing his lips. "And anything on our young imposter? I'm sure Director Sanderson would want a few words with her."

Mitchell shook his head. "Sorry, sir, nothing there. She has probably changed her appearance by now and will be hard to catch quickly. She had too much of a head start. We'll get her though, sir. It'll just take time."

"This one's personal, Tom," Putnum said, eyeing Mitchell. "We need to close the case sooner rather than later. They need to be on their A game, or they will answer to me. Please spread the word to all units to proceed."

The former Navy pilot nodded one more time and went back to the van. Putnum looked back at Fred. "Any words of wisdom, Fred? I just took the leash off the dogs."

Fred smiled. "Not dogs, Admiral. Wolves."

Putnum thought about the old man's comment, then returned the smile. He was right.

The column moved slowly but at a steady pace. They didn't have far to go, and the trail was clear, despite the heavy fog masking their movement. However, that fog also concealed the approach of any hostile force. Jon's biggest concern was the amount of noise the column was making. The people they rescued were not professional military, and while they were doing their best, they couldn't help but make noise. That meant his people needed to be that much more alert.

A call over the radio told Jon that Naylor and Reardon reached the extraction point and everything was clear. He'd picked this spot for two reasons. First, it provided excellent cover if they needed to make a stand, which he guessed they were going to have to. Second, it provided an excellent landing spot for the extraction team. Communication was limited to avoid the kidnappers getting wind of how they were leaving. The entire team knew the kidnappers would be desperate and getting to the boats would be their goal. That couldn't be allowed to happen.

Jon stood looking at the former hostages while they walked past. Demmer gave him a quick smile and mouthed the words "thank you" to him. The Del Monte's and Hennen followed her, and each acknowledged him. Next came Alexander and O'Leary. O'Leary looked at him, smiling like she always did. Summers did find her attractive, and he knew the offer for her companionship was always open, but the cost was too high. He just smiled back, nodding.

Next came Ericson, being carried by Hector and Fortum. Hector started to say something to his uncle, but Ericson cut him off, saying, "Quiet boy! He doesn't have time to talk to us right now."

They moved past, followed by the grandchildren, Fiona, Nancy, Julie, Alex, and Emily. Emily was still carrying a rifle and looked like the proper soldier in her dress.

Jon fell in next to her. "Em, when these guys come after us and we engage them, you stay with your aunts and the rest of the family."

Emily looked over at her uncle and knew not to argue. "Yes, sir. Can I help guard the prisoners?"

"No, you help your dad get the family out. He'll need your help more than me. Becky's going out with you as well."

Nancy looked over her shoulder at her husband, seeing he was watching her. Julie glanced back, too, both acknowledging with a nod. The whole family was going out.

Dartford Island
Adirondack State Park, New York
July 20, 2010
0550 hours

The teams were crowding back into the four boats. They'd spent the last thirty minutes checking their weapons and talking about strategy for their landing. The plan was to pull the hostages out and then stay to track down the remaining kidnappers. They knew the rendezvous point would be protected by the rescue team, but the concern was brought up that only one of the freed hostages was active military and there was only a part-time deputy and the wounded sheriff to represent law enforcement. Skier reminded his teammates that there was a CIA team with them and most of the rescue team had written the book on the types of missions they did.

"They may be retired, but I wouldn't want to be fighting against them."

There was silence when the names of those on the rescue team were revealed. Skier was right—these were the sort of men everybody wanted on their team. Sandy Monroe watched with interest as the names were given to the teams. The reaction was what she expected: silence.

Kingston gave the word, and the boats were started, moved out about fifty yards from shore, and shut down again, drifting. He then went on the radio to say, "Arrowhead to Fort Deliverance, in position."

"Copy that, Arrowhead."

"Falcon to Fort Deliverance, we are airborne."

Kingston knew by the last transmission that things were about to get messy.

Summers' Island
Adirondack State Park, New York
July 20, 2010
0555 hours

The hostage takers were gathered to discuss what needed to be done. The messages the FBI kept sending out asking them to surrender were never really deliberated. They all agreed they needed to make a break for freedom, because there were federal agents dead and people kidnapped, and a peaceful surrender would only lead to an inevitable arrest.

It was obvious to them they had been sacrificed by Kingston in his bid for freedom, and they would be facing life in a federal prison with no chance of parole. They needed to take the assault boats being used for the extraction. Two or three RIBs could easily fit them all, then a quick trip to the mainland under the cover of fog would give them a fighting chance.

They decided the hostages' extraction point was west of them. There were several points on the map that looked ideal. The plan was to overwhelm the small team that freed the hostages and then take the boats. It was a simple plan, but then, the simplest plans were often the most efficient.

They moved out toward the first point, confident they would succeed in taking the hostages and their rescuers by surprise and escape their fate. They were ready for a fight.

Summers' Island
Adirondack State Park, New York
July 20, 2010
0600 hours

The column reached the extraction point without incident. While the former hostages were taking cover in the thick forest that lined the shore, the rest of the team took up defensive positions in anticipation of the kidnappers attacking. Matt, Becky, Sean, and Kevin stayed with the freed hostages and would accompany them back. Abby, Steven, and Nathan were staying with the prisoners, and Abby would oversee arresting any new prisoners until additional law enforcement teams arrived.

Wiedenkeller and Shomakker were setting out some flares attached to trip wires to give them some warning if the kidnappers approached their positions. Nothing deadly, but it would make enough noise and send up a flare to let them know where the hostage takers were. Justin, Ryan, and Kay began questioning prisoners with Abby present to see if any of them knew anything about Richard Kingston's grand plan. Becky attended to Hapke's ear wound, taking the duct tape off his mouth. Abby read them their rights, and then the questions started. They were surprisingly talkative, but nothing of importance was being gleaned by the questions.

Jon noticed Hector moving toward the prisoners. He was being as nonchalant as he could under the circumstances, but it was obvious what he had in mind. His uncle moved up behind him and pulled him down under cover. "You shouldn't make yourself a target when you try to kill him."

Hector didn't even try to deny it. "He killed my dad, Uncle Jon. I need to do this."

Jon looked at his nephew and held out his hand. The young man held his uncle's gaze for a few seconds, then looked down. He produced a combat knife in a scabbard from behind his back, giving it to his uncle.

"Hector, I know what he did, and trust me—his life is not worth ruining yours."

Tears spilled down Hector's cheeks, and he nodded.

"He'll pay, son, but we need to make the people he was working for pay, too."

They were interrupted by a commotion where the prisoners were being interrogated. They both moved toward the noise and found Hapke having a violent reaction to being near Justin. Both his hands and feet were bound with zip ties, but he was trying to kick Justin. Hapke spotted Jon, and immediately stopped resisting.

"Keep him away from me! He's the guy," Hapke said.

"What guy?" asked Jon quietly.

"Your father! He's your father!"

Jon kept a straight face. "I told you, Hapke, my father's been dead sixteen years. We had this conversation, remember?"

Hapke nodded, trying to crawl toward Jon the best he could. He was making a spectacle of himself at this point and had everybody's attention.

Everybody remained silent, watching Jon as he observed Hapke's approach with an unreadable expression.

"I know, but this is the guy! You have to protect me—he's going to kill me!"

Hapke crawled up to Jon, almost knocking him over. Jon put a hand on the man's shoulder, and he seemed to calm down some. "Hapke, this man's my son, and he works for the CIA, so there is a family resemblance. He's asking questions about Richard Kingston."

Hapke looked up at Jon, saying nothing.

Jon cleared his throat. "Hapke, you said the man you saw was dressed in a World War II uniform. This man is not."

Hapke looked at Justin, then back at Jon. His look of panic didn't change. Jon's eyes found Abby's as he motioned for her to come over.

"This is Deputy Crogan," he said to Hapke. "She obviously doesn't look like the ghost you say you saw, and she will keep you safe. You told the two men who found you that you had Hector Romero killed. Is that true?"

Hapke nodded and then started to babble, spilling every detail.

Abby looked at Jon in disbelief. He lowered his voice a little and said, "You know what questions they need asked, right?"

"Yes," Abby said, and she started leading the conversation with the crazed kidnapper in a direction that would answer several important questions at once.

Jon motioned for Hector to follow him, and as they passed Justin, he leaned close to his son and said, "I'd get rid of the World War II uniform before they figure out what you did."

Justin looked blankly back at his father. "I don't understand what you're talking about."

Jon said nothing in response, but his look spoke volumes. Justin gave his father a slight nod and then moved closer to Abby to monitor the questioning. Before they could move back to where the former hostages were under cover, Hector put his hand on his uncle's arm.

"Thanks, Uncle Jon. You're right—he wouldn't be worth it."

Suddenly, there was a popping sound to their east, and a flare soared into the sky above them. Jon looked at his nephew. "Damn!"

Summers' Island
Adirondack State Park, New York
July 20, 2010
0615 hours

The kidnappers were approaching the first point they suspected the rescue team might use as an extraction point when their point man hit the trip wire, setting off the flare. They all took cover immediately, organizing into an assault formation.

They hesitated to make sure everyone knew what to do and then began to move slowly forward. There now was no option but to engage the rescuers, and with luck, they would be in the boats in fifteen minutes. They also decided they didn't need the hostages anymore.

Summers' Island
Adirondack State Park, New York
July 20, 2010
0620 hours

The first kidnapper was sighted just as two more flares went off—this time located up the hill from Jon and his people's position. Panicking, the kidnappers opened fire, having no clear targets, exposing their own positions.

Jon and his people assumed a defensive position in a dense stand of trees and quickly returned fire, inflicting several casualties and causing their enemies' assault to falter. The fog was clearly confusing the attackers, because several fired at their own positions. Added to this, Reardon and Wiedenkeller threw smoke and tear gas grenades at the kidnappers' positions.

Jon keyed his mic. "Arrowhead, this is Pathfinder. We have heavy enemy contact and are requesting an immediate hot extract of noncombatants. We are taking effective enemy fire from our nine o'clock position at approximately one hundred fifty yards. I have twenty-three passengers with two wounded."

There was a crescendo in the sound of the gunfire.

Dartford Island
Adirondack State Park, New York
July 20, 2010
0622 hours

The gunfire was heard first, followed by three beeps, indicating an incoming message.

Jon's voice came over the radio. A calm seemed to come over all four boats, and the personnel on each listened to the incoming message.

"Pathfinder, this is Arrowhead," said Kingston. "We copy you five by five. You're taking effective enemy fire from your nine o'clock position. You have twenty-three packs with two wounded."

Kingston gave the signal, and the engines on each of the boats roared to life.

He kept the radio to his lips, speaking over the engine noise. "We'll be coming from the west and will be doing a four-boat pickup in two boat intervals. Be advised, we'll be dropping off friendlies upon landing."

"Roger Arrowhead, Pathfinder copies. Four-boat pickup in two boat intervals with incoming friendlies. Be advised, the LZ is hot. We'll mark our position with green smoke and strobes."

The boats accelerated quickly, almost to their top speed of forty knots, disappearing into the fog.

Shadow Lake
Adirondack State Park, New York
July 20, 2010
0623 hours

The dozen RIB assault boats had just left the marina when the gunfire was heard in the distance. They were monitoring the radio frequency and heard Jon's transmission requesting a hot extraction from the island. Each boat carried an eight- or ten-man team, and their target was to secure the cabin complex. The rescue team already told them there were wounded kidnappers to take into custody and there were explosive charges needing to be defused. Once they secured the cabins, the FBI teams would link with the other teams on the island to mop up the operation. After all the frustration over the past several days, they were on their way to do what they were trained to do. Once they helped to secure the island, they would take custody of all the prisoners and arrange their transport for interrogation. As the intensity of the firefight seemed to increase, they were ordered to land as soon as possible.

Upton's Marina and Boat Sales
Bluffton, New York
July 20, 2010
0623 hours

Putnum, Mitchell, Fred, and Preston left the Mohawk, walking across the street to the marina to join Sanderson and Cassie. They arrived just in time to hear Jon's transmission and Kingston's response. Everyone turned to look at Putnum as Jon acknowledged the pickup orders.

"They're after the assault boats. You know that, right?" Sanderson asked bluntly. "They'll be desperate to get away, and this is their best chance."

Mitchell eyed Putnum, looking for permission to say something. None was forthcoming, so the CIA man remained silent.

Sanderson added, "I hope your rescue unit has some sort of special training to keep those boats from falling into the hands of the kidnappers."

Putnum still didn't respond, but a hint of a smile crossed his face. Preston leaned over to Fred and whispered, "I assume the admiral is a good poker player, but I'm guessing that expression means he has an ace or two in his hand."

Fred grunted. "The man's a warrior, so there's no fighting fair here. I'm guessing that we're all about to be surprised."

Sanderson turned to look at the two men behind him. His expression conveyed surprise at Fred's statement. When he turned to see Cassie's reaction to the comment, he was even more surprised to see her smile was like Putnum's. She apparently knew something he didn't.

Summers' Island
Adirondack State Park, New York
July 20, 2010
0624 hours

The kidnappers' assault stalled quickly. After taking four casualties almost immediately upon contact, one dead and three wounded—one of which was from friendly fire—they lost the small amount of organization they had in the first place.

It was obvious there were more than six rescuers. The volume of fire coming from the defensive positions was so intense, they were left to assume they were facing an equal number of rescuers, until one of the kidnappers commented that the tactics being used were those common to Special Forces. For the first time, the realization set in they were not dealing with law enforcement.

The smoke and tear gas were starting to do their work. Most of the kidnappers hadn't brought their masks, leaving them with the rest of their equipment at the cabin complex. The coughing and watering eyes caused more confusion when orders about their assault changed. The slight wind cooperated with the rescuers, because it moved the gas into the kidnappers' positions. As a result, one more kidnapper was shot leaving cover to get away from the tear gas.

Summers' Island
Adirondack State Park, New York
July 20, 2010
0625 hours

Nancy watched as the team maintained their volume of fire at the kidnappers' positions, amazed by how unfazed they were. She'd known most of these people her entire life, and here they were, fighting a hostile force, seemingly unfazed by what was going on around them. She was most surprised by her children. Sean and Justin were on the firing line, and Steven was with Nathan and the prisoners. Even Matt and Kevin, who were in a support position guarding the former hostages, seemed more than ready to join in the fight.

The whole situation was surreal.

Nancy was helping Becky and Amy keep the former hostages under cover and safe. She noticed that Amy kept watching Jon as he moved around the various positions. She felt a tinge of jealousy run through her. Here they were, fighting for their lives, and Amy was watching her husband while she wasn't.

"Amy!" Becky's tone was sharp. "You pay attention to what's going on here—not with Jon. We need to be ready to move when the boats get here."

Amy blushed with embarrassment. She was far too obvious and looked at Nancy.

"I'm sorry, Nancy. I just couldn't help it. You're so lucky."

Nancy sensed insecurity in Amy's response. For all her power, she couldn't get the one thing she wanted.

"Yeah, I guess I am pretty lucky."

"Ladies," interrupted Becky, "we need to focus!"

Right on cue, several rounds from the kidnappers struck the tree next to Nancy, and all three women dropped to the ground. Becky raised her head, looking around, making eye contact with Amy. A moan from Nancy made the other two women scramble to where she lay on the ground. She was conscious, but there were several large splinters of wood protruding from her shoulder and neck.

"Damn it, Nancy!" exclaimed Becky as she examined the injury. "Damn it, not you!"

Matt reached them, immediately taking his sister-in-law's hand. A quick look at Becky told him she hadn't decided how serious things were just yet.

"Look at me, Nancy," he said, and she did, her eyes wincing with pain. Matt's voice was even, fueled by confidence. "You're going to be okay. Take a few deep breaths; breathe through the pain."

Sarah showed up with some extra supplies and looked at her mother. Becky smiled at her daughter. "It missed the arteries; she'll be fine. I'll stabilize her, and we'll get her out on the last boat. You get everyone else out first. Matt, you, and Kevin help her."

Both nodded and then disappeared. Nancy seemed to have regained her composure, lying still on the ground. "Damn, that hurts! Did he really tell me to breathe through the pain? I'm not pregnant and giving birth!"

Becky chuckled at the comment while she stabilized the wounds. "Yeah, he did. You've been through childbirth, though, so this should be nothing. Look, Nanc, I'm going to transport you like this because if I just yank these splinters out, I could do more damage. I—"

Jon appeared, looking down at his wife, concern etched into every inch of his face.

"She'll be fine, Jonny," said Becky, working at cleaning blood off her patient's neck. "It looks worse than it is."

"She's right, sailor," Nancy said to her husband. "You work on getting us out of here."

The look on his face changed, and he became cold, detached. Nancy felt a chill run down her back. He disappeared a moment later, and Nancy could feel Becky's eyes on her.

"That was scary." Nancy tried to make eye contact with Becky, but it was hard because of where the splinters were. "I don't think I've ever seen that expression before."

Becky didn't answer her friend. She'd seen that very expression in 1995, just before another group of kidnappers attempted an assault. She had a feeling what was about to happen wouldn't be pretty.

"Arrowhead's a minute out," a voice said over the tactical radio that Becky carried.

"Pathfinder copies!"

Two smoke canisters were tossed out in front of the rescue team's position. They flashed, green smoke beginning to fill the air. Several blue strobe lights were tossed into the landing zone. All stood out in the increasing daylight, even with the fog.

Summers' Island
Adirondack State Park, New York
July 20, 2010
0626 hours

In the last thirty seconds, Hapke's people had taken three more casualties—one of them dead. For some reason, the intensity of the incoming gunfire from the rescued hostages increased, successfully pinning down the kidnappers' main force, but the team closest to the shoreline was making headway. They'd just reported the sound of boat engines, so things were looking up.

When the RIBs landed to take out the freed hostages, they would slide in and take them. The boats wouldn't be heavily manned and should provide little resistance. Their main force needed to keep the rescue team occupied long enough for them not to notice.

It seemed as though their approach was covered from all angles, however. This was less of a race to the boats as it was Hapke's crew launching an assault on the rescue team's defense of the area—and the kidnappers were losing.

Just as the kidnappers thought they might be able to flank the rescue team, another one of their men dropped due to the intense fire. They began to wonder if anyone would be left to use the boats once they had them.

Shadow Lake
Adirondack State Park, New York
July 20, 2010
0627 hours

The four Special Operations Craft were not the Rigid Inflatable Boats the kidnappers were expecting. RIBs had numerous missions in the military, law enforcement, and emergency services in general, where it was the boat of choice. Knowing the odds and what was at stake, Jon had requested and received something different. The four Mark V SOC boats were ideally suited for extracting people out of a hostile environment. Each boat was armed with two GAU-17 miniguns forward, each capable of firing three thousand rounds per minute, two light machine guns amidships, a heavy fifty-caliber machine gun aft, and two forty-millimeter grenade launchers.

Each crew was trained to work under conditions such as this. Landing and extracting Special Forces was their bread and butter. All four of the boats slowed to half their speed—about twenty knots—while they approached. Though the fog was thick, it had started to lift some, allowing for two-hundred-feet visibility. The green smoke and the strobes were visible.

The bows of all four boats plunged to a stop, and all hell broke loose.

The team tasked with taking over the boats took little fire from the rescuers. While they numbered six, they guessed they were facing two defenders and decided not to press their advantage until the boats landed. The advantage would clearly be theirs.

They could hear the boats approaching, and it sounded like they were coming in fast. The fog was starting to burn off some, and they could see out on the lake close to three hundred feet. Four shadows appeared out of the fog so fast, it made most of them jump. The boats came to an immediate stop, throwing water up in front of them. The landing area was obscured by heavy green smoke. Now was the time to take the landing site.

The team leader rose and gave the order to attack. The team complied, laying down heavy fire in the direction of the defenders to pin them down. Within seconds, the return fire was so intense that the entire team was down. The boats opened with all their miniguns, and the sound was terrifying. It was obvious to the remaining kidnappers their last hope of escape just died with the team tasked to take the boats. These were not the RIBs they expected, but something else. Something more terrifying and deadly. To avoid the gunfire, they dropped down to their bellies, lying prone in the grass. They could see the crafts were equipped with a vicious fifty-caliber machine gun, but that of course wasn't what the rescue team was using.

The miniguns, all on their own, blew through the white pines at their backs, splitting the trees in half. They fell, leaning toward Hapke's crew on the ground, but they didn't dare move—every direction led to death.

Summers' Island
Adirondack State Park, New York
July 20, 2010
0628 hours

The RIBs carrying the FBI assault teams landed, and the agents moved into the cabin complex. The sudden sound to their west caused a pause in their progress. The high-pitched whine of the weapons being used carried across the still lake with amazing clarity. It sounded much like the noise a heavy power saw made. There was the chatter of light and heavy machine-gun fire mixed with the unmistakable sound of the six-barreled miniguns. Several in the teams were familiar with the sound of the weapon, and word spread quickly. They feared from the initial sound of the firefight that the kidnappers were trying for the rescue boats. If their landing had been opposed with such strength, it would have been a bloodbath with heavy losses on both sides. That wouldn't be the case today.

Upton's Marina and Boat Sales
Bluffton, New York
July 20, 2010
0628 hours

The door to the showroom had been propped open, so Director Sanderson and his team were able to hear the firefight from their location the moment it started.

Sanderson had just asked his team leader for an update when the rapid fire of miniguns ripped through the fog. He wheeled around and stared at Putnum. "What the hell is that?"

"Minigun," answered Mitchell. "Fires three thousand rounds a minute. You were right; they were going to ambush the assault boats. The boats we sent in are designed specifically for this type of mission. We're also dropping off some reinforcements for our teams on the island."

Sanderson's expression showed he was skeptical. "What kind of reinforcements?"

Mitchell glanced at Putnum, who answered. "Mr. Sanderson, you know the president got approval to use military assets in this case. Two SEAL teams and a New York State Police SORT team are being landed as we speak. Also, EOD units from Fort Drum should be landing on the island any minute to help your people with the explosives."

The unmistakable sound of helicopters could be heard along with the sound of the firefight.

Summers' Island
Adirondack State Park, New York
July 20, 2010
0629 hours

The first two boats came in, firing until the last possible instant. The SEALs off-loaded and went right into the fight. The first boat took Sheriff James, who was arguing the entire time. With him went the children, Sarah, Emily, Julie, Alex, and Kevin. The second boat was loaded with Sue Ellen and Frank Del Monte, Hennen, Alexander, Demmer, Wells, and Rice. Rice also objected to leaving, but Jon made it clear this wasn't an option.

The exchange took less than a minute, and both boats were backing out onto the lake. They took firing positions, replacing the other two boats, continuing the level of fire on the kidnappers' positions. The next two boats came in, dropping the remaining SEALs and the state troopers. Boat number three backed out of the landing area, taking up an additional support position that left boat four to take the remaining passengers.

Josh was carried onto the boat by Hector and Fortum. They were followed closely by Fiona and O'Leary. Nancy was the last one loaded onto the boat. She was carried on a makeshift stretcher. The crew laid her on the deck aft of the helm. She was accompanied by Becky and Matt. As they were loading her aboard, a flight of five Army helicopters roared over their position.

"Eagle One-One to Arrowhead. Do you need an assist after we drop our passengers?"

"Arrowhead to Eagle One-One," answered Kingston, making eye contact with his mother, "we should be all set, but thanks for checking."

"We'll orbit the area for a few just in case."

Kingston acknowledged the pilot's transmission and was given the signal by the crewman in the bow that they were clear to leave. The boat immediately reversed its engines.

Summers' Island
Adirondack State Park, New York
July 20, 2010
0633 hours

When the last boat backed out of the landing area, Jon took a deep breath. Nancy was hurt—not seriously, but hurt, nonetheless. This had been the first time in his career he'd forced himself not to kill the people on the other side of the line. It had always been easy—if they tried to kill you, you killed them. He was always able to back away when the shooting stopped, his father's words ringing in his ears. On several occasions, his father, Ray, had told him, "Learning to kill is easy; knowing when not to kill is the hard thing." For the first time, he really understood what his father meant. They'd hurt his wife, the woman he loved, and all he wanted to do was kill them all. They'd made it personal when they kidnapped his family, and now Nancy was wounded. The basic urge for revenge was overpowering, and he had to fight it.

The three teams that landed blended in with Summers's team like they'd trained together. The lieutenant in charge of the SORT team assigned several of his men to help Steven and Nathan with the prisoners, but otherwise, everyone was on the firing line. As the boats pulled away from the landing zone, the fire shifted from the miniguns to the heavy machine guns, and then stopped altogether when the boats moved out of range. Ellison called a cease-fire, and the silence was deafening. In the distance, the Army helicopters thundered in the sky as they circled the lake north of the island—but even they seemed quiet compared to the volume of gunfire that just stopped.

Nothing happened for almost a full minute, then several of the kidnappers slowly rose from their places of cover and safety with their hands raised. They decided surrender was preferable to the alternative they were facing. More kidnappers rose to surrender.

Jon breathed a sigh of relief; his decision had been made for him.

Summers' Island
Adirondack State Park, New York
July 20, 2010
0633 hours

Five helicopters flew over the firefight at the extraction point. The pilot would later write in his after-action report that he was amazed that any of the kidnappers survived the volume of fire he'd witnessed the boats pouring into the woods. Even through the fog, he was able to describe the tracer rounds reaching out to deal their deathblows to this once grand plan. He remembered the calm of the sailor who had refused his offer for help and the background noise of the gunfire coming over the radio.

Two of the choppers were Apache gunships, and the remaining three were Blackhawks carrying troops. Their mission was to drop an explosive ordinance disposal team onto the island to assist the FBI teams in making it safe. The commanding general of Fort Drum had no intention of leaving the security for one of his crack EOD teams to the FBI, so he detailed two squads of light infantry to be responsible for that duty. The helos came to a hover, one at a time, over the meadow in the center of the island. Each aircraft carried ten troops, and they fast roped into the meadow, the infantry squads first. The whole process took less than ten minutes. The first squad set up a defensive perimeter, with the second squad reinforcing it. The last group to fast rope in was the EOD unit. They landed ready to go to work. The helicopters moved off to the north to orbit there and await further orders.

Shadow Lake
Adirondack State Park, New York
July 20, 2010
0640 hours

The boats moved in formation, but not at their top speed; there could be other boats on the lake carrying assault teams or equipment. Even though the SOC-Rs were equipped with radar, they wanted plenty of time to react if needed. Kingston turned over command of his boat to the regular boat commander, a chief petty officer, and went to check on his passengers. He started with Josh and his mother. Fiona broke down, throwing her arms around her son. Ericson just smiled and put his hand on the younger man's shoulder. He had questions, but they would wait.

Smith was down and next to Becky, who was continually monitoring Nancy's condition.

"Mrs. Summers," she said, loud enough to be heard over the engine noise, "it's Stephnie Smith. Do you remember me?"

Becky had already given Nancy some morphine for the pain, knowing the transport could be problematic, so she was conscious but not entirely coherent. "Stephnie, you made lieutenant commander. Good for you, girl."

Nancy sounded intoxicated, and that drew a smile from Becky, who told Smith she was medicated. That drew a look of concern. "She'll be fine; the wounds aren't life-threatening. The splinters are big enough, though, that I'd like to see them removed in a hospital. Keep any secondary damage to a minimum."

Smith nodded.

"So, Stephnie," said Nancy, slurring her speech and taking the young officer's arm, "have you ever managed to hook up with that dashing Bryan Kingston?"

There was laughter all around.

Summers' Island
Adirondack State Park, New York
July 20, 2010
0645 hours

The radio chatter from all the units now on the island required multiple frequencies to communicate. The teams at the extraction point moved in, taking the remaining kidnappers prisoner. Surprisingly, there were ten who were either not wounded at all or suffered only minor wounds. Four more were seriously wounded and would need evacuation to a hospital. The SEAL team corpsmen were treating and stabilizing them for transport. The remaining seven kidnappers were killed in the assault.

The troopers took the healthy kidnappers into custody and placed them with the others being held by Abby and her team. Abby was surprised when she was told by the SORT team commander they were at her orders. He also told her that the FBI would eventually be taking custody of all the kidnappers. They were surprised to see that three of the people working with Abby were with the CIA. The SORT team commander guessed the FBI wasn't entirely aware the CIA was taking the first crack at their suspects.

Jon and his people collected the weapons and equipment used or left behind by the kidnappers. The two SEAL teams were not reluctant to place themselves under his command, even when he protested. Chief Skier reminded the retired admiral they were experts at gathering information and there was much to be learned from the collected weapons and equipment.

Jon allowed himself a few minutes to regroup and collect his thoughts. Seeing Nancy hurt threw off his usual focused state of mind. The sight of her being carried, wounded, to the boat was almost too much. He'd made it to this point by pure luck and instinct. It was Ellison who called the cease-fire. George was a good friend and saw the disconnect take place. He was just going through the motions.

Jon stood, leaning against a tree, looking out over the fog-shrouded lake. He didn't see Ellison come up behind him.

"Jon, you, okay?"

Jon jumped when his friend spoke. His eyes refocused, returning to the here and now as he smiled and said, "Sorry, George, I was thinking about Nancy. I never dreamed she would get hurt."

Ellison seemed to detect that his friend was returning to normal but wasn't quite there yet. It often took time, shifting from the mindset of survival to ordinary life. This was especially the case when family was involved.

He nodded quietly before saying, "Jon, she's going to be fine. The doctor gave her a shot of morphine just before they loaded her onto the boat. She's probably higher than a kite by now and feeling no pain. The wound looks worse than it really is."

Jon looked at his friend. "It's all my fault, George. This whole mess is my fault."

"Jon, snap out of it. This isn't your fault. Dick Kingston's the bad guy here and is on the loose out there somewhere. Focus, and we'll get him. It may take all of us, but we can and will get him in the end."

"Kingston?" Jon's tone changed as he looked back at his friend. His eyes became cold and hard again. He looked around. As soon as he spotted Skier talking to Sean, Samcevic, and Wiedenkeller, Jon immediately started moving in that direction. As he drew near, they all turned to face him.

"Chief." Jon directed his first comment to Skier. "Pass the word to the team to get everything to Justin and his people first, then to the FBI. We're looking for anything that can connect this to where Dick Kingston might be heading."

"Aye, aye, Admiral."

Skier turned to leave, but Jon stopped him, adding, "Chief, thanks for bringing me back to reality."

Skier nodded, smiling. "Anytime, sir." The SEAL moved off to do as he was told.

"What am I, chopped liver?" asked Ellison with mock indignation.

Jon ignored his friend, turning to Sean and the other men. "Sean, you and Walt go back to the cave and make sure it's secured. I don't want the FBI ruining my hideaway."

His oldest son acknowledged the order and trotted off, with a smiling Samcevic in tow.

Jon then turned to Ellison and Wiedenkeller. "Why don't we go talk to some prisoners? We have a bad guy to track down."

As they moved off to where Abby had the prisoners, Jon touched Ellison's arm and quietly said, "Thanks."

Upton's Marina and Boat Sales
Bluffton, New York
July 20, 2010
0645 hours

The media lined the roadway, as they were barred entrance to the FBI command post. The sound of the firefight and the helicopters roused every reporter within the village, as well as curious onlookers, and brought them out here, all asking questions. It was obvious to even the most inexperienced of them that something was going on and the hostages were either rescued or the unthinkable happened. Either way, there was no sign from the FBI that suggested they were willing to surrender information about what had taken place in the last fifteen minutes.

The overcast started to break up, and the early morning sun was fighting its way through, helping the fog on the bay burn off. The fog on the main body of the lake was still heavy, and visibility was negligible. As if cued by someone directing a movie, a beam of sunlight reached down from the sky and glistened off the water just as the first boat broke through the fog bank. The gathered reporters and spectators gasped collectively at the sight. The first was followed by the second, then the third, and finally the fourth. They stayed in perfect formation, making a wide turn into the bay, throwing up a wall of spray from the placid surface. It was breathtaking.

Rumblings started through the crowd. These were not the same boats that took out the assault teams. Those boats were the rigid hulled inflatable type boats seen being used by the military for assaults and rescues. These were longer and had no visible outboard engines. While the boats that carried out the assault teams carried only the weapons being used by the teams themselves, these boats appeared to be heavily armed. Each appeared to be carrying five heavy guns and the crew to man them. Whispers of military intervention quickly spread throughout the crowd.

When the boats drew closer, there was an increased level of activity, almost frantic, at the marina. FBI agents and medical personnel began to line the docks. TV video cameras began rolling, and reporters began to go live to their networks or stations. Cameras zoomed in on the approaching boats, and a positive speculation began to work its way through the crowd about the outcome of the battle they all heard minutes before.

The boats were quickly approaching the marina. When they were several hundred yards away from the docks, they suddenly cut power, and the bow of each boat dropped and disappeared behind the wave that was put up in front of them as they came to a stop. They didn't stay still long; each boat began to move forward almost immediately, though much slower. They pulled into the marina, and the number of FBI agents and emergency responders blocked any view the media may have had.

Upton's Marina and Boat Sales
Bluffton, New York
July 20, 2010
0655 hours

Sanderson had been standing next to Putnum when the boats broke through the fog.

The older man just smiled and started a casual stroll out to the dock area. One could almost hear the sigh of relief from the gathered crowd along Lake Street. Knowing who was on the rescue craft, agents and first responders began to pour onto the docks in anticipation of the hostages' arrival. A wheelchair and two gurneys were discreetly held nearby, out of sight, until they were needed. They decided to send all the hostages and returning rescuers to Fort Drum, where they could be secured and treated without any interruption from the media. An FBI debriefing team headed by Grey was to be flown to the facility right behind the hostages, leaving Sanderson to deal with the kidnappers who survived. The wounded kidnappers would also be sent to Fort Drum. The base was already locked down and ready to receive their guests.

Mitchell walked up behind Putnum and Sanderson. "Admiral, the Army choppers will be here in less than five minutes to transport the hostages and wounded. A second flight of choppers to transport the FBI team and the assault team to Fort Drum should be here in less than twenty minutes. We'll be on the second flight."

Putnum watched the boats pull into the docks in the marina. "What about the wounded kidnappers and the assault team still on the island?"

"They'll be airlifted out as soon as we get the okay," responded Mitchell without hesitation. "The Army has as many choppers as we need to get them all to Fort Drum."

There was a flurry of activity on the docks, causing Mitchell to stop his report and watch as the hostages were off-loaded from the boats. The two gurneys were rushed down the docks, with the wheelchair right behind one of them. Sanderson watched Sheriff James being placed on one gurney and a woman on the other. Ericson was helped into a wheelchair, and all three were quickly removed from the docks.

The other hostages were escorted past him on their way to the field next to the marina, which was being secured as a landing zone for the helicopters. They all seemed no worse for wear, and most were smiling as they spoke to the medical people who were on-site to evaluate them. He watched as the members of the rescue team stood on the dock, speaking to the boat crews. Hands were being shaken and even an occasional hug exchanged. Young Kingston seemed to be giving orders to one of the boat crews.

Sanderson allowed himself a curious glance at the scene before him.

"This is his command, Gene," said Putnum, watching the same drama play out. "He's been with the Special Boat crews for some time. He's an excellent officer."

Sanderson nodded. "He looks to be one. His men appear to respect him."

"He's flying up to Drum with us to be with his mother and stepfather. Commander Smith has been assigned to help us track his father. We'll all look forward to seeing you there when you're done on the island."

Sanderson turned to Putnum and nodded. He then glanced at two members of the rescue team who were walking by. They were dressed in woodland camouflage, and their faces were painted for the mission. They appeared tired under the weight of their weapons and equipment, but they walked with pride. He couldn't help but smile at them. It wasn't until they returned his smile that he realized they were none other than Kevin Gateway and Matt Summers.

Upton's Marina and Boat Sales
Bluffton, New York
July 20, 2010
0700 hours

The crowd watched the flurry of activity on the docks, and speculation ran rampant when it was clear there were wounded among the hostages. They were even more amazed when Sandy Monroe appeared with Sanderson, who announced a press briefing would be held in thirty minutes.

Numerous rapid-fire questions were directed at Sanderson by the gathered reporters, but before he could say "no comment," they were overflown by the choppers from Fort Drum.

The Blackhawks landed in the field by the marina, ready to take on the hostages, while the two Apache's hovered, as if to provide cover over the entire scene.

Everyone forgot Sanderson's press conference, allowing him the opportunity to quietly withdraw back to the command post. Monroe, silent, moved past her distracted colleagues before they decided to question her. Once loaded, the Blackhawks took off, and they circled north in formation, heading toward Fort Drum and the hospital, with the two Apache gunships flying cover.

Queen Beatrix International Airport
Oranjestad, Aruba
July 20, 2010
0800 hours

The customs agents for the Kingdom of the Netherlands boarded the aircraft to perform a cursory inspection. The man in the expensive suit was obviously an important American businessman to have such a large entourage. All their paperwork was in order, and nothing on the aircraft seemed out of place. There was no cargo, and the few bags they had had passed inspection. He'd piloted his own plane into the airport, providing documentation showing he was renting an estate on the north end of the island on Arashi Beach. It was an exclusive neighborhood where the homes were large, although close together. He had leased one of the beachfront properties.

The woman who appeared to be the man's senior assistant, and, while not rushing them, was trying to conclude the formalities of the customs inspection. She politely asked them if there was anything else they needed, offering to produce more supporting documentation regarding their business on the island. The cell phone of the senior agent chirped, indicating there was a message. A quick check told him another private plane was landing and was also in need of a customs inspection. He smiled at the woman in front of him.

"Everything appears to be in order, ma'am," he said in heavily accented English. "Enjoy your stay in Aruba. I hope your visit isn't all business; we have some beautiful beaches here, and I understand the nightlife can be quite exciting."

The woman returned his smile. "You don't enjoy the nightlife yourself? I'm not sure I could live here and not at least sample the nightlife."

The senior customs agent raised an eyebrow. "Our economy is based on the tourist trade, which leads to the nightclubs and casinos being a bit too expensive for us locals. You enjoy your stay now, miss."

With that, the agent turned, leading his partner off the plane. The woman looked at her boss, who nodded. He turned to another woman standing next to him, kissing her gently on the forehead. The customs agent hadn't noticed the resemblance between the two women, or he would have guessed they were sisters. Different hair color and a pair of sunglasses could do wonders. Kingston put his arm around Andrea Handcock, and they moved toward the open door of the aircraft. Both smiled, walking into the warm Caribbean sun. They were free!

Queen Beatrix International Airport
Oranjestad, Aruba
July 20, 2010
0825 hours

Evans stood at the bottom of the stairs, waiting for the customs officials. He watched their car approach. Looking beyond them, he recognized the private jet from Dulles several hundred yards away, with a number of large SUVs bunched around it. The vehicles were being loaded with luggage, and while weapons were not visible, the men standing about looking formidable were obviously security. Evans watched a tall, well-dressed man and two women get into the first vehicle. Slowly, all the others began entering the other vehicles until all but four were left. Suddenly the vehicles began moving in a caravan toward the exit of the airport's private terminal. The last four men jumped into the remaining SUV, racing off after the rest, leaving the ground crew to take care of the aircraft.

The car came to a stop next to him, and Evans refocused his attention on the customs officials. "Alphonse, so nice to see you again."

"Ah, Mr. Evans," responded the senior customs official. "How nice to have you with us again. Are you here on business or pleasure, sir?"

Evans handed the man his passport. "Last-minute decision, Alphonse." He watched the caravan of vehicles drive away. "I have to say pleasure. I'm meeting an old friend here."

The customs official looked over his shoulder, also spying the caravan. Evans waited to see if he'd say something—and to his delight, the official did. "An American businessman with quite a large entourage. He seems very self-important."

"I recognize the jet," Evans responded, smiling at the official. "He's not a man to be trifled with, for sure. I met him once—a bit ruthless for my taste. Is he staying in one of the hotels on the island?"

The customs man raised an eyebrow, giving Evans a curious look. He glanced over his shoulder just as the last of the SUVs left the airport grounds and then returned his attention to Evans. "Do you think he might be a danger to anyone here in Aruba or be involved in any illegal activity?"

Evans shook his head. "No, my friend. If he says he's here on business, then that's why he's here. My guess is he's here to do some banking. We shared an employer a number of years ago who used one of your fine banks here on the island. I do have some friends who will take an interest in his presence here, however. After all, he has been keeping a low profile for some time now."

Alphonse raised an eyebrow again, hesitating before he spoke. "Thank you for your candor, Mr. Evans. It's always nice to do business with a true gentleman. You don't have to worry, either. Troy Bennett and his party are staying at a rental on the north end of the island by Arashi Beach. They have leased a nice beachfront compound fit for his affluence. He won't bother you that far north."

"I'll be staying at the Marriott. The casino there is calling my name. I left them too much of my money on my last visit to your beautiful island."

The customs official laughed. "Our local economy thanks you, Mr. Evans. You are always welcome to leave your hard-earned money here in Aruba."

Evans turned serious for a minute. "How is the family, Alphonse? The children, they are well?"

The customs man seemed to soften immediately, a smile coming across his face. "They are doing well, sir, thank you for inquiring. My oldest starts university next year. We are very proud of her—she wants to be a doctor."

Evans couldn't help but smile. He reached out and touched the man's arm. "Cherish your time with her, my friend. My daughter has grown up and now has children of her own. She is a doctor. I couldn't be prouder, but I never get to see her."

The government official's look became serious. "My friend, take the word of a humble civil servant. There is nothing more important than your children. You are a rich and powerful man, but maybe not as rich as I. You need to spend time with your child and her family. It will make you whole. Without them in your life, you're missing everything. Take my advice—spend less time here losing your money and spend it on your child and her family."

Evans didn't respond but nodded to indicate he understood. The man's partner came off Evans's plane, giving them the all clear. Alphonse extended his hand to Evans. "We're done here, sir. Enjoy your stay in Aruba. Remember what I said, Mr. Evans. Spend some time with your daughter. You're a good man and deserve to enjoy your life."

The customs official turned, walking back to his car, before Evans could respond. The vehicle pulled away. They hadn't even reached the hangers where the customs office was located and Alphonse was already on the phone with the police, requesting surveillance be put on the address given by the Troy Bennett party. Evans was a man who lived his life on the fringe. He was an attorney from the Bahamas and visited this side of the Caribbean often for both business and pleasure. He'd given tips to customs in the past that paid dividends in keeping Aruba, its population, and its visitors safe. If Bennett didn't come to cause trouble, then nothing would be lost except a few man hours in surveillance—but the fact that someone might be interested in the man's location was enough reason to keep an eye on him. They didn't need any trouble. Alphonse knew he was doing the right thing. He'd do Evans the favor of keeping him abreast of Bennett's movements.

Evans watched the car pull away from his plane, noting that Alphonse was already on the phone, probably asking for surveillance, and he smiled. There was no way he could keep up with watching everything Kingston was up to, so why not have the police do that for him? They were used to being discrete and were equipped to do the job right. He would go to the hotel, rest up, and wait for the cavalry to arrive. Besides, he was guessing Kingston would show up at the casino anyway. It was the largest one on the island, and he'd just escaped from prison after fifteen years. Evans was patient; the man would come to him. The smile on his face faded, thinking about what Alphonse had said about family.

Fort Drum Military Reservation
Guthrie Army Medical Center
July 20, 2010
0900 hours

The medical center wasn't large, but it was secure, being in the middle of an Army base. The base was locked down due to the presence of the hostages. They were being isolated in the medical center for the time being, until space could be made for debriefing interviews elsewhere.

The staff at the medical center was busy with the rush of patients from the scene on Shadow Lake. Most of the hostages were quickly processed and cleared medically, except for Nancy and Sheriff James. Both were sent immediately to surgery, and both were expected to recover fully. Nancy was already out and in recovery, but James's wounds were a bit more serious. They received word more helicopters were on the way.

The wounded kidnappers were already at Fort Drum. The surgeons on base would be busy for some time because the kidnappers were in worse shape—some serious enough they may not survive. Additional doctors and staff were being brought in to help.

Putnum stood outside Nancy's room, watching O'Leary fuss over the sleeping woman. He found it funny, knowing the history. He shifted his gaze briefly when Josh wheeled up next to him in a new wheelchair and said, "So, Admiral, I'm not surprised to find you part of this mess. I'm assuming you're the one who brought clarity to it all?"

Putnum continued to watch the two women in the room. "I'm just another pawn in Richard Kingston's grand scheme, Senator. He couldn't get me because of my protection detail, or I would have been in the same dilemma as you and the others. He went after everyone that was responsible for putting him in prison. We're fortunate no one was killed except for the two men in the first rescue attempt."

"You're not counting the kidnappers, Admiral. Is there a reason for that?"

Putnum looked down at the man next to him, who was also watching the two women.

"The teams that went after George and Jon were all taken alive," said Putnum.

Ericson chuckled. "Just a few bumps and bruises because they picked the wrong old guys to go after. Maybe a little wolf slobber on a couple of them. You have to laugh."

Putnum ignored the comment. "All totaled, we're guessing there was upward of fifty kidnappers involved in this fiasco. Of that number, you have twenty dead, at least fifteen seriously wounded, two of whom may not survive surgery. Fifteen are in custody with either minor wounds—or 'bumps and bruises,' as you call them. Pardon me for not laughing; it could have been far worse."

"Don't misunderstand me, Admiral," said Josh, looking up. "I'm not minimizing the seriousness of all of this. We were extremely fortunate to only have the two deaths on our side of the tally board. As usual, Dick Kingston underestimated a few things. Poor planning on his part."

Putnum didn't answer right away, pausing to consider his response. "I think he planned it well enough. He's free, after all," he said, and Ericson's energy dampened. They stood silently for a few seconds before Putnum added, "That's all this big show was—a distraction to get him out of Leavenworth so he could escape. He couldn't care less about what the tally board says or who's alive or dead. He's free, and that was the sole purpose for this exercise."

Ericson said nothing.

Putnum smoothed the lapels of his jacket, rolling out his neck. When he spoke again, it was with the lightheartedness of discussing the weather. "All that being said, Senator, it is good to see you again. How's Mrs. Ericson holding up?"

Josh sighed, appreciative of the change in topic. "She's doing okay, Admiral. Having Bryan here is helping her forget why this took place. Thank you for that, if you're responsible."

Putnum nodded. "He's a good man, Senator. She has every right to be proud of him."

Both men turned when they heard someone coming up behind them. They weren't surprised to find Mitchell approaching. "Admiral, the team should be landing shortly. They're bringing them here to avoid any unforeseen entanglements with other chains of command."

Putnum nodded. Josh watched the exchange between the two men, deciding he couldn't remain silent. "I'm assuming parts of your plan weren't sanctioned. Is there anything I can do to help with that?"

For the first time in their conversation, Putnum turned, facing Ericson. "Thank you for the offer, Senator, but this is one of those things you should distance yourself from. There are several things going on where the boundaries of propriety might be just a bit fuzzy. You need to be above reproach on any of this."

Josh's expression became very serious. "So there is a plan to bring Dick Kingston to justice?"

Putnum returned the senator's gaze, saying nothing. He then looked at Mitchell, giving him a nod. Mitchell turned and started down the corridor. Putnum followed without saying another word, leaving Ericson alone in the hallway.

Fort Drum Military Reservation
Guthrie Army Medical Center
July 20, 2010
0930 hours

The four helicopters roared in low over the medical center, causing a stir among the small groups of people gathered. The helipad at the clinic had been busy since the hostages arrived. Not every helicopter brought in wounded or injured; several were loaded with federal agents. The traffic had become commonplace. What had really caused the stir was the sudden presence of the commanding general.

When the first helicopter landed, a group of armed men with camouflaged uniforms off-loaded. They moved away from their aircraft quickly and professionally. Their faces were painted, and they looked like soldiers returning from a combat mission. The second helicopter landed, and the remainder of the team off-loaded. This group included one woman. They moved to where the rest of the team stood waiting. When they were all together, they started walking toward the main clinic. There was no question to anyone present who they were and what they had done. It was how they carried themselves. No one moved, they just watched.

As the group neared the clinic, the commanding general and his staff moved forward. When they reached the assault team, the general threw his arms around one of the men. Charlie Naylor and the general were old friends, and it quickly became obvious he was there to pay his respects and nothing more. The fact that the general knew a member of the rescue team had raised his standing among his own people. The rumor going around the base was the team was an ultrasecret unit of the armed forces put together for just such contingencies. The fact the general knew a member of the team had only fueled the rumors. After some quick greetings, the general led the team into the clinic.

Fort Drum Military Reservation
Guthrie Army Medical Center
July 20, 2010
0945 hours

Inspector Preston laughed at the story being told by Kevin while they sat at the table, enjoying a cup of coffee. Most of the hostages gathered in the cafeteria while they waited to be debriefed by Grey and his people. All the members of the rescue team who escorted them out were also there, although they turned in their weapons and cleaned up. All were in civilian clothes and, aside from looking a little tired, seemed none the worse for wear.

The mood in the room was light and jovial while they waited for more teams from the FBI to arrive to speed the debriefing process up. Laughter filled the room, and Preston was enjoying being part of it. There was a sudden shift as the faces looked toward the hallway on the other side of a series of windows. Sarah and her children were up and moving toward the entrance to the cafeteria. Preston turned to watch them meet Sean. He was still in camouflage from head to toe and armed. Sarah threw her arms around her husband, hugging and kissing him. The kids held onto their father as tightly as they could. Others from the rescue team moved into the room while everyone stood and applauded. Preston suddenly found himself facing a man looking quite intimidating with his battle dress and weaponry. Preston smiled, realizing who it was.

"Inspector Preston," said Jon, returning the Mountie's smile, "I apologize for leaving you so abruptly. I'm sure I've broken a number of laws in Canada and will make myself available to you when I'm done with this business."

Preston laughed. "I was just sent to see if there was a connection to your disappearance and the kidnappings here. We've cleared your disappearance—since you're obviously no longer missing—and made the connection. I have no orders beyond that. Besides, chances are pretty good that the two men who tried to kill you will be extradited back here for their connection to all of this. It'll save the people of Canada the cost of a trial and a long incarceration."

It was Summers's turn to laugh.

Preston continued, "My colleagues and I did enjoy hearing about your interrogation techniques. You really intimidated those two; they wouldn't shut up."

Summers smiled. "I don't understand, Inspector."

"Using wolves as an interrogation tool scared the living daylights out of them."

Summers maintained eye contact with Preston, the smile never leaving his face. "You must be mistaken, Inspector."

Preston chuckled. "Okay, Admiral, have it your way. They had gray wolf DNA all over them from urine and saliva. We're advanced in our crime investigation techniques, even in the north woods. Tracks and other wolf sign all over your campsite around the two bound suspects. Impressive. They didn't have much of a chance, did they?"

"A close encounter with wild wolves," responded Summers, feigning innocence that not a single person was falling for. "It sounds like they were very fortunate not to have been hurt."

Preston's only response was a grunt and a smile. It was obvious nothing was going to come out of this conversation. He was just glad the man was on his side. What happened in Canada had nothing to do with luck. If any laws were broken, there was no intention of pursuing prosecution because of the circumstances surrounding this case. The mess here in New York had spilled across the border into his country, and they could conveniently move everything back here and be rid of the entire issue. There were no obvious victims in his country looking to file charges, except maybe the wolves.

Their conversation was interrupted as the former hostages began crowding around the newly arrived members of the rescue team, thanking them. Preston watched as Summers quietly withdrew to the hallway and disappeared.

Nancy woke to find Amy sitting in the chair next to the bed. When she opened her eyes, the senator smiled. "Don't talk. They said you'd have a hard time speaking until you drank some liquids. Do you want to sit up?"

Nancy nodded, opening her mouth to speak, but nothing came out. O'Leary stood, moving to the bed. Using the controls, she moved the bed to a more upright position. She pointed to a plastic water cup on the movable table. Nancy nodded again. O'Leary pulled the table next to Nancy, handing her the cup.

"I'm glad you can't speak yet, because I have something to tell you and I'm not sure I could get it out if it had to be a two-way conversation." Nancy raised an eyebrow as she sipped the water. O'Leary continued, "I'll be the first to admit that when you and Jon separated, I celebrated, just a little bit. Ever since that summer in Annapolis, I've had a thing for him, and I know you know that. I thought for sure when you left him, he'd come right to Becky or me. She knew better."

O'Leary smiled weakly.

Nancy continued to sip her water, staying quiet.

"We talked, you see," O'Leary went on, "and Becky tried to explain, but I was convinced that, if not her, then he'd come to me. But he didn't. He went to commune with nature and play with wild animals. Who would have thought that? Anyway, I want you to know that I get it, and you don't have to worry about me."

A tear ran down O'Leary's cheek, bringing a sympathetic smile to Nancy's face as she raised her hand, indicating she wanted something to write with. O'Leary found a pen and a pad in the drawer of the movable table, giving them to Nancy. She scribbled something on the pad, handing it back to O'Leary.

"'Thanks, welcome to the sisterhood,'" read O'Leary aloud, looking puzzled. The two women looked at each other, and O'Leary began to laugh. Just then, Becky and Jon walked into the room right on cue, catching them off guard.

"Well, it's good to see you awake and happy," said Becky, smiling.

"Oh my goodness!" said O'Leary, gasping at the sight of Jon still in his combat gear and carrying weapons.

Meanwhile, Becky moved right to Nancy's side—her doctor's hat on—and began by checking her friend's pulse. "The splinter just missed the artery, but we couldn't take a chance removing it in the field and causing more damage," she explained, giving Nancy a quick once-over. "The surgery took longer to set up than to perform, but if the artery had been nicked, at least they'd have the tools here to deal with it. You'll be sore for a few days but will be back to normal before you know it."

Becky looked at Nancy before adding, "I found the war hero here pacing in the hallway. He and the rest of the guys managed to escape the FBI and all their questions. Amy, why don't you and I go get some coffee and let these two be alone?"

Without a word, O'Leary stood, walking past Becky and Jon. She hesitated for a second, shooting a glance and a smile over her shoulder at Nancy, and then left the room.

Becky turned to leave, putting her hand on Jon's shoulder. "Don't be too long. Nancy is just out of surgery and needs her rest. Besides, you need a shower and some sleep yourself, cowboy. You smell like you've been in the bush for a while."

The toothy smile appearing from amid the green face paint told Becky everything was going to be okay. She left the room.

Jon walked up to the bed, gently taking Nancy's hand. "How are you holding up, babe?"

Nancy squeezed his hand in response. With her free hand, she motioned to him that she couldn't talk yet and indicated she was still a little sleepy from the surgery. She let go of his hand, grabbing the pad and pen, and scribbled a quick note, holding it up.

He read it out loud. "'Did he get away?'" Jon looked at his wife, nodding. "He did, but this isn't over yet. I have to go away for a while, then everything will be good."

Nancy scribbled another note.

"'More secrets?'" read Jon, raising an eyebrow. "No, no secrets. I'm going after him. He won't get away. I'll be out of the country for a few days."

Nancy scribbled one more note.

"'How do you know where he went?'" Summers smiled broadly as he read. He didn't answer beyond that smile, though. Nancy wrote out another appeal.

"'You don't trust me?!'" read Jon. He shook his head in response. "No, I trust you. I've called in a favor from a dead man. I know exactly where Dick Kingston is. Don't worry, we'll get him. You're better off not knowing what we're up to."

Nancy frantically scribbled on the pad and then grabbed her husband's hand, pushing the pad into it. He read what was printed on the paper and just looked back at his wife. "'See, more secrets!!!'"

Her eyes flashed hatred.

CHAPTER NINE

ENDGAME

Marriott Resort
Palm Beach, Aruba
July 20, 2010
2130 hours

Evans had stayed at this resort before. It hosted the largest casino in Aruba, and he could spend twenty-four hours a day relaxing in the casino or enjoying the first-class room accommodations if he wished to indulge in a quiet evening. The prices were steep, but it was worth every penny. He was currently registered for the governor's suite on the top floor, with access to a private club as well as a view of the beach below and the blue Caribbean.

Sitting in the casino, he positioned himself at a poker table where he could see the entrance and most of the gaming tables. Evans enjoyed poker and was good at it. He usually won enough to come out ahead, but that wasn't why he chose this table—or game, for that matter. Here, he was able to play and keep an eye on the comings and goings in the casino. Arriving at the casino at about eight o'clock, he had spent a half hour looking around and wondering if the people he needed to contact would be coming to this casino. It was closest to where they were staying on the island, and Evans suspected that they couldn't resist going out for the evening after being in prison for so long. He knew they contacted the bank earlier in the day and the transaction would take at least twenty-four hours to complete. It was the same bank they had all used at one time to conceal funds paid by the employer they had shared.

Evans was three hundred dollars ahead due to two of the players at the table being careless with their bets. He almost missed Kingston when he entered, as one of the players was claiming the other was cheating, drawing everyone's attention to the table. Kingston made eye contact with Evans, and there was instant recognition.

Security was at the table shortly after, calming the two men and escorting them out of the casino. Both were Americans, likely tourists, and had been drinking heavily during the game. Security was quick and efficient, hustling both men out. One of the floor managers appeared at the table, apologizing to the three remaining players and offering to move them to other games. The other two agreed because the offer included free drinks for the rest of the evening. Evans turned down the offer, figuring he'd quit while he was ahead. The manager motioned for an employee to escort the other players and then turned back to Evans to say, "I'm so sorry for this, Mr. Evans. Obviously, they were amateurs and poor losers. They are tourists—not even staying here at the resort. Please, drinks are on the house."

Evans waved his hand, dismissing the offer. "It's okay, Albert, I'm staying in the hotel and have free drinks at the club if I want. Nothing to concern yourself about. I have several hundred dollars of their money, and they weren't accusing me of cheating."

The supervisor smiled politely. "Just the same, Mr. Evans, you shouldn't have had to witness that in our casino, much less have it occurred at your table. I ha—" The man pressed on the earpiece in his right ear, then looked at Evans. "Sir, there is a Mr. Troy Bennett in the lounge here in the casino asking you to join him and his party. He says you're an old business acquaintance. He's asked us to remind you the two of you met over a deal involving Philippine real estate."

Evans nodded, handing both the dealer and the supervisor a chip as a tip.

The dealer accepted the tip, but the supervisor protested. Evans held his hand up to stop the protest, smiling. "Stop, Albert, you deserve it. You and the staff here always take good care of me. Could you please be so kind as to cash out the rest of my chips and bring my winnings to the lounge?"

The supervisor nodded, motioning for the dealer to collect the pile of chips in front of Evans. The dealer smiled, taking care of the task. Evans stood up, glancing at the lounge. He saw where Kingston and his party were seated and suddenly felt underdressed, even though he was wearing a pair of dress slacks, a dress shirt with no tie, and a lightweight sport coat. Kingston was dressed formally in a tux, and the two women on his arms were in formal evening dresses. He looked very much the part of a Bond villain surrounded by beautiful women. Evans didn't feel the part of Bond, though; he was used to being the villain, in real life, and didn't see that changing anytime soon. He looked around the casino before heading for the lounge. There was no one he could see fitting the part of the hero. He shrugged his shoulders, moving off toward Kingston.

Fort Drum Military Reservation
Guthrie Army Medical Center
July 20, 2010
2245 hours

Sanderson was furious, moving through the hospital, looking for Putnum. His people had gone to interview the rescue team and found them gone. Not one member of the team was anywhere on the base, and rumor said an aircraft with them on board flew out at noon, over ten hours earlier. There were interviews to be done to close out the case, and that couldn't be completed without speaking to Summers and his team. This wasn't acceptable or professional behavior on Putnum's part.

Sanderson headed toward the main entrance, moving through the lobby, when he stopped short. Coming through the main doors was Putnum, accompanied by the base commanding general, Mitchell, his entire team, and Cassie Summers.

Putnum walked directly to him. "There you are, Sanderson. We need to talk."

"Yes, we do. I—"

"Pack your bags, Gene. You and Cassie are going with Tommy's team."

"What . . . Where?"

"I'm not sure yet, but I need a team ready to move on a moment's notice. Things are moving quickly right now. We sent teams after Kingston earlier today because of a couple of leads that popped up."

"Summers and his team?"

Putnum ignored the FBI agent. "We're hoping for some information in the near future about where our Tina Ramsey impersonator may have gone, and we thought you might want to volunteer for the FBI slot on the team."

A sly smile crossed Sanderson's face. "That billet should go to a field agent with a lower rank than I have."

"True," replied Putnum, remaining serious, "but you were the first FBI agent that came to mind when the topic came up with your boss. It's personal with this one, Gene, and if you want the slot, it's yours. Cassie jumped at the chance to go along. How do you feel about it?"

"I'm in," Sanderson said, not giving the topic further thought.

"Gene . . ." Putnum's voice became quiet. "Justin's team will be taking lead, and he's in charge. We'll probably be going to a nonextradition country, and there could be military intervention required to pull this off. Do you have any problem with that?"

Sanderson shook his head. "Until I met you and this crew, my life was ordered and neat. My goal is to get that back in my life, but having a page of the case left open wouldn't allow that to take place. While I'm not convinced your methods are the best, if I can get a conviction on this woman, that's all I care about. If I have to fracture a rule here and bend a procedure there to get this done, I'm all for it."

Putnum smiled at the last comment. "Careful, Gene, you might never again find that book you've been so proud of following all these years."

Sanderson thought for a second, and it was his turn to be serious. "Like you said, sir, this is personal."

Marriott Resort
Palm Beach, Aruba
July 20, 2010
2145 hours

Evans walked up to the table, smiling. "Mr. Bennett, how nice of you to recognize me— Timothy Gerard Evans, Esquire, at your service."

Kingston stood when Evans approached, taking the attorney's extended hand. He motioned for him to take the vacant seat between the two women at the table. They weren't young, by Evans's standards. The older one was about forty, and the younger one was in her mid-thirties. They were beautiful, nonetheless.

"Mr. Evans, may I present my fiancée, Kellie Rutledge, and her sister Annie? Ladies, Mr. Evans here is an old business acquaintance."

Evans acted the part of the proper English gentleman, taking each woman's right hand, kissing it gently, and acknowledging them by name. Both women blushed as he greeted them, though it showed more prominently on Kellie with her pale complexion. Annie had certainly seen more sun than her sister, but then she hadn't been in a federal prison for the past fifteen years. Evans smiled, thinking about prison—but then, an American prison wasn't like the ones he'd been in. Both he and Kingston took their seats.

"You look very familiar, Mr. Evans," said Kellie. She seemed to be searching her memory for where they had met.

"My dear," Kingston said, smiling politely, "you met Mr. Evans one time in the Philippines in 1994. He accompanied our friend from Japan the very first time we met. His hair wasn't graying around the temples then, and he spoke with an Irish brogue instead of sounding like a proper Englishman."

Kellie smiled broadly. "I remember you now. You were a real bad boy back then—had all the women after you. You've toned down your persona a bit. Are you still a dangerous man, Mr. Evans?"

Evans raised an eyebrow. "That depends on how you define dangerous. Beautiful women such as yourselves may have to worry about me as I pursue you to woo and dine you, but otherwise I'm pretty much harmless. I've retired from my other pursuits. Trying to keep a low profile from our mutual adversaries."

"He's charming," said Annie, grinning. "I like him."

"Careful, sister," warned Kellie, "this one will break your heart. As I recall, he's quite the ladies' man. I'm guessing he hasn't shaken all that bad-boy image."

Everyone at the table laughed politely. The waitress in the lounge brought over an Irish whiskey, neat, for Evans. "Here's your regular drink, Mr. Evans. Will there be anything else?"

Evans returned the woman's smile. "Liesbeth, if you could, please get something for each of my friends here, and put it on my tab."

The waitress nodded. She took their orders and quietly moved off while they carried on casual conversation about the weather and how crowded the casino was. Evans looked at his drink, thinking it was wrong for a British spy. While he wasn't one, he was certainly playing a game of cat and mouse with Kingston. You didn't shake or stir Irish whiskey—it was best when served without ice, and he wasn't a big mixed drink fan. He smiled, comparing himself to the famous British spies of legend. He was more the villain. It suited his character better, like the whiskey.

The rest of the drinks came, and Annie made a toast to being free in the tropics. They all laughed, sipping their drinks.

Then, a serious look crossed over Kingston's face. "I was wondering, Mr. Evans, why is it that you're free when so many of our counterparts on that venture were arrested and imprisoned. Out of curiosity, why are you here?"

Both women looked from Kingston to Evans with an equally serious look. Evans maintained eye contact with Kingston, a hint of a smile showing at the corners of his mouth.

At this very instant, Kingston remembered the stories about this man and how very dangerous he really was.

"You forgot executed."

"I'm sorry?" responded Kingston, puzzled.

Evans didn't answer Kingston right away. The hesitation made the American shift nervously in his chair. "Many of our counterparts were not only arrested and imprisoned, but they were also executed by the Philippine government."

Kingston seemed to settle, and both women looked at Evans with wide-eyed disbelief.

Evans continued, keeping eye contact with Kingston. "I was wounded and arrested by your military and turned over to the Philippine government like everyone else on the island. As a matter of fact, an old friend of yours—a Captain Summers—is the one who captured me."

Kingston immediately flushed with the mention of that name. Evans smiled broadly, not caring if the man sitting across from him knew the mention of his old Academy rival was intentional. It showed there were no secrets here at the table and set the ground rules for the rest of the conversation.

"He's dead now," Kingston blurted out, clearly trying to regain an advantage in the conversation. "I had him killed as part of the diversion for our escape from prison."

There it was. The truth was on the table.

Evans swiveled his drink, watching as the color in Kingston's face started to return to normal after he made this statement. He had to stifle a laugh. "Well, I appreciate the gesture, Mr. Bennett. He was not my favorite person back then."

Kingston nodded to Evans, while Annie added, "They shot him while he was canoeing on a lake in Canada. They're still looking for the body."

"No body?" questioned Evans.

"He's dead!" snapped Kingston, his face turning crimson again.

"I'm just saying . . ." chided Evans, looking as innocent as he could.

"So, how did you end up here?" asked Kellie, trying to change the subject.

"I had made some powerful connections over the years and arranged for an escape from that hellhole of a prison they put me in. The one constant in many of the third-world prisons is the corruption of their officials. I literally just walked away. Being the first of those arrested to escape, the others weren't allowed to be as lucky. Security on them was increased, and they are either dead or still in prison. I don't apologize for that. Like you, I took the opportunity when it arose."

Kingston again nodded, as did his two female companions.

Evans continued, "I knocked around for a couple of years, working in the same business that almost killed me. I finally faked my death, and here I am. I'm here tonight by chance. Ever since I picked up the money deposited by our former employer in the bank here, I occasionally return to gamble, meet exotic people, enjoy the beaches, and even occasionally practice law."

"You really practice law?" questioned Kellie, sounding a little amazed.

"I do have a certain amount of experience with the law." Evans smiled. "A good set of documents and an ironclad background, and you can be and do most anything. I had some powerful enemies looking for me. Not anymore."

Kingston seemed to be thinking about something else while he listened. "Did you speak to our former employers after you escaped?"

Evans looked at Kingston, then shook his head. "There was no need for that. For them, I'm dead, killed in Ireland while being foolish."

"I contacted them this afternoon to renegotiate compensation for our services in that venture in 1995. We've been in prison for fifteen years and have kept certain secrets all this time. I feel that makes us worth a bit more to them. Would you like to be part of that?"

Evans smiled, but not because he was thinking about the offer—to the contrary. He knew the secrets hadn't been kept. Their former employers in Japan didn't know who gave them up and didn't care. Anyone connected with that venture looking to renegotiate payment would find a very willing party to do just that. The problem was the negotiation would be one-sided and final. Evans guessed a hit team was already on its way to the island. He hadn't talked but had dealt with various versions of organized crime all his life. He would not be anywhere near Kingston when they arrived. He shook his head.

"Thank you for the offer, but no. Like so many others, they think I am dead. I'd like to keep it that way."

Kingston nodded. "My friend, how good are these people who helped you with your documents and background story? The reason I ask is because it's only a matter of time before my government finds us and creates, shall we say . . . residency issues for us."

"My people are the best in the world at what they do, but they are expensive. You can find a nonextradition treaty country to hole up in; that would be much less expensive."

Kingston waved his hand, dismissing the comment. "We are headed to Indonesia tomorrow after we go to the bank. We have a place there. I'm looking for some way to get the government right off our trail. Money won't be an object. Can you put me in touch with them?"

"Our little sister is going to meet us in Indonesia," said Kellie innocently. "Like Annie, she helped us escape."

Evans was silent for a moment, thinking about Kingston's request. "Mr. Bennett, I will ask them. Right now, you might be a little too hot. Remember, I bounced around for a couple of years before they agreed to help me."

"Was it worth the wait?"

"The price was high," answered Evans, "but I'm alive and not being chased. I'll ask them, but that's all I can do. The rest is up to them."

"That's all I can ask," smiled Kingston. "We would be in your debt."

"Come on, Tim," said Annie, grabbing Evans by the arm, "show me how good a gambler you really are."

Evans gave Kingston a pleading look. The man just smiled, shrugging his shoulders.

"That's why we're here. We've been away for a really long time. We're here to get our money and be a little stupid."

Evans smiled, surrendering to Annie's wishes, but couldn't agree more with the last part of Kingston's statement.

Marriott Resort
Palm Beach, Aruba
July 20, 2010
2200 hours

They were in place to watch them before they entered the casino. The man playing the slots was running the surveillance. There were three others in the casino besides him. The man sitting alone at the bar in the lounge, quietly looking at a newspaper; the man in the sport coat and dressed like Evans, playing roulette at table two; and the cowboy in jeans and the Western-style shirt, playing poker. Another part of their team was outside, watching the three SUVs Kingston and his party arrived in. There was also a team watching the rental up the coast, where they were staying. It had been difficult on short notice, but they'd managed to rent a home across the road from Kingston's rental and had several vehicles to cover them while they were moving around the island. Every base had been covered.

They counted ten security people covering Kingston and the women inside the casino and five with their vehicles. They guessed another five in the house at Arashi Beach. They couldn't do what they needed to here in the casino because they would have to contend not only with Kingston's security, but casino and hotel security as well. There was too much traffic on the roads this time of year, so that left the house. It would be a tricky assault but could be done.

There was movement at the table as one of the women dragged Evans toward the casino floor. They had been watching him as well.

"Evans and one of the women are moving to the casino floor," the man at the slots said quietly into the hidden mic of his communications set. "Heads up, everyone."

"Understood," answered the man at the roulette table.

"Kingston and the other woman are getting ready to follow," said the man in the lounge. "I'll reposition when they're out on the floor."

"Copy that," responded the man at the slots.

The cowboy didn't respond to any of this, and a quick look in his direction told the man coordinating the surveillance he wasn't in any position to talk. He did deliberately nod to the man in the slots. That meant he'd heard the transmissions and was continuing with his part of the operation. It looked like a long night.

Marriott Resort
Palm Beach, Aruba
July 20, 2010
2210 hours

Evans and Annie settled at a blackjack table and just finished a hand when Evans's phone chirped. He took it out of his pocket, played with the screen for a few seconds, then turned it off and put it away. He looked around the table and smiled. "Sorry, my calendar telling me it's past my bedtime."

There were chuckles around the table.

"I hate these things," continued Evans, "but today, you wonder how you lived without one all the rest of your life."

"I know just what you mean," responded the tourist sitting on the other side of Annie.

"House wins," announced the dealer.

"Damn!" said the tourist.

"You lost?" ask Annie, mockingly. "I thought you would be a hotshot gambler?"

Evans smiled, seeing Kingston take a seat at a nearby poker table. There was another open chair at the table.

"I'm much better at poker."

Annie looked over to the table where her sister stood next to Kingston. "How lucky do you feel?" she asked, motioning toward the nearby poker table. "His ego won't allow him to lose, but I bet you can do it."

Evans smiled, looking from the poker table back to Annie. He stood up, collected his chips, took her by the hand, and they were off.

Fort Drum Military Reservation
Guthrie Army Medical Center
July 20, 2010
2345 hours

With Grey leading the investigation, Sanderson found time to finally get some shut-eye. They found a couch for him in an empty room, and he collapsed into an exhausted sleep. Justin walked in, followed by his boss and the rest of his team. All looked as tired as the sleeping FBI agent. He walked over to where the man was sleeping, kicking one of the legs off the couch.

Sanderson sat straight up, startled. "What the hell—"

"No time to sleep now, Director," said Justin. "We go wheels up in forty-five minutes. You can sleep on the plane."

Sanderson rubbed his eyes. "What the hell are you talking about, boy?"

Justin looked at the FBI agent, not responding.

Cassie came into the room, addressing Justin. "You wanted to see me?"

She looked around the small waiting room; everyone looked beat. Ryan closed the door, and Justin motioned for everyone to sit down.

"We've received information about where our impersonator is headed," Ryan said.

Sanderson was awake and looking impatient. "Where is she?"

Justin again gave the FBI agent a benign look. "Right this instant, I couldn't tell you, but we know she's headed to Indonesia because there is no extradition from that country." There was silence around the room. Now that he had everyone's undivided attention, Justin lowered his voice and added, "Her real name is Melissa Handcock."

"Handcock!" blurted Sanderson. "Any relation to escapee Andrea Handcock?"

Everyone gave Sanderson an irritated look, which he ignored. Mitchell cleared his throat, causing the FBI man to look at his CIA counterpart. Mitchell had to say nothing else. Justin tried not to show his pleasure in Sanderson's discomfort with the situation. "She is the youngest sister of Miss Handcock, and we don't know what name she's traveling under or by what means she's getting there, but we know she's headed to Indonesia to meet her sisters and Kingston."

"Sisters?" questioned both Cassie and Ryan at the same time.

"We also have information that the middle sister in the family, Kimberly, has been involved in the escape. We believe she is responsible for the murder of the team of deputy US marshals in Virginia. We do know she's in the company of her sister and Mr. Kingston. She'll be apprehended with them. Our job is to go after and pick up Melissa Handcock."

"How will we find her?" asked Cassie, almost too innocently.

Justin smiled at his cousin. "Our intelligence has a number of aliases we know they're currently using. We're banking on the fact they bought or rented a place in Indonesia under one of those names. By the time we arrive in the country, we should have the location pinpointed and have a plan for extraction in place. The Indonesian government won't be helpful and, depending on where in the country we have to go, could actually be hostile toward our efforts."

Sanderson had been listening quietly but couldn't contain himself anymore. "Where is this intelligence coming from? How good is the source?" He glared at Mitchell, making the point he expected an answer. "I won't be put off on this—I demand to know! I'm not going to be part of something illegal."

Mitchell looked from Sanderson to Justin and nodded.

"All you need to know, Director," Justin said, "is that this information comes from an extremely reliable source involved in a current operation to track and bring Richard Kingston back into the custody of the United States government. I can't be more specific than that. You and Cassie are involved with our part to ensure that we don't jeopardize the case against Miss Handcock."

Sanderson nodded. "I can accept that. This operation to get Kingston . . . is it a CIA operation and is the FBI involved?"

Justin shook his head. "I don't believe so, and to be honest, you know as much about that operation as we do."

Sanderson looked at Mitchell, who just shrugged his shoulders.

"Get whatever gear you feel you'll need," said Mitchell. "The plane leaves the airfield here in thirty-five minutes."

Queen Beatrix International Airport
Oranjestad, Aruba
July 20, 2010
2300 hours

A call from the home office in Tokyo communicated that there was a mess to clean up for their employer. They worked for people who did some of their banking in the Netherlands Antilles but had no other business interests here. They banked here not because of any special banking laws, but because it was quiet and unassuming on the islands off the coast of Venezuela. It wouldn't be uncommon for tourists from all over the world to visit and use the banks here. Their organization had been doing this for years.

While they exited the small private plane, the leader of the group took a quick look around. Aside from the lone customs agent meeting their aircraft, their arrival was going unnoticed. He was pleased because the type of business they did required anonymity. There was already surveillance going on regarding their targets. His bosses kept a small office here, just in case. The rest of their team would be arriving early in the morning, and the job would be completed by early afternoon. Tourists disappeared all the time, and these were tourists that no one would miss or be looking for. There would be a brief mention of their names in the arrival logs for customs and for the house they rented, but after that, they would just disappear. Considering who they were and what they had done, no one would question that. A boat had been made available to facilitate the disappearance. How convenient to be on an island surrounded by the ocean. The man grinned, stepping off the plane.

Marriott Resort
Palm Beach, Aruba
July 20, 2010
2315 hours

They'd been at the poker table for an hour, and the big winner was the cowboy sitting across from Evans. He'd taken almost every hand over the past twenty minutes. Evans was still ahead a little—he had taken a couple of big pots right after coming to the table but bet more conservatively when the cowboy started winning. The other three people at the table, including Kingston, were a little more liberal in their bets and were in the hole because of it. Kingston was showing his frustration.

The cowboy reminded Evans of one of those bad-boy, country-and-western singers. He had on a neatly trimmed Western shirt with sleeves rolled up, blue jeans, and a pair of well-worn, tan cowboy boots. He had several days' growth of beard on his face, and his long hair was in a ponytail. He had on a tan cowboy hat that was worn low over his eyes, which were also covered by a pair of aviator sunglasses. He didn't speak much, but when he did, it was laced with a heavy drawl.

Evans watched him and could say for sure the man wasn't cheating. He also wasn't just lucky. He was a good, solid card player who knew when to take a chance as well as when to be conservative. Kingston was the big loser at the table, and the cowboy seemed to be taking joy in frustrating the man. Evans guessed his early big hands allowed the cowboy to size up both him and Kingston. Evans was able to pick up on a couple of tells from the man, but they were small, and he guessed they might be nothing more than a ruse to mislead another good cardplayer.

Kingston played his last couple of hands close to the vest, playing a game of catch-up. He was not a bad player and, in some circles, would probably be the best at the table—but not tonight. Evans knew both he and the cowboy were better. The other two players at the table decided to sit out this hand while the dealer began to shuffle. The three of them put down their ante, and each received one card dealt face down.

"I don't trust someone whose eyes I can't see," commented Kingston. "Take those sunglasses off."

"Sorry, Mr. Bennett." The man's drawl was thick. "I don't think that's gonna happen."

"How do I know they're not helping you cheat?"

The dealer looked nervously between the two men. Evans noticed a very subtle signal from the dealer to a nearby supervisor. The supervisor spoke into a handheld radio, and both he and two security guards cautiously moved closer to the table.

The dealer spoke in an even tone. "Mr. Bennett, rest assured—the casino has checked the gentleman's sunglasses, and they are perfectly fine. He was extremely cooperative."

Kingston grunted, looking back over at the cowboy. "I don't even know your name, cowboy. What do I call you? Tex?"

The slight hint of a smile crossed the cowboy's face. "I didn't give you a name because I came here to play poker, not talk. If you must talk, you can call me Cowboy or Tex. Whichever suits you."

Kingston grunted again. It wasn't much, but it was enough to tell everyone he was backing off. Both the dealer and the supervisor let out an audible sigh of relief. Annie squeezed Evans's shoulder. Evans smiled, knowing this was going to be an interesting hand.

The dealer placed the next card face up in front of Kingston. "Queen of spades."

The next card went to Evans. "Five of diamonds."

Finally, the cowboy got his next card. "Ace of hearts."

The dealer looked to Kingston to start the betting. They were using American dollars, and Kingston tossed in a fifty-dollar chip. Evans looked at Kingston for a second and then followed suit. The cowboy didn't hesitate, tossing his fifty-dollar chip into the pot.

The dealer dealt the next card to Kingston. "Jack of spades. Possible straight or flush."

Evans was dealt his card. "Eight of hearts."

And the cowboy again. "King of clubs, possible pair."

Kingston grinned broadly, tossing in one hundred dollars' worth of chips. Evans again looked at Kingston, this time with a raised eyebrow.

He tossed in his chips.   "Call."

Again, the cowboy smiled, tossing in his chips. "There's your hundred, Mr. Bennett. I'll raise you fifty."

Evans could feel Annie squeezing his shoulder again. He noticed Kingston was starting to flush a bit; he was losing his cool. Annie leaned down to whisper in Evans's ear. "He's baiting Troy on purpose. Troy will kill him if he wins."

Evans didn't think so. Something about the way the cowboy carried himself told him that wouldn't be easy. Besides, he knew Kingston didn't do his own killing. He put his hand on Annie's, and she loosened her grip. Everyone tossed in another fifty dollars.

"A king of spades to Mr. Bennett," said the dealer. "A possible straight flush."

Kingston again smiled broadly. When the dealer dealt Evans's card, a woman with curly blonde hair came up behind the cowboy, leaning down and kissing him gently on the neck. She was slender, and the evening dress she was wearing was tasteful but revealed ample cleavage. When she bent over, Evans admired the view and couldn't help but raise an eyebrow in approval. The cowboy gently pushed her away. "Not now, baby. I'm playin' cards here."

"You're always doin' somethin'." The woman's drawl was as thick as the cowboy's.

Evans didn't even notice the card he had been dealt. "Mr. Cowboy, where I come from, a beautiful woman should be appreciated, even when playing cards. Who knows, she might even bring you luck."

If the cowboy looked at Evans, he couldn't tell because of the sunglasses.

"Mr. Evans, sir," the cowboy said, "I make my own luck. Don't need a pretty face to do that for me. I'd also appreciate you mindin' your own business and leavin' my wife be. Now, I'd pay attention to the game if I were you."

The tone was threatening, causing the security guards to take a step closer to the table. Kingston grinned, seeing his opponent flustered for the first time.

"Thank you, Mr. Evans," said the cowboy's wife, "for being a proper English gentleman. I do appreciate it."

"Mr. Evans has a two of clubs and a possible pair."

Evans looked at the dealer, then at the cards, and finally at the cowboy's wife. She was smiling at him, and when their eyes met, his heart almost stopped. Annie noticed the shift in his demeanor and squeezed his shoulder again.

"And that's an ace of diamonds," said the dealer, voice going up an octave in surprise, "a possible three of a kind or two pair."

The dealer looked at Kingston, who was again calm. He was deep in thought, taking in everyone's cards. He absentmindedly picked up some chips while he looked. Finally, a smile crossed his face.

"Gentlemen, it'll cost you two hundred to stay in the game."

Evans again looked at Kingston, then at his cards. He peeked at the card that was face down, then glanced over at the cowboy's wife. She had moved back to a railing behind her husband and was leaning against it, looking inviting. She was just watching him, smiling. He couldn't concentrate on the game for the first time since he and Annie had come to the table. He picked up the overturned card and tossed it into the pot. It was the queen of hearts.

"Gentlemen, I'm afraid I'm out."

Evans sat back in his chair, looking around the table. Kingston stared at the cowboy as if to dare him to accept the challenge. The cowboy seemed expressionless when he matched the two hundred dollars and then raised another five hundred. Kingston threw in five hundred dollars' worth of chips without blinking. You could cut the tension at the table with a knife. The dealer exhaled, then dealt Kingston his last card. When the card was placed face up, there were gasps all around the table.

"Ten of spades to Mr. Bennett, a possible royal flush."

Kingston stared at the cowboy, saying nothing as his last card was dealt. There were more gasps from the crowd gathering around the table.

"Ace of clubs to the cowboy," said the dealer, feeling the pressure, "a possible full house or four of a kind."

There was silence around the table as the two men looked at each other. Annie was now squeezing both of Evans shoulders. He could barely feel it, though, because he was watching the cowboy's wife, who continued to return his gaze, smiling.

The dealer looked at Kingston. "The bet's to you, Mr. Bennett." When Kingston didn't answer, the dealer spoke again. "Mr. Bennett? It's your bet, sir."

Kingston gave the dealer an irritated look, then picked up some chips and placed them in the pot. He slowly turned to look at the cowboy. "That's five hundred dollars for you to look at my card, if you have the guts."

The cowboy played to the crowd of onlookers by not responding for about thirty seconds. He then shifted in his chair, never taking his eyes off Kingston. He slowly picked up the right number of chips and played with them, as if he were contemplating his next move. He slowly placed them in the pot.

"I'll see your five hundred and raise you another thousand."

The crowd stirred, having grown. The word spread there was a big showdown at the poker table. The two men didn't hear the crowd; they were focused on each other. Finally, Kingston broke the silence. "Let's cut to the chase, my cowboy friend. I can see the thousand, and I have another five thousand here that says I have you beat. What do you say?"

The silence was deafening. The two men just sat there, staring at each other. A smile began to creep over Kingston's face; he was feeling confident he had the cowboy. The smile stopped when the cowboy slowly counted out five thousand dollars in chips, placing them in the pot. The cowboy motioned for Kingston to flip over his card. Kingston slowly moved his hand and turned over the card, revealing a four of spades.

"Mr. Bennett has a flush," announced the dealer.

There was no change in expression while the cowboy reached for his card. Everyone around the table was riveted to the scene. The cowboy flipped over his card, and the crowd went wild. He had an ace of spades and four of a kind. He had just won the hand and the pot.

Kingston jumped up from his seat and was met by the supervisor, who stepped forward, whispering something into the poker player's ear. Kingston was flushed again, taking Kellie by the arm and starting for the door. Annie said a quick goodbye to Evans, chasing after them.

With one of the main players in this high-stakes game leaving, the crowd dwindled quickly, and the players still at the table got back to the business of poker. Evans looked around and couldn't find the cowboy's wife anywhere. He collected his chips, excusing himself from the game. He had to find her.

Marriott Resort
Palm Beach, Aruba
July 20, 2010
2345 hours

They watched Kingston storm out of the casino, going directly to his caravan of vehicles. One woman was with him when they entered the middle vehicle, while the second woman was racing to catch up. The security detail quickly made their way out, heading to the vehicles as fast as they could without drawing too much attention.

They were sitting in their car, watching this exodus with anticipation.

One policeman looked at the other. "There must've been a problem inside. Look, casino security is following them out."

The second policeman looked toward the casino entrance, seeing the light-blue sport coats of casino security. They weren't pursuing the Bennett party, just keeping their distance while making sure the group was really leaving. "Why don't you have headquarters call and confirm everything is all right?"

Both were in plain clothes and assigned to keep an eye on the Bennett party because of an alert from customs. There wasn't a lot of information available, and the government was inquiring for more information on Mr. Bennett and the Rutledge sisters. With the number of people in their security detail, they understood why customs might be curious. The two policemen assumed that the security people were armed, even though no paperwork regarding possession of weapons was provided upon arrival on the island. The last of the security people reached the cars, and the caravan started off. Even though they appeared to be in a rush coming out, the vehicles took their time navigating the parking lot. When they turned onto the street, the first policeman hung up his phone.

"It appears Mr. Bennett was a big loser tonight at the poker tables. It looked like he was about to start something, so they asked him to leave. They didn't know he had his own security detail, or they would have called us for help. He lost all his chips in the game."

The other policeman chuckled.

"A sore loser, great. Was the other guy cheating?"

"No." The first policeman laughed. "Some cowboy from America took him for a ride."

"Never play poker with a cowboy."

Both men laughed as the procession of SUVs drove past them. He checked traffic and eased out onto the road, following the last vehicle at a safe distance. Neither officer noticed the sedan behind them go through the same procedure, pulling out into traffic.

L.G. Smith Boulevard
Arashi Beach, Aruba
July 20, 2010
2320 hours

He was just lying down in bed when his cell rang. It had been a long day, and his whole team needed their sleep. He knew the rest of his people would be arriving at the airport early and should get to sleep on the flight. If they didn't, that was their problem.

"Yes?" he said into the phone, recognizing the number as one of the men he had trailing Kingston. "What do you need?"

"The police are tailing our target, sir. They're keeping track of him, too."

He thought for a moment. "How many men?"

"Two men, one car. They are holding back, following the last car. These Dutch . . . they're good, sir."

"Will they be a problem for us in the morning?"

"Yes, sir, I believe they will. Like I said, they're very good."

"How about Kingston—have you lost them?"

"No, sir. We managed to get tracking devices on all their vehicles, as you requested. We know exactly where they are."

He was silent while he thought.

"Keep track of the police and where they end up and let us know here. When we clean this mess up in the morning, we'll kill them as well. The American government will be blamed. When they finally set up their surveillance somewhere, we'll send someone from here to keep an eye on them."

"Yes, sir."

The line went dead. He rubbed his eyes, lying back down on the bed, setting his phone on the night table. This was going to be a messy one. Now they were going to be killing cops. They needed to make it look like the Americans. He didn't think he would sleep now, but he was wrong—he was snoring within minutes.

Fort Drum Military Reservation
Wheeler-Sack Army Airfield
July 21, 2010
0020 hours

The two lines of men marched up the ramp of the C-17 transport while its big Pratt & Whitney engines started to turn. There were sixteen men, all SEALs, who had been part of the rescue the day before. All were armed with their weapons and carried packs full of fresh ammunition and other equipment they might need on their new mission.

Sanderson and Cassie followed them, surprised they were riding a military transport and not something more comfortable. Each was dressed in

BDUs, not looking much different than the special operations troops they were following onto the aircraft. They also carried a small pack with their personal belongings. Neither spoke, but each wondered what they had gotten themselves into.

When they reached the top of the ramp, they were surprised to see the aircraft was also filled with cargo covered by tarps. There was plenty of room for the troops and other passengers on board, but it still surprised the two of them. They were also surprised to see Putnum, Mitchell, and Commander Smith talking to Justin and his team.

When they reached the small group, Sanderson said, "I wasn't expecting anything so Spartan for our flight. It's going to be tough to get any rest on this thing."

There were several chuckles from those gathered. The Navy lieutenant leading the SEAL team came up to them. "Admiral," he said, speaking to Putnum, "the team is on board, and it looks like all the equipment is accounted for. Any orders, sir?"

Putnum smiled at the young officer. "Nothing now, Lieutenant, thank you. The men have had a long day and will have an even longer flight. Make sure they get some rest on the first leg of the trip."

"Aye, aye, sir."

"Mr. Summers here will be in command," said Putnum, nodding to Justin. He and the officer looked at each other. "This is officially a CIA operation. Any problems with that?"

"No problem, sir. I've been brought up to speed on Mr. Summers's record and family history by Chief Skier." The officer turned, then, offering Justin a subtle bow, followed by a handshake. "Mr. Summers, it'll be a privilege to serve with you, sir."

Justin nodded. "Same here, Lieutenant."

Sanderson grunted, rolling his eyes at the exchange.

"Careful, Mr. FBI," warned Cassie. "No making fun of my family, or I'll kick your ass."

Sanderson grinned at the comment. Justin looked confused at the man's reaction to the comment, furrowing his brows. "Why are you smirking, Mr. FBI?"

Sanderson locked eyes with Justin, openly grinning now. "It seems young Miss Summers here was temporarily taken hostage by a gangbanger when this whole mess started. She kicked his ass, putting the FBI agents trying to save her to shame. She claims to have a cousin and an uncle who taught her self-defense. Personally, I think crazy runs in the family and will just keep my mouth shut."

There was laughter all around.

Putnum took the conversation back over. "We know she's headed to Bali at this point. Mr. DePalma, at Tom's orders, has managed to track down reservations for our four fugitives at a resort on Bali. They have rented a villa there for the short term and have made appointments to look at real estate on the island. Looks like their plan is to make Indonesia their base of operations for the near future."

"What about Kingston and the two sisters?" asked Sanderson. "Are they going to be there?"

Mitchell shook his head. "We don't think they'll make it that far. There's an independent operation underway to bring them into custody that's keeping us in the loop. They're currently in Aruba, and I expect they won't get off that island without being taken into custody or neutralized."

"Neutralized?" asked Cassie.

"They have a twenty-man protection detail. If they decide to not go peaceably, the team that's on scene and the Dutch authorities could have quite a gun battle on their hands. It'll be up to them. The team that's there is the best we've ever trained—if anyone can bring them in, they can."

"You said this was an independent operation," Sanderson remarked, "but how can that be the case when we trained them?"

Mitchell said nothing in response, merely eying the director.

Sanderson looked at Cassie and raised an eyebrow. "I'll take that as 'don't ask any more questions,' then."

This was answered by several chuckles within the group.

"One more thing," added Putnum, "it seems that Kingston has contacted his former employers to renegotiate his fee for betraying his country back in 1995. Be on the lookout for hit teams sent by the Japanese underworld. They'll negotiate his fee back to zero because they got burned on that little deal. He didn't give the authorities any information back then, but they don't know that. As far as they're concerned, he's a dead man. I would keep an eye out because they just may have the villa in Bali under surveillance."

Everyone in the group nodded.

"Now, Commander Smith will be going with you to be a liaison with American naval units in the area. There will be no help from local authorities, and the Navy will be the only friendly backup."

Sanderson and Cassie looked at Smith, who smiled back at them and said, "I promised Admiral Summers that I'd keep an eye on you two. He's a hard man to say no to."

The aircraft's crew chief walked up to the group, looking at Putnum. "Sir, we're ready to take off."

Marriott Resort
Palm Beach, Aruba
July 21, 2010
0015 hours

Evans entered his suite on the top floor of the hotel, tossing his key card on the table next to the couch in the main sitting room. Taking his sports coat off and laying it over the back of the couch, he stretched. Evans was tired and needed to get some sleep but couldn't. Searching all over for the cowboy's wife had been frustrating—she'd just disappeared.

They knew each other from a long time ago, and it was evident she recognized him.

He guessed she knew who he was before she'd even come over to the table. If she was who he thought she was, then that meant he knew who the cowboy was too—and why he had taken so much pleasure in tormenting Kingston. Evans smiled at that thought. Kingston was a pompous ass and deserved the humiliation.

His mind shifted back to the cowboy's wife. She was one of the true mistakes of his life. He allowed politics and his former profession to get in the way of his life with her. She was a fighter, and he wasn't surprised she was here with the cowboy—after all, they had known each other for a long time, and this whole mess affected both families. He needed to think. Where would she be? He couldn't think clearly because he was so tired. A little sleep, and he'd be able to track her down. Just as he decided to get ready for bed, a knock at the door made him jump.

He shook his head, checking his watch. It was going on twelve-thirty in the morning.

"Who is it?"

"Room service, sir," replied an accented female voice.

He hadn't ordered anything, so he decided to question what was happening. "I'm sorry, I didn't order any room service."

"A Mr. Fleming sent the order up, sir. It's on his account."

That was the pass phrase for his contact to let him know what his instructions were. He'd hoped to get some rest before they contacted him, but he couldn't ignore this.

"One moment, please."

He had no weapon with him and thus positioned himself so he could force the door closed just in case the person on the other side of the door wasn't friendly. He slowly opened the door a crack and peered through, and there she was: curly blonde hair, exquisite evening dress, and a smile. He opened the door wider, moving out from behind it.

"My God, are you a sight for—"

Before he could finish the greeting, she punched him in the face as hard as she could. The force of the blow moved him backward, causing him to trip over an end table and fall on the couch. A man with a gun streaked past her toward Evans and stood over him with the pistol leveled at his head. The woman shut and locked the door. She then moved over toward the couch, where Evans was wiping blood away from his nose. He then looked up at the man covering him with the pistol as he said, "You wouldn't shoot your father-in-law, would you?"

"You're supposed to be dead." Sean's voice was low, and the tone neutral. Sean showed no signs of putting the gun down.

"To most of the world, I am dead, Sean boy." The Irish accent was back. "But they took my little girl. We can't have that now, can we? After all, you came after her as well—and your children. My grandchildren."

Sean was about to say something when a blonde wig hit Evans in the head. Becky stood there with her hands on her hips. "You ass, letting me think you were dead these past years! I don't know who I'm madder at—you, or that son of a bitch in the cowboy hat!"

Sean looked surprised. "Dad? What does he have to do with this?"

"Who do you think called this asshole?" Becky exclaimed. "The minute the threat showed up against the family, I bet the two of them were on the phone together before he even called me. Son of a bitch!"

Evans smiled at his ex-wife. "You need to leave this business to the professionals, darlin'. In that way, Jonny and I are alike. He has a few more scruples than me. Not many, but a few more."

"What about Sarah? She thinks you're dead," said Becky. "And Ryan— poor boy said he buried you! What about him?"

"I'll find a way to break it to Sarah," said Evans, looking at Sean.

"Don't look at me, man. This is your problem. I value my life. You're already dead—you tell her."

Sean smiled at Evans, but he still hadn't put the pistol away. Evans looked at Becky. "Ryan's a tough kid; he'll understand. Besides, he's been hanging around with Sean boy's dead brother for some time."

"I have a solution," announced Sean, lowering the weapon. "I shoot the Honorable Timothy Gerard Evans here, then Justin, and let you and Mom shoot Dad. Everybody's happy."

The laughter that followed broke the tension.

L.G. Smith Boulevard
Arashi Beach, Aruba
July 21, 2010
0015 hours

A line of SUVs pulled into the walled courtyard of the beach house complex. When the last vehicle entered, the electronic gate closed slowly. From his vantage point in the darkened, second-floor room of the house across the street, he could barely see over the ten-foot-tall wall separating the house from the road.

There were three buildings in the complex behind the wall. The main house, which was substantial, the pool house, and a four-car garage, plus the walled-in courtyard, all looking toward the street. On the other side of the house was a large pool, as well as access to the beach.

It's the perfect vacation house, if you can afford it, he thought, watching the vehicles park. While the occupants got out, he noticed a small car slow down in front of the house and then move on at a leisurely pace. The car had an antenna on the back, and the two occupants had an official look about them. He guessed Kingston was honored by a police surveillance team. Probably the size of his protection detail. While he watched the car move on, he noticed Kingston speaking to one of the women. She and four of the men got back into one of the SUVs and started to back up. Kingston stayed outside with several of his bodyguards, watching the vehicle pull out. It headed back toward Palm Beach. At the same time, he noticed the police car pull into the public parking lot for Arashi Beach just to the north of their location. The man thought if he had the proper orders, this whole nightmare could end, because right now, he had the perfect shot at the back of Kingston's skull. Then everyone could go home.

While he dwelled on his thoughts, another car slowed and stopped at the house next door. The driver and the passenger got out and were met by two more men, who came out of the house carrying duffel bags. Even though it was dark, there was enough light to make out these men were Asian. His window was open to allow the cool breeze off the ocean into the room, and when they spoke, he picked up a couple of words he recognized. Japanese. The men changed spots—the men with the duffel bags getting in the car, while the other two men went into the house.

He watched as the car pulled away, going down the road and turning into the same public parking lot the police had. A bad feeling began to come over him. He picked up his phone, hitting the first speed dial.

"They neatly tucked into bed?" asked the voice on the other end.

He smiled at the expectation. "One of the women and four guards are headed back to you. I'm guessing to make a deal with your friend."

The man on the other end laughed. "Probably. We'll be ready for them.

"Say, guess who the new neighbors are? I'll give you a hint: you speak their language fluently."

"No shit?"

"Yup, the problem is Kingston has a police tail and it looks like they plan to take them out as well."

"That's not very nice, being new to the neighborhood and all. Maybe we'll have to have the *neighborhood watch* introduce themselves."

The man smiled; he liked that idea.

There was a knock at the door, and while Evans went to answer it, Becky ducked into the bedroom suite and Sean into the walk-in closet next to the door. Before he opened the door, he checked around the suite to make sure everything was clean. To his surprise, Becky ran out of the bedroom, grabbing the wig she'd left on the couch and then disappearing back into the bedroom. He heard the shower go on and smiled. She was not hiding but playing the part. This new side of his ex-wife intrigued him.

"Who's there?" he asked through the door.

There was a delay before a female voice said, "It's Annie Rutledge, Timothy. Let me in."

Evans made one last check of the suite and then opened the door. There stood Annie, still in the evening dress. Her smile beamed, but her eyes told him she was here on business. Behind her stood a very formidable-looking bodyguard. As she breezed past him, she gently touched his face. The bodyguard followed her, giving Evans a neutral look. He closed the door and joined the two of them in the open living room. There was singing coming from the bedroom. It sounded very country and western.

Annie looked at Evans and contrived a smile. "You're not alone?"

Evans returned the grin. "You raced out and left me standing there all alone. What's a man to do?"

"Please don't tell me it's—"

Annie was interrupted when Becky came to the bedroom door. She was wearing the robe the hotel provided its guests. The blonde wig was back in place. She gave a surprised look when she saw Annie and the bodyguard, then smiled. "Sorry darlin', I didn't know you had company. When y'all get done doin' business here, sugar britches, I'll be in the shower. Y'all come join me—I'll wash your back."

With that, she turned, the robe dropping to show she was wearing nothing underneath, and disappeared back toward the master bathroom.

Annie raised an eyebrow. "Sugar britches?"

Evans smiled weakly. "Like I said, my dear, you ran out on me."

Annie laughed. "Look, Timothy, Troy would like you to join us for breakfast in the morning. He's very interested in your contacts to create new identities for all of us. We've made some pretty powerful enemies recently and need to start over."

"I've already made the call."

"Tomorrow morning then?" She gave him a devilish grin. "That is, if you're not too tired. Say nine o'clock? Here's the address." She handed Evans a piece of paper with some writing on it. She then wrapped her arm in his and led him toward the door. "Maybe we can arrange for you to visit us in Indonesia when we get there. You can wash my back. I promise it'll be more fun than you'll have tonight."

Evans smiled, knowing this would probably be true but would never happen. He'd already decided he didn't want it to happen. He opened the door, kissing Annie gently on the cheek.

"I look forward to it. Tell Mr. Bennett I will see you later this morning."

Annie smiled and kissed him on the lips, touching his cheek. He opened the door, and she and her bodyguard exited without looking back. The door closed, and Sean came out of the closet behind Evans, his pistol in his hand. When Evans locked the door, Sean put the weapon away.

Becky came up behind them, again wearing the robe, and said, "Patrick, it's not my business anymore, but I would stay away from that woman."

Evans looked at his ex-wife, grinning. "You're still able to turn a head or two, my dear."

Becky was still wearing the wig. She glanced at him, taking it off. "Don't get any ideas, because you're alone tonight. There's a reason I'm your ex-wife."

Evans continued to grin. "For the life of me, I can't remember why I allowed that to happen."

Sean raised an eyebrow. "Enough, kids. We have a job to do."

Outside in the hallway, Rutledge and her bodyguard moved toward the elevators. They were surprised when the man in the cowboy hat came around the corner. The bodyguard's hand went into his jacket out of reflex, but when the cowboy staggered drunkenly, he relaxed, and the hand came back into sight. The cowboy slowed when they approached, tipping his hat. He reeked of whiskey and still wore his sunglasses.

"Ma'am, you were at the game tonight with that Englishman, Ev . . . Evans, I think his name was?"

Annie smiled politely, nodding. "I just left him."

"Damn!" exclaimed the drunk cowboy. "I figured him for runnin' off with my wife."

Annie couldn't help but let out a chuckle but said nothing.

"Ma'am, I wanna thank ya for bein' such a lady and lettin' me know . . ." The cowboy surprised both by tripping and falling into Annie, knocking her purse out of her hands. "Sorry, ma'am, I think I had a tad too much to drink. Let me get that for ya."

Annie and the cowboy seemed to be tangled together as he struggled to pick up her purse. The smell of whiskey was overpowering. She looked at the bodyguard, her eyes pleading for help. He was quick to respond, grabbing the cowboy and pulling him off his charge. The two men seemed to scuffle for a few moments before he was able to push the cowboy hard up against the wall. This was followed by two quick punches to the stomach, causing the cowboy to double over and his sunglasses to fall off. The man slowly slid to the floor, moaning.

Annie collected her purse, looking at the bodyguard. He reached into his jacket again to pull out his pistol. She shook her head. "Never mind that—grab his money instead. Dick will be glad to get his money back."

The bodyguard took his hand out of his coat and kicked the cowboy in the stomach, causing a muffled scream. When he reached down to go through the cowboy's pockets, searching for his earlier winnings, two men came around the corner.

"Hey," said the first man, who had salt-and-pepper hair and a full beard, "what are you doing there?"

The bodyguard recoiled from the cowboy at once and took Annie by the arm, moving her toward the elevators. The man with the beard stopped next to the cowboy, kneeling beside him. The second man followed Annie and the bodyguard. At the elevator, the bodyguard hit the closest button several times and the middle door opened immediately. They both got on. Annie hit the button for the lobby repeatedly until the door closed, leaving their pursuer standing all alone.

A smile crossed his face as he turned, making eye contact with the man with the beard.

"They're gone," said Walt Samcevic, looking down at the cowboy. "You okay? You took a couple of good hits from that guy."

Jon Summers opened his eyes, smiling at the former SEAL. "He punches like a girl, but I think the kick might have broken a rib."

When Jon sat up, he grimaced in pain. Samcevic looked at Naylor, who was returning from the elevators. He was finishing up a call on his phone. "Both bugs are working perfectly. How much damage did he do to Tex here?"

Samcevic chuckled at the reference to Jon's disguise. Both men offered Jon a hand up, which he accepted. When he was up, he leaned to his right and winced. Naylor gave Samcevic a concerned look. Samcevic shook his head, grinning as he said, "The cowboy here thinks the gorilla took out a rib when he kicked him."

Naylor chuckled. "It's a bitch getting old, Jon. Medicare may not cover this. You're not supposed to get kicked in the ribs when you're retired."

"Wait until the doc gets hold of him," Samcevic said, winking.

"She'll be too busy with her ex-husband to worry about me," said Jon, joining in on the laughter. They started to move down the hall toward Evans's suite.

"No, she won't," Naylor countered. "She's a smart girl. She can multitask."

Jon decided to change the subject. "So, how's the new book coming, Walt?"

"Oh, I'm writing fiction now," said Samcevic seriously. "No one would believe this stuff really happened."

"I thought everything you wrote was fiction," commented Naylor.

When the door opened, all three men were laughing, and one was holding his side.

Public Parking Lot
Arashi Beach, Aruba
July 21, 2010
0130 hours

The two policemen couldn't see the house rented by Bennett from where they were parked, but they could see the road. They had seen the SUV return about fifteen minutes before. The problem this far out from the city was how remote it was. While they sat quietly in the car, the officer in the passenger seat shifted nervously.

"What's wrong?" asked his partner, seeing the movement.

"I have to go to the bathroom—too much coffee."

His partner laughed, opening the door. "I need to stretch. Let's go."

Both men exited the vehicle, looking around the parking lot. There were only a few vehicles on the far side. Probably lovers, considering the hour. While the first officer found the cover of a large cactus to relieve himself behind, the second one stretched next to their car. When he did, he saw movement to his left.

There was a man with a gun aimed at his head. The only thought going through his mind was he didn't have time to react and he was going to die. As suddenly as the man appeared, he flew into the air, landing on the pavement, and flopped around. It took a moment, but the officer realized the man had the leads from a Taser attached to him. The man was struggling to get up off the pavement when he got another shot of voltage through the wires. He was back on the ground, twitching uncontrollably.

The policeman started to reach for his pistol when he saw two men with submachine guns, one on either side of him, covering both he and his would-be attacker. A third man handled the Taser on the other end of the wires.

"Nice and easy, partner," said the man to his left, speaking English. "Slowly move your hand away from your weapon. We're on your side. We really don't need anyone getting shot."

He followed directions and was surprised when they didn't search him or take his weapon. A noise behind him caused him to turn. He found his partner returning with two men, similarly armed. The two men were dragging a third, who appeared to be unconscious. His partner joined him while the unconscious man was dropped on the ground next to the man connected to the Taser. Two of the men secured the arms and legs of the attackers with zip ties.

"The guy they dragged in was about to shoot me," said the partner.

The first policeman motioned toward the man with the leads still attached. "Same here."

For the first time, the two policemen noticed that the men who had come to their rescue were all older. They guessed them to be in their fifties or sixties. All were fit and looked to be ex-military by the way they carried themselves. One of the men standing nearby startled them when he spoke to them in Dutch.

"Are the two of you okay? I know you weren't hurt, but I just want to make sure."

There was the hint of an accent—the first officer guessed American—so he answered in English. "We're fine. Are you American?"

A smile was all he got for an answer.

"Are you part of the Bennett protection detail?"

This time, he got a smile and a shake of the head. The policeman gave the man a frustrated look. Ellison grinned back in return.

"May I have a name then?"

"No names," responded Ellison. "All you need to know is we're on your side and these two were going to kill you. They're part of a hit team sent to kill Bennett and his party. They must have seen you tailing him back from the casino and added you to their list of things to clean up."

Both policemen looked troubled and, for the first time, noticed the men sent to kill them were Asian.

"I wonder where they're from?" asked the second policeman.

Reardon and Wiedenkeller were moving the two subdued attackers over to the unmarked police car, leaning them up against the front tire.

Wiedenkeller answered the policeman. "They're Japanese, part of the Japanese mafia."

The two policemen looked at each other and then at Ellison.

"You've been sent here to watch Bennett too. Are you FBI?" asked the first policeman.

Ellison just patiently smiled.

"CIA then?"

Ellison gave the man the same response as the policeman's attention returned to Reardon and Wiedenkeller. They were bringing both of their captives back to consciousness. Shomakker, who was keeping an eye on the perimeter, moved up next to Ellison and quietly said something. Ellison nodded.

"Their vehicle is that car over there on the other side of the parking lot, for when you're working on your investigation. We just need to ask these guys a few questions and then we'll leave them in your care."

Before either policeman could protest, Wiedenkeller began speaking to the two captives in Japanese. After the initial shock that one of their captors spoke fluent Japanese, both men became very defiant, refusing to respond.

"Are you sure you're speaking Japanese?" chided Reardon, glancing over to Wiedenkeller.

"I've been married to a Japanese woman for thirty-five years," Wiedenkeller replied with narrowed eyes, "and I know the language better than these two."

He reached out with his left hand, grabbed the man still attached to the leads, and asked his questions again. This brought a verbal response, but no less defiant than before. This time, the man also spit on the pavement next to Wiedenkeller. The former SEAL looked over his shoulder at Matt Summers, who pulled the trigger on the Taser, sending a shot of voltage to the prisoner. This went on for several minutes, and it wasn't long before both prisoners were giving a fountain of information. Wiedenkeller finally stood, walking over to where Ellison and the two policemen were watching.

"There's eight more in the house down the road, with twenty more men coming in on a private aircraft about nine-thirty. They're coming from Tokyo via LA. They plan on cleaning up the entire Bennett crew all at once with a full assault—kill everyone—and then they're on their way out, all of them using the same plane. The leader of the group is in the house and ordered the hit on our friends here. They had a plan to take out their relief as well."

Both policemen looked at each other and then at Ellison.

Ellison handed the first policeman a piece of paper. "Here's the address my colleague was referring to. It's just down the road and kitty-corner to the compound Bennett's in."

"Does that mean your surveillance is close by as well?" inquired the second policeman.

Ellison smiled again. The members of the team began to cross the road and disappear into the dark night. He looked down at the two prisoners, who were now fearful of being left with the men they were sent to kill.

"I don't know if our friends here speak Dutch, but they certainly understand English."

The response from the two men leaning against the car told the policemen Ellison was telling the truth.

"I know what you have to do," continued Ellison, "and I wish you luck. These guys here mean business and, when cornered, will fight. I know from experience, so tell your bosses not to be too proud about using the Royal Marines stationed here. They're a good group to have at your backs when dealing with these types."

Korps Politie Aruba (Aruba Police Force)
Santa Cruz, Aruba
July 21, 2010
0200 hours

The commander had been awakened at 12:30 a.m. and summoned to the commissioner's office from his home in Oranjestad. He commanded the police precinct in the capitol city of Aruba and was the man who ordered the surveillance on the Bennett party, which was why he was called. Being awakened and summoned to headquarters by the commissioner himself at this hour of the morning, he thought he was going to be in trouble. Quite the contrary. It turned out Bennett was not the man's real name—it was Kingston. They were all watching the news from America about the kidnappings, rescue of the hostages, and escape of the traitor, Richard Kingston. Now his surveillance team had not checked in for almost an hour. He was worried his team was going to be another casualty of Kingston's bid for freedom.

His cell phone rang. He answered, seeing it was his second-in-command.

After a few quick pleasantries, the caller went on to say, "The team radioed in; someone tried to kill them."

"Kingston or his people?"

"No, sir, two professional hit men hired by the Japanese underworld."

"What?" exclaimed the commander.

The man remained calm, explaining the connection between Kingston and the Japanese. He also told him of the rescue by the group of Americans, passing on the thoughts their surveillance team had that they were FBI or CIA.

"The FBI has a team landing in a few hours to help with the capture of Kingston and his party. It would make sense they would have an advanced party here to keep an eye on him if they knew where he was," said the commander. "The question is, why did he come here?"

"We won't be able to answer that, sir, until we have him in custody. Backup is on the way to our team, and we're setting up a second surveillance on the south side of the highway, monitoring all traffic in and out. The commissioner's order calling all off-duty personnel in is underway. We'll be ready."

"Good," said the commander. "We want to hit the Kingston compound about eight o'clock, and that will include the address with the Japanese. I have to tell the commissioner about this development; he may want to involve the military."

The commander looked up when his boss came out of his office. This was going to be a long day.

Marriott Resort
Palm Beach, Aruba
July 21, 2010
0200 hours

Jon sat at the dinette table in the suite, his shirt off, while Becky wrapped a bandage around his ribs. She pulled it tight, causing him to wince.

"That didn't hurt, did it?" responded Becky, giving her childhood friend a look. He didn't answer, so she tugged on the bandage a little harder, causing him to not only wince but grunt. "There, I think that's tight enough. You really need to have those ribs x-rayed. You may have broken more than one, tough guy. You should be in a hospital right now having them treated, not having me wrap them up for you."

There was laughter from the group watching her treat the injury. The laughter only increased when Jon gave them a disgusted look over his shoulder. He returned his attention to Becky and said, "You're enjoying this, aren't you?"

Becky looked at her friend, giving him a wicked smile. "Absolutely! Do you want something to help with the pain?"

Jon shook his head. "No."

"Good," she said, patting his side, causing him to double over and wince. "Then you'll be more alert when I decide to do this. Next time, include me in on the secret."

The group roared with laughter, and Evans tried to come to his defense. "He was only trying to protect you, darlin'."

Becky wheeled around, pointing a finger at him. "And you—"

The phone rang, stopping the exchange. Naylor answered the phone, listening intently to the caller. He acknowledged, hung up, and looked at the others. "Like we suspected, the local police put a tail on Kingston based on the information Mr. Evans here gave the customs people. Our Japanese friends jumped the gun and tried to take out their surveillance team."

"They okay?" asked Becky, looking concerned.

Naylor smiled. "George and the guys helped out."

"But now we have to move up our timetable," said Jon.

"Why?" asked Becky.

"Because, love," answered Evans, "the police will start to lock down the area to collect Mr. Kingston and company, and now the Japanese as well. They tried to kill some of their own; now it's personal. That never changes, no matter where you go."

"We need to get moving," said Jon, standing. He hesitated, feeling the pain from his ribs, then continued. He didn't notice Becky shaking her head.

L.G. Smith Boulevard
Arashi Beach, Aruba
July 21, 2010
0230 hours

They had been packing up all the gear they brought and sanitizing the house since they returned from the public parking lot. They needed to be moving across the street soon, before too many more policemen showed up. And they were coming. Another car took up a position just south of their location, placing itself so it had a good view of the area. There was still a concealed route of escape from the house to where they parked their vehicles in a public parking area at Boco Catalina. They needed to move before more surveillance units arrived, making movement impossible.

Ellison checked everyone's progress and, satisfied they'd covered everything, called the group together. He assigned Wiedenkeller, Matt, and Kevin to carry the gear to the vehicles and then work their way back up the beach to the compound Kingston rented. In the meantime, he, Reardon, and Shomakker would be across the street, working on neutralizing the protection detail. The last thing they wanted was a gunfight with a larger force. They brought measures to prevent that, if possible. A quick phone call told him that Jon and the rest of the team were about ten minutes out, so he sent the group with the equipment on its way. They would meet up with Summers's team and could come up the beach together. They needed to take advantage of the darkness, so both groups exited the back door of the house, leaving in opposite directions.

Public Parking Lot
Arashi Beach, Aruba
July 21, 2010
0235 hours

Three additional cars were assigned with the two plainclothes officers. Two more cars were dispatched to take the two prisoners to the closest police station for further interrogation. They were also in contact with the other unit on the other end of the neighborhood, where their two target houses were. While the situation wasn't perfect, at least it was contained for the moment.

Both policemen were surprised when they were suddenly not only speaking to the commander, but also the commissioner. They had stumbled onto something big and were very fortunate. Everyone guessed the American team that came to their aid was CIA, because the commissioner was talking to the FBI, and they were saying they had no team in place. The CIA was also denying involvement, saying they had no team tracking suspects in the case of Richard Kingston. They repeatedly told the FBI this over the last hour and alerted their assets in the area to see if it was a local operation that stumbled onto Kingston's whereabouts. Neither the FBI nor the commissioner believed them. They were a spy agency, after all.

They couldn't see much, even with the night vision equipment the additional units brought. At one point, one of the officers thought he saw movement, but nothing could be seen when they followed up. They kept in contact with their counterparts down the road and waited for the cavalry to arrive.

Fort Drum Military Reservation
Guthrie Army Medical Center
July 21, 2010
0145 hours

The FBI was given a large conference room in the medical center to use for their debriefings and other ongoing operations. There were a few agents working on various aspects of the investigation, but Special Agent in Charge Grey and Admiral Putnum had the corner of the room all to themselves. They were going over every detail of the last several days to make sure they covered everything, and their case was airtight. The president was on a conference call with them an hour before to both congratulate them on a job well done and emphasize the importance of recapturing Richard Kingston.

They were still under the gun. Catching the imposter who gave up so much of the operation and cost good people their lives was almost as important as catching Kingston himself. It would create some political issues with Indonesia, but neither man thought that too much of a problem, seeing as the State Department hadn't been in contact with them. Someone high up told them to keep their distance.

Trask exhausted himself supervising both the debriefing of each hostage and the interrogation of the captured suspects. He disappeared around midnight to get some much-needed sleep. All the hostages were scheduled to be sent home by noon, so he would be back at work early finishing up with them.

Both men were surprised when the door to the conference room opened, and Ericson was pushed into the room by Bryan Kingston. Bryan was in uniform, though cleaned up after his participation in the rescue. Josh looked rested, having the look of a man full of questions.

"Senator," said Putnum, forcing a smile, "to what do we owe the pleasure?"

Josh acknowledged both men with a nod. "For the record, the boy here is not part of this. He's here as my chaperone, to make sure I behave myself."

Bryan gave the older man an irritated look, saying nothing.

Putnum decided to meet the senator head-on and not mince words. "Doesn't want you to embarrass his mother?" Josh gave him a sharp look, but before he could say anything, Putnum continued speaking. "We've known each other a long time, Josh, and when you're in one of these moods, you tend to be direct. I'm treating you in kind. You want to know about Richard

Kingston and what we're doing about his escape—the official version is that we are following up several leads in the case and expect a quick arrest."

"I'm not the media, W.C. You're not going to put me off on this. With him on the loose, my family is in danger. I expect an answer."

"And the answer you'll get is that we're following up on a number of leads and expect a quick arrest," said Grey, jumping into the conversation. "Richard Kingston's escape is our priority and our primary focus. We have teams all over the world following up on leads, looking not only for him, but for the people who were passing information to the kidnappers. We'll get them all. That I promise you, Senator."

"In the meantime," Putnum said, picking up the conversation, "you, your family, and the rest of the hostages will have additional security. You're right about the threat. No offense, Commander, but you all could be in danger until Richard and his followers are brought to justice."

"Followers?" Josh asked, looking puzzled.

Bryan jumped into the conversation, surprising everyone. "Well, you don't think he did this on his own, do you?"

"What do you know about this, Bryan? What haven't you told your mother and me?"

Josh's questions were more from the surprise of Bryan entering the conversation than expecting an answer. The younger man seemed to have a half smile on his face as he responded. "Josh, I know that Father still has many friends and supporters out there who wouldn't necessarily help him escape but won't help in his capture, either. You know him—he's charismatic and will charm the pants off most anyone who hasn't dealt with him. You need to let them do their job and go about the business of bringing him to justice."

Josh looked at the man who was pushing his wheelchair with renewed interest. "And your friend, Commander Smith—she disappeared quite suddenly. Is she part of this big effort?"

The conversation was leaning too close to the personal side for the naval officer, and Putnum looked like he was about to help with an explanation, but Bryan held up his hand, stopping him. He smiled at his mother's husband. "The answer to that question is yes. I don't know where she was headed, but she left with one of the teams a little bit ago. The answer to the unasked question that you and mother danced around before you went to bed is yes, she's the one. We both have jobs to do and will have to work a few things out. Now that you know that, let me get you back to bed and let these two gentlemen get back to work."

Before Ericson could say a word in protest, Bryan turned the wheelchair around and headed back out the door. Both Grey and Putnum looked at each other, smiling.

L.G. Smith Boulevard
Arashi Beach, Aruba
July 21, 2010
0330 hours

It was like it was planned to happen the way it did.

Wiedenkeller's team met Jon and his team just as they pulled into the public parking area at Boco Catalina. They stowed all the gear they packed out from the house, allowing enough room for everyone when they made it back to the vehicles for the trip to the airport. While they readied themselves for the trip up the beach to meet Ellison's team, Jon, Sean, Samcevic, Naylor, and Wiedenkeller each produced an M4 carbine assault rifle equipped with a noise suppressor, a pistol, a tactical vest, and enough ammunition to fight a small battle. Matt and Kevin each had a tactical vest, a small pack, and a pistol. Becky carried a pack filled with first-aid supplies, and Evans carried a pistol in his waistband.

They slowly moved forward in the darkness, past the public buildings lining the beach. There was no one around to see them moving on the white sand. The weather was overcast, blocking any moon and stars. Jon called a halt when they reached an open area where the police car on the south end of the road was positioned. They took a few minutes to observe the position, using night vision gear to see if they were in danger of being detected. The two officers in the car were focused on the roadway and houses along it—not the beach. All the same, they moved slowly and cautiously.

There were only one hundred meters of open beach without cover from the road, and they moved past that in quick order. As they continued, the cover became thicker and the beach smaller. They traveled quickly, as there were no obstacles. Jon called a halt while they checked out the two hundred meters to the path leading up to the compound rented by Kingston. It took about ten minutes, but they figured out where the sentry guarding the path stationed himself.

They determined he couldn't see their progress if they left the beach, staying under the cover of the trees running from their current location right up to the wall. They moved slowly and quietly inland, avoiding the sentry and detection. Once they reached the wall of the compound, they stopped to take a break and wait for the signal to proceed. They only sat for a few minutes when there were two audible clicks over the communications gear. It was time.

L.G. Smith Boulevard
Arashi Beach, Aruba
July 21, 2010
0330 hours

Ellison and his team moved slowly, crossing the street one at a time. They had the shortest distance to go but needed to avoid being detected by the police on either end of the road, the Japanese next door, and Kingston's security people. They entered the compound next to the one being used by Kingston. This wasn't hard because the compound was smaller, and trees hung over the wall surrounding it.

One by one, they scaled the wall entering the compound. The next wall wasn't as easy to scale, but Reardon found a way onto the roof of the garage, offering them a quick jump into the courtyard of the Kingston compound. The roof also gave them a good view of the security. This allowed them to make their jump when the guards were farthest away and couldn't see or hear them. Reardon went first, then Shomakker, and finally Ellison. Each man was wearing a tactical vest and armed with a rifle, pistol, and knife. All carried a small pack and were equipped with night vision gear. The pool house where most of the security people were sleeping was next to where they dropped in. They slowly and quietly located the air-conditioning system and pulled a canister out of one of the packs, connecting it to the AC using a rubber hose with Snap-on connectors. While Reardon and Ellison kept watch, Shomakker attached the canister to the AC unit. When Ellison gave the nod, he opened the valve, releasing the gas into the AC system. It would take a few minutes to take effect, but the anesthetic inside the canister would ensure an easy takedown of the bulk of the security force.

When the three men moved off to start dealing with the security on duty, Ellison clicked his communications transmitter twice to send the signal.

L.G. Smith Boulevard
Arashi Beach, Aruba
July 21, 2010
0415 hours

When the signal from Ellison came, Jon started to move his team along the wall to the beach entrance of the compound. Wiedenkeller and Samcevic broke off after taking a small pistol out of Matt's backpack. While the rest of the team neared the compound gate, they heard a commotion. It wasn't necessarily loud but sounded like someone scuffling on the other side of the wall. This noise went on for a few moments, and then there was silence. Jon called a halt until the noise stopped, waited a few more moments before moving slowly forward, his weapon at the ready. Suddenly, Shomakker poked his head around the corner, motioning them forward.

As they followed Shomakker, Wiedenkeller and Samcevic appeared, coming up the trail from the beach, dragging the sentry, who was unconscious from a tranquilizer dart. Once inside, they found Reardon securing another sentry with zip ties around the wrists and ankles and with duct tape over his mouth. The man was unconscious, having been on the receiving end of the scuffle they had all heard. Wiedenkeller and Samcevic secured their prisoner in the same manner. Both men were placed under cover, so they would be protected from the rain that was starting to fall. While they moved through the compound, they found three more sentries on duty. Each was rendered unconscious from either the dart gun or a sleeper hold. The team secured each of the sentries like they had the others and moved on.

Shomakker went back to the AC unit, turned off the gas canister, and disconnected it. Meanwhile, Sean, Reardon, and Wiedenkeller all donned gas masks, entering the pool house. The amount of gas used was only enough to put them to sleep for a short period of time. They were told what to look for in the way of side effects when securing the rest of the security force. This included collecting the weapons they were armed with and placing all of them in the main room of the building.

Becky entered the pool house and did a quick examination of each man. Once she was satisfied there were no medical issues with the prisoners, the team turned its focus on the main house and Kingston.

They found the door to the main house locked, but Reardon picked it, opening the door in less than a minute. They'd neutralized eighteen members of the security detail already, leaving two more in the house, and entered quietly, weapons at the ready. Kingston's men had already showed their willingness to kill, and they had to be prepared to defend themselves.

They cleared the first room quickly. It was a spacious living room, well furnished, covering half the first floor. A stairway led to a second floor and they assumed the sleeping areas. While Sean and Samcevic watched the stairs, the rest of the team went about clearing the first floor. In the kitchen and dinette, there was a noise coming from a room just beyond, along with a light coming from what was suspected to be an open door.

The team could hear two distinct voices.

Reardon and Naylor entered the room first, each carrying one of the dart guns they'd brought along. They were followed closely by Shomakker and Wiedenkeller, who were raising their M4s. The room was a den converted into a small security command post. Both remaining guards were seated at a small table, playing cards. One had his back to the door and didn't see the intruders enter. The other did. His eyes showed fear, but that fear caused a delay in his reaction. Two darts hit their marks just as the man facing the door decided he needed to reach for a weapon. The drugs in the darts took effect, causing both men to collapse almost immediately into unconsciousness. These men were bound in the same manner as the others and placed on the floor where they would be safe. Again, the weapons were placed well away from the men. There were two laptops present, and they were taken to be examined later. Matt and Kevin each took one, putting them in their backpacks.

While Sean and Shomakker maintained security of the first floor, the rest of the team slowly made their way up the stairs. Wiedenkeller was in the lead, stopping when he got to the top. Using hand signals, he confirmed they were looking at five doors. Wiedenkeller and Matt took the first door, entering as quietly as they could. It faced the street and was a small bedroom. They checked the entire room in less than a minute, moving back into the hallway to find Reardon, Evans, Becky, and Kevin doing security in the hall-way. They moved on to the next door, which appeared to be the bathroom.

Ellison and Naylor went into the first door on the ocean side of the house. They found it to be the master bedroom with an attached bathroom. There were two people, fast asleep in bed, entwined in each other's arms. Ellison motioned for Naylor to check the bathroom while he watched their sleeping prey.

Farther down the hall, Jon and Samcevic entered the last room on the ocean side of the house. It was a bedroom, and the bed had been slept in but was empty. The door to the balcony was open, with a breeze blowing in off the ocean. Samcevic moved slowly toward the open door, his M4 up and ready to fire. Without warning, a female in a nightgown rushed out of the walk-in closet, pointing a pistol at Samcevic. He hadn't seen her coming, so she had a clear shot at him. Just as she was about to pull the trigger, her legs were knocked out from under her, sending her flying backward. The gun discharged, firing the bullet harmlessly into the ceiling. The woman landed hard, knocking the breath out of her lungs. She suddenly realized there was a second man in the room, but before she could raise the pistol to threaten him, the man's boot came down hard on her forearm and wrist, breaking it and causing her to scream in pain. She released her grip on the weapon. The next instant, the woman was struck hard in the jaw, knocked unconscious.

The gunshot from the other room caused the man sleeping in the bed to quickly roll over, reaching for the nightstand drawer. Ellison responded with two three-round bursts from his silenced M4, causing the top of the nightstand to disintegrate, sending splinters out in all directions. The woman on the other side of the bed screamed, rolling off onto the floor. Even with the noise suppressor on the rifle, in the confines of the room it sounded like a series of explosions. The silence that followed was deafening.

Public Parking Lot
Arashi Beach, Aruba
July 21, 2010
0455 hours

The sound of the single gunshot was unmistakable. It was a bit muffled, but all the gathered officers agreed it had the ring of a 9mm handgun. A quick call was made to the team on the other end of the highway to see if they had heard the same noise, as they were closer to both target houses. They reported that they had heard nothing.

The officer in charge made the comment that they were probably sitting inside their car with the air-conditioning on. He notified headquarters of the incident and was told to standby until they could get ahold of the commissioner.

He was surprised when the commissioner came on the phone in less than a minute. He assured them help would be there in force within ninety minutes and to hold their positions. In the meantime, some extra units were being sent to strengthen the positions on either end of the road. It was briefly explained they were to hit three locations at the same time: the two houses they were watching and a private plane that would soon be landing.

The commissioner explained that the FBI was saying they had no advanced team on the island, so they were guessing there was an American CIA team out there somewhere. The FBI thought the CIA was putting them off by denying they had resources on scene. Their agents wouldn't be in time for the assault on the residences. The assault had been moved up an hour, to seven o'clock local time.

The commissioner hung up. The lead investigator looked at his partner sitting next to him. Their simple surveillance had suddenly become quite complicated.

L.G. Smith Boulevard
Arashi Beach, Aruba
July 21, 2010
0455 hours

The man from the Japanese team watching the compound across the street heard the sound but couldn't quite tell what it was. It could have been a gunshot, but the breeze coming in off the Caribbean distorted the sound. He checked with the other man who was with him in the second-floor bedroom. He hadn't heard the sound.

"What did it sound like?" asked the second man.

The first man didn't answer right away, putting careful thought to his answer. "It could have been a gunshot, but with the wind it's hard to tell.

We didn't bring any recording equipment for this job, so we can't replay it. Too hard to say without hearing it again."

"Any extra movement in the compound?"

The first man shook his head. "Since the rain started, there's been no movement over there at all. I'd be worried about waking the boss over nothing."

The second man thought for a few moments. "It's not enough to wake him. He just got back to sleep. Any word from the parking lot team?"

The first man shook his head. The man leading the operation was known for his temper, and neither of them wanted to be on the receiving end of that. The boss had floated the theory the men at the parking lot were waiting for the police surveillance relief to arrive before they made their move. They decided not to bother their boss. Outside, the rain masked the arrival of an additional marked police unit on either end of the road.

L.G. Smith Boulevard
Arashi Beach, Aruba
July 21, 2010
0505 hours

Naylor came out of the master bathroom. "Clear!"

His weapon was trained on the crying woman curled up on the floor beside the bed. They were all equipped with night vision gear, so all lights were off. Both men heard Jon also say "Clear!" over their encrypted radio channel. He indicated they captured one prisoner who fired the shot and was unconscious. He ordered everyone to hold their positions. Ellison never moved his gaze off Kingston.

"Lights!"

Naylor moved to the light switch by the door, continuing to keep his weapon trained on the woman by the bed. Both men removed the night vision goggles, and Naylor turned on the lights.

Kingston was sitting up in bed, his hand still over what was left of the nightstand. Splinters were protruding from his hand, wrist, and forearm. He made eye contact with Ellison, and there was immediate recognition and a memory going back to 1995, when the marine dared him to reach for the gun in the nightstand drawer.

Ellison said nothing this time, and the look in his eye made it clear to the fugitive that any further movement would be fatal. The color drained from Kingston's face.

"Doctor," Ellison said over the communications network, "you're needed in the master bedroom, please."

"I've got the computers in the last room on the east side," said Matt over the net.

"On my way to you," responded Kevin.

There was movement at the doorway, and Becky entered, followed by Evans. A few moments later, Wiedenkeller entered, weapon at the ready. Becky slowed, looking at Handcock, who was wrapped in a sheet, crying.

"She's okay, Doc," Naylor said, still holding his rifle on the woman. "George just scared her half to death trying to shoot her boyfriend."

Becky laughed, moving past the woman.

"My dear General Naylor," Ellison said indignantly, "if I'd wanted to shoot this asshole, I would have hit him—it's just that he's not worth the paperwork."

There were chuckles across the room.

Ellison then focused on Kingston. "Mr. Kingston, you obviously recognize me. Do you remember our conversation from several years ago?"

Kingston nodded slowly, maintaining eye contact with Ellison the entire time.

"Now, this lovely lady is a doctor and she's going to take care of the splinters in your arm. You do anything to threaten or harm her in any way, and I'll do to your head what I did to your nightstand. Do you understand?"

Kingston nodded again. Handcock began to wail and sob uncontrollably. A cruel smile slowly crossed Ellison's face.

"Tell me you understand."

Kingston's eyes never left Ellison. The marine's smile seemed to unnerve him. "I . . . I understand."

"That's good for you, because you sent someone to kill both my wife and me, and that makes me more than just a little bit angry. You can thank General Naylor here for being the one to keep you alive. Wait a minute," he said, pausing for dramatic effect. "You tried to kill him, too—back in 1995. Maybe this just isn't your lucky day."

Handcock's sobbing seemed to intensify with the last comment.

Ellison glanced at Wiedenkeller. "Master Chief, shut her the fuck up and get her ready for transport."

Wiedenkeller allowed himself a chuckle but immediately moved forward, producing a roll of duct tape as he did. He ripped off a strip and threatened to place it over Handcock's mouth. This quieted her some, but she continued to cry. Wiedenkeller produced some clothing and told her to put it on.

"Transport where?" asked Kingston, trying to sound as if the assault rifle pointed at his head didn't affect him. "You guys don't have the look of federal agents, and I don't see the CIA using you guys for something like this. You're too old."

There were more chuckles in the room.

"Charlie," chided Ellison, "did he just call us old?"

Naylor smiled broadly. "I do believe he did, George. I don't know about you, but I'm just retired, not old. Can I shoot him now that he's started insulting us?"

"Charlie, come now, he is right about us not working for the feds, but I can't let you shoot him—yet. Besides, I was in line ahead of you."

The door burst open, and two men dragged in the limp body of Kimberly Handcock, dropping her at the foot of the bed. The woman had blood on her face from a cut on her lip. She moaned, indicating she was still alive, but said nothing.

"You guys have trouble?" asked Ellison sardonically.

"The bitch tried to shoot me in the back!" ranted Samcevic. "She was hiding in the closet and came out, ready to shoot."

"You did okay and got her before she got you," commented Naylor.

"Wasn't me," answered Samcevic, pointing at Jon. "It was him. She never saw him."

"You've been trying to write about him for years," said Naylor, laughing. "This should be good for at least a chapter in your next book."

Jon gave Naylor an irritated look. Samcevic smiled, shaking his head. "The problem is no one would believe that chapter. Like I said at the casino, this whole thing has the makings for a great fiction story. The whole team is either dead or over the hill."

"And our kids are the CIA team our friend here alluded to," Wiedenkeller said, bursting into laughter while nodding toward Kingston.

Andrea, who was quickly dressing under the close supervision of Wiedenkeller, turned to look at Jon for the first time. They made eye contact, and there was immediate recognition on her part. The hint of a smile crept over Jon's face. He nodded ever so slightly.

"Andrea."

Her eyes were already red from crying, but when she opened her mouth, only a muffled sound came out. As if on command, tears started to flow again, and her legs became wobbly. Wiedenkeller grabbed her to keep her from falling just as she found her voice. "Oh my God! Oh my God! Oh my God! You're alive! How are you alive? *Why* are you alive?"

Kingston turned to look at Handcock and, for the first time, recognized both Summers and Evans. He tried to move his whole body to confront them both, but Becky, who was tending to his injured arm, jerked one of the splinters out, causing him to scream in pain. He saw Ellison move and quickly focused back on him. He knew that if he did anything to threaten anyone in the room, the man wouldn't hesitate to kill him.

"You hold still," ordered Becky, "or I'll create enough pain to bring you to your knees."

Kingston glared at Jon. "You wouldn't do that, Doc. You took an oath. Besides, you're a child of the sixties. An activist for peace and love. You protested and fought your father all through the Vietnam War. You don't have it in you to hurt me."

Becky didn't even look at Kingston as she twisted the splinter she was working on. Kingston screamed in pain, raising his other hand to strike her, forgetting all about Ellison and the rifle. In a flash, Becky had a combat knife to Kingston's throat.

"I may be a child of the sixties and believe in peace and love, but you threatened my daughter and grandchildren, you son of a bitch. I'd just as soon cut your throat as treat your arm. Don't mistake my disagreement with my father's profession as a sign of weakness on my part. He taught me how to protect myself, and if I have to kill you to protect my family, I won't think twice about it."

The color disappeared from Kingston's face. He focused back on Ellison. The marine's finger was on the trigger, and his smile was gone. He looked all business. "Doc," he said quietly, "I was worried I was going to have to protect you from this guy, but I see the general has trained you well."

Becky smiled. The knife left Kingston's throat and returned to the sheath on her belt. Ellison relaxed, and his finger moved outside the trigger guard of the rifle.

Kingston focused back on Summers. "You just won't die, damn you."

Jon moved forward and knelt next to Kimberly, who was coming to. "Dick, you hired the wrong people. If it were up to me, I'd leave you dead on the floor in this room, but promises have been made."

Kingston grunted. "Promises to old man Putnum? You're a Boy Scout till the end, huh, Summers?"

Jon smiled. "You never were a good judge of character, Dick. You just proved that with Becky. You've always allowed your hatred of me to rule your actions when it came to our relationship. Admiral Putnum may have my respect, but you tried to kill members of my family. My respect for him wouldn't stop me from killing you. I gave my word to Fiona not to kill the father of her children."

Kingston's eyes narrowed in what appeared to be genuine confusion. "What?"

Summers only grinned, relishing this moment. "You wouldn't understand that, Dick—the unconditional love of family—because you've never cared for anyone but yourself."

Matt's voice came over the communications network. "Jon, we're in the computer, but we need a password to get into the money accounts."

Ellison answered. "We copied, Matt. Charley, the girl."

"Hustle it up, boys and girls," Shomakker's voice broke in over the net. "We've got more police showing up."

Naylor lowered his rifle and drew his pistol instead. While Wiedenkeller held the woman, Naylor placed the pistol to her head.

"The passwords to your bank accounts," said Ellison, looking coolly at Kingston.

The man—as though determined to prove Jon's point from earlier—just grinned back at him and said, "Go ahead and shoot her."

"What the hell?" Andrea exclaimed with surprise.

"Actually," Kingston amended, "feel free to shoot them both."

Before Handcock could protest again, Kingston screamed in pain as Becky again twisted a splinter in the man's arm. Jon pushed past everyone, making his way over to Kingston, drawing a silenced pistol. He pushed the pistol against Kingston's knee. The prisoner looked into Jon's eyes, panic crossing his face.

"You may not care what we do to them, Dick, but how about I arrange for some pain and a wheelchair for the rest of your life?"

"You wouldn't . . ."

"Dick, your people put my wife in the hospital and threatened to kill the rest of my family. Give you pain for the rest of your life? In a heartbeat—and I'd still be keeping my word to Fiona."

"No . . . no, you wouldn't . . . I-I mean—"

Summers thumbed the hammer back on the pistol.

"No, Jon, don't!" protested Becky as she pulled the last splinter out of Kingston's arm. The man screamed in pain, looking back and forth between the doctor and his old rival. With the last splinter now pulled, she stepped back, satisfied. "I'd tell him, Dick," said Becky, calmly looking at Jon. "The man's certifiably crazy. He's going to pull the trigger."

Summers began to count down from five. When he reached three, Kingston screamed again as Jon pushed the barrel of the pistol a little harder against the man's knee. Before he reached two, the man blurted out, "ANDREA95" as fast as he could. Ellison passed it on to Matt, who, less than a minute later, said they were into the accounts they wanted. As Summers released the pressure on Kingston's knee, the man sighed audibly, closing his eyes.

When Evans laughed out loud, Kingston's eyes snapped open, glaring at the lawyer.

"Ah, Dick, lad . . ." Evans's accent was heavily Irish. "You're upset with me. Well, I promised to introduce you to the people who helped me disappear, and here they are."

"What?" Kingston looked confused.

Evans grinned. "Well, not these very people, except for maybe the good admiral here. I don't know what part he played, but he knew where to find me when my little girl was threatened."

"Little girl?"

Evans waved off the question. "The lovely lady who's bandaging your arm used to be my wife. We all make mistakes, and I treated her poorly, but we did create a beautiful little girl, who married the admiral's oldest son."

Kingston looked around the room and was trying to put the pieces together. All he saw were smiles, and he heard nothing but laughter.

"Before you get all emotional and scream and yell some more," Evans went on, "all you did was align the planets so we were all set against you. I laughed because you're right about Jon here being a Boy Scout. When you gave up the password, I would have shot you in the knee, anyway."

Kingston looked at Evans for a few moments, a look of fear on his face. Everybody in that room knew Evans would've indeed shot Kingston without a second thought—perhaps even before he'd given up the password.

Evans smiled, grunted, and walked over to Summers. "We need to leave, Jon—the hair on the back of my neck is starting to stand on end. Means the police are closing their trap for our friends here."

Summers nodded and gave the order.

Public Parking Lot
Arashi Beach, Aruba
July 21, 2010
0600 hours

The commissioner and the commander from Oranjestad arrived in the same car. The investigators in charge of the scene quickly brought them up to speed, including the fact they heard a gunshot not long before. The commissioner made a call, asking that the assault teams be expedited to hit both compounds and seal off the area so no one could escape. The fact that his people had clearly heard a gunshot raised the level of concern about the operation being peaceful and routine. Aruba was a historically peaceful island, which was one of the reasons it was so successful as a tourist mecca in the Caribbean.

The main concern was with the assault teams coming from the police department's special operations and SWAT departments. They were being backed up by teams of Dutch Royal Marines. This made the entire operation high profile and potentially a media disaster that could cost the island's economy millions of dollars. A team of detectives and Royal Marines were also at the airport, awaiting the 7:30 a.m. arrival of a private jet carrying an additional team of hit men from Japan via the United States. Both Japanese authorities and the FBI were assisting them with tracking the aircraft. This, too, had the potential of becoming a media circus.

The biggest concern was over the mysterious Americans who had come to the aid of their men earlier in the evening. The FBI had provided information that these mysterious saviors were not their people, and the CIA was denying any involvement. They did share that they had teams actively following leads in other areas of the world but none anywhere in the Caribbean. This mystery was a huge concern, because there was an unknown force of very capable men out there that could be an issue. Orders were given to be on the alert for yet another group that could be a potential problem.

C-17 Globemaster III
Approaching Hawaii
July 21, 2010
0020 hours

The white noise of the aircraft's engines put most of them to sleep. They would need the rest for what was to come in the next twenty-four hours. Cassie and Sanderson took the lead of the SEALs, who passed out quickly after leaving upstate New York. They all curled up wherever they could find a comfortable spot. Even Justin and his team were managing some sleep. All aspects of their mission were quiet at the moment.

The laptop sitting on the floor of the plane dinged, waking up Justin, whose head was resting closest to the machine. He looked at the screen to find it was flashing—which meant they had a priority message. He reached over, pushing the enter key. The screen lit up with what looked like an email, the glow coming from the machine lighting up the cabin.

Justin read the message, smiling, not saying anything.

"What's it say?" asked Ryan.

Justin looked around and saw everyone was awake and waiting for his answer. He smiled again, not because of the message itself, but because over the ages, some things never changed. Everyone on the mission was curious.

"They have Kingston."

Cheers echoed throughout the cabin. That meant all that was left to do to close the book on this entire incident was to get the woman they were after. The cheering subsided, and Sanderson looked pleased with himself.

"Leave it to the FBI," he said, "we get it done every time."

Justin looked at Sanderson, grinning sheepishly. "It wasn't the FBI. Their team is just about to land there."

"The CIA, then?" Sanderson guessed, and again Justin shook his head. Sanderson's tone shifted to something with a little less conviction. "Local authorities?"

"The Dutch are just getting their strike teams ready to go in. Police supported by Royal Marines. Apparently, the Japanese mob wants Kingston dead, and they were there, too. Sounds like a real mess."

"The Dutch?" Sanderson looked shocked.

"They're in Aruba," confirmed Justin, grinning even more.

"Aruba! Sweet!" chimed Cassie and Kay together.

"The message is from your father, isn't it?" asked Commander Smith. She stood up and was stretching.

Justin again shook his head and pointed at Cassie. "Her father, Uncle Matt."

"Dads in Aruba? Why? He's not . . . What the . . ."

"He's not alone. Trust me," Commander Smith said, chuckling. "All those old, retired guys and Doc O'Keefe disappeared yesterday. That's a hell of a team."

"My dad?" Kay questioned, looking at Justin.

He just nodded his reply, then turned to face Ryan. "And your father, too."

It took a second to sink in; Ryan looked at Justin, mouth gaping. Justin just smiled at his partner.

"Family business," said Smith. "As in 'don't mess with my family.'"

Justin looked at the officer, grinning at the comment. "That would be correct, ma'am."

Public Parking Lot
Boco Catalina, Aruba
July 21, 2010
0650 hours

They left the compound through the gate leading to the beach. The trip back to the cars was slow due to the police presence along the road. The police were getting ready to move in on the houses between their checkpoints, with more units arriving every minute. The team moved across the open beach in small groups, hiding their weapons and disguising themselves as tourists and fishermen. They were only bringing out Kingston and the two women, leaving the protection detail bound and gagged.

They reached the cars unchallenged and quickly loaded their prisoners. They were about to leave when a convoy of police and military vehicles started by, blocking their exit. One of the cars pulled over and a young policeman dressed in tactical gear walked over to Ellison, Naylor, and Wiedenkeller, who were standing at the rear of one of the cars.

"Good morning, Officer," said Naylor smiling. "Whatever is going on looks serious."

The young man was all business. He spoke in accented English. "Can I ask, what is your business here?"

Naylor put on the charm. "We're just a bunch of retired friends here on vacation. Came up here today to maybe do some snorkeling and diving. We were told this is one of the best places on the island to do that. We wanted to get an early start."

The policeman nodded, looking the cars over. His expression didn't change. "Normally, I would agree with you about this location, but not today. We have some dangerous business about to happen here, and it's best you find another beach."

"Huh? Oh, well . . . okay. Do you have any recommendations, Officer?" asked Naylor, feigning ignorance. "We really don't know the island very well."

Much like before, the expression of the policeman didn't change. His stoicism was the sort that would've made him an expert poker player. "I would recommend you ask at your hotel. I would appreciate your moving on, please. We can't have you here."

The three Americans looked at each other and then back at the policeman.

"Right away, Officer," responded Naylor, looking every bit the worried tourist.

"We don't want any trouble, Officer," added Ellison for good measure. "We're only here on vacation."

Wiedenkeller glanced at his two companions, shaking his head while walking back to the vehicle he was riding in. The policeman raised an eyebrow, but the two men who had been speaking to him smiled, thanking him for his courtesy. They both got into the other vehicle. Both vehicles started up, slowly pulling away and heading back toward Palm Beach and the hotels. The officer made a mental note that the large SUV and the van were packed with people. He didn't think it strange because snorkeling was big in this area of the island. Just not today. Still, that was a lot of people for one diving party. A call from one of his comrades in the car brought him back to the business at hand, and his concerns were immediately forgotten. He started back for his vehicle and the assault on the two houses.

They drove down the road, saying nothing and looking straight ahead. Ellison was driving and checking his mirrors for the position of the van behind him. He was also looking to see if the police suspected anything and were in pursuit. Everything seemed clear. He looked forward again, just as another group of police vehicles raced by in the opposite direction.

"They're going all out for this one," he said, not looking at Naylor.

"Yup." Naylor nodded. "I'm going to guess this island is usually pretty quiet."

Ellison investigated his passengers through his rearview mirror. They were all smiling except for Kingston.

"Not today, it isn't."

Laughter erupted throughout the car.

Fort Drum Military Reservation
Guthrie Army Medical Center
July 21, 2010
0600 hours

Nancy woke up feeling surprisingly alert, considering she was on pain medication. She found herself moving slowly, feeling the bandage on her neck. It was hard to remember what happened during the rescue. Her memories were foggy, but she remembered being wounded and Becky giving her a shot that had to have been morphine, because after that, things got hazy. She thought she remembered a boat ride and a helicopter ride, but she wasn't sure. At one point, she got a flash of a lot of people in surgical masks, but not much more. And hadn't she had a conversation with Amy about her husband at one point? Because of the pain medication, all of it was a blur. She knew she was in a hospital but didn't know where.

"You're awake. How do you feel, Mom?"

It took a few moments for Nancy to recognize the voice of her daughter-in-law. She was lying down on the bed, so her view of the hospital room was limited. Sarah came into view, smiling. She began checking Nancy's pulse and her bandaged wound.

Nancy smiled back and opened her mouth up to say something, but nothing came out. Sarah put a finger on Nancy's lips. "Don't try to talk just yet. Let me sit you up and then we'll get you a drink of water."

Nancy nodded to indicate she understood, and Sarah began to raise the hospital bed to a more upright position. While she worked, she said, "So, I've got a feeling you don't remember much about what happened, do you?"

Nancy shrugged, shaking her head.

"Well," Sarah went on with a smile, "I'll fill you in. Once we got you off the island, you were evacuated here by Army helicopter. You're in the hospital at Fort Drum. They did emergency surgery on you because you had quite the chunk of wood sticking out of your neck."

Nancy nodded. The bed now had her in a better position to see around the room. She could see her grandchildren curled up together on a recliner by the window and her sister-in-law, Julie, lying on a small sofa on the far side of the room. All were sleeping. Sarah handed her a cup of water, and she took a sip. The cool water felt good on her throat.

"All of us were brought here," continued Sarah, keeping her voice low so as to not disturb those currently sleeping, "so the FBI could debrief us away from the media. They shut this place down tighter than a drum—pardon the pun."

Sarah giggled at her little joke, and Nancy smiled. Nancy pointed to Julie.

"She's been in here since you came out of surgery. One of us has been with you the entire time."

"J-J . . . Jon?"

The look on Sarah's face told Nancy she didn't want to hear what was coming.

With a sigh, her daughter-in-law said, "Jon's been here to see you, of course, but he had to take off shortly after your arrival." Nancy raised her brows, confused. "Kingston escaped during his relocation. Dad, Sean, Matt,

Uncle Kevin, and even Mom all disappeared yesterday. They left ahead of the FBI and the CIA, so I'm guessing they had information the authorities didn't."

This triggered a memory of Nancy's that featured Jon visiting her the previous morning, still dressed for combat, and what he told her. Even drugged, she'd reacted badly. Her memory of taking a pen and paper, of writing him that note. . .

Sarah continued, "Sean sent me a text saying he would be in touch, but that's it. Justin, his team, some FBI big shot, and even Cassie left here last night to go after someone connected to the case. Apparently, there was a spy on the rescue operation—they are going after her."

Nancy took a sip of water and risked speaking. "Stephen and Abby?" she asked hoarsely.

Sarah laughed. "Abby will have paperwork to do for weeks; she's the reporting deputy. Stephen and Nathan are securing the island. They're still deputized."

Nancy smiled in response to the last comment. "I want to get out of here and go home."

Sarah fussed over her mother-in-law. "Now that you're awake and coherent, the FBI will want to talk to you. If they're timely in that process, we should be out of here by this afternoon and back on the island by tonight."

Nancy nodded. She was thinking of her family—many of whom were after the people who had caused all this pain. She noticed an envelope on the small night table next to the bed with her name on it. She held it up, showing Sarah.

"It's Dad's handwriting," responded Sarah with a knowing smile. "It's been here since yesterday morning."

Nancy opened it and began to read the letter inside. Tears began running down her cheeks.

Public Parking Lot
Arashi Beach, Aruba
July 21, 2010
0730 hours

The teams had been moving into place for forty minutes, and everything on the road was quiet. They knew where the two target houses were and had enough manpower to hit both at the same time. The one unknown was where the mysterious American team was hiding. They called all the neighboring homes, telling the residents to stay inside and away from the windows. There was no answer from the house next to where the Japanese hit team was staying, so they suspected the Americans were there.

They closed beach access to the entire area just before seven o'clock, using two SWAT teams supported by several police Marine units and the Dutch Coast Guard cutter assigned to the island. All the roads in the area were closed, and units were going house to house in search of any possible escapees from either of their two target houses.

At seven-thirty, the commissioner received word that everything was in place and ready.

He gave the order, and within seconds, teams were through the doors on the beach side of the compound where Kingston was suspected of staying. The team heading in the gate on the street side of the compound immediately came under panic fire from the house where the hit team was holing up. The response from the Royal Marines who drew the assignment of breaching that house was quick and decisive. Cover fire from automatic weapons to pin the unseen assailant down came first, flash bangs were thrown through windows on all sides of the house, tear gas went in, while front and back doors were breached. There was no more gunfire from the house. The team breaching the front gate of the Kingston compound continued as if nothing happened.

The entire operation was over in less than ten minutes. Prisoners were taken from both the Kingston compound and the house across the street. Aside from the effects of the tear gas on the Japanese, there were no casualties. The commissioner was furious that their prime targets, Kingston and the women, were nowhere to be found, and an immediate house-to-house search was ordered. The first house to be approached was the one they suspected the Americans to be in. The police found the front door unlocked and the house spotless; there was no sign anyone had been there. When told that the entire guard force in Kingston's compound was found drugged and bound, the commissioner very uncharacteristically lost his temper. It appeared this mysterious team of Americans not only saved his policemen from being murdered but also eluded his people with the targets of their search. He looked to the sky and screamed at the top of his lungs.

Marriott Resort
Palm Beach, Aruba
July 21, 2010
0730 hours

The vehicles stopped in front of the hotel, pulling into the main parking lot, trying not to look conspicuous. The door of the first vehicle opened, and Evans got out, followed by Becky. Summers exited the other vehicle, walking over to the couple. He took Evans's hand, shaking it, then quickly put his arms around the man, giving him a hug. Becky stood by, looking quite surprised by the display.

"Thanks for answering the call," said Jon, sounding choked up. "Thanks for coming out of retirement. My family needed your help, and you stepped up."

"I worry about you, Mr. Smith," responded Evans in a thick Irish accent. "The whole world's falling to shit, and I'm the first one you call? And look at you, getting all mushy on me."

The two men released and stood back, looking at each other.

Summers spoke first. "Drastic times call for drastic measures."

"So, you call back the dead and come back from the dead yourself. It sounds like you're more into miracles to resolve this intolerable situation than just relying on mortal men and their abilities. Look at this crew you put together. Most are retired, old-school types. Most not only have families but grandchildren. Not your average rescue team. Besides, when your boy married my little girl, we became the same family. So, if they attack you, they attack me and suffer the wrath of both of us. One favor, though, if you can, Jon?"

Summers nodded. "If I can."

"Give me one minute with the bastard and his evil she demons, and I'll save the world a lot of trouble. Promise I'll be quick."

Jon just smiled. "Mr. Evans, you are a respected attorney, retired to the Caribbean. Sorry, they're my demons to deal with, and while what I have in mind will be less final, it'll be more painful in the long run. I couldn't have such a respected member of society as yourself jeopardize your standing because of a weak moment with scum like him. Trust me on this, Dick Kingston has hurt a lot of people over the years and will pay more than he wants to."

Evans chuckled, looking at Jon and then at Becky. "Darlin', I see why you always liked this man. He has a sense of honor and always looks out for the underdog."

"Underdog?" Becky looked puzzled. "Patrick, you've never been the underdog in your entire life."

Evans smiled, looking back at Summers. He pulled a pistol from his waistband, handing it to the American. "Can't get caught with this on me, can I?" The accent changed back to that of a classy English gentleman. "My dear woman, you've mistaken me for someone else. My name's Timothy Gerard Evans, a retired British barrister. This ruffian isn't bothering you, is he? I'd be happy to call the local constabulary for you, if he is."

Jon looked at them both, grinning. "Becky, you have one minute to say goodbye; we have to get out of here before they close the airport."

When Jon got back into the vehicle and sat next to Kingston, he looked through the rearview mirror at his friends. Evans was kissing Becky. A sly grin crossed Jon's face, and he looked at Kingston, who immediately looked down at the floor.

Queen Beatrix International Airport
Oranjestad, Aruba
July 21, 2010
0800 hours

A large private jet had just been cleared to land and was being directed to taxi directly to the commercial terminal on the south side of the airport. It touched down and stopped at the end of the runway, where it then slowly powered up and taxied off, heading to where it was directed. Once the runway was clear, another large private jet was given clearance to take off. The pilot acknowledged and immediately began his roll down the runway.

The jet had just lifted off and was gaining altitude when the airport tower called saying they were closing the airport due to the government having a major security issue they needed to investigate. All outgoing flights needed to be inspected. The pilot contacted the tower and advised them that he was climbing out of Aruban airspace and requested instructions. After several moments of silence, the tower responded for the jet to continue.

Kevin had been sitting in the jump seat behind the pilot and copilot of his company's corporate jet. He breathed a heavy sigh and patted both men on the shoulder. In two hours, they would be in United States airspace and hopefully that much closer to closing the final chapter on this nightmare. He stood, opened the cockpit door, and looked out at the anxious passengers. He gave a thumbs-up, and all but three cheered.

Queen Beatrix International Airport
Oranjestad, Aruba
July 21, 2010
0810 hours

The private jet was surrounded before it came to a stop.

Police and Royal Marines trained automatic weapons on the aircraft, and a voice from the tower told the pilot that everyone on board was to exit the aircraft one at a time, hands above their heads. There were twelve people listed as being aboard, and one by one they did as they were directed. Most were Japanese, but not all. The operation ran smoothly, the suspects not putting up any resistance. A cache of weapons was found on board, and the group was held as potential terrorists. The demeanor of the Royal Marines guarding them shifted when this was announced.

As the suspects and aircraft were being searched, another private jet—this one with US government markings—landed and pulled up to the same area. This jet carried the long-awaited team of FBI agents sent to support local police in the Kingston investigation. They immediately went to work alongside their Aruban colleagues but were disappointed that Kingston and the Handcock sisters were still at large. There were leads to be followed up on the island, and that would take time. While the locals conducted an all-out search for their suspects, they could do nothing but help investigate. The commissioner of police assured them that once the island had been shut down, no one would be able to get off. They were encouraged.

Challenger 850
Over the Western Caribbean
July 21, 2010
0900 hours

The aircraft left Aruban airspace and headed on a course taking it over the Western Caribbean, then over Mexico, with a destination of Los Angeles, California. The plane was owned by a media conglomerate whose current chairman of the board was illegally smuggling three wanted felons back into the United States. Kevin didn't seem to be worried about the consequences. He, Matt, and Sean were in the back of the cabin, working feverously on laptops.

Forward in the cabin, the three prisoners were strapped into their seats on a couch against the starboard bulkhead. Ellison was sitting at the table across from them, staring directly at Kingston. When Kingston would look back at him, Ellison would grin, and Kingston would inevitably look away again. Sitting in the seats forward were Reardon, Shomakker, Wiedenkeller, and Becky. Samcevic came back from the galley with two bottles of beer. He sat down next to Ellison, handing him one of the bottles.

"You know, George, you look happy. No one will know what we did to bring these three to justice. It's a shame, but it's true."

Ellison grunted and took a swig of beer. "I'll know, and that's all that matters. This scum lives off hurting good people and made the mistake of targeting family and friends of everyone on this plane. For a smart man, this wasn't the brightest thing he's ever done."

Samcevic nodded, sipping his beer.

"Besides," continued Ellison, "you'll write some half-assed piece of fiction about this mission that'll sell a million copies and make you rich and more famous. Hollywood will buy the rights and make a sleazy, low-budget B movie that's 'based on real events' starring some candy-assed actor as the hero, and you'll sell more books and become even richer."

"All true," Samcevic replied, chuckling. "All true. It's a good story, and nobody would ever believe it really happened. Maybe you can help me cast the movie?"

Before Ellison could answer, Jon and Naylor walked up from the back of the cabin. They sat next to the two men at the table. Jon and Kingston made eye contact, and you could see the hatred in the latter's eyes.

Naylor took Samcevic's beer, took a sip, and handed it back. "When you cast the movie, I think we should play ourselves. No actor could quite capture our personalities."

The three laughed, then turned their attention to Jon and Kingston, who were just looking at each other. Even the two women took notice of the staring contest going on. Kingston blinked first.

"Your catching me won't change anything, Summers," snarled Kingston. "All they'll do is put me back in prison. At some point, with my lawyers, I should be able to make parole. They can't connect any of this directly to me."

The two women looked at Jon, defiantly grinning. He smiled pleasantly, nodding at the two of them.

"Let's talk about lawyers, Dick. One of the people you tried to kill was the lawyer who saved you from death by lethal injection the last time. How hard do you think your attorneys will be willing to work when they hear that? They also don't work for free. When they find out all your money's gone, they probably won't stick around long."

Kingston looked at Summers, giving him a wry smile. "The government can try to take the money, but it'll be tied up in court so long I'll be out of prison before they can get their hands on it. Besides, it's all in offshore accounts where they can't find it. I wish them luck."

All three of the prisoners glared at Summers.

"Who's talking about the government?" he replied, the comment catching Kingston by surprise. "You're right about them not being able to find them with three hands and a flashlight, and I'm certainly not going to hold their hand while they look."

There were chuckles from behind Jon. He ignored them, keeping his eyes locked on the prisoner before him. "Back on Aruba, when you gave us access to your files, it allowed my brother and my good friend Kevin in the back there," he added, gesturing vaguely to the back of the plane, "to get into a lot of things—including all your bank accounts."

Kingston's eyes widened.

"They're good at breaking down firewalls, security protocols—all of that kind of stuff. Guys like us?" He motioned to the men sitting at the table. "We're good at blowing shit up, but your money would still be safe—but not from guys like them."

Kingston grew pale, looking nervously at the back of the plane. His two disciples looked confused over this plot twist.

Jon's face remained expressionless. "Kevin, how are we doing?"

There was the sound of someone shifting in the rear of the aircraft. Kevin poked his head around the partition that separated the two sections and said, "Matt just found two more banks, one in Hong Kong and one in Switzerland. We don't have amounts from them yet, but we're already moving thirty mil, plus some, out of the other seven banks we've found."

Andrea gave an audible gasp, and her sister muttered, "Oh my God!" under her breath.

Kingston looked genuinely panicked, shifting his gaze from Gateway to Jon and then back to Gateway again.

Kevin went on to add, "And Sean has been sifting through all the other documents in the files. He's been able to find payments to various mercenaries and others involved in this mess. All authorized by our friend here. He even managed to find some digital copies of signed authorizations transferring money to the accounts specifically used by those tasked with the kidnappings. Guess who signed them?"

The look of panic on Kingston's face was replaced with fear.

"When we get over Mexico," continued Kevin, "we'll start emailing that information to the two addresses you gave us, Jon. The FBI and the CIA will be excited over some of the stuff. It's old material, but it closes the loop on a lot left open from 1995 and the Philippines and connects Mr. Kingston here to known terrorists at the time. I think the death penalty might even be put back on the table."

Kingston turned back, giving a terrified look to Jon. There was just a hint of a cruel smile on the face of his old nemesis.

Fort Drum Military Reservation
Guthrie Army Medical Center
21 July 2010
1100 hours

Most of the former hostages were being released from the hospital and heading home. The president himself ordered an air force jet to be dispatched to Fort Drum to fly them all back to Washington. He planned to meet with them before they went their separate ways. The base commander was providing several vans to transport them the short distance to the airfield. They'd gathered in the small cafeteria to wait for that transportation when Admiral Putnum, Glenn Grey, and Tom Mitchell came into the room to pay their respects. They were closely followed by Julie, Hector, Alex, and Emily. Everyone still looked tired, but considering what they went through, it was understandable. They mingled, speaking quietly, hugging each other, and wiping away tears.

Everyone was so busy saying goodbye that no one noticed Josh and O'Leary corner the three men.

"Kingston got away, and I know you have an operation underway to capture him. What can you tell us?" demanded Ericson.

"There'll be a briefing on the flight to Washington, Senator. That should answer all your questions," responded Grey politely.

O'Leary looked at Putnum.

"Admiral, Josh and I have been at this too long and know you'll just be handing us the party line in that briefing," said O'Leary frankly. "We want to know what's really happening. There's been too much movement of personnel since yesterday to be just business as usual. We want the truth."

Putnum held Amy's gaze for a few moments, then turned to Mitchell and nodded.

"We have an operation underway to bring back the suspect who was feeding information to the kidnappers from the command post during the kidnapping. She fled to Indonesia and a team is enroute to take her into custody and bring her back to be prosecuted."

"Her?" asked O'Leary, looking puzzled.

"That'll be part of the briefing on the plane," explained Grey. "We also have an ongoing operation in progress currently on the island of Aruba. Kingston showed up there using an alias. We have good cooperation from the local authorities and the government of the Netherlands. We think he was there collecting money before meeting up in Indonesia with our other suspect."

"But you've lost him, haven't you?" Josh said, more of a statement than a question.

Grey held the politician's gaze, not responding.

"I'll take your silence as an affirmative answer to my question. What are we doing to track the bastard down?"

A grin slowly crossed Putnum's face. Both Grey and Mitchell started to show a hint of a smile as well. Josh shifted in his wheelchair, looking up at O'Leary, who asked the question they were both thinking. "Where's Jon Summers?"

"The whereabouts of Admiral Summers and his friends is currently unknown," answered Mitchell, his smile broadening just a bit. "They left in a rush yesterday—that's all we know for sure."

"Kingston's security detail was taken into custody on the island of Aruba about six this morning, our time," Grey added. "The Dutch authorities found them all bound and gagged. They also took a Japanese mob hit squad into custody. It seems they tried to murder a couple of Aruban cops who were following Kingston. A group of mysterious Americans who they thought were FBI or CIA saved them. We think they're also the ones who gave the Aruban authorities a heads-up about Kingston."

"Let me guess," said O'Leary, "there was no operation underway in Aruba, was there?"

Before anyone could answer, they all turned as Nancy was pushed into the room in a wheelchair.

"As always, senators," said Putnum, "it's been a pleasure talking to you. I'll let you say your goodbyes to Mrs. Summers."

With that, the three men quietly slipped out of the room.

Lembongan, Nusa Lembongan
Bali, Indonesia
July 23, 2010
1100 hours

The policeman leaned against his car, watching the beach and the tourists congregating there. Tourists were good for business, and they came to Bali from all over the world to enjoy the beaches, the ocean, and the attractions. Indonesia also didn't have extradition treaties with several countries, so it attracted the type of people who were running from the police. He didn't mind, because they usually paid well for information and protection from those same police agencies who may be sending people to bring them back to justice. In the case he was working currently, they were paying exceptionally well.

The woman had stopped at the precinct the previous day, speaking to his captain and, in turn, to him. He guessed his captain was paid well, because the amount she was paying him was four times the normal fee he charged. He guessed her to be a beautiful woman by American standards, but he didn't have any feelings about that either way. All he cared about was she was paying in cash and her money was good. She was expecting a man and two more women, probably today, and they wanted around-the-clock protection. They had their own security people, but they weren't arriving until the other three came, so she was paying him extra to stay close.

She was currently on the beach in front of the two villas she rented for her party, wearing a very small bikini, which she filled quite well. She was lying on a chaise lounge, sunning herself. People were strolling across the beach, enjoying the morning sun before it got too hot. Boats moved along the coast, but nothing that raised suspicion.

"Excuse me, Officer," said a female voice. The accent was Australian.

The policeman turned to find a couple standing next to him. He guessed the woman to be in her early thirties, dressed in a tasteful one-piece bathing suit, a big floppy hat, and large, stylish sunglasses. There was a towel wrapped around her waist, and she carried a large bag over her shoulder. The man beside her looked to be at least twenty years her senior. He wore tan knee socks and tan Bermuda shorts, a bright floral shirt, a broad-brimmed golf hat, and dark-rimmed sunglasses. There was an expensive-looking camera hanging around his neck.

"You wouldn't happen to speak English or French, by chance? I can manage a little German, but it's absolutely horrible."

He understood English well and could speak it enough for tourists to understand. He waved his hand at the woman. "English please, miss. No French."

The woman stopped by the rear of his car, smiling at him. "That's wonderful. Did you hear that, Charles? We found an officer who speaks English! How fortunate. Could you tell us if this beach is a public beach?"

"Beach? Public?" The policeman looked confused.

"Yes, is it a public beach or a private one? We don't want to get in trouble for going where we don't belong."

"Private . . . trouble?"

The man gave an exasperated sigh, throwing his hands in the air. His accent seemed thicker than the woman's, but not necessarily Australian. "Look, Officer, we go on that beach, okay?"

The policeman broke out into a toothy grin. "You go beach. Okay. Public beach, not private. Okay. You go swim."

"Isn't that just terrific, Charles—" As the woman turned around to face her husband, they collided, dropping her bag on the ground. She bent over to pick the bag up, showing ample cleavage when she did. The policeman decided that for a Western woman, this one was pretty enough, and he didn't hide his joy at the show.

"My dear, I'm so sorry," said the husband clumsily.

He moved to help his wife, tripping and, in turn, accidentally kicking the bag just under the rear of the police car. When the woman moved to get the bag, the towel dropped from around her waist, exposing her well-formed figure. She was not small like the woman who was paying him, but it was obvious this woman took time to stay fit. The policeman's smile broadened even further as he watched. He was so busy enjoying the show, he missed the quick glance of disapproval from the husband. The wife, having retrieved her bag, was again standing straight up and wrapping the towel back around her waist.

"I'm so sorry, Officer, we must look so clumsy. Just a couple of clumsy tourists."

"Oh no, miss." The policeman was all manners. "You go beach. Have good time, enjoy self."

The couple smiled at the policeman and then moved off toward the beach. The policeman shook his head. Just a couple of rich tourists from Australia. He enjoyed the show and, under different circumstances, might have offered to help the woman more when her husband wasn't around. He shrugged his shoulders. He was being paid well to keep the woman on the beach safe. A quick look told him she was still in her chaise lounge. He looked at her villas and saw no unnecessary movement. His car radio came alive with the report of separatist pirates being sighted nearby. He automatically reached down and touched his sidearm, breathing a sigh of relief at its touch. A quick look around told him all was quiet. After all, they had an agreement with the pirates, and they may be around, but they were paid by the local governments not to scare away the tourists. They were good business for everyone and not to be bothered. He smiled again, thinking about the woman who just left.

Lembongan, Nusa Lembongan
Bali, Indonesia
July 23, 2010
1100 hours

The locked door to the villa was no match for the six armed men. This was the fourth villa they'd forced their way into. They knew what they were looking for but weren't sure which villa they would find it in.

Each wore a scarf identifying them with one of the extremist groups from the islands in this area of Indonesia. To the local police, they were more of a criminal irritation than political militants. They attacked small yachts, raided villages, and acted more like pirates than politically motivated separatists. To most of the world, they were considered pirates and nothing more. Several nearby nations even deployed naval resources to protect their citizens and interests in the area. Still, their trademark scarves were well-known, along with their reputation for violence, which prompted the locals to avoid them whenever they were around.

Two men immediately took security positions—one with a view of the front and one watching the beach, their AK-47s at the ready. The other four began a thorough search. One of the men alerted the others that they'd finally found the right villa. Drawers were emptied onto the floor and suitcases were dumped. They located the safe in a closet in one of the bedrooms. It was locked, but a small amount of explosive was placed in just the right spot. A pop and the door opened, and the contents emptied into a backpack being carried by one of the men. Other items throughout the villa were collected and placed in backpacks to be carried out as well. The entire break-in took about five minutes, and the men were ready to leave. They were just waiting for the signal from their approaching escape boats. They gave the signal over a small radio and waited patiently.

Lembongan, Nusa Lembongan
Bali, Indonesia
July 23, 2010
1106 hours

The couple moved onto the beach, away from the policeman. The woman stifled a laugh as they walked toward their target.

"What a pig," said Sanderson, the accent gone. "He's a disgrace to his uniform. When you bent over, it was all he could do to keep his hands off you. I almost punched him out."

Smith first blushed, then giggled. "It's nice to be working with such a gentleman. These third-world types tend to like Western women. There's a big market in human trafficking of Western women out here. So, I am serious when I say it's nice to have you here. Either way, the show I gave him served a purpose."

"Like what?" Sanderson glanced quickly over his shoulder to make sure the policeman was still leaning on his car. "All this spy shit is new to me. Makes me nervous."

Smith smiled at her companion. "It's new to me, too. They never let me into the field except to investigate. This is kind of fun. I left the good policeman a gift under his car. You did well for such a straitlaced fed, Gene."

Sanderson smiled. "So, you're not going to tell me what you did?"

Smith couldn't help herself and giggled again. "You're better off not knowing—it was probably illegal."

Sanderson laughed. They focused on the woman in the chaise lounge in front of them.

"Do you think she'll run?" asked Smith.

A cruel smile crossed Sanderson's face. "I think she'll try."

Lembongan, Nusa Lembongan
Bali, Indonesia
July 23, 2010
1108 hours

Melissa Handcock relaxed in the chaise lounge, enjoying the sun and peace of the beach. To everyone here, she was Wendy Rutledge and was waiting for her sisters and her brother-in-law to arrive. She saw the news of the incident in Aruba a few days earlier but received a message that Kingston and her sisters were safe and enroute. It was on the news that they evaded capture while members of the security detail were in custody. The message calmed her because it was in the code Kingston insisted they learn. They should arrive today or tomorrow, according to what was sent.

Melissa peered up and down the beach. There were tourists everywhere, but it still wasn't overcrowded, like going to a public beach in the States. There were just people out enjoying the sun and surf on their vacations.

She took note of three people walking toward her on the beach. There was a young man who was good-looking and probably European, based on the style of his swim trunks. On either side of him was a young woman in a bikini. One was Asian, with long dark hair, and very pretty—she looked familiar. The other was white, with strawberry-blond hair. She, too, looked familiar. All were wearing sunglasses, and she tried to picture what they looked like without them. Glancing in the other direction, she noted that no one was coming her way.

She removed her sunglasses and looked back at the trio approaching her. They appeared innocent enough, but something about them told her these were no ordinary sunbathers. The white woman took off her sunglasses and met Melissa's gaze. *Cassie Summers!*

Without hesitation, Melissa was out of the chaise lounge and running toward the villa. She stopped when she saw the couple approaching her from that direction. Even with the disguise, she recognized Sanderson; he and his companion moved toward her at a determined pace. Melissa hesitated, trying to decide where to go. She turned to head in the direction away from all five of her pursuers, only to find that Cassie had beat her there.

Melissa balled up her fists and struck out at the attorney. Cassie easily blocked the blow, landing a punch with her right fist squarely on Melissa's jaw, knocking her into the sand. Ryan and Kay were on their knees next to her, flipping Melissa over and pinning her arms behind her back. Ryan produced a zip tie and secured her wrists.

Cassie looked surprised. "Where were you hiding that?"

Ryan looked up and innocently shrugged. This brought a laugh from Kay and chuckles from Sanderson and Smith.

Cassie blushed. "Never mind, I don't want to know."

**Lembongan, Nusa Lembongan
Bali, Indonesia
July 23, 2010
1115 hours**

All the policeman's senses came alive. They were kidnapping the woman! He shouted at the people attacking his employer, but they ignored him completely. Panicked, he drew his handgun, taking several steps forward. The Australian woman he was admiring earlier looked over her shoulder. She appeared to be smiling. As he was about to shout a command for them to stop, there was a popping sound followed by the roar of his car's gas tank exploding. The force of the explosion threw him about ten feet. He could feel the heat from the burning gasoline on his back.

He landed hard, his breath being knocked out, momentarily paralyzing him. He slowly started to rise, seeing his handgun several feet away. His ears were ringing; he could only hear bits and pieces of what was going on. It sounded like screams and gunfire. Before he could focus on what was happening, bullets started landing in the dirt and sand all around him. His training kicked in, and he scrambled for cover behind several nearby trees, leaving his handgun on the ground where it had landed. Bullets still impacted the area where he was hiding, but he managed to peek around the cover of the trees. He counted six pirates moving out onto the beach toward the ocean. That meant more were on the way in; no one would be safe.

**Lembongan, Nusa Lembongan
Bali, Indonesia
July 23, 2010
1116 hours**

Ryan gave an irritated look in the direction of the policeman when he finished securing the zip ties. "Damn, the copper woke up and is headed this way."

"Focus on what you're doing," Kay reminded him. "We want her ready to go."

"I paid him well!" Melissa Handcock blurted out as she struggled. "He's my protection!"

Smith smiled at the comment as she turned back to glance at their prisoner. This drew a harsh glare from both Kay and Ryan. It was Sanderson who first noticed the remote in his partner's hand. It looked like a garage door opener remote. Smith's smile seemed to broaden as she pushed the button. Almost immediately, the policeman's car erupted into a ball of flames, knocking the man to the ground. Kay looked at Ryan and grinned.

"Why didn't I think of that?"

They pulled Handcock to her feet, double-checking to make sure her hands were secure behind her back.

"You placed something on the car's gas tank?" Sanderson's question to Smith was more of a statement than anything else. His brows were raised in a rare display of his approval. Smith gave him a smile and then a wink.

"While he was admiring my assets, I left him a gift to remember me by."

"How thoughtful," Ryan chimed in as they started moving Handcock toward the water.

"Remind me not to play poker with you," responded Sanderson, and before Smith could respond, gunfire broke out by the villas.

Kay looked at Ryan and smiled. "Pirates!"

"Pirates!" echoed a panicked Handcock.

Ryan winked at Cassie, who also looked panicked. "Yo ho!"

Cassie blinked back at him, a war taking place within her that Sanderson—who pulled off his sunglasses to gape only at the pirates— seemed to share. But after everything they had been through, the group was riding a new high. There wasn't room for fear; there was only the sense of true freedom. It felt, Cassie thought, almost like taking flight.

"No wonder they refuse to go into retirement," Cassie muttered, thinking of Jon, Evans, and even her father. "This is so cool!"

Lembongan, Nusa Lembongan
Bali, Indonesia
July 23, 2010
1120 hours

When the police car exploded into flames, the six pirates moved out of the villa and started working their way toward the water. They appeared to be firing their weapons indiscriminately, but a professional soldier would have seen through that ruse. Two were firing wildly into the air, causing most of the commotion—forcing the hundreds of tourists to run for cover. Two more were firing at specific targets, including the policeman. This was clearly meant to keep them pinned down, not harm them. Their fire was quite effective and ensured they would have witnesses to what was taking place. The last two weren't firing their weapons at all. They panned 360 degrees around their team, looking for any actual threats to engage. A serious look at this tactic would show this was not a random attack by amateur pirates.

Two small fishing boats were headed into shore, their big outboard engines roaring. They were long and narrow, and each carried two men, both armed and wearing the same trademark scarfs as the men in the villas. There were small boats scattered about just off the beach, so the men in the bow began firing their AK-47s at them. This guaranteed the desired effect of sending the craft running in the opposite direction.

The pirates on the shore quickly surrounded the small group that had taken Handcock into custody. Screams could be heard from the women, and both Sanderson and Ryan were seen being knocked to the ground. They were then pulled to their feet, and all were herded toward the water. They reached the water just as the two fishing boats reached the beach, the men in their bows jumping out and firing wildly into the sand around them. Their prisoners were loaded onto the boats, and they were pushed off the beach. The big outboards roared again, and the boats sped out to sea.

Lembongan, Nusa Lembongan
Bali, Indonesia
July 23, 2010
1130 hours

The policeman peeked out from behind the trees when they were pushing the boats back out to sea. He saw the woman he was supposed to be watching in one of the boats with the Australian couple he spoke to. They were all taken prisoner and would no doubt be held for ransom or killed. These pirates were nothing more than animals.

Sirens signaled approaching reinforcements and the need for him to account for himself. He rose quickly, moving to where his pistol lay in the sand. He picked it up and fired it at the retreating boats. They were out of range, but now he didn't have to explain why he hadn't fired his weapon. He might even be treated as a hero if there weren't witnesses to prove otherwise. The pirates, after all, had blown up his car. The first police car arrived, and the officer jumped out and began running to where he was standing. He put his empty weapon back in its holster and turned to face his colleagues.

Bali Sea
Bali, Indonesia
July 23, 2010
1200 hours

They had traveled in silence ever since leaving the beach. Handcock found it interesting that her initial captors had stopped fighting the pirates so quickly. They certainly were more heavily armed, but she guessed that the people who took her down on the beach were trained CIA or FBI agents. Cassie and Sanderson were with them after all. It was bad luck for all of them to be taken by pirates. Maybe not for her. She guessed she could negotiate her way out of this by paying her own ransom, and they would probably kill the others. The pirates, after all, were driven by the quest for money and routinely ransomed prisoners. She looked over her shoulder at the man seated behind her, who appeared to be the leader.

"You speak English?"

The eyes behind the scarf blinked back at her and seemed to twinkle. She guessed there was a smile there as well.

"I can pay my own ransom. I have access to lots of money. I'll pay you well."

"Mon . . . money?" the man replied.

Someone sitting behind the man laughed. Handcock smiled dismissively, looking into the man's deep-blue eyes, trying to read them. Cassie, who was sitting in front of Handcock, grunted her disapproval. "You think money will buy your way out of this?"

Handcock glared at Cassie, whose expression was so serious that Handcock couldn't help but laugh. "These people thrive on negotiation and being paid well for their hostages. Your bosses won't negotiate for you and your friends—but I can broker a deal that'll make me free and ensure your bodies are never found. It's basic economics."

"Money!" said the man with the twinkling eyes.

"You see, Cassie? Basic economics. Anything for the almighty dollar."

Handcock watched as the man seated in front of Cassie took off his scarf and tossed it overboard. From the back, he didn't look Indonesian; his hair was too light. For the first time, she noticed he looked taller than most Indonesians she'd met.

Chief Skier turned around, grinning at her. "We're in international waters—time to ditch the disguises."

The man in the bow immediately took off the scarf and let it fly overboard. He was African American. Blue eyes! The man behind her had blue eyes; Indonesians didn't have blue eyes.

Cassie was the one smiling now. "Miss Handcock, I'd be interested to hear how basic economics works in this case."

Handcock turned to find the scarf off the man with twinkling eyes. Justin sat there, smiling broadly, looking back at her. "Miss Handcock, I'm glad you could join us. If it were up to me, I'd leave you out here for the sharks. But fortunately for you, both my cousin and Mr. Sanderson have more ethics than I do. They may even read you your rights."

Mohawk Tavern and Grill
Bluffton, New York
July 24, 2010
1835 hours

Nancy and Karen Summers decided to have everyone into town for dinner and made reservations at the Mohawk for the evening. Abby was finally getting some time off from her newfound full-time job as a deputy. Since Nathan and Stephen were still the protection detail for the family, getting together was easy. The news came on, and Fred asked the bartender—his grandson—to turn the volume up so they could hear the reporter. Sandy

Monroe was now in New York City and was covering for the regular evening anchor. A still picture of Melissa Handcock appeared on the screen behind her.

"The FBI announced today the arrest of Melissa Handcock in connection with the kidnappings of several members of the House of Representatives and Senate. Miss Handcock has been accused of posing as a federal prosecutor, passing on rescue plans to the kidnappers, and aiding in the escape of her sister Andrea Handcock and Richard Kingston."

A still picture of Kingston and Melissa's two sisters appeared on the screen behind Monroe.

"Kingston, Handcock, and the third sister, Kimberly Handcock, are still at large, having narrowly escaped arrest on the island of Aruba three days ago."

The television switched to footage of armed police pulling suspects out of a beachfront compound in Aruba.

"Aruban authorities had received a tip about suspicious activity and made almost thirty arrests, including members of Kingston's entourage and members of a hit team sent to kill him. Before his escape from federal custody earlier this week, Kingston was serving a life sentence for treason and murder for the 1995 attempted takeover of Philippine territory by Japanese organized crime interests. Unconfirmed reports have the hit team originating from Japan.

"Kimberly Handcock is the prime suspect in the escape of her sister and Kingston, as well as the murder of a team of deputy United States marshals. Witnesses have confirmed both Kingston and the Handcock sisters were indeed in Aruba and believe they slipped away just before their compound on the north side of the island was raided. The FBI has come under some criticism regarding their handling of this case. They were defended today by Senator Josh Ericson of Hawaii, himself a former hostage earlier this week."

The scene changed to a studio shot of Josh.

"The FBI and other federal agencies are putting everything they have into this investigation, calling on resources from all over the world. The incident in Aruba shows that the number of places Richard Kingston and his accomplices try to use to hide is shrinking daily. It's only a matter of time before they bring him to justice. I have every confidence that this case will be resolved quickly and efficiently."

The picture switched to a grainy video of chaos on the beach, filled with the sounds of gunshots and screaming.

"In unrelated news, yesterday, Indonesian pirates took several vacationers hostage off a public beach near Bali. A total of six tourists were taken, including three Americans. The tourists were taken away in small fishing vessels, which were intercepted by an Australian frigate and helicopter that were on patrol in the area to prevent just such incidents. The hostages were all freed and taken to Australia for medical treatment. Indonesian authorities say they believe several of the tourists were Australian citizens. A Royal Australian Navy spokesperson said the freed hostages were in excellent shape, but that they had been thrown overboard by their captors in their attempt to escape. All ten of the pirates were killed in the ensuing pursuit and firefight. In other news . . ."

"I'm so glad I spoke with Cassie earlier today," said Karen, looking relieved. "That one girl looked an awful lot like her. At least I know she's safe."

Bill Gateway managed a smile. Fred noticed and leaned over. "What's so funny, old warrior? You know something the rest of us don't?" Gateway said nothing and just looked at the old Indian, giving him a slight nod of the head. "Unrelated?"

Only Nancy noticed the two old men smiling and seemed to understand.

Office of the Director
FBI Headquarters
July 24, 2010
1835 hours

The director of the FBI was famous for remaining calm in the face of the most frustrating of circumstances, so when he lost his temper over the money missing from the Kingston accounts, it was quite out of character. They recovered approximately three million dollars from the account Melissa Handcock had direct access to, but all the other accounts were emptied. He looked directly at Sanderson. "So you're telling me, Gene, that over thirty million dollars has just disappeared? What do your CIA contacts have to say about this?"

Sanderson wasn't in the mood for an inquisition but knew better than to protest. He was just tired from all the traveling in the last twenty-four hours. He and Cassie were both placed in the back seat of Navy fighters and flown back to Washington to report to their superiors. Cassie had been ecstatic about the flight. He was sick most of the way. Justin and his team were tasked with returning their prisoner to the States and were scheduled to arrive in Washington sometime the next day. He would have normally complained about this, but having worked with the team, he knew they were more than capable.

"Sir, the CIA is as puzzled about this as we are. They got access to the files at the same time we did, and we're pretty sure that Kingston didn't have time to transfer the money before he fled Aruba. The police there were at the banks by noon that day and had the accounts frozen. According to what we initially saw, the accounts were already empty. Miss Summers and I couldn't follow up on that because we were put on a Navy aircraft for a flight back."

The director nodded, looking to Grey, who was also at the meeting.

Grey jumped right in. "Our teams have followed up in Aruba, and Kingston is definitely not on the island. We followed up on every flight that left that day. The Dutch have sent extra manpower to the island because of the size of this investigation."

"Any idea who the American team worked for? The team that saved those two Aruban cops at the compound?"

Grey shook his head, making eye contact with Sanderson, who grunted before saying, "Nothing official, sir."

Noticing the exchange between the two men, the director of the FBI decided to press the issue. "You two seem to know something no one else does. It's time to share it. Unofficial information at this point in the investigation is better than no information."

Sanderson smiled, nodding toward Grey. "I'll let Glenn float our theory. He can retire faster than you can fire him."

Even the director smiled at the comment. Grey cleared his throat and began his explanation. "Sir, as you know, we were assisted greatly by a group of retired military people Kingston targeted along with the hostages. They were commanded by retired Rear Admiral Jonathan Summers."

The director nodded. "I saw the list, Glenn. There were several flag officers in the group. What's your point?"

"I'd bet money, sir, that they followed Kingston to Aruba and grabbed him before the authorities could spring their little trap."

"The two cops described the group as having a military bearing," interrupted Sanderson. "It all fits. These guys go in and grab Kingston and his girlfriends and scoot before the Aruban authorities knock down the doors. A twenty-man protection detail was neutralized without a shot being fired. Who does that kind of thing except special ops people?"

The director wasn't entirely convinced. "How'd they know where to track Kingston? What'd he do, put out an ad?"

Sanderson grunted again. Grey answered, "Sir, who the hell knows? These guys are that good. They tried to get George Ellison at his horse farm in Virginia, and he captures the men sent to kill him and delivers them to the brig at Quantico via the base hospital. They try to kill Jon Summers in the Canadian north woods, and he captures them and uses wolves to interrogate them. I have a Mountie sitting in your outer office who would just love to talk to him about that."

The director's eyes widened. "You're joking, of course." The silence that followed told the director they were not. A concerned look briefly crossed his face, brows furrowing over his dark-brown eyes. "You're serious?"

"Yes, sir," said Sanderson. "You have no idea unless you've seen these guys work."

The director hesitated, tapping a folder sitting in front of him.

"Then maybe you can make some sense of this," he said, gesturing to the folder. "This came in just before you got here, and we haven't had time to confirm or chase any of this down. It looks like the money may have been transferred to a not-for-profit foundation for veterans and their families. We're trying to find the connection to Kingston or the Handcock sisters, but nothing yet. The foundation is run by a man named Gateway."

The two men couldn't conceal their shock.

The director stared back at them. "What?"

"You said Gateway, sir?" asked Sanderson, a grin starting to form as he glanced at Grey.

"Yes, a William Gateway. Agents are trying to find his connection to Kingston and how he's getting Kingston's money." Both agents began to laugh, causing the director to go red in the face. "I don't see the humor, gentlemen!"

The director's anger didn't seem to affect the two.

"No disrespect intended, sir," said Sanderson, trying to stop laughing.

"You see, sir," Grey said, feeling more in control, "General William Gateway must be in his nineties by now. His connection to Kingston is that he was one of the veterans captured in the 1995 Philippines incident. His granddaughter is married to Summers's son. That money is gone, sir."

The director raised an eyebrow, looking at his watch.

"I've been called to a meeting about this money. I want you two to come with me and bring your Mountie. No one there will believe me, so they need to hear it from you."

Winnebago Motorhome
Leavenworth, Kansas
July 24, 2010
1800 hours

After getting off the aircraft at a small airport in the middle of nowhere, they traveled several hours. Kingston and his two counterparts were blindfolded, with duct tape placed over their mouths. The prisoners' wrists and ankles were tightly bound, limiting their movement. Sheltered in the rear bedroom with the door closed, they could feel the RV slow down, speed up, or occasionally stop. They couldn't hear much other than the sound of traffic and mumbled conversation from the front. The RV stopped for what seemed to be ten minutes or so, and they heard different voices from outside the vehicle, but soon enough, they were back on their way.

They had reentered the United States through Los Angeles, where they stayed in confinement for two days. They were questioned by Jon, Ellison, and Naylor about their activities and the planning of the kidnappings and escape. The former rescuers were trying to make sure all threats to those targeted by Kingston had been neutralized. They were treated well, but their accommodation was Spartan, at best. Kingston knew both the women had been talkative with their captors, but he refused to answer questions. He suspected he would be able to beat any new charges because this entire operation was most likely off the books and illegal. He guessed there would be no new convictions from any of this.

The sound of the door opening and the blindfolds being removed startled all three. It was Jon and Ellison, both dressed in polo shirts and slacks. Each was armed with a handgun and had a badge on their belt. Kingston found this curious but decided not to ask any questions, because he didn't expect the answer to be truthful.

Andrea asked instead, prompting a smile from Jon. "It's a necessary disguise, my dear. It's almost time to say goodbye."

"You're not going to kill us, are you?" Kimberly asked, voice shrill.

Ellison grunted. "By all rights, we should save the taxpayers the money of paying for your cowardly existence."

Jon chuckled. "You'll have to pardon George. He looks at things much more simply than the rest of us. In this case, I have to say I agree with him, though. It sure would save a lot of time and trouble, not to mention the money . . ."

Each woman's eyes went wide.

"Don't worry ladies," Jon replied. "We're not like you and your boyfriend here. You'll all end up dying in prison after a long and lonely life."

Kingston grunted, rolling his eyes.

Jon turned, facing him now. "Don't think you'll get a bunch of new lawyers to fight all of this. You're all broke. Every penny from every hidden account is gone. It's all been reappropriated and given to people much more deserving than you three. That means all of you will get some poor, under-paid public defender."

For the first time, Kingston's expression showed concern.

"Dick, we've been telling you this the last couple of days, and apparently you weren't taking us seriously. There's no more money. What we didn't take, the feds did. They also announced they arrested Melissa."

Both Handcock sisters gasped.

"It seems some pirates kidnapped some tourists who were, in turn, saved by the Australians. She should be in Washington by tomorrow."

"You son of a bitch!" Kimberly hissed.

"Easy now," said Summers, chuckling, "you and Melissa may just face the death penalty for what you did. Maybe your boyfriend, too. You guys killed federal agents. I know they frown on that and even tend to take it a little personally."

Kimberly said nothing, turning very pale.

Summers looked amused, keeping his focus on Kingston.

"So, Dick," he continued, "we really are here to say goodbye. You've hardly spoken a word since we left Aruba, but that's okay. With your new public defenders, feel free to drop our names. We don't plan on denying anything. If they decide to press charges, we'll both plead guilty. Hey, we might even be on the same cellblock. We'll have lots of time to talk then. Just think of all those hours of conversation you, George, and I can have! After all, look at all the memories we can share. I mean, you'll be in solitary for the rest of your life for your protection, so who better than an old Academy buddy to share all that free time with?"

The RV stopped and was turned off. Kingston still said nothing, but there was a look of terror in his eyes that was more pronounced every time Summers spoke. Ellison just sat there, grinning at him.

Kingston shifted nervously and finally spoke. "You keep him away from me. He's nuts. I don't want him anywhere near me."

"Dick, he's not crazy, he's a marine," smiled Summers. "You see, he gets upset when people turn traitor and put innocent people in harm's way—especially other marines. You did that, Dick, and if you've got the impression that he doesn't like you much, you'd be right. I know this all sounds rather simplistic, but George here is a sensitive guy—wears his feelings on his sleeve, so to speak. You sent some marines out to die in 1995. They didn't, but that's irrelevant. He holds a grudge. While I promised your ex-wife I wouldn't kill you for your kids' sake, he made no such promise. Unlike you, Dick, he's an honorable man. You can count on him following through with any promise made to you."

Ellison leaned forward, close to Kingston. Kingston shifted nervously.

"Boo!" Ellison blurted out suddenly, causing Kingston and the two women to jump. Kingston was visibly shaken, and the two women began to cry.

Becky came into the bedroom, giving both Jon and Ellison a cautious look.

"George," she said evenly, "stop scaring the prisoners."

"You spoil all the fun, Doc," said the retired marine, smirking.

Becky was dressed the same as the other two, right down to the sidearm. Pushing them aside, she moved in to perform a quick check of each prisoner. She carried in a blood pressure cuff and took readings from each of them and checked their pulse and general condition. This took about fifteen minutes.

Wiedenkeller came back and told them all it was time to go. Both he and Ellison left the RV, leaving Jon and Becky alone with the prisoners.

"They're all in good shape," said Becky in her most neutral tone. "Their blood pressure is a little high, but then again, you and George have been terrorizing them."

Summers chuckled, stepping out of the room. Kingston took advantage of his absence. He leaned forward, close to Becky's face. "You're not like them, Doctor." His voice was smooth and flowed like honey. "You can get us out of here, and I can still make it worth your while."

Before he could continue, Becky drew her pistol, putting the barrel flat against his forehead. He could see the hammer was cocked and the safety was off.

"This has been your trouble all these years, Dick," said Jon, who'd returned when he saw the movement. "You continually misjudge people. You appropriately took the Flower Child here to be a pacifist. You were one hundred percent right on that."

Kingston looked into Becky's eyes and saw no remorse or fear—only a deep, dark well of cold determination. He knew there would be no hesitation. She was going to kill him. He'd fully lost all control, all power, over the situation.

"I have to say, Flower Child, that was one of the smoothest draws I've ever seen. Cleared the holster, hammer cocked and safety off in one graceful motion. Almost like you've done that your whole life," said Jon. "You see, Dick, she may be a pacifist, but she's a devoted mother and grandmother, and you endangered her family more than once. She's also an Army brat, brought up around weapons. I'm sure that's the reason she was such a good pacifist."

Jon gently put his hand on Becky's shoulder. "Becky, he's not worth it; you'd never forgive yourself."

Becky's eyes softened, and a smile slowly crossed her face.

Kingston blushed with embarrassment.

"Was it really that good?" she asked Jon, smirking as she lowered the firearm, putting it back into its holster.

"You have no idea." Jon laughed. "Almost better than sex."

Becky looked up at Summers, who was grinning. He winked.

The Oval Office
White House
July 24, 2010
1930 hours

Inspector Scott Preston, Royal Canadian Mounted Police, was in over his head while he explained the details of their case in Ontario to the president of the United States.

When he'd boarded the plane several days earlier, he had no idea the case would land him here. At least he wasn't alone. Tommy Mitchell, Gene Sanderson, and Glenn Grey were there with him, covering their part of the investigation. Putnum was there with his boss from NSA, as were the directors of the FBI and CIA, as well as the attorney general. He was feeling pretty good about closing out his end of the case. The FBI and the CIA still had three of their primary suspects at large, with no solid leads regarding their whereabouts. No, he was feeling better than pretty good—he was bordering on excellent.

The president had been listening, stone-faced, until Preston reached the part about finding wolf DNA on the suspects. He raised his hand, stopping the inspector. He didn't speak immediately but tried to absorb what he'd just been told. "So, you're saying Admiral Summers used the wolves he was studying to interrogate the men who tried to kill him, Inspector?"

Coming from the president of the United States, the question sounded different than it did from everyone else who'd asked it over the past several days.

"Yes, sir, Mr. President. That's correct."

Again, the president didn't speak right away. It was obvious he was contemplating what he had just heard. Eventually he scoffed and said, "Inspector, you're joking, right?"

"No, sir, I'm quite serious. He used the animals in some way to get the answers he wanted. We don't know how or what he did. We only have the suspects' version of this, and they were blindfolded."

"Suspects?" questioned the president.

Preston didn't like being questioned in this way but knew he had to tread lightly.

"Yes, sir. These two men admitted to trying to kill Admiral Summers. He is definitely the victim in this case, sir."

The president looked around the room, not believing what he was hearing. He received nods from both the directors of the CIA and FBI that the story was true.

"Summers was the victim. Yeah, right," he replied sarcastically. "I don't believe that for one second."

But before he could say anything else, there was a knock at the door and one of his secretaries poked her head in. "Sorry to disturb you, Mr. President, but we have a call you need to take."

"Not now, Betty," the president said, irritated. "We're in the middle of something here."

"Sir," she said firmly, "it's Admiral Summers on the line for you."

The room immediately became hushed as everyone exchanged looks.

The president looked at Putnum. "You know him best, Admiral. Any guess as to why he's calling?"

Putnum held back a smile, shrugging his shoulders. He knew everyone in the room had an idea as to why Summers was calling, but he wasn't about to be their spokesperson. When the president still didn't take the call, awaiting an answer, he said, "No idea, sir."

The president looked at Putnum, his expression making his distrust clear.

The president looked back to the secretary, who said, "Line one, sir."

The president rose slowly, walking to his desk. He looked around the room one more time before pushing the button on the phone. "Good evening, Admiral. I have you on speaker with the attorney general, the FBI, the CIA, and NSA. I also have Inspector Preston of the Mounties here. I assume the reason for your call has something to do with Richard Kingston and the Handcock sisters still being at large?"

"Yes, sir, it does."

"I'm guessing everyone here in this office feels you had something to do with what went on in Aruba. Anything you wish to share with us about that?"

"Yes, sir, I'd be happy to. I have to say that Aruba has some of the nicest beaches I've had the opportunity to be on. I recommend it highly to all of you as a vacation spot."

The president began to laugh. Everyone in the room joined him.

United States Disciplinary Barracks
Fort Leavenworth, Kansas
July 24, 2010
1945 hours

The duty sergeant sat at his desk, working on the schedule for the following week, when his captain walked in and said, "Do you know there's an RV in the parking lot out front?"

The sergeant nodded, looking at a clipboard on the desk in front of him.

"Yes, sir, I do," he replied. "We had some marshals bring in a prisoner. They must have parked it there after they brought him in."

"Any paperwork on the prisoner?"

The sergeant checked the clipboard and the in-basket on the desk. "Nothing yet, sir. They must still be processing."

The officer didn't think anything of it, as it was routine to have US marshals bring in and transport out prisoners. He picked up the phone on the sergeant's desk and punched in a number. While they waited for someone to answer, the sergeant brought the security cameras covering the parking lot up on his computer. The RV was parked away from the other vehicles in the lot. Both men were looking at the computer when someone answered.

"Yeah, this is the duty officer. I'm looking for those marshals that brought in that new prisoner . . ." He paused, listening to the person on the phone. "What?"

The captain's face became very serious.

"Are you sure?" the officer asked. A moment later, he hung up the phone and looked at the sergeant.

"Who told you the marshals were bringing in a prisoner?" asked the captain.

"There was a call from the main gate, sir. The RV and a chase car. They checked the paperwork and cleared it directly here. They said the paperwork was in order. Why?"

The captain looked down at the computer screen and the RV sitting by itself in the lot.

"They haven't seen the marshals."

Before the sergeant could respond, the phone rang. He picked up the phone, identified himself, and seemed to snap to attention in his chair.

He offered the handset to the officer. The captain replied, "Take a message, sergeant; we really need to solve this mystery immediately."

The sergeant thrust the phone at the officer. His tone was more an order than a request. "Sir!"

The captain took the phone, giving the sergeant a look that said they weren't done with the matter. He identified himself to the caller and went pale at what came next.

"Captain, this is the president of the United States."

United States Disciplinary Barracks
Fort Leavenworth, Kansas
July 24, 2010
1955 hours

The two rows of twelve armed soldiers each left the main entrance to the disciplinary barracks. All were armed with rifles and in full riot gear. At least a quarter of the responding soldiers had been fitted with remote video gear and were being monitored in real time by both the command at the disciplinary barracks and the White House. Each column was headed toward the RV from a different angle to surround it. Sirens could be heard in the distance, getting closer every second. The entire base had been put in lockdown within seconds of the president's call, and a response team was being sent like they were dealing with an inmate riot. The White House had been given a set of coordinates and the frequency of a GPS tracker. Both had led them to the RV in the parking lot.

The two columns proceeded forward. They were being led by the captain who had taken the call. Every soldier had their weapons at the ready while they moved into position around the parked vehicle. They were positioned back far enough to protect themselves from any typical IED explosion but close enough that they could effectively open fire on anyone in the vehicle. They were assured the vehicle was clean, but procedure and training told them that it was always best to assume otherwise.

The captain and four men moved forward in tight formation to the door of the RV, which was located about halfway back on the passenger side of the vehicle. Like the officer, each man was a combat veteran of either Iraq or Afghanistan, and one had EOD experience. When they reached the door, the duty sergeant's voice came over their com gear.

"Sir, they knew where to park the RV. We have no direct close-up footage of these would-be marshals exiting the RV. We have one view from a distance, and they appear to get out of the RV and get right into the fly car. They didn't appear to rig anything as they left."

The captain tapped one of his men on the shoulder, and he moved forward, checking the door. After a minute, the soldier gave the officer a thumbs-up, indicating everything looked good. The captain gave the signal to move to the next step. While they came prepared to blow the lock on the door, the soldier decided to try the door handle first. He found it unlocked, gently turning it, opening the door just enough to check for wires or other signs of booby traps. Finding none, he again signaled the officer the all clear. The captain and his team readied themselves to enter the RV, while everyone watching took a deep breath.

The door was flung open, and the four men entered, two headed forward toward the driver's area and the other two toward the rear. The two who went forward quickly called an all clear, while there was a flurry of activity from the two in back.

In the rear bedroom, they had found three individuals secured with flex-cuffs around their wrists and ankles. Another four soldiers moved in to help bring out the three secured prisoners as the first vehicles of the response team began to arrive. Heavily armed soldiers dismounted the vehicles and began to form an outer perimeter.

With the second team of soldiers in the van, they began to bring the prisoners out one by one, starting with Andrea Handcock. The flex-cuffs securing her ankles had been cut off, and she struggled to walk with a soldier holding each arm. They gently placed her face down on the pavement, her wrists still bound behind her back. She was followed by her sister and then by Kingston, the soldiers treating each in the same way. Medics with the response team rushed forward and began checking each of the prisoners over.

The medic checking Kingston backed away from his charge, looking up at the captain.

"Sir, er . . . uh . . . this man shit his pants. He . . . uh . . . stinks, sir."

The captain smiled. "I'd like to think it's from us coming through the door, soldier, but for some reason, I don't think so. Get him checked out, then get him inside and cleaned up."

The medic responded in the affirmative and went about his business. The captain and one of the soldiers went from prisoner to prisoner to prisoner, holding up a picture next to each to confirm their identity. When that was done, he supervised the loading of each of the prisoners into separate Humvees for transport into the disciplinary barrack's prisoner intake facility. While they were taken away under heavy guard, he was connected to the White House.

"What's the news, Captain?" asked the president.

"Sir, we've visually confirmed their identity. They're under heavy guard on their way into prisoner intake, where we'll do fingerprint and DNA confirmation. They're in our custody, sir, that's for sure."

The president gave an audible sigh of relief. "So, it's over?"

"Yes, sir, Mr. President, it's over. The emergency response team from the base is here, and there's no way Mr. Kingston or the Handcock sisters can escape."

A private came over and said something quietly to the captain.

"Captain," asked the president, "is there any sign of Admiral Summers or his team? Have you found them on the base?"

"No, sir, we haven't found any sign of them." The answer was quick and with a tone of frustration. "We had the base locked down within a minute of your call, sir. If they were still on the base at that time, there is a minimal chance they were able to get off. We did find the car they used to leave from here when they left the RV. It's clean, sir—no prints, nothing."

The president was silent.

The captain continued, "Sir, it's like they just disappeared. No trace anywhere. You said they were all retired from the military. What'd they do when they were in?"

There was a chuckle over the phone. "Son, I'm afraid that's above your pay grade. Have the base security keep looking, but I'm going to guess they won't find them. This is what they do. Call me back when you get the other confirmations, Captain. And tell your people job well done."

"Thank you, Mr. President."

The line went dead, and the captain looked around at the men standing near him. The manhunt was over. They had taken three of the most wanted fugitives in the world into custody, but they hadn't been the ones to capture them. Someone brought them onto a military base, passed heavy security, and left them there to be found. There would be hell to pay for someone breaking into one of the most secure facilities in the nation. That wasn't his issue, though; it was his people who had ended it. He thought about the people who did this. The president referred to them as retired. Wasn't retirement supposed to be quiet and relaxing?

★ CHAPTER TEN ★

TRUTH

Summers' Island
Adirondack State Park, New York
July 30, 2010
0830 hours

Matt and the family had arrived back on Summers' Island the evening before, the FBI having finished up their investigation and released the property back to them. He and the family spent the night on the island for the first time since the kidnappings, and with the help of friends, were going to start repairing any damage.

They were having breakfast when Hector left the table and went out on the front porch. He leaned on the railing, looking out over the lake. It wasn't long before he was joined by his sister. Julie, sitting with Matt and Karen, watched her children with a pained expression on her face.

She looked at her brother with pleading eyes. "I wish there was something I could do or say to make things better for them." Julie nodded at her children. "Ever since we found out their father was murdered, things just haven't come together for us as a family. I keep thinking I've failed them in some way."

Matt looked at Karen, who motioned for him to go ahead and take care of this. He rose from the table, taking Julie's hand and leading her outside. Hector and Alex looked surprised to see them. Matt suggested they all sit down.

"You guys mad at the family?" he asked evenly.

Both answered by shaking their heads.

"Mad at your mom?"

Again, they shook their heads.

"What's the problem, then?" Matt's tone was even and paternal. "We're family, after all, and work through this stuff together."

"He murdered Daddy and he's still alive," said Alex. "Why couldn't he die?"

"He also hurt this family by being part of this Kingston thing," Hector broke in, "and will try to get off by saying he's crazy because Grandpa's ghost threatened him. It's not fair—he'll get away with it."

The smile that crossed Matt's face drew a response from his sister.

"What's so funny, Matthew? I don't think it's funny that he'll get off using Dad's ghost as an alibi. He needs to pay for Hector's murder."

Matt looked at Julie, holding up his hand to stop the coming tirade. "Easy, girl. What would you say if I told you it was Dad's ghost that got the confession from Hapke?"

Julie and her children all looked at each other in confusion.

"I'd say you're as crazy as he's trying to make himself out to be," said Julie.

"If this were a normal situation, I would agree with you. Hector and Dad were close; I know Hapke was told that years ago, and he's the type of man who would never forget. When Hector was killed, Dad was all over the investigation because he never believed it was an accident. I believe Hector told him more than any of us realized. Karen and I had our hands full with Dad to the point I called Jon for help. Even though Hapke worked for a different department, he was on the drug task force with Hector and would have known Dad's feelings about this."

Matt saw a tear starting to run down Julie's cheek. He gently wiped it away. He shifted the conversation, saying, "Dad's uniforms are kept in storage here. When Hapke was captured, it was by Ray Summers in World War II period uniform."

All three looked surprised. Hector started to say something, but Matt held up his hand.

"Sean and Justin drew straws; either one could pass for Dad at their age. Justin took Hapke down in the woods alone. Whatever he did, he scared the living daylights out of the man. Jon didn't help when he whispered something in the man's ear after he was a prisoner. With their history, I'm sure he was the premier diplomat. He hasn't stopped talking."

"What do you mean by that?" asked Hector.

Matt smiled weakly. "He's given up two other people who are being charged with your dad's murder. These two arrests are leading to who knows how many dealers involved in the sale and distribution of drugs in the Rochester area. There are lots of arrests taking place right now, and a big dent is being put in the upstate New York drug trade, all because of the information he's giving them. The man just can't stop talking. It seems he's found someone he's more scared of than the cartels and gangs."

"Who's that?" asked Hector.

"Your grandfather's ghost."

The laughter started slowly and then overtook them. Julie was finally able to say, "Dad is still watching over all of us, even after all these years."

Her older brother just smiled.

**Camp David
Thurmont, Maryland
July 30, 2010
0830 hours**

The morning dawned bright, with only a slight breeze to temper the already rising thermometer. It was going to be a hot and muggy day in the mountains. Fortunately for those gathered around the table, all were headed back to Washington—and the comfort of their air-conditioned offices—after one final meeting. The president entered the room, and they all rose, except for the man in the wheelchair.

"I want to thank you all for coming this morning," said the president, smiling warmly as they all sat down. "I know you weren't given much of a choice and it meant rising early."

The president looked at each of them, smiling his genuine appreciation. Sitting at the table were Ericson, O'Leary, Alexander, Hennen, Del Monte, the attorney general, the director of the FBI, the director of the CIA, and Sanderson.

"I wanted to brief all of you on the investigation into your kidnapping and the arrests that have been taking place. I believe it's important that you have all the information."

"Sir," interrupted Congresswoman Del Monte, "I think it's important to take into consideration the men and women who rescued us. They were retired military and civilians who put their lives on the line for us. We need to protect them, Mr. President. I know my colleagues here would agree."

There were nods of agreement from around the table. Ericson spoke next. "I personally know all of them, and they didn't hesitate to come to our aide when we needed it. They're dedicated to this country and stepped up when they didn't need to. Sue Ellen's right, sir, they need to be taken care of."

O'Leary started to say something, but the president held up his hand, stopping her. He looked at the attorney general. "Eric, it's my understanding that any civilians or nonsworn persons involved in something like this would face criminal charges."

O'Leary began to object, and the president cut her off, saying, "Let the attorney general answer the question, Senator O'Leary."

The attorney general smiled. "That's correct, Mr. President, they would. But Deputy Director Sanderson can explain better what took place during the rescue and about all who are facing charges."

All eyes turned to Sanderson, who cleared his throat before giving his report.

O'Leary looked anxious but calmed when Ericson put his hand on her shoulder. His gaze told her he, too, was concerned, but they needed to listen.

"The rescue of the hostages," started Sanderson, "was affected by a joint task force of law enforcement, military, and intelligence assets. This effort was supported by the FBI, New York State Police, the Franklin County Sheriff's Office, as well as units of the Tenth Light Infantry Division out of Fort Drum and the Navy's Special Boat Squadrons."

There was silence as the former hostages took a few moments to look at one another, acknowledging what hadn't been said. They all looked to Ericson, who they knew would ask the question. "So, you're telling us, Director, that there were no civilians or retired military personnel involved in our rescue? What about CIA? Did they or NSA have any people involved in the rescue?"

Ericson's expression was serious but not hostile.

Sanderson smiled pleasantly. "The bulk of the rescue team were personnel attached to the Franklin County Sheriff's Office—at least Sheriff James has assured us of that fact. As for CIA and NSA, they were extremely helpful, sending us expert support for this incident. The CIA loaned us one of their teams that specializes in this type of operation overseas. They were invaluable." Sanderson raised his eyebrows, as if to ask if there were any questions, only to continue before any could be asked. "Now, CIA tracked the fugitives' movements. We're not sure how they did it, but their information was accurate."

Sanderson looked at the director of the CIA for comments. The man just raised his hand and shook his head, saying nothing.

"An operation was mounted on two fronts to take Richard Kingston and the three Handcock sisters into custody. I will admit that there was some trickery on our part when it came to dealing with the local authorities in both cases, and we have apologized to both countries officially. The team in Aruba was able to save two police officers who had been targeted for execution by organized crime. They have asked to decorate the team involved. Because the operation was covert, we have offered to pass the medals on with their thanks."

O'Leary interrupted Sanderson by saying, "I've been to Aruba, Mr. Sanderson, and while the island is quite lovely, their police force is extremely efficient and there is no organized crime problem there."

"So, you're not recommending I take the family there for vacation?" quipped Hennen.

The smile never left Sanderson's face.

"I never said it was their organized crime problem," he said, checking his notes. "The group was from a foreign country. Not ours, thank God. They were quite surprised when the Dutch Royal Marines came through the door to take them into custody."

Laughter filled the room.

"Mr. Kingston and Andrea and Kimberly Handcock were taken into custody there, along with twenty others. Melissa Handcock was taken into custody in Indonesia in another covert operation."

"No extradition treaty," stated Ericson, and Sanderson nodded in agreement.

"Our investigation determined that Indonesia was the destination for the other three fugitives as well. They were in the process of purchasing property there, presumably to avoid extradition back to the United States. Not a bad plan, if they could've pulled it off. Fortunately, after Melissa Handcock was kidnapped by pirates along with several other tourists, she was rescued by the Royal Australian Navy and remanded to our custody."

Ericson laughed, drawing everyone's attention.

Sanderson continued to smile as he addressed Ericson. "Is there something you'd like to ask?"

It was Senator Alexander who spoke. "I've been around this game a lot longer than anyone in this room, Director Sanderson. I know, as do my colleagues, that what you're giving us is the truth according to the United States government. The truth you want out there. I'm guessing our pirates in this case were members of a fraternity that Senator Ericson hails from."

Ericson chuckled and nodded in agreement.

Alexander continued, "Mind you, Director, we have no problem with that truth, as long as you know we all understand what really happened out there."

"This all took money for Kingston to pull off," Sue Ellen Del Monte interjected. "Any idea what happened to his accounts? We can't have him buying his way out of prison with another escape attempt like this one."

For the first time during the interview, Sanderson looked a little nervous. He glanced at his boss and the director of the CIA, who both nodded for him to respond.

"When we took Melissa Handcock into custody in Indonesia, we were able to get a list of accounts. We've recovered a little over 1.5 million dollars from one account in an Indonesian bank. There were ten other accounts from banks all over the world that, at one time, contained over thirty million dollars in assets."

"At one time?" asked Hennen.

Sanderson shifted his weight and hesitated before saying, "The money was withdrawn from all the other accounts on the day Kingston and his two accomplices were captured in Aruba and transferred to a charitable trust on the West Coast. From there, the money was disbursed to a little over two hundred individuals or families. Once that was completed, the fund was closed within twenty-four hours. All quite legal and untouchable. The other thing is that we can't trace any of the money back to Kingston. He's broke. Everything is gone, every penny."

It was quiet around the room. Ericson broke the silence. "Did your team in Aruba have the same account numbers?"

Sanderson looked serious. This time, his smile was gone. "We don't know."

A sly smile crossed Ericson's face, as if he knew something no one else did.

O'Leary grinned. "Well, we know who was there, don't we?"

"We sure do," replied Ericson under his breath.

"The fund was administered by an old friend of both of yours." Sanderson looked directly at the two senators. "General William Gateway."

"I know him," said Del Monte. "My God, the man's in his nineties. What would he be doing running a foundation stealing money from someone like Kingston?"

"Bill's not a thief," Alexander said in defense of Gateway, "and there must be some good reason he's involved in the foundation. Director Sanderson, have you had the opportunity to follow up on this foundation?"

Sanderson gave him a confident nod. "Yes, sir, we did. I'll start by saying that none of this money has gone to General Gateway or any of his family."

Puzzled looks crossed the faces of the gathered members of Congress. This seemed to amuse both the president and Sanderson.

"This will make more sense as I explain," said Sanderson. "After we traced the money and where it ended up, we identified one common denominator with each recipient. They, or a member of their family, were victims of the crimes committed by Richard Kingston. Both Gateway, his children, his grandchildren, and his great-grandchildren were all victims. From what we've been able to determine, none have received any money from this foundation."

Ericson looked concerned. "I know for a fact that some of those victims' names are attached to classified military operations. I'm curious as to how you've been able to determine all the people on that list were victims of Kingston's treachery?"

Sanderson's smile seemed to broaden with the question. He really enjoyed this part of the briefing. "We involved the Pentagon, Senator, and whenever we had a name that didn't seem to make a connection, they checked and made the connection. They shared no details, so secrets are safe and still secrets. All of you are on the list."

The look of shock on each face showed they were not aware. Sanderson continued, not allowing time for reactions or questions.

"Within the next day or two, each of you should receive an envelope from the Foundation for Forgotten Victims. I can't say what's in the envelope coming your way, but each of you was on the list of those receiving disbursements from the monies taken from Kingston's accounts."

The room was completely silent. The gathered members of Congress looked at each other, speechless. It wasn't often this group was at a loss for words. They would usually be involved in a lively debate, but today they were all silent.

Sanderson's look became serious again as he said, "I must ask all of you if you know the whereabouts of Admiral Jon Summers. The FBI has some questions we'd like to ask him."

"I know he's not on that list," Ericson stated bluntly.

"Correct, Senator, he's not on the list. To our knowledge, he received no money from the foundation."

"Then why do you want to talk to him?" asked O'Leary defensively, tears starting to form in her eyes.

"He should get a medal for what he did," stated Alexander flatly, with Hennen and Del Monte nodding their agreement.

The president leaned forward. "Unfortunately, that's not why we're looking for him."

Mohawk Tavern and Grill
Bluffton, New York
July 30, 2010
0830 hours

Justin and Kayli sat at the counter, talking to Stephen, Abby, Maggie, and Fred. Abby was in full uniform, now working full-time as a deputy. Stephen and her brother Nathan had finally been able to give up the special deputy status, going back to their normal lives in town.

They all laughed at something Maggie said, only for Stephen to become serious, looking at his brother. "Do you have to leave so soon? You just came back to all of us, and now you're running off to who knows where."

"We're just taking the van back to our shop," said Justin, chuckling. "We leave later this week for the Caribbean to debrief some people on what happened in Aruba when they grabbed Kingston. We'll be back after that, and we all have some time coming. I'll be back here on the island then."

"At least we know you're returning. Say, how did Dad figure out you were alive? Mom will probably shoot him."

Kay laughed. "I'd like to say it's because he got sloppy or lazy, but your brother isn't either of those things. I'd have to say your father is very determined. He's also very intimidating when he wants to be. I can't imagine anyone keeping a secret from him for long."

It was Stephen's turn to laugh. "No shit."

Justin nodded while everyone else laughed. "He knew for some time—and I'm guessing Mom knew he was onto something. She's the one person he couldn't keep a secret from."

"And that's why they separated," said Maggie. Her laughter stopped, replaced by a look of sympathy. "It's a tough business keeping secrets among family; sometimes it's necessary, but it's always a nasty business."

"Where is your mother anyway?" asked Kay. "I know she was released from the hospital. Is she on the island or did she go back to Rochester?"

"All I can tell you is that Uncle Matt, Aunt Karen, and I went to pick her up and Dad had already been there. They've disappeared. They're totally off the grid. The neighbors in Rochester haven't seen them, and they haven't contacted anyone in the family."

"I know the CIA and the FBI both want to see your father," Kay interjected, chewing on her lower lip. "In the worst way."

"They won't find him," Fred said, smiling. "He was brought up like he was a member of the Wolf Clan of the Mohawk Nation. He's taken your mother somewhere safe and has an angel looking over them. They'll only find him when he's ready for them to."

"Fred, you make him sound like a legend," Justin responded doubtfully. "With all of the resources out there looking for him, he can't hide forever."

"But look at what he's done in his career," Kay argued. "All the people whose lives he's affected. The work he did in the teams, the mission in the Philippines, his intelligence work, and now this. To many in the Special Forces community, he *is* a legend. Look at who came to help him without being asked."

"He's a human being, Kay," said Stephen, "and a damned lucky one, at that."

Abby punched Stephen hard on the shoulder.

"Ouch, what was that for?"

"Get used to it, little brother," Justin said, laughing. "I have the feeling the two of you will be sharing moments like that for a long time to come."

There was quiet recognition of the young couple until Fred said, "You young warriors all did well, but you still have much to learn."

Justin gave the old man a look of disbelief.

Fred focused his gaze on Justin. "Your grandfather was my good friend. A white man, yes, but one who accepted all people for who they were. He was a true warrior because he knew that peace is the ultimate goal for all willing to fight for what they believe in. He and I taught that to your father and your uncle, and both learned those lessons well. Both have done well in life. Each took a different path to achieve their goals while staying true to what they learned. Defend the weak from those who would take advantage. Be true to nature; take only what you need. Be true to the clan, or family; they come first. Provide for them and keep them safe.

"You all learned those lessons and proved yourselves well against a cunning and formidable enemy. Now you need to learn how the Great Spirit and the Spirit of the Wolf protect all of you. For each of you it will be different, but each must move to the next level. You must learn to trust, to believe, and to allow something greater into your life and everything you do."

"Wow," said Kay, "it's like listening to my mother about Japanese culture."

"Then she's a very smart and wise woman," said Maggie with a smile.

Fred looked at Stephen. "It's like knowing when a shadow passes over the moon that everything is going to be all right. Everyone would be safe."

Stephen smiled back at the old man. "Like a man in a parachute silhouetted by the light of the moon?"

Fred nodded, eyes twinkling. "The Spirit of the Wolf passing across the moon. When they asked me to negotiate, I warned them on the island not to anger the spirits. They didn't believe me. The Spirit of the Wolf protected you, my granddaughter. The Spirit rained death down on them. You returned to us safe."

Abby looked as if she were about to say something but decided not to. The old man continued, "They angered the spirit of my old friend, your grandfather, and look at what happened—he returned and brought fear and intimidation to your enemies, crippling their leadership. In that process, he helped to right a wrong done to your family with the killing of your uncle Hector. My old friend lives on and continues to fight the good fight."

A strange look crossed Justin's face. Then he smiled. "Thank you, Yoda."

There were soft chuckles from those gathered.

Fred looked at Justin, smiling gently. "You don't believe, young man?"

"Yes, sir, I do. More than you know."

Justin reached into his jacket, pulling out a sheathed World War II bayonet. He placed it on the counter and slowly slid it across to the old man. The old Indian put his hand on Justin's and just smiled.

United States Disciplinary Barracks
Fort Leavenworth, Kansas
July 30, 2010
0830 hours

Cassie stood next to her boss, Assistant United States Attorney Trask, and FBI Special Agent Grey. They were surrounded by heavily armed soldiers and FBI agents for the transfer of the prisoners. The government was taking no chances on Kingston and his confederates getting away again. Several armored vehicles were present to deter anyone foolish enough to try to affect an escape from the middle of an Army base. The four prisoners, all in leg and arm shackles, shuffled out to the armored van that was to take them to the nearby airfield. They were loaded into the van one by one. Each wore a long face, unhappy about their situation.

Cassie watched each of them board the van and was surprised by how little compassion she felt for them. They had tried to hurt her family. They had kidnapped her sister, aunts, and cousins and had tried to kill her uncle. They deserved what was happening to them. She felt ashamed about that, however, and it must have shown.

"Don't feel sorry for them, Cassie," said her boss. "They wouldn't feel a bit bad about those they killed or wounded if their little plan had succeeded."

Grey grunted in response. He added, "The man has no loyalties. He even gave up his own people to get away. These three women may think he cares, but he'd give them up in a heartbeat if he thought it would get him out of here. The sad part is, even though they're sisters, they'd cut each other's throats to be alone with Kingston. It's really sick."

Watching the scene in front of her, Cassie responded, "That's the problem—I don't feel any remorse about what's happening to them. I'm afraid that makes me as bad as them."

Grey motioned them forward to the open rear door. The Army officer in charge asked if they were set to proceed. Grey checked each of the prisoners before he said he was set.

"You do know our rights were violated, Special Agent Grey," said Kingston, a smirk on his face.

Grey gave the order to proceed, then turned to face the prisoner. "That's why these two are here—to make sure that doesn't happen. After all, our most important goal at this point is the preservation of your rights."

"You do have a sense of humor," said Kingston with a sneer. "Both of them are biased about the four of us."

Grey managed to smile. "I don't think you'll find anyone in the US Attorney's Office who won't be at least somewhat biased about your case. Quite frankly, you're lucky anyone has agreed to work with you at all."

Kingston grunted. "It may be hard for you to believe, but we're victims here. You need to be looking for her uncle," he said, nodding at Cassie. "He's the real villain, stealing millions of dollars for himself."

Trask smiled and responded to the prisoner. "Admiral Summers received no money. We've followed the money trail. The money miraculously turned up in a charitable trust and has been distributed to victims, and the families of victims, who have been connected to the crimes you've been accused of committing. We'd love to talk to Admiral Summers, General Ellison, General Naylor, and the rest, but they've all disappeared. The FBI investigation may show criminal proceedings need to be pursued against them. In that case, I promise you a new cellmate."

The color drained from Kingston's face. He looked down at the floor of the van, becoming suddenly silent. Cassie gave her boss a surprised look as the soldiers closed the doors on the prisoners. There was a distinctive sound of heavy metal as the doors were secured, giving the sense of finality to the prisoners' situation.

Cassie looked at the van and then back at her boss, her face similarly drained of color.

He smiled weakly. "Sorry, Cassie, we really do need to speak to your uncle. He and the men he was with have quite a bit of information we need for the investigation, and they possibly have a few things to answer for. I can't promise there won't be criminal charges."

"I can," responded a grinning Glenn Grey.

"Because you're an old friend?" asked Cassie hopefully, but Grey shook his head.

"No, because he would truly love to be Kingston's roommate for even ten minutes."

"He wouldn't need that long," commented Cassie.

Nothing else was said between the three as the van began to move.

Trask chuckled. "Let's hope we never have to find out. Where are they going?"

Grey shrugged. "Don't know—it's a big secret. The trial will be public, and I'm guessing the death penalty will be put back on the table."

Trask nodded in agreement, saying nothing in response. Both men noticed a tear rolling down Cassie's cheek.

"You okay, young lady?" asked Grey, putting his hand on her shoulder.

She wiped the tear, nodding. "My uncle Jon shared with me something my grandfather once told the family when they were asking about his experiences in World War II. He said learning to kill was easy, learning when not to kill was much harder. I think I understand that now. It's what separates us from people like them."

She put her arms around the FBI agent, giving him a hug.

She realized they were different from Kingston and the Handcock sisters. They were allowed to leave alive to face their fate. That wouldn't have been allowed if the roles had been reversed. Both men nodded at what she'd just said. They understood all too well how hard it was.

O'Malley's Tavern
Virginia Beach, Virginia
July 30, 2010
0830 Hours

The SUV pulled into the lot and parked next to the red compact sedan. There were two other cars parked next to them. Cory Hayes knew them to belong to the early prep crew working for his wife. She managed this O'Malley's, having worked there for years. He got out of his vehicle, stretching. A deep breath told him he was only a few blocks from the ocean. He looked around, seeing all the signs it was going to be another scorcher. The wind blew his hair across his forehead, causing him to involuntarily brush it back with his hand. He smiled. The breeze would make the day bearable this close to the coast.

Morning traffic was busy on both Laskin Road and I-264. He'd been on his way to work when he got the call from his father-in-law to meet him at the tavern. He thought it strange, this impromptu outing, because Tom Mitchell was a family occasions and holidays type of in-law. He'd call once a week on the weekend to keep up with the grandchildren—otherwise, he kept to himself. Mitchell had been this way since his daughter married Cory. Cory didn't take it personally. There had been someone else in Shelley's life before Cory, and his death had hit everyone hard.

The second thing Cory found strange was that when he called in to tell his boss he would be late, the commander already knew. Cory taught survival, escape, and evasion techniques to pilots and aircrews at the Oceana Naval Air Station just on the other side of I-264. His time in the teams qualified him to teach the pilots, and his students always did well when they went to the service schools for those topics. He didn't do much in the way of field training anymore, due to the wounds and injuries he'd received on his last mission. He'd lost some close friends on that mission and still experienced nightmares and bouts of insomnia as a result.

While he watched the traffic coming off Laskin Road onto Regency Drive, he saw a familiar car. It had been over a month since he had spoken to Mike Skier, and since he didn't believe in coincidences, he guessed his driving by was no accident. It only took a minute for Skier to maneuver his car into the plaza housing O'Malley's and park next to Cory. Skier quickly exited and the two men embraced.

"Good to see you, brother," Cory said, looking at his old friend in his summer whites and patting the man on the back. "I figured you to be off to some exotic climb where the wind blows sand into everything you own."

Skier smiled, releasing his old teammate. "Nah, just got back from the steamy jungles in the exotic Pacific. Bikini-clad women, umbrella drinks, and white sand beaches. First class all the way."

Cory cocked his head slightly, eyeing Skier. "I saw that blurb in the paper and figured that to be a West Coast team. How'd you guys manage that gig?"

Skier ignored his friend, reaching into the car and putting on his uniform cap. For the first time, Cory noticed the young officer on the other side of the car. Skier smiled as Cory's body unconsciously came to attention. Some things one just never forgets.

"Cory, this is my CO, Ensign Eddie Johnston. Skipper, this is an old teammate of mine, Cory Hayes."

Johnston came around the car and took Cory's outstretched hand.

The young officer smiled. "The chief has mentioned you before. He says you teach escape and evasion to the pilots at Oceana. How do you like it?"

"It's okay—not as exciting as being in the field, but it allows me to keep my hand in and feel like I'm contributing. I'm here to meet my father-in-law. What brings you guys here?"

Both men looked at each other, shifting nervously. Cory's curiosity was piqued, but before he could ask another question, a dark SUV pulled up in front of O'Malley's. Two men in civilian clothes got out of the front seats. They had the look of military people, but it quickly became obvious they were a protection detail for someone. The driver moved to the front of the SUV, his eyes constantly moving, looking for any threats. The passenger went to the back door of the SUV, opening it. To Cory's surprise, an admiral with four stars on his collar got out first. He was followed by Tom Mitchell, who was in his old Navy uniform showing the rank of captain. He was followed by a woman lieutenant commander. As she got out of the SUV, yet another officer in a Corvette pulled into the lot and parked. His presence didn't seem to surprise or bother the security people.

Mitchell came right over to his son-in-law. He returned the salute from the two men in uniform and then shook Cory's hand. "I'm glad you could make it, Cory. This is important to both Shelly and you."

Cory looked puzzled and motioned to everyone in uniform. "Why all the brass?"

"They're here for moral support—something I think I'll need before this is over."

"Tom, what's wrong?"

Mitchell ignored the question and went right to introducing the other officers. "Cory, this is Admiral Putnum. He's the deputy director of the NSA."

Putnum shook Cory's hand. "It's nice to finally meet you, young man. Tom speaks highly of you."

Next, he introduced Stephnie Smith and Bryan Kingston. Cory thought it funny that an officer from Naval Intelligence and another from the Special Boat Squadrons were together until he was told they were newly engaged to be married and were going to introduce Kingston to her grandfather after this meeting.

"So your grandfather lives here in Virginia Beach?" asked Cory.

Smith nodded and smiled at Kingston. "He left the Navy here at Little Creek and stayed. He's an ornery old chief petty officer who's overprotective of his granddaughter. He'll love Bryan, but he has to go through the motions and put on the show."

They all chuckled politely.

"What did he do in the Navy, Commander?" asked Cory as they all walked toward the door to the tavern.

"You may know him, Mr. Hayes, if you go to the reunions," said Smith. They walked through the front door, which was held open by Skier. "His name's Lewis Burke."

Cory visibly stumbled at the mention of the name. Commander Smith was related to one of the original Navy SEALs, and Cory's reaction showed his surprise.

"Daddy," said Shelly Hayes, meeting them just inside the door, "what's all this about?"

Shelly stopped fast when she saw Putnum walk in behind her father and Cory. Mitchell made quick introductions, and Shelly asked them all to sit at the bar and offered them some coffee. Cory disappeared into the kitchen as everyone settled onto a bar stool. He returned a minute later with coffee, and everyone settled for the business at hand.

"So, what's so important that we're doing this on my busiest day of the week and you have all this extra help?" asked Shelly.

Mitchell's look was serious, and he had difficulty starting. He took a deep breath and finally jumped in. "Like I told Cory, they're all here for moral support. I think I really screwed up, baby. I mean, big-time. They're here to help explain, and maybe even protect me a little."

Shelly and Cory were standing behind the bar next to each other. They instinctively held each other's hands, faces warped with worry.

"Daddy, what did you do and who did you screw up with?"

Mitchell swallowed. "The two of you."

There was silence for a few moments before Mitchell continued. "Several years ago, after you two married, I had something fall on my lap at the agency. It was an opportunity and probably the hardest thing I've ever had to do in my whole life."

Shelly looked curiously at her father. She noticed his hands shaking.

"Daddy, what's wrong?" Her voice broke over the words. Mitchell looked at Putnum, who just looked back, his eyes telling him to just move along.

"Shelly, honey, it's about Justin."

"What about Justin?" Her brows furrowed. "They found his body?"

Mitchell hesitated one last time. "Well . . . he's . . . he's alive."

There was silence as both Shelly and Cory looked at Mitchell in disbelief.

"He escaped," Mitchell went on. "They held him in secret for several years after he had been reported as KIA. I can't go into detail, but he has been working with my operation for the past few years. I'm so sorry I kept this from you, baby."

Shelly half laughed. "That's not funny, Daddy. Really, that's not funny."

No one at the bar laughed, and Skier couldn't even maintain eye contact with her.

Shelly's tone went from flabbergasted disbelief to one of anger. Her eyes flashed, chin wobbling as she addressed Skier. "Are you part of this, Mike?" she asked almost harshly. "I expected better from you."

Skier looked at Putnum, who nodded. This was not missed by Shelly. She looked from Putnum to Skier, waiting for her explanation.

"You guys heard of that mess this past week up in New York?" asked Skier.

They both nodded, and Cory asked, "That was you guys?"

Skier shook his head and almost smiled. "No, the actual rescue is a ghost story for another time. A bunch of over-the-hill retirees who wrote the book on what we do are responsible for that."

Shelly's eyes seemed to grow as a thought came to her. "The only names we saw in the papers here had the politicians listed as hostages. They didn't list the locals. It was Summers' Island, wasn't it? Justin took me there once when he was alive."

No one answered, so Skier continued, saying, "We went in on the extraction. We ran into a CIA team that worked for your dad that was there to support the FBI. That was the official story, anyway. Justin was the team leader. Kay was there, too. She's part of his team."

"She's working as an analyst for the CIA?" Cory said thoughtfully. "But she doesn't have the background for field operations."

Skier looked at his old friend. "She suited up and went in with the rescue team. She was with us on the second part of the mission as well. You've got to remember who her father is. Justin led the second part of the mission."

"Like old times?" Cory's question seemed to be open-ended on several levels.

Skier made direct eye contact with his former teammate. "No, not like old times. Justin, he's . . . he's more driven, more focused. He's still a ball-buster, don't get me wrong, but the circle of people he trusts is smaller. A lot smaller. Considering what he went through, I'm not surprised. I'm not even sure the Teams are inside that circle anymore."

It was quiet while everyone seemed to absorb Skier's answer. Mitchell was looking down at the bar in front of him, avoiding any eye contact with his daughter and son-in-law. When he finally looked up, he found Shelly glaring at him. Her face was flushed, and her fists were clenched.

"Kay too!" Her tone was venomous. "We haven't seen her in over a year, and she was distant then. Now we know why."

"Baby, I couldn't let—"

Shelly moved so fast, no one had a chance to stop her. She grabbed onto her father's collar with one hand, pulling him toward her while hitting him squarely in the face with the other. She quickly landed two punches. Before she could land a third, Bryan grabbed both of her wrists and started to pull her over the bar. She was screaming, out of control, and as she came over the bar, she tried to kick her father. Johnston pushed Mitchell out of the way while Skier intercepted and blocked her kicks. The commotion was loud enough to bring the two security men in from the outside, their hands on the grips of their weapons, but not drawn. It also brought the prep crew out of the kitchen.

The two blows that Shelly had landed caused a bloody nose. Now both blood and tears flowed freely down Mitchell's face. Putnum, Smith, and Cory were doing their best to control the blood, but not before some made it to Mitchell's white uniform. Shelly was calming down to the point where

Kingston and Skier let her go, and a young waitress on the prep crew took her to the ladies' room.

Mitchell was given a towel from behind the bar, with which he was now controlling the bleeding. "Cory, I'm so sorry. You guys were married, moving on, and so happy after everything the two of you went through. I couldn't turn that upside down. It killed me not to tell you. Kay was having problems, too, and I suspect that's why she stopped calling."

As Cory and Mitchell started to talk, Putnum moved around behind the bar. He motioned for Smith to lean closer. He whispered something in her ear, and she nodded. She walked by Kingston, taking his hand and squeezing it. Everyone in the room saw the look and smile they exchanged. She then walked directly to the ladies' room.

Shelly was at the sink, throwing water on her face. The young waitress was standing by the far wall, trying to look supportive. She looked very uncomfortable, so when Smith nodded toward the door, she wasted no time in leaving. Before the door was even closed, Shelly said, "I don't need your lecture on all this being secret, Commander. I know the drill."

Shelly's voice was angry as she leaned on the sink basin, glaring at Smith's reflection in the mirror. Smith leaned casually against the wall and waited patiently before responding, visibly calm despite the conflict. "Actually, I think this whole secret thing sucks."

"You have no idea," responded Shelly bitterly.

Smith seemed to ignore the projected attitude. "Yeah, it hurts too many people I care about. I'm glad all this happened. Now, maybe we can get some normalcy back."

"I don't understand." Shelly sounded annoyed, but her attitude was softening. "You're not making any sense."

"At the start of my career in the Navy, I worked as Admiral Summers's aide. I was with him when Justin disappeared. It devastated the family. I know you and Nancy spent a lot of time together grieving. I was there, in the background, watching every day."

Shelly remained silent, remembering the commander as an eager young officer serving in her first posting out of the Academy.

"The admiral knew about Justin; he called him when this all went down. I'm guessing the CIA told him that Justin survived to keep him from blowing a lid off one of their best teams."

Shelly grunted, a slight smile emerging on her face. "His reputation scares them—of course they told him. He's a kind, caring man who looks out for his family."

"Just like your father."

"What did you say?" The angry tone returned. "My father *lied* to me. Justin was alive, and he never told me. I deserved to know. He lied to me!"

Smith took a deep breath. "He never lied to you."

"Yes, he did!"

"It was the admiral who told you Justin was dead, not your father. Your father was with you when you got the news, we made sure of that. We knew you would need each other with that news. Your father just never told you when Justin was found alive. He didn't lie, there is a difference."

Shelly glared at Smith, thinking about what she said.

"I don't agree with his choice, but he didn't lie. He was doing what he thought was best. You and Cory were just married and the happiest you'd been in a couple of years. Because of Justin's skills, and the fact he didn't exist anymore, the agency put him to work. This made your father happy because you and Cory have been happy all this time. It's driven him crazy keeping this secret from you, but seeing how happy you've been, he felt it was worth keeping it. I can't speak for Justin, but I would guess he feels the same. Hell, the only way Kay could keep from telling you was to avoid you altogether."

A tear was slowly running down Shelly's cheek, and her lip was quivering ever so slightly. She suddenly started to sob uncontrollably. All her emotions came pouring out all at once, and she threw her arms around Smith and cried. This lasted for several minutes before Shelly started to regain some control. There was a box of Kleenex by the sink, and she was liberally using it to control the tears. Smith said nothing more; she just supportively smiled and motioned toward the sink. Shelly again threw some water on her face. As she was drying her face and hands, the door opened, and Putnum walked in.

"Do you often walk into the ladies' room, Admiral?" asked Shelly as she threw out the paper towel she had been using.

He smiled, handing her a glass. Shelly smelled the liquid—it was whiskey. She downed it in one quick swallow, making a face as she did. It burned going down, causing her to cough. Smith moved forward to help, but Shelly held up her hand, stopping her.

"Sorry," she said, catching her breath. "I'm used to serving whiskey, not drinking it. I know it's supposed to help in a situation like this, but now I'm not so sure."

Putnum gave her a grandfatherly smile. "Give it a few minutes to kick in, young lady."

Putnum looked at Smith, who just nodded to the unasked question.

"I'm going to be fine, Admiral," said Shelly, noticing the exchange. "One question, though."

Putnum looked at the young woman and raised an eyebrow.

"When will I get to see Justin?"

A sympathetic look came over Putnum's face. "We can arrange that in time, my dear. Right now, I think you have some other things to focus on."

Nothing more was said between them. Shelly looked back into the mirror at herself. Her eyes were still red from crying, but the tears had finally stopped.

"I need to see Daddy," she suddenly said, walking past the two officers.

Putnum looked at Smith, nodding his approval. She just smiled in return, opening the door and holding it for him. They both walked back to the bar. Mitchell, Shelly, and Cory were all hugging. They all had tears running down their faces, but there were also smiles.

Evans Residence
Nassau, Bahamas
July 30, 2010
0830 hours

Evans sipped his coffee by the pool, deep in thought. His life had not returned to normal like he'd hoped it would when he resumed his daily routine. Being close to his family and not being able to see his daughter and son to let them know he was alive hurt. But in the back of his mind, he knew not telling them was the right thing, as it kept them safe from his past. The problem was being right was keeping him from sleeping and causing him untold agony. He was currently alone in the house. He employed a staff of two. A husband-and-wife team took care of the cooking and cleaning and worked as general household help. He gave them the day off to deal with some family errands. Nothing was going on, and he felt the need to be alone, so here he was, by the pool.

He heard the doorbell ring.

"Damn," he muttered under his breath.

He looked out over the beach and the ocean that was his backyard. He was really enjoying the solitude and didn't feel like answering the door. They didn't get many visitors here, and he wasn't expecting anyone. He guessed it was some type of delivery and decided to ignore it. He took another sip of coffee, closing his eyes and feeling the sun warm his skin and the air around him. He could hear the breeze rustling the leaves on the trees and the waves lapping up on the sand.

The doorbell rang a second time and then a third. Irritated at being disturbed from his peaceful meditations, he rose, swearing under his breath. When he entered the house, the doorbell rang again and again.

"Damn it, I'm coming, you bastard!" Evans snapped, taking a deep breath and trying to control his temper. "Stop ringing the bloody doorbell—I'm coming!"

When Evans reached the door, the bell rang three more times.

As he opened the door, he said, "I told you to stop ringing the god-damned bell!"

At first, Evans thought he was the brunt of a jokester, seeing no one at eye level. But then, when he glanced down, he found two children standing in the doorway, looking up at him. He immediately recognized who they were and was overwhelmed with emotion. Both were smiling back at him innocently.

The little girl said, "You have a potty mouth. You shouldn't talk like that, you know. You might have to eat some soap."

Evans laughed as he knelt and said, "Now, who told you that?"

"My grandpa," said the girl proudly, "and he said *you* had a potty mouth. You know you really shouldn't talk like that. He told us to make sure you behaved."

Evans smiled as he touched the little girl's cheek. "I'll try and work on that, young lady. Your grandpa wouldn't happen to be with you, would he?"

The boy giggled, answering for his sister. "Nah, just Mom and Dad and Grandma. Grandpa and our other grandma are on a trip together. Uncle Ryan came with us, though. He's here to work."

Evans looked up, seeing Sarah, Becky, and Ryan standing about halfway down the walk. Becky and Sarah were holding each other, beaming at the interaction between Evans and the children. Ryan looked serious, but even he couldn't help but be touched by the innocence of the scene.

"Grandpa said you might like to be our other grandpa," blurted out RJ Summers.

"Yeah," his sister jumped in. "He said that Mommy and Grandma would like that a lot."

Evans cocked his head to one side, giving the little girl a serious look. "And what do *you* say, young lady? Would you like that?"

Patty put her hands on her hips, giving Evans a good once-over. She then glanced at her brother and reasoned, "Grandpa likes him, so does Dad . . ." She looked back at Evans, her lower lip curled, indicating she was giving the question a lot of thought. She finally nodded her head and said, "You'll do."

"Well then," responded Evans, grinning, "do I get a hug?"

Before he'd finished the sentence, Patty jumped forward, throwing her arms around his neck, with RJ right behind. They hit him with so much force, they almost knocked him over. He hugged them back, a tear in his eye. He managed to stand up, holding Patty in his right arm, with his left holding RJ. Before he could react, Sarah came up and gave him a hug, kissing him gently on the cheek as she whispered in his ear, "It's good to see you, Daddy. I'm not letting you disappear on me this time."

She took Patty from him, walking past her father into the house. Becky followed Sarah, but not before she'd put her hands on either side of Evans's face, kissing him gently on the lips.

"Thanks for having us, Patrick."

"Have *you?*" he quipped, winking. "Where are you staying?"

Becky scoffed, kissing him again. "I have it on good authority you have room. Come on, RJ. Let's you and I go explore this big house." RJ walked off with a big grin as Becky led him through the door.

Ryan was behind her, still looking quite serious. There was a moment of silence before he said, "I was at your funeral."

"So was I." Evans smiled weakly. "I filled in the grave with dirt. It was necessary to protect you."

"And them?" Ryan motioned toward Becky, Sarah, and the two children.

Evans slowly nodded. "And them. I see you met your sister."

Ryan looked at his father, and a smile finally came to his face. "There are a lot of secrets in this family. It appears I may have come by my lunacy honestly."

They both laughed, and Ryan added, "Justin and Kay will be down in a couple of days to help with your debriefing."

Evans's look became serious. "Does Justin know?"

Ryan laughed. "I don't know for sure, but I have to guess he doesn't."

"Don't tell him, then—let's surprise him."

"Welcome to the loony bin."

Ryan moved into the house with the others. Evans looked down the sidewalk and found Sean helping Bill toward him. Sean smiled broadly as they approached, but Gateway gave him a disgusted look. As they walked past Evans, the old man said, "I thought you were dead!"

Evans grinned, shaking his head. "Some things never change. Nice to see you, too, General. I was dead until about ten days ago."

Sean chuckled. "Yeah, it's been quite the month for resurrections."

Evans closed the door as the two men moved past. Sean found a comfortable chair for the old man near the window in the spacious living room that looked out over the patio and pool where the rest of the family was. Sean looked at his wife's grandfather, telling him he'd be back after checking on the rest of the family. Gateway nodded, saying nothing. He looked uncomfortable being in Evans's home, so the host decided to try something. It only took a minute, but he appeared in the chair next to Gateway, placing a drink on the table between them. He had one for himself in his hand.

"What's this?" asked the older man.

"Scotch—neat, as I remember. You'll find this to be top-shelf liquor. Very smooth."

Gateway looked at Evans and just grunted. "A little early in the day for this, don't you think?"

Evans found the statement amusing and gave his guest a smile. "Fifteen minutes ago, I would have agreed with you. Right now, it just seems like the right thing to do, no matter the hour. Besides, what is it you Americans say? 'It's five o'clock somewhere.'"

Gateway grunted again. He looked hard at the man sitting next to him. "I'm told you tracked this bastard after he escaped. I'm also told that you were in Bluffton as well."

Evans nodded.

"Why?" asked Gateway.

Evans looked at the old man, holding his gaze. "For the same reason you were there, General. This was about family. I wasn't a good father or husband. It was a chance for me to make things right. Besides, I left that old life behind years ago. Retired, if you will."

For the first time, a smile crossed the old man's face. "Hell, boy, everyone involved in this seems to be retired from something. A little old-school justice seems to have won the day. No matter how I feel about you, I want to thank you for the part you played in rescuing the family and bringing that bastard to ground."

Evans nodded again. A twinkle seemed to appear in Gateway's eyes.

"Say, I hear you're a pretty decent lawyer now. You know, I just may need some legal advice. It appears the United States government is looking at a charity I head."

The two men looked at each other. Gateway picked up his drink and held it out. Evans took his and they touched glasses. Both men took a sip.

Algonquin Park
Ontario, Canada
July 30, 2010
0830 Hours

The sun glistened off the water as Inspector Preston raised the high-powered binoculars to his eyes. The canoe he was looking for drifted in the calm waters of the bay across from the cabin they were using as their base of operations. The cabin was on a small island on the west side of the lake and was one of about a dozen or so scattered around the body of water. They were allowed access by the lease holder, who was away for a couple of weeks. Preston didn't think they would need it that long, but he planned on enjoying the assignment while it lasted.

A noise behind him heralded the approach of one of his coworkers. A quick glance told him it was his female counterpart, Leslie Matthews, and she was bringing him a mug of hot coffee. She was a lifesaver. He put down the binoculars and took the mug, sipping the hot liquid.

"Mmm . . . That's good. Thanks, Leslie."

She picked up the binoculars, looking at the canoe across the lake. "Is that our boy?" she asked, and Preston nodded, taking another sip of coffee. "Who's in the canoe with him?"

"His wife."

Matthews adjusted the binoculars. "I thought they were separated."

Preston smiled. "They must have made up."

Matthews laughed quietly. "What are they doing there?"

"Good God, woman, you ask a lot of questions."

Matthews turned, grinning. "I'm a cop—it's my job to ask questions."

Preston couldn't resist smiling as he chided his colleague. "Then you're not a very good one. Check the shoreline in front of the canoe."

Matthews shifted her gaze, and almost immediately, Preston saw her body stiffen. He grinned, knowing what she was seeing. She leaned forward, as if that would afford her a better view, and continued to adjust the binoculars. "Oh my God," she said, the words barely a breath. "What the hell . . . I mean, are those wolves?"

"You know, Matthews, you should be a cop." Preston chuckled. He downed the last of the coffee as Matthews gave him a look.

"Are you going to tell him today he has to go back to the States because his government is looking for him?" asked Matthews, getting straight to the point. Preston raised an eyebrow. He shook his head, and she ignored his look of disapproval. "I'll tell him if you don't—then we can get back to civilization."

Preston smiled as the third member of their detail, Ian Britton, joined them. He looked at Ian with his brows raised, nodding at Matthews. "Ian, Matthews here wants to let our subject know he has to go back across the border."

Ian was a big, serious-looking man. He smiled slightly as he spoke, and something about the smile looked unnatural on his face. "That would be unfriendly—and we do have a reputation of being friendly here in Canada. There's no indication he's wanted criminally. The orders say that their CIA just wants to talk to him. Why rush? Besides, Matthews, this is what we do. It's our heritage, chasing people all over the north woods."

Matthews scoffed, shaking her head. "You two may like all this rustic living, but I'm a city girl. Traffic, crowds, smog—all the good things in life. All this clean air is disturbing my delicate system."

Preston laughed. "Okay, feel free to go over there and tell him he has to leave and go back across the border, Matthews. Just remember, those wolves you were just looking at are the same ones he used to question those two jackasses who tried to kill him." Matthews visibly shivered. Britton laughed as Preston added, "He's also the guy who snuck onto one of our military bases, hitched a ride on one of our military aircraft, parachuted onto that island in New York State, and helped rescue his family. You saw the report I submitted and know what he did there. If you want to go pick him up and ask him to leave Canada, please, feel free."

Matthews smiled weakly, looking at the other two Mounties. "Now that I think about it, I'm not in that big of a rush to get out of here."

"He knows they want to talk to him; give him a couple days, and he'll head back himself. Give him some time to rest and recover from his little adventure. I think he's earned it."

"Besides," said Britton boldly, "look what he left us. He plans to visit."

Britton produced an unopened bottle of Kentucky bourbon from behind his back.

"How do we know it's from him?" asked Matthews.

Britton, smiling broadly, pulled a note from his pocket and started to read: "'Inspector Preston, our last meeting was brief on that southbound aircraft. I feel I owe you a drink and an explanation. We'll be by this evening to share this bottle.'"

"How do we know it's from him?" asked Matthews again.

A grinning Britton handed Matthews the note. "He signed the note."

"I'll be damned . . . How'd he know we're here?"

Preston took the binoculars from Matthews and handed her the empty coffee mug. "You can ask him tonight, Matthews. Looks like we're having company for dinner."

All three of them heard a noise out on the water and turned to see three red canoes moving swiftly over the calm surface.

"They're from the boys' camp on the other side of the lake," commented Matthews.

There were three people in each canoe—one adult in the stern and two boys. The crew of each canoe paddled in unison, not changing sides. Preston thought they knew what they were doing. He looked through the binoculars to see what was on the bow of each canoe. The name of the camp shone brightly against the red background, arched in white. Preston smiled and lowered the binoculars. He thought of the man across the lake and shook his head. Of course, it wasn't a coincidence.

★ EPILOGUE ★

STRENGTH

Algonquin Park
Ontario, Canada
July 30, 2010
0830 Hours

The alpha drank slowly from the lake and then raised his snout in the air as the breeze shifted ever so slightly. There was a familiar smell of human beings. He recognized the one scent belonging to the man who had been watching and following them. He was no threat to the pack. The second scent was new. Human, just softer—female. A low growl from behind him told him his mate had picked up the scent as well. This was followed by the growls from several other pack members while they moved slowly forward from the cover of the tree line.

Four young pups played with the alpha female, not paying any attention to the new scents in the air. Their mother didn't move, taking notice of the drifting canoe just offshore. She, too, recognized the one scent. That human was not a threat, but the other was unknown. Her senses were alert to any danger that might threaten her young. The members of the pack that came out from the cover of the cedar trees lining the lake took positions that would ensure the safety of the cubs. Several raised their snouts into the air, searching for any other new scents. There were none.

The canoe drifted quietly about fifty feet from the rocky shoreline. The woman leaned back into the chest of the man, both sitting on the bottom of their vessel. The man, facing the stern, leaned his back against the bow seat, the paddles stowed under the thwarts. The two sat quietly, in awe of what they were watching. They, too, sensed the shift in the gentle breeze that was now coming out of the southwest. They saw the alpha male raise his head and then look directly at them. He was magnificent. At his side, the alpha female lay, watching the pups play, oblivious to the world around them. Ever so slowly, three adult wolves moved out of the forest, forming a semicircle around the mother and pups. Movement on the inside of the tree line indicated the presence of other members of the pack. After a few minutes, the alpha female rose and led her pups down to the water to drink. They followed their mother, took their time drinking, and when they were done, they followed her back up the gentle slope, where they continued to play.

One by one, the rest of the pack made their way down to the lake to drink under the watchful gaze of the alpha male, who maintained his watch on the drifting canoe. As they finished drinking, each member of the pack moved back up the hill. Most disappeared into the trees, but several lingered near the alpha female and the playing cubs. When the last had finished their drink and headed up to the safety of the forest, the alpha male remained by the lake for a bit. He casually took another drink. There was no fear, no aggression, no threatening posture—just a certain confidence. He slowly turned, moving up the hill, lingering near the alpha female. He nuzzled her, and then she led the cubs into the forest. One by one, the remaining members of the pack followed, leaving the alpha male by the tree line. He knew the pack was at the top of the pyramid. A family, and their strength was each other, working together to survive in an unforgiving but beautiful land. The alpha knew this strength was paramount in their day-to-day struggle to stay on top in this environment. He quietly disappeared into the forest.

In the canoe, the female pushed gently back into the male. His arms were wrapped around her, and he squeezed her, gently kissing her on the cheek. They understood too.